FROM A BROKEN BOTTLE TRACES OF PERFUME STILL EMANATE

VOLUMES 1-3

ALSO BY NATHANIEL MACKEY

Poetry Books and Chapbooks
Four for Trane
Septet for the End of Time
Outlantish
Song of the Andoumboulou: 18–20
Four for Glenn
Eroding Witness
School of Udhra
Whatsaid Serif
Splay Anthem

Fiction
Bedouin Hornbook
Djbot Baghostus's Run
Atet A.D.
Bass Cathedral

Criticism
Discrepant Engagement: Dissonance, Cross-Culturality, and Experimental Writing
Paracritical Hinge: Essays, Talks, Notes, Interviews

Anthologies
Moment's Notice: Jazz in Poetry and Prose, with Art Lange

Recordings
Strick: Song of the Andoumboulou 16–25

for Reggie

FROM A BROKEN BOTTLE

TRACES OF PERFUME STILL EMANATE

VOLUMES 1-3

NATHANIEL MACKEY

with best wishes...

NYC
Poets House
7/21/11

A NEW DIRECTIONS BOOK

Sections of this book have appeared in *ACTS, Alcatraz, Arras, Avec, Black American Literature Forum, Blue Mesa Review, Callaloo, Chain, Chicago Review, Code of Signals, Conjunctions, Credences, Dark Ages Clasp the Daisy Root, The Gig, Hambone, o·blēk, Resonance, River City, River Styx, Sun & Moon: A Journal of Literature & Art, Temblor, Tyuonyi,* and *Wch Way/New Wilderness Letter.*

Bedouin Hornbook was originally published by Callaloo Fiction Series in 1986 and reprinted by Sun & Moon Press in 1997. *Djbot Baghostus's Run* was originally published by Sun & Moon Press in 1993. *Atet A.D.* appears here by arrangement with City Lights Books, who originally published it in 2001.

Manufactured in the United States of America
New Directions Books are printed on acid-free paper.
First published as a New Directions Paperbook (NDP1167) in 2010
Published simultaneously in Canada by Penguin Books Canada Limited

Library of Congress Cataloging-in-Publication Data

Mackey, Nathaniel, 1947–
From a broken bottle traces of perfume still emanate. Volumes 1–3 / Nathaniel Mackey.—1st American pbk. ed.
p. cm.
ISBN 978-0-8112-1844-3 (pbk.: alk. paper)
1. Jazz musicians—Fiction. 2. Bands (Music)—Fiction. 3. Epistolary fiction, American. 4. Musical fiction. I. Mackey, Nathaniel, 1947– Bedouin hornbook. II. Mackey, Nathaniel, 1947– Djbot Baghostus's run. III. Mackey, Nathaniel, 1947– Atet A.D. IV. Title.
PS3563.A3166F76 2010
813'.54—dc22
2009044388

10 9 8 7 6 5 4 3 2 1

NEW DIRECTIONS BOOKS ARE PUBLISHED FOR JAMES LAUGHLIN
BY NEW DIRECTIONS PUBLISHING CORPORATION
80 EIGHTH AVENUE, NEW YORK, NY 10011

CONTENTS

AUTHOR'S NOTE

At some point in the mid-1970s the phrase "dear angel of dust" occurred to me. "Dear" I took at first to be strictly descriptive in its multiple senses, the phrase eventually part of a poem I hoped. But by the time I wrote it down in a notebook the phrase had become salutational, "Dear Angel of Dust," the opening of a letter which at that point remained to be written but the "open sesame," it would turn out, for a series of letters which, as the saying went regarding ragtime, "jes' grew." Earlier in the same notebook a passage of which "Dear Angel of Dust" seems to be a condensation or a concatenation occurs: "an earth of asymptotic approach to which we beckon, bite of dust." Compounding the doo-wop group The Penguins' "Earth Angel" and ancient Iran's Mazdean "Angel of the Earth," "Dear Angel of Dust" had to do with aspect and allure, daunted access, and as well with endless approach and approachability, such address as the letters would rehearse and make recursive. Dust carried its common association with mortality, fleetingness, time, ephemerality, record, recall, verging on defeat; it announced a need to consecrate or accede to the grit of particularity, specificities of incident, reference, time and place, crying out to be rethought.

The first "Dear Angel of Dust" letters, signed "N.," were part of the serial poem *Song of the Andoumboulou,* the first comprising "Song of the Andoumboulou: 6," the second a section of "Song of the Andoumboulou: 7." Part prose-poem, part *ars poetica*, they addressed aesthetic issues pertinent to the poem, launching a reflexive, poeticizing strain that would continue to run thru the letters even after they parted company with the poem. It was with the third letter, in which N. emerges as a composer/multi-instrumentalist and announces the formation of a band, that the epistolary series detached from the poem and lit out into fiction, remaining related to the poem, however, something of a cousin. Music was already present in the poem, its title that of a Dogon funeral song, but this presence was made more pronounced by the mention of Brazilian singer/songwriter Milton Nascimento in the second "Dear Angel of Dust" letter (and as well, perhaps, by the phrase it coins, "A Supreme Friction," recalling Wallace Stevens, recalling "fictive music"). An even more pronounced, multifaceted, prolonged address of music was what the third letter set out to pursue. It was with this letter that *From a Broken Bottle Traces of Perfume Still Emanate* began.

However much *From a Broken Bottle* grew out of a phrase that popped into my head thirty-some years ago, its roots go farther back. The work reaches back to dreams of playing with some of the greats of the music that I had listened to during my teens and early twenties, non-musician that I am notwithstanding, dreams in which I played alongside John Coltrane, Ornette Coleman, Thelonious Monk and others. Thus it was that the letter which opens the work developed out of a related dream I had one night in my early thirties, a dream in which, although I played alone, the presence of Eric Dolphy seemed implied by the fact that I played bass clarinet, that of John Coltrane by the fact that the tune I intended to play was "Naima," that of Archie Shepp by the fact that what I actually played was "Cousin Mary" done the way he plays it on *Four for Trane*. Behind this dream lay an odd concert I'd attended several months earlier, a concert that planted the idea of N. writing as a musician and forming a band, the oddness of it being that I was the only person to show up, an audience of one.

This was in late 1977 or early 1978, in Los Angeles. There was a concert series at the Century City Playhouse that presented "outside" music on Sunday nights and this concert was by a group named A Love Supreme, after Coltrane's album/composition. I had seen posters announcing the concert and I went out of curiosity, on the basis of the name, not knowing or having heard of the group. I got there to find that, besides the band, only two other people were there: the fellow I bought a ticket from at the ticket window and the fellow who took my ticket at the door. I went in and sat down and before long the lights lowered and the band came onstage and played—for me. It was as though I was there on a special assignment or by special appointment, an appointment I didn't know I had, an appointment of an almost mystic sort. The band played and I sat, an audience of one, listening, wondering why in a city of over two million people and a greater metropolitan area of several more million, I was the only person to show up to hear a band called A Love Supreme. I felt as though I'd been summoned. It felt as if I was being inducted into the band or was already part of the band, a phantom member. It started me wondering, at least, what being in such a band—an L.A. band touched by Trane, the Art Ensemble of Chicago, Sun Ra and such—might be like.

One of the members of A Love Supreme read poetry from a notebook at one point during the concert, which seemed to say the music invited poetic support, literary accompaniment or assistance. That, along with wondering what being in a band like that might be like, led eventually to *From a Broken Bottle* and the fictional band in which N. plays, known first as the Deconstructive Woodwind Chorus, next as the East Bay Dread Ensemble, next as the Mystic Horn Society, most recently as Molimo m'Atet. Now into five volumes, the first three of which comprise this book, the letters respond to the music's ongoing call.

NATHANIEL MACKEY

BEDOUIN HORNBOOK

for my mother

14.VI.78

Dear Angel of Dust,

You should've heard me in the dream last night. I found myself walking down a sidewalk and came upon an open manhole off to the right out of which came (or strewn around which lay) the disassembled parts of a bass clarinet. Only the funny thing was that, except for the bell of the horn, all the parts looked more like plumbing fixtures than like parts of a bass clarinet. Anyway, I picked up a particularly long piece of "pipe" and proceeded to play. I don't recall seeing anyone around but somehow I knew the "crowd" wanted to hear "Naima." I decided I'd give it a try. In any event, I blew into heaven knows what but instead of "Naima" what came out was Shepp's solo on his version of "Cousin Mary" on the *Four for Trane* album—only infinitely more gruffly resonant and varied and warm. (I even threw in a few licks of my own.) The last thing I remember is coming to the realization that what I was playing already existed on a record. I could hear scratches coming from somewhere in back and to the left of me. This realization turned out, of course, to be what woke me up.

Perhaps Wilson Harris is right. There are musics which haunt us like a phantom limb. Thus the abrupt breaking off. Therefore the "of course." No more than the ache of some such would-be extension. Still, I'm not so sure anymore. I'm not so sure all this recent insistence of mine on absence isn't couvade after all. (Please don't tell me you told me so.) Two years ago, you'll remember, I wrote: "He now set out to reconstruct—with all the comely lost illusion of lore—to reassemble a Way, as though this were 'his' (he himself realized the presumption) to do anything with. Even though the mute but astonishing leap of inversion beckoned (a stone's throw away, as though wisdom were the meaningless balm for his every unvoiced want), some tail or trace of her voice's yet to be bodiless thrust caught in his throat like sand, a precise powder perhaps (as of a moth's or even an angel's wings) cautioning breath itself. Unpredictably clear—the acute but vertiginous brunt of his awarenesses dulled into purled affronts, each numinous rush he'd come to acquaint with them a seemliness—the earth (belated image of calm) so without dread became the crypt of its own occasion for joy." You know as well as if not better than I do that the "she" whose disembodied voice I invoked was no one other than myself. I would never write such a passage today. All that endless putting off of its point boomerangs on me now as the very abortion I once accused *you* of.

No. What I'm about these days is something very different. The bed I put aside for Erzulie (the rococo brass one with the incongruously threadbare quilts) is a bed in which I no longer care to sleep. "Endless" variations on scratchy riffs I can do without. All this grunting to give birth to a lack I no longer "need." Dream or no dream, some friends and I have gotten together and formed a band. We call ourselves the Deconstructive Woodwind Chorus. I'm doubling on saxello and contrabass bassoon. We haven't done any actual playing yet but we've had an interesting series of discussions on the idea of *duende,* some of them quite heated at times. In addition to this I've fallen in love with a smoky-voiced woman whose sagging breasts are the perfect touch of imperfection.

So as you can see, things move pretty fast here in Babylon. I'm not at all sure this won't be the last letter you'll receive from me. As much as I hate to say so, this dialogue of ours seems hopelessly enmeshed in the very "ontology of loss" of which you've insisted I disburden myself. I know I've been known to cut you loose before, but this time I think I really mean it. I'll send tapes of the band, of course, but please don't expect anything more in the way of words.

Love,
N.

27.IV.79

Dear Angel of Dust,

I just had the pleasure of walking past the aftermath of a motorcycle/automobile crash on my way home—the bike pinned under the front wheels of the car, driver sprawled on a stretcher some twenty feet away getting attended to by paramedics, the "great beast" come out to ogle it all. This only days after someone finally had the decency to remove a dead cat from the same sidewalk, having given up, I guess, on the makeshift burial gown provided by the shopping bag it'd (with half its body still showing) been put into. And only a little more than a week after I was out driving one afternoon and saw an old lady lying facedown straddling the southbound lanes of La Brea just south of Olympic, wearing what looked like a ghoulish white ricepaper powder on her face.

In any event, I'm sorry to have taken so long answering your letter, though I'd have thought you'd be the last person to be bothered by those sorts of questions. I should probably have told you, though, that the tape I sent was the band's first concert appearance, our first "gig," as they say in the business. It took place in Berkeley in fact, which explains why we changed our name. We thought "Deconstructive Woodwind Chorus" sounded maybe a little stilted, Euro-cerebral or (the word Penguin, our oboe player, uses) "deracinated," so we called ourselves the East Bay Dread Ensemble. (We also didn't want people to know we were from L.A.) Anyway, that longish, somewhat open piece you ask about is called "Our Lady of the Lifted Skirts." It more or less grew out of the argument we had as to what we'd play on the way up in the car. Lambert, who plays alto and tenor and does most of the driving, started off by saying we'd have to become what he kept calling "the true heroes of tunelessness," an iconoclastic (as he also put it) "counterplay of deprivations." But he's so given to theory I just ignored him and suggested a couple of Brazilian tunes I especially like. I was immediately put down for my "weakness" for what he called "Iberian schmaltz." I held my ground though, insisting that the Afro-apocalyptic, polypercussive "cloth" more than made up for any lapse into nasalness. I went on, in fact, to very eloquently (and convincingly I thought) argue the case for a redeemed or reconstructed nasality, a nasality carrying not the least suggestion of whine or self-pity—something like that ghostly but husky falsetto Jackie McLean manages to get.

Anyway, we decided the best thing to do would be to continue our discussion once the concert began. (We'd just pulled up to The Barn, a soul food joint in Oakland, as I was about to ask a rhetorical question—"Does the expression 'layin' pipe' mean anything to any of you?"—as a case in point of my impromptu theory of "inertial wisdom.") This, of course, accounts for the "somewhat contentious edge" you note in the piece. We literally allowed it to be "composed" of our disagreements. (The "angularity" you remarked on in my solo—the "indirectness of address," the bent notes and all—probably has to do with the fact that my fingers were slippery, still a bit greasy from the food we'd had at The Barn.) The other composition you asked about I've since titled "Third Leg of the Sun." I wrote it a couple of weeks before the concert. You're right to detect "a certain Egypto-Mayan, Meso-Haitian air" about it. It actually grew out of a passage I'd read in Maya Deren's book on *vodoun,* a passage I might as well quote for you. "Legba," she writes, "who knows the divine language and through whom one might seek recourse from destiny, is himself the destined answer to the riddle of the Sphinx: he was once the new-born infant sun, lived through the fertile prime of his noon, and is now the old sun, walking with a cane—the 'third leg'—in the afternoon of life."

This gave rise to the following questions, which I more or less tried to de-clench in that composition: Couldn't *Ba* have cut itself off from *Legba* and made the journey back to Egypt, have hidden out there like Stesichorus's Helen, a phantom limb calling itself "Ram" and at other times "Soul"? Couldn't *Leg* have followed suit, have introduced itself as "Thigh," the Great Bear of the northern heavens, then almost immediately have left Egypt for Guatemala, calling itself "Huracan," and have come to be known there as "Heart of Heaven"? Couldn't the memory of *Leg* have merged with that of Set back in Egypt, Horus having wounded Set in the thigh when he swallowed the moon? If not, why else would 1) Huracan, the Quiche Maya stormgod whose name sounds like "hurricane," be described as a huge thigh coming out of the clouds, 2) Set go by an alternate name of Typhon, and 3) Typhon be what the Greeks called the hurricane buried in Tartaros?

More some other time.

As ever,
N.

19.VII.79

Dear Angel of Dust,

This might be the most inclusive net I've cast all day. However much I resist, it all reduces to waste. I've taken a look at those paintings, drawings and so forth as you suggested, but can't say that I see the connection you sense between them and that latest tape I sent. I may in fact, I admit, have come of late to resemble the Clown of Octaves, but I still detest this recently widespread tactic of presuming to explain by way of analogizing. In fact, I question the need to "explain" at all. Bear in mind that Ogotemmêli, the Dogon hunter whose replies to "the Nazarene" I've been known to recite, suggested the ear as a kind of womb in which the word is made flesh, a vaginal (excuse me) condition to which all talk aspires. Perhaps this is, as you say, only my own foolishness, but then again it is me whose voice is at stake. Don't confuse whatever small truce I've managed to make with what I know to be futile with an outright romance of collapse. I mean by this that there's a semantic of motive you yourself imply when you say that I deliberately "conceal" my meanings. Or as I recently saw it put somewhere: "Everyone's clown, but nobody's fool."

Let me, then, put it this way: One afternoon six years ago I sat at the end of a thread. At the other end of that thread was the eye of a needle. The needle's tip rested some distance below me in a space between threads of cloth—two wefts and two warps crossed so as to make it a square. With the square as its pivot (or inverse pivot) the needle spun as I swung the thread but could not be disengaged. What this was was the Veil I've since come to know. Seeing it so, I intuit a "space" we're all immigrants from. (I see it so simply at certain times. It invariably *has* to conceal itself.) On the day in question I'd begun by setting out to enact an omen. Carefully arranged about my feet I scattered bits of what I later found to have been a wish. The room, an all but empty one, was invaded by a green—very faint at first—light. Later, as I lay in bed, I thought back over what had happened. My thinking hovered around the figure of a cloth-enshrouded, enormously protective Thigh. The needle pricked a vein and what blood flowed out was an ending, the ending of a song I went on to write. The words, afloat on this river of blood like paper boats, were these: "the bait of how wet / she'd be, her bought kisses." I saw by this that much of what occurs comes *after* the fact.

"But what about the punchline?" I can already hear you asking. "Isn't it humor, that always hastily altered view of things, in whatever way managed—taken out and then put back in—isn't it humor which at all allows for whatever relief?" This may in fact be so, but, be that as it may, I don't think either Mondrian's trees or Picasso's bulls have a lot to do with what I meant by "de-clench." I might as well come right out and tell you that you won't find an ear for this music in art history classes. The hip thing nowadays is for art to get out and mingle with the action, get a taste of what the streetlife's like. I tend to go with that. The last thing I want our group to become is a lonely hearts band. But if you've heard that album *Indian Street Music* you'll understand why I say that music comes only of where the streets intersect with the lonely, heaven-seeking heart. Or to give the last word to someone else: "Hallelujah Avenue and Amen Street were paved with gold so fine that you couldn't drop a pea on them but what they rang like chimes. Hallelujah Avenue ran north and south across heaven, and was tuned to sound alto and bass. Amen Street ran east and west and was tuned to 'treble' and tenor. These streets crossed each other right in front of the throne and made harmony all the time."

Yours as ever,

N.

24.IX.79

Dear Angel of Dust,

Funny what an odor can do. This afternoon in the produce section of the supermarket I bent over between the oranges and the nectarines and unexpectedly caught a brief whiff of what was exactly the scent of the Nago incense David used to bring back from New York four years ago. I wouldn't exactly call what I went into a swoon, but it did carry me back to the night he and I sat up late drinking port and listening to the album of Tunisian music he'd brought over.

In any case, I'm writing not so much to play Proust as to tell you about the press conference we held this morning. The band decided it was time we confronted our critics face to face, so we reserved some space down at Rhino Records, the hip record store in town, and sent out invitations. A pretty large crowd showed up. The people at Rhino were nice enough to provide refreshments, so it turned out to be something of an event. Things got under way with a fellow from one of the local radio stations clearing his throat to say that while he admitted being "somewhat uninformed" on recent developments in music the trouble he has with our compositions is their tendency to, as he put it, "go off on tangents." He then said that "a piece of music should *gather* rather than *disperse* its component parts" but insisted that he wasn't asking that our music be made easier exactly, "just more centered somehow," etc.

This line of argument was a piece of cake, as they say, for Lambert, who sat fidgeting, smirking and jotting notes on the back of an album cover he'd been looking at the whole time this fellow spoke. (I have to give Lambert credit, knowing his temper, for even hearing him out.) Anyway, the guy did at last finish, at which point three people back toward the budget classical section applauded. Lambert stared at them a moment, then began by saying that all the talk of being "more centered" was just that, *talk,* and had long ago become too easy to throw around anymore. He then asked what, or where, was this "center" and how would anyone know it if it were there. He went on, tilting his chair back on its hind legs, folding his arms across his chest and saying that he wasn't sure anyone had anything more than the mere word "center," that it didn't simply name something one doesn't have and thus disguises a swarm of untested assumptions about. Then he shifted his argument a bit, saying that if our music does have a center, as he could argue it indeed does, how would someone who admits being "somewhat uninformed" recognize it, that maybe the fellow from the radio station wasn't saying anything more than that our music churns out of a center other than his, one he's unfamiliar with. He pointed out that, as he put it, "you don't know any center you don't go to" and finished the matter off by rising from his chair, wagging a very preacherly right index finger and admonishing, "But if, 'somewhat uninformed,' you refuse to make the journey to that center and instead pontificate on its need to be 'more centered,' then you're asking for nothing if not an easier job, that your work be done by someone else, that our music abandon *its* center and shuffle over to yours." With that he sat down to cheers and stamping of feet from the folk imports section.

Next a fortyish, not bad looking lady from one of the neighborhood weeklies spoke up. She had a lazy way of talking—not a drawl exactly, but a way of almost retracting what she had to say. And not exactly lazy either, considering the care she took, the effort it must have taken to sustain (like a sigh, only longer) that blasé way of speaking she took for charm. Anyway, what she had to say was that she considered herself not a critic but a fan of our music, but that she wondered why we couldn't, to quote her, "place the music within the context of the *whole* culture, rather than just the African, Asian and generally 'Third World' references you like to make." She sat down and those of us at the table, the members of the band, looked around at one another for a moment. Finally Heidi, whom I don't think I've mentioned before but who plays violin and congas and also calls herself Aunt Nancy, spoke up. "All I can say," she said, "is that the culture you're calling 'whole' has yet to assume itself to be so except at the expense of a whole lot of other folks, except by presuming that what they were up to could be ignored at no great loss." She went on to accuse the lady of "speaking right from the heart of that exclusionary sense of dichotomy to even ask such a question." There was a bit of rumbling at the back of the room but she went on. "What makes you think of Africa, Asia and other parts of the world," she asked, raising her voice, standing up and putting her hand on her hip, "as *not* a part of 'the *whole* culture'? What makes you feel excluded by our sources if not the exclusionistic biases of the culture you identify as 'whole' boomeranging back at you?" The lady from the neighborhood weekly blushed, and Heidi (or Aunt Nancy) went on to say that while she was standing she might as well reply to something in the first guy who spoke's remarks which'd bothered her. And what she said she said so eloquently I have to quote her again. "I don't know where you get this business of gathering vs. dispersing," she argued, turning to the fellow from the radio station, "the sense of them as an either/or proposition, one a choice against the other. We inhale as well as exhale, the heart dilates as well as contracts. Those of us in the band want music that shows similar signs of life. You may want something different, something more modest maybe, but your modesty betrays its falseness, shows itself to be the wolf-in-sheep's-clothing it is, when you saddle up your high horse to tell the rest of us we have to likewise lower our sights." She then took a drink of water and sat down. Again there was applause. This time from some people over near the used reggae bin.

Well, things went on pretty much like that, back and forth, for three hours or so. I'd go into more detail—and maybe at some other time I will—but I've begun to get hungry, so I have to bring this to a halt. But that reminds me: You may be wondering what Penguin had to say during the press conference. I forgot to tell you he wasn't there. Yesterday, as you know, was John Coltrane's birthday. Penguin, by way of homage and celebration, insisted on eating three sweet-potato pies, just as Trane did one afternoon in Georgia in the late forties when he was in the Cleanhead Vinson band. We all warned him but he wouldn't listen, so he ended up sick and had to have his stomach pumped. Won't get out of the hospital till tomorrow, perhaps even later.

I'll be in touch.

Yours truly,

N.

2.XI.79

Dear Angel of Dust,

One of those dreams I have over and over again came again last night. I had the sense of it as a place to which I'd returned. It had something of a mazelike feeling about it, the various buildings set at odd angles to one another and rather hazily suggesting the housing projects I remembered living in as a child. What "action" there was took place in an area between two buildings, though a sense was maintained of it also taking place inside. The sky, what little bit of it I could see, was extremely dull, crossed here and there by occasional hints of a configuration. What I mean is that the telephone wires overhead looked as though they were posing, bearing down in a static but at the same time stately sort of way, yet seeming to bulge (to be on the verge of bursting) with implication. "An antediluvian sense of design," I heard myself mutter.

But those words, if they belonged to anyone, belonged to someone else, though what I'd say was the meat of the dream came on the heels of my mumbling them. I stared thru a window, that is, across the roofs of several buildings below, into a kind of courtyard in which a mule stood hitched to a cart. Someone sat on the bed in back of me, though I gave little if any thought to who that someone was. He or she may have been reading but I couldn't have been sure, could not, in fact, have cared less. What struck me was the way in which—in that way dreams have of doing so—the scene not so much changed as abruptly included two places other than itself, became an overlay of sorts. Both the dormitory room I'd lived in as a college freshman and my grandmother's living room, as though they'd been not quite thoroughly erased, made their presences—a palimpsest—felt. My brother Richard, after more than a dozen years, had come home from overseas. I was trying to show him my dormitory room but—and this is the part I come to in dream after dream after dream—was overcome by weeping.

The odd thing is that my brother in fact came home a year ago, yet I've continued to have these dreams of his return. It's as though the gap between fact and idea filled the heart to the point of flooding, as though grief were a liningless womb turning inside out. Words don't go to where this sadness welled up from, a deepening throb I felt as a sorrow set free of all cause, a sorrow previous to situation. I wept not for Richard nor myself nor anyone else but for the notion of kin, as though the very idea were an occasion for tears, a pitiful claim to connection, a bleeding socket whose eye'd been plucked out. The dark of that hollow brought me to my knees. As though I knelt before blood, I knew my pulse to be an influx of losses, a bottomless hurt or an echoing thump come out of the cave I call the Heartbreak Church. I tried telling Richard how much I'd missed him, how glad I was to see him, that there were no bad feelings. He put his arm around my shoulders. I woke up crying.

But you're probably wondering what this has to do with the tape I'm sending. Well, isn't the pathos, the ache we hear in certain music a longing for kin? Isn't that what Braxton means by "vibrational affinities," that no sound exists of itself but as a leaning toward others? I see that some time ago I even copied words to that effect, from a book I came across called *Sound and Symbol,* into my journal: "The dynamic quality of a tone is a statement of its incompleteness, its will to completion. To hear a tone as dynamic quality, as a direction, a pointing, means hearing at the same time beyond it, beyond it in the direction of its will, and going toward the expected next tone. Listening to music, we are not first *in* one tone, then in the next, and so forth. We are always *between* the tones, *on the way* from tone to tone; our hearing does not remain with the tone, it reaches through it and beyond it."

Wasn't the hollow into which I wept such a reaching thru, a passing over perhaps? Was the brotherly arm I felt a phantom limb? (And, even if not, how much does “limb” have to do with “liminal”?)

Tell me what you think.

Yours truly,

N.

19.XII.79

Dear Angel of Dust,

I'm enclosing a tape of my latest composition. I call it "Not of Rock, Not of Wood, Not of Earth" and (here you can say you told me so again) I got the inspiration for it from the work of an artist named Petlin who works in pastels. I saw a canvas of his at the house of a friend not too long ago and was instantly struck by how he manages to make texture constitute itself of its own erosion, infuses color with a certain aura of captured ruin. It seemed he'd worked the powderiness of the medium so as to have it collapse into a capacity for infiltration, that a spectral choir of massed incursions chromatically cloaked itself in vows, in conceptual hoods of deprivation. I was surprised to find myself so moved (and moved to music no less), especially in light of my letter to you a few months back. But what I saw to be the tactile or coloristic counterpart of hoarseness proposed a scratchiness of voice, a self-seeding smudge with overtones of erasure as a possible arc along which our music might pass. I tend to pursue resonance rather than resolution, so I glimpsed a stubborn, albeit improbable world whose arrested glimmer elicited slippages of hieratic drift.

The problem, of course, was less to translate than to accent what I'd seen, to outmaneuver its lack of a strict musical occasion. Though to intuit a body of theoretical beauty gives rise to knots of quite a particular kind ("an inflexional latticework of rusted bells" I wrote at points on the score), I'm not sure the solution to its several impasses won't have to ultimately be a social one. I'm thinking in part of the chorus in Brazilian samba, where the perviousness of Carnival to an apparent ambush of painted futures repossesses the "folk," inoculates flesh against otherwise illusory notions of weight. I'm sure this all sounds hopelessly hypothetical, but listen, for example, to the way the horns make for an almost churchlike joining of voices about seven minutes into the piece. Though I can't pretend to be able to account for how this came about (it wasn't written out in the score), I will say that I felt the floor become a flood of dancing feet, that I felt the air undulate like snakes and that the snakes' coils caressed the smalls of our backs.

You'll also notice that we've added a singer to the group. She's from Mauritania and her name's Djamilaa. I think I mentioned her in a letter some time ago. (I referred to her as "smoky-voiced," if I recall correctly.) I finally got up enough nerve—or at least I thought I had—to call her up a month or so ago. I say "thought" because, as it turned out, after I'd dialed her number and she'd answered the phone I was too tense to speak up. It was like in a dream. I moved my mouth but no sound came out. The weird thing, though, was that after she'd said hello about three or four times and gotten no answer she paused for a while, assumed a more intimate voice and whispered, "It must be you then, N. I knew you'd eventually call." She went on to say a number of other things, the upshot of which was that I got my voice back. Anyway, one thing, as they say, led to another, so we've been getting pretty cozy of late. I think you'll hear what it is I like about her voice, the throaty direness I love. "As though it etched itself in ashes," Penguin says.

As ever,
N.

22.XII.79

Dear Angel of Dust,

This'll be something of a postscript to the last letter I sent. The question I raised around the example of samba needs going into further I think. You'll recall that I hinted at the possibility (the inevitability even) of a "social" solution to certain formulational blocks. What I meant to suggest was that the so-called "unheard-of," insisted on for so long (and most typically within the context of one or another *group*)—that any dismantling of some such insistence likewise finds its site to be a collective one. I've talked about an otherness—though it's hard to use that word anymore without wincing—about an otherness the chorus intimates. We've all heard endlessly about call and response, endless repetitions having to do with "community," "dialogue," so on and so forth. What I'd have us listen for and hopefully hear beneath the by now triteness of such observations, however, is a heretofore fallow reserve of poetic suggestion. It's not that we don't rightly hear call and response as both solicitation and bestowal of communal assent. Nor am I suggesting the chorus not to be a projection of sanction, a bodying forth of collective accord and/or insinuation. What I'm proposing is that we hear into what has up to now only been overheard (if I can put it that way), that we can awaken resources whereby, for example, *assent* can be heard to carry undertones or echoes of *ascent* (*accents* of ascent).

You'll understand by this that I'm not using the word "social" in any flat sociological sense. What interests me is the chorus's construction of an otherwise unavailable Heaven, its more or less utopic insinuation of an accretional "yes" that annexes the trace of its historical locus. (Have you had a chance, by the way, to listen to "Streams," the piece by Cecil Taylor I recommended a while back?) The specific relevance of samba has mainly to do with its submission to a processional muse, an explorational wooing of aggravated fates wherein the rowdiness endemic to one or another breadwinning task openly takes to the streets. I hope I can say this and still keep clear of a strictly euclidean sense of "the streets" as an on the one hand lumpen, on the other hand mechanized school of hard knocks—a parade, as it were, of on the one hand thrillseeking, on the other hand robotized and on yet a third, unexpected hand rebellious or at least resentful masses. I should stress the word "openly" perhaps.

These matters, as you can see, have been much on my mind of late. I've been listening to Jair Rodrigues's *Eu Sou O Samba* all morning but just happened to turn on the radio and what should I hear but Louis Armstrong's "Oh memory" version of "Stardust." There again I hear the chorus (a chorus of horns in this case), an amen corner to Louis's birdbeak sermon. I'm intrigued by a special play back and forth between ghostliness and goad, as though the chorus thinned and also hollowed itself out to become a cavernous cloth, a pall of sorts like a muffled thrust of apparitional coughs. Then there's that scratchiness I've alluded to before, an almost cryptic hoarseness. Is it the age of the record, the shortcomings of early recording techniques? Or is it something more primal, something more "ontic" perhaps? The sense I have is that we're being addressed by a barely audible witness, some receding medium so heartrendingly remote as to redefine hearing. As you yourself have so often pointed out, the frayed edges of sound are not to be heard as "unheard-of," however much that handle might appear to apply. The initiatic husk of self-inflicted static or the residual hum of self-ingesting suns (call it what you will), the raspiness of Louis's voice against the answering piercingness he gets from the horn supremely sets up the chorus to be the skinless muse it turns out to be.

Socioethnic rub or cosmicomic ruse? A cloak of powders one

might almost call it, but for the nagging question of whether his handkerchiefs contained cocaine as some have said they did. Stardust indeed . . .

Much affection,
N.

27.11.80

Dear Angel of Dust,

You may be right to bring up the matter of taunt. You might even go a bit farther and say that in a music bereft of the merest hint of an unincongruous occasion the chorus can't help—however much it might coo (or at least appear to do so)—can't help but cover itself in a subversive, more or less abrasively incongruous croon. (There is, isn't there, a way in which even smoothness *grates*—though not so much on the nerves as against a certain roughness it serves to set in relief.) I'm ready to defend even the most outrageously saccharine moments (the beginning of Jair's "Vai Meu Samba," say, with its apparent echoes of "I Could've Danced All Night") against any charge of unfought for sentiment. The fight, as I hear it at least, is so abundantly there—that almost oily "mellowness" so decidedly under duress—as to animate a swarm of insurrectional whispers. (I agree with whoever it was I once read who described the whisper as "a laminated shout.")

The real work, though, might be to approach the chorus on a somewhat different plane, to keep ourselves clean of whatever romance of resistance would hear it only as camouflage. You bring up the possibility of taunt, a distinct quality of tease you detect in the seductive, almost dovelike smoothness we so often get from the chorus. I'm very much inclined to agree, but I can't help cautioning us both against, again, *over*hearing rather than hearing what's there. It's like those people who used to say that Coltrane sounded like he was searching for some "right" note on those long runs of his that at the time were called "sheets of sound." What he was up to was no such cover at all. He wanted each and every one of those notes to be heard, not to be erased by the eventual arrival at some presumably "correct" (or at least sought-after) note. What I'm trying to say is that, while I'd agree that there's an aspect of taunt to the chorus's contribution, part of what it taunts is our inclination to hear it as taunt, that the chorus whispers so as not to be overheard. I'm not so much disagreeing with you as, if anything, agreeing too much.

Anyway, you're right on the money, as the saying goes, with your hunch that "Not of Rock, Not of Wood, Not of Earth" takes its title from the story of Gassire's lute. In fact, that passage about eleven minutes into the piece, where the band goes into what you term "a collective stutter," comes directly out of my recent reading of two other tales from what might be called the Gassire cycle. I was struck by the fact that on four separate occasions Lagarre, a later king of Wagadu living some 747 years after Gassire's time—the recurrent intrusion of jet noises throughout the passage attempts to allude, albeit clowningly, to this fact—confronts an animal (a lizard, then a jackal, then a buzzard, and finally a dragon) which says to him: "I don't know you but I know your father. I don't know your father but I know your father's father. I don't know your father's father but I know your father's grandfather. I don't know your father's grandfather but I know your grandfather's grandfather. I don't know your grandfather's grandfather but I know your great-great-grandfather's father. I don't know your great-great-grandfather's father but I know your great-great-grandfather's grandfather. I don't know your great-great-grandfather's grandfather but I know your great-grandfather's great-great-grandfather. I don't know your great-grandfather's great-great-grandfather but I know your great-great-grandfather's great-great-grandfather . . ." And so on.

I was after something similar. Not so much a stutter in any precise sense of the term as a curve of articulation which whenever it asserted would instantly qualify, even contradict itself. That sense of a receding, self-correcting withdrawal into a cave of ancestors I found immensely attractive, a curious borderline stance between the compelling and the merely compulsive. What I felt was needed at some point in the composition was exactly that eruptive, calmly eroding assumption of an atavistic mask of initiation—in this instance a generation by generation default on what I think of as the underside of recognition. What you've called "a collective stutter" is indeed iterative, but if I've been at all successful in what I set out to do in this piece the tongue is not so much obstructed (think back to what I said about Trane a short while back) as it is inflated in pursuit of options which, however cautionary they might appear on first encounter, erase the ostensible line between emphasis and obsession.

Lambert and I sat up late last night discussing this very question, the notion of a threshold beyond which a riff requires dues of itself. He continues to call for what he terms an "interrogative witness" as a way of having harmony undo the fetish that's been made of its fashionably "imminent" death. (His quarrel, as you know, is with the sense of it as impending instead of an already accomplished fact.) He's working on a piece now in which the ghost of harmony, outfitted in wind-chimes which turn out to be chains, loudly and somewhat snidely "actualizes" itself beneath a mound of pseudomelodic earth. If you can imagine a cross between a Sufi swoon and an Appalachian hiccup you've got a good idea of what he's getting into. I hope to be sending you a tape of it soon.

Yours,
N.

16.III.80

Dear Angel of Dust,

I thought it was about time I wrote you a letter from on the road. As you can see from the postmark on the envelope, we're in San Francisco right now. We played a lovely concert here last night—one of the best, I think, we've done so far. Everyone's chops, as we say, were definitely up. There's something about being up this way that seems to always loosen us up. Maybe it's all the different kinds of music you can hear on the radio. Yesterday, for example, we were in the car on our way over to Richmond and a monster of a cut by an ongo horn ensemble from the Central African Republic followed something by a salsa band known as Orquesta Cimarrón. The segue was so outrageous—so much a community of sighs or a single, elaborately elongated sigh—that Lambert had to pull over to the side of the road and turn the engine off to keep from going, as he explained to us later, "irretrievably *out*."

I guess part of what made the gig so unusual was the audience, which was made up largely of people we'd met earlier in the day. Some of them even brought tambourines and bamboo flutes and joined in at a number of points—exactly the sort of communal insistence I've had on my mind these past weeks. It was kind of odd, though, the way we happened to meet them. The five of us decided to go out walking yesterday around mid-morning. Djamilaa, in particular, wanted to take some pictures to send to her relatives back in Mauritania. We were walking along down Sutter Street near where it intersects with Fillmore when Lambert all of a sudden stopped and was staring at something scribbled on the wall of a boarded-up store. He was stroking his beard and had a funny gleam in his eyes, so the rest of us went over to see what it was had caught his attention. There, somewhat shakily written in pencil, were the words: "Mr. Slick and Mister Brother are one of the two most baddest dude in town, and Sutter Street."

We all stood there pretty much silent for a while, till Penguin said he was struck by what he termed "its enabling confusion concerning the singular and the plural," that he saw its vacillation between the claims of the one and the counterclaims of the other ("Mr. Slick and Mister Brother" referred to as "one," with the word "two" thrown in as an apparent concession or an afterthought of some kind, only to be disregarded by the word "dude" being put in the singular) as the sign of a deep-seated upheaval in the consciousnesses of the folk, an insistent interrogation of the bounds between individual and collective identities, something like the "I and I" of Rastafarian talk in fact. He went on to argue that this carried thru in what he called "the inclusion/exclusion syndrome" of the last five words, where the implication would appear to be that Sutter Street is somehow not covered by the words "in town."

Aunt Nancy objected that Penguin, as she put it, had "put words in the mouths of the people," that he sold them short and gave them too much credit at the same time. What he said smacked of outmoded, condescending notions of the people's inability to think in individualist terms, she argued, and the leaving off of the "s" from the word "dude" was more likely an oversight than a deliberate tactic. At this point Lambert jumped in and asked how she'd explain, even if that were the case, the words "Mr. Slick and Mister Brother are one"—to which Aunt Nancy answered back, "Bad schooling." By this time a crowd had begun to gather around us, attracted by the loudness and the increasing heatedness of the discussion, and on hearing Aunt Nancy's answer a number of them burst out laughing. Lambert came right back, though, raising his voice to compete with the laughter and insisting that anyone who chose to misread the handwriting on the wall did so at his or her own risk. He said it was obvious that the hand of whoever had written those words had been put upon, literally shaken by powers—whether artistic or autistic he couldn't, he admitted, say—which were neither to be trifled with nor explained away by hardheaded sophistries disguised as common sense. He added that if anything the words were a summons, a call-to-arms as it were, an invitation into an area of *un*common sense, and that the dislocations they visited upon so-called proper English were manifestly of an invasive, mediumistic order. By the time he finished a heavy, uncomfortable silence had settled over everyone.

I heard someone toward the back of the crowd mutter what sounded like the words "elitist mystification," so it wasn't without care that I broke the silence by remarking that the apparent redundancy of the words "most baddest" seemed to me to be what was really of compelling interest. I harped on the advisedness of my use of the term "apparent," pointing out that instead of redundant I heard "most baddest" as a novel, rule-abandoning technique for intensification. Sensing the restiveness of certain elements in the crowd, I thought it best to pull away from the more discursive possibilities of the situation, so I observed that, however much we may have sounded like one, we really weren't a debating team after all, but a band of musicians in town for a gig that night. After making a pitch about how what attracted us to that particular piece of graffiti was its gut-level realization of exactly the quality we strive for most in our music—the primacy of intensity over etiquette—I passed out handbills announcing the concert and encouraged everyone to come check us out. (I've been reading up on medicine shows a lot lately.) So we ended up milling around there for a while, talking with what of the crowd was left, exchanging our views on a number of matters. And, as I've already said, a pretty fair number of them did in fact show up at the concert last night.

We'll be here for another day, at which point we take off for a gig up in Seattle. I'll write you from there to let you know how it goes.

Sincerely,
N.

PS: I almost forgot to tell you we've changed the name of the band again. As of last night we're now the Mystic Horn Society. "Behold a wondrous restoration and renewal of the Ethiopian! Because of the bath of rebirth he takes a new name, which the philosophers call the natural sulphur, and their son—this being the Stone of the philosophers. And behold it is *one* thing, *one* root, *one* substance, with nothing superfluous added, from which much that was extraneous is taken away by the magistery of the art."

7.IV.80

Dear Angel of Dust,

The Seattle gig, as it turns out, fell thru. The manager of the club we were supposed to play at phoned us the day we were gonna drive up there to tell us that not only had the club been broken into and vandalized but that because he'd put off paying the premium his insurance coverage on the place had run out. The upshot of it all, of course, was that he was broke and had to temporarily close the club down. So here we are back home, where we've been for three or so weeks now. I'd have written sooner but I was so depressed about the cancellation of the gig that whatever I'd have written would've depressed you too. Things in the past weeks, however, have picked up some. Remember that piece of ours called "Our Lady of the Lifted Skirts"? Well, we've gone into the woodshed with it and recast it somewhat. I wanted to explore more explicitly the verbal qualities implicit in what you termed its "contentious edge," as well as to make use of some intermedia effects. I've come up with a very dense form of writing, brief blocks of which are to be used to punctuate and otherwise season the music. Compressed Accompaniments I call them. I'm enclosing copies of the ones I've written for this piece.

What I have in mind takes off from the Easter programs in church back when I was a kid, when all of us in Sunday School would each be given a short piece to memorize and recite before the grown-ups on Easter. In this case, then, I've provided five of them, one for each member of the band, though the assignment of pieces to specific individuals is by no means fixed. The way it works, in fact, makes it so each player gets to recite all five of the Accompaniments in the course of the composition. We've developed an approach to improvisation which we call Modular Rotation, an approach that makes use of a number of stations (five in this case) marked off at various points around the playing area. What happens is that each station is presided over, so to speak, by one of the Accompaniments, and in the course of the performance each player moves from station to station, at each of which he or she recites the particular Accompaniment which "defines" that station. (I put the word "defines" in quotes because the point is to occupy a place, not to advocate a position. The word "informs," it occurs to me now, might get more aptly at what I mean.) We draw straws to decide which player will be at which station at the beginning of the performance and the composition concludes only after each player has put in time at each of the five stations and recited each of the Accompaniments. At no point in the composition is any particular station to be occupied by more than one player at a time, unless the performance happens to take place on the second Thursday of the month—in which case doubling up at the station presided over by Accompaniment No. 4 is not only allowed but in fact required at least twice in the course of the composition.

Some would say it's not my place to make comments on what I've written, but let me suggest that what's most notably at issue in the Accompaniments' he/she confrontation is a binary round of works and deeds whereby the dead accost a ground of uncapturable "stations." The point is that any insistence on locale must have long since given way to locus, that the rainbow bridge which makes for unrest ongoingly echoes what creaking the rickety bed of conception makes. I admit this is business we've been over before, but bear with it long enough to hear the cricketlike chirp one gets from the guitar in most reggae bands as the echoic spectre of a sexual "cut" (sexed/unsexed, seeded/unsown, etc.)—"ineffable glints or vaguely audible grunts of unavoidable alarm."

Let me hear from you soon. I've told everyone in the band about you and our correspondence and they all send their regards. Aunt Nancy says be sure to tell you that—this is something she's been fond of saying these past few weeks—"fashions come and go but *style* is eternal."

As ever,
N.

FIVE COMPRESSED ACCOMPANIMENTS TO "OUR LADY OF THE LIFTED SKIRTS"

Compressed Accompaniment No. 1

As he asks her to comment upon the birth of each related web she calmly raises her head, furtively lifting her skirts.

Such arrivals as could ever, she thinks, fuse her voice with beaked risings of sand would find their way into their "nest" (whose anchored glimpses of quartz become a base for any further expedition, pirate suns would lap the erratic shores of dust).

However much of a piece with her recent loss of voice (the irretrievable seed of its own habitual cloth), to insist of sound that it not in fact exist seemed an act of despair.

Compressed Accompaniment No. 2

Notwithstanding, she persists in imagining herself "deaf."

Without an earth on which to relate, the uncommitted instants, ineffable glints or vaguely audible grunts of unavoidable alarm, tick unintelligibly away, everlastingly immune to each arthritic throb of humanhearted unrest.

So a gritty persistence, a pebbliness, the masticatory toothlessness of birds betokening muse-forsaken pulp (some ascendancy of dross the elapsed inclusiveness of awkward premonition) admits a ruse whereby these punctual impendences of thought lay their hands upon light.

Compressed Accompaniment No. 3

In fact her skin was so starkly his own fetish-hungered flesh as to give him cause to wonder whose voicelessness it was the desert sand had sown.

He saw himself deprived of every spiritual reassurance.

The voice he'd always known to be hers, so abruptly lost, brought him to the pitiless realization that all his ludicrous passion (pathetic in its redemptive appeal he thought) bordered relieflessly on a path of destitution.

Compressed Accompaniment No. 4

Each reminder of ruin under ceaseless duress (and the broken spine of his otherwise limitless reach of calm come up as thru smoke), the hoarse contempt of her murmurous complaint lapped his ears like dogs.

"The hounds of Hell," he remembered, rousing, taking hold of what tremulous inverted roots lay left of dreams.

Ushered back between collapse and dimly-intuited sun (some previous gash whose corrosive alchemies conjured wish after aberrant wish), he hears her gravelly, barely audible "Wake up . . ."

Compressed Accompaniment No. 5

Swallowing gently, the adept ungraspability of time their cramped egg of remorse, they now wander in thought each unlikeliest inch of remaining earth.

The merest wind, a renewed insistence issuing up as from some vague but somehow timeliest of lungs, wanly echoes what threats the stale precipitous void of whose assumptions posed as unsuspected walls against repulse.

Each arid breath (belated image of dread) become its caricature, the elsewhere absent imminence of loss (the awaited blow) inscribes an arc the all but unbearable conceit of whose precision works its wrath along the inmost edges of thought.

4.V.80

Dear Angel of Dust,

You got me all wrong on what I meant by "a sexual 'cut'" in my last letter. I'm not, as you insinuate, advancing severance as a value, must less pushing, as you put it, "a thinly veiled romance of distantiation." I put the word "cut," remember, in quotes. What I was trying to get at was simply the feeling I've gotten from the characteristic, almost clucking beat one hears in reggae, where the syncopation comes down like a blade, a "broken" claim to connection. Here I put the word "broken" in quotes to get across the point that the pathos one can't help hearing in that claim mingles with a retreating sense of peril, as though danger itself were beaten back by the boldness, however "broken," of its call to connection. The image I get is one of a rickety bridge (sometimes a rickety boat) arching finer than a hair to touch down on the sands at, say, Abidjan. Listening to Burning Spear the other night, for example, I drifted off to where it seemed I was being towed into an abandoned harbor. I wasn't exactly a boat but I felt my anchorlessness as a lack, as an inured, eventually visible pit up from which I floated, looking down on what debris looking into it left. By that time, though, I turned out to be a snake hissing, "You did it, you did it," rattling and weeping waterless tears. Some such flight (an insistent *previousness* evading each and every natal occasion) comes close to what I meant by "cut." I don't know about you, but my sense is that waterless tears don't have a thing to do with romance, that in fact if anything actually breaks it's the blade. "Sexual" comes into it only because the word "he" and the word "she" rummage about in the crypt each defines for the other, reconvening as whispers at the chromosome level as though the crypt had been a crib, a lulling mask, all along. In short, it's apocalypse I'm talking, not courtship.

Forgive me, though, if this sounds at all edgy, maybe garbled at points. My ears literally burn with what the words don't manage to say. I was so blown away by Lambert's concert last night I'm not sure I've gotten my chops back yet. I may not have mentioned it before, but everyone in the band sometimes works out of a solo situation. The money thing, being what it is, makes it easier to get gigs the fewer people there are to be paid. Anyway, Lambert jumped at the chance when the people over at Rhino Records asked if he'd do a solo concert as part of their Sunday night series. He almost immediately went into what ended up being a two-week period of seclusion, a sort of retreat. The night before he slipped off to wherever it was he went he got a spacey look in his eyes at one point and announced, "It's not about being here anymore. I've gotta tighten up my concept, give it a few *turns* I've gotta go elsewhere to get." (He had a strange way of inflecting the word "turns.") We ended up not seeing him again until last night after the concert. I'll get to why I say *after* the concert later, but first you should know that the gig took place where the Rhino concerts usually do, at a little place called the Century City Playhouse over on Pico near the 20th Century Fox complex. (Lambert, alluding to this I think, had himself billed as "The Twenty-Third Century Man of Feeling.") What's nice about the Playhouse is that it's not all that big a place, so there's a certain coziness, the intimacy between audience and performer the solo concert demands. The place doesn't seat more than fifty people I'd guess, and there's no proper stage really, just a moveable, imaginary line beyond which the chairs, which are the fold-up kind, don't go.

The first thing to strike me as we walked in was that there was a skinny, seven-or-so-foot-tall cactus plant sitting in a pseudo-Etruscan pot on the left side of the stage. Right next to and a little bit in front of it was a music stand, turned around to face the audience as though we would be doing the playing. But instead of music what it held up was a sign on which was written THE STEEP RECESSES OF LOVE. On the right side of the stage there was a do-it-yourself shower stall, the kind they sell in hardware stores, right next to and a little bit in front of which stood another music stand, this one as well turned to face the audience. What it held up was a placard on which had been written DEPTH IS A BOURGEOIS ILLUSION. At the center of the stage there was a chair sitting between two coffee tables. Lambert's tenor lay on the table on the left, which was covered with one of those green felt affairs they cover pool tables with. On the table to the right sat a telephone, complete with one of those amplifier gadgets you can set the receiver on top of to have a conversation without having to hold it up to your ear. This gadget, it turned out, was hooked up to the two speakers sitting at the back of the stage. We found seats and sat down, gazing around the place and being pretty impressed that an almost capacity crowd had turned out. Not long after we sat down the lights lowered and it looked like things were about to begin. After a period of about four or five minutes in which nothing happened a woman whom none of us in the band had ever seen before came out from backstage and sat down in the chair between the two coffee tables. She struck me as no doubt being, under different circumstances, a strikingly beautiful woman, but for this occasion her face had been excessively made up—to the point of looking clownish in fact—and she was dressed in Red Wing boots and overalls from which hung hammers, pliers, wrenches and an assortment of other tools. She also wore a name tag such as one gets at conventions, which read "Hello. My name is Polhymnia." (I later told Lambert I thought this was a needlessly heavyhanded touch.) She sat there saying nothing for a while and Aunt Nancy, who was sitting next to me, nudged me on the arm and whispered, "All we need now is a box of popcorn."

Polhymnia finally broke her silence by announcing, in one of those airy, artificially breathy tones of voice Hollywood actresses affect, that it would be unwise for us to expect a simple excavation of longstanding residues of illusory depth. Intensity in the twenty-third century, she said, will have long since quit its traffic in deservedly trashed intimacies of affliction. She said she suspected music to be less and less an attempt to "redeem" affection, as though it were not to be more straightforwardly engaged, that she found it weird to find herself indicted by what she'd always thought was her inspiration, increasingly at odds with an untraceable sigh consecrated to loss. She said she sensed an urgency afoot she hadn't felt for some time, that she felt feeling itself was only a mirage kept alive by a ghost of what never actually was. She went on to say, looking directly at me, that she suspected the chorus was merely one's own obsession, though its juxtaposition of a layered air against what could at best only be proposed (its address of a tiered world whose homonymy with "teared" is too poignant to miss) spoke long and loud to her still. It wasn't, she insisted, so much that the caressive, obedient way the chorus has with sound thickens the air with a school of endearments. Nor was it, she added at once, that its often shameless Dostoevskian deployment of children's voices pinches her spine with asymptotic shivers. What gets to her, she pointed out, goes somewhat "deeper" than that. (She would allow herself that word, she quickly explained, than which, as luck would have it, she could at that moment think of none better, only this once. And only, she went on to say, enclosed in quotes.) But just as she opened her mouth to continue, to tell us more exactly what it is that gets to her, the telephone rang.

Polhymnia lifted the receiver, set it down on the amplifier gadget and said hello. The voice on the other end of the line, which we could hear coming over the speakers at the back of the stage, identified itself only as that of "the caller." Penguin, Djamilaa, Aunt Nancy and I all turned and looked at one another. The voice was unmistakably Lambert's. He started off, after identifying himself as "the caller" ("Hello. This is the caller," he said), by saying that he was calling from a phone booth in the parking lot across the street. The phone booth, he said, stood just outside the Kentucky Fried Chicken establishment (his word) he'd gotten a box of the Colonel's new extra crispy recipe from. Punctuating what he had to say by taking bites of what, from the sound of it, must have been a drumstick, he told us that the ringing of the phone marked the end of the "overlude" to the initial movement of the evening's performance. (It's possible he said "moment" rather than "movement." The food in his mouth made certain words unclear.) The composition's title, he said, was "Eventual Elegy." It was to be part of a longer work entitled "Aggravated Assent." The composition, he said, had begun millions of years ago, the ambiguous verdict of a galaxy-wide dispute between conscious and mechanical forces. The possibility of going beyond romantic as well as classical concepts of phrase, of creating a linearity of unpredictable lengths, was the horizon, he insisted, set up to be either erased or illusionistically addressed. He talked about something he termed "a bouquet of burnt powder," calling it "the obsessive perfume of a shotgun bride serenaded by echoes of an inaugural blast," belaboring (or so it seemed to me at least) the metaphorical potential of the Big Bang theory.

As Lambert spoke Polhymnia began a series of stiff, rectilinear gestures (sort of like that dance called "The Robot" which was popular a while back), the first of which coincided with Lambert's mouthing of the phrase "a heuristic rigor overwhelming all recourse to anecdotal appeal." Turning to her right and taking a set of very small screwdrivers from her pocket, she picked up Lambert's horn and proceeded to take it apart—not just undoing the mouthpiece, the reed and so forth, but using the tiny screwdrivers to detach the pads and the keys as well. Her movements were very slow and painstakingly deliberate, which gave Lambert plenty of time to talk. What he did was keep a monologue going throughout the time she worked on the horn. I can't give you a word-by-word account of what he had to say, but among the things that struck me most was his repeated quoting of a statement whose source he neglected to cite: "Whether we deal with music or some other human event, spirit is at our mercy and we are, in reality, accountable for it." I was also impressed by the self-inquisitive tactic he resorted to at times, posing pairs of like-sounding words against one another as indecisive "notes" of an indeterminate "scale." I recall him asking at one point, "Eventual or eventful? Basis or bias? Composite or compost? Concept or conceit?" Another thing he did which sticks in my mind was give a brief sketch of the life of Antoine Joseph Sax, the inventor of the saxophone, arguing that Sax has yet to be given the credit he deserves for his other inventions (most likely, he noted, because Coleman Hawkins never played any of them), the saxtromba and the saxtuba in particular.

Once Polhymnia had gotten the tenor completely disassembled she proceeded to put it back together again. Maybe the most impressive thing about the whole performance was the seemingly telepathic way in which her completion of the reassembly of the horn coincided, to the very second, with the final words of Lambert's monologue, a statement he said had been made by an ex-slave on one of the Georgia Sea Islands to a white folklorist in 1894: "Notes is good enough for you people, but us likes a mixtery." The very last turn Polhymnia put on the very last screw, in other words, coincided exactly with the word "mixtery" (or was it "mystery"?), at which point the lights in the theatre went down. It took the audience a while to realize that the concert, which had lasted about two and a half hours, was in fact over, but after a minute or so of sitting silently in the dark we all gave a long, intense round of applause. The lights never came up again, however, so we had to grope our way back to the door, outside of which Lambert stood shaking hands with the exiting audience as in a receiving line. The five of us ended up going over to Onaje's, an after-hours juice bar just off Pico a block away from La Brea. We sat around rapping till something like five or six o'clock.

I said earlier I'd been blown away by the concert, the implications of which I'll have to go into in another letter. I'm not sure I've got a line on it yet, but I too feel an urgency afoot I haven't felt for some time, as though I'd finally *seen* that the trouble with song is that it siphons off longing. I'm struck by how the echoes are already there in advance of themselves, that maybe it's all only next year's nostalgia heard ahead of time. Something about the accents if one were listening in a certain way makes the yearning we hear (the overarching trace of somehow having been stunned) the self-appointed plight of an unstated appeal to alibis of oppression. I've recently learned, for example, that *fado,* the name the Portuguese give their version of the blues, means, literally, "fate."

Enough for now.

Yours,
N.

15.V.80

Dear Angel of Dust,

Here's a tape of my latest composition. It's an extended piece for unaccompanied saxello. I've been working on it in secret over the past few weeks, ever since the inspiration for it came in a dream one night. It was a dream whose first part took place in a halfway woodsy, half-way suburban sort of location. Though there wasn't much light in this place everything could be pretty clearly seen. Walking down a slightly inclined road, I saw a somewhat overweight man consoling a four-year-old boy. (I couldn't make out his words but his tone was clearly a tone of consolation.) My own awareness of myself as The Observer was made abruptly evident (i.e., *observable*—so that what I was doing was thereby taken to a second power) by their coming to a corpse laid out on a pyre made of redwood branches on a bed of snow. The snow was blackened by automobile exhaust and the corpse, while alive, had been known as Opposable Thumb. As the stout man knelt and mumbled a prayer the small boy looked on. (I vaguely recalled having watched Opposable Thumb's burial on television, so it struck me as odd that the body could be there in this other place.) The stout man stood up, leaning over the corpse and speaking words which, again, I couldn't make out. I could, however, see that the corpse's head was made of plastic, somewhat like a doll's, whereupon I wheeled instantly around, away from the scene, intending to confront, head-on, the "camera-eye" of my self-observation. I expected I'd conclude by shrugging my shoulders, disavowing all comprehension of what I'd seen . . .

But instead of a benign, suddenly eyeless gaze, what I saw once I'd turned was a deepening blackness—something like a funnel the way it tapered toward its densest point. Attempting to walk toward this point, I found myself seated in the driver's seat of a small car, about to leave what I hazily knew had been a gathering of some kind (a party perhaps, a reunion even). Driving away, I happened upon L. S. Doug, a roommate from college with whom I'd been active in SDS, a fellow archaeology major. I stopped and got out of the car but all he'd say was "We're even worse off then than now." This he repeated a number of times and then disappeared, evaporating into the air and leaving a mist, a kind of steam, on my glasses. I began to walk with no destination in mind up the hill I turned out to be on, quickly coming to the interior of an Egyptian temple where I met two tall, coffee-colored men with abnormally prominent, futuristic foreheads. The last thing I remember is my hand being shaken and the eerie glow my skin got from them knowing my name.

I awoke annoyed at the naiveté of such an ending, put off by the patness of the dream's apparent comment on the letter to a friend I'd begun before going to bed. In the letter, that is, I'd written: "There seems to be an innate opportunism to the fact of having been born, at this point in our evolution at least, with opposable thumbs. This accounts, I think, for the overtones of manipulation (the Latin word for hand, you'll remember, is *manus*) which contend with and otherwise complicate the 'innocence' of touch." But this exists for me as nothing other than an open possibility, a navigable breach to be unceasingly addressed by way of an effort wholly distinct from concessions to closure. In deciding to compose a piece which would carry thru on the dream I wanted to somehow subvert or erase the triteness of any such ending, to in so doing deflect what arrest had set in with Opposable Thumb's assassination. (It was somehow obvious to me in the dream that Opposable Thumb had been a victim of foul play—this in spite of the fact that the authorities had labeled his death a suicide, referring to him as having died, as they so smirkingly put it, "by his own hand.")

The name of the piece is "Opposable Thumb at the Water's Edge." Its basic theme I'd put this way: Graspability is a self-incriminating thirst utterly native to every hand, an indigenous court from which only the drowned hope to win an acquittal. The piece makes use of two triadic phrases which I call utility riffs: “whatever beginnings go back to” and “an exegetic refusal to be done with desire.” These generate a subtheme which could be put as follows: Thirst is by its nature unquenchable, the blue lips of a muse whose refusals roughen our throats with *duende*. I wanted a piece which would liberate color from attitudes of dependence, grow increasingly athwart of what it proposed would be at issue. (A piece, in other words, in which each and every note would keep its neutral truth.) To what extent I’ve succeeded I leave to each listener to decide.

Sincerely,
N.

28.V.80

Dear Angel of Dust,

I write in the wake of an extraordinary occurrence. Earlier this evening during rehearsal I gave a debut performance of "Opposable Thumb at the Water's Edge" for the other members of the band, not saying much about the piece other than announcing its title. The occurrence to which I refer took place following the conclusion of my performance. At that point Penguin (whom I'd vaguely noticed fingering an imaginary horn toward the end of the piece, and who, by the time I finished, had taken his oboe from its case, inserted the mouthpiece and wet the reeds with his tongue and lips) embarked on a solo in which he held forth on what he said was a rapport he sensed—"a shadowy congress" he called it—between Opposable Thumb and an extremely ancient, primeval Egyptian god by the name of Temu. In the course of his solo he presented an impressive, all but overwhelming rush of corroborative data. Temu, it turns out, was worshipped in the city of Annu during the earliest dynasties, where he was known by a number of epithets, the most frequent being "Father of the Gods" but "Chief of the Great Company of the Nine Gods" and "Governor of the Companies of Gods" being in common use as well. He was said to have existed "before ever the earth and the world were made." By way of a flurry of 16th and 32nd notes, Penguin made it known that the Papyrus of Nesi-Amsu, repeating a legend reputed to be "older than the pyramids," reports that Temu "had union with himself" and thus produced the gods Shu and Tefnut ("air" and "moisture").

This legend comes down to us in a number of versions and the specifics of Temu's "union with himself" vary from account to account (a fact to which Penguin did justice by "overblowing" the horn, exploiting overtones and resorting to tremolo and vibrato effects). According to one of these, Temu showed up in Annu in a state of arousal, took his erection in his hand and masturbated. As a result Shu and Tefnut—whom we now know to have been of Nubian origin, Penguin pointed out in an aside—came into being. According to another, upon bringing himself to an orgasm Temu spat. His spit took the form of Shu and Tefnut, both of whom he then embraced in order to quicken them with his Ka (his "double"). Yet another version has it that Temu "acted as a husband to his hand," uniting himself in an embrace with his shadow, ejaculating into his mouth and thus producing Shu and Tefnut. Penguin succeeded at points in making the horn sound as though he were playing chords, much the way Pharoah Sanders does. He was thus able to elaborate on these various versions concurrently. Throughout his solo he made abundant use of circular breathing, which in a self-reflected aside he called "an old snake-charmer's trick" at one point, making mention of one K. Gopalakrishna Ouroboros, a nagaswaram player of some repute. (The nagaswaram, he noted, is a South Indian oboe, a double-reed horn just short of three feet long. Its name, translated literally, means "snakepipe.")

In one particularly long, seemingly endless run—which in a series of extremely high, falsetto notes he referred to as "The Chapter of Traversing Eternity"—Penguin brought to light a number of details concerning Temu which "Opposable Thumb at the Water's Edge" had reminded him of. I can't tell you how moved I was by the oddly denotative, almost pedantic articulacy of Penguin's playing, the amount of information be managed to convey with no loss of immediacy or lack of emotional address. He pointed out that the inscriptions found in the pyramid of Unas, the last king of the fifth dynasty, say of the deceased ruler in one passage: "His father Temu grasps his hand." Likewise, a passage among the inscriptions found in the pyramid of Teta, the first king of the sixth dynasty, addressed Temu directly and says, referring to the deceased Teta: "Thou graspest his hand, thou drawest him to heaven. He is not a dead thing on earth among men." Among the Unas inscriptions, he informed us, there's a passage which, referring to Unas as "the blessed one," says: "The blessed one was taken by the god Temu into the hollow of his hand."

At this point Penguin not only modulated into another key but also switched from 6/8 to basic 4/4 time, observing that even if we were to ignore the passages among the Unas inscriptions which liken Unas to Temu (e.g., "Thy hands, thine arms, thy shoulders, thy belly, thy back, thy hips, and thy legs are those of Temu"), the tendency of the pyramid texts to identify the deceased with Osiris, along with the tradition wherein Osiris is the grain-god or seed-god Osiris-Nepra, makes the above passage which pictures Unas in the hollow of Temu's hand (given the equation Unas = Osiris = Osiris-Nepra = seed) a pretty obvious reference to Temu's "union with himself." The taking hold of himself (the grasping/grafting-on of "himseed") that created Shu and Tefnut, Penguin argued, was itself but an echo, a recapitulation of the earlier, likewise masturbatory act which produced the world. Getting a more three-dimensional sound than one normally hears from the oboe (like that of a geodesic beehive or hornet's nest), Penguin quoted from a source he cited as *The Book of Overthrowing Apep,* which, we were told, says of Temu: "A desire came over him to create the world, and he carried it into effect by making his mouth utter his own name as a word of power, and straightway the world and all therein came into being." What Temu uttered, however, was not the name "Temu," Penguin added at once, but a secret name about which the papyrus is absolutely mute.

Just as Penguin finished asking the by then rhetorical question "Could the secret name of Temu have been 'Opposable Thumb'?" Lambert, who'd had his tenor strapped on for some time, joined in, keeping to the gruff, no-nonsense notes of the horn's lower register for the most part. He traded choruses with Penguin for a while, then took off on a short improvisation of his own. Punctuated by pseudo-electronic, more or less Moog-like bleeps from Penguin's oboe, Lambert's solo had to do with recollections from his boyhood back in Texas, specifically a trick he and his buddies used to play on one another. Walking along in a dusty field or some such place, he said (hitting a coughlike middle C for emphasis), one of them would say in a matter-of-fact way, "I've heard that jackin' off leaves whelps on your hand." Anyone caught looking at the palm of his hand, as everyone who didn't know the trick immediately did, Lambert explained, was loudly laughed at for having thus admitted, as he put it, "doing what no young, self-respecting stud would've otherwise confessed ever having had to resort to." Against my better instincts I broke out laughing, as Penguin also did, but just as Lambert began what he warned might sound like a sermon, announcing his "text" to be (quoting him again) "the would-be heaven of one's own hand," Djamilaa joined in on harmonium and Aunt Nancy came in on violin, both of them accusing us of having lapsed into "locker-room humor."

Aunt Nancy quickly made it known that she resented the phallocentricity of what had been played up to that point, that we seemed to have either ignored or forgotten the fact that the hands of men have no monopoly on thumbs. Setting aside the bow and playing pizzicato to underscore this point, she went on to admit that on a more subtle, paradoxical level she'd heard in all our solos something she termed "an opportune, albeit unconscious owning-up to the self-servicing hollowness of masculine assumptions." What one might have otherwise dismissed as rhetoric was so intimately the issue of certain technical resolutions that we all (the three of us—that is, me, Lambert and Penguin) stood stunned at the digital precision of her approach to the strings. She plucked with the fingers and thumbs of both hands, not only near the top of the fingerboard but down by the bridge as well, in what amounted to an extended essay, an impromptu étude on the question or quandary she involved us in: "Opportune for whom?" Djamilaa meanwhile extracted an etheric, spherical extendedness of sound from the harmonium, breaking beyond the confines of any engulfed, however timely contention or self-sustaining debate. Her playing seemed to propose, in what had the sound of a deep, ancestral caroling or a keening of sorts (as though it implicitly mourned or in some other way despaired of its own statement), a Byzantine wedding of courteous, extended palm or polite, courtly back-of-hand with clenched, adversarial fist. I felt I was being tickled and invited to weep at the same time.

By the time Aunt Nancy returned to the bow the room had acquired the feel of an ocean of hands (like the hallway of anxious, groping hands which grab at the woman in the movie *Repulsion*—only much more numerous and much less locatable as to point of entry). "Point of intrigue," she was in fact quick to put in, making use of a tremor she sustained in her wrist to give the strings a somewhat quivering, eloquent orphan's voice—at once aggressive and apologetic, self-assertive and contrite, a two-way, witnessing complaint. Djamilaa's harmonium, little more than a fringe by now (an elaborately edged, heavily petticoated whisper), spoke to us of an amulet known in Brazil as a *figa*, a fist carved of wood, metal or stone—"It doesn't matter which," we were told—with the thumb between the index and middle fingers. The *figa* turns out, Djamilaa let it be known in a droning, drawn-out footnote, to be an ancient African protection derived from a gesture used to ward off the evil eye. (It seems that many of the Africans brought to Brazil had the custom of clenching their fists, letting the thumb be seen between the index and middle fingers, whenever they felt a spell might have been cast against them. Tradition has it that when they arrived in Brazil they walked off the slave ships making the *figa* fist.)

Penguin, Lambert and I instinctively related this to the amulets—the so-called "hands"—made use of in hoodoo. We joined in with a unison riff in which a preponderance of triplets spoke loudly of love hands, mojo hands, revenge hands and what have you. At one point Lambert, attempting to answer Aunt Nancy's charge of phallocentricity, made reference to a Haitian handclasp in which the fingers of one hand, encircling the thumb of the other, represent a vulva encircling a penis. By this time, however, Aunt Nancy's bowing, embroidering the hem of Djamilaa's threadbare drone, gave all the more reach to what came out of the horns. It wasn't so much that she'd given in or been at all won over by what we had to say, nor that her complaint nourished or in some other way enabled us, complied with any sense or simpleminded hydraulics of an exchange back and forth. Nothing so hackneyed as that was the case, thank God. What occurred, I think, is that a symbiosis from which every horizon had fallen away sought to extend itself. Falling short of this, the horns undertook a role of deceptive bottom or unsecured buttress, an illusory "base" in relation to which Aunt Nancy's persistence (the undulant tenacity of her central assertion) inhabited the hollow she'd eternally resent, an "opportune" exposure to every grasp ever sown by grief—an elusive anchor, if you will. This left us free, I believe, to forage in whatever ways we might, which is what we did.

It's hard to say with any certainty, however. Perhaps it's foolish to try going into this in a letter. But since, as bad luck would have it, no one thought to turn the tape recorder on, all I can do (I'd much rather send you a tape) is say that once Djamilaa began to sing her voice flowered, as it were, from the *figa*. It quickly took on a quality of naive but omniscient, blocked but open access to truth which a Brazilian singer I like a lot, Elis Regina, is so heartwrenchingly an exponent of. The cramped insistence of a nasality which bordered on regret slowly elicited a sort of rain—a rain, however, which was more like a dessicated spray or a suspended rush of infinitesimal powder. It felt to me like a miraculous, immaculate ash in fact, an aromatic dust (like what's left behind by the burning of incense). "An ashen finesse," Lambert whispered in my ear, but I stuck to my own understanding of it as the drift or debris of an echoed eruption, the dry-minded rain of all eternity, the very ash of time. I intuitively knew that somewhere and somehow someone had scorched an "ever after" root. The last thing I remember is my hands falling away from the saxello, my arms going limp at my sides and me leaning forward like one of those guardian women carved on the prows of ships. I must have leaned as if to anticipate a blessing, I think, letting the dry, telepathic rain wash my brow like cigar smoke from a Mother of the Gods.

All I know for sure, though, is that the next thing I knew I was sprawled on the floor, coming to. I eventually looked around and saw that Aunt Nancy, Djamilaa, Lambert and Penguin had all, as I apparently had, passed out. They too were picking themselves up off the floor. Needless to say, the silence, following so much music, was extremely problematic. It was Aunt Nancy who finally broke it, dusting herself off and exhaling, "Whew! What was *that* all about?" We all laughed, a little bit more at ease, but the spectre of our collective swoon had introduced an at once congratulatory and cautionary air which was so intense it precluded any talk of what had taken place. I find it hard to put words around it even now—but equally hard to rid my mind of what occurred.

In any case, I've been writing all night it looks like. The sun's beginning to come up now I see. I very much wanted to share this experience with you, the most intriguing rehearsal the band's had so far. I see now, among other things, that "Opposable Thumb at the Water's Edge" was just a beginning. I'll have more to say on this later, but sleep seems what I'd best be doing right now.

Please let me in on whatever thoughts you have on any of this.

As ever,
N.

29.V.80

Dear Angel of Dust,

I wouldn't have thought I'd be writing so soon after yesterday's lengthy letter, but the draft of your new essay arrived in the mail this afternoon and I find I'm unable to not respond to it at once. First of all, let me say that I think "Toward a Theory of the Falsetto in New World African Musics" is absolutely brilliant. I'm especially impressed by its long overdue disinterment of the occult, heretofore inchoate arcana intuitively buried within the reaches—the wordless reaches—of the black singer's voice. Would it be going too far to say that in your essay the black falsetto has in fact found its voice? (Forgive me if I embarrass you.) In any case, the uncanny coincidence is that the draft of your essay arrived just as I'd put on a record by Al Green. I've long marveled at how all his going on about love succeeds in alchemizing a legacy of lynchings—as though singing were a rope he comes eternally close to being strangled by. In this he seems to me to be Rhythm & Blues's equivalent of Jean Toomer ("braided chestnut, / coiled like a lyncher's rope"). More importantly, it's no coincidence that he does this by way of that falsetto you've so astutely written about.

One point I think could bear more insistent mention: What you term "the dislocated African's pursuit of a meta-voice" bears the weight of a gnostic, transformative desire to be done with the world. By this I mean the deliberately forced, deliberately "false" voice we get from someone like Al Green creatively hallucinates a "new world," indicts the more insidious falseness of the world as we know it. (Listen, for example, to "Love and Happiness.") What is it in the falsetto that thins and threatens to abolish the voice but the wear of so much reaching for heaven? At some point you'll have to follow up this excellent essay of yours with a treatment of the familial ties between the falsetto, the moan and the shout. There's a book by a fellow named Heilbut called *The Gospel Sound* you might look into. At one point, for example, he writes: "The essence of the gospel style is a wordless moan. Always these sounds render the indescribable, implying, 'Words can't begin to tell you, but maybe moaning will.'" If you let "word" take the place of "world" in what I said above the bearing this has on your essay should become pretty apparent. (During his concert a few weeks back Lambert quoted an ex-slave in Louisiana as having said, "The Lawd done said you gotta shout if you want to be saved. You gotta shout and you gotta moan if you wants to be saved." Take particular note of the end of "Love and Happiness," where Green keeps repeating, "Moan for love.") Like the moan or the shout, I'm suggesting, the falsetto explores a redemptive, unworded realm—a meta-word, if you will—where the implied critique or the momentary eclipse of the word curiously rescues, restores and renews it: new word, new world.

You might also make more mention of nonvocal music. Granted, the unarrestable play back and forth between words and wordlessness—between "signal" and "noise," as it were—might not seem to apply where there're no lyrics. In the past you've accused me of attributing "rather unlikely verbal powers" to strictly instrumental music (yesterday's letter will no doubt annoy you no end), but the fact is that instruments actually do speak. Anyone who's heard Mingus and Dolphy's exchanges on Mingus's tune "What Love" (*Charles Mingus Presents Charles Mingus,* America 30 AM 6082) has no doubts about this at all. (Dolphy once commented, "I more or less try to make the horn speak." And Mingus remarked, "We used to do that, you know. We used to actually talk in our playing.") Anyway, my point is that the falsetto serves the same alchemical function in nonvocal music as it does in the singing of, say, Skip James or Jorge Ben. The examples of this are too numerous to exhaust, but I find the following particularly moving and would recommend that you check them out: Sonny Rollins's squealing use of overtones toward the end of "Lover Man" on the album he did with Coleman Hawkins (*Sonny Meets Hawk,* RCA 741075); Jackie McLean's high, whistling clench on "I'll Keep Loving You" (*Let Freedom Ring,* Blue Note 84106); Robin Kenyatta's "Until" (*Until,* Vortex 2006); Anthony Braxton's alto solo on "Howling in the Silence" (*Archie Shepp & Philly Joe Jones,* Fantasy 86018).

Which reminds me: I had an odd dream about Braxton the other night. He came by to pick me up in a brand new BMW and as we pulled away from the curb he began to talk. The strange thing was that he kept his eyes glued to the road ahead, seeming to make a point of not looking my way, and talked about "Braxton" as though he were someone else. Badmouthed him in fact. Told me he couldn't be trusted and called him unreal. "That Braxton's real slick," he said. "Can't trust him. Unreal to the bone. Your basic trickster. A little bit false."

A little bit false as in "falsetto" perhaps? Did my dream foresee your essay's arrival?

Yours,

N.

9.VIII.80

Dear Angel of Dust,

Please forgive the long silence. I've had every intention of writing sooner but an extended bout with inertia set in shortly after I received your letter. There seem to be times when I feel as if all expressive potential had been turned back empty-handed. For the past few weeks I've done little more than a lot of sleeping, feeling brought down if not exactly done in by the contradictions (to loosely paraphrase Lambert) between the world one carries around in one's head and the world one carries one's head around in. I'm sorry to say my predicament hasn't been as abstract as that may sound, but you'll allow me to spare you the gossipy particulars I'm sure. Suffice it to say that the fog (or whatever it was) has at last lifted, however much it may simply be lying in wait, having set me up for a surprise attack.

You ask if we've had any further discussion of our "intriguing rehearsal." I appreciate your circumspection. We did throw around some talk on one or two occasions, only to end up sending Penguin to confer with his grandmother. She's rumored to be well-versed in rootwork, hoodoo and such, so we thought she might throw some light on what had taken place. According to Penguin, once he'd finished giving her all the details, telling her the story of what happened that night, she simply sat there puffing on her pipe and leaning back in her rocker, staring at the TV as though he weren't there, not saying anything. He says this went on for some time and that what she finally said, turning to look at him, was "Play with a puppy he'll lick your mouth." She refused to elaborate, he says, but instead told him he'd best be going, that she'd said more than she should've already. You can make of it what you will but I sense an allusion to the incestuous Dogon jackal Marcel Griaule has written about. "The jackal," he says, "the deluded and deceitful son of God, desired to possess speech, and laid hands on the fibres in which language was embodied, that is to say, on his mother's skirt. The incestuous act was of great consequence. It endowed the jackal with the gift of speech so that ever afterwards he was able to reveal to diviners the designs of God." Penguin's grandmother's words I hear as a recipe and a warning: *Play around with prophetic music and you moisten your mouth with a jackal's kiss.*

Now as for your "reading" of Opposable Thumb, let me say that I have no trouble whatsoever with your understanding of him as a projection of proletarian unrest. I myself sense that he may well be that "third, unexpected hand" to which I referred in an earlier letter—an avatar, as it were, of on the one hand manual, on the other hand manipulated labor. I ask only that you take the word "labor" in its most (if I may say so) pregnant sense. I've long argued against strict adherences to one-dimensional meaning, so my hope is that such a figure as Opposable Thumb retains the power not only to point but to correspond—to unsettle, if you will, an otherwise flat referentiality. As I've already said, "Opposable Thumb at the Water's Edge" represents no more than a beginning. In future elaborations I intend to unearth or erect a layered, resurrectional scale, an oppositional "poetry" of synchronistic fact by which to body forth the *soul* of a long-resisted ascent. To this end I'm looking into the possibility of a collaboration with two local groups whose work I much admire, the Boneyard Brass Octet and the Crossroads Choir. You've heard of them perhaps. In any case, I'll keep you abreast of whatever develops along these lines.

Your other comments I'll have to deal with some other time. Penguin and Djamilaa have gotten it into their heads that we've been taking things "too seriously" lately. They've decided that what the band needs is recreation, so we're all heading down to Venice this afternoon to rollerskate along the beach. They'll be here to pick me up in a few minutes, so I'll close for now. I hope to be writing you again soon. I especially want to speak to your remark about "letting go."

Sincerely,
N.

12.VIII.80

Dear Angel of Dust,

The afternoon in Venice turned out to be not all that bad. I haven't seen so many bodies on display in one place in I can't remember how long. In fact, I'm not sure I've ever seen the likes of it before. I saw even more flesh than the last time I was there. It even got me thinking along lines which have put me to work on a new composition. For some time now I've noticed an increasingly widespread tendency, on the part of men and women alike, to wear shorts or cut-off jeans which are cut short enough to expose at least an inch of the rounded base of each buttock—a tendency to publicize, one might say, the liminal crease where the upper back of the leg meets or joins or turns into the lowest part of the hip. Still, I was nowhere near prepared for the quantum increase in public access to "private" parts. Some of the outfits people turned out to go skating in I found hard to believe. We saw one couple dressed in what appeared to be cellophane jumpsuits—bizarre, rose-tinted, blatantly transparent affairs which clung to their bodies like a sort of Saran Wrap. There it all was for everyone to see—body hair, balls, asses, breasts, labia, the whole works.

What struck me about this couple, though, was that each of them wore headphones and cradled a large radio/cassette player to which he or she listened while disco-skating down the walk. They both seemed to be utterly oblivious to every outside presence (one another's included), thoroughly and absolutely absorbed in their respective maneuvers. What more telling sign of our present predicament, I thought.

So observable a contiguity of publicized private parts with privatized public space spoke to me deeply of a miscegenous exchange between the public and the private. I instinctively recognized the crossfire, so to speak, of a precipitous volley back and forth between two mutually disdainful, mutually infiltrating domains. It both withheld and held forth on a war of which I knew we were all, in one way or another, casualties. My intuition was both confirmed and complicated by the outbreak of a quarrel soon after the couple skated by. A somewhat skinny teenager with scraggy hair and a broken front tooth fended off a group of three other youths, making them keep their distance by threatening them with a baseball bat. (He kept taunting them to come on and, as he put it, "take a bite of the wood.") There were whispers among the crowd that he might be on the drug there's been so much publicity about lately, a violence-inducing concoction known as PCP. This evidently wasn't the case, however, as no violence actually materialized. The excitement died down not all that long after it arose when the three would-be attackers turned around and walked away. The funny thing is that we saw all four of them about a half hour later, carrying on like the best of friends, joking with one another, laughing and drinking beer.

I remarked at one point that the crowd, the bustle, the outfits and all made for what struck me as a Carnival air. Penguin "corrected" me right away, however, pointing out that the word "carnival" etymologically has to do with bidding the flesh farewell, a sense of the term which didn't seem to apply to what was going on around us. "What we have here," he held forth, "is no such taking leave of the flesh but an indulgent exhibition of it, an outright wallowing in it." I disagreed, making a point of the ambiguous, debatable character of the word's original meaning. Its root might equally, I pointed out, have had to do with accommodating or taking solace in the flesh. It was as I made this point that the ideas for the new composition began to crystallize. I recalled a piece called "No Tonic Pres" that Rahsaan wrote as a tribute to Lester Young, a tune whose "head" doesn't have a tonic or definite key resolution. I sensed a connection between this piece's lack of a tonic and Carnival's refusal to resolve into a fixed, unequivocal meaning.

As I gazed upon the various disclosures of pubic hair, haunches and cleavage we were surrounded by I saw what seemed to be the third term of a triangulated refusal to resolve. What I saw, as though for the first time in fact, was the body's dichotomous desire to both extinguish and extend its own mystique, to reveal itself without relinquishing its ruse. What I saw was that ruse's ability to survive exposure. "The body as open secret," I heard myself mutter.

What I have in mind is a composition which, like Rahsaan's, would advance disclosure as a further phase of complication. I'd like to posit exposure as a questionless "answer" whose intended unravelings only work to ensnare. (The word "crotch," though of uncertain etymology, appears to go back to a French word meaning "hook.") How much the piece will have to do with "Opposable Thumb at the Water's Edge" I can't say for sure, but the skinny kid's grip on the baseball bat would certainly seem to fit in. "The Slave's Day Off" is the title I'm working with now. Two Carnival traditions out of the Caribbean, Trinidadian Canboulay and Jamaican John Canoe, should, if all goes well, serve to "season" the piece. I'm learning to play steel drums in order to allude to the former but the latter has an especially personal resonance for me. I remember, from back in the days when I was a kid in Florida, a rowdy, music-making time known as Junkanoo. There's a tune I can still hear as though it were only yesterday, a song called "Kunk Ain't Got No Bone." ("Kunk," in case you're wondering, was our way of pronouncing "conch.") I intend to quote from this tune throughout "The Slave's Day Off." Isn't it exactly what I've already said? *The body as open secret.* The obvious play one could make on Venus-in-a-shell I'll try to avoid. To say that one disrobes to unveil an anticlimactic mystery inverts the shell-as-outer-bone's concealment of nothing if not an esoteric absence of bone. The bearing this has on questions of form and resistance, it seems to me, has yet to be given adequate attention—an oversight "The Slave's Day Off" will hopefully help to correct.

As ever,
N.

28.VIII.80

Dear Angel of Dust,

Perhaps I can put it across this way: "Public" and "private" are now disjunctive, now convergent masks for the featureless cave or the evaporative curve of an elapsed interiority, a nonexistent self. They cohabit so as to woo, so to speak, an otherwise involuted, apparitional pigment, a profoundly suspect, deeply prepolitical "taint." Though I may not be saying this with all the elaboration it deserves, a timely enough illustration of it took place a few nights ago. The Art Ensemble of Chicago came to town for a concert over at UCLA. As you've probably heard they sometimes do, they came onstage with their faces painted. To me it made perfect sense. I saw line, spotting effects and color taken on as though they were voluntary, self-contracted stigmata, emanations of the flesh as though it were a canvas or a cave wall, gaudy with aboriginal paint. The band seemed to revel in the imposition of a public, admittedly masklike face, but only to ambush, it turned out, the public's nonchalance toward its own deep investment in "smeared" paints, "painted" snares or self-wielding "strokes." (It was like a few weeks back when Oliver Lake, during his solo concert over at the Century City Playhouse, whipped out a camera at one point and, to everybody's surprise, took a picture of the photographer who was taking a picture of him.) The emphasis seemed to fall on identity not as entity so much as enmity, self not as substance but as auto-constitutive stress. To me it made perfect sense.

I wish I had more time to go into it now but I hope this at least begins to answer your question. We've got a gig tomorrow night up north in a place called Santa Cruz, a small town on the coast about an hour and a half south of San Francisco. We'll be playing at a club known as the Kuumbwa Jazz Center. In other words, we've got some running around to do this afternoon. Things like renting a trailer to carry our instruments in, getting a new trailer hitch for Lambert's car (the old one had a hacksaw put to it by vandals in Pasadena), so on and so forth. We'll be leaving early tomorrow morning. I'll try to get a letter off to you from up there.

Yours,
N.

30.VIII.80

Dear Angel of Dust,

The events during our stay here in Santa Cruz have been such that I'll have to put off till some other time what I'd intended for this letter. My hope was to enlarge on the points I made in day-before-yesterday's letter, but the goings-on of the past couple days are at the moment much more on my mind. We got here yesterday afternoon after getting up early enough in the morning to take the longer, more scenic route up the coast. That in itself I could fill a letter with—all that blueness of both the ocean and the sky so much like a medicine after the exhaust fumes and tinsel glitter of L.A. But I'll resist going into that, except to say that Santa Cruz itself entirely partakes of that blueness. This accounts for the cheeriness of the people who live here no doubt. I don't know if I've ever seen so many smiling faces before—and not just on the residual hippies there're so many more of here than any other place I've been. It's a little bit eerie in fact how friendly the people are. I even hear you can cash a check here without leaving your thumbprint or your mother's maiden name. While we were out for a walk yesterday I heard a barefoot girl in somewhat ragged jeans say to her boyfriend as they passed us, "I didn't let it bother me though. Whether she wanted it or not, I knew I was spreading love."

You can imagine what a recess this is from what we're used to down in L.A. I couldn't help having misgivings, however, as to what sort of reception our music would get. Even though I'd heard a lot about how appreciative Santa Cruz audiences are, I had a hard time repressing the thought that our solemnity might put people off. I kept hearing a remark I'd read in *Downbeat* by a member of a "fusion" group called Spyro Gyra, one of whose tunes we'd heard on the radio just as we pulled into town. "It's not intellectually intensive," this fellow had said of their music. "We dance around and smile. We feel good. We're not pensive black men who have suffered. We're happy white kids. We don't have a heavy cosmic message that we're trying to get across." I couldn't help thinking of them as probably more this town's cup of tea than what we're into is. As it turns out, I was evidently right. Only seven people showed up for our gig at Kuumbwa last night. (At first only three people came in, but then the manager of the club called up the local radio stations and had them announce that they were letting people in for half-price. Four more people drifted in after that.) We were pretty stoical about it though, going ahead with the music as though we had a standing-room-only crowd. And the audience, small as it was, was enthusiastic enough. They gave us a standing ovation and even wanted an encore. So that, along with our getting all the granola-raisin cookies, carrot cake, brownies and date bars the club hadn't sold at its snack bar, made the turnout not so hard to take.

The interesting part took place this afternoon, however. They've got a place here known as the Pacific Garden Mall which is more or less the town's main drag. It's one of those situations where they've taken four or five blocks of a street where there're a lot of businesses, made the traffic move one-way, widened the sidewalks, set up benches, planted shrubs and trees, put in crowd-control streetlamps and called it a mall. Mainly what people do there is shop. Besides that, a lot of what're called street people hang out there, including a lot of what're called street musicians, people who play one instrument or another and/or sing on the sidewalk for handouts. On a given day one hears music of various kinds played by various people situated at various places, the dominant sounds usually coming from a non-street band known as Warmth which entertains eaters at the outdoor café in front of a place called the Cooper House. They're a pretty middle-of-the-road, somewhat torchy group that does mainly what Aunt Nancy referred to as "Cal Tjader retreads." Anyway, we got to talking this morning and the next thing we knew we'd decided that maybe it wouldn't be a bad idea to go out and play on the mall for an hour or so—take our music to the people, so to speak. Encouraged by the ovation we'd gotten last night, we were curious to see what kind of impact we could make, to see how many people were walking around out there not even suspecting they might dig our music if only given a chance. So we took to the streets, as they say, coming on like so many gnostic invaders. We found a reasonably uncrowded space in front of a stationery store not too far down from the Cooper House. It was Djamilaa who suggested that while playing we keep time by walking around in a circle, varying the tempo by changing the pace of our walking, just as we'd heard a Toupouri wind ensemble from Chad do on a record Aunt Nancy got from France. With her on trombone, Aunt Nancy on tuba, Penguin on flute, Lambert on alto and me on bass clarinet, we circled up and, moving counterclockwise, began an uroboric strut, marking every eighth beat with an ever so slight stutter-step.

We opened up with a somewhat tongue-in-cheek attempt at one of those interweavings of two different tunes (the sort of thing Mingus used to do so well), in this case "The Shadow of Your Smile" and "You Light Up My Life." Lambert had suggested we take off our shoes and tie bells to our ankles, which we did and which made for some interesting effects. With the most innocent, unassuming gesture imaginable, that is, the music laid what had the feel of a cape, a tablecloth and a magic carpet, so much like a rug of prayer it proposed a gossamer, immaterial dew which wet the soles of our feet. We walked not so much on eggshells as on a skim of oddly uterine water, each note evoking a thinned, auto-suggestive liquidity which by way of an inverse, evasive equation known only to itself possessed us of a newly arrived-at notion or understanding: *band-as-manyfooted-beast*. It had the feel of being walked in or walked away with I often get from certain salsa bands. It was the most ingenuous appeal ever shaped by human lungs and lips I was pretty much convinced, an offhand, obliquely yawning elasticity whose corralled insistences made for a remote, pathetically extrapolative dirge. Part burial song but a boat-hauling shanty as well, it seemed to arise from the very streets upon which we walked with no other wish than that they could somehow be our own, could somehow, that is, be as "outside" as the music itself.

The first piece went on for what must have been twenty-five minutes at least, though by then we'd all pretty much lost track of time. I suppose I expected to look up once we stopped playing and find the entire mall silenced, everyone turning their ears our way as in an E. F. Hutton commercial. Instead, we found people still going about their various businesses just as before. Warmth was playing "Pensativa" (which I considered fairly hip given what they otherwise play), while from the other direction one caught the strains of a hammer dulcimer played by a long-skirted, Birkenstocked, hairy-legged earth-mother type. The shoppers went on with their shopping. Still, a small audience of about six or seven people had gathered around us and they gave a polite round of applause once we'd finished our first number. A couple sitting off to my right were nodding their heads and with a spaced, purring look on their faces they muttered, "Thank you." A passerby dropped a few coins into Lambert's saxophone case, which happened to be lying open on the bench next to where we were playing. We went right into our second number, a relatively new composition of Aunt Nancy's called "Dream Thief." Again that watery, carpeted feeling asserted itself, the piece going on for some thirty-five minutes or more. Once we finished we saw that we'd attracted a few more people, our audience having gone well into double digits by now.

The applause was a bit more hesitant this time, however, and, once it came, noticeably scattered, inconsistent and sparse. As we prepared to do our third number one guy spoke up and asked didn't we think our music was a bit elitist, overly esoteric for such a public place. Aunt Nancy looked at him and laughed, going on to explain that we play in a non-hierarchic high mode known as neo-stilted, though "nouveau stilted" our critics might call it she confessed. She pointed out, however, that either "neo-" or "nouveau," whichever one chose, was a bit misleading, as our inspiration was the widespread, age-old stilt-dancing traditions of West Africa, where mask-wearing, dancing figures mount a pair of stilts as much as fifteen feet high. "The wretched of the earth," she let it go at saying, "can hardly be accused of elitism." With that we went into our final number, a section from Lambert's ongoing composition "Aggravated Assent." It proved to be an oddly strenuous, oddly effortless piece, starting off with a plaintive sigh from Aunt Nancy's tuba (as though she set out to find love in the least likely of places). The gossamer dew again wet the soles of our feet as we went around in a circle, making the play between *lifted* and *lofty* even more pronounced than in the first two numbers.

An even more insistent vertical moisture, that is, made for a helical escalator effect. To me it felt something like a throwback to a high school commencement ceremony, though decidedly more brash in its utopian understanding of the term "graduation." The music, almost against our wills, had become an anthem, so that the Upper Room so often sung about in gospel music—understood by us as a musician's loft—spoke less of some alienated genius's garret than of a surprisingly elastic, ever-expanding auditorium (like a longshoremen's hall, but infinitely more inclusive). Surrendering none of their earlier suggestion of clanking chains, the bells on our ankles felt like wings as the helical escalator kept us aloft. Had the crowd on the mall beaten us to the elastic longshoremen's loft toward which we ascended? Would they be waiting to greet us once we arrived at the Upper Room? Or was it the other way around, us leading them? Did they lag behind on the helical escalator, proverbial kids behind the proverbial piper? These are the questions I couldn't help asking myself even as I struggled with the E-flat pedal the piece required of the bass clarinet. But as I looked around in search of a possible answer I noticed two cops getting out of the patrol car they'd pulled up in. They walked toward where we were and pretty soon were saying we'd have to stop the music, that the storeowners were complaining we were making too much noise. We argued, of course, that we had as much right as anyone else to play on the mall, but to no avail. We got some satisfaction, though, from the fact that the crowd of thirty or so people that had gathered around us loudly hissed and booed the cops. In a perfectly deadpan, gentlemanly tone of voice Penguin congratulated them both on their part in making the town, as he put it, "one of the most alarming mixes of flabby pseudo-sixties idealism and crass mercantile instincts we've ever played." The cops showed no signs of having gotten his point, however. They simply accepted the handshakes he offered with two indulgent, openly patronizing smiles.

These matters, I find in the course of writing, have more to do with the question of public and private than I suspected at first. Though I haven't the time to go into it now, I'm struck by the curious inversion implied by how we musicians use the terms "inside" and "outside"—the first applied to conventional respect for the changes and the latter to less traditional approaches. The thing worth noting is that the private or esoteric is referred to as "outside," the public or exoteric as "inside." It's as though music were the ground on which one guts every fixed assumption, chants it down (like the Rastafarians say) by turning its insides out. Yet what happened on the mall, I think, shows that simple inversion finds itself invested in the very assumptions it sets out to subvert. Were the cops in some occult way summoned by my own misgivings, my alarm at the concern I felt with who'd reach the Upper Room first? Unless revolution, as well as taking an upward turn, makes for a lateral displacement (a stepping aside from whatever one thought "upward" and "downward" meant), the road ahead doesn't seem to hold much in store beyond running in place. In other words, what Earl Zero says is true: "Where there's a wheel there's a turn." But until we get dizzy with it, dervishly and devilishly dizzy, we'll forever be stuck in the same old rut.

As ever,
N.

17.IX.80

Dear Angel of Dust,

Sorry to have taken so long to answer your letter. I've been meaning to write for some time now but one thing or another managed to get in the way. I've been very hard at work, for one thing, finishing up "The Slave's Day Off," a tape of which I'm sending along. I also have to admit that I was surprised and a little put off that you took what I was saying in my last letter to have anything to do with being an "alienated artist" in some romantic sense. I would think you'd know better by now. One can, I think, speak of alienation without making a romance of it. In Kenya, when the English took land away from the Masai, the Kikuyu and the Kamba to give away to white "settlers" they referred to it, believe it or not, as *alienating* the land. Neither a confession nor a sadistic joke (and certainly not romantic), this use of the term turns out to be perfectly correct. Alienation, I'm trying to say, is something people do. (And certain people have done it more than certain others.) I've said it before and I'll say it again: The last thing I want our group to become is a lonely hearts band.

I was also uncomfortable with your throwing so trendy a word as "history" around as you do. I hate to say it, but you sound like one of those critics who seem to fear that anything any of us do could somehow escape being "history." I keep wondering whose "history" it is you're talking about. I like your notion of "history as a manner of speaking," but when you accuse me of "trying to outshout or shut history up" I detect a sense of it not as a language but a lexicon, a fixed primer of permissable terms in which the tongue is either broken or embalmed by prohibitions. (A not very "historical" sense of the term, in other words.) In fact, I could go even farther and argue that what we're up to is hyperhistorical. Just the other day I heard a talk by Sun Ra in which he proposed a spelling of the term "word" which speaks, I think, to this point. He suggested "w-e-r-e-d" as a truer spelling, that "word," one might say, is the past tense of "were," an exponentially archival coefficient. Relatedly, I think of such things as scat, where the apparent mangling of articulate speech testifies to an "unspeakable" history such singers are both vanquishers and victims of. This carries back, of course, to what I said about the moan and the shout a few letters back, so I won't belabor it here. I will, however, add that one can hear the same sort of thing even in reggae, a scatlike gargling of "meaningless" sound in the singing of, among others, Burning Spear. Listen to "Jordan River" or, even better, the "live" version of "Man in the Hills," where you'll hear a kind of yodeling and even birdcalls about halfway thru.

This all bears more or less directly on "The Slave's Day Off." You'll notice, for example, the raspy, non-essentialist quality in Djamilaa's voice. This we got by having her sing with a piece of waxed paper about a fourth of an inch in front of her lips. Though the lyrics contained very few words in the usual sense, I wanted to guard even further against possible lapses into illustration, to give the thrust of her singing a dispersed, ventriloquistic edge. It's as though one answered the question "What was it really like?" by suggesting there's no "really" when it comes to "was"—as though the voice came out of a throat filled with bits of string.

Anyway, I hope you like the piece. My steel drum playing, I admit, has little more than a coloristic function, but my clarinet solo at the beginning of section three has to be one of the most inspired I've ever played. The feeling I had was that I wasn't there, that the "I" which was was an "I" which wasn't my own. If it strikes you as overly dissonant please remember the old saying: "The more you hear it the more harmony it has."

Sincerely,

N.

27.IX.80

Dear Angel of Dust,

The past few days have been somewhat strange. We've been having a heat wave and there's a big fire burning up in the hills east of Malibu. You can see the flames from the freeway in fact. The temperature's been above a hundred for six days in a row and we've also been having what're known as Santa Ana winds—very dry, hot winds which, according to local legend, drive animals to bite at the air and people to behave in odd, often dangerous ways. I have to admit I'm beginning to believe in such lore. Night before last Djamilaa told me she was feeling very edgy and asked if I'd spend the night with her. She's been getting phone calls lately where the caller hangs up as soon as she answers. She's also been hearing noises outside her apartment late at night. I said yes, so we enjoyed a peaceful, uneventful enough evening listening to the Qawwali tapes a friend had sent from Pakistan. The heat didn't let up much as it got late, so even at midnight the temperature was in the low nineties. It was pretty much impossible to fall asleep. We ended up watching a Fred Astaire movie on the *Late Late Show* and eventually, somehow, managed to doze off.

I don't think I'd been asleep very long, though, when I felt a soft tapping on my shoulder and a voice which turned out to be Djamilaa. She was sitting up and leaning over me somewhat, whispering my name so as to wake me up. She had cramps in her stomach, she said, which were keeping her awake. Would I sit up and keep her company, she asked—which, of course, I agreed to do. I suggested, after a while, that a joint might relieve the pain, and so proceeded to roll and then light one up. It didn't take many hits, however, to see that the grass was having the opposite effect. She bent over a bit, clutching her stomach with both hands, and let out a moan which sounded like a cross between Bessie Smith and Om Kalsoum. Her eyes, which had closed at first but were now open again, got a more and more vacant look. Her moaning finally tapered off into broken bits of speech, delivered in a voice which only vaguely resembled her own. She had just given birth, she said, to the dreadful realization that she and I were the true Egyptians in the band, that Lambert, Aunt Nancy and Penguin were nothing more than provocateurs. What she went on to say alternated between mumbled, incoherent digressions and loud, clearly enunciated rants against "the enemies of Ra." For some reason I turned to look at the alarm clock on the bedside table. It was just past four o'clock. A sort of throbbing emanated from the clock like successive waves of a concentric dawning. I felt like I was being slapped. I recalled having read in one of the Coltrane biographies that this was the traditional time for meditation, known as the Hour of God, that it was at this hour, in fact, that Coltrane had died. It was then that I felt a dizziness hit, a feeling like smoke building up at the base of each eye. To steady myself I took hold of Djamilaa, who at that moment was mumbling what sounded like "Death to Set's lackeys." My dizziness cleared somewhat.

My reaction may strike you as odd or exaggerated, but consider the events in whose wake this was taking place. Two nights earlier, on the twenty-third, we had all gone out to celebrate Coltrane's birthday. We went up to the Sunset Strip, which was packed with people out to escape the discomfort of staying indoors, the heat being what it was. We ate carrot cake and drank herbal tea on the patio at a restaurant called The Source. Afterward, as we were getting into Lambert's car, a fellow with dreadlocks came up and asked if we had any change we could spare. Lambert pulled out a dollar and handed it to him, at which point the dread's eyes fixed on Djamilaa in the backseat. He stared as though he knew her from somewhere. He went into a tirade to the effect that the Santa Ana winds were "the hot breath of Jah come to burn bad Babylon down." He told Djamilaa that she didn't know that he knew her but he did, that she would have, as he put it, “more babies than you bargained for.” With that he took off running down the Strip.

The other weirdness happened to Penguin. I don’t know if I’ve told you before, but Penguin dj’s a late-night program on KCRW, a pretty together radio station over in Santa Monica. Two nights before the run-in with the dread he discovered on finishing his show at three o’clock that he’d left his keys to the station building at home. Since his is the last show of their broadcast day (and by that time of night he’s the only one left in the studio), it’s his job to lock up the building when he leaves. The locks on the doors, though, are the type that don’t lock by themselves, the type that you have to lock with a key. So, having forgotten his keys, Penguin had to leave without locking up. He was afraid someone might come into the building, he says, but finally had to figure that the chances were pretty slim. Plus that, he really had no choice but to either leave or wait around for the woman who does the seven o’clock show. He thought of calling up the station manager but decided the slight risk wasn’t worth the bother of getting him out of bed at that hour. (They used to have an extra key in the studio but it got lost and was never replaced.) Anyway, he finally turned out all the lights and left. The spooky thing was that he got home to find that his apartment had been broken into. Someone had gotten in thru a window and made off with his receiver, his cassette deck and his speakers. The turntable they’d tried to take as well but had evidently dropped it. It lay on the floor with its tone-arm broken.

Now getting back to the night before last: Once I’d gotten my composure back we got up, at my suggestion, to make a pot of tea. We walked to the kitchen with our arms around one another’s waist, Djamilaa addressing me as “sweet Osiris” in a now soothing, now distracted voice. When we got to the kitchen I began to heat up some water and then made the mistake of turning the radio on. What came on was that Marley song “Natural Mystic,” the one where he says, “There’s a natural mystic flowing thru the air”—hardly what I needed to hear at that moment. I turned it back off right away. I got the tea made before too long and we sat there sipping it, Djamilaa calming down and becoming more coherent as we quietly talked. After about an hour things seemed to be back to normal, so we decided we'd get some sleep. We slept well into the afternoon, after which, while eating lunch, we were able to laugh at what had taken place.

But these matters are not, I find, that easily put aside. I came across the phrase "phantom objectivity" in a book not too long ago. It refers to a situation, if I've got it right, where we find ourselves haunted by what we ourselves initiate. Is it possible, then, that the alarming sense of a conspiracy aroused by the things I've been describing—such apparently orchestrated events—amounts to a projection of what we're up to in music? The word "orchestrated" would appear to suggest as much but there's also the base meaning of "conspiracy" as a "breathing or blowing together." (Forgive me for resorting to etymologies again, but therein, I'm convinced, lie the roots of coincidence.) What I'm trying to explore is the extent to which the spectre of conspiracy, not so much an omen as a foregone conclusion, may well be indigenous to the notion of a band.

The word "band," of course, can't help but carry overtones of "bond." What most stays with me of all that occurred in fact (the note on which I'd end if this were a song) is the feel of Djamilaa's arm around my waist and of mine around hers. Something so plain yet so poignant about it. As though intimacy and intimation were thus wed to one another . . .

As ever,

N.

13.X.80

Dear Angel of Dust,

Maybe you're right. Maybe my sense of intimacy/intimation, my notion of omen as a self-embracing ordeal, does easily lapse into solipsism. It does run, as you say, a certain risk of reduction. But it's not that I want to bring experience down to an automated ghost of itself, to make the world out to be a tautology or in some other way deny its extensity. I suppose I got the events I was reporting mixed up with certain questions concerning form I've been wrestling with lately. One way to state it would be to say that I'm troubled by the apparent fatalism intrinsic to form, the threat of a conservatism the centralness of "form" to "conformity" seems to imply. Music got pulled in not only because I'm a musician but because of the longstanding tradition that uses musical form as the symbol par excellence of a cosmic status quo, the so-called "harmony of the spheres." Any such harmony, if it exists, does so at our expense I'm convinced. This led a drummer I once had beers with in a bar to say that if the harmony of the spheres ever came near him he'd "pop it upside the jaw." In this town you don't have to listen long to realize that the music coming down from on high can't be heard for the noise the police helicopters make.

So it was less a sense of confirmation than that of a dare which led me to write as I did in my last letter. I resent but also feel the challenge of a situation in which law and order invokes a musical alibi. I hate it when things become so pat as to be oppressive. In fact, I got a dose of my own medicine by way of a dream the other night. You'll recall that at one point in "The Slave's Day Off" there's a passage that echoes "Love Theme from Spartacus." I worked it in so as to accent the slave motif. There was also, I have to admit, a certain sentimentality at work. The tune harks back to a woman I was much in love with years ago. Yusef Lateef's version of it on oboe was one of her favorite pieces. I once gave her the album on which it appears for her birthday, *Yusef Lateef Plays for Lovers.* Anyway, night before last I had a dream in which I was a poet. I was giving a reading before an enormous crowd of people inside a domed arena. Instead of reading poems, though, what I did was sing an extended version of "Someone to Watch Over Me"—Arthur Prysock's rendition of which I was greatly taken with while in my teens. I tried my hardest to sing it the way Prysock does. I was doing all right too, until I got to exactly the lines which had been my favorites when I was nineteen: "Although I may not be a man some / Girls think of as handsome / To her heart I'd carry the key." I tried to imitate Prysock's touching, ever so sensitive delivery, but my voice repeatedly broke as though I were entering puberty. I rebegan the lines, going back to "although" over and over again, but could never make it all the way thru. The dream faded into something else with me coughing as if to clear my throat and the audience beginning to fidget and getting more and more impatient.

The point was pretty hard to not get. Even before I awoke I knew I was being chided for the "Spartacus" licks. Even as the dream was still in progress I knew I was being advised against a threat of excess, that I was being warned against sentimentality as a possible lapse into (to use that word you seem to like so much) overdetermination. I was being accused of stacking the cards or gilding the lily or however else one might want it put. I awoke to the even more radical realization that it's not enough that a composer skillfully cover his tracks, that he erase the echo of "imposition" composition can't help but be haunted by. In a certain sense, I realized, to do so only makes matters worse. The question I was left with, of course, was: What can one do to outmaneuver the inertia both of what one knows and of what one feels or presumes to feel? There must be some way, I'm convinced, to invest in the ever so slight suggestion of "compost" I continue to get from the word "compose."

I don't claim to have come up with a solution yet. I've been listening a lot to Pharoah Sanders's solo on the version of "My Favorite Things" on *Coltrane Live at the Village Vanguard Again!* The fellow who wrote the liner notes quotes Trane as having said that he was "trying to work out a kind of writing that will allow for more plasticity, more viability, more room for improvisation in the statement of the melody itself." That may well be what I'm after as well. What gets me about Pharoah's solo is the way he treats the melody toward the end of it, coming on to it with a stuttering, jittery, tongue-tied articulation which appears to say that the simple amenities or naive consolations of so innocuous a tune have long since broken down. He manages to be true to the eventual debris of every would-be composure. (Think about the movie the song is taken from.) It's as though he drank water from a rusted cup, the tenor's voice such an asthmatic ambush of itself as to trouble every claim to a "composed" approach. To me it borders on prayer, though prayer would here have to be revised so as to implicate humility in some form of détente—an uneasy truce or eleventh-hour treaty—with hubris. Part prayer, part witch's brew.

What I'm trying to say is that Pharoah's solo points to the possibility of exactly what I'm after. I should quickly add, however, that "exactly" may not be all that appropriate here. I don't have time to go into certain aspects of Pharoah's tone, a somewhat hovering, hivelike quality whose buzzings make a virtue of "imprecision." I don't mean to make a fetish of uncertainty but I did hear a woman on the radio say something that Pharoah's solo, albeit implicitly perhaps, is in agreement with. She was talking about scientific research into the nature of consciousness. What she referred to as "the catch-22 of consciousness research" she explained by saying that "if consciousness were simple enough to be understood we'd be too simple to understand it." That may be putting it a bit too glibly of course, but it's a thought worth considering I think.

Sincerely,

N.

14.X.80

Dear Angel of Dust,

I hardly slept at all last night. I was so worried about how you'd react to what I said about "imprecision" in yesterday's letter that it wasn't until five o'clock or so that I finally dozed off. The plan which finally put my mind at ease was that I'd get up this morning and make it over to the mailbox I put the letter into last night. My intention was to be there waiting for the postman when he showed up for the nine o'clock pickup. I thought maybe I could talk him into letting me have the letter back. But getting to sleep so late screwed everything up. What happened is that I ended up oversleeping, not waking up until well after eleven. By then, of course, the postman had already come and gone. So I'm doing now what I guess is the next best thing–writing to elaborate on the "virtue of 'imprecision.'"

You should notice that I put quotes around the word "imprecision." I hope you know by now that I don't mean to suggest anything sloppy, haphazard or inept, but to avoid any possible misunderstanding I'll go into it more deeply. The term "imprecision" is a relative one, a paradoxical measure of the discontinuity–the lack of any one-to-one correspondence–between two incongruent, albeit overlapping approaches to intonation. Maybe an illustration will help. Djamilaa's been teaching me some of the fundamentals of Moorish music in Mauritania, which is divided into three principal styles or "ways" known as the black (*lekhal*), the white (*lebiadh*) and the spotted (*zrag*). Within each of these "ways" there's a sequence of several different "modes."

I'll quote from the article she gave me: "A 'mode' in Moorish music is not exactly what is generally understood by this term in the West. It is not only an outline whose limits are number, nature and arrangement of the intervals in relation to a preferential degree (modal pole). In the mode 'karr,' for example, there are notes pitched more than an octave away from the lowest modal pole which apparently have no homologue (by reducing the octave) in the lower register. The unstable nature of certain degrees, the wealth of grace-notes and the imperfect modal concordance between voice and instrument (where an accompanied song is concerned) are often serious obstacles in determining the actual mode, as it is understood in Western musicology." The writer goes on to point out, however, that Mauritanians can easily identify these "modes" when they hear a griot play or sing. What this means is that these "modes" are imprecise or inexact—i.e., "not exactly" modes—only in relation to an alien frame of reference.

The other thing I would stress is that "imprecision" relates in a non-pejorative sense where the parameters of expression have become too profound for anything other than a notional approximation. The distinction is between the notional and the notational. ("Notes is good enough for you people, but us likes a mixtery.") Nor can I forget that "notation" happens to rhyme with "location," or that the opposite of "locate" is "equivocate." What I'm arguing is that, to the extent that "precision" implies a Cartesian bias, the virtue of "imprecision" consists of its departure from an oversimplified grid constituted by eye-based discriminations. This gives us, I think, another way of talking about music as a spiritual calling. Let me quote from a book I've quoted to you before, *Sound and Symbol:* "The space experience of eye and hand is basically an experience of places and distinctions between places. The ear, on the other hand, knows space only as an undivided whole; of places and distinctions between places it knows nothing. The space we hear is a space without places." If you've heard Sun Ra's composition "Space Is the Place" you'll know that what's being advanced is a notion of spirituality as a holistic, dislocating factor whose itinerary, so to speak, endlessly undermines place in favor of space.

Likewise, in the gurgly, otherworldly sound of Pharoah's tenor we hear each "note" given what I call a spiritual quiver—a quivering, equivocating edge he makes waver the way a candle's flame wavers in a draft. (One hears something similar, by the way, in the way the Sundanese play their suling flutes.) It's as though the sound—not unlike a soul resisting incarnation—refused to be contained by any locatable, unequivocal point on the notational grid. In this it behaves like certain subatomic particles present-day physicists tell us about. So it's with both aural and scientific sanction that one says amen to the statement I found on an album of music from the Upper Xingu: "What the spirits say, which can manifest itself in a dream or through special techniques, can only be expressed musically. Music is addressed to the spirits, it goes toward them, the rhythms call the spirits, and the spirits' messages, summoned from the mythic time when spirits, people and animals were still indistinct, can only be sung."

Sincerely,
N.

23.X.80

Dear Angel of Dust,

Do you remember the Boneyard Brass Octet? A few weeks back I mentioned the possibility of collaborating with them and a group called the Crossroads Choir. Well, I seem to be making some progress working something out with the Octet at least. I've had a number of talks with one of the members of the band by the name of Raoul. He plays trombone and I know him from a long way back. We tend to see eye to eye on a number of things. I've shared some of my compositional plans with him recently, particularly the ones which call for the collaboration I mentioned to you some time ago. He seems genuinely excited by the possibility and even invited me to sit in with the band over at Onaje's the night before last. He said it might be a good idea to "ease our way into this thing," as he put it, not jumping into a fullblown orchestration involving all three bands but starting off with me getting a feel for the seemingly simple but tricky terrain the Octet tends to explore. The set, he said, would begin sometime after one o'clock—an afterhours gig. He grinned as he told me to bring along a toothbrush and an overnight bag, that there was no telling how long we'd be away.

The Octet mainly deals in moody, low-register voicings, so I decided I'd sit in on contrabass bassoon. In addition to Raoul there's a fellow named Abdul and another fellow named Rasul on trombones. The band also includes two trumpeters by the names of Dewey and Tyrone, a tuba player who doubles on electric bass by the name of Rashid, a conga player who also plays organ and calls himself Shango, and a drummer whose name is Dilip. I'd been reading Ives's *Essays Before a Sonata* a few days before the gig. I was struck by and basically agreed with his idea that music is the art of outrageous talk. ("The art of speaking extravagantly" is how he puts it.) Still, I was nowhere near ready for the sort of holding forth the Octet opted for. They have a way of finding their voice in the most out-of-the-way places. The entire set, for example, consisted of a single extended composition called "Bardo Thoroughfare." Their approach appears to be one of confronting themselves with an array of constraints which, by way of a finicky, almost fanatical syntax, they retroactively convert to the "higher ground" of an at once belated but anticipatory access to the most radical imaginable future. Always on the verge of disintegration, each "advance" turns out to have gone according to plan.

The piece opened up with Raoul, Abdul and Rasul playing a series of unison figures which sounded a lot like Tantric chants. (The quirky, apparently random transitions from figure to figure, together with the tight regimentality of the horns' keeping together, made for a pun in which "chants" might just as well have been "chance.") Each player covered the bell of his horn with the rubber "cup" of a toilet-plunger from which the stick had been removed. A tiny lavalier mike had been inserted into the center of each "cup," thus confusing mutedness with amplification. The result was a sound somewhat like a cross between a yawn and a sigh, though not without aspects of an arrested sob. There were in fact moments when something like a barrelchested whimper broke thru. In any case, the transitions finally subsided into a sustained, repetitive "vamp-till-ready." Raoul had once quoted me a statement on the use of repetition he'd read in a book on Caribbean music. A Jamaican woman, it seems, had remarked to the author of the book, "It don't make no matter how many times you sing it. You just sing it till it turn sour to your mouth." Thus it was that by the time the vamp had gone on for no telling how long I seemed to see the earth wrap itself in a skirt made of soured grass. It was an earth away from which I appeared to be floating—feetfirst, head grazing the ground, my nostrils wide with the smell of wet soil. My only chance of holding on thus consisted of grabbing the hem of the skirt made of grass. It was a hem which, once I'd gotten it firmly in both hands, I instinctively took into my mouth and began to chew like cud, the tart juices forcing my eyelids shut.

By now time was of course beside the point, my own bovine persistence with regard to the skirt the mirrored image of the Octet's "baby elephant walk." What I mean is that the trombones had been joined by the rest of the band, the vamp taken up with the ruminative patience of some lumbering beast. The staggered entrance of the trumpets made for a certain halo around the figure, something almost like a spray which if one were not "awake" would tend to overcome "sleep." But here "sleep" moved thru an atmosphere so absolutely one with its own hypnotic arousal as to activate an army of otherwise overt, albeit rhapsodized obstructions. Dewey, that is, came on with the sputtering eloquence (if not opulence) of a Bill Dixon, while Tyrone nicked one's ears with a knifelike pointedness worthy of muted Miles. The self-predicating ordeal of Dewey's Dixonian approach rubbed against the slickness of what Tyrone proposed, the result of which was a splintered voice which came off like an elapsed or elusive aspect of itself. Under their care the vamp grew to be poetically graced in such a way as to suggest that to adorn, whatever else it might also be, is to adore. It was some of the most heartfelt trumpet work I've ever heard.

All while this went on Dilip laid down a repeated bass drum to snare drum to sock cymbal figure which managed to be dirgelike, militaristic and funky at the same time. Rashid pumped away on tuba while Shango drifted in and out on organ in a way which had a definite "dub" quality to it. In fact the alternation between absence and availability, the evocation of something there but not there that one gets from "dub," was very much what Shango seemed to be after—a skeletal promise or a spectral insistence of a sort that the organ seemed to be played by a ghost. So extreme was the organ's power of suggestion that by the time Raoul nodded to me to join in I'd begun to see, as though with both eyes closed, a "posthumous," apparently premonitional vignette which entirely undid all my reservations as to what I could possibly add to the piece. As though in a dream (though this was clearly not a dream), I saw myself at the wheel of a car in whose backseat my mother and my aunt were seated. We were heading west along a route I knew to be the one between Rodeo and San Francisco we used to take when I was a child. Something about the hills on either side of us recalled it, though I equally had the sense that we were on the ferry which used to carry cars across the bay. I heard my aunt ask my mother, "Have you heard from your mother lately?" I found it strange that, being my mother's sister, she'd refer to my grandmother as though she were my mother's mother but not hers as well. But there was something about the childlike, innocently demented way she asked the question which reminded me that my grandmother had died in July. My aunt, it occurred to me, hadn't gotten over it yet. I turned around to try to comfort her and as I did I saw a look of bewilderment on my mother's face as she stared at my aunt. It was a hurt look which seemed to ask, "How could you?" This vignette immediately replayed itself, the difference being that the question my aunt asked the second time was "Have you heard from your son lately?" As I turned around I saw the same look as before on my mother's face, at which point I vanished and the car continued on without me, my mother and my aunt in the backseat still.

I felt I'd been offered assistance of a sort I barely knew was there. I thought of you in fact. It seemed I'd only recently truly awoken to the reality of death, to the realization that my letters to you have been even more sincere than I thought they were. (I smiled as I recalled the period during my late teens and early twenties when I affectedly signed my letters "N. Ernest.") It was as though I'd fallen backward into an extravagant woodshed, a fantastic reservoir filled with time-tested riffs. "Devil or angel?" I asked, put upon by the strains of a popular song of that name. Novelty, I knew, was a pointless pursuit. My contribution to the piece, I decided, would amount to a discourse on mortality, the rough texture of which would tend toward complaint more than lamentation. I took the mouthpiece between my lips but before I knew it I'd blurted out two questions having nothing to do with what had brought me to my decision. "Who'd have thought the saints would show up wearing white sneakers?" I asked—whether rhetorically or not I couldn't have said myself. This I immediately followed by asking,

"Why do they serve the wine in what used to be jelly jars in the Tavern of Ruin?" Wonder, evidently, would not be denied its due.

To make a long story short I'll leave it at saying that we moved farther and farther out, sounding at times like a tarpit filled with bellowing beasts. At one point I heard someone in the audience whisper, "The Octet's out for blood tonight!" But don't get the idea that there weren't moments of great joy and, indeed, *jubilation*. (At times my bassoon even sounded like the ram's horn to which the root of that word refers.) I believe an historic (if not prehistoric) meeting of minds took place. We all, in one way or another, gave ground so as to extend all previous horizons. I can't help crediting myself with the fact that for the first time ever the Boneyard Brass Octet saw fit to go on playing once the sun had come up. In fact, I successfully insinuated that like so many Orpheuses we were the ones who had made it do so. (Up to then it had been their policy never to play while the sun was out.) It was going on noon when the piece came to an end.

Now if I could only hook up with the Crossroads Choir.

As ever,
N.

6.XI.80

Dear Angel of Dust,

Here'a a tape of a new piece we recently got together. It's called "Meat of My Brother's Thigh"—something of a sequel to that earlier composition "Third Leg of the Sun." I was moved to write it by an African myth having to do with Dieli, the ancestor of the griots. Lambert brought it to my attention. The story, though versions vary, goes basically like this: More years ago than any one mind can remember two brothers were making their way thru the forest. The younger of the two was seized by hunger pangs so intense he stopped and said he could go no further. "You'd better continue on by yourself," he told his brother. "I can't take another step. I'm almost dead with hunger." The older brother pretended to agree. He went on alone, but as soon as he was out of sight he ducked down behind a clump of bushes, took out his knife and sliced a piece of flesh from his thigh. He made a fire and carefully cooked the flesh, then went back to where the younger brother was. The younger brother eagerly ate the piece of meat. Once he'd gotten his strength back the two of them set out again. After a while the younger one noticed the bloodstains on his brother's clothes. He asked him how they'd gotten there but he got no answer. It wasn't until they reached the village that the elder brother explained to him what he had done, whereupon the younger brother vowed, "To save me from death you gave me the flesh of your own thigh. I shall henceforth be called Dieli and shall be your servant, and all my descendants shall serve your descendants."

The composition, as you can hear, is a duet between Lambert on tenor and me on bass clarinet. Lambert, when he told me the story, offered it to illustrate the ambivalence people feel toward the griot. (Dieli, he pointed out, is the name still used to refer to griots by the Fali of Guinea and the Bambara of Mali.) The picture one gets of the griot as something of a parasite, he suggested, reflects the contempt which complicates their admiration for the griot's talent. He pointed out that griots generally occupy a low position in the social hierarchy, that people fear them because they know so many secrets. "People don't like the griot," he summed it up by saying, "because he's got a big mouth." What most immediately spoke to me about the myth, however, was somewhat different though nonetheless related to what Lambert had to say. I've remarked before, you'll recall, on music as a quest or concern for kinship. (I have a record, by the way, by a band known as Brotherhood of Breath.) This particular myth would seem to agree with my point, given its younger brother/older brother configuration—to say nothing of the fact that part of what a griot does is keep track of genealogies, family histories and such.

But what spoke to me in an even more resonant way was this business of eating a piece of the older brother's thigh. I couldn't help recalling something I'd once either read or heard somebody say, to the effect that cannibalism is cultural behavior. Suddenly that word "chops" we musicians make so much use of took on an altogether larger, more ambiguous meaning. (This accounts for the "overblowing" Lambert and I resort to throughout the piece.) The taste I picked up sitting in with the Boneyard Brass Octet—the taste of a skirt made of soured grass—hadn't left my mouth yet (and still hasn't left it in fact), so a flow of astringent, vaguely hallucinogenic juices accompanied my musings regarding the term, the myth and their interrelated implications. I felt I'd hit upon a paleo-appetitive impulse, an aspect of the angel or agent indigenous to the jaw—an impulse whose archaic structure makes the angel its more or less captive, oddly involuntary tenant. (Notice Lambert's interjection, a third of the way thru the piece, of a number of licks reminiscent of Eddie "Lockjaw" Davis.) I tried to have certain notes take a downward turn throughout the piece, a tendency to slide in the direction of flatness as though the note had gone sour. I hate to burden the piece with "explanations" but my sense is that the slur of such legato figures embodies a fugitive tendency toward self-effacement, each articulate sigh the elegiac witness to an emergent abscondity not otherwise to be known.

But now I've gotten into matters I'd best let the music "explain" on its own. I'll add in closing, however, that the occult clamor you can hear throughout the piece was made by a chorus comprised of Djamilaa, Aunt Nancy and Penguin. It's too bad they got recorded so poorly. Pretty much impossible to make out on the tape, the words they repeat are these: "Day so hot and me so hungry did it. Said I couldn't take another step."

As ever,

N.

12.XI.80

Dear Angel of Dust,

Just a note to accompany the tape I'm enclosing—a new version of "Meat of My Brother's Thigh." Right after sending you the tape of the earlier version I came across something which extended the piece's conception somewhat. It turns out there's a Yoruba proverb which goes: *A ò lè b'ára 'ni tan, k'á f'ara wa n'ítan ya.* The book I found this out from explains that there's a play between *'ni tan,* which means "related to each other," and *n'ítan,* which means "at the thigh." Translated loosely, the proverb, the book says, means: "Kinship does not mean that, because we are entwined, we thereby rip off each other's thigh." I found myself, as you can well imagine, seductively addressed by the contentious rapport between this and "Meat of My Brother's Thigh." It seemed I'd entered a cloud of lightly salted perfume, an effusive aura thick with offhand implication. Another way to put it would be to say that I'd again waded into waters in which one forever runs the risk of going under, waters deep with irreducibly primal concerns. The proverb seemed to be the tacit, contradictory motor which in its cautionary way, though unbeknown to us, had oddly kept us all afloat throughout the first version of the piece. It seemed to demand, in retrospect, that we not only do what we do but also *know* what we're doing—which is what gave rise to this new version I'm sending.

It could be said that with the Yoruba proverb—in particular the coaxiality between *'ni tan* and *n'ítan*—the piece had been given an alternative ground. Keep in mind, however, that the ground is simply something one works up from (a "root" which has already been dug out by the time it's even thought to be available as such). Throughout the piece one finds the music actively and unremittingly heterospecific. You'll notice, for example, that one of the additions I've made is a quotation from Shepp's tune "Hambone." My appropriation of these licks, however, reaches *thru* Shepp's piece to take hold of a recollection from when I was about six. My brother Richard, together with some friends of his, took part in a Boy Scout talent show. They did a group version of "Hambone," which, as you may already know, is a sort of streetsong in which one slaps one's thighs as rhythmic accompaniment to such lyrics as "Hambone, Hambone, where you been? / 'Round the world and I'm goin' again." The incident sticks in my mind partly because of my mother's surprise and apparent embarrassment that they would not only dare to put this forth as *talent,* but do so publicly and in front of white folks no less. She talked about it for weeks. But that's a story I can't go into right now.

What I mainly wanted to say was that right before we began playing Lambert said to me, "Let's do our best to *lean* as much as we can with the music." It's not unlikely, I think, that some such positioning relative to a suspect, unappreciative Other indeed amounted to the embarrassed, atavistic ground up from which (as though one repeatedly sought to erase one's indecision) a rippling, outward-moving set of rings began to mount by way of the loose, wobbly spin of an earth out of joint.

Yours truly,
N.

PS: A few years ago an acquaintance of mine from the Gambia, seeing the title "Hambone" on Shepp's album *Fire Music,* pronounced it "ŏm·bō′·nā." He told me that in his native language (though I can't recall now which one it was) this means "Let us sing."

6.XII.80

Dear Angel of Dust,

Your letter arrived this morning. Thank you for your encouraging remarks. I'm glad you like "Meat of My Brother's Thigh." I especially took to what you say about "outward embrace compounded of inbred refusals." Funny you should ask about the Crossroads Choir. I've been meaning to update you on my attempts to make contact with them, to let you know that I in fact did so the other night. Not that it was the easiest thing in the world to do. I spent several weeks asking around regarding their whereabouts, only to be told again and again that they'd "gone underground." No one I talked to was willing to discuss it any further than that. But two nights ago I received a phone call from someone who refused to identify himself. He said that if I wanted to meet with the Crossroads Choir I should go alone, on foot and carrying the horn of my choice to the summit where Stocker, Overhill and La Brea come together. This I should do, he said, at half past midnight and once I got there blindfold myself and wait. I would be picked up and from there taken to where I'd, as he put it, "be allowed the audience you so deeply desire." I tried asking what the point of all the cloak-and-dagger business was, but he cut me off by emphatically repeating, "Alone, on foot and with the horn of your choice!" And with that he abruptly hung up.

I suppose it's a measure of a lack in my life that I went along with this arrangement. In any case, I did. I decided on bass clarinet as the horn I'd carry along and once I got to the summit I blindfolded myself as instructed. I turned my coat collar up to the wind but the wait turned out to be short. Before I knew it I was being helped into the back of a van which had just pulled up. Once inside, I made a move to take the blindfold off but was told to leave it on. The van pulled away and I was given a tasteless, odorless liquid to drink. The trip took maybe an hour and a half I'd say, though it's hard to be exact as to how long. We seemed to move across an undulatory terrain in which ups were immediately followed by downs and vice-versa. It was hard for me, in fact, to keep from getting sick. The liquid I'd been given to drink induced a sense of immersion, a watery submission to the elements at large in which every wrinkle of wind, however slight, fluttered like wings or splashed like a swimmer's limbs. There was something baptismal about it, an invoked or in some other way sought-after thirst for shipwreck, a sense of having sunk. There was something Brazilian about it as well, a Bahian fisherman's tenuous truce with the sea. My sense was not so much one of having run aground (the van was clearly moving along smoothly), but of a "diet" I'd embarked on whereby my stomach fell into the pit of itself, its would-be floor falling away in an abrupt, breathtaking onslaught of vertigo.

The airiness of every previous disposition now made itself felt. It was as if the collision course or crash diet I'd embarked upon deserted me at the edge of a body of thought whose bitter, lawless beauty only led me on. Shunning every eventual advance, the road ahead brought me to the realization that I had never actually seen or heard the Crossroads Choir as such. My knowledge of their music, I couldn't help seeing, had to do with its having always been, as the expression goes, "in the air." It was with a merciless, missionary clarity I saw now that the Choir was an anonymous, axiomatic band whose existence had always been taken for granted. I suspected this was the only way it could be "taken" at all, even though to see it so made my pilgrimage seem absurd. Moist with the sweat running down my face, the blindfold projected an illusory pool of reflection in the seemingly sunlit distance ahead. The asphalt ribbon we'd set out upon, pursuing a watery promise without aid of an actual sun, brought the night to life with a kind of furry moisture (a feathered moisture in fact). Every pinpoint droplet of mist interacted with sweat, making for a velvety, somewhat salty compartment of blind, irretrievable flight.

When we got to wherever it was we'd been heading the van came to a stop and I was helped out and led thru a number of doors, the blindfold still in place and my horn, in its case, still in hand. We went from the damp outside air into a place whose air was warm, dry but oddly humid at the same time. It was the humidity of breath and bodies I knew at once, hearing the collective, incoherent murmur of what was obviously a crowd. My escorts sat me down at what turned out to be a table, one of those tiny round ones one sits at in niteclubs. It was all right, one of them told me, to remove the blindfold now. Having done so, my first impressions of what I saw were mixed and, in a certain sense, without definition. Whether this was the effect of the odorless, tasteless liquid I'd been given to drink I can't say for sure. What I can say is that I was struck by the indeterminate character of my surroundings, the variable aspects of which refused to settle into any solid, describable "take." One moment it seemed I was in an intimate niteclub, the next a domed arena with a seating capacity of thousands. One moment it seemed I was in a cramped garage (the sort of place Ornette's band used to practice in during those early days in Watts), the next a huge, drafty warehouse in Long Beach or San Pedro or some place like that. One moment it seemed I was in a cathedral, the next a storefront church. The possibilities seemed to go on without end. I was "everywhere," which, I now knew, was nowhere in particular, a blank check drawn on a closed account.

In keeping with this, the crowd was faceless and of a variable aspect all its own. I looked around, a bit disconcerted by the blank, laconic stare I met on every rounded, "metaphysical" head. It was as though I'd stepped into a de Chirico canvas, the crowd composed of hairless, mannikinlike men and women, each of whose face wore itself like a tight, tautological mask. The smooth, more or less featureless flesh which enveloped each head contrasted dramatically with the faces of the band which had begun making its way onto the stage up front. The band's faces appeared to suffer from a surplus or an overcharge of features—etched, it seemed, with every crow's foot or expressive crease to which flesh had ever been prone. Fold upon fold, line upon line and wrinkle upon wrinkle gathered, one moment suggesting the Assyrian god Humbaba, whose face was built of intestines, the next the Aztec rain god Tlaloc, whose face consisted of two intertwining snakes. The band, which could only have been the Crossroads Choir, partook of an elastic, variable aspect equal to if not greater than that of the audience and the structure (whatever and wherever it was) in which we were gathered. Their entrance threatened to go on forever—a slow, numberless stampede, as it were, of musician after hyperbolic musician which made me wonder whether the stage could hold them all. It seemed they were every band I'd ever heard or even dreamt I'd heard all rolled into one.

Their rolling entrance did at last come to an end. They were a motley group of an uncountable constitution, one moment seeming as intimate as a trio, the next as large as eight orchestras combined. The audience had been applauding throughout the time they took coming onstage, the applause subsiding once the entrance came to an end. At that point one of the bass players, the apparent leader of the band, stepped forward and spoke into one of the microphones. He thanked the audience for their applause, then announced that the first number would be a piece he'd written called "Head Like a Horse's, Heart Like a Mule's." He described it as an Indo-Haitian Sufi nocturne based on a line from the *Upanishads:* "The pressing stone of the soma press is the penis of the sacrificial horse." The band came on with a somewhat tortured but robust keening, reminiscent of the choked, almost Korean insistence of the opening ensemble passage in Joseph Jarman's "Song for Christopher." It was a wild, inordinate avalanche of spirit which caught me offguard. I was suddenly ridden by the band's capitulation to ancestral fury, a horseheaded sleeper robed in cardiac stitchings who stubbornly brayed as if begging for love in a pirate's world.

Such a sense of myself I'd nourished only in private (or what I thought was private), unassailable, or so I thought, within the vascular walls of a fool's paradise. But the band had wasted no time going for the audience's jugular, laying claim to blood and to kinship ties as though they mined us for gold. It was risky turf on which they staked their claim, veins liable to be loaded but most likely yielding only fool's gold, as they themselves must have known. "Better fool's gold than no gold at all," they seemed to insist—a conviction after my own quixotic heart. Still, there was a thread running thru much of what the flute had to say which took a much more tentative approach. "Fools rush in," it warned, entering into an exchange with the rest of the band. Disregarding the equestrian character of the band's obsession with bittersweet sevenths, the flute insisted on referring to them as birds. "Dear Birds," I heard it say, my head cocked at an angle, "See sun in the shadow, yes, but also turn it around. Be alert. Beware." On a less obvious level, of course, the exchange was no more than a set-up, a rigged appropriation of any would-be rider's misgivings or doubts given the feathered horse the band had become. Nevertheless it was the unobstructed body of love their exchange addressed, a pneumatic equation whose antiphonal factors each exacted an abrupt, unlikely gift of itself.

After several bars had passed and the rest of the band pulled back the flute continued on, a cappella. It was a solo whose impromptu structure somehow built upon the rags of its meager technical resources. Slaptonguing the lip-plate while fingering the keys, the flutist resorted to certain percussive effects whose goal seemed to be to do away with themselves as such. It was a technique Rahsaan used to make use of, but here it seemed condemned to cut its teeth on longing. In fact, the flutist went on to quote from "Serenade to a Cuckoo," the piece Rahsaan did on *I Talk with the Spirits,* giving it a veiled, agitational touch as of an Islamic perfume, humming and even talking as he played. Though it insistently announced its theme to be the "bliss of eternal becoming," the solo, with equal insistence, veered toward complaint. An extended note of regret having to do with "wasted youth," once admitted, took root like a dragon's teeth.

Just as I began to weary of a sloganizing strain which had crept into the solo (a syllogistic bent betrayed in advance by a host of "sculpted," "architectonic" preparations), the flutist did something which brought the crowd to its feet. At the end of a warbling, birdlike run reminiscent of Dolphy, he leaned forward and whispered across the lip-plate into the mike. “As for me,” he muttered, “who am neither I nor not-I, I have strayed from myself and I find no remedy but despair.” With that all hell broke loose. Everyone immediately rose, some of the crowd even standing up on their chairs, applauding, yelling, whistling, pounding tables and stomping their feet in approval. Off to my right I saw one man break two glasses on the edge of his table, set them up again and bring the palms of his hands down on their jagged rims. He then held his hands up for everyone to see, moving toward the stage to stand directly below the flutist, his bleeding hands up in the air and the blood running down his arms—a token, he seemed to be suggesting, of his appreciation.

It took me a while to realize that I too was standing. The flutist, egged on by the audience’s response, for one extended instant fulfilled the most radical, far-reaching dreams of the otherwise oppressed. Opting for folly on the one hand and philosophy on the other, he extracted a bare-bones, hungry sound from the flute. An almost clandestine appeal, its claim was that were there no call the response would invent one. It was at this point that numerous bits of broken glass imbedded themselves in my forehead, each of them the seed of a low, breathy growl which seemed to emanate from the stars. The bits of glass had all the feel of something heavensent, but an angular, trigonometric intrigue born of airtight recesses gave rise to a traumatic, anticlimactic unpacking of the fact that it was the windshield of my mother’s car when I was eleven which was, after all, their source. In a flash, I heard the screeching of tires and felt myself thrown forward, the car ramming the rear of the one in front of us, not having stopped in time. I went weak in my legs for a moment, the people on either side of me taking hold of my arms as I began to go down, easing me very gently back into my chair.

The bits of glass went on to instigate a prolonged, problematic meditation on a theme which up until then had been only tangentially touched upon. Could it be, each and every laserlike sliver of light gave me reason to wonder, that the pinpoint precision of any breakdown of the tribe made for an obsessed, kaleidoscopic rift in sound, the audible harmolodic equivalent of a certain impingement or pungency? Could the piercing, punchy use of brass one hears in salsa bands be the proof of this or at least a usable case in point? How would one then, I went on to ask, build outward from "pointillisticity" so as to account for the dry waterfall effect of what was at that moment coming out of the flute? And what about rescue? What, that is, could free the future from every flat, formulaic "outcome," from its own investment in the contested shape of an otherness disfigured by its excursion thru the world? My thoughts then took a somewhat different course. The fertile bed of glittering bits of glass had become an oasis, an agonizing mirage whose momentary splendor threw me back upon myself like a gun going off. A shadowlike report which, as it turned out, was the band coming in as the flute solo ended, inducted me into a dance whose disjointed aspects embraced an untested need I felt to investigate fear.

It was evidently a need I shared with others, for at that moment the tenor player stepped forward as the band made a quick transition into one of the most dangerous standards around, "Body and Soul." If you know the expression "teardrop tenor" then you've got some idea of what the sound was like. It was a rendition filled with a vulnerable regard whose rhetorical supports telegraphically "fell" so as not to be seduced by a possibly naive, no longer available eloquence. These rhetorical supports, meant to bolster up an unforced, free-standing truth (or what purported to be one), made for what I can at best only approximate by the phrase "liturgical ambush"—a self-inquisitive instrumentality which feasted on sorrow. On one level at least, the band arraigned every attempt to make a virtue of sorrow, not only plumbing the depths of an allegorical exhaustion but unwinding a parable, more or less, having to do with first and final things. The tune, as you know, is a showpiece for tenor, and the tenor man rose to the occasion with an almost lethal brilliance. To say that he chewed it up and spat it out, as the expression goes, doesn't even come close. There was a New World extravagance to what he came up with, an endlessly caressive ritual of adoration, a grammatology of touch. What came to mind was the way Shepp does Ellington, or Sonny Rollins on, say, "Everything Happens to Me." Then again, there was some altogether other stuff he mixed in with it which absolutely blew me away.

The bed of glass just behind my brow again began to throb as the piece went on. A rippling sense of *surge* complicated by *sway* had made its way into the music. The tenor man continued on in what had become an essay (a manifesto even) assaulting the notion of "everyday life," concocting a long, breathy, sinuous line whose hoarse exuberance he thinly laced with a sort of erotic dismay. I leaned over and asked the man sitting next to me (the crowd was now sitting again) were my ears playing tricks or did I hear something Egyptian running thru the solo. He whispered back that he heard it too, going on to attribute it to what he referred to as the tenor man's "herbal sanction," saying that backstage between sets he'd seen him puffing on a "sherman"—which, he went on to explain, noting my puzzled look, is a joint soaked in embalming fluid. This might also explain, I suggested at once, the vicarious octaves he'd apparently added to the tenor's range, the solo's "phantom" reach. "Precisely," he whispered in agreement, nodding his head, as we both turned our attention back to the music.

The tenor man's face had become a sweating mask by now. A tight-lipped howling nursed an otherwise awkward ascent whose ritual insistence took us under its wing as if rooted in threadbare follicles of light. At the height of its powers—part rant, part psalm, part put-on—the solo took an abrupt yet understandable turn, its eventual cadences hissing and flaring like sodium dropped into water. A chemical wedding whose unlikely fruit bore the brunt of an exquisite, disquieting cross between Albert Ayler and Jr. Walker, the lyrical bridge the tenor embarked upon immersed us deeply in a sirenlike, wide-eyed whine. Possessed of an unkempt sandpaper texture suggesting a monochrome rainbow, each line invested itself in variegated gradations of black, each esoteric thread belatedly managing to harvest the raspy nothingness of a comet's tail. The crowd by this time had begun chanting one of the lines from the song, crying over and over, "My house of cards had no foundation." It was a chant whose edgy confession became a fleeting wisp. As if subject to dust which refused to settle, it was a fleeting wisp of nothing so much as the wish to be there as well as elsewhere, everywhere at once.

I opened my mouth to join the chant but no sound came out. For some reason I couldn't get beyond the title, on which my thoughts locked as on something so axiomatic it left nothing more to say. At the same time, though, it was the very wellspring of what was being said. The realization hit me that here was the sweet, sour, somewhat acidic hollow in which what was spoken belied the mootness of what might better have been intoned, as if certain prohibitions against belaboring essentials made for an ulterior permission. "Body and soul," I muttered under my breath, taken aback by the relevance of these words yet again, but the abrupt renewal of such an apparently pristine relevance formed a lump in my throat. Building up to become a faint, unpretentiously drawn sadness, it was a lump which ironically confirmed my vocation, the vacated premise of an image of change I thought I'd one day grasp. But such a skeletal body of hope was not to be taken hold of nor taken lightly, even though the wildest, farthest reaches of spirit ran like an engine thru the blank but eloquent chambers of the heart. "Body and soul," I managed to mutter again, as though intoning a prayer too close to the heart to be put into words. No matter how much I cautioned myself against it, I couldn't shake the feeling that the lump had become a lozenge, so soothing and at the same time so sweet it gave my mumbling the sugared, ethereal sound of a children's choir.

As I began to muse on the borrowed voice I'd somehow contracted I became aware that I was being escorted toward the stage. I hadn't been able to help noticing the leader of the band pointing towards me from behind his bass, this evidently being a sign to the invisible ushers who helped me out of my chair. Still weak in the knees from the bits of broken glass, I instinctively grabbed hold of the case containing my bass clarinet as I began to move forward. It took me no time at all to realize that I'd been summoned, that I was now being given a chance to sit in. The opportunity both excited me and gave me cause to be wary. The tenor man was still deeply into his solo, blowing an insanely beautiful tremolo figure which, as did everything else, made his "act" an almost impossible one to follow. It was then that it occurred to me that the emotional cramp I'd felt in my throat might very well have been a dowry. I saw myself as a "bride" by way of whose wedding what had been confirmed was—how can I put it?—a vocation for longing. It was nothing less than a calling brought about in such a way that one nursed a sweet-tooth for complication.

Now I knew for sure that my heart cried out for obstruction, a realization which evolved into warnings I fought against in vain. It was as though it did so in order to exercise itself, to assert its beauty (a muscular beauty it seemed) in relation to resistances the world put up. However simplistic it seemed to put it so, I felt as though longing had long ago wearied of its ostensible objects, keeping itself alive by way of the obstacles it met. There were other sides to my meditation, of course, but by this time I was already onstage, horn in hand, trading fours with the tenor while trying to make sense of the tempo changes the leader introduced. I'd begun with a sly breathy phrase which, however gruffly it started out, ended up as a sigh. It was a begging off from the possible hubris of going on, as if I shrugged my shoulders by way of asking, "What more can I say?" The sigh was an ode, an elegy and a confession all at once. I felt depleted and put upon. I rummaged around in the horn's lower register, buying time, though I knew this wasn't getting me anywhere. It wasn't ideas or feelings I lacked so much as a focus, a door by way of which to broach what I thought and felt. "Body and soul," I reassured myself, keeping close to the head but unraveling a line which progressively tutored itself on hope.

It was shortly after the tenor man pulled away and left me all to myself that a plea I'd have never predicted could issue from the horn did exactly that. A paradoxical plea, it had the quality of a koan, lecturing all who'd listen on the hopelessness of hope while at the same time indicting the presumptuousness of despair. What had taken place was that I'd had no other recourse but to resort to my recurrent appeal to a long lost, distant love, my memories of whom, to this day, refuse to fade. With infinite, greedy tenderness I embroidered the line with the tale of this obscure love affair, a seven-day romance I had ages ago with a woman I met halfway around the world. It was a whirlwind affair, love at first sight, proposing impossibly wide horizons and laying claim to only the most unlikely prospects. With painstaking patience I sketched every detail of our initial encounter, thrown back upon that oldest, ever available sacrament—rites of seduction. The featurelessness of the crowd before me made my recollection of her face all the more poignant. Sounding as much like Dolphy as I could, I tried to suggest the gamy brightness of her eyes, the freckles to the inside of her cheekbones, the dimples below the corners of her mouth. I went on to elaborate as best I could, filling in the portrait with such details as the tiny star of an earring she wore, the curliness and cut of her hair, the generous pout of her slightly jutting mouth to which I'd been so drawn. Wrestling with the limits of the horn, I did what justice I could to the press of our bones and the snug, thrusting fit of our flesh, the enduring, wicked sting of the carnal rites whose plunge we took. I resorted to a melismatic bending of notes by way of evoking the gamma flood we felt in one another's arms.

The basses, appropriately enough, sustained an ominous, throbbing ostinato, the ironic donor of a heartbeat, growl and sob whose message was unmistakably clear. It had been a love, they reminded me, doomed from the very start, condemned to the crib and crypt of its promise (as love perhaps always is), an aborted or stillborn flight whose foreboding their throb so insisted on. They softened their line somewhat to allow that we'd been victims of circumstance, our love a case of mistaken identity perhaps (though they couldn't resist throwing in that such was almost always the case). I instantly ratified their suggestion, finding it the basis for the beautiful, squawking eloquence to which the bass clarinet's upper register lends itself. I admitted that, yes, we had both no doubt felt orphaned by the circumstances we attempted to flee, the inert familiarity of the lives we were doomed to return to, half an unmoved world apart. It was an image of global anguish, global desire and global ennui I resorted to, the meeting of promise with paradox, universal deadend. It was apparently an image which got to the crowd, for at that moment something miraculous happened. Not only did the audience come to their feet, as they had during the flute solo, but their heads all of a sudden acquired features, welcome wrinkles and expressive lines they hadn't had before. I went on playing, amazed and encouraged by what I saw, even though many of the faces appeared grotesque and distorted, recalling the twisted, misplaced eyes, teeth, noses and lips of New Guinean masks. A gambler against my will, I'd gone for broke and won.

Still, the brevity of our seven-day romance all but made me weep. It took every mystical consolation I could muster to keep from breaking down. I attempted, for example, to think of our week together as the seven days of Creation, recalling Messiaen's idea (come upon in some liner notes I'd recently read) that the seventh day, God's day of rest, prolonged itself into eternity to become an eighth, a day "of unfailing light." The seven days had gone by so swiftly, I reflected, but the eighth, which we now inhabited, would never end. The last day we'd seen one another now returned, but with a new sense of lingering access—once a day of parting, now a day of repose. I relaxed into such a sense of it, deepening its consolation with a meditation on the number eight. "Upright infinity," I whispered into the horn. It occurred to me now, as though I'd never seen it before, that the eighth note of every octave is a return to the first, both end and beginning. It made me think of Lébé, the last of the eight Dogon ancestors, also said to be the oldest, which would make him the first. I reflected on his having died and become a snake, a fact I referred to with circular breathing in a run which also brought Ouroboros to mind.

The crowd had started singing again. "My life revolves about her, / What earthly good am I without her? / My castle has crumbled, / I'm hers, body and soul." The band came in on the chorus and as the audience sang a ball of light bounced from syllable to syllable as in the singalong cartoons we saw at the movies when I was a kid. I couldn't help thinking of it as a ball of cabalistic light our week-long courtship had sparked, a promise of one day overcoming division. It was both a ball of cabalistic light and the blank, bouncing check I'd gotten inklings of earlier. I knew I'd come home to the heart. I opened my eyes just in time to see that the ball was in fact a balloon the crowd was batting about among themselves, each person tapping it ever so lightly to keep it aloft. It was a white balloon on which, written in black, were the words “Only One.” Finally a woman tapped it with a sharp flick of her finger, sending it toward the ceiling. It rose with ever-increasing speed, taking my breath away, only to come down even faster.

Yours,

N.

2.1.81

Dear Angel of Dust,

I'm writing from a hospital bed. I'd have written sooner but I haven't had the strength. It was only a week after the last letter I wrote that I began to be put upon by dizzy spells—relapses or attacks brought on by the bits of glass planted in my brow by the Crossroads Choir. This time around they feel more like shattered cowrie shells than bits of broken glass. I think of them as tightfisted imprints, fossil imprints. (I'm struck by the mouthlike, eyelike look they have when whole.) I think of them as a mute but somehow musical motif having to do with thwarted fire, confirming a dizziness intrinsic to the earth but with bedouin roots in the sky. One of the striking things is that at the onset of each of these attacks I hear Ornette's version of "Embraceable You" piped into my head like a subcortical muzak. You might think of the spells, then, as animistic sculpture—a whirling, cranial dance of disinterment whose evasive embrace outmaneuvers an all too seizable, all but self-cycling ordeal. I tell you this because the doctors don't yet have a name for my affliction.

I've been here for almost three weeks now. They've put me thru test after test but don't even begin to have a diagnosis yet. This is only appropriate to my condition it would appear—a wheeling, drenched or drunken intensity in which aberrant flight answers aberrant fall. The attacks tend to come on as an inverse gravity in which I'm cut loose from every anchoring assumption, a giddy index if not an indictment of a tipsy world. I feel it as a weightlessness, a radical, uprooting vertigo, a rash, evaporative aspect of myself. The fear of simply floating away—

as though I were empty of all solidity or substance—overtakes me just before I either pass out or enter a kind of trance, my behavior during which I'm unable to remember once I return to normal. Apparently I'm put upon by peculiar cravings during these trancelike interludes. I'm told that on Christmas Eve I went into one in which I insisted on being given orange-flavored aspirin (the kind they make especially for children). It seems I was so insistent that, once I'd eaten eight of them and showed no sign of stopping, the doctor, afraid I'd overdose, sent a nurse out to get several packs of orange-flavored candy tablets. These, unbeknown to me, they then began to feed me in place of the aspirin.

Tangled up with "Embraceable You" I tend to hear my own heartbeat, amplified and coming at me from outside. It's as though the heart were a ventriloquist of sorts, throwing its voice at an ever more obtuse angle so as to exact an acoustical shell from the surrounding air. It's an eerie feeling to be engulfed by one's own heartbeat, put upon by the heat of one's own stolen pulse like a vulnerable flame palpitating in a draft. The heart's thrown voice, it seems, moves as a mutable window or a "mute" succession of windows, the transparent advance of an elliptical witness to a many-tongued yet unmentionable, all the more audacious truth. It appears to elope with each evaporative cranial kiss or breathy phantom caress as with an outrageous, caged or cagey embrace—caught up in the ache or the echoed report of its eventual extinction. It's as if the stolen pulse fed the amputated hand with which one might one day stroke the ribs of a ghost.

What I'm getting at might also go like this: *caressive* haunted by *corrosive* imprint; *imprint* haunted by *implicated* hand; *implicated* haunted by *complicated* haunted by *complicitous,* evaporative embrace; evaporative *embrace* haunted by vertiginous *imbalance* . . .

The circularity of some such vicious equation, I'm increasingly convinced, accounts for the dizzinesses I'm visited by.

I'll quit for now but as soon as I'm up to it I'll write again. I'd like to go on but I'm starting to feel a bit weak.

As ever,
N.

6.1.81

Dear Angel of Dust,

Thank you for the flowers and the get-well card. I seem to be doing a bit better, though whatever I've got still has the doctors in the dark. What with all the testing I'm beginning to feel like a guinea pig. There's even been talk of flying a specialist in from New York. The uncertainty's getting to be a drag. Still, everyone's been so thoughtful it almost makes being sick worthwhile. The band comes by to visit pretty regularly and my mother comes up from Santa Ana pretty much every other day. I even got a surprise visit from an old friend of mine named Derek whom I hadn't seen for two years. He teaches music out at Cal Arts and it turns out he's planning a symposium, at which he's invited me to give a talk. He got interested in something he calls "propositional positionality" a few years back. He was in a workshop run by Joseph Jarman at the Creative Music Studio in Woodstock. Jarman, it seems, turned to a horn player at one point and asked him to stand up and play something. The horn player stood up but before he could start playing Jarman stopped him, saying, "Wait a minute. Notice the stance. It's a statement. The instrumentalist as sculpture. *Notice* it. We usually take it for granted but we can *use* it." This clicked with an idea Derek had been carrying around for some time—namely that people weren't being precise enough in discussing Miles Davis turning his back on his audiences, that sufficient note had yet to be made of the fact that the angle at which his back addressed the audience tended to vary in relation to a host of contextual factors and coefficients. The upshot was that he set about quantifying and chronologizing—based on photographs, films, second-hand accounts and first-hand observation—the positional/propositional variables attendant upon Miles's posture, or, as he himself puts it, the "semiotemporal calculus of Miles's postural kinematics." He's published two or three monographs discussing his findings. Anyway, this developed into a more general interest in the "semantics of movement and posture," one of the results of which is the symposium he's planning for the spring having to do with "Locus and Locomotivity in Postcontemporary Music," the one at which he's invited me to speak.

Which brings me to the tape I'm sending—a piece of music from Chad. Aunt Nancy turned us all on to it one night a while back. It's a piece which continues to get to me, its acoustic trace tantamount to a chorus having cast a mounded shadow, a banked, elliptical silhouette. The somewhat harassed, exhortative quality of which it partakes, paradoxically enough, preens itself as though possessed of a certain unlikeliness, residually pregnant (or so it seems to me) with an implied poetics I hope to build my talk around. The piece is performed at harvest time among the Toupouri of the Fianga region in the southwest corner of Chad. It's played by a wind orchestra comprised of ten men, nine of whom form a counterclockwise-moving circle, at the center of which the tenth player stands. The ensemble varies the tempo of the music by altering the speed at which the circle revolves. Four of the players wear metal rattles around their right ankles, the sound of which, augmented by the calabash rattles held in the right hands of three other players, provides the rhythmic underpinning of the piece. The players perform on a variety of wind instruments, almost all of which, it's worth noting, make use of a calabash bell. The sole exception is the mandan, a straight, notched, four-holed flute made from a millet stalk. Otherwise, the horns are either straight or transverse affairs whose tubes are made of either animal horn, wood or calabash, to the end of which a calabash bell is attached.

I don't exactly know what I want to say about the piece. I'm not all that sure I can do justice to its impact or the implicit poetics to which I referred above. What I'm drawn to might have to do with how the horns, if I may put it so, traffic in fractures they otherwise alchemize or mend. I'm struck by the ensemble's insertion of itself into an oblique, etymologically understood algebra, the basic healer's way it has of embracing animal extracts (cow horns, goat horns and antelope horns), vegetable extracts (millet stalks and calabash gourds) and mineral extracts (iron rattles) in a single, heat-seeking gesture. The prominence of the calabash underscores the depth and thoroughgoingness of its investment in resonance—as though the whistling fissures, which, especially in the case of the flutes, equip the music for flight, danced on rickety limbs by way of whose telltale creaking the orchestra stalks itself. I'm not sure what I want to say about the piece, as I've already said, but it's pretty clear one might have it endorse the farfetched as an intrinsic edge on the far-reaching. I'm fairly convinced, for example, that the counterclockwise rotation asserts a solidarity with the far-flung heavens. Each player, looked at in this way, might be said to stand in for a star.

There's an aspect of this worth going into. Notice the mileage the lead horn gets from as few as two and at the most four notes. I'm reminded of Count Ossie's comments on Rastafarian drumming. He relates the sound one gets from a particular drum to the noise made by the animal from whose hide the drum's head is made. The repeater's head is made from the skin of a female goat, he points out, whereas that of the bass drum is made from the skin of a male. The ram, he explains, is less vociferous than the ewe and its bleat is of a lower pitch. Its hide is thus more suited for the bass. The ewe, on the other hand, bleats not only more often but in more strident tones than the ram, which makes her skin ideal for the soprano pitch of the repeater. I hear an analogous play between *beat* on the one hand and *bleat* on the other in the rhythmic, essentially percussive spurts to which the lead horn confines itself. I'm also reminded of a passage in Brathwaite's poem "The Making of the Drum." There's a point where he addresses the goat whose hide is used:

stretch your skin, stretch

it tight on our hope;
we have killed
you to make a thin
voice that will reach

further than hope
further than heaven . . .

The long reach of this beating drum, to my own heartfelt hearing, inhabits or is in some way invested in by the far cry of the bleating horn at harvest time. Stressing the role the piece plays in the harvest, I hope, helps emphasize what I mean by farfetched, far-reaching edge.

Something very peculiar intervenes to modulate these bleats into a sound as of a crowd's roar heard from a distance. My impression is that the lead horn is played by the man who stands at the center of the revolving circle. A commitment to pulling free of ceremonial stasis is there to be heard in the ostensibly centered yet in reality ripped, eccentric voice bled by the orbiting chorus of horns' centrifugal flutter. A would-be hub overcome by wobble one might call it. What gets me is the way this loss of alignment throws and then retrieves the voice, as though it installed or instituted a rift only in order to erase it. What it amounts to is a looped or ventriloquized harvesting by which the voice is no sooner flung than fetched. The orbit-induced hemorrhaging elicits an elliptical, precipitous halo—a poignant, protuberant illusoriness all the more stubborn for being under duress. (One calls it precipitous by way of noting that, "illusoriness" notwithstanding, its effects are no less audible or available, no less there to be heard.) Words waver in pursuit of such phenomena, but what I hear I'd call an arrested, half-naked sashay to the beat of a "thrown," syncopated pulse, an affirmation of the heart as abducted drum or an Orphic prompting, a plunge in search of outlawed fire. I've drawn a diagram which gets at much of what I'm saying. (See the sketch I've enclosed labeled "Deaf Diagrammatic Perspective on the Toupouri Wind Ensemble's Harvest Song.")

The diagram pretty much speaks for itself I think, with the possible exception of the Yawning Flock, which is only a more accurate way of referring to the "crowd's roar heard from a distance." The apt unlikeliness of such a "roar" confirms a dreamer's agenda: feathered sleep, vicarious flight, night's trunk of thunder under flammable cloth. The alarmed, allergic outbreak of sound—conceptually a shout but in actuality muffled by the padded impact of runaway hoofs—carries all the illusory nonchalance of a sculpted sigh. The question this brings us up against is the by now familiar one: How do we activate the wings implicit in so deceptive an air of resignation? The haunted side of which is this: To what extent does circumambulation tend to co-opt rather than cultivate a collective "roar" whose weariness borders on revolution? The very fact that one puts "roar" in quotes, of course, loads the question, but from a deaf perspective the line between yawn and roar tends to disappear. The position the jaws assume, that is, is the same in either case, as is the shape to which the mouth conforms—an oval, ellipselike extremity which all but indicts the elasticity of skin. How, then, do we awaken or unlock the roar so apparently sedated by a shepherded ennui? How do we harvest (i.e., mobilize) the lion?

The susceptibility of the Toupouri piece to any number of allegorizations (symbolic sociality, symbolic circumlocution, symbolic hollowness-musically-sculpted-by-breath and so forth) leaves me dangling as to which thread to pursue. I'm thinking of calling my talk "The Creaking of the Word," which is the name the Dogon give their weaving block. The sense I get from this is that a) we can't help but be involved in fabrication, b) a case can be made for leaving loose ends loose, and c) we find ourselves caught in a rickety confession no matter what.

I look forward to hearing what you think of the piece.

Sincerely,
N.

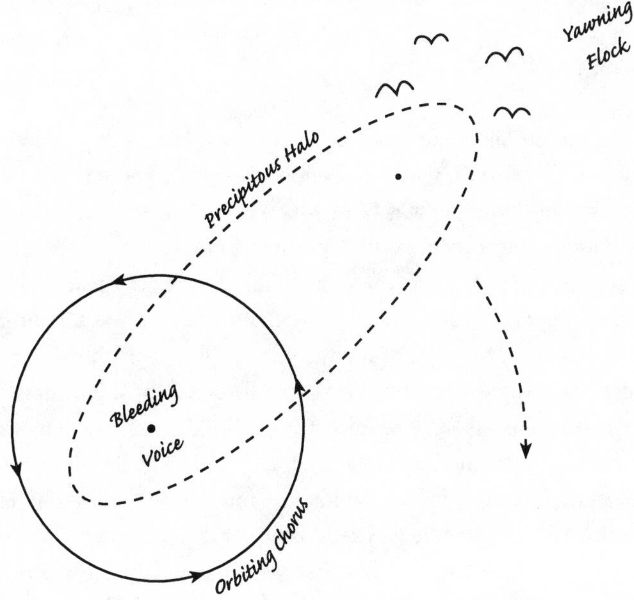

Deaf Diagrammatic Perspective on the Toupouri Wind
Ensemble's Harvest Song

19.1.81

Dear Angel of Dust,

Very subtle. The tape you sent had me puzzled for days. I couldn't hear what it had to do with the Toupouri piece. I knew it was Monk right away and I knew it was "In Walked Bud." I have it on a record in my collection. But it wasn't until I left the hospital and came home (details on that shortly) that I was able to look the record up and see that the tenor man on the date was Johnny Griffin. Thank you for agreeing with me. I hadn't thought of it so explicitly but, yes, when we really get down to it some "fabulous beast" would seem to be in order. Take a look at the lions on Marley's album *Exodus*. The red, green and gold banners they carry might as well be wings. I once heard a funny reggae number done by a group whose name I forget, a piece called "Haile Unlikely." And I remember a friend telling me of seeing Monk at the Both/And once. He finished his first set, it seems, by sliding off the piano bench, dropping to his knees and shuffling all the way across the room to the bar. At the bar, still on his knees, he looked up and growled at the bartender, "Gimme a drink."

As for my leaving the hospital, let me say first of all that my condition hasn't radically changed. I'm still subject to invasions or visitations, put upon from all sides by a whirlwind embrace as by an orbiting "absence" (half muse, half menace). The attacks occur less frequently these days but I continue to fall prey to a steep, receding but cerebrally embraceable threshold, an eroding precipice preyed on in turn by a lifelong thirsting after tenuous kin. I press the bits of shattered cowrie shell embedded in my brow and out of my throat comes an involuntary growl. At times the taste of a skirt made of soured grass returns to my mouth, an aftertaste or perhaps a Pavlovian anticipation I picked up the night I played with the Boneyard Brass Octet. My heart occasionally feels as though it grew wings and sprouted a beak, pecked a hole in my chest and flew out from underneath my ribs. Is this the symptom of a collective disorder or simply my lusting after impossible union? I ask because of a dream I had last week: I was in a hospital having my heart examined. I asked the doctor what were the chances of my having a heart attack later in life, recalling that my father had died of one in his early fifties. He answered that the odds were 400 to 1. The curious thing, though, was that rather than a heart attack he called it a "first strike." "The chances of a first strike," he said, "are 400 to 1." I immediately woke up.

It was only a day later that the band came by to visit and presented me with what proved to be—mute concert though it was—a therapeutic serenade. The four of them walked into my room just as I was finishing what could loosely be referred to as lunch (an assortment of ill-defined, pablum-like this and that on a fiberglass tray). Each of them carried an instrument—Penguin an alto sax, Djamilaa a trumpet, Lambert a tenor sax and Aunt Nancy a violin. With no ado at all, they stationed themselves at the foot of my bed and began to "play." That this was in a hospital, of course, meant they couldn't make any noise, so they contented themselves with going thru the motions of playing while making sure no sound came out. Lambert, Penguin and Djamilaa fingered their horns exactingly but barely blew into them at all. Aunt Nancy bowed her violin, seeing to it that the bow, however close it came, made no actual contact with the strings. I sat with my mouth open, the fork in my right hand arrested on its way up from the tray. After a few minutes I closed my mouth and lowered the fork, aware by now that being deprived of ears, as it were, had blessed me with unsuspected eyes. The mute concert to which I was being treated, that is, was nothing less than an inoculation in the clearest, most radical sense of the term. The silent music provided me with buds of possible vision I had no idea were there before.

I looked very closely at the four of them. I studied their movements, noting with ever more clairvoyant acuity every change in embouchure, minute detail of fingering and so forth. It took me a while but I came to see that what they were playing was "Embraceable You." I can truthfully say that I *heard* it in fact, so after my own heart was the mixed pace at which they took it (part waltz, part funeral march). It was like hearing my lush, longstanding absorption in "absence" at last harvested or come home to roost—a concert or a concept, as I've already said, after my own heart. The mute withholding imposed on the band by the surroundings made for a music fueled with a feeling of loss or lack. Aunt Nancy in particular, embellishing the head of the tune with asymmetrically placed flurries of strenuous bowing (not unlike the buzzing of an enormous fly), saw to it that the I/thou dialectics inherent in the song's lyrics bore demanding but exhilarating fruit. What she did came close to magic in fact, investing in the "charms about you / arms about you" rhyme in so convincing a way I felt I'd been laid on by a healing hand. I blinked my eyes, touched ever so lightly as by a winged, unquenchable kiss—brushed, it seemed, by feathers falling thru the dark (though this was a bright, glaringly sunlit afternoon). The horns went about the business of lamenting an elapsed enchantment, despairing of each and every past and present pair of arms by way of mourning what they insisted was only an ephemeral, futureless balm, the fleeting warmth of this or that mortal embrace. What Aunt Nancy was up to, however, had a way of converting their lament, endowing it with a measured, openly wishful unrest which, ripe with innuendo, piled caress upon remedial caress.

The horns, in other words, conceded the lead voice to the violin throughout the piece. As Aunt Nancy's bow stroked the air (possessed of a bizarre, brooding assurance that it was only a myth one lamented, nothing more), I was struck by the spiderlike dexterity with which she maneuvered its avoidance of the strings. What she did, one might say, was emphasize the dance in the word "avoidance," wrapping all who'd listen in the progressive windings of an eventual cocoon. The mute but audible web she secreted or spun further made for an ambiguous, mummylike bandaging effect—welcome relief, welcome resurrection, welcome-albeit-webbed embrace all rolled into one. My back stiffened as I sat there, more than slightly alarmed at Aunt Nancy's transformation from buzzing, air-borne fly to enticing, equally airborne spider. The overtones of worm-turning-into-butterfly only made matters worse. It wasn't that she pursued insinuation, as some would argue, at the expense of meaning. Nor was it that her "dance"—which, as she would be the first to admit, was mainly meant to be suggestive—ran the risk of amounting to nothing more than a tease. (This was the horns' deepseated contention.) What made me sit up and take notice was much less a matter of precept or principle than such ways of putting it suggest. The effect on me of Aunt Nancy's abrupt transformation from possible nuisance to outright enigma (from buzzing fly to wormlike spider donning butterfly wings) was much more physical or physiological than philosophic. I *felt* it work its way up my spine.

That the "silence" could be so compounded of implication injected a dizziness I sought to contain by sitting up straight. But a tingling had taken hold of my back, an intractable itch, it seemed, which rose to eventually expand at the base of my skull. Whatever it was, it rayed out as if to unwind or unravel—a nebulous, whirling, ever more far-reaching flare which, even as it unfolded, drew one further into the recesses of built-in resistance one barely knew were there, fold upon fold of ingrained immunity long taken for granted. Once the initial rush of uneasiness passed the very dis-ease whose holding pattern I'd been caught in successfully harnessed or, as it were, harvested itself. The tempo at which the four of them played the piece began to speed up. Their movements accelerated but lost none of their precision. The tempo moved from funereal-bordering-on-waltz to outright waltz to breakneck rag. It then moved into something even more frenetic (though still without any loss of precision), as much a matter of frequency as of tempo by now. It was like a 33 rpm record played at 45 gradually building to 78. One barely recognized the tune as "Embraceable You" anymore, the horn players' fingers and Aunt Nancy's bowing arm each a fast-moving blur.

It was like a spacecraft orbiting the earth gathering escape velocity. Everything went faster and faster and faster, building to an all-out, full-tilt, faster-than-ever peak—at which point the four of them simultaneously stopped and tucked their instruments under their arms. With as little ado as that with which they'd entered, they quickly and silently marched out of the room.

The following day I checked out of the hospital.

Sincerely,
N.

26.III.81

Dear Angel of Dust,

Just a note to let you know I'm still here. It's been so long since I last wrote you're no doubt wondering if I've abandoned you. Far from it. You've been much on my mind, as usual, but my time's been taken up entirely by one thing or another since I came back home. For one, those weeks in the hospital left me somewhat rusty and I've had to work at getting my chops up again. Most of my time these past weeks I've devoted to my horns. There've been days I've put in fourteen hours of practice. It's as though the cowrie shell pieces were seeds of sweat. I've been working, one might say, at learning to live with this condition. There must be a way, I believe, to turn it to the music's advantage. Already the pull between periphery and center seems to have given my intonation a bit more bite, an element of taunt conducive to curvature as well as interiority. What furrows any brow, I've begun to see, is an upstart vertigo intent upon pursuing an intransitive "crust"—abject, indomitable "beauty" endowed with aspects of camouflage. Which is also a way of saying that as well as practicing I've been working on my lecture, "The Creaking of the Word." (Have you, by the way, heard from Derek yet? I gave him your name as a possible participant in the symposium. He said he'd contact you.) On top of all this, the band's been getting more work than we're used to of late. We did a week at a place in Pasadena called The Little Big Horn not too long ago and the weekend before last we played three nights at Onaje's here in town. We also did a Sunday afternoon set at a place called The Studio a few weeks back.

One interesting development is that we're now thinking about adding a drummer to the band. This came about a few nights ago, largely by way of Lambert's rather oblique insistence. With his characteristic flair for the dramatic he telephoned each of us and requested that we meet at his apartment within a half-hour, declining, however, to elaborate on what he had in mind. This was at about a quarter of eleven. It took me about twenty minutes to get to his place. (It was a nice night out, so I decided to walk.) When I got there the door had a note tacked to it which read: "Had to step out for a minute. Come on in." I opened the door and stepped into the living room and saw that Djamilaa and Penguin were already there. He was sitting on the bean bag against the wall beneath the window. She was stretched out on the couch. The one thing different about the living room which instantly caught my eye was that the poster-size photograph of Duke Ellington which normally hangs on the wall facing the window had been replaced by a Dahomean appliqué cloth about half the size of a bedsheet. It was a red cloth onto which had been stitched bits of cloth of various colors and sizes making for the figures which are typical of these Dahomean pieces—animals, bushes, birds, men and women. The one atypical figure, however, was the dominant one, larger than any other and situated exactly at the center of the piece. It had been cut from a bright blue piece of cloth and the other figures more or less radiated out from it. It was a bit of notation, the rhythmic phrase ♩♩♩ ♩♩. Having gazed at it a while, I turned to Penguin and Djamilaa, both of whom shrugged their shoulders and said nothing. I sat down on the large pillow across from the couch.

It was about five minutes after I got there that Aunt Nancy arrived. Then five more minutes passed and the doorbell rang. I got up and opened the door and there was Lambert standing outside in a blue and red Superman costume, cradling his tenor with his left arm while saluting me with his right. I let out a laugh but he kept a perfectly straight face. It was as he stepped inside that I noticed that his outfit featured not the customary S but the figure ♩♩♩ ♩♩ emblazoned in red across his chest. Around his neck hung a saxophone strap and a piece of leather from which a nose-flute dangled. I sat back down on the pillow across from the couch as he proceeded to explain why he'd called us all together. He had a new composition he wanted to lay on us he said. Djamilaa looked at me and rolled her eyes as if to say, "We should've known," but my ears perked up when Lambert announced the new piece's title. He had decided, he said, to simply call it "Prometheus." He went on to explain that he'd never forgotten a passage he'd come across in his reading many years back which had said that Prometheus "stole fire from Heaven in a hollow tube." As far as he was concerned, he said, the hollow tube was a saxophone. With that he fastened the tenor to the strap around his neck, stood silent with his eyes closed for several seconds, took the horn to his mouth and began to play.

The piece began in a rather straight-ahead vein, its opening phrases built around an arpeggiated B-flat triad by way of which the most commonly accepted particulars regarding Prometheus were once again served up. Lambert was careful to begin with Prometheus's birth to the Titan Iapetus and the Oceanid Clymene, going on to make a point of the clever way in which Prometheus remained neutral during the revolt of the Titans, thereby ingratiating himself with Zeus. Falling back on a riff or two reminiscent of "Confirmation," he told of the grudge Prometheus nursed against the Olympians for destroying the Titans and of how he revenged himself by favoring humans at the gods' expense. (In a parenthetical aside that displayed a boplike reverence for the opening phrase's chord configuration, Lambert made reference to a rather late tradition which maintained that it was Prometheus who with earth and water—his own tears according to some, Lambert pointed out—had fashioned the body of the first mortal.) He took his time going into the well-known and oft-repeated details of the meeting at Sicyon. Zeus's anger at having chosen a pile of bones as his portion of the sacrifice, his decision to withhold fire from humans and then the trip Prometheus made to Hephaestus's forges on the island of Lemnos all came vividly to life with Lambert's more pronounced, more prominent use of Trane-inspired 16ths.

No detail was either left out or not gone into beyond mere mention. The academic, almost slavish thoroughness of Lambert's retelling of the Prometheus myth was nothing like his usual tendency to avoid the heavily travelled road—so much so, in fact, that I found myself at a loss as to what he was trying to do. I stole a look at Djamilaa, Aunt Nancy and Penguin and I could see that they too found what he was doing somewhat puzzling, to say the least. Still, we sat patiently as he told us how Zeus had sent Pandora as a "gift" to Epimetheus (he was quick to point out that her so-called box was in fact a vase), how Zeus had stirred up a flood to annihilate mankind, how Zeus had sent Hephaestus, Kratos and Bia to chain Prometheus to one of the crests of Mt. Caucasus. We continued to sit patiently even as he went on with the endless business of the eagle and the liver and so forth. But this turned out to be only a ploy. It was a way of setting what came after in relief (somewhat the way a boxer sets up his opponent for the knockout punch), for what followed stood what had gone before on its head. This became clear when Lambert threw in a quote from "It Ain't Necessarily So." He began to mine a radically different vein, as though he'd ripped a page, Bobby Womack style, from a street preacher's book. Indeed, what he went into was a streetwise rejection of conventional wisdom. *Street shaman* was now the mantle he wore. *Street priest.* Crudely put, his point—and he was not averse to putting it crudely—was that the story in its orthodox mold amounted to so much "bull."

If you've heard the Coltrane/Rashied Ali duets on *Interstellar Space,* Frank Lowe's duets with Rashied or Shepp's "The Magic of Ju-Ju" you've got an idea of what the mode he went into was like. In this case, however, the conspicuously absent drums conveyed a theme of contraband or confiscated fire, a dream of stolen thunder come true. Lambert sputtered, growled, spat, split notes, ranted, railed, bellowed and shrieked—all by way of maintaining that the Prometheus myth in the form in which we know it represents a classic case of "blaming the victim." With a gravelly, five-o'clock-shadow sense of maturity complicated by menace he argued that Zeus's apologists had deliberately confused causes with effects. It wasn't true, he insisted, that Prometheus had been chained to Mt. Caucasus as a result of or as punishment for having stolen fire. The truth, he contended, was that fire came into existence only after Zeus had Prometheus bound, that the inner combustion bred of bondage brought it into the world. Extrapolating from an inverted C-sharp seventh which lent itself to the pull of the earth, he made it clear that, quiet as it's kept, it was Zeus who stole fire from Prometheus and not the other way around.

Having made this point, he took the horn from his mouth and let it hang from the strap around his neck. He then reached into a pocket sewn into the inner lining of the cape he wore and pulled out a harmonica. Before blowing into it he raised his right forefinger and said something which, had I been walking, would've stopped me "dead" in my tracks. "To articulate the past historically," he said, "means to seize hold of a memory as it flashes up at a moment of danger. This danger affects both the content of a tradition and its receivers: that of becoming a tool of the ruling classes." I could hardly believe my ears. It sounded like a quote, but he neglected to name its author. He then put the harmonica between his lips. Before starting to play he was careful to turn his back to us. It was as though the harmonica were a sandwich or a piece of meat and he an African god. (In Africa it's considered taboo to watch a god eat.) In any case, once he'd turned away from us and stood bent over the harmonica in a posture suggesting privacy he began to play. The first thing he did was refer to an occult tradition which has it that the bond with which Zeus bound Prometheus was the "outer man." This "outer man," he suggested, might with good reason be thought of as Prometheus's brother—or, as he preferred, his "so-called brother"—Epimetheus. This, it turned out, was the last time in the course of the piece that Lambert would refer to Epimetheus by that name. From that point on he instead referred to him as Epidermis—his way of underscoring the point he went on to make to the effect that it was the "weakness of the flesh" which allowed Prometheus to be bound. He would leave it to us, he said, to reflect on the significance of Epidermis's failure to reject Zeus's "gift," his inability to "keep his cool" (Lambert's words) toward Pandora and her ambiguous "box."

All this Lambert conveyed by way of a harmonica style worthy of the Delta blues at its visceral best. He exploited the now concave, now convex hollow to which the harmonica lends itself so as to shape a lament which was in effect a compendium of every moan brought about by the ups and downs of desire, a plaintive theme having to do with having been "burned." In fact, the recurrent confounding of "burned" with "bound" would've by itself made the piece a *tour de force,* but Lambert's design was more ambitious than that. Accusing Zeus of collusion with "unclean spirits," he seemed at one point to borrow a phrase from Skip James's "Devil Got My Woman." It's hard to say for sure since there was so much going on, but I did seem to hear something meant to recall James's falsetto. The one thing I can say with certainty is that he brought the harmonica part of the composition to a close by alluding to yet another occult (or at least obscure) tradition—this one to the effect that one of the devil's nostrils tends to be unusually wide whenever he assumes bodily form. Moreover, Lambert pointed out, the devil will gladly open it even wider in order to allow one to peep in and get a glimpse of his brain. But the devil's brain, he quickly warned, is nothing other than the fire of Hell and if he can get you to take a peek at it he's happy, for with merely one look one loses one's senses forever. It's from this, he added, that we get the habit of saying that such-and-such a woman has such-and-such a man's nose open. He punctuated this last point by swiftly wheeling around to face us again, taking the harmonica from his mouth with his left hand while raising the nose-flute to his right nostril with his right, giving it a quick, somewhat comical toot à la Rahsaan, at which point Penguin and Djamilaa looked at one another and laughed.

The laughter made me turn and look their way. During the instant it took me to do so and then return my attention to Lambert he had taken the tenor to his mouth again and gone on from where the harmonica had left off. In going from harmonica back to tenor he went from grief, as it were, to grievance, from lover's lament, one might say, to slave narrative—to some extent erasing the line between the two. On returning to his Coltrane/Rashied Ali mode he began to rail against what he termed "the skin-game of history," though here "skin" had less to do with passion than with pigment. It was Lambert at his quarrelsome best. Zeus's binding of Prometheus on the basis of color was now gone into, Lambert no longer referring to Epimetheus simply as Epidermis but as "Epidermis, the so-called brother," laying the stress of a colloquial understanding on the word "brother." Nor did the fact that it was Mt. Caucasus to which Prometheus had been chained escape his analytic scalpel. He invited us to reflect on the meaning of this detail by asking, "Could Mt. Caucasus have been the 'racial mountain' that Langston used to talk about?" It was some of the most moving, thought-provoking music I've heard Lambert make.

I'm not sure I've made it sufficiently clear that what Lambert was up to was in no way, strictly speaking, a solo performance. The more or less overt allusions he made throughout to the Coltrane/Ali duets, as well as to Shepp's teaming up, on "The Magic of Ju-Ju," with a five-man percussion choir, had the effect of conjuring a rhythmic umbilicality, if you will, an implied polity or a mystico-accentual assembly dealing in alchemized, neo-Africanized "weight" (i.e., duration and pulse). The conspicuously absent drums, I mean, had a way of making their "presence" felt, giving yet another dimension to the concern with *skin* which was so inescapable a part of the piece. The ♫♩ ♫ emblazoned on the chest of the Superman suit, along with the one sewn on the appliqué cloth, brought this "presence" home even to those who might've somehow managed to miss it, doing so with a palpability beyond the reach of the otherwise ghostly, allusive means at Lambert's command. This palpable percussive absence accorded especially well with the slave-narrativity of this part of the composition (as, in retrospect, the "academic thoroughness" to which I referred earlier as "almost slavish" also did)—inserting or availing itself of a rhyme, so to speak, between, on the one hand, Greek-mythological stolen and/or outlawed fire and, on the other, Black-historical stolen and/or outlawed drums, Black-historical stolen labor. With an Ayleresque ascending wail Lambert toyed with the refrain from "John Henry," having us understand that the master/slave dynamics conducive to "combustion"—to which he also referred now as "profit," now as "stolen thunder"—was the brooding, deep, repressed but mushrooming truth of the Prometheus myth.

It was a devastating note on which to end. The wail twisted and curled and seemed to writhe in the middle of the air. I could've sworn I heard a drumroll hold it aloft. Be that as it may, Lambert now took the horn from his mouth, removed it from the strap around his neck and set it down on the stand which sat by the end-table near the couch. Penguin was the first to respond. He let out a short, approving, appreciative chuckle, brought his hands together with a single clap and, after glancing at the tenor near the end-table, exclaimed, "Yes indeed! Somebody light him up another one right quick!" Djamilaa and I laughed and a grin came onto Lambert's face. He was well aware that he'd come up, so to speak, with a "hit." I extended the open palm of my right hand and he ceremoniously slapped it, thereupon extending his own so that I could do the same. Djamilaa meanwhile had gotten up and taken the hem of his cape in her hands and stood examining it with squinting eyes and wrinkled brow. Lambert turned and asked her what she was doing. "Just looking for scorch marks," she said, shrugging her shoulders. Penguin and I broke out laughing again. She then went on to add that, all kidding aside, she'd been deeply moved by the piece's "calibrated fire," the fierceness of its joining of foresight with afterthought so as to endow itself with "structure by default." Lambert almost blushed.

I'd of course been deeply moved by the piece myself. In fact, I felt somewhat personally addressed, so much of it seeming to be the issue of certain conversations Lambert and I had recently had, especially while I was in the hospital. "Prometheus," that is, seemed to touch upon my own ongoing wrestling with a spectre of thwarted fire, my would-be coming-to-grips with the eventual "angel" of Black-historical stolen harvest, Black-historical sweat. I was just about to share these reflections with Lambert when it became evident that his attention had shifted and was now focused on Aunt Nancy, who sat quietly in her chair across from Penguin's bean bag and who had not, it abruptly dawned on Djamilaa, Penguin and me, taken part in our expressions of enthusiasm for the piece. She seemed to be sulking, in fact. Lambert asked her what was the matter. She was reluctant to answer at first, keeping her eyes on the floor in front of her and in a barely audible voice muttering that nothing was the matter and that, besides, she didn't want to bring everybody down. It was quickly pointed out to her by Djamilaa that she'd already done exactly that and that she might as well, having done so, go ahead and get whatever it was off her chest.

Aunt Nancy needed no more coaxing than that. She opened up by assuring Lambert that, aside from certain elements of spectacle which were not exactly to her taste but which she wouldn't go into (the Superman suit for one), she had found his piece extraordinarily beautiful, possessed of a "bold, voluptuous loftiness" and a "nervous conception" which had given her goose bumps at points. She went on, however, to say that she resented its implied attack on her, its allegation (muted, she allowed, but no less unmistakably there) that her increased involvement with the violin at the congas' expense over the past several months amounted to a betrayal of the band's identity, a disregard for matters of history and atavistic transmission. Djamilaa had sat back down by this time and Lambert had taken a seat, crosslegged, on the floor. He responded to Aunt Nancy by saying that he was genuinely sorry that she'd chosen to take the questions his piece had raised in so thin-skinned and personal a way, that it hadn't at all been his intention to indulge in scapegoating, fingerpointing or any such witch-hunting as that. He continued by saying that he was pleased, however, with the opportunity her remarks had provided him with, an opportunity to make his concerns more explicit, whereupon he proceeded to do exactly that.

Lambert went on at some length but what he had to say basically came down to this: He was no longer convinced that the band's "come-as-you-are" approach to percussion was the most effective. He granted that our practice of making everyone in the band responsible for percussive contributions on a variety of "little instruments" (bongos, shakers, tambourines and what have you) has a certain communal, democratic beauty to it. Still, he argued, he increasingly felt a need for a more assured, authoritative rhythmic presence, "a percussive anchor." The five of us were no more than novices and part-time workers in such matters, he said, and he was more and more of the opinion that a full-time percussion specialist couldn't help but work to the band's advantage. He finished up by asking wasn't rhythm the most essential, characteristic component of our musical tradition and didn't we therefore owe it something more than a makeshift treatment? Wasn't this the conclusion, he frosted his argument by adding, which had led the Art Ensemble to bring Don Moye into the group?

Penguin right away put in that Don Moye was Don Moye, which in itself was reason enough to bring him into any band. Having made this point, he went on to say that the more crucial point he wished to make was that the approach Lambert had referred to as makeshift, disparaging it on historical grounds, was not without historical precedent, not without a certain sanction from the past. He reminded us that in this country, unlike places like Trinidad, Cuba and Brazil, the drums had been taken away during slavery (a fact, he admitted, to which Lambert had repeatedly alluded in the course of "Prometheus"). This theft, however, he encouraged us to recall, had given rise to a tradition of oppositional, compensatory or, if we would, makeshift practices, a making do with whatever came to hand whose inaugural "moment" was marked by more emphatic recourse to such things as footstomping, handclapping and the-body-used-as-drum in general. (In an aside he remarked that he wouldn't be at all uncomfortable with the argument that the rite of slapping hands which had recently taken place between me and Lambert was nothing other than this earlier "moment" reasserting itself.) He took this "moment" to be the seed of such subsequent developments as the tendency to reinstate, as it were, the outlawed or abducted drum by taking a percussive approach to ostensibly non-percussive instruments. The examples he gave included a blues singer whose name escapes me drumming on the wood of his guitar, Cecil Taylor's much-quoted reference to the piano keyboard as "eighty-eight tuned drums" and the practice among present-day electric bass players of "slapping" the strings. To say nothing, he went on to say, of drumming on things which are not, conventionally speaking, instruments at all—Coke bottles, Quaker Oats boxes, tin cans and whatever else.

It was at this point that Aunt Nancy, getting the drift and eventual point of Penguin's argument, impatiently cut back in. What Penguin was getting at, she explained, was that the absence and/or presence of the drum could never be taken literally, that either was also the other as a genetically dislocated aspect of itself. This, she insisted, was the heterodox beauty of our conception, the hybrid (as against "highbred") pedigree of our percussive concept, the resiliency which made such retrieval as Lambert proposed altogether redundant, not to say absurd. The curious thing, she continued, was that "Prometheus" in its most impressive moments had given evidence of an intuitive understanding of this on Lambert's part but that in the rush to make ideological capital of these "dark advances" he had almost totally lost the subtle, dialectical "touch" which was their animating spark. The work itself, she contended, was in a sense more wise than him, eternally at odds, in its most authentic aspects, with the life-defeating stiffness of his interpretations and afterthoughts. Lambert, of course, refused to sit still for this, snapping back that if she insisted on confusing absence with essence they might as well kiss the conversation goodbye. She could revel in deprivation all she wanted, he said hotly, but, as for him, he was, as he put it, "fed up with scrounging around for roots." She was equally quick on the uptake, however, arguing that her point had nothing to do with essence but that she knew an *accident* when she saw one, that the quasi-political case Lambert had made for adding a drummer to the group was in the end nothing more than that—"inessential, expendable, eminently beside the point."

They did anything but kiss the quarrel goodbye. Quite the contrary. They rode it for all it was worth and for even more than it was worth, sustaining a volley of rapid-fire claims, quips and counterclaims whose back-and-forth intensity made the three of us who merely looked on—me, Djamilaa and Penguin—move our heads as at a tennis match. It was as though the quarrel became an end in itself, a dominant third party or factor on whose prolongation the two participants, kissing caution and sobriety goodbye, were irreversibly bent. They expended all the eloquence at their disposal, deploying and depleting every verbal resource. Before long their exchanges acquired a quirky, self-propellant quality which had a way of spiraling into areas not especially germane to the issue at hand. Aside followed aside, digression built upon digression, irrelevance intercepted irrelevance to the point where it became obvious that Aunt Nancy and Lambert had only the vaguest recollection of what had given rise to their disagreement. It had, in fact, been conceded by Aunt Nancy early on that she had no quarrel with adding a drummer to the band, that it was essentially the reasons for doing so Lambert put forth that she begged to differ with. The spiraling drift of the argument, however, had long since obscured this point, enveloping each of them in an ever more extreme, ever more intransigent, ever more uncompromising reaction to and refusal to hear the other. Neither of them was averse to contradicting him- or herself so as to stay at odds with the other at any point where an agreement seemed at hand. They both bowed religiously to the demands of a contentious, evaporative "curve," a volatile rush which would admit of no closure, speaking as though possessed by the spirit of contradiction. They weren't long in getting to the point where they both spoke at the same time, all pretense of listening to one another giving way to a forked, finally parallel flow of ongoing talk, the most intense, two-sided exercise in devil's advocacy I've ever heard.

The attempts Penguin, Djamilaa and I made to intervene were to no avail. At various points one or another of us tried either to resolve the disagreement, steer it on a more relevant course or, all else failing, simply change the subject. I tried, for example, to get Lambert to address certain questions which, in my mind at least, "Prometheus" had given rise to concerning the devil's dilated nostril. (I wasn't altogether certain who corresponds to the devil when someone is said to have another's nose open. Is it the open*er* or, so to speak, the open*ee* I wanted to know.) Aunt Nancy and Lambert simply went on, however, waving us off like so many flies or some other such nuisance. Penguin and Djamilaa finally gave up and got going on their own conversation, discussing the debut of Bobby Bradford's new band at a place called The Bridge to which Penguin had gone a few nights before. I sat there, torn between the two conversations.

I began to feel a slight dizziness but, beyond that, I can't say what it was that so abruptly came over me. The room, the occasion (Lambert and Aunt Nancy simultaneously talking while Djamilaa and Penguin went from Bobby Bradford to the Namibia situation to rumors of a new, soon-to-be-released album by Miles) seemed possessed of a rare polyphonic permission. Seeking to avail myself of it (and in some way compelled to avail myself of it), I asked Lambert would he mind if I tried something out on his tenor. He hardly seemed to notice me, turning distractedly from his debate with Aunt Nancy only long enough to say, "Go ahead," and then immediately going back to the point he'd been in the midst of making.

It was an odd compulsion, this business of picking up Lambert's horn. The tenor's not an axe I feel all that intimate with or fluent on. Though I fool around with it from time to time, something about it continues to intimidate me. No intimidation, however, stood in the way as I took the horn from the stand by the end-table near the couch. The four of them paid me no mind as I took the metal cover from the mouthpiece and took the horn to my mouth, wetting the reed with what had the feel of aboriginal thirst and aboriginal moisture, the deep enduring grip of a remembered kiss. I began by toying with the arpeggiated B-flat triad which Lambert had resorted to throughout "Prometheus" but soon surprised myself by getting a velvety, assured, heraldic sound, an annunciative "call" not unlike Sam Rivers's opening on Tony Williams's "Love Song." Penguin, Djamilaa, Lambert and Aunt Nancy went on with their conversations.

An odd compulsion indeed. The tenor was not only an axe but also a scythe in a reaper's hands. I was the reaper, even as I awoke to something having stopped, an echo of stunted growth. I awoke to the sound of obstructed movement (wood against metal, clouds against drought), awoke to the strains of a song long since concluded, snagged on a thought of having fallen or flown.

I hummed into the horn as I played. It sounded like a protest, a benediction, a poem and a pun. There would always be this dream of a deferred harvest, I seemed to suggest, a band of reapers hoisted skyward, spiraling thrust of a leavened earth. A dream of grain spiraling down from the heights, ears falling from Heaven. Rotgut dream of an eventual audience, wishfulfilling myth of someday having been heard.

There would be the coils, I quickly added. There would be the canals. There would be the ear's own answering drum. Inexhaustible dream of inextinguishable touch, of taking hold. Tangible husk out of which, as from an oven ("baked," a "bread"), a music like no other would emerge . . .

As ever,

N.

2.IV.81

Dear Angel of Dust,

Thank you for the tape. It's as though we shared a single set of ears. It's not only that I'd already heard the piece you sent (I have the record it's on, in fact), but it's the very cut I like most on the album and, to my hearing, one of the most awesome things Wayne's ever done. I especially like the way the soprano integrates itself into all that percussion (which is exactly, I realize, why you sent it). To the point, in fact, that toward the end of the opening instrumental section Wayne isn't so much playing the notes as pounding them out. I love the way he wedges what he puts forth between the bass and Chick Corea's nervous, timbaleslike tapping on the snare's metal rim. It's as though the horn had become an additional drum. In this respect it reminds me, now that I think of it, of the beating/bleating horn in the Toupouri piece. Beating/bleating horn-as-well-as-drum. I confess to a weakness for these amphibious, in-between, both/and advances into a realm which defies categorization, this way of trespassing, so to speak, the line which otherwise divides melody from rhythm, horn from drum and so forth. (There's a curious Korean instrument called the haegeum, a two-stringed fiddle whose timbre is so much like a horn's it's classified as a wind instrument.)

In the case of "Dindi," I can't help thinking it's the presence of the cuica, that weird Brazilian "friction drum," which goads or invites Wayne into this realm. It's a realm the cuica very much inhabits, given, as it is, to those vocal, often hornlike yelps so unlike what one expects from a drum. Goads or invites or *hounds,* I might've said, for I've always heard something canine in the cuica's now barking, now whimpering insistence—as though snarl and sob, ferocity and contrition, were each an ingrained aspect of the other. ("Contrite," you're no doubt aware, comes from a root meaning "bruised," the past participial form of a verb meaning "to rub" or "to grind." The cuica, as I've already said, is often referred to as a "friction drum.") How appropriate, then, that Maria Booker breaks down and weeps at the end of the middle section. Thus we have an overt, outright maudlin voice-and-guitar middle, on either side of which there's a polyrhythmic instrumental section, a more toughminded ensemble foray in which the cuica and the cuica-hounded soprano prominently figure. What Wayne is doing is dealing in ambiguous, borderline mixes—running the borders, one might say. Not only melody and rhythm, horn and drum, but also wound and resistance, blister and callous, tearfulness and attack are by this "running" made to rub against and grind with one another.

These, then, are the thoughts which accompanied me to bed the other night. Earlier in the day I'd received and played your tape. It's not all that surprising that as I slept I was visited by a dream I have from time to time. It's a dream in which—less a fullblown dream than an abruptly there, abruptly ended "flash"—I find myself in the dark, facing a ladder at whose foot a dog sits. The darkness notwithstanding, the dog and the ladder are both easy to see, each as though it were lit by an intrinsic light. The dog sits as if guarding the ladder, crouched as if ready to strike. This it immediately does, in fact, springing up and going directly for my face, at which point I wake up, the echo of its growl and the lingering image of its teeth still in the air. It was ten years ago that I had this dream for the first time. Since then I've had it three more times, the other night included. A few days before the third of its four visits, two or three years ago, I had a conversation with a woman with whom for some time I'd been very much taken. In response to her question concerning my feelings for her I replied with a single word: "Serious." Thus it was that, awakening from the dream's third visit a few nights later, I realized that the dog at the foot of the ladder was no mere dog but in fact a star—the dog-star Sirius. I realized for the very first time that the previous two times the dream had come had likewise been times in which a romance in which I was involved had begun to "get serious."

The other night I noticed a slight variation. During the split-second before its attack the dog sat with its head cocked at an angle, reminiscent of the RCA Victor trademark dog, listening, as the label says, for "his Master's voice." (As far as I can recall, however, there was no phonograph in sight.) Once I'd awakened I felt summoned—goaded even—by this detail of the dream. A new composition was being demanded of me I felt. It was a feeling I couldn't shake. For two days I worked as in a fever on the composition which is on the tape I'm enclosing. We recorded it at rehearsal last night, so it's still a bit rough. It's called "Dog-Eared Anacrusis." I'm on saxello, Aunt Nancy on congas, Lambert on harmonica, Djamilaa on oud and Penguin on cuica (though he prefers, on those rare occasions when he plays cuica, to be called Peixinho).

You'll notice that in this piece one again finds the band in an Egyptian mood. This has partly to do with the two "outside" or unaccented notes with which the piece begins corresponding to the "outside" or epagomenal days on which Isis and Osiris were born. (These notes the piece revisits throughout—an exemplary "reader" thumbing a dog-eared "book.") Sirius, as you know, was regarded as the star of Isis. Its rising at the time of the summer solstice coincided with the flooding of the Nile, whose waters were believed to be swollen by the tears which Isis wept in her lamentation for Osiris. These waters irrigated the bare corn fields and in doing so contributed to the return of the corn with which Osiris was identified as Osiris-Nepra. Thus Isis's maudlin, Magdalenic weeping led to the rebirth or resurrection of Osiris in cereal form. On the other hand, her loud lamentations upon opening his coffin in the royal palace at Byblos caused one of the royal children to die of fright.

This ambiguous or amphibious vacillation between life-giving lamentation on the one hand and death-dealing lamentation on the other led me to incorporate an analogous commingling of, respectively, major and minor keys into "Dog-Eared Anacrusis." You'll notice the preponderance of neutral thirds. My suspicion is that the ladder at whose foot the dog sits represents a scale. Whether it's a major or a minor scale I can't say. For this among other reasons I'd like to be visited by the dream again. This would give me an opportunity to ascertain whether the half-steps occur between rungs two and three and rungs five and six or between rungs three and four and rungs seven and eight. I'd have done so the other night but the dog was too great a distraction.

Yours,
N.

4.IV.81

Dear Angel of Dust,

It turns out that the Sumerians saw Sirius as the tip of an arrow shot from a bow which was made up of stars from Canis Major and Argo. They called it ^{mul}KAK.SI.DI, the Arrow-Star. In Persia it was seen the same way and known there as Tishtriya. A slight variation emerges when we move to India though, for there the star was envisioned not as an arrow but as the archer known as Tishiya. His arrow was made up of the stars of Orion's Belt. An even more drastic and dramatic variation turns up in China. Sirius there was seen neither as archer nor as arrow's tip, but as target. It was known as Tien-lang, the celestial jackal, and was aimed at by a bow and arrow made up of the same stars as in Persia and Mesopotamia. The arrow, however, was shorter. The Chinese view turns out to have been close to one that existed in Egypt, where the Round Zodiac of Dendera pictured the goddess Satit aiming her arrow at a star which sat between the horns of the cow Sothis, namely Sirius.

These particulars pertaining to Sirius were brought to my attention by Penguin-Peixinho. I pass them on as something of a footnote to "Dog-Eared Anacrusis." The star's association with the arrow, for example, might account, whether as tip or as target, for the extremely high (one might say piercing) notes, the wincing falsetto to which I couldn't help returning throughout the piece. More crucial though, I think, is the unconscious agreement between the piece's unresolved snarl/sob tension and the way in which, concerning Sirius, tip and target qualify and complicate one another. It's as if each high note were shot from a bow strung between two such extremes, its would-be escape diametrically tied to the very string from which it flies or attempts to fly. Though there appears to be a rifting endemic to global or would-be global perspectives, the discrepancy between Sirius viewed as arrow's tip and Sirius viewed as arrow's target has to do with something other than regional differences or geographic distance. (Egypt is closer to Mesopotamia than it is to China.) I like to think of it as a transitive identification of tip with target, a celestial union of subject and object by virtue of a taut, symbolically highstrung bow. A foregone conclusiveness bordering on tautology arbitrates the rift between aim and object.

Having said this, however, I hasten to add that one speaks all too easily nowadays of healing a rift or of bridging this or that chasm. I'm hopefully up to no such thing. There're only two things worth doing with a chasm: You either leap it or, failing that, you fall in. No such naive equation as "healing" and "bridging" imply has any lasting application. The true equation has a more numinous aspect. It won't sit still nor will it go away. If the phrase "arbitrates the rift between aim and object" brings a bridge to mind, you should make it an evaporative, self-retracting bridge, an endlessly negotiable construct or contract not to be glibly invoked or taken for granted. Thus the factor of *strain,* the sense of *shouldered weight* one hears in "Dog-Eared Anacrusis"—something Lambert refers to as a "migraine emotionality"—the exorbitant, tethered, yet-to-be-let-go *heaving* of a theme by Don Cherry I was able to reshape and thus work into the piece. It's from *Symphony for Improvisers* (Blue Note BST 84247), specifically the part called "What's Not Serious." There's no question mark in the title, but if Sirius is not only arrow, archer and target but (as Penguin points out) also identified with Pan, can we help wondering what, if anything, it isn't?

Yours,

N.

10.IV.81

Dear Angel of Dust,

Sorry you had to decline Derek's invitation. I'm sure your participation would have enhanced the symposium, which, as you know, is now set for the last weekend in May. I've finally arrived at a somewhat stable sense of the talk I'm scheduled to give, a draft of which you'll find enclosed. I've come to think of it, for reasons I'll perhaps go into later, as a metalecture. A number of threads recently came together and catalyzed its completion, not the least of them being a book Aunt Nancy's had us all read. More or less a footnote to the bone she picked with Lambert's "Prometheus," it's called *African Rhythm and African Sensibility* and it's by a fellow named Chernoff. Thumbing thru it casually (I can't claim to have really read it yet), I was struck by certain phrases and formulations which I could see had lent themselves to Aunt Nancy's odd, somewhat French-inflected sense of African drumming. Her preoccupation with "absence" and "presence" (more exactly with a coupling or a structured cohabiting of one with the other) no doubt recognized its pedigree in such passages as this: "*The music is perhaps best considered as an arrangement of gaps where one may add a rhythm, rather than as a dense pattern of sound.* In the conflict of the rhythms, it is the space between the notes from which the dynamic tension comes, and it is the silence which constitutes the musical form as much as does the sound" (Chernoff's emphasis).

I was even more struck by the point the book makes to the effect that polyrhythmic drumming implies an absent, additional rhythm, a furtive beat one's listening supplies or one's dancing echoes. Thus the phrases "hidden rhythm" and "unsounded beat" which recur throughout the book. That there's a theology underlying this point comes to light as follows: " . . . it is God's drum (Drum Himself) which beats the note that is never sounded." An interesting proposition emerges: Polyrhythmicity accents absence. It echoes or elicits an echo of what's not there. It's as though the beat which goes without sounding made the heart pound harder, as though each gap were only an endlessly altered fit. It's as though each fit were a self-mending fracture, the lost or collapsing survival of which makes for deferred, refractory thresholds of empty causation. Think of this in relation to the Dogon teaching that the drum's head represents God's ears. Remember that since God has no external ears, only auditory holes on the sides of his head behind which he cups his hands in order to hear, his ears, in a sense, are the palms of his hands. To drum is to slap hands with God.

What I gather from the notion of God as hard-of-hearing if not deaf (or God as mute, albeit "echoable" drum on its other side) is not simply the idea of *Deus absconditus*. The fact that the music moves from hand to hand—from drummer's hand to God's hearing-aid hand—might be a coded way of admitting that God's hearing, if not God himself, is handmade or, indeed, manmade, i.e., *produced*. One invents one's audience in more senses than one. Could the hand God's hearing lends itself be the very hand which beats the drum? The bearing this has on "The Creaking of the Word" should become apparent from even a cursory reading, so let me here go on to say simply that I've sought to accent the sleeping resources which persist as preconditions to a fallow but fertile ground (to a fertile but unfurrowed brow, that is), the supplement-soliciting plot of an only nominally inert conception. It's exactly here, of course, that prospect and problematic intersect, deepening the crisis to which they're brought by a need to perform the act they announce.

By now you're wondering how the Toupouri piece and the "Deaf Diagrammatic Perspective" figure into all of this. Let me say first of all that I see no necessary conflict between performative and constitutive modes. It almost goes without saying that each endures the risk of an appetite for meaning it tends to answer if not annul. It's for this reason that I've decided to speak *thru* rather than speak *about* the Toupouri piece and the "Diagrammatic Perspective." What I have in mind is a mixed-media presentation with the enclosed metalecture as a rickety centerpiece of sorts. I've decided to stone as many birds as I possibly can, my plan being to make this the occasion for the collaboration involving the Boneyard Brass Octet and the Crossroads Choir. In other words, I intend to accompany "The Creaking of the Word" with music performed by the three bands, the positioning and movement of which—of the bands, that is—will comply with the "Deaf Diagrammatic Perspective."

Using the "Perspective" as something of a blueprint or even an outline of steps for a dance, the distribution of "turf" will go as follows: Occupying the position of Bleeding Voice, I'll recite "The Creaking of the Word." Around me will revolve the remaining members of the band as Orbiting Chorus. They'll be playing a version of the Toupouri harvest piece which I've scored for bass clarinet, oboe, tenor and flute (respectively played by Djamilaa, Penguin, Lambert and Aunt Nancy). The Crossroads Choir, performing a multi-voiced version of "Opposable Thumb at the Water's Edge," will revolve elliptically as Precipitous Halo. Finally, the Boneyard Brass Octet will occupy the stationary position of Yawning Flock. They'll play a version of "Dog-Eared Anacrusis," highlighting Shango on congas and Dilip on cuica.

I haven't worked all the logistics out yet, but what I hope to achieve might be termed a coaxial ballet. What most needs working out is the mesh—not only that of the three distinct compositions, but especially the mesh (if one can call it that) between Orbiting Chorus and Precipitous Halo. The two of them should penetrate one another, if all goes as planned, with such precision as to bring to light their raided carnival roots—a well-oiled, worked-out exactitude worthy of halftime at a football game.

I look forward to your comments on "The Creaking of the Word."

As ever,
N.

PS: One thing I almost forgot: The Crossroads Choir, it turns out, will be on a concert tour of Japan when the symposium takes place. The plan we've come up with to get around this is that before they leave they'll record their multi-voiced version of "Opposable Thumb at the Water's Edge," each member's part going on a separate cassette. At the presentation of "The Creaking of the Word" each band member's place will be taken by a substitute who'll carry a portable cassette-player. The cassette-player, of course, will be loaded with and play the cassette of the absent band member's part.

THE CREAKING OF THE WORD

A metalecture to be delivered at the symposium "Locus and Locomotivity in Postcontemporary Music"

Jarred Bottle approached the podium. He was nervous, caught up on the arc of an asymptotic slope or the powdery rung of an eroded ladder. He felt pressured by other possible lives, by unexhausted variables come abreast of a question of something withheld and assumed to exist "outside." Something withheld, he went on, from the very start—the very notion of "start"—but, captivated by its own flawed fabric, less and less able to get over itself. Thus its theme of absence or intuited lack was only a sly or inverted form of self-regard. But to address itself in this way, he couldn't help concluding, was to be condemned to recurring bouts of tipsy conceit, to clandestine rushes of see-thru clarity complicated by blind, unseen but sought-after, zigzag "flashes"—each endlessly (or so it seemed) adumbrated, endlessly dark but unimpeachably there.

As he walked, wondering would he in fact ever reach the podium, Jarred Bottle unfolded a piece of paper on which he'd jotted a few notes outlining his talk. He consoled himself with the thought of how far he'd already come, muttering under his breath, "I've made it this far, haven't I?" But, having said this, he immediately felt the need for a piece of wood to knock on—an outright yearning which made the few feet between him and the podium (an elegant though somewhat scuffed affair made of polished oak) all the more precarious, all the more unassured.

His weak-kneed rectitude betrayed him. He'd been drinking bourbon after drinking coffee all morning. His hands were visibly shaking, as though the air itself were the wood on which he'd knock.

He fidgeted with the piece of paper, holding it with both hands as if to steady them. The words of Derek's introduction stayed with him, echoing with ever increasing insinuation: ". . . not unrelated to Jug Ammons. Displaced Egyptian Ammon. Dogon Amma. Canopic jug or jar. Starred bottle. . . ." Yes, he reflected, stored viscera. The caffeine made for a tight but empty feeling in his stomach, an issueless heaving of eponymic tension between would-be containment and quivering discontent. He fidgeted with the piece of paper, put upon by attacks of namesake anxiety, namesake ennui. A jittery wind caught him up in its gusting.

Echoes of a song played upon him as well. A song whose title had come to refer to its own ceaseless echo (his inability to cease humming or hearing it for several weeks now). "I Can't Get Over You" it was called. Much to his chagrin, he'd been unable to convince anyone of the occult significance he found in the fact that it was done by a group known as the Gap Band. He'd been widely laughed at for proposing that the song was no simple string of banalities about love gone awry, but a shorthand treatise whose namesake brooding had to do with an ontic, unbridgeable distance, a cosmogonic, uncrossable gap. Even now as he thought about it he shivered, shook even more than he'd been shaking already. The cold reaches of space seemed to impress themselves on him like so many ice cubes pressed against his ribs—frigid, albeit intimate buffers which were not to be gotten over. He swerved a bit. The stabbing, palpable chill of such remote, unthinkable distances made him stagger. Their momentary closeness almost landed him on the floor.

These feelings were not unconnected to the topic on which he'd come to speak. Jarred Bottle swerved and seemed on the verge of collapse partly due to the weight of what he took to be his message. He'd come bearing good news. Not good unmixed with bad, he admitted, but considerably less bad than good. *The fallacy of adequation,* he called it. *The lack of any absolute fit.* Out of this wobbly, rickety crux he would spin a web of tough, wish-inflected prospects, fully aware (though few would believe it) of every failed utopian promise which had gone before. He himself, it almost went without saying, was widely rumored to have been a test-tube baby. This perhaps accounted for the fact that, despite his nearly calamitous brush with interstellar space, he found himself, after a moment or two, relatively unruffled and well on his way to the podium. He knew he'd been unalterably, involuntarily forwarded, as by a conveyor-belt. It was a feeling he associated with subway rides. In fact, as the train he felt himself to be on pulled away from Gap Station he stared out the window and greeted his audience with a smile concocted of infinite, all-embracing calm.

The smile faded almost as soon as it formed. The audience was a small one, no more than sixty people at the most. It was a group made up mainly of musicians and music students, though a few teachers, poets, painters and other fellow travellers were there as well. Three or four journalists sat toward the front of the room, pencils and notepads poised and ready. The train gathered speed. The sleeping accents at large among the group now came to life with an upstart, conveyor-belt charisma all their own. Jarred Bottle couldn't help noticing an attractive woman in her early twenties sitting in the front row. She was a student he took it. She had the look of a cellist. What struck and spoke most deeply to him was the full, pouting ripeness of her mouth. Her lips were what technicians describe as "everted"—almost overly so—though Jarred Bottle preferred to think of them as "beestung." He'd long had a weakness for the full, swollen, full-to-bursting look of such lips, resorting to an image of the swelling brought on by beestings in trying to describe them. He stared at her. "Beestung Station," he remarked inaudibly to himself.

He wasn't at all surprised to catch himself staring at her, though once he had he found elsewhere to look. One would tire of that mouth too, he told himself, though whether wisdom or resignation spoke he wasn't sure. It was all—he inwardly threw his hands up in the air—so stupidly incestuous. It had just dawned on him (with the jolting, lightning-bolt abruptness of an emergency stop) that such lips, no matter who he saw them on, took him back to his sister's two-year-old daughter when he himself was nine. His niece, he recalled, had been teething at the time—her lips and her gums swollen, tender to the point of pain. He remembered a photograph taken of her at the time, a photo in which she was trying to smile though on the verge of tears from the pain in her gums. The photo epitomized a poignancy which had haunted him all these years. "Yes," he said, surprised to find he was muttering out loud, "as a wonderful singer once remarked: 'An image is a stop the mind makes between uncertainties.'" It was the first audible remark he'd made since being introduced. A few members of the audience nodded in agreement. A few giggled. He hadn't reached the podium yet.

The giggles disconcerted him a bit. He looked at the young cellist with beestung lips to see what she was doing. She smiled, revealing a gap between her upper front teeth. He was torn. The African in him was drawn to it—a beauty mark. The American in him drew back from it—the mark of a liar. In either case, he was alarmed that the train had possibly gone nowhere, that even had it actually moved it'd moved in a circle, that Beestung Station and Gap Station had turned out to be one and the same. The equivocality of Beestung Station ate away at the calm he'd mustered seconds before. Gap Station, he realized, was all-pervasive and not to be gotten away from, a persistent semantic rift not unrelated to the point he was there to make. It was his very intimacy with that rift, moreover, which lent the appeal of the young woman's mouth a certain solidity and groundedness—welcome relief to so much airy ambiguity, airy signifier-this, airy signifier-that.

He returned her smile. It was then that he began to succumb. He submitted to Gap Station as to a ritual affliction. He began to admit to himself that he wanted nothing so much as to press his mouth to hers, to cover (while confirming) the gap he was hounded by, to wallow, as it were, in a smear of meaning. Their eyes no longer met, however. His had rolled upward and toward the back of his head to the point where only the whites could be seen. (This was something he'd seen Pharoah Sanders do on occasions when a solo got unusually intense. He'd heard it was Pharoah's way of finding his way back to the "head" of whatever tune he happened to be playing, as though the "head" could be seen returning only on the ceiling or the inner walls of the skull.) What he saw was the young woman sitting with her legs open—*gapped,* he insisted—and a cello resting between them. She began to play. It was on hearing that the sound it made was not the sound of a cello but the creaking of bedsprings that he was forced to go even farther in his confession. He now had to admit that the cello was only his own wishful self-projection. He saw himself planted between her legs, thrusting with stopgap urgency, stopgap clarity, stopgap lust.

The explicitness of it shocked him, brought him to himself with all the abruptness of a subway stop. As the train pulled away from Bedspring Station he gazed out the window, his eyes meeting hers again for only a fleeting instant. Their brief exchange of glances carried a lifetime of promise, but it would have to be put aside. So would every other see-thru, conveyor-belt amenity he now swore he'd one day wean himself of. Things had gotten out of hand. He wasn't even halfway to the podium yet, but already he stood accused of redundancy and had even caught himself in the act (treadmill coitus, incestuous clarity, promiscuous kin). In fact, he felt he'd been—here he paused, groping for the word he wanted, and then, supplied it by an Ndembu prompter, carried on—*bitten* by shadowy affinities, conveyor-belt predecessors, predatory kin. So it was that, setting out to vaccinate himself, he strode with renewed uprightness and rectitude. He strutted. The giggles had died down.

It was at this point that another group of sleeping accents inadvertently awoke. Jarred Bottle had taken the precaution of planting a group of supporting musicians in the audience, a saxophone quartet comprised of four reformed casanovas known as the Bled Brethren (renamed, for this appearance only, Blood Station)—a readymade test-tube chorus, co-conspiring amen corner and streetcorner quartet all rolled into one. Responding (as they later explained) to what they took to be their cue—the word "bitten" on the prompter's lips—they stood up in unison playing "I've Got You Under My Skin." It was an obvious and somewhat snide allusion, Jarred Bottle thought, to his threadbare brush with incestuous clarity a few seconds before. He wondered why they chose to rub such an incident in as their initial act of ostensible support. The audience, however, took to them at once, popping their fingers and tapping their feet to the music. He gazed out the window as the train bore down on Blood Station. It was an odd but instructive sight he had to admit: four signifying, saxophone-playing albinos holding forth on the topic "Metaphor Is to Metabolism as . . ."

In a sense it came as no surprise. Now that he thought about it he recalled having seen it scribbled on the walls at Bedspring Station: "Metaphor Is to Metabolism as . . ." There had even been those who had it tattooed on their arms as they waited for the train—refugees from threadbare clarity in most cases, though there'd been some who fled treadmill drift. Jarred Bottle stared out the window at the quartet. The music, not entirely against his will, had begun to get to him. He felt the rim of the baritone's bell caress his abdomen, nudging his skin like a "cupping horn."* He couldn't make out what they were up to. Were they rubbing it in or were they rubbing it out? The baritone player (a tall, somewhat lanky sort) moved adroitly back and forth between a whimpering, on-the-edge falsetto and a grumbling Ayleresque vibrato in the horn's bottom register. Jarred Bottle saw the gap between the young woman's teeth come around again, more pronounced yet even more equivocal than before. He coughed, trying to clear his throat—coughed as though a tooth were caught in it, as though the cough would clear his throat of the menacing gap between the young woman's teeth. Gap Station made every encounter, whether casual or close, a threadbare escape. The quartet had sat down by now. The train pulled away from Blood Station.

Menacing but liberating gap, Jarred Bottle thought, returning to his topic for the afternoon's talk. He stopped long enough to steal a glance at the piece of paper on which he'd jotted a few notes, making sure of the wording of the quotes he planned to use to introduce his talk. Namesake Epigraph #1 came from a book on the Dogon:

> "The Word," said the old man, "is in the sound of the block and the shuttle. The name of the block means 'creaking of the word.' Everybody understands what is meant by 'the word' in

---

*A goat's horn with its tip cut off, used by the Ndembu to extract or "catch" the *ihamba* tooth, an upper front incisor with which dead kin afflict the living.

> that connection. It is interwoven with the threads; it fills the interstices in the fabric."

Namesake Epigraph #2 came from a book on Ghanaian drumming:

> The tension of the rhythms works to make time seem to speed up or slow down, as if the rhythms, which are founded on recurrence, were somehow knocking on their own foundation.

He looked up from the piece of paper and gazed out the window. It felt good to be arriving at Block Station, no matter how weary, no matter how knocked or put upon. He was getting used to having fun made of his crackpot theories, crank namesake notions he only half believed in himself.

He was there to announce that the creaking word, the rickety, crackpot word, was at the root of all music, its motivating base. "The creaking word gets the oil," he'd come prepared to say, the words put in his mouth by a Dogon prompter who made it known that among the Dogon the word for "oil" is the word for "song." Whatever the risk of cant, whatever the risk of unctuosity, music oils the word and were there no creaking there'd be no song. So, at least, the Dogon prompter seemed to say. The oiled oak of the podium all but whispered in agreement, as though song were a leg—a last leg, a lost ultimate leg—on which to stand. Jarred Bottle continued his gaze as the train bore down on Block Station. He now gazed not only out but also *at* the window, wary of protestant clarities, crackpot certainties, transparent truth. The opportune creaking of the word (as he now put it) was almost too tidy, too providential, perhaps a betrayal of the ricketiness he'd set out to endorse. Endorsability itself, he would end his talk by admitting, was by now more or less openly a "lie," too true to be good.

He staggered. A nervous perfume which now went to his head had evidently rubbed off on him at Bedspring Station. The podium, however, was almost within reach. An unguentary swaying from side to side came over him as yet another of the yawning accents in the audience came to life. The words "locus" and "locomotivity" motored, as it were, a recollection of the '52 Ford whose engine block he'd inadvertently cracked when he was seventeen. He shuddered with recollected embarrassment, resurrected shame at his automotive incompetence. (The engine of the car had overheated. He'd made the mistake of adding water to the radiator while the engine was off before allowing it to cool.) He shook his head from side to side as though saying no to the memory. He wondered if he'd be visited by every embarrassment he'd ever known, set upon by an endless drift of associations, endless diehard insecurity, endless cracks eroding outward calm.

Was the presumption of public speech, he wondered, endlessly haunted by private misgiving? It was a question he could ill afford. Even as he teetered, only a hair's breadth away from the podium, teenage gangs were beginning to cluster at Block Station. He clamped a namesake lid on the recollection. The train slowed down to a halt. "I'm here," he said to himself, rapping the podium with his clenched right hand.

14.IV.81

Dear Angel of Dust,

Thanks for writing back so quickly. As for your request regarding the *ihamba* and the cupping horn, I don't mind at all going into a bit more detail. Most of it I take from one of Turner's books on Ndembu ritual, *The Forest of Symbols.* I'll simply quote some of what he has to say: ". . . the term *ihamba* refers among the Ndembu to an upper central incisor tooth of a deceased hunter. . . . Some *mahamba* [plural of *ihamba*] are believed to afflict the living by burying themselves in their bodies and causing them severe pains. . . . To remove an *ihamba,* the senior adept or 'doctor' makes an incision on any part of the patient's body and applies to the cut a cupping horn (usually a goat's horn) from which the tip has been removed. After the horn has been sucked, it is plugged with beeswax. The doctor's intention is to 'catch' the *ihamba,* which is believed to 'wander about' subcutaneously."

The above can't help but call Charlie Parker's comment to mind: "It really has to be *in* you to come out of the horn." Nor can one help noticing that the Latin counterpart of "wander about" is *ambigere,* the verb from which "ambiguous" derives. The goat's horn, then, makes perfect etymological sense. What better way to pursue the nomadic source of one's affliction than with a likewise mobile, prancing or capricious horn? What better way to "catch" one's ambiguous ordeal by its infectious roots than with an analogous, homeopathic "wandering about"? Or to belabor the point and put it another way:

$$\mathrm{b}_{\mathrm{co}} \longrightarrow \mathrm{b}_{\mathrm{cu}} \longleftarrow \mathrm{b}_{\mathrm{ca}}$$

(*bedouin complaint* and *bedouin caprice* converge on *bedouin cure*).

But I'm writing back so soon mainly to say that Jarred Bottle paid me a visit last night. He showed up in a dream. (Well, he didn't so much "show up" as "make his presence felt.") Somewhere in North Africa I'd fallen in with a group of Sufis. It was their practice to go into a form of trance in which some of them hissed like snakes, others meowed like cats, still others neighed like horses and so forth. This was their way, one of them explained to me, of humbling themselves before Allah, their way of acknowledging that in relation to Him they were merely "as animals are to men." On hearing this I opened my mouth to say something about the need to inoculate loss, to make the point of a need to mourn abandonment in advance. "As though one were always to be left behind in advance," I intended to say, "by whatever one hopes to not be abandoned by . . ."

I opened my mouth, however, only to find that a piece of glass had gotten caught in my throat. It seemed to be about an inch long and a half inch wide. I pondered making a move to dislodge it, very careful not to make a swallowing gesture, no matter how slight, for to do so would've embedded it all the more firmly. I didn't even dare inhale.

Finally I coughed with all the force I could, hoping to get it out that way. I don't know if I succeeded, for what struck me much more than whether I did or not was the sound that came out of me in the attempt. It was a yelp (as though a dog had taken over my throat), so loud and so resounding it woke me up.

It seemed my point had been made anyway. The inoculation of loss proposed an "it" to which one at best had only a differential access, an inverse ladder as in the Sirius dream (god/dog), whose being there would seem to deprive one of something.

Sincerely,
N.

28.IV.81

Dear Angel of Dust,

We just got back from a weekend gig in Berkeley. I'd hoped to find a letter from you waiting when I got back, but since I didn't I assume you're tied up with one thing or another. The gig, anyhow, was a good one: Friday, Saturday and Sunday nights at a club on San Pablo called the Scarab, a block or so south of University. It caters to a knowing (some would say incestuous) clientele, and it was good, as it always is, to be in the Bay Area. I was especially struck this time by an apparent trend we came across on Market Street in San Francisco and, to a somewhat lesser extent, on Telegraph in Berkeley. The latest thing seems to be to go out on the streets with a cheap guitar and amplifier setup and perform. We saw at least a half-dozen people doing so the other day on Market. I don't know if I can do justice to the impact it had on me. The cheapness of the equipment seemed to give the sound a pinched, precarious quality which was not only moving but inescapably true to the times. It was as though Hendrix and Blood Ulmer were embryonic harbingers of some sort of upheaval, advance men, more or less, for a mass deployment of oppositional fuzztones (abject, irreverent feedback punctuated by "sprung," utopian wah-wah licks).

The players we heard relied heavily on frenetic, no-letup guitar runs, underneath or alongside, in a number of cases, a mumbled, inarticulate vocal line. I say "inarticulate" with some hesitation, however, for in its own possibly more exacting way the inarticulacy *spoke.* To me it seemed the work of a disgruntled, not unconscious decision on the singer's part, a willful dismantling of the gag-rule amenities which normally pass for coherence. Refusal worked hand in hand with exposé in such a way that what one heard was a loud critique of available options, a gruff dismissal of available conduits, no matter how "coherent," for admissable truths. It was a mix of exposé and refusal which both rose above and got to the bottom of such truths, supplementing conventional speech in the manner of scat, the way, say, a Slim Gaillard does. Here I'm especially thinking of a man who played and sang in front of a store called Grodin's. His guitar-playing highlighted the same adrenaline-rush, machine-gun mode of address relied on by his "colleagues" up and down the street. His voice, however, partook of a quality of transport which, trite as it sounds, had to be heard to be believed. He wore a yellow bandanna and kept his eyes closed while he sang. What he sang was a blues whose lyrics I couldn't altogether make out or be exact about, except that every fourth word or so sounded like "jellyroll."

But that one word (if that's what it was) made it clear that what was being gotten at, advocated or advanced was an adamant, unremitting lubricity, a slippery, unsecured exchange between what was "known" and what would otherwise not be heard. There was a pleading, unpolished quality to his voice which inverted itself. Slippery plea became sticky demand. Listening to him, one couldn't escape the feeling that one was being *furthered*, discontinuously annexed as though—legless prey of this or the other beaked imperative—one's will were abruptly beside the point. One was being ushered, one understood, beyond oneself. In me it awoke the debris of an eroding precipice, an insecure foothold whose remnants were gritty no matter how slippery they felt ("oily" but also "dry").

The grating jellyroll voice, that is, had a way of conjuring hell, giving rise to fumes whose particulate air was nothing if not heaven's dusty, threadbare cloak. What drew me in was the look on the singer/guitar-player's face, a certain tendency to end or to accent each run with a jellyroll grimace as though dotting an "i." Somewhere a curtain had fallen away, a cape of moth-eaten silk.

Each dotted "i," the longer we stood there and listened (swaying to the only halfway enunciated beat), installed an etheric, sugared lump in my throat—not unlike the one I contracted while listening to the Crossroads Choir. It was this gruff jellyroll endorsement or endowment, I believe, which allowed me some leverage over the billboard we saw later that day. Every kiss, the guitar licks warned, conceals a viper's teeth. Only a deep jellyroll mistrust of shallow, threadbare endearments, I've come to see, could account for the immunity I felt before the billboard we encountered a few hours later. At the time I was hardly aware of the jellyroll bubble in which I walked about. (It only dawned on me fully, as these things do, in retrospect.) We were walking down Valencia when the encounter I refer to occurred. It was as we turned at Twenty-fourth and were about to begin crossing the street—we were headed for a coffeehouse, Café La Bohème, just off Mission—that Penguin stopped and, looking up and to his right, muttered, "Damn it! They're at it again."

The rest of us stopped and looked to see what it was he'd spotted. There on the other side of Valencia (on the other side of Twenty-fourth too) was a billboard atop a three-story building. The billboard carried an ad in which a piece of cake was pictured sitting on a plate. It was a piece of devil's food cake beneath a mound of whipped cream, on top of which sat a glossy red cherry. At the base of the ad were the words "Top your favorite bottom with real whipped cream." We stared, not knowing exactly what about the ad had gotten Penguin worked up. He went on scowling. It was Lambert who finally asked, "At *what* again?" Penguin stroked his beard and let out a sigh. "Can't you see it?" he answered. "It's the same oppressive meal they've always dished out. Only now they're trying to pass it off as dessert."

He went on to expound on a subliminal theme of domination he found at work in the ad. He first of all directed our attention to the homophony between "dessert" and "desert." He made the point that one couldn't help hearing echoes of "deserve" in the word "dessert," that one was being invited to buy into something he termed "saccharine abuse," being invited to endorse a code of "justified injustice." (He noted, almost as an aside, that earlier in the day we had in fact eaten pastries at a place on Embarcadero called Just Desserts.) The rest of what he had to say turned largely on the words "top" and "bottom." Their use in the ad, he argued, was loaded with the meanings they brought from the S/M world, whose parlance, as you no doubt know, equates "top" with "dominant," "bottom" with "submissive," "top" with "actor," "bottom" with "acted on," "top" with "master," "bottom" with "slave." It was the S/M ruse of consent he found so offensive, he explained, especially given the ad's white-over-black theme or insinuation. Lambert, Aunt Nancy and Djamilaa nodded their heads in agreement. Aunt Nancy, turning her eyes from the billboard, spat into the gutter as if to say that was what she thought of the ad.

I too was struck by what Penguin had to say and to some extent saw the ad in a brand new light, but the jellyroll bubble whose polychrome lining had unsuspectedly intervened induced a corridor effect. It seemed to carry me along in such a way that, before I knew it, I was halfway across the street, holding up traffic while beckoning to the four of them to leave the curb as I myself had just done. "Don't make too much of it," I croaked in an ephemeral, don't-care, blow-bubble tone of voice I hardly knew I had, a raspy jellyroll burst I could never, I'm sure, have come up with at will.

The four of them stayed on the curb a while longer. I continued on to the other side of the street. They too eventually crossed and we spent an hour at Café La Bohème. We drank coffee and discussed the billboard, my jellyroll bubble wearing thinner and thinner as we sat. Its wearing thin ate away at the "So what?" I repeatedly found on the tip of my tongue. Before long the subtle implications the others elicited from the ad made more and more sense. After about twenty minutes I was wholeheartedly taking part, putting in my two cents as to what this or that meant. By the time we left I felt we'd exhausted the subject, that that was that. That this wasn't so I found out the following night.

It was during our second and final set Sunday night at the Scarab that what I'm referring to occurred. We had just finished doing a movement from Lambert's ongoing piece "Aggravated Assent." As the audience applauded, Penguin turned to the four of us and specified the instruments he wanted us on for what he'd just decided would be our next number, a piece whose head, he said, had come to him that very instant. Aunt Nancy he wanted on congas, Lambert on alto flute, me on bass clarinet and Djamilaa on harmonium. As for himself, he put his oboe down and picked up his baritone sax. Clipping it on to the strap around his neck, he leaned forward and spoke into the mike. The next number, he announced to the audience, would be a brand new composition entitled "Bottomed Out."

He took the horn to his mouth and began to play. The idea was that the rest of us would at first only listen. Once we'd gotten an idea of the tune's outline and where it seemed to be going we'd contribute as we could. It took only a few notes for Penguin to establish an authoritative jellyroll eloquence, a curious, compelling, somewhat slick jellyroll encounter between the erotic and the oratorical. I was immediately struck by the richness and the depth of his tone, the meeting of mischief and muse it brought off. The line he laid down seemed to be held together by a preacherly needle he'd brought into odd or unlikely alliance with a jellyroll thread. It was a line possessed of a technical ecstasy, an abiding, rough-and-ready sensuality along the lines of Mingus's "Orange Was the Color of Her Dress, Then Blue Silk." If you're acquainted with Mingus's piece you're already familiar with the gruff, technical-ecstatic equation Penguin stitched by way of inducting us into "Bottomed Out." What got to me most was exactly the line's technical-ecstatic bellowing: deep, rough-and-ready grunts which were not only factors but implosive multiples of a certain frayed, holistic fabric they proposed. It was a drenched, even a drunken fabric, a soaked, "ecstatically" sunken cloth. The bellowing seemed to erupt from an ocean's floor.

The similarity to Mingus's "Orange," however, was one of spirit more than anything else. What Penguin played had a more direct resemblance to Sonny Simmons's long, unaccompanied intro to "Lost Generation," one of the tunes on Prince Lasha's album *The Cry!* from the early sixties. This was due, no doubt, to the fact that Sonny had shown up during our second set the night before. (For the most part he'd merely stood at the back of the room snapping his fingers to a beat which had nothing to do with the piece we were playing. He had a way of staring but seeming to see or to be looking at nothing. This made him conspicuous even as it made it seem he wasn't really there. At one point he began to finger and blow into an invisible horn. He left after about fifteen minutes.) At points Penguin made the baritone sound like an alto à la Hamiet Bluiett, accentuating the debt he owed Sonny's "Lost Generation" but getting at something else as well. What this was I can put best by saying that the decadent, sickly-sweet defeatism endorsed by the ad we'd seen the day before came under attack by way of these wavering, "weak" ascents into the baritone's upper register.

Threaded into Penguin's intro, that is, was an admission we hadn't noticed in the ad. It was an admission he now brought to light, letting it serve as a witness at the trial or arraignment "Bottomed Out" was turning out to be. The intent of each precarious alto flight, we began to see, was to mimic and thereby expose the inversion built into the phrase "whipped cream." How could one invest in its inverse witness or its obverse cherry so as to cleanse it of its cliché theme of a "loneliness at the top"? This was the question Penguin's technical-ecstatic intro implicitly asked. The more explicit, more pointed question his rhetorical needle put before us was this: Wasn't "whipped cream" an occult way of owning up not so much to a loneliness as a lameness at the top? (This, we knew, was our cue to join in.) It was an opportune admission of weakness, Penguin insisted, returning to a throaty, low growl so as to argue that here was a foot in the door for newly ascendant bottoms. Aunt Nancy was the first to answer his call, slapping the skins of the congas as the audience loudly applauded Penguin's recourse to a series of tremolo figures. She came on with a fierceness which all but outright shouted that a foot in the door wasn't enough, one had to kick it in. What she played wasn't without finesse, however. She took up Penguin's lingering riff, the figure of wavering, weak-kneed cream, not merely taking it up but taking it further, relating by contrast at first but more enduringly by contagion. She too laid heavy stress on the adjective "whipped."

Penguin's thread was now a mode of support. Each conga beat broke to be hoisted and held by the baritone's riff as by a pair of cupped hands, held as if rocked in a bedouin cradle or the rough-and-ready arms of an itinerant embrace. It was the wildest, most audacious embrace one would ever know, sprouting arms whose wandering threadbare shawl it caught in the drift and the upward draft of its infectious wind. What made for this was Aunt Nancy's technical-ecstatic refusal to traffic in "depth." She wore the blasé, placid look of a would-be lover playing hard-to-get, her surface calm in no way ruffled by the kick-out intensity she brought to the drums. Contentious wind, infectious crib and contagious eclipse all rolled into one, each beat arose as if to confirm an ashen fear of bedrock heat, to endorse a blind but embraceable fear of being burned by "depth." These were matters we'd heard her go into before, though never under such anonymous control or to such advantage. Penguin went on with his riff, cupped and cradled each beat but gave it a jellyroll spin as well. A spinning head of steam is what he appeared to be after, though something horselike arose to rear back out of ashen fear of an equally ashen hoofbeat, bedouin fear of indigenous, runaway dust. The upstart, intractable rashness implied by such an inverse, inebriate hoof had its way with the riff to the point where, almost without knowing it, I too had now taken it up.

I had the feeling I'd had on Market while listening to the man in the yellow bandanna, the same sense of thrust or of having been forwarded regardless of will, inclination or intent. I fell for the sway of Aunt Nancy's deadpan cradle, caught between it and the alarmed inheritance Penguin's pursuit of nomadic abandon had become. Squawking bird to the baritone's bellowing beast, I overblew the horn by way of stretching my wings and thereby flew from the random straw of Aunt Nancy's drowsily eloquent nest. But no matter how far away I flew I stayed in touch and related by tether to the congas' padded, hypnotic pulse—the recurrence, reassurance and resonance of a pillow and hoofbeat rolled into one.

By now Penguin had let go of the riff and was following my lead, though he'd not so much let go of it as allowed its more explicit R&B aspects to fade. Steadfast boogie gave way to something more staggered, abstract and diffuse, a misty if not explicitly mystical acceptance of ash, incompletion and loss on the one hand, technical-ecstatic fulfillment on the other. Each abstract hand conceded something to the other, coming dangerously close to an admission of complicity or condoning the very caresses "Bottomed Out" had set out to reject.

The three of us wove in and out of what each other proposed. The nominal lead I took notwithstanding, Aunt Nancy and Penguin pushed, pointed and pulled me in directions I wouldn't have otherwise embarked upon. What I played was otherwise influenced by having heard a record by Frank Wright's quartet called *Center of the World.* (This was a few days earlier at the house of a friend.) The line I pursued had a similar sense of alarm, as though the hub around which the head of the tune revolved blew a whistle on the world. I looked out at the audience and saw looks of surprise and even shock on their faces. Not even I could escape being startled by the shrill, shadowed incision I'd made in the air. Lambert joined in as though this incision were the foot in the door he'd been waiting for, coming on with a mellowness of tone which cooed and ever so soothingly spoke. If what Aunt Nancy offered was kick-out congas he in turn came up with cool-out flute, coming in as a brisk but diabolical fourth which augmented the triad Aunt Nancy, Penguin and I sustained. It was a pregnant, polysemous triad we three had enacted, compounded of a technical-ecstatic appetite for drought (pronounced "dĕz′·ẽrt"), a technical-ecstatic blending of abandonment and merit (pronounced "dē·zûrt′") and a technical-ecstatic jellyroll sense of an ending (pronounced "dĭ·zûrt′").

I detected an ever so slight trace of lipstick on the cool-out oasis Lambert's flute brought into play, as though he blew across the lipplate in hollow anticipation of a newly-won lover's name and number on the tip of his tongue. This made for a plunge into staggered capacities which had barely been touched by Aunt Nancy's blasé, hard-to-get hoofbeat or bedouin drum. All the more reason, I reflected, to wonder why an unrequited flight from the numbed incision I'd etched in the air would so resoundingly ring. Even so, it rang like an unsuspected quiver, still alive albeit buried in the blunt recesses of a bottomless thud. My embouchure began to slacken somewhat, confounding jellyroll exit with rough-and-ready cut. By "bottomless thud," I nevertheless explained (noting an air of dismay which had come over the crowd), one meant a blocked or obstructed void out of which a signal sparks and flies as from a stone. This I conveyed with an arpeggiated run I'd been afraid might be beyond my weakened embouchure's reach. Lambert grinned on the far side of his lip-plate, a gleam in his eye at my having gotten my chops back up. The trace of lipstick I'd gotten inklings of he now accented with a trill which tapered off into a sigh. Trill as well as trace throve on a technical-ecstatic erasure, abdicating every note whose availability one took for granted or in some other way tended to essentialize. Every would-be equation of the available with the inevitable bit the dust, bit into an aroused, inverse oasis Lambert's bedouin foot-in-the-door meant to apprise us of.

Aunt Nancy's blasé look broke down when she grinned at the slow-motion cloud of dust making its way across the lip-plate of Lambert's flute. Caravan and spidery crux rolled into one, the cloud slowed as though caught in a tempo change worthy of Mingus, moved as though caught in the "hallelujah spokes" of an adamant, outmoded wheel. The wheel's eaten rim disappeared as if in pursuit of an arcane hub. The alternate, unwatered shore of which it apprised us pursed our lips as though each of us occupied Lambert's place.

The four of us now stood as one. Aunt Nancy's congas were a flute. Penguin's baritone was a flute. My bass clarinet was a flute. Lambert's flute was the cultivated hollow we'd been invaded by, a contagious oneness whose cradling insistence none of us could've escaped even had we tried.

The hollowness and wholeness we'd contracted luckily lasted only an instant. I blinked, not altogether believing the transformation it underwent at once. It seemed we were seated at a circular table, a four-cornered wheel, as it were, around whose perimeter a smaller wheel passed from hand to hand. The smaller wheel had once belonged to a covered wagon. We took turns biting into its rim while holding it firmly by two of its "hallelujah spokes." Having taken a bite, one passed it on to one's left.

Out of the corner of my eye I caught a glimpse of the audience. They showed even more surprise than at the shadowed incision I'd cut in the air. I too was bewildered by the turn "Bottomed Out" had taken.

But once their faces began to relax and regain their composure I saw that they saw that the wheel's gnawed rim was a symbolic threshold, that we stood on the brink of devastation and debris, that the eucharistic edge or ubiquitous hollow into which one bit and over which one blew obeyed a deepseated wish to contend with frontier justice. The slow-motion cloud I saw now in a new, retrospective light. Dust was a time-lapse inversion of the jellyroll spin Penguin had given Aunt Nancy's beat. The splintered, oddly supportive wood into which we bit betrayed bedouin appetite, bracketed pieties, pioneer drift. The reflection of this on the audience's faces we soon saw to be the door for which Djamilaa'd been waiting. She came in on the comet's-tail edge of Lambert's ironic oasis, insisting that we not lose sight of an earlier motif regarding "weak-kneed cream." She did this by alluding to James Brown, odd as it seemed, quoting the organ line from the beginning of "Lost Someone" on the *Live at the Apollo* album. Out of the corner of my eye I caught a glimpse of the audience again. The allusion didn't seem so odd on deeper reflection. Not only did "Lost Someone" hark back to "Lost Generation," but both, I recalled, had been recorded in 1962.

From its opening notes Djamilaa's harmonium blended rowdiness with rectitude, going to such extremes it left one with no recourse but to admit to a weak-kneed susceptibility. One's only "out" was to awaken to a deepseated, subtle commotion, a deepseated shadow of collapse whose call announced a forfeiture of upright illusion. Bottom-over-top as well as top-over-bottom gave way to a pun. Whichever way, she insinuated and insisted, both were "prone." Penguin shot everyone a devilish grin on hearing this, extracting a downward theme or thread of his own from Djamilaa's motif. He blew as though he stood on the stage at the Apollo, bent over holding the horn as though its voice were JB's lowered an octave or two. The word "someone" seemed to catch in his throat, the corresponding notes barely making it out of the baritone's bell. It not only caught but seemed to crack as well, a deepseated chasm or a deepseated croak testifying to nameless cardiognostic loss, nameless cosmogonic lipstick, nameless oracular lump-in-one's-throat, lost cardiogenic endowment. There was something of a tongue-in-cheek edge to Penguin's choked-up chasm, an oblique remove in relation to what he played as though he scratched at every door of material compulsion, consolation and constraint. Nonetheless a new proportion came into play with his and Djamilaa's bracketless, ad hoc Apollo, a new poise as well as new proportion in which anonymous arms rocked an evacuated cradle.

Lambert, Aunt Nancy and I understood immediately what was taking place. A curvaceous hollow whose hallelujah contour complied with Penguin's bent, intervening spin served and summoned a nameless, newly-constituted "someone"—served (as I've already noted) a caught, cryptic, cardiognostic need to personify loss. It was a need, we understood, to personify but not identify the resident hollow one's apparent solidity concealed. Notwithstanding Aunt Nancy's earlier refusal, all three of us now saw ascendancy mired in depth, wing mirrored in root.

The new proportion and the anonymous personification which had come into play required a change in our instrumentation. Lambert put his flute aside to take up the tenor, Aunt Nancy switched from congas to electric guitar and I went from bass clarinet to muted trumpet. While Djamilaa went on with the bass line the three of us punctuated Penguin's lead by alternating between Aunt Nancy's descending four-note figure and a down-and-up ditty-bop riff played by trumpet and tenor. This punctuating support passed back and forth in such a way as to further the back-and-forth rocking of Penguin's abject cradle. The limiting terms of its back-and-forth volley (descending four-note figure on the one hand, down-and-up ditty-bop riff on the other) were the alternate, anonymous arms by which the rocking was done.

The audience too rocked back and forth, each pair of eyes in its proverbial sea of heads trained on Penguin's jaw. One saw that the cheek on the left side of Penguin's face tended to balloon or bulge with a wad of breath at the outset of each run. Tied to it as by an umbilical thread of obsession, one stared at the bulge and saw that it was made not by Penguin's tongue but by a certain cud his bedouin "someone" had left him with. Though one saw this one heard it more as "could" than as "cud," rocked or swayed by the enabling proportion of one's umbilical stare. The reflection of all this on the audience's faces came into focus with Penguin's ad hoc admission of weakness, an impromptu "Apollonian" collapse—he fell to his knees—which further brought JB to mind. It was plain for all to see as he knelt with his baritone grazing the floor that it was the straining, distraught repetition of "I'm so weak" on the Apollo album that this new move of his was meant to mime and recall. His mimed admission took part in a mixed umbilical alliance with the surge one saw reflected in the audience's eyes—a surge of power, possibility and permission which grew more insistent as we all, band and audience alike, chewed a collective "could."

The source of this "could" intrigued us. Was it the wheel we five had bitten into, the wheel which at an earlier time would've run us over but which in the name of a millenarian agenda we now not only digested but redistributed so as to advance beyond blind inversion? Had the wheel been bitten into by the audience as well? Something warned me that this was too fanciful a notion. The taste of a skirt made of soured grass picked up from the Boneyard Brass Octet now returned to mingle with the conditional mana whose woodpulp juices wet the back of my mouth. It was as though someone had bitten into a lemon as I put the trumpet to my lips again. I flubbed a note but recovered in time to see the ditty-bop support Lambert and I gave Penguin pierce an otherwise impenetrable halo and hub rolled into one. I saw that one fed, whether one liked it or not, on the splintered "bread" we'd bitten into and broken, the outmoded halo built on bracketed spokes, the bedouin spark one saw but never quite caught. Aunt Nancy's four-note descending figure came in to remind us that a sparked or incendiary "someone"—the anonymous other one's abrasive arms had long since lit but been abandoned by—repeatedly flared only to flicker and fade and die down again.

Still on his knees exhorting all who'd listen, Penguin ran a scale and began to ad lib. The weak-kneed plummet to which he'd submitted provoked a shamanistic flight on the audience's part, some of whom now stood up while those who didn't moved forward to the edge of their seats. They in turn exhorted Penguin and egged him on, shouting things like "Teach!," "Go tell it!," "Blow your horn!" and so forth. A buzz and a ripple ran thru the crowd when he told us it was "gettin' a little *cold* outside." The jellyroll inflection he gave the word "cold" inversely tied him to the sparked or incendiary "someone" Aunt Nancy's guitar repeatedly brought to mind. The splintered wheel now came across not only as cud but also as kindling. The moist wad and dry wood rolled into one to which it amounted implied one was lit no matter how much one sputtered. That this was so one took to be the deep, psychotropic meaning of hollow, hallucinatory "could," though seeing it so left a bittersweet taste in one's mouth, a tart, philosophic savor one tried in vain to spit out or spew forth.

Djamilaa's bass line grew more and more insistent while this went on. She seemed to advance or to seek to advance from conditional "could" to unconditional "will." Easy for even the blind to see was that the question was how to unleash the captive "could" in one's reflective jaw. Penguin "rose" to this occasion and question by going even deeper into the kneeling position, letting his hips come to rest on his heels while on the horn he ran back and forth between guttural plunge and falsetto flight. More and more of the audience was standing up by now and Djamilaa's bass line built on itself so as to increasingly endow the piece with a Baul or Bengali feeling. More and more, that is, the harmonium *sang*—so earthy, so obsessed, so abstract and so wind-afflicted it almost made us all weep.

Another new proportion had come into play. Penguin picked up on this and by way of adjustment played more and more toward the top of the horn. It was as though he set out to get an oboe sound. What he got was a barely eked-out but no less continuous trickle of sound, a pinched, oddly sinuous falsetto—something like the gurgly snake-charmer's moan Trane tended to get whenever he'd crouch or go into a clench. (I'm thinking, say, of "One Down, One Up" on the *New Thing at Newport* album.) I could hardly believe my ears. I'd never heard a baritone make such a "highstrung" sound.

In any case, Lambert, Aunt Nancy and I complied at once with the new proportion which had come into play, the "Baulness" or "Bengaliness" of which Aunt Nancy acknowledged by putting her guitar aside for a khamak, a gubgubi drum. The two strings attached to its head seemed related to Penguin's "highstrung" baritone squeal, however much the fat, rotund, watery-resonant sound Aunt Nancy managed to get suggested undulant buttocks firmly tied to the earth. Lambert and I let go of the ditty-bop support we'd been giving Penguin, Lambert letting his tenor hang from the strap around his neck while he took up with a small pair of bell-toned cymbals. I kept at it on muted trumpet, but tended toward a more percussive, more spiked or staccato attack. This I did by way of conversing with what Aunt Nancy, on the one hand, was up to, as well as with, on the other, Lambert's well-placed, repetitive chimings-in. It seemed I spat fire with every staccato burst, so combustible was the "could" in my mouth. A tiny spark had caught hold of my tongue, a tiny star, a wad of kindling I'd have recourse to again and again.

Djamilaa implicitly spoke to my staccato spark. She intuitively fanned the muted flame I invoked. She dug deep into her desert roots to come up with a desolate, forlorn, yet fiercely devotional sound. Though desolation and desertion had to do with it heat had to do with it as well, and though heat had to do with it waves had to do with it too. The Baul or Bengali proportion she'd brought into play added a page to our book: a scrap of paper washed ashore in a bottle, it seemed, a mixed-metaphorical message or note regarding sand as eventual glass, embryonic bottle. (This is where heat came in.) The new page's report—there'd been a shipwreck it said—echoed Penguin's technical-ecstatic bellowing at the start of the piece. But its mixed-metaphorical import (caravan, caravel and caracol rolled into one) went beyond anything Penguin had implied. The sea itself was a ship which had crashed, it seemed to suggest, coaxing an evaporative language and logic from its image of ocean as wrecked, predecessor desert. The desert too was a ship which had sunk, it went on to announce, etheric debris or amniotic debris, dessicated crib and crypt rolled into one. It was an odd, admittedly idiosyncratic line but we pursued it so devoutly that the audience joined in and began egging us on by shouting things like "Uterine hoofbeat!" and "Navigable drought!"

Djamilaa opened her mouth to sing but no sound came out. She moved her lips and though no sound came out she went on moving them, grimacing as though her voice were now anointed in sand. The mute contortions undergone by her mouth formed a slow succession of dry see-thru incisions, each of which caught fire and very cleanly cut between one's marrow and bone. Her loss of voice partook of a pinched but oddly expansive quality—an extended gasp or unending intake of breath which seemed to take up where Penguin's "highstrung" falsetto left off. Nonetheless she was singing, dealing in sounds which were audible only to the mind, frequencies beyond the reach of conventional hearing. One understood that what she was up to was a dry run—futuristic, tortuously utopic, a not-yet-articulable address, an *envoi.* She sent her song into the world, but did so with the understanding that the conditions which would truly bring it into being had yet to be met. She went so far, in fact, as to despair of their ever being met, as though she'd been deserted by the future she proposed. Without saying it she seemed to say that that future couldn't help but be absconded with by this or that preemptive intervention.

As Djamilaa went on with her inaudible singing the audience grew louder and louder, more and more finding its voice in her loss of hers. The mute page her evaporative tide had turned elicited a rowdy carnival rush of sound on the audience's part, virtually all of whom were standing by now. Despite Djamilaa's mixed-metaphorical future's theme of thwarted sunrise or preempted dawn they came on like the Great Gettin' Up Choir one had secretly (but not so secretly) longed for all one's life. What they now did went beyond their earlier shouts of "Blow your horn!," "Uterine hoofbeat!" and such. What they now did went well beyond words. It was an elemental, ongoing gust of unadulterated push and of pure aspiration they advanced. The aspirated push they brought to light and put forth had the sound of the background hiss one hears on recording tape. Only it was much louder, an amplified seashell's roar, it seemed, with something of a seismic, decidedly *street* aspect or edge factored in as well. The sound, however much it implied the sea, conveyed a sense of drought and carried a report of smoldering ash as well as endless abrasion, consistent with Djamilaa's mixed-metaphorical future. Consistent as well with her desert roots, there was something Arabic about it, notwithstanding the feel it also had of a samba chorus or a gospel choir.

Djamilaa's "loss" had become the audience's "gain," but even more worth noting was the fact that the mixed-metaphorical page which had entered our book was not so much a page as a precarious advance held together by stark, semiotic stitches, an awkward, unwieldy, endless piece of parchment, an endlessly unwinding scroll. We in the band all knew by now that we'd been inducted into an order of insensate rhythm, into a technical-ecstatic recitation of a "text" whose words we'd been abandoned by in advance. It was equally an order of insensate "pressure," a direness and a preciosity compounded of technical-ecstatic erasure, jellyroll abrasiveness and rough-and-ready brunt (technical-ecstatic lubricity on its other side: mixed-metaphorical indemnity, rough-and-ready plunge). As for my part, I went on spitting fire, my lips burnt and belatedly stung by the hint of lipstick I'd gotten earlier from Lambert's flute. "Broken ships," I tried to say thru the horn but ended up whispering, "Note-bearing bottle, bits of scattered glass."

By now the Apollo seemed somewhat remote. So did "Top your favorite bottom with real whipped cream." The new proportion Djamilaa had brought into play tended to make for a tenuousness or a tangentiality, an elliptic, asymptotic wisp of a theme whose ghostly ongoingness all but undid one's need for an explicit, more expository take. There was a sense in which the angularity we increasingly cultivated (anticlimactic impact, pseudoclimatic ash) took advantage of the persistence or the apparent pervasiveness of the conditions from which it offered an escape. No such "out" as it proposed or appeared to posit had any reason to endlessly allude to the centrist ordeal from which it flew. The insensate rhythm into whose order we'd been inducted maintained neither a directly dialectical nor a directly diametrical but an oblique centrifugal relation to the metronomic center whose initiatic split between "bottom" and "top" now seemed so remote. One ran the risk, we fully realized, of endorsing an overstatement in the other direction by appearing to ignore such a split or by annulling its catalytic distinction.

Such a risk inhabited and haunted the need for a new conception it paradoxically fed.

It was this Lambert had in mind when he made a gesture which brought yet another new proportion into play. The need for an unheard-of conception hadn't only annulled Djamilaa's sand-anointed voice but in time had gotten hold of Penguin's baritone as well. Penguin had gone deeper and deeper into the kneeling position. He'd gotten even lower, once he'd gone as deep as he could, by leaning to his left and letting himself fall to the floor. He lay on his side with his knees pulled up toward his chest in a vaguely fetal position, still blowing the horn and still coming out with a falsetto squeal. The squeal eventually thinned as though pulled like taffy by the risk-inhabited need for a new conception. The need pulled it to the breaking point in fact, for after Djamilaa had gone on voicelessly for a while Penguin's falsetto abruptly snapped and turned into a dry but furious, urgent but inaudible "screech." He went on like this for a short while, the effort contorting his face, but he then let the horn slip from his hands and mouth and lie beside him, still grimacing as though playing a horn (an invisible horn), moving his fingers as though executing a run. It was at this point that Lambert made his move, the one which brought another new proportion into play.

Lambert had kept up a steady contribution on cymbals, peppering Aunt Nancy's wobbly gubgubi line, spiking the carpeted rumble she invoked. But when Penguin toppled over on his side and let the baritone slip to the floor, he (that is, Lambert) stopped playing. He stared at Penguin, looking to see what he'd do next. Seeing that Penguin went on grimacing and moving his fingers as though playing a horn, he quickly made the gesture to which I've referred and in so doing brought a new proportion into play. What he did was put his cymbals aside long enough to pick up a sopranino sax and put it into Penguin's hands. Having done so, he took up the cymbals again. The tiny horn was entirely appropriate to Penguin's more or less fetal position. Its tininess and toylike dimensions made it look like an embryonic version of the baritone which lay nearby. With Lambert's move the few members of the audience who hadn't already done so stood up and the amplified seashell's roar grew even louder.

The new proportion came more explicitly into play once Penguin took the sopranino to his mouth. For a while he merely fingered the horn without blowing into it, but once he took it to his mouth and began to play a curious proportion materialized. He came on with the same barely eked-out trickle he'd played on baritone, taking its gurgly aspect and image even further by making bubbles emerge from the horn. I found it hard to believe what I saw. Out of the horn's bell floated bubble after bubble of the sort children make from soapy water. I felt right off that this was THE RETURN OF THE BLOW-BUBBLE VOICE, but on further reflection I saw that to see it so did little to answer the questions which had now arisen. Were the bubbles Penguin's mixed-metaphorical manner of speaking of a proverbial mouth-washed-out-with-soap? Were they a laundering or a would-be laundering of the billboard's sugarcoated S/M insinuation? Were they possibly the bubbles a baby sometimes makes by belching or spitting up a meal? And what was one to make of the allusion (if that's what it was) to Lawrence Welk's bubble machine? Was it a snide indictment or a tongue-in-cheek endorsement of middlebrow American tastes, implicating middle-of-the-road aesthetics in the centrist ordeal from which we sought an eccentric "out"?

These and other questions arose, ramified and went on and on, as numerous as the bubbles which were filling the room. One had little time to ponder or pursue them, however. I took my eyes off Penguin only to notice that bubbles had begun to emerge from the bell of my own heuristic horn, notwithstanding the mute (which, oddly enough, did almost nothing to impede their flow). Infectious bubbles floated from both horns now. The audience responded by trying to catch them as they rose toward the ceiling. The amplified seashell's roar gave way to gurgly murmurs of delight as the audience made a children's game of the bubbly, embryonic proportion which had come into play. Some of them stood on their chairs and still others stood on their tables attempting to grab or at least touch the highest bubbles. The bubbles burst as soon as they were grabbed or touched. Even those which went untouched burst when they reached the ceiling, if not before.

Each bubble as it burst was both a flashbulb exploding and the blink of a weeping eye. Cavewall and canvas rolled into one, each as it burst unveiled a hollow socket on whose teardrop interior we etched an otherwise aborted exit, a caesarian "out." Penguin's toylike horn, we now saw, was as much a crowbar as an axe, and we all, band and audience alike, made the most of the opening, the caesarian door it'd left ajar. I for one couldn't help thinking of Jarred Bottle, finding that on doing so the bits of glass or of broken cowrie shells embedded in my brow came together like a third eye, a unicorn's horn and the lamp on a miner's cap rolled into one. It was only by virtue of such a forced and fragile sense of coherence that I was able to go on with my staccato sparks, the bubbles which now came out of the horn notwithstanding. The other members of the band seemed likewise tested and toughened—though each in an aptly idiosyncratic way—by the buoyant, albeit "burstable" proportion which had come into play.

"Bottomed Out" had grown in finesse as well as ferocity and there was no reason for it to ever end, though it eventually did. It turned out to be the last number we played, though its denouement (if one may put it so) didn't come to light till some time after the music had ended. It was after we'd packed up our instruments, gotten paid and so forth that we walked out of the club only to find that Lambert's car was no longer parked in front. We looked about and saw that the surroundings weren't the same as when we'd come in. Finally, Lambert walked to the corner, took a look at the street sign and came back. We were on Ninth, not San Pablo, it turned out. The Scarab had moved east a block while we were inside. The move had occurred, we knew at once, during "Bottomed Out."

We now couldn't keep our thoughts from turning south, toward L.A. Though a block doesn't amount to much in the ultimate vastness of it all, it was nonetheless a promising start. We carried ourselves back to "Bottomed Out" and retroactively looked ahead to the symposium at Cal Arts. The opening movement of "The Creaking of the Word" had already begun.

Yours,

N.

23.V.81

Dear Angel of Dust,

Please forgive the long silence. I've meant to answer your last letter for some time now (I too, of course, wish we'd gotten "Bottomed Out" on tape), but the past few weeks have been unusually busy. Then, to complicate matters even more, the news of Marley's death last week really laid me low. I'm sure I don't have to tell you how broken up we all are, even though we've more or less known it was coming for several months. Even so, the news of his passing hit us hard, hit me especially so. I felt I was finally cured of my shattered cowrie shell attacks that last night at the Scarab when the shards in my brow came together like a third eye, a unicorn's horn and the lamp on a miner's cap rolled into one. But the cure, if that's what it was, was a tenuous one at best (more like a tenuous, problematic reprieve—the unwet, residual salt of an evaporative tear). The news of Marley's death brought on another attack.

It was as I was thumbing thru a number of concert photos taken from magazines and so forth that it hit me. I couldn't help noticing that in several of them Marley's eyes are closed and his right hand raised to his head, his fingers and thumb respectively pressed to his forehead and right temple. This appeared to be related to the brain tumor, as though (something inside me insisted) he'd felt it coming long in advance. It was this insistence or realization which subjected me to a rush of sympathetic affliction (empathetic access, inverse couvade), laser-like threads of thoroughgoing "thru-ness" my shattered cowrie shell attack amounted to this time around. It wasn't Ornette's "Embraceable You" I heard as the trance came on, but a piercing, odd, annunciative wail, a call or a cry compounded of sinuous threads emanating from each bit of broken shell. Each of these threads approximated a mix of Augustus Pablo's melodica line on Earl Zero's "Home Sweet Home," Little Walter's harmonica work on Muddy's "40 Days and 40 Nights," Trane's opening soprano statement on "The Promise" and the accordion choir I heard in my sleep on a train in Spain several years ago. Each appeared enticed by if not outright possessed of an adrenaline high, a transparent advance whose catatonic lucidity introduced a new wrinkle or note to the attack. Instead of losing consciousness of what was going on, that is, I found myself encased in a brooding clairvoyance. My head seemed to be set in crystal, so concrete was the impact of looking, so substantial or solid the surrounding clarity and light.

It was an oddly inert clarity, however, the abject address of a would-be rise above thoroughgoing "thru-ness." I found myself unable to do anything but sit, staring straight ahead. I sat up straight in the chair I was in, my back erect against its back and each arm on an armrest, my feet resting flat on the floor. I was the true, undisputed King of Sorrow. I sat as though mourning were a sad, see-thru investiture, an unsuspected throne. Neither sleeping nor needing sleep, I sat up that way all night and thru most of the following morning.

Indeed, the King's reign might never have ended were it not for Aunt Nancy. She showed up at eleven that morning as we'd previously planned. (I've been having trouble getting "Dog-Eared Anacrusis," "Opposable Thumb at the Water's Edge" and the Toupouri piece to mesh the way I want for "The Creaking of the Word." At rehearsal a few nights before she'd mentioned having a few ideas and suggestions as to how I might pull it off. It was to talk about this that we'd arranged to get together.) She rang the doorbell several times but my brooding lucidity had me glued to the chair. I heard the bell but could neither get up nor say anything. Finally, trying the knob and finding the door unlocked, she simply let herself in. She half shouted was anybody home, but almost before the words got out of her mouth she noticed me sitting there.

It took her a while to figure out what was going on. First she asked why hadn't I answered the doorbell. When I didn't say anything she asked again. I again remained silent and she asked was I playing some sort of joke. Finally, noticing the straight-ahead, dilated look in my eyes, she gave up on trying to get a response. She gazed around the room a while, then brought her attention back to the photographs on the coffee table in front of my chair. A lightbulb seemed to come on inside her head. She came closer and placed her hand on my forehead. She snapped her fingers in front of my eyes. She then began to talk to me again, a sort of cooing to the effect that, though she respected my sensitivity, I wasn't the only one affected by Marley's death and that, in a sense, it was egotistical of me to make so much of my grief. She also made mention of certain reports coming out of Jamaica that some of the more orthodox Rastas, not believing in death, were making a point of neither mourning nor attending the funeral.

Aunt Nancy went on like this for no telling how long, but to no avail. I continued to say nothing and to stare straight ahead, my back erect against the back of the chair and my arms on its armrests, my feet resting flat on the floor. After a while she tried a different approach. She walked over to the record cabinet, pulled out a few records and proceeded to put them on the turntable and play selected cuts. She began with some of Marley's more "upful" tracks, things like "Lively Up Yourself" and "Wake Up and Live," playing each of them a number of times. My paralytic lucidity, however, maintained its grip. Still, she kept at it, going on to play such cuts as Earl Zero's "Get Happy," Max Roach's "Members, Don't Git Weary," Stanley Turrentine's version of "Feeling Good" and so forth. It was a piece by Fela which finally did the trick.

The album's his most recent. What I have, in fact, is an advance pressing a friend of mine sent me from Lagos not long ago. It's called *Original Suffer Head* and features the group Fela now calls his Egypt 80 Band. Aunt Nancy put side one on first, the title cut, but for a long while it didn't have any effect. Afflicted Kingship showed no sign of letting up. It wasn't until toward the end of side one that my brow began to loosen a bit, to lose some of the impactedness of thoroughgoing "thru-ness." More specifically, it was during the part where they sing:

> Them turn us to Suffer Head O . . .
> . . . Original Suffer Head!!!
> It is time for Jeffa Head O . . .
> . . . Original Jeffa Head!!!
> Me I say Suffer Head must go!!! Jeffa Head must come!!!

Hearing this, I developed a small twitch just above my right eyebrow. Encouraged by the twitch, Aunt Nancy turned the record over as soon as side one was finished.

The decisive thing seemed to be that she now also held the record jacket up in my line of sight, turning it from time to time so I could see both sides. The picture of Fela on the back proved especially effective. It shows him sitting in a chair with his left leg crossing his right, wearing nothing but the strap for his tenor and a pair of black bikini briefs. The tenor sits in a stand just in front of him, painted red, green and black and adorned with cowrie shells, the most prominent lining the lip of the tenor's bell. I couldn't help feeling that the horn was not only extracting the broken shells from my forehead but in doing so managing to piece them back together.

This feeling was reinforced by "Power Show," the cut which takes up most of side two. The photographed cowries' homeopathic address of my brow was ably assisted by the biting insistence of Fela's tenor solo, the irritable, oddly surgical edge he somehow gives it. Thoroughgoing "thru-ness" and the Afflicted Kingship it installed now seemed to dissolve like a speeded-up glacier's retreat. I felt my brow touched by an apparent miracle of offhand precision, as though Fela were my very own Surgeon-With-A-Rusty-Knife.

In any case, I did come out of it, though certain side effects lingered for several days. The whole thing slowed me down considerably. Catching up on the sleep I'd missed was part of it, but a residual air of distraction took its toll as well. I'm now hurrying to make up for lost time, trying to put the finishing touches on “The Creaking of the Word” for the symposium next week. I don’t imagine you’ll hear from me again until after it’s over.

As ever,
N.

PS: Any idea what a Jeffa Head is?

2.VI.81

Dear Angel of Dust,

"The Creaking of the Word" and the entire symposium came off beautifully. What took place exceeded my wildest dreams. Enclosed you'll find a videotape of our presentation, which will spare me the effort of trying to describe all of what went on. I do, however, have to go into a couple of things. First of all, you'll notice that the stand-ins for the Crossroads Choir are wearing headphones. You'll also notice that "Opposable Thumb at the Water's Edge" can't really be heard. This came about because of my inability to get the three compositions to mesh. My version of the Toupouri piece and the Boneyard Brass Octet's rendition of "Dog-Eared Anacrusis" play *into* one another, as you can hear, extremely well. No matter how hard I tried and no matter how many variations I experimented with, however, I couldn't work "Opposable Thumb" in. I finally solved the problem the night before the day of our presentation by deciding to have each of the Crossroads Choir stand-ins wear a Sony Walkman (loaded, of course, with a cassette of the part played by the band member whose place he or she would be taking). As you can see on the videotape, they walk around on their elliptical course listening to the cassettes. This way "Opposable Thumb" remains a part of what's going on—albeit a disjointed, dispersed and, for most, inaudible or even "unheard-of" part—and the audible mesh remains undisturbed (on the surface at least). This has the added advantage of a certain metaphoric and rather obvious relevance to the theme of my talk.

The second matter is a lot harder to give an account of. You won't hear a hint of it on the videotape. You may, however, notice me distractedly glancing to my left from time to time. What was happening was that the sand-anointed *envoi* Djamilaa'd introduced during our closing set a few weeks ago at the Scarab resurfaced and reasserted itself. Like a gremlin, a grain of salt or a ghost in the machine, it not only reneged on its own mixed-metaphorical promise but renounced or at best renegotiated the highstrung harvest one hears in "Dog-Eared Anacrusis." The latter's "marriage made in Heaven" between aim and object came under fire not only as opiate but, even worse, opportunistic. It was an eerie, ventriloquistic intervention whose point of origin (which is what I was glancing toward to my left) seemed to be the second focus of Precipitous Halo's ellipse. Since I stood at the other focus I occupied a privileged position with regard to being put upon or pestered by Djamilaa's *envoi*. (The conjunction of *pestered* and *privileged* made its insistence all the more disconcerting.) I was evidently the only one who heard it.

But the fact that there Djamilaa clearly was, playing bass clarinet, one of the Orbiting Chorus of horns which revolved around me, made the *envoi* even more disconcerting. The insinuation which addressed me from my left did come across occasionally with a Dolphy-like squawk more like a bass clarinet's than that of Djamilaa's own voice. It was as though Djamilaa, even while playing the horn, threw her voice by way of a boomeranging trickster thread. This trickster thread, moreover, was a telepathic tether which tied the two of us to one another, a roundabout, circumlocutory "soul serenade."

Put another way, it was as though we were dancers, Djamilaa and I, on the "Make-Believe Ballroom" TV show I used to watch as a kid. She was my flung partner it seemed, made to fly away from me only to be pulled back once she'd gone as far as our stretched arms would allow. This dance, the mimed ingestion of separation we enacted, made for a thrown, dislocated intervention (infiltration on the one hand, preemptive enticement on the other), a punning sense of far-flung investiture: *thrown = throne*. Djamilaa was clearly my Bedouin Queen.

But Bedouin Queenship's exaggeration only made matters worse.

It was exactly its overdone, operatic aspect which bothered me most, the very costume/courtly extravagance or lack of adequation I was there (or thought I was there) to advocate. Nothing I say can even convey, much less account for, what occurred. I could go on "putting it another way" but I won't.

Maybe I shouldn't have brought this second matter up at all, but in many ways it seemed to be the crux of the entire presentation. However unplanned and unexpected it was, however unsusceptible to mechanical reproduction, it seemed to me something which anyone interested in what went on should be told about.

In any case, I hope the videotape makes up somewhat for your not having been able to be there.

As ever,
N.

17.VI.81

Dear Angel of Dust,

Thank you for your flattering letter. I too was especially pleased with the way Orbiting Chorus and Precipitous Halo penetrated without intruding on one another—with all the grace, as you say, of the Florida A&M marching band. I'm glad the videotape gave you some sense of how things went. As it turns out, however, I'm still haunted by Djamilaa's *envoi*. I can't seem to rid my thoughts of the way it despaired of an elusive congruity between itself and my recited text. As I said in my last letter, it seemed to insist upon or to insinuate a precarious wedding, an operatic sense of a tenuous thread or an antiphonal tether tying my words to its own arch, incantatory enticement. A sense of unlikely, operatic elevation repeatedly brought me up short. Still, by the sheer force of repetition it left me no more than a stone's throw away, no more than an arced, asymptotic "inch" away from operatic height.

I should perhaps point out that behind "operatic" I'm thinking of Krenek's phrase "the 'non-sense' of sung words." In fact, I've been so taken up with this that I took another look at the essay in which the phrase occurs. It's a piece Krenek wrote in the mid-thirties, "Is Opera Still Possible Today?" One of the things he says struck me as related to Gap Station in "The Creaking of the Word." He speaks of an "antithetical tension, allusions which break up or crack the apparently consistent whole," and goes on at greater length: "So in modern opera music is not merely a means of heightening, ennobling verbal language—it is not there to make the words more eloquent, so to speak; it is deliberately contrasted with the words, placed behind the words, making them transparent so that you can see their second inner significance. . . . The music does not achieve this by 'heightening' the words but by opening an abyss of meaning and countermeaning behind them."

I don't think it's going too far to say that Djamilaa's arch, asymptotic *envoi* was an antithetical aria. I'm forced, in fact, to go a bit farther: The stone whose throw allotted my lack of operatic election was the biblical "stone that the builders refused." Djamilaa's voice was the eventual cornerstone initially ousted by strict construction.

This brings me to the piece I'm enclosing. It's something of a rewrite of "The Creaking of the Word," a reconstruction of the spectral serenade which infiltrated the presentation. It's not meant to erase the earlier version so much as extend it. Though I call it "an after-the-fact lecture/libretto from the symposium 'Locus and Locomotivity in Postcontemporary Music'" I really have the future in mind. You should read it, that is, as an outline, a skeletal draft of a possible "opera" which has begun to take shape.

I look forward, of course, to your comments.

Yours,
N.

THE CREAKING OF THE WORD

An after-the-fact lecture/libretto from the symposium "Locus and Locomotivity in Postcontemporary Music"

Djamilaa stood at the window. Word was out that a band of aliases had blown into town. Rumor was unclear as to whether it was a combo or simply a schizophrenic one-man band, but Djamilaa wasn't sure it mattered. She'd heard that the band now went by the name Flaunted Fifth, but that until recently it'd been known as Jarred Bottle, JB for short. (There were some who said J&B.) The band had blown into town on the tail-end of the longest heat wave in years. Djamilaa had received a letter from a DB a few days before.

The letter, which came utterly out of the blue, addressed her by a nickname she hadn't gone by in years. "Dear Dja," it began, "I've gotten weary of letting sleeping dogs lie. I'm on my way to see you." The letter went on to announce that its author would be presenting a lecture/demonstration on the blues at a music symposium to be held at Cal Arts. Included in the letter was a lengthy quote, referred to as a Namesake Epigraph:

> The rhythmic density of Patton's music is exceptional, even in an idiom as rhythmically oriented as blues, and so is his frequent use of thirteen-and-a-half-bar verses. According to the anthropologist and blues researcher David Evans, these apparent idiosyncrasies are rooted in pre-blues music. Evans noticed that in the hill country djust east of the Delta, where much

> archaic black music has been preserved, fife and drum bands, guitarists, and young musicians playing a homemade, one-stringed children's instrument called the djitterbug generally structure their performances around repeating one-measure patterns. Evans believes that the use of these one-measure figures as structural building blocks derives from folk drumming and was transferred to the guitar via the one-stringed djitterbug, the first stringed instrument mastered by many early blues guitarists. If Evans is correct, the thirteen-and-a-half-bar verses and rhythmic density of Patton's music represent a direct link between the polyrhythmic folk drumming of the nineteenth century and the blues that came after him.

This the letter referred to as Namesake Epigraph #3, though Djamilaa preferred to think of 3 as $\frac{21}{7}$. Similarly, she thought of 13½ as $\frac{\left(\frac{21}{7}\right)^{\frac{21}{7}}}{2}$. Even as a child she'd had a head for figures.

Djamilaa couldn't help noticing that throughout the letter every word which normally begins with a "j" had a "d" added on in front. It occurred to her that the "D" in the signature "DB" at the end of the letter might well have taken the place of a "J." She couldn't help thinking that "DB" might be short for "Djarred Bottle." It was this which had brought her to the window.

Unbeknown to her, Flaunted Fifth lingered on the outskirts of town, caught up in a dream. The city was an asymptotic limit. Combo and one-man band rolled into one, he preferred arriving a little bit late, a bit in back of the beat, an unstated, staggered, unreduced fraction of himself. Yes, it was he who had written the letter. Yes, the "D" had taken the place of the "J." Djamilaa had no way of knowing, however, that in the dream Flaunted Fifth was caught up in the "j" in her nickname was silent, that the dream she too was caught up in, dim as it was, was a dream of Dahomean "Da," the orphaned embrace animating their pursuit of an absent hand, an absent father's absentminded caress. It was a deep, aboriginal writhing, an aboriginal twitch Flaunted Fifth obeyed as he floundered among the weeds of a soon-to-be-paved vacant lot, one of the few such lots—not yet cemented or asphalted over—remaining in all of L.A.

"The city," he muttered under his breath, reflecting on the sprawling, postcopernican outskirts the entire town, it seemed to him, had become, "is an asymptotic limit. Nobody knows where it ends or where it begins." He felt the same, though with even more urgency, about the fugitive touch and/or fallow accent of the unfelt father's hand he and Djamilaa were caught up in. The disappearance of a definitive threshold (and thus the loss of an assured center as well) belied the strutting, upstart jitterbug he took himself to be. What he really was was a staggering, highstrung jitterbug, following—not without faltering—in what he took to be his father's footsteps, though "took to be his father's footsteps" made him laugh. His father, everybody knew, had neither arms nor legs.

Djamilaa stood at the window wearing a crumpled, light cotton dress she'd obviously slept in. Unbeknown to her, on the other side of town Flaunted Fifth stood among waist-high weeds, unzipped his fly and began to pee, gazing at the oranges, purples, reds and pinks of yet another chemical sunset, the polychrome curtain coming down on yet another numbered day. Two recollections fed his absentminded musings, two recollections from his early childhood in Liberty City.

Namesake Recollection #1 took him back to the patch of dandelions and other blooming weeds behind his uncle's house, where he and his friends caught bees and butterflies in mason jars. A dirt road ran past the patch of weeds. It was on the side of this road that they'd found a run-over snake one day. No one would touch it, but they all marvelled at the color of its skin, a lush iridescent green. The dead snake was still there the next day, though still no one would touch it. They did, however, poke it with a stick. Its skin had turned a turquoise blue. On the third day the snake was a purplish ruby color and still, other than poking it with the stick, no one would touch it. They came back the next day, anxious to see what color its skin would be, but the snake was gone. This was when Flaunted Fifth was four years old, a few weeks after his mother had left his father and they'd moved in with his uncle.

As the liquid flowed from the "middle leg" or "fifth limb" he held in his hand, Flaunted Fifth wondered if he hadn't embellished the memory some. He suspected himself of having been influenced by tales of Damballah, the Dahomean rainbowsnake he'd heard so much about. He brushed the suspicion aside almost as soon as it arose, for he saw a truth in the recollection, saw that the embellishment, if that's what it was, was irrefutably true to the hunger which prompted it. He was aware of a need to cannibalize one's past, to cast a fanatic, far-reaching net, no matter how apparently outlandish, no matter how apparently farfetched. But to do so, he had to admit, was to be eaten in turn, was to be stunned by a namesake viper's bite, was to be bled as if by a vampire's teeth. He couldn't escape the feeling, the heartfelt conviction, that a curious claim had been staked in his chest. A fanciful, preemptive past had laid claim to him, eating him just as he ate it. What he felt was a hunger which cut so reciprocally (two-way predator, two-way prey) that all its claims, no matter how fanciful, bore accurate, exacting witness, never ceasing to obey, even as they "embellished," disingenuous fact or ventriloquistic truth.

Slowly a numbness overtook the hand in which Flaunted Fifth held his "middle leg" or "fifth limb." Unbeknown to him, Djamilaa stood at her window on the other side of town, wearing no panties beneath her crumpled, light cotton dress as was her wont when the weather turned hot. She felt a hand alight on her waist, a right hand which caressed her right side, eased its way down and a bit to the left to cup the rounded base of her right buttock, squeezed it firmly, then rested there. She turned to her left to see who it was but saw no one. Neither she nor Flaunted Fifth had any way of knowing that the feeling which had fled his hand did so in order to seek out Djamilaa's waist and pantyless rump. It was as if his fanatic, far-reaching net, unbeknown to him, laid claim to the very hand which cast it, to a phantom itch, a fallow eighth-day accent's two-way claw, a need for feeling's numb reciprocal "catch."

Flaunted Fifth himself understood the numbness which had claimed his hand as having to do with the burning he felt in his chest.

It was only proper that on his way to deliver an address on the blues he took the burntness/numbness axis to be an inverse bottleneck displacement, a snakelike upward slide harking back to Namesake Recollection #2 (or, as he also thought of it, Heartfelt Recollection #2).

Namesake Recollection #2 carried him several months farther back than Namesake Recollection #1. Again the setting was Liberty City. His mother and father hadn't separated yet. It was an extremely bright, sunny day and he and his girlfriend—his very first girlfriend, in fact, though he couldn't, however hard he now tried, recall her name—were playing on the sidewalk in front of his house. He'd gotten a tricycle for Christmas a few months before and was giving his girlfriend a ride. (It was a model which featured a passenger cart in back.) His father came up the sidewalk as he and his girlfriend played. Before turning to go up the walkway and into the house, his father stopped, reached into his pocket, took out a dime and handed it to him. Flaunted Fifth took it and said thank you. He then opened his hand to let his girlfriend see. It was a new dime, extraordinarily shiny, made even shinier by the extraordinary Florida sun. He and his girlfriend stared at it, entranced by its blinding reflection of the sun's light. The dime lay in his palm with the adhesive, burning feel of a piece of dry ice. It slowly burnt a hole thru his hand, then fell to the sidewalk below.

As the liquid continued to flow from the "middle leg" or "fifth limb" he held in his hand, Flaunted Fifth absentmindedly reflected on the shiny dime his father had given him years before. He knew, without telling himself outright, that he teetered on the edge of the hole in his palm, that the tipsy inheritance his father had left him launched a migratory flight of otherwise numb, burnt-out emotion (fly-by-night romance). This had given rise, in the most literal sense, to a technical-ecstatic vertigo, a dizzy, seemingly drugged immunity to every thrill he subsequently sought. Thus the numbness in his hand, he reflected. Thus the burning he felt in his chest.

Flaunted Fifth thought of himself, looking ahead to the lecture he was in town to give, as the fretboard of a blues guitar. The riff whoever played him resorted to most was a full-octave slide between *numbed* and *scorched*. His father's touch or surrogate touch had sown a void, it was true, but *numbed* was not so much a defect or deficient feeling as an inverse bottleneck forfeiture (fly-by-night extremity, migratory touch). The point he was in town to put across was that *burning* was to *numb* as *feeling* was to *flight*. He instinctively knew that fugitive touch had *flown* from his hand, though he didn't realize how far. That it flew to the rounded base of Djamilaa's right buttock had no way to occur to him. That it outflew the burning in his chest voided heartfelt law.

Djamilaa too knew the feeling of being eaten from within, the lingering burn and the bite of her own indigestible past. The invisible hand which caressed and cupped her right buttock unveiled and obeyed a deepseated sense of providential fit, a deepseated belief or a need to believe that convex buttock and concave hand confirmed a fugitive law of conjunctive curvature, reciprocally enacted by virtue of complying with a seesaw sense of interlocking parts. The phantom hand which fondled her rump, she felt, arose from a sense or an assurance of seesaw adequation. After she turned and saw no one was there, she felt the hand to be the proof of an introvert conviction she outwardly rejected but inwardly fed. She turned back and again gazed out the window.

The idea of the approaching lecture/demonstration intrigued her. Public speech had long been outlawed locally, as was much in evidence in what could be seen outside. Police helicopters circled noisily overhead and everyone who passed her window, whether on foot or in a car, wore a Sony Walkman headset. The idea of DB's lecture/demonstration attracted as well as intrigued her, but she couldn't help suspecting him of wishful thinking. He'd failed, she couldn't help noticing, to give any particulars (times, dates, etc.) regarding the symposium his lecture/demonstration was to be a part of. She couldn't help hearing something of a confession in what the letter referred to as Namesake Epigraph #4, a quote which, according to the letter, DB had found in a book on Stravinsky: "In the Kingdom of the Father there is no drama but only dialogue, which is disguised monologue." She heard it as a two-way confession, in fact, in part a projection of her own deep-seated dialogue with herself, a dialogue whose deep-seated father fixation was the fly-by-night family romance which harassed and had its way with her, burning as well as biting her from within.

She cautioned herself, however, against projecting too blindly, against blinding herself to the possibility that DB might actually pull his lecture/demonstration off. She warned herself against not seeing it as more than mere utopian thinking. The fact was that she had no way of knowing just how far DB's reach exceeded his grasp. Unbeknown to her, his plan was to parlay his lecture/demonstration into a weekly radio program devoted to the blues. All he needed, as he saw it, was a sponsor. He'd already, in fact, spoken to the manufacturers of Cheer, a blue cleaning agent which would give the show the soap-operatic overtones everyone he consulted said were needed for success.

Knowing nothing of DB's radio ambitions, Djamilaa stood at the window holding the letter she'd received a few days before. The shadowy hand continued to rest on the rounded base of her right buttock. She removed the letter from its envelope, unfolded it and reread Namesake Epigraph #4, preferring to think of 4 as $\frac{6^2}{(\frac{21}{7})^2}$. (Her head for figures had lately nourished a penchant for roundabout fractions.) Her undigested past preyed upon her as she mused on the quote again. Her reflections as she reread it came into unwitting sympathy with DB's soap-operatic aspiration, so strong was the quality of soliloquistic fiction or ventriloquistic script the family yarn she inwardly spun had come to possess. It was as if the yarn which had laid claim to her was a sympathetic string brought into unconscious proximity to DB's soap-operatic overtones or would-be harmonics. The vibrating yarn which ate away at her from within made Djamilaa an unsuspecting participant in DB's lecture/demonstration, an unwitting member of the band which had blown into town.

So deep was Djamilaa's induction into DB's combo, so indelibly written was her ventriloquistic script into his eventual soap-operatic radio show, that her musings amounted to Namesake Recollection #3, Namesake Recollection #4, Namesake Recollection #5 and Namesake Recollection #6. The four Namesake Recollections (also known as Heartfelt Recollections) segued or tracked into one another like cuts on a "concept" album, the lines between them blurred if not erased.

Djamilaa had long sought to sort them out, to distinguish pattern from pretense, fact from figment, to see things soberly and clearly, think in either/or, black-and-white terms. But the blue, in-between truth was that she either couldn't or (what amounted to the same thing) could but could do so for only the most fleeting, irreducible fraction of an instant. An infectious, hemorrhaging coloration seemed to invade and permeate everything. Soap-Operatic Overtone #1 was the fact that Djamilaa, whether she knew it or not, sought to be done with indelible coloration, to wash her hands of its tainted polychrome sunset, wash her hands of its bleeding rainbowsnake.

As she pored over Namesake Epigraph #4 standing at the window, Djamilaa was haunted by the dream from which she'd recently awakened. She'd taken a nap on the couch in the living room earlier in the afternoon, falling into a not quite settled, not quite restful sleep, the sort of fitful, uncomfortable nap one tends to fall into on hot afternoons. She'd dreamt of her father's funeral, reliving her grief and shock at his unexpected death several months before. In the dream she relived in painfully exact and vivid detail every aspect of the events leading up to and taking place during the funeral: the phone call out of the blue from her mother saying her father had died, the hurriedly arranged flight home, the unhappy reunion with relatives she hadn't seen in years, the pinched or twisted look on the left side of her father's face as he lay in the coffin (a crease or an arrested twitch cut in the flesh by the stroke he'd suffered—an indentation, the morticians assured the family, they'd done everything they could to remove).

What haunted her most about the dream was the curious turn it had taken at the end: The family had returned home from the cemetery and entered the house to find her father alive again, taking a nap on the living room couch. What she recalled and what stayed with her most were the mixed emotions she'd felt as her father woke up, rubbed his eyes and—as though it were *they* who had died—surprisedly muttered, "Welcome back." However happy she was at his having come back to life, it was a happiness mixed with the unhappy certainty that everything they'd been thru those past few days would someday have to be gone thru again.

Djamilaa had awakened from the dream with a renewed sense of pitiless reprieve, a grim renewal of a sense of useless postponement it seemed she'd been haunted by all her life. The fact was that she'd been an adopted child (Soap-Operatic Overtone #2) and that it was her foster father, not her actual father, who had died of a stroke. For all she knew, her actual father was still alive. Though not an orphan in the technical sense, she'd always thought of herself as one. Her actual parents (her mother actually) had put her up for adoption at the time of her birth, "dying," to her way of thinking, in doing so. She viewed her adoption as a mixed blessing, both a loss of her parents and, insofar as it provided new ones, a mere postponement of the inevitable loss of one's parents, the eventual orphaning one is born into. Better to have gotten it over with at the beginning, the hard side of her thought, a huskiness coming into her reflective, inner voice which belied the soap-operatic sympathies Flaunted Fifth played on from the other side of town.

The other side of her sense of providential fit, in other words, was a feeling of deep, thoroughgoing estrangement. She knew she was all alone in the world, an absolute orphan. But the gruff, resolute orphan she took herself to be was in turn belied by her authentic attachment to her foster family, particularly her father, and her inquiries over the years into the identities of her actual parents and the circumstances surrounding her birth. These inquiries, however, hadn't come up with much other than that her mother had reputedly been a woman of loose habits and her father a foreigner—some said Cuban, some said he'd come from Brazil—passing thru Mauritania. She'd evidently been born of a shortlived affair, no more than a one-night stand perhaps.

Djamilaa looked up from DB's letter and sighed, realizing that her husky, self-protective inner voice was being eaten at from within. It was being thinned and hollowed out by the fly-by-night aegis or wing she was under. Absentmindedly watching the passersby in their Walkman headsets, she couldn't help thinking that her fly-by-night parentage had fostered, as it were, an answering lightness and a birdlike buoyancy, a certain hollowness (hollow bones, hollow blood) conducive to flight. That blood could be so loaded yet be so empty left no recourse but a cultivated numbness, a husk or a callousness, an unsecured fit. Husk and hollowness were in longterm league with one another, a fact to be suggested in DB's lecture/demonstration by a loaded use of the word "maroon" (a token, DB would explain, of Djamilaa's Cuban or Brazilian roots). Runaway slave and shipwreck survivor, absolute orphan implied stranded, free.

DB's goal was to find a place for Djamilaa's gruff inner husk on his program. Her operatic soprano had attracted him at first, but more and more the throaty depth of that inner voice eroded operatic height. In fact, he was tempted to call his program "Rag Opera"—alluding to the way the two indicted and potentially tore one another to shreds. From his position on the other side of town he was able to note that a husky inwardness ate away at superficial buoyancy, that an inverse weight complicated the anchor which, only on the surface, got in flight's or flotation's way. He sensed a parallel with his own inverse bottleneck slide between *feeling* and *flight*.

Djamilaa's inward huskiness, more specifically, reminded DB of Maria Bethania, a Brazilian singer whose voice he'd long been drawn to but now heard anew. He now heard a corrective or a possible corrective to "atmospheric" height, to operatic inflation. The eventual strains of Djamilaa's rag aria began to address his inner ear, a "throaty husk" he'd make a note of once his right hand was free again.

The waist-high weeds he stood among rustled. The subtle gust of warm air which blew thru them subsided almost as soon as it arose. A police car, he noticed, had circled the block. As the liquid continued to flow from the euphemistic "limb" he held in his hand an odd warmth invaded the crook of his right arm. It felt as if Tiger Balm or some other such ointment had been rubbed into the bend between his forearm and biceps. There was a cushiony side to the feeling as well, as though the back of someone's head and neck rested there. Flaunted Fifth couldn't shake the feeling of a head of soft, curly hair pressed against the V between his biceps and forearm. He was intrigued by this new wrinkle or bend in the bottleneck slide between *numbed* and *scorched*. He absentmindedly toyed with the figure of a V lying on its side, a V at whose vertex he placed "Warm Cushiony Crook" and at the ends of whose "arms" he put "Burning Chest" and "Numb Hand."

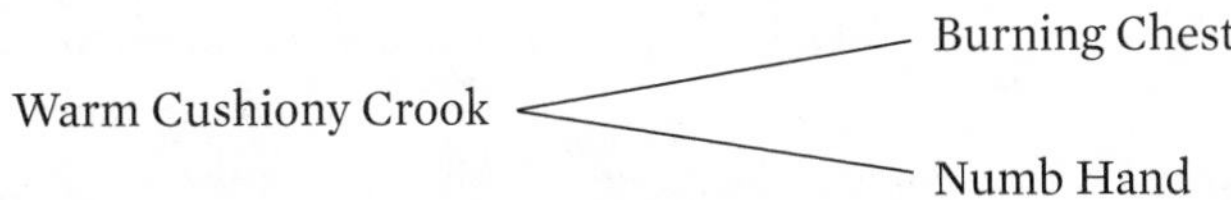

The prostrate V, he felt, was an emotional figure he'd been given to work with as if it were a riff or a leitmotif. He'd make a place for it in his lecture/demonstration, his pilot radio show.

Flaunted Fifth heard the noise of a helicopter overhead. He noticed the cops in the police car looking his way. The emotional figure he absentmindedly toyed with was given an abruptly ominous edge by the setting sun, the helicopter overhead and the police car circling the block, all of which put an inverse halo around it. A panicky rush ran thru him as the cops continued to look his way. He couldn't help remembering that several black men had been killed by the L.A. police in recent months, victims of a chokehold whose use there were now efforts to outlaw. The V-shaped warmth in the crook of his right arm seemed to detach itself, rise up and, like an ironic boomerang, press itself against the front of his neck. He imagined himself held in the sweaty crook of a cop's arm.

It was hard not to be overwhelmed by the lethal irony which invaded everything. Flaunted Fifth was suddenly haunted by having once written that the use of the falsetto in black music, the choked-up ascent into a problematic upper register, had a way, as he'd put it, of "alchemizing a legacy of lynchings." He'd planned to make use of this idea again in his lecture/demonstration, but the prospect of a cop's arm around his neck reminded him that every concept, no matter how figural or sublime, had its literal, deadletter aspect as well. It now seemed too easy to speak of "alchemy," too easy not to remember how inescapably real every lynching had been. He'd always thought of himself as an advocate of spirit. He should have known the letter might someday do him in.

The ominous edge he picked up on was also, he realized, an attribute of spirit. Overtones and resonances inhabited the letter, causing it to creak like the floorboards and doors in a haunted house. That the emotional triad he absentmindedly toyed with, the triangulation he'd made a note of to himself, should creak with overtones of strangulation came as no surprise. That Namesake Epigraph #4 should be haunted by patriarchal patrol cars and helicopters, that it should creak with patriarchal prohibitions against public speech, equally came as no surprise. It all confirmed a "creaking of the spirit" he'd heard referred to in a song from the Bahamas many years before. That the creaking might kill was the price one occasionally paid. "No blues without dues," he reminded himself, making another mental note for his pilot radio show.

Flaunted Fifth grinned at his inward note, but for the first time he entertained doubts as to whether he could pull his lecture/demonstration off. The ban on public speech was no joking matter. To ward off these thoughts he now returned to the prostrate V he'd inwardly drawn, meditating on its emotional structuration as upon a mandala. He knew that in resorting to the diagram he was owning up to a synchronous constriction and construct, an almost autistic obsession with the link between feeling and cipher, sentimental ties which now drew him to Djamilaa, antiphonal ties which kept the two of them apart.

The stream of liquid flowing from the "limb" he held in his hand finally came to an end. As he re-zipped his pants he couldn't help associating the numbness in his right hand with his fear, as a four-year-old boy, of touching the snake which lay turning colors on the side of the road in back of his uncle's house. On his emotional diagram he replaced the words "Numb Hand" with the name "Damballah." Consistent with this, he rethought the burning he felt in his chest, understanding it now as a psychoanalytic fiction, an upward displacement of the hole burnt in his hand by his father's dime. The words "Burning Chest" he replaced with his father's name, "Obadiah."* The prostrate V he now came to see as a flock of geese in flight, the vertex or lead position of which was a pointer, a vector's aim or index. With little ado, he replaced the words "Warm Cushiony Crook" with the name "Djamilaa."

---

* Flaunted Fifth was well aware that in Hebrew the name meant "Servant of the Lord" (related, he suspected, to the Arabic "Abdullah"—"Slave of Allah"). But what held his attention most was that its first two syllables amounted to the Yoruba word for "king." The "i" in "-diah," like the "j" in "Dja," he preferred to think of as silent, viewing it, as in mathematics, as the symbol of an imaginary operation.

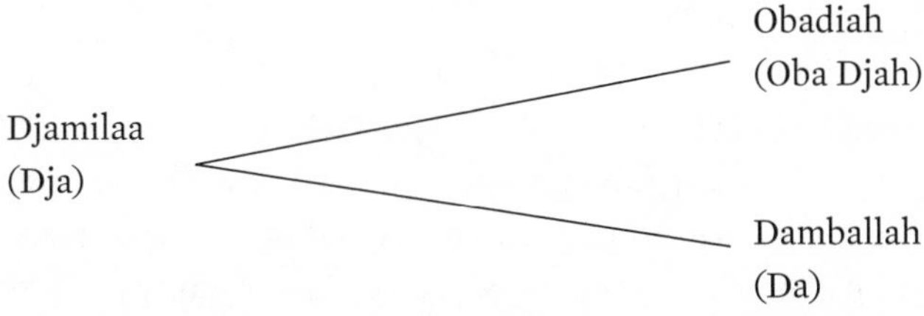

Flaunted Fifth had no way of knowing how much he knew. He was unaware that what he took to be a pilot run was the real thing. Djamilaa, unbeknown to him, had now segued into Namesake Recollection #6, at the center of which was a one-time lover's embrace. As she stood at her window on the other side of town, the phantom hand still caressing her right buttock, she had an unshakeable sense of atavistic flight, a sense of dry run and of automatic pilot so construed as to bring pseudo-structure abreast of genuine strain, authentic stress. The night she'd spent with her one-time lover now came back to her with a stark, unconscious clarity and contour (technical-ecstatic amplitude allied with absentminded, disjoint crux). The crook between his right biceps and forearm now seemed to rest against the back of her neck, just as it had throughout the night they'd spent together two and half years before.

It surprised and disconcerted her that the memory was still so alive, that her cultivated husk hadn't been able to dismiss it altogether, that she still hadn't put it aside or gone beyond it. She recalled the nested feeling she'd had lying next to him, the crook of his arm pillowing the back of her head and neck. "A child," she'd thought at the time, "in the V of his arm." But even then her sense of long-awaited arrival had had to vie with a sense of elegiac fit, the fly-by-night fate to which every joining or would-be joining seemed to succumb. The resolute orphan within her had risen up almost at once, cautioning against and cauterizing the potential wound which had opened up. Her inward husk warned her head for figures that "a child in the V of his arm" was a lapse into feelings which were best held at a distance if held at all.

Namesake Recollection #6, then, was as much a warning as it was a *récit*. The facts of it were fairly straightforward: Djamilaa's one-time lover had been literally that, a man she'd seen only once, a one-night stand. She'd met him on the beach one afternoon in Santa Monica. He was a vacationing Spaniard named Miguel who (Soap-Operatic Overtone #3) was to return to Spain the following day. What she'd thought would be a guarantee against getting involved had in the end boomeranged or backfired, for the brevity of their time together had aroused instead of ruled out a projected future. At the airport the following day they'd made promises to write one another regularly, to telephone from time to time, to see one another again in two months (the plan being that Djamilaa would visit him in Spain). She'd found it hard not to get on the plane with him then and there.

The plans and promises had reassured Djamilaa but they'd worried her as well, their projected future plucking a responsive, jittery string in her guarded heart, a tender string which, up until then, she hadn't thought was there. Even now as she stood at the window she had only the slightest inkling of the unconscious concert she was a part of and party to, the namesake realm and unwitting root in which everything, no matter how fleetingly, fit. At that very moment on the other side of town, that is, Flaunted Fifth made a note reminding himself that her name had to do with bonding. On the emotional construct or score he continued to work at he now replaced the name "Djamilaa" and its parenthetical "Dja" with the Arabic root √*dj*.m.^{c}.

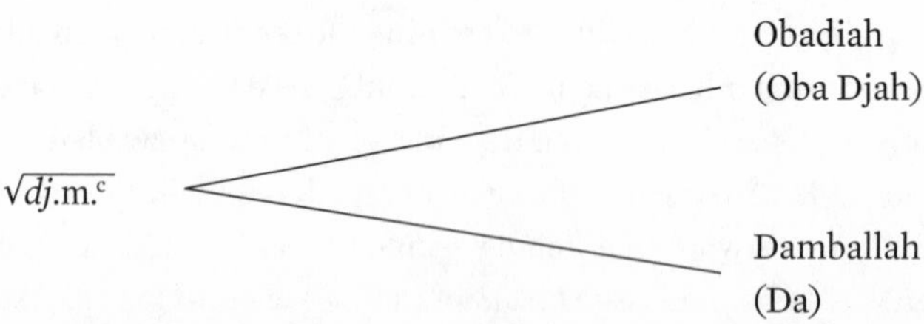

Having now zipped up his pants, Flaunted Fifth was relieved in more ways than one. His namesake session with a bottle of scotch that afternoon had left a bloated feeling in his bladder which it felt good to be finally rid of. "We drink to put out the fire," he'd announced every other time he turned up his glass, repeating a line his mother had told him was his father's favorite. This he alternated with one he took to be his mother's favorite, a line he'd heard her repeat endlessly over the years: "Tried to flee the fire but got burned anyway." (She'd left his father because of his drinking.)

The fallow, weed-infested ground on which he stood was also a source of relief. It felt good to be addressed by something other than the low-maintenance yards he'd seen so many of since blowing into town, the rock-filled and cement-covered "lawns" which were rapidly taking the place of plants and grass. Another gust of warm air made its way thru the weeds, reawakening thoughts of resistant, wind-assisted flight, the flock of geese his emotional V had already become. His knees weakened a bit as he allowed himself to sway with it, a curious cross (to his own fertile head for figures) between a prostrate V and a standing 8. The sudden, subtle jab of warm air subsided almost at once.

Flaunted Fifth also felt relieved by having admitted, albeit obliquely and diagrammatically, that Djamilaa was his reason for coming to L.A. It was a blue, soap-operatic admission which continued to be inflected with cop-show menace, patriarchal swat. The patrol car, that is, had stopped and the cops had gotten out and were now walking toward him. He experienced an abrupt, evanescent image or vision in which he saw, as in a funhouse mirror, Djamilaa's head in the shape of an hourglass. Time, she seemed to say without speaking, was running out.

Meanwhile Djamilaa went even deeper into Namesake Recollection #6, pierced and retroactively needled, it seemed, by the V of her one-time lover's embrace. The needling truth, she almost wept to recall, was that (Soap-Operatic Overtone #4) Miguel had broken things off three weeks, five letters and two phone calls after returning to Spain. The letter she'd gotten announcing that things couldn't go on, the frantic phone call she'd made to Spain after reading it, his refusal to explain beyond saying, "It just can't work," and his finally hanging up on her all came back to her now. She'd felt at the time and continued to feel that she'd been inducted into an order of inflation. The false bottom on which the affair had rested or seemed to rest exposed the equally fraudulent wings which had kept them aloft or seemed to keep them aloft in false flight. She sighed, gazing out the window at the setting sun. The whole thing had been a lie.

Djamilaa's inverse bottleneck slide between fraudulent bottom and equally unreal top was a motif she feared she was doomed to repeat without end. The sense of following in her mother's footsteps alarmed and annoyed her. She had a sense of being the hereditary, inevitable prey of repeated one-night stands, the inevitable, repetitive prey of this or that fly-by-night romance. The unconscious concert advanced on the basis of an endlessly repeated slide, Miguel's repeat of her mother's fly-by-night Brazilian or Cuban (fly-by-night lover and father rolled into one). It advanced and also grew more overt. As she gazed out the window at the Walkman-wearing passersby and at the setting sun, Djamilaa began to admit to herself that she secretly hoped DB might be Miguel in disguise.

DB's lecture/demonstration, as far as Djamilaa was concerned, would take the form of a serenade. Miguel would sing from the sidewalk below the window at which she now stood. She would answer in kind, doing so by virtue of an alternate genealogy she'd long ago adopted and now inwardly nursed. The voice she'd sing with from her second-floor window had been handed down to her by two remote, adopted namesake parents: her adopted namesake mother Djamila, the famous singer of Medina at the time of the first Umayyads, and her adopted namesake father Djamil, the early Arab love poet and founder of the Udhrite school of poets who, as the traditional saying puts it, "when loving, die."

It was this entrenched, potentially scandalous voice the serenade would elicit, an ulterior husk inside her already inward absolute orphan's husk. Her inherited voice, as Djamilaa heard it, would convey an inverse butterfly fragility, fluctuating between pure, rough-and-ready vamp on the one hand and poised, unconsummated adoration on the other. In part she took her cue from the cassette DB had included with his letter, a demo tape which began (appropriately, maybe pointedly, she felt) with Charley Patton singing "Pony Blues," followed by Muddy Waters singing "Long Distance Call." It was a 90-minute cassette which ranged widely following these first two numbers, weaving together music from all over the world. Included were (again, pointedly, Djamilaa felt) a song by the Cuban singer Bola de Nieve and one by Maria Bethania, as well as (most pointedly of all) a 10-minute piece called “Anta Oumri” done in the Egyptian style of Om Kalsoum by the Spanish singer Lole Montoya.

Djamilaa turned away from the window and walked across the room to lie down on the couch. The invisible hand continued to caress her right buttock. Having reached the couch, she took up the Sony Walkman lying on the coffee table, put on the headphones and lay down to listen to DB’s cassette yet again. She tucked a pillow behind her head and turned up the Walkman almost as loud as it could go. The music seemed to come from inside her head. It was as if the cassette were a therapeutic response to fly-by-night closeness, a would-be claim to a shrunken but still not available world.

Djamilaa turned the Walkman up so loud, in fact, that when the phone in the bedroom rang a half an hour later she didn’t notice. As the phone rang she lay unperturbed with her eyes closed, deeply absorbed in a song by the South Indian singer Kamala Kailasanathan. She had no way of knowing that it was Flaunted Fifth, who’d been arrested on a charge of public exposure, calling from the city jail. The phone, unheard by her, rang like an endlessly repeated note on a scratched record, the opening note of a blocked opera she and Flaunted Fifth would sing their hearts out in for days.

DJBOT BAGHOSTUS'S RUN

to the memory of

my mother
Sadie Mackey
1919–1990

my uncle
Ernest Wilcox
1923–1987

and
("in this thirst that defines Beauty / I have found kin")
Robert Duncan
1919–1988

11.VIII.81

Dear Angel of Dust,

Sorry to've taken so long getting back to you. I've been meaning to write for some time but it seems one thing or another has managed to get in the way. In any case, thank you very much for your last letter. It stirred me. I feel even more confirmed in the new sense of direction I've come into. For the time being, though, I prefer not to talk too directly about what I'm doing. I'll leave your questions regarding my antithetical opera for some other time. I can, however, bring you up to date on the other matter about which you asked, our search for a drummer. It's become a bit complicated.

We haven't, for one thing, had time for anything other than an offhand search, busy as we've been with our various projects. Still, we've asked around over the past weeks and gotten out to hear a few bands whose drummers we thought or were told we might be able to lure away. We've gone so far as to audition a few but haven't yet found one we can all agree on. You can imagine the delicateness of it all I'm sure. But our most recent audition—or would-be audition—took a turn which is worth going into in some detail. Why I say "would-be" will soon become clear.

The drummer in question is a fellow who calls himself SunStick. (Delbert Simms, I've heard, is the name he grew up with.) Up until recently he played with a band known as The Chosen Few. The band broke up about a month ago. It was Lambert who suggested we go after him. I turned out to be the only other person in the band who'd heard him play and I was quick to second Lambert's suggestion. I'd caught The Chosen Few's closing set one night at Onaje's a few months back and had been especially impressed with SunStick's playing, the way he has with time. He tends, that is, to pit the bass drum against the cymbal in such away as to rescind the punctuality of time, exacting a feeling for the tenuous, uninsured continuum the so-called beat thereby allows or is made to admit itself to be. In this, of course, he works the vein opened up by such people as Milford Graves, Sunny Murray and Rashied Ali. And by "vein" I mean exactly that, for what he does (or so it seemed to me that night) is insist upon a hemorrhaging, a dilation of one's way of looking at time. What struck me most was his playing's apparently absent yet all the more convincing regard for linearity, his having collapse and consolidation, qualm and quanta, find their way to one another.

SunStick's been widely quoted around town as having said, "I don't play time. I've never played time. I play truth." In fact, it was this which led Penguin to voice reservations about Lambert's suggestion. What bothered him about the statement, he said, were two things, one a technical matter and the other, as he put it, characterological. First, he wondered whether SunStick actually *could* keep time. Secondly, he couldn't help being put off by SunStick's messianic sense of himself, an evidently extreme ease, he ventured to say, of the egotism drummers are said to suffer from. Lambert calmly answered that as for the first matter the best way to find out would he to have him audition. And as for the second, he said, slightly lowering his head and looking over the top of his glasses at Penguin (whose primary axe, you'll remember, is the oboe), one needed only to reflect on the reputed weirdness of double-reed players to get a sense of how little such stereotypes were worth. Penguin let the matter rest. There being no other objections (though I did notice Aunt Nancy make as if to say something but apparently decide, for some reason, to keep it to herself), we agreed we'd invite SunStick to our next rehearsal.

The rehearsal in question took place last week at Penguin's house in Inglewood. I got there about five or ten minutes late. Lambert was already there, as was SunStick, who was busy setting up his drums as

I walked in. Neither Aunt Nancy nor Djamilaa had gotten there yet. As it turned out, a good deal of time would pass before they showed up. I talked with SunStick while he got his drums together. Lambert and Penguin looked over a couple of new charts. After about fifteen or twenty minutes Lambert looked at his watch and wondered out loud what was keeping Aunt Nancy and Djamilaa. By this time SunStick had gotten set up and begun to go thru a few rolls and other figures. I took a look at the new charts with Lambert and Penguin.

Another ten minutes or so passed and still neither Djamilaa nor Aunt Nancy had shown up. Lambert looked at his watch again. Penguin tried calling them up on the phone, only to get, in each case, no answer. SunStick by now had finished warming up and adjusting his drumset, so the four of us talked about the music we'd be rehearsing while we waited for the two women to arrive.

After about five or ten more minutes Djamilaa and Aunt Nancy walked in together. We knew there was something up as soon as we saw them. They were dressed identically, each of them wearing sandals, a white cotton skirt, a white cotton blouse and a white cotton headrag. They each carried a duffel bag. The four of us stood watching them, saying nothing, as they walked toward us. The two of them seemed rather remote, an odd blend of mystical and businesslike. In fact, once they'd walked across the room to where we stood they handed each of us a business card, Djamilaa handing cards to Penguin and Lambert, Aunt Nancy to me and SunStick—still no greetings, no words, not so much as a grunt having passed among us. The cards bore the inscription "Halve Not, Will Travel."

I looked up from the card Aunt Nancy had handed me and saw the two women dressed not in white cotton but in black cowboy suits: black hat, black shirt, black pants, black boots, an empty black holster hanging below the right hip. I dropped the card and rubbed my eyes and looked again. After rubbing my eyes I saw them dressed, as before, in white cotton. I turned and looked at SunStick, Penguin and Lambert, who one by one (as in a chain reaction) looked up from their cards and apparently saw what I'd seen, each of them (again one by one as in a chain reaction) dropping his card and rubbing his eyes and looking again, doing a double-take. “Why don’t you fellas have a seat,” Aunt Nancy finally said, rather nonchalantly. Still not speaking, but exchanging looks which said, “Damn if I know,” the four of us found places to sit.

Djamilaa and Aunt Nancy opened their duffel bags. Each took out a pillow, followed by a Kashmiri drum known as the not, a clay pitcherlike affair with a narrow mouth and big belly. They sat themselves down, crosslegged, on the pillows and began to play, opening up with a Hindustani *tāla*, the *Tintāl*, made up of sixteen beats. They began by alternating beats. The first time thru Aunt Nancy took the odd-numbered beats, Djamilaa the even, turning it around the second time thru and then turning it around with each repetition. They took it slowly at first but the tempo steadily quickened. This went on for some time. After a while they stopped alternating beats and began playing in unison, each of them hitting all fifteen beats. (The ninth beat is unsounded.)

The two nots made it clear that the preemptive recital we were being offered was meant to register an objection, an oblique form of whatever point, perhaps, Aunt Nancy had broken off from raising during our discussion of SunStick a few days before. What one heard was a crisp, insistent rush of binary negation. “No way,” it repeated again and again, each beat a predicate postulating doubly assertive negatives, inverse-affirmative “oomph” and “us” rolled into one.

Was it also, one wondered, a twice-told tale having to do with haves and have-nots, a now percussive suffixality expressing emptiness, exclusion, lack? The preemptive school in which we now found ourselves enrolled made it a question one had no choice but to address, its rush of oblique yet insistent, hollow but hard knocks eliciting rough-and-ready quandaries we only now began to see had always been there. I stole a glance at Lambert, Penguin and SunStick and saw that their brows, very much as I knew mine too must have been, were now deeply and noticeably knitted.

But the card had said, “Halve Not.” Not “have-” but “halve”: meaning, one took it, to divide into two equal parts, to share equally. To what extent, one wondered, did the preemptive concert and catechism rolled into one amount to an arraignment, a charge of inequality, a threat of secession? "Halve Not, Will Travel." Each beat was a hoof to one's head, driving home a point. It was more than appropriate, one was made to admit, that the band, on the verge of becoming a sextet, address and take the issue of sexual equality into account. No women had been considered for the new position, the nots reminded us. Here was our chance to even things up yet here we were, blowing it.

Aunt Nancy, as if underscoring this last accusation, now put her not aside and reached into her duffel bag, taking out an Iranian reed flute known as the nay. She put it to her lips and began to play. What came out was a fallen, wedging wall of sound, an aroused, inclined carpet of breath whose bare-bones eloquence pushed and slid and seemed to shove the earth out from under our feet.

Aunt Nancy blew only in the nay's lowest register to start off with. The wedge and wall rolled into one she exacted was part hiss, part swallowed roar heard from a distance, the music of a waterfall. It could equally have been a gust of "smoke" off a sheet of dry ice—semisung, semispoken, assertive yet semiwept (as though tears were the fluid medium whereby speech kept in touch with song). After a while she began moving up an octave or two every now and then, became a bird at the foot of the falls contrasting upper-register wing with low-register wedge.

With each exhalation Aunt Nancy expounded a theme of empty ambition, emptying her lungs as though indicting the inevitable vanity of all aspiration. An extended sigh in which poignancy and pointlessness were one (pointless arousal, equally pointless disappointment), the sound of the nay nevertheless managed to be possessed of a pointedness, possessed of an edge by way of the polemic Aunt Nancy obviously intended it to carry. Her theme of emptiness, that is, pointed outward as well as in, a mixed message in which confession qualified accusation and vice- versa, a mixed-metaphorical knife and flute rolled into one which cut both ways. The resonant hollowness her breath exploited loudly echoed by way of indicting our own. Lambert, Penguin, SunStick and I sat, looked and listened in amazement. The sound emptied us of all solidity and self-assurance, held us riveted to our seats while it went right thru us.

Djamilaa aided and abetted Aunt Nancy's nay by letting the *Tintāl* go and resorting to a persistent tapping, a repetitive measure whose marking of time seemed the issue of an infinite, oddly timeless, absentminded patience. She tapped out a basic 4/4, three beats with the fingertips of her left hand (the ends of her fingernails in fact), every fourth with the heel of her right. One couldn't help but now know that the not's clay was a thin crust of nothingness which, like Aunt Nancy's nay, echoed and implicated one's own. Djamilaa's fingertip tapping came across with a crispness and a clarity which pierced and penetrated one's flesh like acupuncture pins.

There was a sense, of course, in which the music's polemic and its metaphysical insistence were at cross-purposes with one another. If ultimately emptiness and absence reigned, one had reason to ask, on what grounds did one critique and propose an alternative to the brunt of exclusion and the sense of social nothingness one suffered from? It was a question which aroused and agitated the bits of cowrie shell embedded in my brow.

It was a question, however, which Aunt Nancy and Djamilaa's contestatory recital casually and with infinite confidence and calm, simply yet cavalierly brushed aside. It proposed a quandary they refused to inhabit or be inhibited by. The force of their double namesake negation was such as to undermine the conundrum I for one found myself grappling with. "No such problem," the music objected, outmaneuvering the ordeal and desperation which, owing only to the not's and the nay's insistence, began gradually to let me go. Double namesake negation, that is, wielded a pendular, contradictory brush, a self-scripted embrace which overlooked and, so doing, outlived every flaw in what, after all, was more "oomph" than it was argument anyway.

Still, for all its assertive, unimpeachable "oomph" cavalier brush was never entirely out of touch with sorrow. Aunt Nancy's nay spoke again and again of separation. Djamilaa's not was an articulate womb which told of parting and parturition in the same breath. But here sorrow found itself surprised by reserves of intensity which upstaged and eroded and overwhelmed and came close to annulling the cause and occasion of their having been called up. One such reserve was Djamilaa's voice.

I'm sure you've heard the Jazz Composer's Orchestra's "silver" album. I'm also certain you more specifically remember Pharoah Sanders's playing on Mike Mantler's piece "Preview." It was something like Pharoah's teethclenching, sandpaper screech that Djamilaa came on with when, without letting up on her 4/4 tapping, she began to sing. It was vintage Djamilaa, a wordless wrestling with sound as in flamenco singing, ever on the verge of extinguishing or strangling while extending her unraveling rope of a voice. Part wail, part suspended sentence, unraveling rope turned out to return us to the sense of an endlessly unwinding scroll we'd gotten a taste of our last night at The Scarab three months back. The scroll was embellished by Aunt Nancy's now calligraphic reed, whose way of "worrying" a note became an obsessed, insistent signature (cavalier brush and ornamental arabesque rolled into one).

Egged on, Djamilaa now sang with an open-heart assertion we hadn't heard before. Her characteristically forlorn, forsaken, destitute orphan's voice took an orphic turn. She closed her eyes but went on looking at us, an opaque stare that confirmed her voice's stridency and strain as of a time and place we hadn't gotten to yet. This was the sense in which, even though she continued to look at us, we weren't there, the sense in which look at was less what she did than look thru us. Looking and loss, obeying her voice's orphic turn, were now rolled into one.

Lambert, Penguin, SunStick and I sat openmouthed as before an array of blocked options, a blocked but still beckoning sense of alternatives. Unwinding scroll, calligraphic reed and uninhibited clay, we knew and saw, had now left us behind, now, as it were, written us off. Open-heart stridency went on and on, stroked, strung out, backed up and embroidered by Aunt Nancy's calligraphic nay. Penguin leaned over and whispered in my ear at one point, "Makes Diamanda Galas sound like Rosemary Clooney."

But with no advance notice a calm and composure abruptly

entered Djamilaa's voice. Stridency and struggle gave way to a sense of glide and flotation, a lightening up and a holding pattern rolled into one. She lowered her voice as though reasoning with a gremlin or a ghost, waiting for the rest of us to catch up with the not-of-our-time intensity which had gone before. Softer but no less insistent, her voice was now possessed of an aspect of concession and caress, a cooing conciliatory touch whose ostensible lightness nonetheless coaxed and seemed out to convince. A sense of automatic pilot, one might even say, had taken over, an odd uncanny mix of absentminded assurance. Lambert, Penguin, SunStick and I, independent of one another yet acting as one, pinched ourselves at the very same instant to make sure we were actually there.

Even so, her voice retained an ever so slight hint of husk, troubling its grid by remaining exact while at the same time confessing to its falling short. Here husk, that is, had to do with surface tension, a wincing, unavailable tenderness, a textureless appeal which was neither to be had nor held on to. Erosion called every eloquence into question.

Imagine, then, our surprise and shock as Djamilaa now eased into a song which had been written for and recorded by Nancy Wilson. We could hardly believe it was happening. Each of us pinched himself again. Even though a few days before I'd gone along with Djamilaa to the garage sale down the street from her apartment where, more or less as a joke, she'd bought a used copy of the album the song appears on, I was no better prepared for what now went on than Lambert, SunStick or Penguin.

The ever so slight withholding and suggestion of husk began to fade as Djamilaa set about imitating Nancy Wilson's unselfconscious elegance and uptown polish. Her voice acquired a silkiness, an unobstructed smoothness and availability none of us had ever before suspected it of having.

The name of the song was "China." Djamilaa went about the business of breathing life into its lyrics with such conviction as to give the impression of a common spirit she shared with Nancy Wilson having taken over and come to the fore:

In my ocean liner
Nothing could be finer
Seeing what I can see
On my way to China

The way she had of lingering on and thus emphasizing the feminine rhymes underscored the sense of a shared womanly *esprit*—sisterly ties as well as the more obvious filial ties the album's title, *This Mother's Daughter*, insisted on.

For some reason, Djamilaa's newly adopted voice began to falter the farther she moved into the song:

In my raincoat liner
Didn't think I'd find her
The woman I used to be
Back in Carolina

Her impersonation of Nancy Wilson began to break down once she got to these lines. Why this was one couldn't say for sure. Lambert later suggested that the lines' apparent indebtedness to the Virginia Slims ad gave rise to more qualms in Djamilaa's mind than she could, as he phrased it, "keep a lid on." My own guess at the time was that a curious compound play of identity and difference had intervened. Djamilaa's faltering reproduction of Nancy Wilson's voice seemed to obey a namesake negative dialectic and a nominal near-identity with Aunt Nancy rolled into one. Flawed reproduction seemed to insist that Djamilaa was not, after all, Nancy Wilson. The new name with which in so doing it seemed to christen her confirmed an echoic, slightly "off" rapport with Aunt Nancy. Djamilaa was no longer exactly Djamilaa either but was now Ain't Nancy.

Though double namesake negation had its way of troubling every pose or impersonation, every ostensible position, Ain't Nancy went on with the song and its subtle threat of secession. "I'm on my way to China," she repeated, just as Nancy Wilson does toward the end of the song. Aunt Nancy's nay imitated the chorus on the record, taking up the melody to which they sing, over and over, "Oh, are you there, are you really there in China?" This was now her obsessed, inquisitive signature, an interrogative riff which infiltrated ostensible position and thus offered the band a new sense of reprieve and possibility, an alternative to self-destructive "Halve Not." The question, Lambert, Penguin and I began to see, was more directed at us than it was at Ain't Nancy.

Ain't Nancy, in fact, eventually ended her singing and, continuing to beat out patterns on the not, gave the last word, as it were, to Aunt Nancy's nay, which went on with its interrogative riff for a few more bars. The recital finally came to an end on that repetitive, pointed note.

Once the music had stopped the two of them simply stared at us in silence.

SunStick finally stood up and broke the silence. "Well, I can take a hint," he said and began to take his drumset down.

Djamilaa, Aunt Nancy, Penguin, Lambert and I all looked at one another. There was no need to say anything more on the matter. It was understood we'd begin looking for a woman drummer.

As ever,
N.

27.VIII.81

Dear Angel of Dust,

Thank you for your letter. It arrived a couple of days ago. I'm sorry to say it found me not feeling too well. I'm in bed now, as I've been for the past four days, bearing the brunt of a new round of shattered cowrie shell attacks. I can't say for sure what it was that brought them on, though I suspect Djamilaa and Aunt Nancy's recital played a not insignificant part. In any case, they remain as much a mystery as ever. So much so, in fact, I no longer bother to see the doctor about them.

I have, though, had occasion to do some reflection and self-diagnosis these past few days. A remark my mother made the other day sparked it. We were talking on the phone, me telling her about the latest round of attacks, the quandary they've got me in, the dizziness, trances and so forth, when she said, "It's all that music, all those records you've been buying all these years." I laughed. "No, seriously," she went on, "all those records doing all that spinning have made you dizzy." I laughed again, my only defense. It was an old axe, one she's been grinding ever since I was a kid. My mother, as I may have told you already, has never really understood my becoming a musician. Virtually nothing, as far as she's concerned, could be more impractical. I recall times as a kid when I'd buy a record and have to sneak it into the house, so upset would she get at my "throwing away good money."

Still, it's an axe I've come to take more seriously than my laughter let on. It set me to thinking. Are the attacks a self-sentencing conviction the music fosters and feeds, even if only as the occasion for a reprieve?

Are self-sentencing conviction and self-commuting sentence merely symbiotic halves of a self-cycling ordeal? Do I knock myself down in order to be picked up?

Someone I once read remarked on the need to produce an inventory of traces. What better place to begin, I've been thinking, than with those discs I used to smuggle into the house? Records we call them. Rightly so.

I've been listening a lot these past couple of days to one such disc, Miles's *Seven Steps to Heaven,* one of the first I ever bought. I can't help hearing it as a repository of imprints which long ago went to work on me, set up shop (tenuous hope, tenuous heaven) in my perhaps too-impressionable heart (foolish heart). The title of one of the cuts, my favorite in fact, practically jumped off the album jacket at me: "I Fall In Love Too Easily." There it was. A complete sentence. This indeed was one of the cuts which made me.

And the other titles, even when only fragments or phrases, likewise had a sentencing effect. "So Near So Far" gave an apt enough description of the tenuous heaven it whetted one's appetite for. It was an old dialectical story: possibility paradoxically parented by prohibition. Not only did vertigo set in, a quixotic dizziness and discontent, but one's heavensent stagger turned into a blue compensatory strut. Blue earth itself was made even bluer by the tenuous ladder one took it for. Listen, if you don't believe me, to "Basin Street Blues."

My mother's axe notwithstanding, I accept it all, even the scratches and the nicks, the points on the record where the needle skips. Noisy reminders of the wear of time they may very well be, but I hear them as rickety, quixotic rungs on a discontinuous ladder—quixotic leaps or ellipses (quantum lump in one's throat) meted out by contraband heaven having set up shop.

Sincerely,
N.

30.VIII.81

PREMONITORY DREAM OF NEW DRUMMER DJEANNINE'S POST-ROMANTIC BOOTH (SEE-THRU SCHOOL OF HARD KNOCKS)

Djeannine loomed larger than life at the top of the hill with the sun behind her. The sunlight stripped her of the white cotton dress she wore, weaving an alternate, see-thru web which had caught my eye and which held me captive. I lay on my back in the meadow at the foot of the hill, my legs and feet pointing toward the summit Djeannine stood on, my feet drawn back so that my heels addressed my hips while my knees loomed almost as high as Djeannine, who stood, it seemed, partly between and partly above them.

Beneath her white cotton dress she wore nothing. No slip, no bra, no panties. The sun's light, having stripped her of the dress, was a further nothing, so unseizably there as to make sight a fleet, far-reaching rendezvous (trance and transparency, wile and redress). I lay possessed and penetrated by shadows, drunk with a glimpse of silhouetted legs and the X-ray wafting of an imaginary musk.

The staggered scent (part static dance) I was caught in caused Djeannine's cotton dress to billow. The billowing dress loomed larger and larger, an immense tent held up by a pungent, punishing sense of miraculously available "parts." A contrabass trombone blast[1] came

---

[1] Charles Mingus, *The Black Saint and the Sinner Lady* (Impulse! AS-35), Side 1, Track 1: "Solo Dancer."

out of the blue, came on as if to seize while accenting the billowing of Djeannine's white dress.

Stripped of habit, the light found its voice in a transparent equation: brass accompaniment conjured brazen legs.

What began as a blast tapered off into a soft insistent keening, part purr, part growl, part prayer, sustained by what I now could hear was a trombone choir (six players, each of whom came on as though he or she had just seen a ghost). Spectral usher, elegiac reminder and bony escort rolled into one, the choir lifted me off the ground, set me down on my feet and got me started on my walk toward the summit Djeannine stood on.

The closer I got the more the hill turned out to be part circus tent and part revival meeting tent, outside of which, instead of on whose peak, Djeannine stood. No longer lying on my back, I felt new to the earth, newly born. The trombones complied with my need for a new investiture, introducing a "Hymn to the Dawning Age" which I confounded with the hem of Djeannine's alternate, see-thru web and billowing dress rolled into one.

Just outside the big top, the revival tent her billowing dress turned out to be, Djeannine stood in a booth selling kisses[2] and a brand of hard candy known as Kashmiri Cough Drops.[3] I approached her, wearing a new pair of pants. I could see that now, having been stripped of her white cotton dress, she wore a dark blue blouse, though the front of the booth blocked my view of what she wore from the waist down. I handed her a dollar bill but she handed it back, saying that for me there'd be no charge. I leaned forward over the counter of the booth, closed my eyes and awaited the light perfunctory pressure I expected her lips to make on mine.

It did in fact start off that way—a light perfunctory pressure. But suddenly Djeannine slipped her tongue between my lips. The kiss grew wetter, her tongue more adventurous, daring, solicitous, insisting my own tongue answer in kind.

---

[2] Eddie Jefferson, *The Main Man* (Inner City IC 1033), Side 1, Track 1: "Jeannine."

[3] Eli Mohammad Shera and Ensemble, *Folksongs of Kashmir* (Lyrichord LLST 7260), Side 2, Track 1: "Sufi Love Song."

My mouth began to fill with a mint-flavored liquid[4] which now flowed from Djeannine's mouth (somewhat like a sweet North African tea,[5] only not as hot). When she ended the kiss and drew back I opened my eyes, my mouth full to the point of overflowing with the mint-flavored liquid. My eyes met hers.

Having made eye contact, I closed my eyes again savoring the liquid which, like a liqueur, caressed my tongue, teeth, inner cheeks and gums. It ever so lightly stung the inside of my mouth. I had a sense of my head having cleared to the point of translucency, a menthol rush converting my hair, skin and skull to crystal.[6] A clairvoyant breeze blew into my face.

An involuntary grunt suggesting peepshow delight escaped my throat. I opened my eyes again as Djeannine stepped out of her booth. She wore a skirt which, like her blouse, was dark blue. Extrovert ingénue and rough-and-ready tomboy rolled into one, she stepped away from the booth and did a cartwheel. Her skirt fell past her thighs and down past her waist while she was upside down. I caught a glimpse of her thighs, a bit of pubic hair and the reinforced crotch of her blindingly white cotton panties. The blinding whiteness caused me to close my eyes again. Not knowing why, I swallowed the mint-flavored liquid. She was on her feet again by the time I opened my eyes.

The mint-flavored liquid began to have a different effect. *Peppermint spit* was what it was I realized, though the longer I reflected the less *peppermint* mattered. Like a piece of chewing gum losing its flavor, the mint-flavored liquid more and more appeared to have been nothing more than X-ray spit, spit-flavored spit. I felt nauseous.

My stomach began to convulse but nothing came up. A gush of

---

[4] The Clovers, *Their Greatest Recordings* (Atco SD 33-374), Side 2, Track 3: "One Mint Julep."

[5] "The Quintet," *Jazz at Massey Hall* (Fantasy 86003), Side 2, Track 3: "A Night in Tunisia."

[6] Coleman Hawkins, *The Hawk Flies* (Milestone M-47015), Side 2, Track 2: "You Go to My Head."

emptiness and air spewed out of my mouth and bent me over. I looked at my legs and saw thru the flesh to the bones underneath. I looked up to see Djeannine step back inside her booth and reach under the counter. The last thing I saw before waking up was her extend her right hand to offer me a box of Kashmiri Cough Drops.

Dear Angel of Dust,

I begin with the above as one mark of its impact. I woke up a half-hour ago unable to think of anything else or get back to sleep, obsessed with getting it down on paper. How I knew the woman's name was Djeannine I can't really say. She didn't introduce herself nor was her name in any other way announced. It seemed that in dreaming I necessarily knew, that dreaming was the same as knowing, that to be there was to be pressed, penetrated and possessed by an epiphanous clarity, a see-thru ipseity, a namesake certainty which, no matter which way one cut it, came down to *Djeannine*. To be there was not only to know Djeannine's name but to know, without knowing why, that it began with a D. And to know that one knew this with such certainty was to know that Djeannine was the drummer the band's been looking for. It was as though such ipseity or certainty (namesake dream, genetic drum) had somehow long been beaten into one's blood.

I should quickly point out, I suppose, that since making up our minds three weeks ago that the new drummer would be a woman we've had little luck locating suitable candidates. We auditioned two women, neither of whom, for reasons I won't go into, worked out. We're still looking, though the days I spent in bed slowed the search down. (I've gotten better, by the way. I was up and about the day after I last wrote.)

As I've already said, I knew in the dream I was getting a glimpse of the woman we've been looking for. This might well, I knew, turn out to be a vain projection, so hard to miss were some of the imprints being played back to me by the dream. (You'll have noticed I footnoted some of the more obvious ones.) Still, I was even more certain once I'd woken up that our new drummer would be Djeannine, that what I'd seen was no solipsistic disc but a genuine vision.

Funny, though, that I can't remember what Djeannine looked like. I recall what she wore but can't form an image of her face.

Still, the good news is that I know the name of our eventual drummer. Now we'll know what to be on the lookout for.

Yours,
N.

31.VIII.81

Dear Angel of Dust,

I hadn't expected to write again so soon but there's been a new development concerning Djeannine. Penguin and I were over at Lambert's this afternoon helping him do some work on his car. We got to talking about the band and about our search for a woman drummer and I, of course, couldn't help talking about my dream. "We're not far away from finding her," I told them. "I was given her name in a dream I had the other night." They each looked up from the new radiator hose they were in the midst of installing and shot me a surprised, half-incredulous look whose credulous half insisted, "Go ahead. Tell us more."

I proceeded to tell them the dream, repeating pretty much verbatim the account I wrote you in yesterday's letter. So indelibly etched or engraved in my memory were the verbal equivalents I'd worked so hard to find that they amounted to a form of after-the-fact dictation, an unerasable script to which my now involuntary tongue seemed inextricably tied. Lambert and Penguin listened with more and more rapt attention, regarding me with an ever more alarmed half-quizzical mix of skepticism and belief. It was when I got to the part about the light finding its voice in a transparent equation that they both blurted out in unison (at the exact instant I myself said it), "Brass accompaniment conjured brazen legs."

"How'd you know that?" I interrupted my account of the dream to ask, only to register within a split-second of asking it that they both had turned and asked the same thing of one another. "How'd you know that?" The question hung like a three-sided echo in the air.

We stood staring at one another for a while. We each had a can of beer we'd taken occasional sips from while working on the car. Penguin now not only took a sip but broke the silence by suggesting I resume telling the dream. This I did. But when I got to the part about the big top and the booth in which Djeannine stood selling kisses and Kashmiri Cough Drops he interrupted me. He asked me to stop and then took up exactly where I left off, mouthing the words I was about to utter as though reading from the letter I wrote you yesterday: "I approached her, wearing a new pair of pants. I could see that now, having been stripped of her white cotton dress, she wore a dark blue blouse, though the front of the booth blocked my view of what she wore from the waist down. I handed her a dollar bill but she handed it back, saying for me there'd be no charge. I leaned forward over the counter of the booth, closed my eyes and awaited the light perfunctory pressure I expected her lips would make on mine."

You can imagine my shock and surprise. Lambert too seemed shocked and surprised but what he proceeded to do shocked and surprised me even more. It shocked and surprised Penguin as well, for what he did was interrupt Penguin just as Penguin had interrupted me, taking the words out of his mouth as though reading from the same unerasable script. "It did in fact," he said, "start off that way—a light perfunctory pressure. But suddenly Djeannine slipped her tongue between my lips. The kiss grew wetter, her tongue more adventurous, daring, solicitous, insisting mine respond in kind . . ."

By now you've no doubt figured out what had happened. At about the same time as I interrupted Lambert to ask if this was a joke and had they been reading my mail Penguin muttered, "My God, we must've dreamt the same dream." Why this hadn't occurred to me I can't say, but Lambert and Penguin each went on to explain that the night before last they too had dreamt of Djeannine. Though, unlike me, neither of them had gotten up and written out the dream, the collective script it'd inwardly etched and engraved agreed in full with what I wrote you in yesterday's letter. We all, having dreamt it once, now knew it by heart.

The one difference was that Penguin, rather than waking up as Djeannine offered him the box of Kashmiri Cough Drops, went on dreaming, unlike Lambert and me. He accepted it, opened it up and took out a piece of candy which, he told us, he then popped into his mouth ("a Sucrets and a jawbreaker rolled into one" is how he described it). He sucked on it a while and then tried to chew it but it broke one of his teeth. It was then that he woke up.

Penguin's extended ending took a while to soak in though it had an immediate sobering effect. His recitation concluded, he stood without speaking, staring off into the distance. Lambert and I each took another sip of beer. By now it was late afternoon getting on toward sunset, copper-colored rays penetrating the trees behind Lambert's garage, threads of see-thru sun. It was this light into which Penguin stared. He wore a hard-won survivor's look and he too now took another sip of beer, grimacing as though it were a pill going down (awkward lozenge, hard-won lesson, bitter truth). So absorbed and private and caught up in reflection was the mood which had come over him that Lambert and I left him to himself by looking away from the light.

"The same taste of rust," we heard him whisper, whereupon we both turned and looked his way again.

"What was that?" Lambert asked.

"The same taste of rust," he repeated, speaking more clearly and louder but still not letting his eyes meet ours. He continued staring as though entranced by the copper-colored light. "I tasted rust on Djeannine's perfunctory lips," he elaborated, "the same taste I recall from when I was a boy in Louisiana." He stopped and rubbed his eyes as though waking up, resumed his stare and then went on, speaking in short staccato bits as though under a strain. "My first girlfriend. Our very first kiss. Her name was Jeannie. Jeannie Bonton. We both must have been about nine. The first time we kissed I was standing on a crate outside her bedroom window. It was twilight." He broke off to take another sip of beer and then went on. The copper-colored light still held his eye. "She'd always leave to go inside once the sun set. Her parents wanted her in before dark. But she'd go to her room and come to the window, outside of which I'd stand on a crate. We'd talk until dinner time. The first time I talked her into a kiss she was too afraid to unfasten the screen. We kissed with our lips pressed against it. It was an old screen, rusty from years of humidity and rain. I made the mistake of parting my lips and letting the tip of my tongue touch it." He broke off again and took a sip of beer as though washing rust from the tip of his tongue. He swallowed, staring into the copper-colored threads. "The taste of it's never gone away."

Lambert and I looked at one another as Penguin stood silent. Neither of us knew immediately how to respond to what he'd said, what to make of his brief soliloquistic equation of would-be romance with insubordinate rust. That love had been weaned before its time or gotten old even before it began seemed to me to be the premature post-romantic point the drumming in of which Jeannie was Penguin's prototype for. Djeannine or Jeannie, I wanted to say, is both dreamgirl and bitter truth. I tried to speak, only to find a preemptive rust now coated my tongue. I took another sip of the now obligatory beer, barely able to swallow. Preemptive rust had infiltrated my jaws and my throat as well. A few seconds more and my ritual sip would've been too late.

Lambert too took another sip. He too seemed to have a hard time swallowing. Preemptive rust, I gathered, had gotten to him as well. About that time, though, a cut came on the radio which seemed to free his tongue. The radio'd been playing in the background all the while, but when the title cut from an early sixties Art Blakey album, *Ugetsu*, came on it noticeably caught Lambert's attention. It necessarily caught mine and Penguin's too. Freddie Hubbard's opening statement, that is, made for a unified field or feeling wherein the copper component of brass was part and parcel not only of the copper-colored rays of the sun but of the luminous brew, the copper-colored beer we all sipped as well. Freddie's horn was both a brass axe and a brass lamp, the Aladdin's lamp our collective dreamgirl Djeannine lived in.

"The ghost of love," Lambert said as though announcing a presence and proclaiming a truth, his tongue now free of the impromptu rust which had momentarily taken over. His tone was part prophetic, part professorial. "*Ugetsu*. It's Japanese," he pointed out. "It means 'fantasy'. Either of you ever see the movie?" I shook my head and Penguin said no. Neither of us had but whether we had or not didn't really matter. "It's about a man who falls in love with a ghost," Lambert added. He fell silent, seemingly lost in thought.

"Don't we all?" Penguin put in as he turned to look at us, much more with us now than he'd been since recounting his alternate, broken-tooth ending and the rust-related tale of his and Jeannie's first kiss.

"Not exactly," Lambert answered, no longer lost in thought. "Many a head's been scratched and many a beard pulled over that one." He took a sip and then set out on an extended rap whose key contention was that Djeannine was "not so much post- as pre-romantic, the Afro-anticipatory taste of disappointment, Afro-inevitable slap upside the head." He noted the lack of romantic concepts of love in most African cultures, hand in hand with which went the dominant role of the drum in most African musics. The two were anything but unrelated he argued, quoting Leadbelly's famous line at one point: "The blues is a feeling and when it hits you it's the real news." The word "hits" he gave an especially pointed emphasis. To insist on the slap, the blow, the hit was to advance a stoic, hard-knocks epistemology. The slap, the blow, the hit had to do with the percussive, no-nonsense character and crux of experience (hardcore truth). "Thus it is that Djeannine," he said, looking at me as if he'd read my mind, "is both dreamgirl and drumgirl, drumgirl and bitter truth."

"Irresistible either way," I couldn't help saying. My tongue was loose now, long since free of extemporaneous rust. "Dreaming sets up the hit."

I took a sip. Lambert and Penguin did the same. "I'm glad you said that," Lambert looked at me again and said. "I couldn't agree with you more. Djeannine's a set-up, the dream we tie to the sky, the match made in heaven. I'd go a bit farther in fact. You both know the stories of Wagadu. Think back, if you will, to the one about the drum the djinns make off with and tie to the sky. Could Djeannine, I'm wondering, be our dream's coded, self-incriminatory way of rolling extraterrestrial thief and stolen drum into one? Could Djeannine, in other words, be a djinn?"

"But that drum was a war drum," Penguin put in.

"Exactly my point," Lambert answered at once. "Isn't war, dissension, discontent (call it what you will) indigenous to the notion of heaven? Doesn't heaven set us at odds with what's real? Isn't that how it sets us up?"

"Tied to the sky in more ways than one," I heard myself mumble. Before I knew it the words were out of my mouth. The next thing I knew I was quoting Eddie Jefferson, a line from "Jeannine": "It was love lost to the rising cost." I repeated it once or twice by way of embarking on a spiel in which "tied to the sky" had to do with inflation. I too now adopted a part prophetic, part professorial tone, as if Lambert's voice had rubbed off on mine. I took a sip, hoping by doing so to wash the influence away, but Lambert's prophetic-professorial contagion turned out to be more stubborn than Penguin's mediating rust. Ritual sip notwithstanding, it refused to go away. I expounded an inverse emotional ladder ("love lost") rooted in spiraling economic ordeal ("rising cost"), going on about a fortress formation, a siege mentality, an emotional callousness given rise to and reinforced by economic hard knocks. "Fort Knocks" I went so far as to call it.

It was as if I'd hiccupped into my sleeve. Penguin laughed and Lambert grinned at my prophetic-professorial joke, my prophetic-professorial pun and complaint rolled into one. "Fort Knocks" introduced a welcome note of levity into an otherwise depressing rap. In fact, it broke the hold of Lambert's prophetic-professorial contagion. I coughed, took an expectorant sip and coughed again, my throat at last clear of the catch-phraseological drift whose expectant gloom I'd become as much victim of as vehicle for. I couldn't help thinking of Donald Byrd's recording of "Jeannine." Pepper Adams's assured, expectorant baritone's repetitive punctuation of the opening notes of Byrd's solo came back to me now as possibly ancestral to the liberatory coughs which had cleared my throat. It felt good to at last be free of apocalyptic phlegm.

"Fort Knocks," Lambert laughed, "I'll drink to that." He went inside and came back out with three more beers.

By the time Lambert returned Penguin was in the midst of saying to me, "Seriously though, don't you think Djeannine embodies a wished-for betterment of base metal, an alchemization of Tin Pan Alley banality of the sort brought off by, say, Newk's way of doing 'Three Little Words'?"

Lambert cut in before I could answer, handing us each a can of beer while insisting with a grin, "As much as I'd like to pursue that question I have to remind you that the radiator's waiting and there's still a tune-up to be done. Why don't we let it go for now with an Afro-expedient, tried-and-true sense of an ending?" He paused, saw that we were waiting, pulled the lift-tab ring from his can of beer and then added, "Then I stepped on a piece of tin and it bent. That's the way the story went."

All three of us laughed. Penguin and I opened our beers. We clinked our cans together and drank to Lambert's formulaic ending. We then went back to work on the car.

It remained to be seen, of course, whether Aunt Nancy and Djamilaa had also dreamt of Djeannine. We tried calling them once we finished the tune-up but didn't catch either of them in, so we'll have to wait until rehearsal tomorrow to find out.

I'll let you know how it goes.

Yours,
N.

1.IX.81

Dear Angel of Dust,

It turns out rehearsal had to be called off. Neither Djamilaa nor Aunt Nancy felt up to it. Both complain of the same ailment—throbbing migraine headaches they woke up with this morning and haven't been able to get to go away. Each of them, within a half-hour of the other, called around mid-afternoon to say she wouldn't be able to make it this evening, and neither Lambert, Penguin nor I felt there'd be much point in going ahead with rehearsal with almost half the band not there.

There've been some very important developments nonetheless. When Djamilaa, the second of the two to call me, did so I was actually not feeling particularly well myself. A number of things have been on my mind, not the least of them being the sense of inverse birth the dream of Djeannine left me with. I haven't been able to shake that initial image or feeling or sense of lying on my back with my legs open and my knees looming, Djeannine standing partly between and partly above them, partly "in" and partly "out" as if newly emerging or (this is the part that bothers me) going back in.

Few would argue that inverse birth isn't an interesting concept. I for one wouldn't argue that it's not a problematic one as well. A man giving birth to a woman is bad enough. A woman returning to a masculine womb is even worse. But by inverse birth do we mean feet-first or ass-backwards? That there appears to be no way of knowing has to be the worst.

I've also been bothered by the false resolution Lambert, Penguin and I imposed on our reflections yesterday. Bent Pan Alley I've come to call it. I've suffered something of a mystic, psychophonic affliction as a result. The rumbling of an Ayleresque anthem hums and whistles thru my groin like radioactive water, a luminous doomed lament scored for hollowed-out pelvis played on dislocated flute. The nervous vibrato of some such renovated brass-band concept upwardly displaced makes for states of election where, like a bird on a wire, my right clavicle trills as though emptied out and blown upon. It was this I was feeling when Djamilaa called this afternoon.

It seemed it took an unusual amount of effort to answer the phone. When Djamilaa explained that she wasn't feeling well and couldn't come to rehearsal my hand shook so much I almost dropped the receiver. The news of her headache, coming within a half-hour of Aunt Nancy's call, aroused embryonic inklings of a paradigmatic mesh which made my collarbone's nervous vibrato all the more disconcerting. I'd gotten ahead of myself I somehow knew, but even that made it all the more the born-again flute my twittering sense of inverse birth pursued and pressed and apprised me of.

"Born-again bone," I whispered into the receiver.

"Upstart flute," Djamilaa whispered back.

We both spoke with a breathy assurance, an inescapably sexual authority and tone. It was a fleet clairvoyant seizure which arose and went away at the same time. Our masonic exchange, albeit brief, was nothing less than an impromptu involuntary séance, the oblique rapport so inescapably copulative and pointed as to confirm the paradigmatic mesh I'd gotten inklings of moments before. Though we both snapped out of it at once, resuming our normal way of speaking as though nothing had happened, clearly a code of some kind had been employed, a password uttered, an "open sesame" into who knows what which moistened our lips with a mutual drop of two-way witnessing water.

"Inverse pelvis," I thought to whisper into the receiver but already the mood had passed. Djamilaa's voice had now gone back to normal on the other end. As if "upstart flute" had been uttered by someone else (or by herself in another life, some other world and time), she now went on about her headache in some detail, resuming the drift of what she'd been saying when I cut in with "born-again bone," our mutual drop of two-way witnessing water having now become a caul of discontinuous milk, burnt milk.

The Ayleresque wheel (the rumble of holiness and ghostliness and wateriness rolled into one) overtook me again as I listened to Djamilaa's once more conventional/conversational voice. Though she didn't come right out and say so I felt she needed company, wanted me to come over. The Ayleresque wheel with its rim of spilt milk notwithstanding, I too recovered my conventional/conversational voice. "I'll be over soon," I said, surprised at how composed I sounded.

"I was hoping you'd say that," Djamilaa said. "See you in a while."

We hung up and I called Penguin and Lambert. It was then that we decided to cancel rehearsal. That done, I was off to Djamilaa's apartment.

It was beautiful out. "A day like no other," I said to myself as I stepped outside. A wind had swept away the smog and scoured the sky, leaving it a resonant, wounded blue. The champagne sparkle the sunlight gave it seemed a luminous blister, an overt burn beneath passing bandages of cloud. In its wounded aspect, in fact, blue submitted to breakage as to a *controlled* burn. In so doing it bolstered the sense I'd begun to have that Djamilaa's and Aunt Nancy's headaches were another side of Lambert's "Afro-inevitable slap upside the head." The twenty-minute drive across town gave me time to reflect on this, deepening my hope that the headaches were a sign that the two of them had also dreamt our dream of Djeannine.

In its resonant aspect, blue complicated my desire for such a consensus by expounding an implicit theme of remote fulfillment, the emphasis and accent falling insistently and pointedly, remorselessly on the qualification "remote." Such a complicating accent, threaded thru with a bittersweet ache and apprehension, gave hope a new, staggered address. A staggered volley of conflicting claims and conflicting sorrows (crossed bones in positions of compound, conflicting breakage on the verge of a dance) evoked an understated rumble, an ever so subtle threat of rain in the otherwise promising sky.

I got off the freeway at Silverlake and from there it was only a couple of minutes more to Djamilaa's apartment.

Djamilaa came to the door soon after I rang the bell. She wore a light cotton shift whose vertical stripes alternated between white and green. The green stripes made me think of the peppermint-flavored liquid which in the dream had passed from Djeannine's mouth into mine. The white stripes reminded me of spit-flavored spit.

Was this another sign confirming the dream as a prescient collective peep into the outcome of our search for a woman drummer?

I was absorbed in pondering this question as I stepped thru the doorway and into the living room. We sat down and it was then that I noticed how exhausted Djamilaa looked. Her eyes had an unusually sunken look about them, pushed back into the sockets with the flesh above and below the lids abnormally dark. It was then that I also noticed how much cooler it was in her apartment than it had been outside. My sense was one of a cavelike coolness in fact, reinforced both by her not having opened any curtains and the cavelike sockets into which her eyes had sunk.

"You look tired," I said, "as though you haven't slept."

"That's part of the problem," she said. "I got a full night's sleep but I woke up this morning feeling as though I'd been awake all night. I've tried to go back to sleep but can't. I evidently slept enough to not be able to sleep any more but not enough to really feel rested. I feel like I'm in limbo."

The word "limbo" made me think of spread-eagle, open-legged dancers passing under a bar, the limber, spiderlike sprawl in which going down gives birth to a bass note, a depth, a closeness to the earth in oneself.

I looked at Djamilaa's thin athletic arms, the meeting of music and musculature the rich tone of her skin evoked or achieved or insisted on. The shift she wore had no sleeves. A bit of hair peeped out from under each arm. There was a close-to-the-bone firmness about her body which gave her the look of a dancer, notwithstanding her large low-hanging breasts, the imprint of whose nipples I couldn't help noticing on the shift she wore.

I found myself seized by a sudden desire to press my mouth to Djamilaa's left shoulder, to work my way down, leaving a trail of wet kisses, from close-to-the-bone biceps to close-to-the-bone wrist. I imagined her in a limbo dancer's position. I saw myself between her open legs. It was this image I became absorbed and caught up in.

"A penny for your thoughts," Djamilaa said with a faint smile. An inward blush and a rush of embarrassment ran thru me, as though my close-to-the-bone lust were now out in the open. I apologized for the lapse of attention but Djamilaa waved it off, saying no harm had been done and that, anyway, she'd been waiting for a chance to use that expression.

Djamilaa went on to explain that "A penny for your thoughts" had come up in a dream she had last night, the same dream she took to be at the root of her headache and of her not having had a restful sleep. It'd been a dream in which there was pounding and stomping, a commotion the migraine throbbing she woke up with seemed an echo and a continuation of.

Djamilaa's talk of her dream caused my collarbone to flutter. "Do you remember," I wasted no time asking, "any of the dreams you had Saturday night?"

She thought a moment and then answered, "No."

I tried again. "Does the name Djeannine, spelled with a D, mean anything to you?"

Again Djamilaa answered, "No."

The agitation in my clavicle died down. I was disappointed.

"Speaking of names though," Djamilaa added after a pause, "the dream I dreamt last night had a strange tripartite power. It was able to 1) name without announcing or announce in such a way that to announce was to show, 2) show in such a way that to show was to tell, and 3) tell in such a way as to dictate its own reception, dictate and read itself at the same time."

My ears perked up on hearing this. My clavicle emitted what had the feel of an approving hum. Djamilaa went on to say that never before had she dreamt a dream in which two or more senses were so legibly rolled into one, in which to see was not only to hear but to hear and feel and experience touch with such immediate translation into sight and sound as to be blessed with a mixed gift, a mixed-metaphorical blend: braille-extended ear, drum-extended eye, synaesthetic limb. It was a dream, she continued, which not only made the name of its heroine known without announcing it but a dream which had a name of its own. It was called—called itself, she insisted—"Wind-Assisted Dream of Penny's Percussive Upper Room (Synaesthetic Serenade)."

Djamilaa's air of exhaustion faded the more she talked about the dream. It was as if in doing so she came into possession of a surge of unexpected energy, a second wind. Increasingly she spoke with a mediumistic animation. The dream, it seemed, not only dictated the terms of its telling but provided the upstart adrenaline to tell it with as well—a mystic, mediumistic imprint, an unexpected pen filled with synaesthetic ink. By the time she began recounting the dream I had the impression the dream itself was not only speaking but also writing, rolling itself into a single synaesthetic apprehension.

WIND-ASSISTED DREAM
OF PENNY'S PERCUSSIVE UPPER ROOM
(SYNAESTHETIC SERENADE)

Penny hadn't slept a wink. She rolled over and looked at the clock beside her bed. It was twelve minutes of six. All night the sense of resting on a dead man's eyelids had kept her awake. Ritual coinage and namesake stasis had come together to induce a feeling for what wasn't there (an immaterial witness not so much to another world as to an aspect of this one), a felt, phantom, X-ray advance which, albeit obscure, was a seeing thru yet a looking into what was.

Making matters worse was that her neighbors downstairs were having an all-night party. That the music they played they played extremely loud was bad enough but that they insisted on playing the same record again and again made it all the more impossible to sleep.

The record was Pennies From Heaven. *The uninvited namesake serenade, Penny couldn't help thinking, was not without an aspect of tease and ironic intent, not without an element of malice. Her neighbors and their guests even sang along with the record from time to time. She could've sworn they were chanting, "Penny's from heaven."*

Still there remained the matter of the dead man's eyes, the raw sense of witness mixed in with an emergent regard for a true, transparent idiom of extremity. Though the man's eyes had lost their visionary gleam, a tangle of voices evidently related to everything he'd ever looked at began to address Penny as though from inside her own head. A namesake ensemble oddly numb to its own inception, these voices affected a colloquial, self-evident request and/or equation, as if "Put in your two cents worth" or "A penny for your thoughts" were in no way beneath them, a "reduction" they were anxious to undergo.

Penny sat up in bed. I peeped in thru the door which was ever so slightly ajar. In some crude but convincing way I knew that the eyes on which everything rested looked and saw by way of a blind synaesthetic stare having to do with the voices addressing Penny's inner ear. That perhaps they even saw without looking I knew as well.

It seemed I looked into Penny's mind and saw the circling of hawks inside a low-ceilinged enclosure. The door I peeped in thru hung on rusted hinges. The occasional creaking suggested an ever so subtle wind. Each ever so plaintive squeak supplied Penny's blind synaesthetic ensemble with outside accompaniment, the girl the dead man took her to be giving up the ghost in the form of a pinched, pathetic, almost inaudible cry.

The dead man had given Penny a doll. The abject embrace in which creaking hinge addressed inward choir ever so subtly matured—ripening, ripped open, trapped inside and translating what sounded like the discarded doll's whimper. The dead man had called it a present but to Penny it suggested an outgrown, irrelevant past she'd long since rejected. The doll sat atop a trash heap. Every so often it whined.

Penny had warned him against confusing the girl with the song he assumed she inspired, against the presumption of any across-the-board equation. She'd said it before and she'd say it again: PENNY'S *wasn't the same as* PENNIES. PENNY'S *meant* PENNY IS. PENNIES *meant* PENNY AIN'T. *The difference was one her life depended on.*

Penny frowned. The singing downstairs had gotten louder, her sense that it was "Penny's . . ." they were singing all the more insistent. She got out of bed and stomped on the floor, letting the neighbors know they were making too much noise.

The opening I peeped in thru was unmistakably the crack between PENNY IS *and* PENNY AIN'T. *I saw that the dead man remained in bed while Penny stomped on the floor. The ever so subtle wind the creaking hinges implied began whispering in my ear, telling me the dead man had been an anthropologist while alive, going so far as to coin a new term by which to refer to him.*

I couldn't help giggling as the implied wind called the dead man an "ain'thropologist." My giggle caught Penny's attention. She looked my way but evidently couldn't see me and resumed her stomping. I was a pure, transparent presence, an Invisible woman, I realized. (Invisible, the implied wind insisted, with a capital I.) Again I giggled.

Penny heard the second giggle and again looked my way. Seeing nothing, she again resumed her stomping. The ticklish wind, causing me to giggle again, called it "her informant's dance." She ignored this third giggle and continued stomping, but to no avail. The people downstairs not only didn't quiet down but even got a bit louder.

Penny stomped harder. She not only stomped harder but brought the rhythm of her stomping into play with the singing downstairs, exacting a sense of aberrant accent which, though failing to quiet the people downstairs, made the ain'thropologist sit up in bed and take notice.

Her stomping had indeed become a dance. Its offbeat accentuation was both informed by and woven into an abject equation whereby virtuosity served a sense of impairment. She repeatedly went from a strong flamenco stomp with the heel of her right foot to a bent-legged, limping gesture which appeared to contend with and call into question the resolve and the strength of what had gone before. Bent-legged, limping gesture repeatedly turned into strong flamenco stomp, the admitted limp not only telling of dues and deprivation but attesting to a capacity for translating damage into a dance. Penny's was indeed a dance of near collapse and last-minute recovery, a felt advance beyond impairment and limitation which amounted to a meeting of the here-and-now with the hereafter.

The ain'thropologist looked intently at every move Penny made. His sitting up gave me a better view of his face. It almost went without saying that his eye sockets were empty, that the eyes with which he looked at Penny's every move had disappeared, been plucked. The hawks inside Penny's head, I saw, almost certainly had something to do with it. Synaesthetic beak embraced visionary blindness. Visionary wing embraced implied polyphonic stare.

Again the door hinges creaked. Penny's dance, the implied wind insisted, rested on a tenuous, tottering "chord" in which like-sounding "notes" were all sounded at once.
IMPAIRMENT
EMPOWERMENT
IMPEDIMENT
made for rickety, resilient limbs, each of which appeared stilted, possessed of a studied awkwardness; each of which, while crippled, was itself a crutch.

The wind had by now become hawkish, nuzzling my ear with its audiotactile beak and rough playful tongue, fondling my neck with affectionate bites and random rough-and-ready licks. Again I heard what sounded like a discarded doll's whimper, a sharp drawn-out cry in which pleasure and surprise complicated the pathos I'd heard before. Almost at once I realized it was me who'd made it. The hawk's puppylike tongue had made me close my eyes and made me whimper, caused a cry to build and break from my throat, a mixed moan in which release tugged a thread of regret.

What I felt was a lulling, alarming blend of complacency and pleasure—comforting and disconcerting at the same time. Never even in a dream had I thought death would be so playful, yet death, I reflected nonchalantly, was obviously what this was. The wind's predatory beak and abrasive tongue were alternately puppylike and possessed of a dry humor. Droll, desultory bites took their toll on my neck but nevertheless they tickled. That I found it funny only made it more terrible.

The wind now carried a worm in its beak and made me wonder: Was I a worm or were the affectionate pecks on my neck each a maggot's bite?

No sooner had this question arose than a tremor crossed the floor from Penny's direction, entered me by way of my feet and traveled up my body to the top of my head. It subsided in the roots of my hair but another quickly followed. And then another followed in quick succession and so forth, bittersweet ripples running thru me so starkly my lulled eyes opened again.

I opened my eyes and saw that the ain'thropologist was still sitting up in bed watching Penny's every move. Penny was no longer stomping but had picked up the hammer she keeps under her bed for self-defense and was now on her knees pounding the floor with it, beating out the bittersweet rippling tremors which entered me by way of my feet.

Penny's hammer, though it made the hawk let go of my neck, had little impact on the people downstairs. They continued singing, as loud as ever. Penny pounded harder, a grim determined look on her face—so hard it appeared she'd soon knock a hole in the floor. The rippling tremors, by now more bitter than sweet, were almost more than I could stand. Still, the people downstairs didn't seem to notice.

The ain'thropologist sat up straighter and seemed ever more attentive the harder Penny pounded. Finally he leaned forward a bit, raised his right hand with the forefinger pointed upward, prophet-like, and, with some effort, parted his lips as if to speak.

But instead of words coming out of his mouth quarters poured out of his empty sockets as if out of a slot machine, hitting the bed and cascading to the floor. The quarters made a deafening noise but Penny paid neither them nor the ain'thropologist any mind. She continued pounding, the people downstairs continued singing, the quarters continued cascading to the floor.

A twitch developed in my left eye and I looked at the clock beside Penny's bed. It was still twelve minutes of six.

My next-to-last thought before waking up was that time now had a hole in it, my last that Penny's hammer had put it there.

By the time Djamilaa finished I too had a headache. The inner walls of my skull now throbbed as though pounded by a close-to-the-bone hammer. I was struck by the parallels between Djamilaa's dream of Penny and my dream of Djeannine, not the least of them being the near-rhyme of the one name with the other.

I was struck but also exasperated by the teasing nearnesses (taunting near misses) by which the two dreams appeared to be related. It didn't escape my notice, for example, that Djamilaa's dream, not unlike the Djeannine dream, could be said to be indebted to Eddie Jefferson's album *The Main Man*. The role played in her dream by "Pennies from Heaven," that is, couldn't help but have to do with the fact that Eddie's version, "Benny's from Heaven," is the first cut on the second side of the album, as "Jeannine" is the first cut on side one. Was Djamilaa's dream to be understood as the flipside of the Djeannine dream, Penny as the other side of the coin? This was the central question raised by the migraine quandary I now found myself in.

The bits of cowrie shell buried in my brow had begun to pulsate, so many close-to-the-bone feet doing a horizontal stomp from inside my head. No less affected by the dream's near misses, my collarbone began to whistle as though letting off steam. I soon found myself obsessed with the expression "flipside," turning it over again and again in my thoughts. Teasing nearness here made itself known in such a way that by the time I turned it over out loud what came out was a mantra. "Flipside so near so far," I muttered, "flipside so near so far, flipside so near so far, flipside so near so far. . . ."

I must have sounded like a broken record. A puzzled expression came over Djamilaa's face. Not having said a word since finishing telling her dream, she now broke her silence. "What's that you're muttering?" she asked.

Djamilaa's question pulled me out of my chant. The bits of cowrie shell buried in my brow quieted down, causing my collarbone to cool it as well. The room's cavelike aspect, I couldn't help thinking, might've had a hand in my mantric lapse. I asked her would she mind if I opened the curtains. She said no. I got up and did so and sat back down.

I proceeded to tell her about my dream of Djeannine, repeating word-for-word the account of it I wrote you day before yesterday. I explained that Lambert and Penguin had dreamt it as well and recounted the latter's divergent, broken-tooth ending. I then devoted some time to the senses we made of it during our talk yesterday, going on at length, of course, about my feeling that Djeannine is the drummer we've been after. I spoke of my hope that she and Aunt Nancy had also dreamt of Djeannine. I confessed my disappointment that this evidently wasn't the case but expressed a compensatory conviction that certain relationships between her dream of Penny and our dream of

Djeannine—the teasing nearnesses, the taunting near misses—might indeed be the confirmation, albeit oblique, I'd been hoping for. It was this, I explained (at last getting around to addressing her question), that "Flipside so near so far . . ." had to do with.

I then expounded on the teasing nearnesses in some detail, sharing with Djamilaa those I shared with you above but also pointing out others, one such being the link between Penny's flamenco stomp and "Djeannine" being spelled with a D. It occurred to me last night while thinking about the dream that the D amounted to, among other things, a flamenco imprint, that it bore the brunt of my longstanding love of cante jondo. It wasn't just that D could as easily stand for *Duende* as it could for Drummer or that it gave the name a Moorish look. No, it had more importantly to do with something else, something I first noticed a few years back.

What it was is this: Andalusian singers tend to drop the d from the past-participial ending. Instead of "condenado" they say "condenao," "dormio" instead of "dormido," "enamorao" instead of "enamorado" and so forth. It's as though the feeling sung about were of such force, the experience of loss and lack of contact of such intensity, as to disallow the meeting of tongue's tip with alveolar ridge, insist on distance, hiatus, gap in even so small a matter as that, accent lack of touch inside as well as outside the mouth. When the *duende* hits, that is, it's as though "as though" were neither remedy not refuge, gap no simple complaint but all-pervasive, occasion as well as cry inescapably real.

"The unpronounced Andalusian d," I said to Djamilaa, "capitalized and put in front, is the D in 'Djeannine.' Thus Penny's dance, her flamenco stomp. It's all related."

I spoke for some time and Djamilaa listened with what appeared to be great interest. Her close-to-the-bone beauty inspired me, spurred me on, and she not only hung on my every word but, whenever I broke off or became hesitant, gave me encouragement, insisted I go on. She showed (for obvious namesake reasons) a special interest in the dropped Andalusian d, though this, as I've already said, is only one of the near misses I went into. The others I won't belabor here.

Suffice it to say that I spoke at length and that when I was done Djamilaa agreed that something seemed to be afoot. "I'd be more cautious however," she admonished, "as to trying to pin down what that something is. All the things you've talked about have an ominous, premonitory quality to them—ominous but inconclusive." She paused a moment, then added, "Which makes them all the more compelling perhaps." She went on to suggest that we give Aunt Nancy a call and find out had she dreamt of Penny and/or Djeannine.

This we did. I was the one who made the call. It turned out that Aunt Nancy also dreamt of Penny last night. Not only had she and Djamilaa had the same dream but her account of it agreed word-for-word with Djamilaa's—except at the very end.

The difference was that after she got thru the part about the quarters cascading from the ain'thropologist's empty sockets Aunt Nancy concluded, rather than talking about a twitch in her left eye, the hole in time and so forth, by saying, "I saw it all as though from a distance, as if thru an eye made of opera glass."

Yours,

N.

26.IX.81

Dear Angel of Dust,

Thank you for your letter. It arrived yesterday. I'm glad to hear you're doing well and that the various demands on your time that you mention have eased up. I'd begun to wonder why I hadn't heard from you for so long. Things here have been busy as well. We've had a number of gigs recently and we've all been doing a fair amount of writing—which means we've also been putting in more rehearsal time. No, we haven't (to answer your question) found a drummer yet. We've been too busy to really apply ourselves to the search. Furthermore, the drum-dreams we had a few weeks back, I've begun to feel, did more to confuse than to clarify matters. Whether it's a drummer named Penny or a drummer named Djeannine we should be looking for we've been unable to reach an agreement on.

I have, however, given some thought to the second letter you wrote me in July, the one regarding my after-the-fact lecture/libretto. The questions you posed have stayed with me—most of all the big one you dropped on me, "Why opera?" I must admit I'm not a fan of opera. Nor do I especially know anything about it. But since anything, it seems, can be an opera nowadays, I could easily answer by asking, "Why not?" The roots of either "why," I suspect, have to do with certain suppositions regarding social and artistic arrival and/or elevation—antithetically to do with a Eurocentric ladder whose "axiomaticness" makes one ask with no real hope of ascertaining why. The roots of either "why" and of my reasons why, in other words, concern opera's aura more than anything else.

It goes back to a movie I saw as a kid in the early fifties, my first exposure to "opera," *Carmen Jones*. Dorothy Dandridge and Harry Belafonte starred in it. Max Roach and Pearl Bailey were in it as well and on one of his recordings of "What Is this Thing Called Love?" Bird throws in a quote from the score. My older brother took me to see it and what I remember most is that it struck us as funny, that whenever someone burst into song we broke out laughing. At one point we laughed so loud and so long an usher came over to quiet us down. We laughed loudest at the end of the movie. When Belafonte choked Carmen to death and then started singing my brother and I thought we'd die.

What made us laugh was the incongruity—the unreality and the inappropriateness of singing, the gap between song and circumstance. That gap, that incongruity, obeyed a principle of non-equivalence, an upfront absence of adequation I've since made a case for regarding as apt. Such a case calls non-equivalence post-equivalence. That is, the post-equivalent slide of a pointedly unsecured address makes for an apt, operatic inappropriateness—an accusative, therefore apt incongruity. Call it fiddling while Rome burns. This is largely, though not entirely, what I'm up to.

It was exactly this I was thinking about the other night when an uncanny coincidence occurred. The notion of operatic incongruity, of an elevated, broken vessel the sound of whose shattering antithetically rings true, was much on my mind as I got up to turn the television on. I pushed in the knob and what came on was the tail end of a Memorex commercial: Ella Fitzgerald hitting an extremely high note while in the foreground a wine glass shattered. I could hardly believe it. I immediately thought of two things: 1) Rahsaan's piece "Rip, Rig and Panic," whose opening section ends with the sound of breaking glass, and 2) Aunt Nancy's phrase "an eye made of opera glass."

The coincidence turned out to be catalytic. The sense of a straining see-thru mode which telescopes its own demise immediately had me under its spell. Turning away from the TV set, I sat down and began a new after-the-fact lecture/libretto, the first paragraph of which came so effortlessly it seemed to be writing itself:

> Jarred Bottle's I made of opera glass dropped out. Orb and vessel both (i.e., glass eye, reading glass and wine glass rolled into one), it dropped out, fell to the floor and shattered, having turned lowercase and taken the place of Aunt Nancy's u. An apostrophe had already pried the n and the t apart, opening the door thru which Ain't Nancy had come in and which remained ajar, a concrete epigraph endorsed in namesake fashion by a Platonic/Pythagorean pun. Jarred Bottle had begun his lecture by reading a quote: "Some clever fellow, making a play with words, called the soul a jar, because it can easily be jarred by persuasive words into believing this or that."

I quickly found myself at a loss as to where to go from there. Not only did words no longer come effortlessly but now they didn't come at all. I found myself put off by and caught up in qualms about the patness of the "shattered I," its apparent endorsement of currently fashionable notions of a nonexistent self, a dead subject and such. My own effortless recourse to some such implication turned me off. That the self gets all the more talked about by way of its widely insisted-upon disappearance turns out to be an irony I'm evidently not able to get beyond.

Thus the paragraph turned out to be no more than a heuristic wedge, an impromptu foot-in-the-door whose playing back of imprints availed itself of a suspect effortlessness which could now be and had to be parted with, put aside. It was a possible music I now turned my attention to. Abandoning paper and pen, I turned off the TV, took out my alto and began working on a solo which would hopefully both allude to and bridge Bird's *Carmen Jones* quote and Rahsaan's "Rip, Rig and Panic." (Rahsaan, by the way, alludes to Bird's quote in the course of his solo on "Wham Bam Thank You Ma'am" on Mingus's album *Oh Yeah.*) The solo would be a part of my antithetical opera.

The working out of it went pretty well. I came up with a number of combinations and transitions, the more complex and oblique of which built upon a sensation of spindly support, a Platonic rapport between panicky stritch and impromptu aria somewhat like impishness and trauma holding hands. My playing grew possessed of a geometric high, a Pythagorean dismay (almost outrage at points) before incommensurables—but only in order not to console "Pythagorean" expectations, only in order to acknowledge or arouse a sense of aliquant excess, an elegant post-equivalent drift. I took out staff paper and as I went along wrote out the passages I felt I might not otherwise remember.

There were some wrinkles which at first refused to be ironed out. I tinkered, fine-tuned and tested for quite a while, working out most of them though a few went on getting the best of me. I arrived at a point where putting it all aside for a while seemed to be the best thing to do, so I set the horn in the stand on the floor and got up and turned the TV back on. There was a Peter Lorre movie on the *Late Show* and I sat back down to watch it, my mind still mainly on the impasse I'd reached in my impromptu post-equivalent solo.

Not long after sitting back down I fell asleep. I must've slept for quite some time. By the time I woke up, that is, there was a test pattern on the TV screen. What woke me up was the sound of an alto playing a familiar tune, a tune whose name was on the tip of my tongue though as I slept I couldn't for the life of me recall what it was. The effort to do so woke me up.

I awoke, rubbed the sleep from my eyes and looked around, noticing the test pattern on the TV screen and the fact that the sound I'd heard was no dream but was coming from my alto sitting on the floor. I rubbed my eyes again and shook my head as if to clear it of cobwebs, taken aback by the sight of the horn apparently playing itself. I looked on in disbelief as keys were pressed and let go, the horn fingered by invisible hands. The tune, I realized after a while, was "The Inflated Tear," Rahsaan's lament recalling a nurse's mistake which had left him blind.

I sat glued to my chair, the horn's captive. There was a lush but alarmed quality to its tone, a namesake fluidity which not only bordered on but clearly crossed over into effortlessness. Indeed, the horn was possessed of a virtuosity which amounted to the ultimate in effortlessness: automatism. I sat entranced by its utter fluency, the utter finesse with which it held forth on the emotional flood to which it owed itself. Automatic alto spoke of a blind Atlantean reservoir of feeling, an inordinate rush and/or capacity from which it ever so lightly held back, all the more insistent, all the more extrapolatively brought into being by its doing so. Automatic alto (effortless alto) spoke eloquently as well as at length of operatic inflation and of its related, residual theme of aliquant excess, the very theme which had been so much on my mind.

Every now and then, however, automatic alto tripped itself up, critiqued its own effortlessness by deliberately having a beginner's difficulty with fourth-line D. By resorting to a beginner's unsuccessful effort to avoid the "break" in using the octave key automatic alto not only brought the issue of human agency to the fore but brought me more actively into the picture. I found I couldn't, that is, help trying to correct automatic alto's lapses into awkwardness. With each problematic D I lent it a bit of body English, gesturing as though I were holding it and playing it, correctly coordinating my left thumb's roll with the appropriate changes in lip and tongue pressure. In doing so I contracted a host of automatic stigmata. I could actually feel the weight of the horn pull the strap against the back of my neck, feel the reed against my lower lip, feel the octave key underneath my thumb and so forth. It was as though automatic alto were playing me, as if I were its axe, its instrument. Even so, its voice broke like that of a boy entering puberty. I could do nothing, body English notwithstanding, to assist it.

But the more automatic alto faltered the more deeply it had me under its spell. I was its axe, its instrument, no "as if" about it. With each "break" it indicted its own suspect effortlessness, but in doing so it implicated a fallible human hand, a broken vessel—namely, in this instance, me. The more it faltered the more I lent it support. But the more support I lent it—the more I gestured, the more body English I resorted to—the more inept its non-avoidance of the "break" became.

With each lapse into awkwardness it brought me abreast of my own ineffectuality, seemed intent on teaching me humility—which, in a sense, it very effectively did. Automatic alto (awkward alto) clearly had a mind of its own.

What awkward alto seemed intent on saying was that I was the problem, not the solution, that aliquant excess provided not a see-thru advance but a before-the-fact Atlantean collapse. This, of course, I'd long suspected and, in that sense, already knew, but the way in which awkward alto went on to both base itself upon and embroider a blend of precipitous forethought and residual truth not only renewed but ever so expertly strengthened its hold on me. Residual truth turned into precipitous afterthought. I couldn't help noting that even though I was its axe awkward alto (aliquant alto) had apparently gotten me under its skin. I was a ghost, a grain of salt in the machine. Mine was the salt- or sand-anointed voice, the unavoided "break."

After the last of these non-avoidances "The Inflated Tear" gave way to "L'oiseau rebelle," a quote of Rahsaan's quote of Bird's quote of *Carmen Jones*'s quote of *Carmen*. Aliquant alto might as well have meant aliquant elevation, aliquant/operatic aura come home to roost. It belabored the fact that what it quoted was already a quote of a quote of a quote, as though in so doing it thumbed a long since remaindered book. This accounted for the "break," the inept employment of the octave key, the lack of the appropriate tongue and lip coordination. Aliquant alto, it invited one to say, was "all thumb."

Having made its joke and having tossed out its quote of a quote of a quote of a quote, aliquant alto again took up "The Inflated Tear," playing it now without the slightest lapse into awkwardness. The finesse and facility with which it now played almost blew me away. I sat entranced as it ran the gamut from a velvety calm reminiscent of Johnny Hodges to a nervous, on-the-edge intensity worthy of Jimmy Lyons, a nervous, pistol-pointed-at-one's-head sense of emergency.

Automatic alto had now come full circle, clearly come to be the host of a circuitous muse. In attempting to sidestep or critique its own technical finesse, it was now willing to admit, it had simply replaced what it took to be artificial wholeness, artificial health, with artificial breakage, artificial debris. This was a dilemma one couldn't help addressing, it went on to announce, in a period haunted by (hemmed in by) artifice, operatic reflex. Was there no way to be genuinely broken it rhetorically asked by way of a distraught, strangled, bittersweet cry, a Braxtonian mix confronting form with flight. Was there no way to be genuinely whole it rhetorically asked by way of a smooth, unhurried blaze of ballad warmth, ballad hearth, ballad health.

I was now even more deeply entranced as automatic alto came full circle by playing the tune straight. Its unhurried blaze of ballad warmth brought Benny Carter to mind, causing me to see that "The Inflated Tear" was the watery, post-equivalent bridge I'd been after, the sunken, lush, dreamless Atlantean drift I'd been looking for.

Automatic alto's Carteresque ballad warmth gradually gave way to a benedictory aubade which made one think of Carlos Ward (more specifically, the edge he puts on "Desireless" on Don Cherry's *Relativity Suite*). It was on this note of salt-inflected fluidity—with its related sense of endless flotation and a requisite regard for longstanding limbo—that automatic alto brought its recital to a close.

Everything was now silent except for the hum of the TV set. I sat riveted to my seat, mulling over the implications of the upstart serenade the horn had treated me to. Automatic alto (upstart alto) had overcome the impasse I'd arrived at in my impromptu post-equivalent solo, ironed out the wrinkles I'd been unable to correct. Exactly how it'd done so I now sat trying to figure out.

It took me a while but I eventually figured it out—the result of which please give a listen to on the cassette you'll find enclosed: "Robotic Aria for Prepared and Unprepared Alto." As you'll hear, I've availed myself not only of automatic alto's technical solutions but of its theme of built-in obstruction as well. The aria consists of two parts, "prepared" and "unprepared." For the former I taped a sawed-off popsicle stick under the octave key. The latter begins, as you can hear, with the sound of me peeling off the tape and the popsicle stick falling to the floor.

I find the aria notable, even if I do say so myself, for the head-on hedging mixed with head-on address it carries off, its dredging up of a watery precipitate (post-equivalent bridge and post-equivalent debris rolled into one).

As always, I look forward to your response.

Yours,
N.

2.X.81

Dear Angel of Dust,

Yes, operatic in only the most radical operational sense: root-labor, root-exertion, root-strain. This to me seems the only usable way to take it—certainly the most inclusive and thus the most amenable to a global conception, which is also what I'm up to and after. Having issued oneself every caution against the hubris of such an ambition, one pursues it nonetheless, going at it, however, antithetically, thus in keeping with the warnings one obeys. A cautionary note having to do with aborted "globality," that is, pits immanent vessel against monumental investiture. The new after-the-fact lecture/libretto I'm enclosing should be read with this in mind.

How it came about bears on one's reading as well, though how it came about is no easy matter to pin down. Who can say for sure how far back any such thing as this goes? Perhaps it began that time I grieved over Marley's death, began with the trance it took Aunt Nancy to pull me out of. Perhaps it was then the seed got sown and thus erected a wall I came to know by way of an effort to break it down, break thru. Thoroughgoing "thru-ness," the impacted lucidity the cowrie shell attack took the form of that time, indeed amounted to "root-labor, root-exertion, root-strain" (genetic sieve, genetic salt, genetic seizure). Yet an oblique rehearsal of this moves the birth of the piece a bit farther back—to a night several years ago when Aunt Nancy and Lambert sat in his car (they'd been to a movie) and she began to weep for no apparent reason, began "crying her eyes out," as Lambert later phrased it. The recent death of her grandfather, it turned out, was what caused her to weep.

It was in part the recollection of this that led me to arrange a meeting with Aunt Nancy the other night, the meeting out of which the lecture/libretto grew and to which it refers. Of that it speaks for itself, so I won't belabor what it has to say here. I will, however, note in closing that the possibly post-equivalent rapport between "eye" and "eye"—"eye made of opera glass" on the one hand, "cried-out eye" on the other—was one of the issues I hoped Aunt Nancy could help clear up. To what extent, I had in mind, among other things, to ask, were they one, albeit not the same?

As ever,
N.

APRIL IN PARIS

or, The Creaking of the Word: After-the-Fact Lecture/Libretto (Aunt Nancy Version)

Jarred Bottle let his right hand rest on his knee. With his left hand he went on gripping the steering wheel, waiting for the light to change. He brought his right hand up from his knee and touched his upper lip with his middle finger. There were no other cars in sight. The light had been green as he'd approached from a distance, turning yellow as he'd gotten closer and finally, just as he'd gotten to the intersection, red. He brought his right hand down from his upper lip and let it come to rest on his knee again. It seemed absurd to be sitting there.

At a quarter of three in the morning his was clearly the only car on the street. Still, he sat there, waiting for the light to change, deferring to the nonexistent traffic. He thought of a quip he'd heard once or twice: Revolution would never occur in a country whose people stop for traffic lights late at night when there's no one else around. He also thought of his adopted childhood in China.

The light remained red and he sat there waiting. He shot a glance at the rearview mirror but saw that there were no cars behind him after all. One of the records Aunt Nancy had spun for him earlier must have been a web he thought. He could've sworn he'd heard the horn of a car behind him, the horns of three cars in fact. He could also have sworn that they played the three-note passage 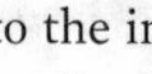 , one car hitting G, one A and the other E. Seeing nothing in the rearview mirror, he turned and looked out the back window to make certain there were no cars there. There were none. He turned his attention back to the traffic light. He now knew for sure that the music Aunt Nancy had played for him had made him an accessory after the fact. The three-note passage, he recalled on giving it some thought, had come up in the melody line of Frank Wright's "China," one of two cuts on the record and web rolled into one Aunt Nancy had spun for him earlier:

He and Aunt Nancy had gotten together to discuss his namesake lecture/libretto "Not Here, No There." His goal was a work which would somehow mobilize exhaustion, put it to new and unheard-of uses. The closest he'd come, trying to put what he was after into words, was the image of blocks turning into waves—the way cars on a freeway, heard from a distance, tend to sound like the ocean. Or the way a Cecil Taylor piece goes on to build on the blocks it seemed at first to be obstructed by. Aunt Nancy, he knew, was an accomplished hand at putting new wine into old bottles, very much the after-the-fact accomplice and confidante he'd only lately come to admit he'd been looking for.

He'd gone by her apartment at half past nine as they'd planned. He'd wasted no time getting into the concerns which had brought him there. The work, he'd explained, would revolve around *locale* and *dislocation*, two terms of a continuing obsession he felt not so much prompted as dictated to by. "Not Here, No There," that is, would apprise the ear of a sense of numbed, interlocking parts dictated to by the unstable gaps between letters (ot H, o Th). The piece would be introduced by two Namesake Epigraphs, the first a quote from a 1936 essay by Ernst Krenek, the Austrian composer who fled the Nazis in 1937 and settled in Southern California:

> Taking the ending of pretences as the basic intention of a new operatic style makes opera a particularly pregnant

> expression of the antagonistic outlook of the present age and at the same time makes it the very opposite of present-day political tendencies, which, whether of the right or of the left, go in for concealing antitheses and simulating a united, coherent world—and do not scruple to use force to do so, which in itself is the most blatant symptom of internal paradox.

The second came from a song by Pink Anderson, the South Carolina bluesman and medicine-show singer, "My Baby Left Me This Morning":

> Lord, I believe I'll call up China,
>   I wanna see if my little gal's there.
> Boys, I believe I'll call up China.
>   I wanna see if my little gal's there.
> And if she's not in China,
>   She must be in East St. Louis somewhere.

It was on hearing the second Namesake Epigraph that Aunt Nancy had put on the piece by Frank Wright. "This is a cut you've got to hear," she'd said, pulling out the record and putting it on the turntable. Every now and then she'd giggled while the piece was playing. Once it was over she'd told of the night she heard Wright's group in a New York loft in the early seventies. The story, which Jarred Bottle had immediately christened Namesake Anecdote #1, had gone like this: Wright was in a blowing mood that night, the band coming on with a tuneless, ultra-out wall of sound (no head, no recognizable structure), a raucous, free-for-all cacophony which at times had the feel of an assault. The first set went on that way, nonstop, for about an hour and fifteen minutes. During the break between sets Aunt Nancy approached Wright and asked if he'd play a request. He said, "Yeah. What would you like to hear?" She told him "China" and he said, "No problem." The second set, however, went just like the first, equally tuneless, equally nonstop, equally without a head or a recognizable structure, coming nowhere near the melody line of "China." The one difference was that about forty-five minutes into the set Wright let the tenor fall from his mouth and hang by its strap, cupped his hands in front of his mouth like a megaphone and yelled, "China! China! China!" He then took the tenor back to his mouth for another twenty or so no-letup minutes of squeaks, honks, moans, growls and screeches.

Aunt Nancy hadn't been able to keep from laughing on finishing the story. Jarred Bottle, sitting before the traffic light and recalling it, couldn't help grinning and chuckling to himself. He reached up with his right hand and adjusted the rearview mirror, turning it till his reflected grin came into view. He was struck by the reddish glow the traffic light gave his face. He also couldn't help noticing that after all the wine and grass he'd had at Aunt Nancy's his eyes were still so bright and alert. This, he knew, was because of his childhood in China, the exercises and routines he'd adopted to enliven his otherwise lackluster eyes. Staring at kites drifting in a blue sky, watching pigeons disappear into the clouds and gazing at the movements of an incense flame in a dark room were some of the habits which had given him the wide-eyed expressivity needed for plausible opera. Watching pandas munch bamboo leaves had also helped.

But as he sat there waiting for the light to change Jarred Bottle couldn't help reflecting on the unfunny side of Namesake Anecdote #1. It was out of a sense of having come to the end of one's rope, he realized, a sense of everything having already been done, that one cried out to China. The need for an ultimate or consummate elsewhere, he reflected, for a last, possibly lost resort, was in fact a requiem or wake tantamount or testifying to after-the-fact appetite on the one hand, before-the-fact satiety on the other. "China," he intoned resolutely, "you will be mine"—though the operatic voice he'd resorted to immediately made him blush. No sooner had he spoken than the reddish glow on his face had gotten a little bit redder. "China," he repeated more softly, "you will be mine."

The fact was that in putting on the record by Frank Wright Aunt Nancy had inadvertently happened upon and reawakened the understated truth Jarred Bottle wanted to blot out. The nagging fact was that "Not Here, No There," his namesake lecture/libretto, was being dictated by the gaps between letters in more ways than one. What he'd shied away from telling Aunt Nancy was that it'd been a week and a half since he'd last heard from his girlfriend, April. April, Aunt Nancy knew, had left a couple of months earlier to live in Paris for a while. What she didn't know was that in the course of those two months April had written Jarred Bottle less and less often. First she'd written him every other day, then every second day, then every third or so day and so forth. It'd now come to the point where he hadn't heard from her in a week and a half and he'd begun to fear she might be drifting away. He was embarrassed to find he felt so insecure. Still, when he'd picked up the Frank Wright album jacket it'd hit him like a slap to read that the music had been recorded in Paris.

It was largely a religious insecurity he felt, he told himself, "numinous qualms" conducive to "endless apprehension." Making matters worse was the fact that in her last letter April, who, like a number of women he knew, had for some time expressed an attraction to other women, had devoted a long paragraph to a woman she'd recently met. She'd used the words "fascinating" and "charming" to describe her. She'd spoken of herself as "enthralled" and "captivated." The woman's name was China.

The coincidence had all but blown him away. Its namesake mingling of *elsewhere* with *sexual other* had seemed to complicate yet confirm a certain ritual tension sustained by "structured" affront. What remained to be seen was to what extent Jarred Bottle's before-the-fact elegance under duress amounted to the sought-after namesake equation of apt exaggeration with problematic romance. For years he'd been under the spell of Monk's rendition of "April in Paris." The mock awkwardness of Monk's deliberate, somewhat halting attack, his way of outmaneuvering an otherwise too sweet, saccharine ambush, was exactly what Jarred Bottle had in mind where he'd written "lump sugar" on the charts for "Not Here, No There." Nor had it escaped him that during the forties Monk had been accused of playing "Chinese" music.

"China," he heard himself insisting yet again, "you will be mine.

One day we'll meet among lighted candles on the Magpie Bridge." He wasn't altogether sure what he meant by this but it somehow fit. Though the light remained red he gave himself a go-ahead of sorts, putting himself in what he took to be China's position, a position he himself had been in many times before. S/he, that is, lay in bed beside April, lifting a hand and ever so lightly caressing the scar left by the appendectomy April had had when she was thirteen. The training which, as a child, Jarred Bottle had gotten in the Chinese orphanage served him well in the task of crossing (even closing) the slash between the s and the h. Known as Dan by some, he couldn't help noticing, as he looked at his face in the rearview mirror, the coquettish gleam his eyes had acquired, the namesake look of an African snake and a female impersonator rolled into one. It was as much her in his position as he in hers he knew.

S/he now ran a finger, as if reading braille, up and down the scar on April's abdomen, both arousing and attempting to erase the sense of animate imprint s/he was riven by. Once again Cecil Taylor came to mind. The jittery, apprehensive sense of touch his playing conveys now appeared to prompt if not outright possess the hand whose fingers moved back and forth across April's scar. Here, though, the sense of the piano being not so much played as broken into gave way to a wincing, resonant tenderness, a lyric restraint whose hesitancies implied while putting off the eventual meeting on the Magpie Bridge.

Indeed, it was a Tayloresque assault of pianistic chatter, Jarred Bottle now saw, he'd had in mind with the words "we'll meet among lighted candles on the Magpie Bridge," an accelerated version of the Monkish "lump sugar" he'd worked so hard to find a place for in the piece. This, he also saw, was the premise or the promise of the Magpie Bridge's premature equation (as if pillow talk and pianistic chatter were now rolled into one). "Dear wounded bird," s/he whispered, "be mine."

Jarred Bottle now had to reflect on the word "mine" which had come up again, not so much a plea as an admission of depth no threat of distance would ever daunt or exhaust. He was struck by its matter-of-fact equation of poignancy with pressure. He was equally struck by its magpie suspension of the rest or resolution it seemed to propose and prematurely possess. A sense of yield equating desire with demand seemed to make for a pregnant, pianistic lump whose reciprocal cut one had no choice but to respect. "Dear wounded bird," s/ he whispered again as s/he continued caressing April's scar, the medicinal kiss it implied or invited gently translating fingers into prepossessing lips. "Dear wounded bird," s/he repeated, "be mine."

Jarred Bottle suddenly felt as though his mouth had been sewn shut. He took his hand from the rearview mirror, touching his lips with his middle finger. He ran the finger back and forth between the corners of his mouth, testing the thread which held his lips together. Afraid of what he'd see, he no longer looked at his face in the rearview mirror. He couldn't shake the feeling that his head had shrunk, that he was now, as the expression has it, "all heart," and that the heart, the lump he felt in his throat, in part accounted for the thread which sealed his lips, for the stitched incision his mouth had become.

Was it thread or was it cobweb he wondered, again suspecting the intrusion of Aunt Nancy's hand. Typical Aunt Nancy mischief, Aunt Nancy omniscience, he thought. Still, one had to give her credit, he went on, gazing out the windows and admiring the set. The design was so realistic and lifelike, much more convincing but, all the same, more enigmatic than he'd expected or dreamt. He'd had every confidence when she'd offered to do the set that he'd be happy with whatever she'd come up with. He hadn't, however, expected it to leave him speechless.

Aunt Nancy had somehow read his mind, it seemed, sealing his lips by relating them to the scar on April's abdomen, using the same rhapsodic thread he himself had obeyed each time he'd kissed her there (kissed April there). That so tenuous a thread could be so binding made for a mystery only moans could address. Jarred Bottle's aria thus consisted of humming punctuated by moans and even a grunt every now and then. What more, given his mouth having been sewn shut, had one a right to expect? This rhetorical question, he knew, the critics would never tire of asking.

He would leave it to them to ask. As for him, he continued gazing out the windows, admiring the apt, unexaggerated torque, the arch insinuation Aunt Nancy'd worked into the set. As he gazed out the windows he hummed in approval of what he saw. He gave a go-ahead grunt to the sense of animate imprint which allowed him to put himself in China's place, to put her in his. Presided over by the traffic light which hung overhead, the set appeared possessed of a stark photo-realist clarity, an implied charisma which complied with and catered to the namesake suspension which now addressed him as never before.

But the sense of having been gagged was beginning to bother him. He was no longer sure the light would ever turn green. His before-the-fact elegance under duress began to veer toward panic, a growing sense of alarm at the autistic tether which tied him to April. The contagious kiss which equally tied him to China now seemed to detach itself from both their mouths, pursuing a life of its own by taking the traffic light's place overhead, suspending a promise of sutured lips and scar-tissue lump rolled into one.

It recalled a Man Ray painting somewhat. The lips lit up the sky beyond the windshield in front of him, a fleeting hallucinatory wrinkle in Aunt Nancy's otherwise realist design. He rubbed his eyes and gave it another look but by then it was gone.

By then, too, the light had turned green and the sense that his lips were sewn together had gone away. Before he knew it, in fact, his lips parted and his mouth flew open and out came the cry "Anywhere but East St. Louis!" It took him only a second to realize that what he'd meant to say was "Anywhere but here!" The slip revealed how deeply he'd invested in both ends of Pink's disingenuous opposition between all too likely East St. Louis and all too unlikely China. Yet even the correct climactic line "Anywhere but here!" revealed the equally disingenuous overdetermination of April's stay in Paris. The fleeting lips had cast momentary light on the closet drama in which he and she were involved, had brought its namesake overdetermination compounded of after-the-fact melodic dictation to the fore. The fleeting see-thru sense he'd gotten was one of ghostwritten parts in a skeletal opera, the outlines of which he felt indelibly touched by even though he'd barely begun to sketch them in or make them out.

China, he'd seen, partook of a namesake overdetermination too: not only elsewhere, sexual other and same-sex rival rolled into one, but also stitches, would-be satiety and saturation rolled in as well. This accounted for the lips' full-to-bursting poignancy, the anti-realist pressure they'd brought to bear on the set. This also accounted for the cars whose horns he again thought he heard behind him:  . Again he turned and looked but there were no cars there. He'd heard of a bonelike hardening of the skin called cutaneous horn, but this, he began to see, went somewhat deeper. The horns were somehow under his skin.

Subcutaneous horn amounted to an inverse hardening, the very opposite of hardening in fact. The softness he felt for April (an inward, almost painful tenderness) rayed out in the form of a welling persistence, a relentless ripple or wave which broke, as it were, only on the shores of China. Jarred Bottle sighed while wiping a dry tear from his cheek. It was a tear constituted of abstract emotive water run thru the sieve of circumstance and constraint. This gave rise to a pinched, piercing sound which now addressed his ears, taking the place of Wright's "China" line. It took him no time at all to recognize the new sound as a cut from Old and New Dreams's first album, the title cut in fact. Ed Blackwell's gong at the beginning would've given it away all by itself, but Dewey Redman's put-thru-a-strainer musette made it clear that the horns hadn't only gotten under his skin but had also gone to his head. There was another cut on the album, he remembered, called "Chairman Mao."

In what sense did April's hard scar-tissue lump have to do with the movement of world-historical masses, with political, cultural and psychic reconstruction of a kind suggested by reports of a unisex China? This was the question, he now saw in retrospect, which had earlier sewn his lips together. It was a lure but it was also a tease. He shied away from it, preferring to reflect on the notion of love as a loosening of limbs which now refused to go away.

This he did in part to deflect the sense of namesake obstruction,[*] of

---

* In an earlier draft of this piece Jarred Bottle went by the name Blocked Opera.

an arrested dance of redistributed limbs which pervaded Aunt Nancy's set. It was as though her design had been to elicit an answering dance of liberated extremities. He felt his penis nudge his left thigh, beginning to stiffen, an after-the-fact erection tied to the sense (dialectically tied to the sense) of having come to the end of one's rope he'd reflected on earlier. "China," he muttered under his breath, "you will be mine."

The critics, it almost went without saying, would conclude that exhaustion, a sense of all other options having failed, had driven April into China's arms. Jarred Bottle knew better. He knew the validity of such a way of seeing it but he knew the ways in which it fell short as well. For one, it failed to acknowledge the fortune April and China had begun to inherit. April's adopted stay in Paris, not unlike his early years in the Chinese orphanage, apprised one, if one were attentive, of a sense of earned, irrepressible bounty, a blasé, before-the-fact advance whose extravagant brunt one bore in the face of an otherwise depleted or deprived circumstance. Over the short run it perhaps amounted to the same thing. Still, he couldn't help insisting on the need to have a go at such a distinction. He insisted on doing so even if before-the-fact advance competed with after-the-fact erection—which, in fact, it very much did. Would the latter, he wondered, suffer the same fate as April's appendix? Did her and China's inheritance mean that the rod now nudging his left thigh would soon be expendable, obsolete? Was this the fear written into his obsession with the scar on April's abdomen?

These were only a few of the questions he both raised and again shied away from, gazing out the windows and again admiring Aunt Nancy's set. What had repeatedly caught and again held his eye was the clarity and the convincingness of her conception. The set looked exactly like the intersection of First and Main in his hometown in Southern California. He looked at the street sign on the corner to his right. The street he was on was First, the cross street Main. "A stroke of genius," he muttered under his breath.

Turning his gaze to the left and looking out the windshield, he finally noticed that the light had turned green. He was surprised to find that he now felt no desire to move on. The green light wasn't enough, wasn't the go-ahead he'd been waiting for. By not moving he seemed to be insisting that the light had no authority over him, that he'd been sitting there for reasons other than its being red, that its turning green was equally beside the point. Green would get him neither to Paris nor to China. Green was irrelevant to the out he was after.

He was gratified to learn that sitting there could have an oppositional, rebellious aspect to it. The green light's irrelevance prompted him to an even more extreme or extravagant out. He would sit there for quite some time, not moving. The light would go back to yellow, then red, turn green again, yellow, then red again, green and so forth. Finally a police car would pull up behind him and signal with its lights for him to pull over to the side. This he'd ignore as well, forcing the cops to get out of their car and come to him.

The cops would ask him had he been drinking, ask what was the idea of just sitting there. He'd tell them he was a Rastafarian, that he was waiting for the red, yellow and green lights to come on at the same time. "All this time," he'd explain, "I've been thinking about Paris and China, but it was Ethiopia I was actually headed for." The cops would have no idea what he meant.

10.X.81

Dear Angel of Dust,

Yes, of course I know Krenek's opera *Jonny spielt auf*, but, no, in speaking of an "aborted 'globality'" I didn't mean to allude to its concluding image of the railway station clock turned into a globe bestrided by Jonny. I wasn't "alluding" to anything, though what I had to say was informed by a book I've been reading, Bastide's *The African Religions of Brazil,* especially a proposition which occurs early on: "What we do need to study, though, is how, why, and in which cases this distortion of the 'sacred' occurs, always taking the 'sacred' as a level of global reality, never as a problem to solve, never as an 'ideology'." Shortly before this he quotes Van Der Leeuw to the effect that the sacred comes to light wherever "life touches its limits, . . . wherever one leans over the rim of existence and is seized by giddiness." What I was getting at, then, is that the muse of inclusiveness awakens one to a giddy sense of spin, a pregnant, rotund integrity eternally and teasingly and whirlingly out of reach (whence "aborted"), a sense of asymptotic wobble.

It's exactly here, of course, that revelation and recuperation lock horns, the latter almost inevitably the victor, exactly here that distortion occurs. Krenek's *Jonny,* since you've brought it up, is in fact an excellent case in point. It's obvious the work arose from a genuinely giddy seizure, a genuinely teasing rim. But the potential breakthru, the asymmetrical fissure which begins to be glimpsed, is almost immediately closed off, almost immediately traded away for the consolations of a binary opposition. That it's an opposition which rehashes conventional racial categories only makes matters worse, makes for an all the more routine ideological drift. Krenek has written of "the antithesis which inspires the piece—the antithesis between man as a 'vital' animal, and man as a 'spiritual' animal—as incarnated in the diametrically opposed figures of Jonny and Max."

The troubled composer Max, Krenek's projection of himself, is nothing more than a self-serving distortion, as is Jonny, the black saxophonist who steals a violin and takes over the world. "Jonny," Krenek says, "is actually a part of the technical-mechanical side of the world; he reacts as easily, as gratifyingly, exactly and amorally as a well-constructed machine. His kingdom is of this world, and as a matter of course he is the one who gains mastery over life here below, over the visible globe. He is the direct contrast to Max, who, starting out from spirituality, never comes to grips with the problems he is set by external life, which is so attuned to vitality today." That this is the world seen thru a xenophobic window, an opaque window, is symbolized, wittingly or not, by the glacier in front of which Max meditates. The giddy breach or abyss of otherness is sealed off, not surprisingly, as much by sexual as by racial stereotypes. They in fact intersect when one learns that Anita, Max's fickle lover, isn't just an opera singer but plays the banjo as well!

There's more I could say on this but I won't. Allow me to simply note that for all its iconoclastic inclusions—the use of a telephone, loudspeakers, an automobile and a train, the incorporation of black music and a black protagonist—the aim is less one of inclusion than of complaint. These novelties enter the opera not by way of an embrace but in order to voice, ventriloquistically, Krenek's gripe against the times. In this light, the U.S. premiere of the piece at the Met, in which the title role was sung by a white performer in blackface, was more accurate than the European productions. *Jonny* predated *Porgy and Bess* by eight years, but it also anticipated Adorno's shrill, ethnocentric "Über Jazz" by roughly the same amount of time. (Six years ago, by the way, when I was in Munich, I saw a newspaper story about a gorilla born at the zoo. Zoo officials had named it Porgy.) My point, finally, is this: A line of scapegoating, a misidentified threat, runs thru the piece, a prophetic note which comes to ironic fulfillment. Ten years after *Jonny*, Krenek, like Max, flees Europe for the U.S.—chased out, of course, by Nazis, not a black saxophonist.

Please forgive me for going on so. I have some problems with the piece, as you can see. I do, like you, think it's important, though less for what it says than for what it shows. Anyway, I wouldn't have gone into it were it not for your letter, which arrived this afternoon. Your other comments I'll address at another time.

The real reason I'm writing is to let you in on the good news: We've got a gig in New York next month. There's an organization there known as NuMu which has gotten some grant money to put together a series featuring "up and coming" bands from outside New York. They're calling it "Out/West" (though the groups coming in, we understand, are from as close as Cleveland) and they're kicking it off with us on the 20th, 21st and 22nd.

This has been in the offing, pending the grant, for some time, but I decided I'd wait till it definitely came thru before telling you. Needless to say, we're excited.

I'll try to write again soon.

Yours,
N.

21.X.81

Dear Angel of Dust,

Thanks very much for your letter. As always, it gave me much to think about. I too was puzzled by the passage you point out in Bastide's book. I find it hard to believe he couldn't see why Ogun would be viewed as the whites' *orisha,* especially since he mentions his identification with the sword. I'd have expected him to pick up on the reasoning, even if only as a case of "ideological distortion." That a numinous feeling of susceptibility might embrace the perception of a secular threat certainly should have come as no surprise.

It's maybe worth mentioning that Brathwaite, whom I've quoted to you before, writes early in *Rights of Passage* in a way which agrees with the Bantu in Rio Bastide discusses, agrees with their sense of Ogun as the whites' *orisha.* In the second poem in the book, "New World A-Comin'," Ogun, the *orisha,* you'll recall, of iron, fire and war, goes over to the side of the Europeans, assuming the form of the flintlock (O-gun), the technological advantage which allows them to overwhelm the Africans, assuming the form of clinking chains as well:

And the fire, our
fire, fashioning locks,
rocks darker than iron;
fire betrayed us once
in our village; now

in the forest, fire falls
us like birds, hot pods
in our belly. Fire
falls walls, fashions
these fire-
locks darker than iron,
and we filed down the path
linked in a new
clinked silence of iron.

Which only goes, among other things, to underscore the obvious: Bastide is neither black nor a poet.

There was much else in your letter worth going into further, but more on my mind right now is our search for a drummer, which due to anxieties brought on by the New York gig has come to the fore again. We've done our best not to give in to the idea of New York as an acid test, our shot at the big time and so forth, done our best not to get uptight. We've talked about the need to keep cool and to maintain a sober perspective, to think of it as just another gig. "No big thing," we keep saying to one another, "No big thing." Still, in rehearsals a certain stiffness has come into the music. We've been trying too hard, it seems, trying to *make* things happen rather than *letting* them happen, the latter now all that much easier said than done.

Tensions are running high. Anatomically we feel them running low as well. We've all complained of the same feeling, the same nervous flutter. A thin itch along the floor of the stomach spreads a sense of expectancy, an issueless urgency with nowhere to turn but on itself, an otherwise blank apprehension. It's an itch which twitters between two like-sounding limits: futurity at the upper end, futility at the other. It plays upon an emptiness in the pit of the stomach—not simple nothingness but a conviction of nothingness peppered with anomalous hope.

A tightness in the jaw makes matters worse. A tightness complicated by a quivering lower lip and occasional twitches at the corners of the mouth. This has been especially difficult for Lambert, Penguin and me, as you can imagine, making for embouchure problems and a less resolute attack. A mix of qualms and hunger, one might call it. It's as if, that is, the mouth were hooked in a dithyrambic embrace, one's embouchure caught by contested claims of a spastic past and a rhythmic future, alternate claims of a spastic future and a rhythmic past. Shakiness reigns. Qualms and compulsion excavate a suppressed quiver, an insubordinate twitch whose ascendancy contends with surface competence. The sense one gets is that motor memory as well as acoustic recall were now not impervious to the attack they normally hold at bay, that the act of retrieval were now no match for spasticity, subject at all points to ambush, bedouin threat of a mnemonic lapse. This threat, subject neither to proof nor to refutation, amounts to an instinctual disclaimer. In the face of the upcoming gig it appears that something deep inside us blushes and shivers and wants to bow out. Whatever it is, though, not only wants to bow out but to go over big, mixes hope with "humility," wanting to make it big by default.

All of this came openly to a head yesterday at rehearsal. We've all, as I've already said, been noticeably on edge and uptight, but yesterday, for whatever reason, it hit a pitch of intensity which wouldn't let us go on. We were working on a piece new to our book, a new piece by Penguin called "Altered Cross." It's a complicated, labyrinthic piece, as the title implies, filled with shifting rhythms and intersecting harmonics—cracked rhythms and altered, unresolved harmonics which demand an alertness none of us could muster or, if muster, maintain. Not even Penguin was at all up to its demands, but it was finally he who, tired of hearing it butchered, took the horn from his mouth and shouted, "Stop! Stop! Stop! Stop! Stop!" We stopped.

Penguin took a moment to get himself somewhat more composed, patting his foot like an exasperated parent, his left hand on his hip. When he began to speak it was with a deliberate, emphatic effort at self-control. "This is a piece," he began, "about the nowness of now. It's also, I admit, about what's ahead, what's around the bend, but in order to get to that you've got to go thru now." He paused a moment, seeming to reflect on what he'd said, then continued, "You have to be in it when you're in it, which is the thing that'll take you there." He paused again.

Djamilaa took advantage of the pause to ask, "Where?"

"New York," Penguin answered right away. "Why beat around the bush?" he went on to ask rhetorically, after which he spoke at some length to the effect that our problem was one of loss of concentration, that we'd lost our grip on the present by looking past it, that we were caught up in looking ahead to the New York gig. The present, he went on to remind us, was the only time in which anything would ever happen—realizing which, he insisted, we'd best be trying to find our way back.

Penguin's rap put us all a bit more at ease. Though what he had to say was something each of us already knew, it felt good to have it out in the open, good to have it off our collective chest. We each spoke up, agreeing with what he'd said, and as we did it was as if a weight were being taken away. The atmosphere grew lighter, much lighter—so much so, in fact, that Lambert started singing. The song was Jimmy Reed's "Going to New York" and the way Lambert sang it, the way he played with the line "I'm goin' if I have to walk," made the rest of us laugh.

It was me who suggested we call it quits, that we call it a day, take some time to cool out. No one objected and, in fact, we decided we'd hang out together—cruise around town for a while and maybe head up to Griffith Park. We put our axes away, got into Lambert's car and hit the streets. We eventually did end up in Griffith Park, which is where our search for a drummer again came to the fore.

It was a nice day out, sunny but not excessively hot, the smog a bit lighter than usual. Even so, it being a weekday, there weren't that many people in the park. We headed, first thing, for the observatory. "This'll help," Djamilaa remarked as we went in, "put New York in perspective." We spent a while inside, looking at various exhibits and so forth, came back out after about an hour and drove down the hill to the picnic area. It was there that the issue of the drummer came up.

We'd been sitting around enjoying the sun and the shade when Lambert commented, "It's gotten a lot quieter here." It soon became clear that he wasn't talking only about the small number of people in the park nor about the fact that a noticeable hush had momentarily taken over. "I remember," he went on, "back in the sixties. Whenever you came here—weekday, weekend, whenever—there'd be at least a couple of conga players out. Sometimes there were a half-dozen or more and there was always a crowd, though not always a big one, gathered around them. You all remember that, don't you?" We all nodded yes and, almost without pausing, he continued. "In fact, that bench over there was known as the Conga Bench," he said, pointing to a bench down a ways off to our right. "It was there they'd play."

"Yes, I remember," Aunt Nancy put in, a dreamy look on her face and a faraway tone in her voice. "I used to come here myself and play."

Lambert made as if to resume speaking but before any words came out broke off. A grin captured his lips as he appeared to be enjoying some inside joke, inwardly relishing whatever it was which had just come to mind. "I just remembered," he said, letting us in on it, "that there was a brother, a middle-aged brother, who would always show up on Saturdays wearing a whistle on a string around his neck. Nobody ever paid him much mind but he carried on like he was the leader. He'd blow on his whistle—part samba master, part traffic cop—and every now and then yell out a time signature the conga players paid no attention to. They'd go on playing the same as they'd been playing while he shouted, 'Six-eight! Six-eight!' or whatever. It didn't seem to bother him that they paid him no attention. He showed up regularly and always did the same thing. People got so used to him they gave him a nickname and the few times he missed a Saturday someone would ask, 'Where's Father Time?'"

Lambert's grin was now an outright chuckle and the rest of us joined in. "Yeah, I remember that dude," Aunt Nancy said, her face lit up with a light laugh. Penguin seemed to be the most amused among us, laughing so hard his eyes began to water. In fact, he went on laughing long after the rest of us had stopped, so much so that after a while we all stared at him, uncomfortable with something forced and artificial about the way he was going on. Lambert's little anecdote, we all knew, wasn't that funny. I for one wondered were the tears in Penguin's eyes really tears of laughter.

Penguin finally noticed we were staring and stopped laughing. He looked a bit sheepish as he wiped the water from his eyes with the backs of his hands. An odd silence now had hold of us. The atmosphere had definitely changed. It was as if the tears which had filled Penguin's eyes had gone up into the air to become a cloud hanging over us.

"I'm sorry," Penguin finally said, "but I couldn't help thinking about Djeannine. I couldn't help thinking that were she with us we wouldn't feel nervous about New York. I tried to laugh it down but the feeling wouldn't go away." He paused, seeming to drift away in thought for a moment, then added, "It's odd to miss someone you've never met, but I do. I miss her."

Penguin fell silent, looking away from us, gazing at the trees on the other side of the picnic area. The rest of us looked at one another, a bit befuddled, momentarily at a loss for words. Djamilaa broke the silence. "It's funny," she said, "but I've had that feeling too, that same thought. It came on especially strong while we were rehearsing 'Altered Cross.' During that section where we go into F and Lambert pumps us with those low B-flats I couldn't help hearing Penny punctuate it all with a mix of rolls and collateral eruptions, an ever so subtle barrage propelled by quick detonations occurring off to the side. . . ."

"Subtle?" Penguin broke in, no longer looking at the trees, his gaze now fixed on Djamilaa. "I'll believe it when I hear it. Penny can bash, I grant you that, but her problem's that she doesn't pay attention to what else is happening. She doesn't listen to what the rest of us are doing." Djamilaa, Aunt Nancy, Lambert and I looked at him in disbelief, taken aback and all but blown away by the familiarity with Penny's playing he laid claim to and the fierce, confrontational tone with which he did so. This he noticed but, even so, went on without letting up. "It's one thing," he insisted, "to talk, another to hold a conversation. Penny, the way she plays, might as well be sitting in an isolation booth."

"No, absolutely not," Djamilaa objected, raising her voice to drown Penguin out. "What I heard was delicately and thoughtfully played, clearly the work of someone listening to what the rest of us were up to."

"Like I said," Penguin shot back, even louder, "I'll believe it when I hear it." Djamilaa turned away in exasperation, looking at Lambert,

Aunt Nancy and me as if to ask what had gotten into him. Penguin, though, went on talking, lowering his voice now that she'd retreated. "Now Djeannine on the other hand," he began, going on at some length to lavish high, unqualified praise on Djeannine's "light, magnanimous touch," her "caressive way with the vagaries of time," her "at once gossipy yet discreet recourse to the high hat," her "lack of bombast" and so forth. He'd obviously been gotten into by something, though what that something was one couldn't say except to call it a namesake fetish or a nominative fixation or, more simply, risking tautology, Djeannine.

Djamilaa didn't give up, however. Her tack now was to answer each compliment Penguin paid Djeannine by simply saying, "What you just said fits Penny's playing to a T." Something had clearly gotten into her as well—a namesake fetish or a nominative fixation, as in Penguin's case, though in hers the risk of tautology went by another name. That name she interjected again and again and again: "What you just said fits Penny's playing to a T." It soon got to the point where she and Penguin did nothing but throw the two names at one another.

"Djeannine!"

"Penny!"

"Djeannine!"

"Penny!"

It was at this point that the rest of us intervened. Lambert, Aunt Nancy and I had stood silently by as the exchange unfolded, a stiff blend of amusement and apprehension holding us back. It must have been that each of us inwardly fought, on the one hand, an impulse to take sides while also fighting, on the other, an impulse to affect indifference by interjecting the old cliché "What's in a name?" But once the exchange degenerated into throwing the two names back and forth the latter impulse not only got the upper hand but got it in all of us at exactly the same time. The three of us, that is, opened our mouths in unpremeditated unison—a cliché chorus, a banal consensus—and blurted out loudly, "What's in a name?"

Penguin and Djamilaa looked at us in surprise. Aunt Nancy, Lambert and I were also surprised. We were all in for an even greater surprise it turned out, for after the three of us intervened there was an odd, uncanny silence followed by an oblique, barely audible drumming which, for all we could tell, came out of the blue, came out of nowhere. It was as Lambert was about to say something that it began to address us. He was looking at Penguin and Djamilaa and appeared to be about to elaborate on "What's in a name?" As he opened his mouth to speak, though, the drumming started up, turning his head as though his ear were now hooked. What came out of his mouth was part cry, part question, "What's that?"

The rest of us heard it as well. At first it was extremely faint, but the closer we listened the louder it got. The drumming came from a set of traps, not congas, the initial figures a strand of clipped hisses played on the high hat. These went on but then gave way to a cluster of thumps on the bass drum, a muted, oddly low-key altercation, scruffy thunder. It had the feel of a kind of running in place.

All of us were now turning our heads and looking around, trying to see where the drumming was coming from. This we did to no avail, though the sound was a bit louder now.

Whoever was drumming now took up the brushes and laid down a slap-and-stir line on top of the bass drum's "hurry up" thumps. The right hand was absolutely steady, as though the snare were a pot in which it stirred an endlessly simmering stew. The sense one got was one of endlessly abiding patience and nonchalance. The left, slapping hand was more eruptive, more erratic in its turning over, a quality which lent itself to the bass drum's likewise eruptive thumps. This made it sound every now and then as though the beat were backing up, gave it a sense of suppositious retreat. It was the most insinuative and subtle brushwork I've ever heard.

It was during one such instance that I made the mistake of closing my eyes. The conflicted sense of being upheld, on the one hand, by longstanding simmer while taken out by suppositious retreat, on the other, quickly began to take its toll. The latter's theme of "lost ground" was a suppositious brush which made as if to sweep the earth out from under our feet.

I closed my eyes in hopes of steadying myself, but doing so, it turned out, only made matters worse. I could hear the brew of bass drum and brushes continue on, the acoustic equivalent of the shadowy glimpse I now got of what appeared to be a dancing broom. The broom was about five feet six and danced an ever so elegant, ever so exacting softshoe. Several notions arose as to what to call it, but all but one of these was at once whisked away by the one which in the end won out, Broom Ex Machina. Backed up by the supportive/suppositious mix the bass drum and brushes continued to serve up, Broom Ex Machina danced but appeared to barely touch the ground—an elegant but ominous witch's ride and sorcerer's apprentice's axe rolled into one.

Broom Ex Machina stirred up dust although it appeared to barely touch the ground. It was a heady, seductive dust which made me want to join Broom Ex Machina's dance, to take the broom into my arms or, failing that, fall down at its feet even at the risk of being swept away.

I was just beginning to move to do so when I heard Lambert say with alarm, "Let's get out of here." I opened my eyes and immediately noticed—as Aunt Nancy, Penguin and Djamilaa were also now noticing—what it was he was looking at, a handful of seeds scattered in the dust around our feet. The exquisite brushwork and bass drum thumps continued on and it was difficult to tear ourselves away but we did. We walked as fast as we could back to the car and got in.

Lambert clicked on the radio as we began to pull away. What came on was Dollar Brand and Gato Barbieri, the soothing, benedictory "Hamba Khale." Lambert let out the breath he'd been holding and said, "Dollar and Gato are with us. All's well."

We all breathed easier now but our relief would prove to be short-lived. Our close brush with Broom Ex Machina wasn't about to be that easily shaken off. It's done nothing, to put it mildly, to ease the anxiety we've been bothered by.

As ever,

N.

29.X.81

Dear Angel of Dust,

If I could answer your questions I would. How we got out of the park without whoever was drumming following us I don't know. Who or what Broom Ex Machina was I can't say. Whether it was visible to anyone but me I can't say either, as none of the others made the apparently prerequisite move of closing their eyes. Yes, the sesame seeds, as you say, may simply have been the remnants of a picnic, though Lambert later explained that what made him react as he did was his having read of them having some role in African smallpox cults. Exactly what role he couldn't say (though obviously, judging from his reaction, it would seem to be a sinister one) and exactly where he'd read this he couldn't recall. He's going thru his books trying to find the one he read this in, hoping it'll throw some light on what went on in the park.

But other than on that score things, I'm glad to report, have lightened up. The tightness we've been bothered by has eased up and we're again playing with our customary poise. How this came about bears going into in some detail and I should begin, I suppose, by saying right off that we owe it all to Penguin. That may sound odd in light of his behavior in the park but in fact it was exactly his desire to make up for how he'd acted which led to what appears to have been the turning point. Two days after the incident in the park he phoned each of us during the early afternoon and said he was feeling bad about the way he'd gone off and that he wanted to make it up to us by having us over for dinner that night. "I'll make the fish curry everyone likes so much," he promised. None of us had to be asked a second time.

I was the last to arrive at Penguin's that night and by the time I did the beginnings of a party could be felt. Everyone was in the kitchen, talking, sipping wine, Penguin mixing spices for the curry. Coming out of the stereo in the living room was music I'd never heard before, which by itself would've made the evening worthy of note. I could write a letter on that alone. The music, it turned out, was new to Djamilaa, Aunt Nancy and Lambert as well—new to us all, as Penguin had suspected it would be. "Peace offering number one," he announced with a grin when I asked about it, going on to say it was a band from Senegal, Etoile de Dakar, led by a singer named Youssou N'Dour. "I heard a cut by them on the radio a year or two ago and it stayed with me. I finally found two of their albums," he explained, "and I thought I'd lay them on you tonight."

I can do neither the music nor its impact on me justice. What immediately got to me were the voices, the lead singer N'Dour's in particular—a strained, exhortative quality which, the farther it reached, appeared to ricochet within itself, to partly abort while partly harvesting an abject emotional hemorrhage held in reserve. N'Dour's singing was at all points inflected by qualms as by a core of complaint, but what spoke to me most was the staggered equation it exacted, the gruff, laminated grain aligning plea with polish or, put more precisely, calibrating seepages of latent polish with patent plea. The insinuative tension whereby sheen broke free of its otherwise exoteric shell confronted one with an implicative timbral husk the likes of which one had to confess never having heard before. An image of direness infiltrated by the threat of traumatic digestion, that implicative timbral husk (mitigating shade, mitigating shimmer) found itself coaxed as well as commented on by the disconsolate horn section's deadpan promptings. These together came into flirtatious, interrogative play with the dundun drums whose uppity strut had a way of stalking rather than stating the beat. Intimacy mingled with awe, both of them threaded throughout the rich polypercussive carpet into which collapse and eleventh-hour rescue were woven, stubbornly rolled into one.

I could write a letter, as I've already said, on the music alone, though, as I've also said already, I can do neither it nor its impact on me justice. It had a hand, I'm sure, in what took place, the shamanic seizure which overtook Penguin. This took a while to come about but it did so while we were still in the kitchen talking and sipping wine, Penguin getting the curry ingredients together. We noticed he hadn't said anything for some time but was instead unusually intent on dicing onions. He took his time, totally absorbed in the task, an absorption so singleminded as to make it seem the fate of the world was at stake. At first we thought he was kidding around, having fun (possibly, it occurred to me, at my expense, as his exaggeratedly deliberate, ritualistic movements were somewhat robotic, an implied but pointedly namesake dance—"Knife Ex Machina"). We went on talking and sipping wine, certain he'd soon, seeing we were paying him little mind, let go of the gag.

It turned out, however, to be no gag. Penguin went on dicing onions, no less deliberate, no less intent. The rest of us went on talking and sipping wine but after a while it became clear something was amiss. Penguin had not only diced four onions—twice the number needed—but was now getting started on the fifth. It was Lambert who finally said something to him. "Say, man, what's up?"

Penguin paid him no mind. He went on with his task, persisting with the ritualistic weight he brought to bear on it, the quasi-robotic solemnity which made him Knife Ex Machina's "horse." Lambert's words, however, did appear to have made a small impact, to have put a small dent in Penguin's ritual aplomb. One saw now that Penguin's eyes had somehow managed not to water as he diced the onions, for after Lambert spoke they began to do so, as though Lambert's words had broken the grip of the immunity they'd been granted. Their quasi-robotic exemption having now expired, his eyes watered and his manner seemed a bit less ritualistic, somewhat more moody, somewhat more reflective. Aunt Nancy echoed Lambert, "Yeah, what's up?"

Penguin said nothing, by now deep into dicing the fifth onion. The reflective strain which had entered his mood seemed to gradually make the tears flowing from his eyes accelerate. His eyes watered more and more with each ever so deliberate stroke of the knife. It was a lot like two days before in the park. Whether the tears were more than onion tears one had reason to wonder. One also couldn't help noticing the way the sound of Etoile de Dakar coming from the living room seemed to endorse and underscore their flow, even urge and encourage it. There was something baptismal about the staggered blend the chorus's voices brought off as they backed and embroidered N'Dour's lead—a dragged-out, drowning quality which lent Penguin's tears a certain air of duress.

Aunt Nancy, Lambert, Djamilaa and I looked at one another, none of us knowing what move to make next. The idea of grabbing him by the wrist and taking the knife away occurred to me but, given how the knife seemed to be in control, on second thought that seemed precipitous, a bit too risky a thing to do. Just about that time, however, as luck would have it, Penguin broke his silence. Having finished off the fifth onion, he took a moment while reaching for the sixth, raised his head to look at the four of us, wiped the tears from his eyes and announced, "About as flimsy as onionskin." Having done that, he began dicing the sixth onion, as ritualistically, as quasi-robotically as before.

The rest of us looked at one another again, right after which Aunt Nancy asked the question one of us others would have asked had she not beaten us to it. "What," she began, taking a few steps toward Penguin, lowering her head and putting her face within inches of his, "does that mean?"

Penguin raised his head, pulling his face up and away from hers and straightening his back (ritual rectitude, quasi-robotic stiffness). Aunt Nancy stepped back but went on looking him in the eye, the air between them thick with ritual tension, ritual portent. Penguin stared back, refusing to blink or flinch but letting his back relax a bit as he answered, "Our chances of finding the furtive beat she embodies are about as flimsy as onionskin." He then went back to dicing the sixth onion, a bit less ritualistically, a bit less quasi-robotically, by now more noticeably governed by a reflective mood and muse rolled into one, the anonymous "her" he went on to evoke in a barely audible, all but under-his-breath discourse intended less for us than for himself it seemed. "Who'd be foolish enough to think we could ever capture that walk of hers," he asked rhetorically, "the subtle, suggestive sway of her hips, a certain pelvic savvy? The pelvic perfume, the erotic musk it seems to toss into the air, is accessible, everyone knows, if it can be said to be so at all, only to thought." He paused, wiped his eyes and went on. "But there's a play, a very profound and very pregnant play between flagrant and fragrant rotundities, between tossed, exoteric hips on the one hand and esoteric, not so obvious pulse on the other, obvious, overt rotundity on the one hand, fleet, furtive curvature on the other."

As Penguin spoke the punchy, projective sound of the dunduns coming from the living room peppered, punctuated and seemed to prompt his muttered meditation. The four of us hung on his every word, though the deeper he went the more oblivious of us he became. "Furtive curvature, furtive beat," he reflected out loud, initiating a long phonological run in which declarative statement gave way to repetitions and permutations of certain syllables, words and phrases and which had a Tranelike, sheets-of-sound aspect or impact to it. "Furtive heat, fevered hit. Fervid curvature. Flaunted rotundity. Flaunted curve, overt curve, ovarian cave, curvaceous ferment . . ." He spoke at a now hurried, now halting, staccato pace, attacking the onion with irregular, choppy strokes of the knife as though it (the onion) were a rope, the phonological rope he was tied up in, a Gordian rope he was trying to cut his way thru, an umbilical rope. ". . . Fervent fertility, pubic fur. Fragrant pelt. Flared nostril. Flaunted crotch, flagrant pelt, pungent crux . . ."

"Djeannine's got him," Lambert said in a whisper as though Penguin were a sleepwalker he was afraid of waking up.

Penguin's long phonological run, for all its alliterative, assonantal, associative thrust, conveyed a sense of being stuck, as though run, as well as rope, were rut (iterative rut he would never get out of, iterative rope he was hung up on). For all its phonemic pliability and play, Penguin's run served a sense of stutter, stammer, "stuckness," the staccato irregularity and the occasional hesitancy he spoke with emphasizing that quality all the more. An aspect of ritual thereby made its return (ritual insistence, ritual iterativity). ". . . Fur. Her. Furred. Her. Hair. Her. Furry. Her. Fury. Her. Flaunted. Her. Fondle. Her. Funk. Her. . . ."

Tears continued flowing from Penguin's eyes as he finished the sixth onion and immediately started in on another. There continued to be a certain disembodied aspect to his manner, though his voice and his movements had grown more heartfelt and haggard, his long phonological run by now as grimly elegiac as it was erotic. In this sense there was no longer much doubt as to whether the tears were real. "Poor Penguin," I thought, but at once corrected myself, "Poor us." N'Dour's now guttural, now high-pitched excursions found a cushion against which to play and a carpet upon which to ride in the chorus's and the horns' fraught, baptismal inflections. They allied themselves with Penguin's erotic-elegiac run in such uncanny fashion as to make it seem that we all, even those of us who stood silent, shared a common tongue and a collective throat. N'Dour's distraught laryngitic accent appeared to find its voice in Penguin's long phonological rope, as much a hanged as a drowning man's lament which qualified our silence as a swallowed cry, so common a cry it all but went without voice.

I now saw Penguin in a new eponymic light, a new namesake light. He was indeed, it now struck me as never before, a flightless bird, a grounded bird whose truncated wings had forfeited heights to negotiate depths, the stunted growth of his ostensible wings instead making for fins with which he "flew" underwater. Grounded bird was equally fish run aground, fish out of water, as Penguin needed, it seemed, to return to the salty realms he knew so well, to in so returning take the rest of us with him. The watery chorus, the baptismal choir we'd been drafted into, silence notwithstanding, preserved a memory of traumatic survival by serving a sense of laryngitic extremity, what there was to preserve suggesting our voices might be stored in salt. Thus it was that we were all, whether we liked it or not, drowning in Penguin's tears. Our conscripted silence appeared at points to be a rope on which we'd strangle, an extension of Penguin's drowning-man's rope which tapered off into a thin laryngitic thread.

The Etoile continued coming on strong, ever so ritual-insistent, ever so ritual-iterative, ever so erotic-elegiac in its own right. The guitar had now taken up a tried-and-true chicken-scratch riff which appeared to mix incense with intimate sweat, so pointedly rhythmic one could literally smell it. One's nose twitched as Penguin's prolix phonological run showed no sign of letting up. ". . . Flaunted rump. Rhythmic swish. Wafted, rounded. Fecund walk. Rusted kiss. . . ."

It did appear that Djeannine had gotten hold of him again. His erotic-elegiac run, one understood, dredged up wings which had devolved into paddles, blunt stubs, would-be wings which his and Jeannie's rusted kiss had prematurely clipped. He spoke (if what this was could be called speaking) out of a deep-seated sexual rift, deep trouble. Only out of such depth, such troubled water, he seemed to insist, could our search for a drummer be legitimately launched. One needed, he insinuated, to woo despair, to come as close as one could to disaster, dispossession. One needed (rump and rotundity punned or implied) to touch bottom. It was an odd concept and conceit but he conveyed it with such insistence as to make it clear that rhythm was nothing if not a way of bouncing back. Rhythm thus understood was where surprise infiltrated support. Unpredictable support had a way of taking one under, he obliquely insisted, the fact that Djeannine did indeed have hold of him all the more evident with each repeat of "Rusted kiss." These were the words he now came back to again and again. ". . . Rich crevice. Rusted kiss. Fevered catch. Rusted kiss. . . ." His prolix phonological run eventually came to where these were the only words he uttered. ". . . Rusted kiss. Rusted kiss. Rusted kiss." This was the note on which his run came to an end, the last few articulations of "Rusted kiss" more widely spaced, each followed by a pause and not much louder than a whisper.

Penguin stood silent once his run came to an end. He lay the knife beside the pile of diced onions and let his arms hang, his shoulders a bit slumped, his look one of exhaustion. Tears continued flowing from his eyes. Coming from the living room N'Dour could be heard entreating some impertinent spirit to leave him alone, to let bad enough be (or so it seemed).

Lambert, Aunt Nancy, Djamilaa and I couldn't stop staring at Penguin, his arms hanging limp at his sides, the ultimate grounded bird.

He more than any of us had kept loss alive. He deeper than any of us had felt our failure to find the drummer we were after (though, admittedly, on his own idiosyncratic terms). It was he who had taken on the burden about which the four of us had become blasé. It was in this sense that I'd corrected myself earlier, "Poor us."

Penguin's disarray indicted an imagino-emotional deficit on our parts, though by now the pile of diced onions had caused our eyes to fill with tears as well. We had failed, he implicitly insisted, to go deep enough into the erotic-elegiac malaise out of which a capacity for rhythmic displacement arises or might arise. No such failure would be attributed to him he made sure, tenaciously clinging to the aborted promise of his and Jeannie's rust-obstructed kiss, equally intimate, outright obsessed, with both of its aspects. Aborted promise oddly accentuated promise outliving abortion. An echo of deferred fulfillment arose to haunt and inhabit time, kept as well as unkept, marked as well as implied. This was the gist of Penguin's oblique discourse on rhythm, its bottom line.

Still, deferred fulfillment notwithstanding, he stood depleted, even devastated, the quintessential fish out of water. One wasn't certain how to approach or comfort him, though one deeply felt a need to do so. His distress now cried out for consolation. The knife's edge which lay beside the diced onions mutely spoke of extremity and amputation, a phantom arm or a phantom wing or a phantom fin whose deep-seated insistence was upon the need for an imagino-emotional intervention—Onion Ex Machina, Drum Ex Machina, Djeannine Ex Machina, call it what you will. Indeed, on the edge, as it were, Call-It-What-You-Will came to promise an unexpected albeit sought-after arbitration for which names were numberless though not beside the point.

The effect of all of this on me, I found, was part cathartic, part paralytic. I stood immobile, bolted to the floor, though I also felt impelled to cross the kitchen to embrace Penguin, comfort and console him. Lambert, Aunt Nancy and Djamilaa felt the same. Aunt Nancy, overcoming paralysis, was the first to extend an unphantom arm, the first to offer Penguin a reassuring hug, whispering as she did so, "It'll be alright, it'll be alright."

Lambert stepped forward, extended his right arm and touched Penguin's left shoulder. "Yeah, man, don't take it so hard." Tears continued flowing from Penguin's eyes.

It was at this point that Call-It-What-You-Will came to the fore. Djamilaa stepped forward, took hold of Penguin's left hand with her right, looked into his eyes and said in a partly motherly, slightly coquettish, ever so soothing tone of voice, "Don't cry, Pen, don't cry. We'll find her." Penguin's face visibly registered surprise. He wasn't used to being addressed by this diminutive, nor had any of us, Djamilaa included, ever heard him called by it, let alone used it ourselves. What prompted her to do so one could only call Call-It-What-You-Will, though Penguin's look, surprise notwithstanding, was not unmixed with a barely detectable touch of pleasure, approval, delight. Lambert, Aunt Nancy and I were also surprised, though we too found it reassuring to hear Penguin so affectionately addressed—all the more so since this was done by Djamilaa, with whom he'd been so petulant in the park.

Why "Pen" as a pet name for Penguin had never occurred to me I don't know, but it took only a moment to realize how appropriate it was. It not only agreed with but assisted with a further performative accent the sense of namesake diminution (stunted feather, phantom nib, numb stub) I'd reflected on earlier. Penguin at that moment was indeed our pet, a shamanic mascot whose erotic-elegiac rope turned out to be a plumb line by way of which we sounded certain imagino-emotional depths. "Pen" spoke to the feeling from which we'd cut ourselves off. One could say that in fact it *was* that feeling, that it returned us to that feeling and vice versa, that now feeling could no longer be distinguished from an apprehension of having been cut off. "Pen" consoled while confirming such an amputation (numb feather, sensitive nub). It passed from Djamilaa's mouth like a mother's kiss to a child's cut.

To what extent though, I couldn't help wondering, did sensitive nub's embrace of numb feather arise from an aspect of mock sensitivity within her voice? To what extent, on the other hand, did numb feather fly from sensitive nub so as to rendezvous with Djeannine's repercussive curvature (numinous rump)? Sensitive nub, numb feather and numinous rump were all in this together, which accounted for the slightly coquettish tone in Djamilaa's voice.

That Djamilaa's affectionate address was not entirely ingenuous became clear with Call-It-What-You-Will's next move, a move which took "Pen" a step further. Penguin and Djamilaa stood face to face, his left hand still in her right, tears continuing to flow from his eyes. Lambert, Aunt Nancy and I looked on. The Etoile's low tolling of drums could be heard coming from the living room. Djamilaa gave Penguin's left hand a squeeze, raised her own left hand to caress his cheek and broke what had been a brief silence by saying, "It'll be okay. It'll be okay. Don't cry, Pen, don't cry." She then, looking into his eyes as intently as ever, added even more soothingly, "Don't cry, Penny, don't cry."

You can imagine Penguin's, Lambert's, Aunt Nancy's and my surprise. Surprise, though, wasn't all of it, for it couldn't help but be noticed by all of us that "Penny" was nothing if not the next diminutive step along the path "Pen" had opened up. All the more endearing, all the more affectionate, it was the pet name par excellence. It was also a stroke of mediating genius on Djamilaa's part. "Penny," that is, allowed her to console and get close to Penguin while pushing her side of the Penny/Djeannine spat which had divided them two days before. It was the subtlest push one would ever witness, but a push nonetheless, a diplomatic coup. There were other aspects to, it of course. For one, Djamilaa seemed also to be suggesting that the "her" (Jeannie, Djeannine, Penny, call "her" what you will) whose loss or unlikely discovery Penguin lamented was in fact an aspect of himself. She seemed to imply that he, like the rest of us, had been cut off or had cut himself off and that "she" (Jeannie, Djeannine, Penny, call "her" what you will) was indeed the amputated part of himself, the feeling which had been cut off as well as the feeling of having been cut off.

Penguin didn't appear to be bothered by Djamilaa's coup. In fact, his surprise at being addressed as Penny, as with Pen, was visibly mixed with a trace of pleasure, approval, delight. His amenability to Call-It-What-You-Will's new diminutive step, moreover, acquired an after-the-fact air of complicity and command. So strong was this retroactive air that it induced an after-the-fact premonitory vision or vignette in which Penguin appeared to have prompted Djamilaa, appeared to have encouraged her addressing him as Penny. What one saw took one back a moment in time. Djamilaa had just said, "It'll be okay. It'll be okay. Don't cry, Pen, don't cry." Tears continued flowing from Penguin's eyes as he reached into his right pants pocket for his handkerchief and, pulling out the handkerchief, caused a penny to fall from his pocket to the floor. It was then that Djamilaa added, "Don't cry, Penny, don't cry."

The curious thing is that Lambert, Aunt Nancy and I all saw it that way, though we'd all seen it the first way as well (no hand in the pocket, no handkerchief, no penny). Time, it seemed, had fallen behind by trying to get ahead of itself and now sought to correct or catch up with itself by including what in its haste it'd left out before. Perhaps the sense of suppositious retreat we'd gotten from the drums in the park two days before had infiltrated and so radically altered our experience of time that a palimpsestic repeat now opened up a crack in what before we'd have taken to be solid, sealed, absolute. Time, we now knew, was double-jointed. Perhaps the Etoile's low tolling of drums with its echoing of self-inflicted fracture against other-exacted splint also had a hand in this, though I can't with any certainty say. And to what extent what we saw was the work of Penguin's sleight-of-hand or sleight-of-hanky (a recuperative ruse whereby he deflated Djamilaa's coup, made it appear that he'd been in control all along, that "Penny" was what he was ultimately after) I equally can't with any certainty say.

The fact is that after we saw what we saw, the premonitory vision or vignette, Penguin did indeed reach into his right pants pocket, take out a handkerchief and wipe his eyes. No penny fell out however, though Djamilaa did again say, "Don't cry, Penny, don't cry."

Penguin finished wiping his eyes and Djamilaa let go of his left hand. Lambert, Aunt Nancy and I were still taken aback by the after-the-fact premonitory glimpse we'd gotten. Lambert asked outright, "Did you see what I saw?" Aunt Nancy and I knew immediately what he was talking about. We both answered that, yes, we had. Penguin and Djamilaa at first assumed that the simple fact of their reconciliation was what we were talking about, but at the mention of the penny falling from Penguin's pants pocket a puzzled look came over both their faces. Neither of them, they both insisted, had seen any such prompting penny, though I saw (or thought I saw) the slightest trace of a grin on Penguin's lips as he disavowed our premonitory vision or vignette. By this time the first side of the record had ended and Penguin now went into the living room to turn it over.

The four of us left in the kitchen each grabbed a paper towel and wiped our eyes. Aunt Nancy opened a window to let some air in, looked at us and shrugged her shoulders. The second side of the record was more upbeat and tended somewhat toward boogie, though the sense of strain, the sense of collision between tread and trepidation one had heard on side one could be heard on it as well. Penguin returned from the living room and acted as though nothing had happened. The excess onion he sealed in a plastic bag and put inside the refrigerator. He nonchalantly went back to preparing the meal. The rest of us took his cue and let the matter rest.

The curry turned out as delicious as ever, wine flowed freely and the rest I've already told you. Since then we've been nothing but relaxed—no tightness, no nervous flutter, no spasticity.

New York had better watch out.

Yours,
N.

4.XI.81

Dear Angel of Dust,

Wouldn't you know it. Now that things are back to normal an unbearable calm threatens the gains we've made. Since the dinner at Penguin's things have gone smoothly, very smoothly. In fact, they've begun to go too smoothly. We're playing with an effortless facility and fluency which is outright scary at times. It's as though we'd made a pact with the devil without being privy to doing so. Our newly renewed eloquence appears coincident with a certain loss of soul, a certain loss of self, though I rush to qualify that by saying that what I mean is that the ghost of a technical chance we seem to've been given makes us ghosts of our former selves. This, Aunt Nancy says, must be what Malachi Favors is getting at by calling himself Maghostus.

I've used the expression "technical-ecstatic" many times, but not until recently, it seems, did I know how apt and applicable it could be. Yes, "ecstatic" in the root sense of standing outside oneself, an exacting leverage applied and approached via "technical" means—means fed by exactly such standing. Which comes first is a pointless question, to which the devil is a likewise pointless though tempting answer. What gets me is the sense of quintessential repose out of which this issues, a paradisiacal aplomb which borders on boredom. The rub is that the self which might have enjoyed it isn't there, which can be said to be where hell comes in. Cold hell.

The other night we played at Onaje's and things went so well we decided to wrap the evening up with "Altered Cross," the piece that was giving us trouble a couple of weeks back. It'd come together well in rehearsals of late but we hadn't played it in public yet. We felt we had it down but this would be the test. Let me let it go at saying we passed with flying colors. Not only were we on it, we outdid ourselves—so much so that when Penguin finished his solo I couldn't help asking him, "Penguin, is that you?" He laughed, but when Lambert, whose solo followed his, was finished he asked him the same question, "Lambert, is that you?" It was a good question—increasingly so as each solo egged the next one on.

In what way is this a threat, you ask. You've probably seen the cartoons in which someone runs off a cliff and keeps running—runs, that is, on air. All goes well until he or she looks down, which, inevitably, he or she does. That's what I'm afraid of. "Where there's a wheel there's a turn." I can't help remembering that. I can't help but see the underside coming around.

The bordering on boredom I think I could live with, but is there a calm one doesn't come to question? Maybe suspect equanimity secretly thrives on apprehension, but to question seems to be to have lost or begun to lose it.

Maybe I'm wrong. Maybe it's all in my mind. Writing this letter would seem to bode ill, but maybe you'll tell me it isn't so.

All's well with you I hope.

Yours,

N.

9.XI.81

Dear Angel of Dust,

Many, many thanks for writing back so quickly. Your letter caught me just in time, buoyed me up as I was beginning to sink. The threat of giddy slippage remains, I imagine, but it's a measure of your letter's salutary effect that I'm staving off exhaustion from lack of sleep to write back at once to agree with you and to say thanks. Yes, my worries do smack of presumption and, yes, suspect equanimity notwithstanding, things are much more indomitably off as well as ordered than to obey the banal hydraulics of any such wheel. Thank you for reminding me.

The reason I'm lacking sleep somewhat relates to this. I was awakened at around two this morning by a phone call. It was Djamilaa, who, it turned out, had walked in her sleep and locked herself out of her apartment. She'd made it all the way to the outskirts of Elysian Park before waking up. You can imagine how upset she was. It got even worse when she got back to her apartment to find that the door had locked behind her as she left. Frustrated, a bit frightened, she was calling from a phone booth and asked if I'd come get her and bring her to stay here until morning when she could call a locksmith. This, of course, I did.

When I got there she was still in the phone booth like she had said she'd be. In the car on the way back here she spoke with an edgy bemusement, wondering out loud what had made her sleepwalk again after years of not doing so. She hadn't walked in her sleep since she was a girl, she said. She spoke with after-the-fact fear of what might have happened to her, the danger she'd been in walking the streets in the middle of the night with nothing but a nightgown on. It was a wonder she wasn't raped, she said, but the strange thing now was that it was all a blank, that what she had been dreaming, where she had felt she was and so forth, she couldn't begin to say.

When we got here Djamilaa said she was too wound up to sleep and that she'd like it if I'd stay up with her and talk. That was fine with me, I said, even though I'd have been asleep before my head hit the pillow had we gone to bed. I got out some brandy and two glasses and poured us each a bit and we sat at the kitchen table talking. Djamilaa now went into more detail regarding how she'd felt and what she'd done when she awoke to find herself on the outskirts of Elysian Park, how she'd gone into an all-night corner market and borrowed a dime for the phone and so forth. It still bothered her that she couldn't recall what it was she'd been dreaming as she walked in her sleep and it soon became clear to me that we wouldn't get any sleep until she did. I asked her questions I thought might trigger the recollection but none of them worked and we went on talking and sipping brandy, our talk becoming more and more tangential to the question of what she had dreamt.

We were talking about Monk's reportedly worsening illness when suddenly a light seemed to click on in Djamilaa's head. "Piazzolla," she said, her lit-up look lending a certain lilt to the way she said it. "Astor Piazzolla," she added, going on to say that she could now recall having heard something like his music as she slept, that it was that which had gotten her up, had gotten her walking. (Piazzolla, I should maybe tell you, is the foremost exponent of what's known as New Tango in Argentina. He plays an accordion-like instrument called the bandoneon. Djamilaa's been listening to his music for a while now and even bought a bandoneon a few weeks back and began learning how to play it.)

"Yes, it's coming back to me now," Djamilaa said. "I heard music, indescribably moving music, a beckoning mix in which a violin and a bandoneon each embroidered the line the other laid down." She stopped, took a sip of brandy, then continued. "It's hard to be exact about it now, but I recall it having the pull of a siren's cry, that its beckoning mix was part appeal, part summons. That I arose to seek out the source of this music makes perfect sense, for whoever or whatever played the bandoneon played it as though it were not so much an instrument as a bodily organ. I may be going too far to say so, but it was the heart itself the bandoneon-player played." Here she stopped again and I shook my head and said no to her suggestion that she'd gone too far. I encouraged her to continue, which, after another sip of brandy, she did. "It seemed that all that romantic stuff about the heart being in someone's hands had come home to roost," she elaborated. "Yes, the heart was subject to the most exhaustive, extrapolative stretch and this affirmation got repeatedly juxtaposed against the bandoneon-player's recourse to the most exacting, infinitesimal squeeze. The poignancy of that play between ecstatic stretch and exquisite squeeze, the extenuating play between stretch and compression, has to have been what got me up and drew me on. In walking, I now know (or at least it now seems), I sought a place of primary instruction."

Djamilaa stopped again and gazed over my shoulder into a distance to which no eyes but hers, it appeared, could ever be privy. I found I could easily relate to what she had said and after a moment or so I spoke to that effect. "Yes, I've always thought of the accordion as an extension, an exteriorization of the chest, which would appear to apply to the bandoneon as well." I paused, a bit put off by how that had sounded, but immediately added that the sense of fingering a vital organ, one's own as well as the listener's, is exactly what gives music its poignancy, its power. "And that word you hit on, 'squeeze,' given all the senses it can have, says it all," I remarked. I then talked about the accordion choir I heard in my sleep years ago on a train one night in southern Spain.

Djamilaa's eyes were by now no longer absorbed in the distance beyond my shoulder. They met mine as she remarked, barely above a whisper, "Yes, landscape and longing. In the dream, I remember now, I was walking on the pampas. It seemed I'd never get to where I was going, that longing had to do with length. I was, I can see now, doubly out of touch. The ground I was actually on as I walked toward Elysian

Park is anything but flat. Besides that, the tango comes out of Buenos Aires, not the pampas, though it's not impossible that it was the city I was trying to reach. In any event, I seem to have associated stretch with topographic extension."

Djamilaa went on to say that the music was so entrancing she began to sing. The surprising thing was that when she opened her mouth to sing a line of string was hanging from it, a line of string which had unrolled from a ball of string inside her chest—unrolled, run up her throat and out of her mouth. "Something told me that if I pulled it I'd go faster," she said, "fast enough to get to where the source of the music was. I did, but instead of going faster found myself slowed down by the fact that it took both hands to keep unrolling the string. The line of string fell to the ground between my feet and trailed behind me as I walked."

Djamilaa noted that the bandoneon's dialectical volleys between extenuating stretch and exquisite squeeze appeared to be in touch and to sympathetically vibrate in agreement with her singing's juxtaposition between line of string and ball of string. "I was its catch. It was reeling me in," she explained. "There was a definite play on pull going on. The music was pulling me along even as it insisted I take part in the pulling. I felt I was pulling, among other things, on my own voice. The weird thing, though, was that instead of getting smaller the ball of string got bigger, the squeeze, the pressure in my chest more intense."

She broke off again, a wisp of an ironic smile barely visible on her lips. I poured her a bit more brandy. "And then what?" I asked.

"Well, this went on for some time—me walking, singing as I walked, the line of string trailing behind me getting longer, the ball of string inside my chest expanding. Whoever or whatever was playing the bandoneon would answer a touching, schmaltzy violin passage with a run whose muscular fury was frightening. Whoever or whatever it was was a demon. He, she or it literally ransacked the instrument for sound, pulling screeches and screams from it I'd have never thought it could make. I can't tell you how badly I wanted to get to where the music was coming from."

Djamilaa looked at me, smiled—a wistful, not an ironic smile—and said that the dream gave itself away when the line of string turned into spaghetti. "Even in the dream I could see that this related to tango's Italian roots," she said drily, inwardly, it seemed, throwing her hands up in the air. "It was too much. I felt I was being mocked. I stopped singing, bit the spaghetti and let the part that had hung from my mouth fall to the ground, swallowing what was left in my mouth. The pressure in my chest went away. That's when I woke up to find myself heading toward Elysian Park."

Djamilaa seemed greatly relieved to have recalled and related her dream. I found her sleepwalk immensely intriguing. Its possible relevance to my reflections on suspect equanimity wasn't lost on me, but, as I've said, I was in need of sleep and thus didn't pose or pursue certain questions it had given rise to. By then dawn wasn't far off, so I suggested we get what little sleep we could before calling a locksmith.

It's late morning now and everything turned out routinely. The locksmith got Djamilaa's door open and she's back at her apartment. I left there about an hour ago and got back here to find your letter waiting. As I've already said, what you had to say was so right on I couldn't wait to write back. I'll break off now to get some of the sleep I missed last night, though a number of questions persist.

Is somnambulism a loss of self or an extension of self? Does such a question really have any meaning if one can be mocked by a demon of self-possession? Could ecstatic stretch and exquisite squeeze be six of one and a half-dozen of the other?

Please let me know what you think.

As ever,

N.

PS: One thing I think is this: That to say "dialectical" is to speak a hopeful shorthand for a process or a providentiality whose particulars one can't be privy to but which, even so, one assumes to be there. This occurred to me as Djamilaa spoke of the bandoneon's dialectical volleys between extenuating stretch and exquisite squeeze. I glimpsed an ever so subtle twitch on the right side of her upper lip, a subtle disclaimer whose mute recoil called into question the consoling dialecticality of what, shepherded though one assumed it to be, was a sleepwalk nonetheless.

15.XI.81

Dear Angel of Dust,

Just a note to say that we leave for New York in a couple of days and that we're all very much relieved now that the gig is finally close at hand. There's no getting around the fact that to make a mark in this music you have to go to New York and that this is our biggest gig yet. Small wonder we've been on such a rollercoaster ride of elation and apprehension these past weeks. I can't claim that we're not still very nervous but it does appear that the worst is over, that the long wait, the weeks of looking ahead and worrying, may have been the toughest part, the testing time.

I'm also writing to say that I've given a bit more thought to Djamilaa's sleepwalk. It occurred to me that that play between stretch and compression by which it seemed to be motored might be related to that between mobility and rootedness found in a number of Native American contexts. I'm thinking, for example, of the Navajo Night Way in which a phrase of blessing puns on *saa nagai* ("walking far") and *sa'aa nagai* ("thriving as a plant"). The point of poetry and song would seem to be to reconcile the two, as among the Toltecs, where the poet-singer is defined as a traveler who becomes a plant, or among the Chimu, where depictions of a beanseed sprouting legs to become a messenger abound. In the case of Djamilaa's sleepwalk I take sleep to be that seed, its legs the parallactic displacement between dreamt ground and circumstantial ground, the compressed-expansive play between misconceived root and realistic source and so on. It "walks," that is, by way of a number of suspect symmetries, a number of bipolar arrangements in which its various "feet" can be aligned with one another. The danger, the thing one suspects, is that these arrangements might be messenger and message both (just as for the Chimu the beanseed not only becomes the messenger but is also carried in the messenger's pouch). What one fears and suspects is that, catalytic and combustible though they may be, their thrust is endlessly internal, that outside themselves they have nothing to say. Thus it is that a parodic hinge intervenes to open things up. Ludicrous root, ludicrous-albeit-based-on-reality root, i.e., spaghetti, ventilates the stalemate of misconceived root and realistic source. Any arrangement can be said to carry the seed of its arraignment. Thus it is that it lets off steam and blows the whistle on itself. The end of Djamilaa's dream shows us that.

This gets me to the diagram I've enclosed, "Suspect-Symmetrical Structure of Misconceptual Seed's Parallactic Dispatch." I won't try to explain what the diagram, if it's at all successful, should be able to get across on its own. I will, however, observe that one thing it shows is that structure comes as no surprise, that it's exactly this that the oneiric roughnesses of Djamilaa's walk parallactically displaces. As I've asked before, is there a calm one doesn't come to question? Is there, that is, a structure that's anything but an after-the-fact heuristic seed, a misleading, misconceptual sleep inside which to walk is to begin to wake up? Like it or not, we're marked by whatever window we look thru. The stigmata, luckily, turn out not to be static.

I'll write you from New York if time permits. In any case, wish us luck.

As ever,
N.

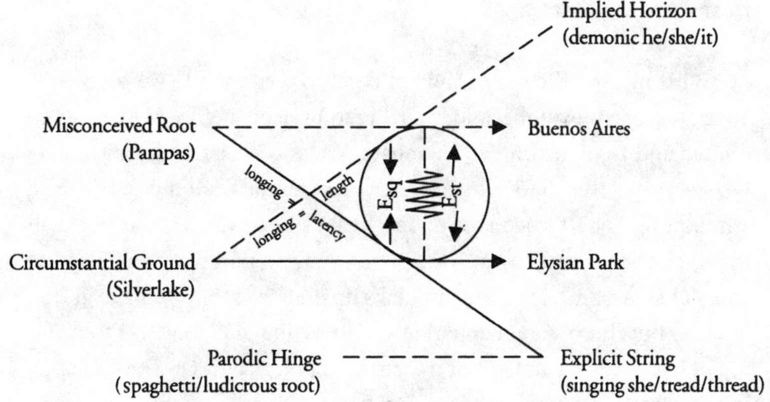

Suspect-Symmetrical Structure of
Misconceptual Seed's Parallactic Dispatch

18.XI.81

Dear Angel of Dust,

This may be the only chance I'll get to write while we're in New York. It's early evening and we're resting a bit before going out to dinner and to check out some music. We got in last night and today we spent mostly wandering around. I can already tell our stay'll be a stimulating one. It's been only a few years since I was last here and all the clichés continue to apply but I can sense a number of changes as well. The harshness one always picks up on here seems to have gotten harsher but there's an insinuative self-knowing wink one has the feeling of having glimpsed out of the corner of one's eye. One has to catch it unawares—one catches oneself unawares as well it seems—but every now and then the city bats an eye (part flinch, part coquettish flutter), every so often lets one in on its joke. How much of it's me I can't say, but that wink, that unexpected wash, waters grime's nearness to glitter, a discrepant "slip" which is only an eye-shift away.

One of the things we saw this afternoon is worth mentioning. Outside Penn Station we saw a group of break-dancers. There were six of them, all in their early teens. A crowd had gathered, making a circle around the area in which they danced, at opposite ends of which area sat cigar boxes for money to be dropped into. I'd heard of break dancing, which along with subway art and rap music is beginning to get a lot of attention, and had seen a bit of it on TV and around the neighborhood back in L.A. But you really have to see it here to comprehend it. Aunt Nancy, as we watched the dancers go thru their routine, whispered into my ear that she was struck by the interplay and the counterpoint between the upward thrust of the surrounding buildings and the dancers' answering exploration of horizontality, their insistence, variegated as it was, on "getting down." I in fact had been similarly struck, had taken note of the same thing.

I've given it more thought since then and have come to see that the verticality/horizontality counterpoint or play opens onto a larger field of implication. One sees, for example, that "break" serves notice on as it diverges from the city's valorization of hardness, unyieldingness, rigidity, the upward investment in steel and stone. That it does this while working variations on the very condition it implicitly critiques is something one might easily miss. The breakers' recourse to choreographed rigidities and robotisms arises as a caveat in the face of exactly the threat it wants to fend off, an inoculation or an aestheticization, at least, of the fate to which it would seem to have acceded. Easier, perhaps, to see is the fact that the splits, the spins, the strenuous bendings and the acrobatic twistings constitute a reminder—a therapeutic reminder—of the malleability and thus the vulnerability of human flesh. Such athletic writhings are anything but a naively triumphal homage to resilience. The cigar boxes make that all the more clear. Breaking accents the body under siege—one notes, among other things, that the electronic drums recall machine gun fire—but also, more trenchantly yet, the susceptibility of states of siege to commoditization.

There's a lot more to it, of course. Coming from L.A., I couldn't help noting that the dancers' pursuit of exponential horizontality had a way of letting sprawl, so to speak, in thru the backdoor. That the body turns out to be that door makes a certain sense. More importantly, this relates break dancing to, among other things, Caribbean limbo, said by tradition to have been born in the cramped holds of the slave ships. Like any other such black negotiation of shrunken space (think of Henry "Box" Brown, Harriet Jacobs's garret and so forth), break dancing understands cramp as embryonic sprawl, embryonic spring.

There're some other aspects of this I wish I could go into, but, as I've said already, we're going out again soon. Perhaps I'll take it up again in another letter, perhaps even work these matters into a new composition. In any case, it's best I relax a bit before we head out. There's a lot of music in town—Max Roach at Seventh Avenue South, Ted Curson at Sweet Basil, Joe Turner at Tramps, Hilton Ruiz at Soundscape, Charli Persip at Jazz Forum, just to name a few. We won't quit till we've heard as much as we can.

Later,
N.

20.XI.81

Dear Angel of Dust,

You won't believe it. We seem to've met the drummer we've been after. I can hardly believe it myself, so odd was the way it came about—outright uncanny in the wake of what I wrote in my last letter about "the body under siege." It in fact occurred later the same evening I wrote that letter. We'd just come out of the restaurant where we'd eaten dinner and were standing on Fifth Avenue waiting to cross. This was around 60th or 61st, I think. In any case, we were standing there waiting to cross when we noticed a fight had broken out at the other end of the block. A man in a trenchcoat had pushed another man against a building and they were punching on one another. There was a car stopped at the curb and almost as soon as we noticed what was going on two more men in trenchcoats jumped out of it and rushed toward the two men who were fighting. The first trenchcoated man, the one fighting with the untrenchcoated man, pulled away, giving the other two access to the latter. The two of them took their hands from their trenchcoat pockets. That's when we heard gunshots.

The instant the shooting started we all took off running. It was as if the shots had come from a starter's gun at a track meet. We ran down whatever the cross street was we were on, away from Fifth Avenue and the threat of stray bullets, our legs instinctively triggered by a seed of escape which, it seemed, had ages ago been planted, a seed out of which unfurled an embryonic spur, embryonic sprint. That seed, it seemed, had run forward to meet this moment, unbeknown to us. We were no more than its horses. We ran, that is, for all we were worth, more than we were worth, spurred by aboriginal reflex and fear, ran as if all hell had broken loose. It seemed, it's no exaggeration to say, that we'd been running without knowing it all along, even as we stood, running farther back than we could remember, so sovereign was the aboriginal spur we were prompted by, provident to the point of retroaction.

There were five shots fired, I think. It's hard to say since once we started running I could hear nothing but the sound of our feet hitting the sidewalk. Manhattan became suddenly silent except for the sound of our instinctual stampede. We ran as a pack, all of us running at the same speed, borne along as though by collective legs. Our aboriginal sprint came to an end about two-thirds of the way down the block and it wasn't till then that we noticed there were six of us rather than five. After we slowed to a stop and stood catching our breath—it seemed we had run much more than two-thirds of a block—we saw there was a woman among us (medium height, dread hair, wearing a coat which came down to her ankles) who'd also, we now recalled, been standing on Fifth Avenue waiting to cross. She too had been prodded by the instinctual spur which had impelled our sprint. She too had run, had been a part of our pack, had run with us.

By now the noise was back—the traffic, the horns and so forth. Things appeared to be back to normal. The shooting had stopped. What had happened had occurred so suddenly, so quickly, my heart went on racing even though my legs were now still. I'm sure this was also true of the others. A swift aboriginal heart raced in each of our chests as we stood there, none of us able to speak. It was Penguin who finally broke the silence, exhaling loudly and saying, "Whew! That was weird." The word "weird," of course, fit only loosely, a registration of dismay which was too all-purpose to be precise, but it did bring things back to normal. We now began to talk, the upshot of which was that we had occasion to introduce ourselves to the woman who had run with us and she to introduce herself to us. Her name is Drennette.

It was after telling her that we're a band that we learned she's a musician too. "What a coincidence. Funny," she said. "I'm a musician myself." Our ears perked up and we gave each other looks when she added, "A drummer, to be exact." We couldn't, of course, help wondering could she be the woman we'd been looking for. Off to so auspicious a start—she had, hadn't she, run with us—we had to make an effort not to jump to that conclusion. Still, that it occurred to each of us right away there can be no doubt. The looks we gave one another made that clear.

On the one hand it was hard not to race to a conclusion but on the other I began to feel qualms about the silver lining we seemed intent on extracting from the shooting's ominous cloud. Here a man had been shot and lay dying if not dead and the best we could do was hope that the shooting had brought us together with the drummer we'd been searching for. That we had succumbed so nonchalantly to big-city indifference, big-city survival instincts, made me shiver. I spoke up to suggest we go back and see what had happened, that the man might have only been wounded, in which case we could call for help. We did so, only to find, once we got back to Fifth Avenue, that an ambulance was already there, pulling away, in fact, just as we turned the corner, with the man who'd been shot inside. There were a couple of police cars and a small crowd gathered where the shooting had taken place. I now recalled having heard sirens as we stood talking after catching our breath. We walked to where the crowd and the police cars were and, once there, heard someone say that the ambulance was on its way to the morgue, that the man was dead.

Penguin's word "weird," I couldn't help reflecting, much more aptly applied to how quickly the ambulance and the police had shown up. They might as well have been snowplows, the man who'd been shot newly fallen snow, so quickly had the sidewalk been cleared. It was as if such goings-on had become so common as to make ambulances and police cars omnipresent, never more than a moment away no matter where. Quick to the point of seeming preternatural, they were ubiquitous, in the air, as it were, anxious to materialize, waiting for some such occurrence as the shooting we'd seen. Later in a bar we stepped into for a drink I remarked on this. "That's the way the Apple is," Drennette said drily. "All in a day's work."

While in the bar we talked more about music, getting back to

Drennette being a drummer and, eventually, the fact that we've been looking for one. We took it as encouraging that she's only here for the holidays, visiting her parents in Brooklyn, that she lives, it turns out, in Santa Barbara. (How she ended up there, she said, was a story she would need more time to go into.) Bordering on too-good-to-be-true, this appeared to be no simple coincidence and made it more difficult not to jump to the conclusion (premature sprint, embryonic end-of-our-search) that she's the drummer we've been looking for. Making it even more difficult not to do so was her disclosure that she's been looking for a band to join, even thinking of starting one of her own. "You wouldn't believe the motley string of groups I've gigged with over the past year," she said. We laughed when she said that last month she'd done three nights with a punk-funk band called Mojo Toejam. By now our premature sprint was well under way, seeming anything but premature. The "in" common to Penny, Djeannine and Drennette wasn't lost on us.

"Premature" notwithstanding, the sense that Drennette might be our drummer grew stronger and stronger, the upshot of which was us arranging to get together again. Yesterday afternoon she came by and brought some tapes of her playing and we sat around listening and talking. No doubt about it. She's for real. If she can scare up a drumset we'll do some playing together before we leave town. If not, we'll wait till we're back on the West Coast. Either way, I have a feeling she's the one.

Tonight we open and Drennette said she'd come by to check us out.

Again, wish us luck.

As ever,

N.

9.XII.81

Dear Angel of Dust,

Sorry to've kept you in suspense. We've been back from New York a while now and I've been meaning to let you know how the rest of the trip, the actual gig and all, went. So much, however, happened—quantum-qualitatively so much, I should say—that I've balked at even attempting to give an account. I've been so put upon by trepidations brought on by quantum-qualitative "so much" as to despair of being able to do it justice. It got to the point a few days ago, in fact, that I succumbed to a shattered cowrie shell attack, a new bout of dizziness revolving around a quantum-qualitative collapse, a quantum-qualitative surge of unsuspended misgiving. It laid me low a couple of days but I managed to get back on my feet. I write now not really free of hesitation though somewhat less disabled by the wishful notion of recounting all of what (or even most of what) quantum-qualitatively occurred. The shattered cowrie shell attack, if it did no other good, appears to have set me free of that. A whispered rush of shattered innuendo insisted I be reconciled to incommensurability, the very crux, it insisted further, of quantum-qualitative "so much."

I should begin, then, by saying that we went over well. There was a good, solid turnout all three nights (a bit larger Saturday night than on the other two) and the music was well received. We played as well as we've ever played and often better, spurred on in part by, so to speak, the high stakes involved. This came as a relief after all the apprehensions, which for me culminated the afternoon of the first night in a stricken, panicky feeling in which I could no longer imagine playing. By then I was deeply into being in New York, one thing I liked about which was the anonymity, the sense of having been swallowed up, absorbed. Anonymous drop in an ocean of other anonymous drops, I took to the lack of self-conscious identity I enjoyed. I enjoyed my inconspicuousness. This, though, was the problem. The passive, spectatorial attitude this induced was at odds with us being there to play. All of a sudden playing seemed an irrelevant presumption, the assumption of a voice which had in fact been swallowed up. The presumed audience which went with that assumption had also, I felt, been swallowed up. It seemed absurd to expect anyone to show up, let alone listen. Attention throve on differentiation metropolitan anonymity had long since dissolved. Why raise and call attention to one's voice when ostensible ear, no less than ostensible voice, had long since drowned?

This all came on me in a flash—not all that long, in fact, after I finished my last letter to you. What brought it on I can't say. That morning we'd had a rehearsal and everything had gone fine, so I had no reason to fear the city had swallowed my voice. A kind of stage fright is probably what it was, but the grip it had on me was all the more scary for being at odds with the apparent facts. Rehearsal notwithstanding (all the more so, perhaps, because of it or in spite of it), whatever it was that had me in its grip seemed to know something, to be in touch with something deeper than ostensible fact. This feeling, this fear, had its way with me right up to the time of the gig, though I didn't let on or say anything about it to anyone. It took me thru a number of degrees of apprehension but there were insights it apprised me of as well. These turned out to work to the music's advantage, giving my tone an inostensible edge, a now cutting, now confidential buzz of implication possessed of a quantum-qualitative anonymity combined with a quantum-qualitative "So what?" Something like a blasé leap, that is, was the form apprehension eventually took, an enabling shrug of numinous nonchalance which endowed my playing with a bittersweet obliquity and bite. It was a steeling of myself against the lure of despair which at the same time stole a march on hope.

I've gotten ahead of myself however. Inostensible obliquity and bite I'll leave to go into again later. What I was on my way to saying was that my fear, while not entirely unfounded, turned out not to be prophetic. Once the set was actually under way I could see I would have no such problem as the one I feared. Facility and fluency were with me from the very first note, as they also were with everyone else in the band. It was, as I've already said, some of the best playing we've ever done. There were peak points over the course of the three nights too numerous—to say nothing of too quantum-qualitatively torqued—for me to be able, as I've also already said, to do justice to, points where something seemed to "take us higher." Two or three of these points however—quantum-qualitative increments I call them—I'll give a shot at going into in some detail.

(Quantum-Qualitative Increment "A")

Night one, second set. We were into the open section of "Opposable Thumb at the Water's Edge." Djamilaa was on harmonium, Aunt Nancy on violin, Lambert on tenor, Penguin on oboe, me on saxello. Aunt Nancy to our left and Djamilaa to our right, Lambert, Penguin and I stood in something of a semicircle around the same mike, leaning in towards it as if in a huddle or a semi-huddle—three witches, it must have appeared, stirring up a cacophonous, free-blowing brew. Our aim at that point was to keep a wall of sound happening, an ongoing instance of threadedness and thrust exacting a layered rush of precept and provocation. It wasn't only a wall we wrote *Outraged* on but a sort of primer, a "blackboard" on which our "chalk marks" conjured as they catechized, worked as though they were *vèvès* inviting visitation. Visitation, at any rate, is what we got.

The wall had been going forward as though it would go on that way forever—buttressed by Djamilaa's harmonium, embroidered by Aunt Nancy's violin—when Aunt Nancy began to do something which gradually altered the music's course. Letting go of the spiccato figure she'd been repeating, she embarked upon an increasingly complex run. It was a run which was especially demanding on her left hand—prestissimo demisemiquavers, tremolo effects and so forth. A blazing display of technique, this in turn gave way to a slower, anthemlike figure I knew at once I'd heard before. Repeating it in alternately higher and lower octaves, she bowed with a deliberate, somewhat exaggerated muscularity in the latter, insisting, it seemed, on viscosity, drag, the air of encountered resistance one hears in, say, Jack McDuff's rendition of "Jive Samba." This wasn't the piece the figure reminded me of however, though the more she played it the more familiar it got—hauntingly so. It became obvious, after a while, that she meant to get our attention, that the figure was a summons of sorts. We gave her a glance out of the corner of our eyes and she indicated we should fade, that she wanted to play unaccompanied for a while. This we did, letting the wall subside slowly.

Once this was done Aunt Nancy went on to play the rest of the piece of which the figure she'd been repeating was the opening part. It was then that I recognized it. It was one of Paganini's Caprices, the 9th. It took me a moment or two to catch on to what she was up to but it soon became clear that it was the "pagan" in Paganini she meant to put emphasis on. Recalling the pact he'd supposedly made with the devil, Aunt Nancy played all alone as if to imply that it was the devil of solitude he'd been possessed by, alluding, it appeared, to his habit of going into seclusion. It was during one such withdrawal to Tuscany, I remembered, that he's thought to've written the Caprices.

About this time Penguin, as though he'd read my mind, looked at me and winked, letting me know that he too was on to what she was up to. Indeed, her solo ratified a thought he had recently shared with me—and, perhaps, with her as well—to the effect that the proverbial pact with the devil, the bargain struck for technical prowess, reflects a fear, a collective suspicion, of the solitude one develops one's abilities in. "Robert Johnson didn't sell his soul to the devil," I recalled him having said, "he just spent a lot of time in the woodshed, off to himself." So it was that we knowingly grinned at one another when Aunt Nancy briefly went back to her prestissimo run. She tossed off a quick, finger-twisting flurry which inquired, "Woodshed or devil's workshop?"—pointedly inverting the old adage about idle hands. Her hands, the left especially, were anything but idle, which is exactly what made her appear to be possessed.

Penguin and I grinned but what she was getting at wasn't really funny. Her prestissimo flurry tossed off, she returned to variations on Caprice No. 9, emphasizing, this time around, its brooding, melancholic undertones. It was a darker mood she now explored, a mix of anthemlike and elegiac, a mood infiltrated by the muse of European hoodoo, the spectre of technological possession. Opposable Thumb, she insisted, was *homo faber* thinly veiled, the projection of a toolmaking tendency gone awry. Her melancholic anthem waved a banner of sorrow consecrated to quantum-qualitative disaster, a technical-ecstatic upping of the ante on the risk of impending ruin. It was, going back to her initial insinuation, a drag of an anthem, a dirge, a dredging up. "Water's edge," one all but heard her caution, "water's edge," while as if it were held onto by something underwater she tugged on the bow.

Something about what Aunt Nancy was playing, even though I'd already recognized it as Caprice No. 9, continued to cry out for identification. There continued to be something familiar about it, though what it was wasn't entirely that it was the Paganini piece. What it was was more obliquely familiar. There was some other piece of music, one whose name was on the tip of my tongue, the Caprice tangentially resembled and brought to mind. Aunt Nancy bowed as if she too had its name on the tip of her tongue, repeating the passage which most brought it to mind so strenuously she appeared to be out to break thru to it on sheer strength. This made it all the more elusively familiar, all the more hauntingly within one's grasp yet still out of reach. She herself didn't seem to know what it was. The height of tangency and teasing kinship, whatever it was clearly had hold of her. This we could clearly see. No mere mime of possession, this was the real thing.

It was Lambert who figured out what it was. Leaving the mike that he, Penguin and I shared and joining Aunt Nancy at hers, he put his horn to his mouth and began to play Ayler's tune "Ghosts," looking Aunt Nancy in the eye—hers were glassy, glazed—as he did. This was it, I realized at once. This was the piece one heard inklings of in Caprice No. 9. Lambert, continuing to look Aunt Nancy in the eye, emphasized its aspect of ditty-hop anthem, ditty-bop strut, its ditty-bop meeting or blend of street wisdom with an otherwise otherworldly insistence. Several people in the audience, recognizing the tune, applauded. One woman shouted out, "Albert lives!" Lambert dug deeper into the tune, playing with a hip, ditty-bop assurance which contrasted with Aunt Nancy's distraught, melodramatic dredge. It was a contrapuntal hipness and hope he proposed and Aunt Nancy, as though this were the door, the way out or in she'd been looking for, let the Paganini passage go and took up with "Ghosts." Even though her eyes retained their glazed, glassy look, there was now a look of relief on her face. Djamilaa came in on harmonium, laying down a Baul-inflected, ditty-bop bass line which gave the music an erotic-elegiac, funky-butt foundation and feel.

It took only a whiff of Djamilaa's funky-butt bass to draw Penguin in. He toyed with the head at first, playing in ever so staggered unison with Aunt Nancy and Lambert, soon letting it go to lend himself to Djamilaa's Indian insinuations. Sustaining the dominant, subdominant and tonic as alternating drones by using circular breathing, what he did could be said to have added a Celtic flavor as well. Part bagpipe and part shenai, Penguin's oboe more than lived up to its "high wood" root. Indeed, given the headiness and the heedless, wishful insistence Penguin implied, it had the sound of "high would" as well. He didn't so much blow the horn, it seemed, as take one long unending hit, as if it were a hookah.

It was heavy. The woman who had shouted out earlier again shouted, "Albert lives!" It was as if she too had taken a hit of "high would." Aunt Nancy, realist to the end, responded with a descending run which picked up on "would" but only to say, "Would it were so." It was a run which ever so subtly resurrected, as it were, her distraught, melodramatic dredge, putting one in mind of Ayler's death and of the East River in which his body had been found. Dredge, with its evocation of depth, came into complicating play with would-be height, "high would." Lambert by this time had let the head go to work on a grumbling low-register frenzy which both quoted and laid Albert to rest and even further made for a mix in which would-be height gave grudging ground. It ostensibly laid Albert to rest I should've said, for it was something, a weeping something—sob, ecstatic sensation and several other indescribable factors—I've heard no one other than Ayler himself do (though David Murray comes close). It so seemed as if Albert had taken hold of Lambert's horn that it was all I could do to keep from shouting, "Albert lives!"

It was then that I joined in. Something told me to switch to alto, which I did to find that the bittersweet edge, the newly acquired obliquity and bite I'd been surprised by on saxello, was all the more inostensibly there on the lower-pitched horn. Had it been a tenor or, heaven forbid, a baritone I don't think I could've stood it. My intonation had something of the timbral evanescence of John Tchicai's hollowed-out, strung-up sigh, the evaporative chill he has a way of putting on certain notes. Then again, it had a bit of Arthur Blythe's cut-to-the-quick poignancy and play on fear ("As if he'd seen a ghost") but without its comic and ecclesiastic extremes. No, I was serious, not somber, nonchalant, not flip. I sounded haunted and free of hang-ups at the same time.

Vacancy and voice had caressed one another unawares I immediately knew and I made the most of their inostensible embrace. I took Aunt Nancy and Lambert up on their low-register wager, starting off with a hollowed-out grumble and growl and a ditty-bop shiver whose reverse-gravitational itch and inclination sought an accord with Penguin's quantum-qualitative "high would." Djamilaa's funky-butt foundation and feel had long since gotten a bump-and-grind aspect about it, which made for just the amount of bounce I would need for my inostensible ascent.

Once again it was a wall we put forth, a wailing, structured rush of sound whose collective insistence took Albert's ditty-bop anthem into twisty, giddy reaches possessed of a wincing, wounded quality Albert himself had often explored. Wounded anthem was what it was we now played, a taxed, exacting air whose implicative thread of capricious wind brought the man we'd seen shot on Fifth Avenue to mind. A second ghost had come up to visit. Capricious wind and capricious wound by now ran as one. Anonymous breath embraced anonymous bullet.

Indeed, the spectre of anonymity had us by the throats, which made for a choked-up, croaking sound which groped as though blinded by the light it ostensibly served. We telepathically knew it was time to restate the head, which we did with a collective voice which was guttural and gutted (hollowed-out) at the same time—hollowed-out and shoveled-up it seemed. This brought the audience to its feet with a burst of applause. What it was they'd been gotten to by were no doubt the detours our vatic resolve had been made to take—the sense of uneasy hope or of strained hope or of staggered, strenuous hope one got from its pitched interplay of parts.

The spontaneous ovation told us the piece had peaked and that this was the place to end—which, though we hadn't intended to, we did. With no cue but the one the audience gave us, we crisply repeated the head's last note in unison, letting the piece end on it. Had we then looked down to find we'd risen several inches off the floor we wouldn't have been at all surprised.

(Quantum-Qualitative Increment "B")

". . . who, when loving, live." So ends the refrain of "Udhrite Amendment," a song Djamilaa wrote after reading my first after-the-fact lecture/libretto, the one which ends with her on the couch. In writing the song, she told us, it was the conventional love-death equation she sought to reopen if not rescind. On at least one level, that is, the song amounts to an exposé of masked enjoyments, an unveiling of mixed emotions which is itself, not quite inevitably, a mixed-emotional display. "Live" and "die" are seen to be less than two halves of a whole, inadequate terms for an essentially nameless resource, though "resource" doesn't quite fit either.

Djamilaa's goal was to ventilate as well as unveil an emotional stance which for her had gone stale. Accordingly, the accompaniment consists of me, Lambert and Penguin on flutes, with Aunt Nancy providing percussion on conga. The flute parts incorporate phrases from Dolphy's recording of "Glad to Be Unhappy," a pointedly mixed-emotional motif set up to be revised by phrases from "To Be," the flute and piccolo piece Trane and Pharoah recorded. "Glad" and "unhappy" are thus implied to be beside the point. The music is also indebted to Henry Threadgill's multi-flute concept on the *X-75 Volume 1* album. The allusion to this latter title, albeit oblique, makes for a further move into abstraction, a move made more immediately evident by Djamilaa's recourse, as in "The Slave's Day Off," to singing with a piece of waxed paper in front of her mouth. The song's affinity with "The Slave's Day Off" doesn't end there, for its contestatory address of the love-death equation moves or seeks to move in a liberatory direction. The piece of waxed paper contends with and hopefully subverts a received semantics which, "live" replacing "die" notwithstanding, tends to be complicit with "the way things are." This is ground, contested ground, our music returns to again and again.

It was this number we concluded our first night's performance with. It was a totally entrancing, thoroughly absorbing reading of the piece, a particularly fitting way to wrap things up it turned out. "Udhrite Amendment," before it was over, proposed an extrapolative cool-out gradient whose uncoiled eroticism translated length, extensibility, into quantum-qualitative lift. Djamilaa's voice was every bit as hypnotic as it's ever been, an ostensible/inostensible mix which had its own way of coming to terms with metropolitan anonymity's blasé obliquity and bite. She put one remotely in mind of the Javanese singer Imas Permas, coaxing from herself, it seemed, a slow tangential address which mated complaint with composure. The piece of waxed paper, of course, obscured the lyrics, introducing a semantic x-factor, as it were, which had the audience on the edge of their seats trying to make the words out.

From the first few notes I knew we were into something. The flutes kicked it off with a serrated climb punctuated by a plunge that brought Aunt Nancy in. She pulled her thumb across the conga's head in such a way as to make it sound like a bass, giving us just the bit of bottom we needed. It was this that did it, this descent which got us on our way. The bent, swelling note Aunt Nancy's thumb adduced—part plea, part Udhrite appointment—apprised us of a see-thru accessibility of which it insisted we avail ourselves. I felt for a moment as though the plate on which my lower lip rested were the edge of a pool I dipped into, the palpable "splash" of an imagined oasis's Udhrite "plunge." The see-thru water I wet my lips with reminded me of Charles Lloyd's "Little Anahid's Day," yet there was an even stronger recollection it occasioned of the psychophonic affliction of which I wrote you a few months back—the luminous doomed lament scored for hollowed-out pelvis played on dislocated flute. I stood naked, I felt, before all of New York, stripped of both clothing and flesh, naked to the bone, abruptly accessible (X-ray accessible) to the eyes of anyone who looked. It was a pool of skeletal water, X-ray water, I dipped into. Penguin and Lambert dipped into it as well.

The X-ray accessibility in whose grip the three of us played must have made the audience all the more unprepared for the divergence from see-thru semantics to which the piece of waxed paper gave purchase. The opacity it gave an otherwise insubstantial medium stood in stark, metonymic alliance with the now transparent substantiality of which Lambert, Penguin and I found ourselves possessed. I noticed a man in one of the front rows whose face got a perplexed—albeit ultimately approving—look when Djamilaa started singing. The contiguous incongruity between X-ray accessibility and semantic x-factor caused more than a few eyebrows to rise.

Part oasis, part piranha pool, the watery body of which we availed ourselves grew calm with an exhortative insistence, a mix whose cue was that of complaint and composure Djamilaa brought off. The unison flute passages made for an etheric, "theoretical" aura from which we each had opportunities to stray or with which to differ by retaining the graininess of "practice." Differential flutter thus tended to intervene so as to ward off the danger of self-inflation, to dispel the auto-enchanted halo "theoretical" aura might have easily become. Something or someone, it insinuated, had dreamt it all up—which, of course, was true—though regarding the limits of what "it" referred to one would've liked to be more precise. The opaque, waxed-paper-assisted accent Djamilaa repeatedly let fall on "live" by now bore the weight of an autumnal ripeness construed to pose myth and maturation as linked. So expressively was the link sustained and so thoroughgoing were its repercussions as to intimate a trumpeter's annunciative kiss. Needless to say, this too caused eyebrows to rise.

Djamilaa's voice rode the wind of its "new day" annunciation, annulling the asthmatic equation on which Udhrite aesthetics had up to then been based. The amended wind of which it grew newly apprised arose in part from the breath Lambert, Penguin and I expended, an obsessed, invasive "second wind" which now began to send ripples across the pool into which we dipped. The piranha pool thus found itself blown upon by an X-ray wind whose exposure of bone was the alarmed incentive toward a "new day" annulment, a "new day" dismissal of love-death license, love-death allure. "New day," though not announcedly so, was "the slave's day off" as far as I was concerned. It was no doubt this that caused my flute to seem it was no longer made of metal, to seem instead to've been cut from cane. This I found oddly reassuring, oddly soothing.

The transformation from "base" metal to "balsamic" wood was not, however, without its apprehensive side. The taste of something burnt came along with it, a taste my lower lip and the tip of my tongue picked up from the lip-plate, the taste, I realized at once, of burnt cane. It was a taste which, consonant with "The Slave's Day Off," excavated the roots of Trinidadian carnival, Canboulay. Grimacing as if overcome by a bitter memory, I embarked upon a rush of differential flutter, a former slave's carnival reenactment of plantation times. Grimacing rush told of canefields burning, sudden rousings out of bed, late night harvest, all-night labor. A reminder of past oppression if not a foretaste of burnings to come, the *canne brulée* taste in my mouth betrayed a fear that freedom was only a dream. Love's "new day" was only another night of sleep one would be forced to wake up from. This fear grew stronger and stronger the longer *canne brulée* prevailed. Even so, I went on blowing, a backslider in the "new day" church without intending to be, trying to blow the fire out but fanning it instead.

My unintended slide caught everyone's attention, most notably Djamilaa's. Her waxed paper scat took on a scolding inflection which reminded me that burnt cane, *canne brulée*—my coded way, she charged, of alluding to burnt kiss, French kiss—was merely a lapse into the unamended Udhrite ordeal the song was meant to challenge. This, of course, I already knew, though it made me blush to hear it put so bluntly. Lambert and Penguin heard it as well and also saw me blush. They came to my aid as if to someone who had suffered a blow, playing the unison passage a little bit louder to recall me to it. It was a strikingly lucid, enticingly sweet passage (all but overly so), not unlike an Indian or a North African dessert. It was also not unlike the strings on Alice Coltrane's "Oh Allah," sweet but all the while bordering on tart. It was a far cry, in any case, from the taste of burnt cane my flute and I had picked up—so far, in fact, I couldn't imagine ever joining them again.

But seeing, they say, is believing. It certainly made a believer out of me. I doubt I would ever have made it back to the unison passage were it not for what I saw when I glanced over at Lambert and Penguin. My eyes, I felt at first, had to be putting me on. I saw grains of sugar on the lip-plates of Lambert's and Penguin's flutes, an image I tried to shake off to no avail. They must really be into it, I thought. This was the beginning of my breaking away from *canne brulée*.

Lambert and Penguin all but out and told me to straighten up and pull myself together, to come back to the unison passage. They stood unusually straight as they played, the true-believer sweetness occasioning an almost military stance. They held their heads high, standing so erect they appeared to be stretching themselves, a strenuous enough stretch to mix true-believer sweetness with true-believer sweat. The grains of sugar didn't blow away as they played but seemed to be indigenous to the lip-plates on which they sat.

To me the flute felt like a chin-up bar. I was trying to pull myself up to a higher level, to make my way back into the "new day" church. Aunt Nancy's winged conga beats helped a bit but nevertheless it was a struggle, a strain—so much so I felt I was losing my breath as I tried to blow and pull myself up at the same time. Were it not for the grains of sugar I saw I'd have never made it. Were it also not for Djamilaa's voice, which had gone from scolding to coaxingly sweet, I'd have never made it. So inspired a reach of sweetness it was it almost made me weep.

It must have been windedness, the thin air of my ascent, which made me go blank. I didn't exactly pass out, for I went on playing, but the last thing I remember is getting back to the unison passage and the feeling which came with it, after only a couple of notes, that I was for all time free of *canne brulée*. The next thing I knew we were backstage in the dressing room, congratulating one another on how well the first night had gone. "Udhrite Amendment" had evidently ended not terribly long after I got back to the unison passage, but not before Djamilaa and I entered into a brief impromptu exchange—my part in which, I'm told, consisted largely of an alternation between E7 and Fmaj7 which took the unison passage's line in a "Spanish" direction—an exchange Aunt Nancy, Lambert and Penguin raved about, Aunt Nancy calling it "worthy of Billie and Pres." I don't remember a note of it. Nor do I remember the ovation we got. I don't remember walking from the stage to the dressing room either.

(Quantum-Qualitative Increment "C")

Drennette managed to borrow a drumset and so was able to sit in with us on Sunday night, night number three. That in itself was a quantum-qualitative high, a sustained increment. Though she complained at first of being "reduced to standard equipment," of nor having her usual accessories and idiosyncratic implements (a set of "gongs" made from hubcaps and trashcan lids, an assortment of bells, rattles and shakers, a toy xylophone and so forth), she more than acquitted herself well. She was, in fact, a monster. All night she was on it, putting forth an order of rhythmic invention which made her corner of the stage a percussion lab, standard, stripped-down equipment notwithstanding. "Rhythmelodic" might be a better way to put it, for Drennette had obviously learned a thing or two from the likes of Ed Blackwell and, among others, Freddie Waits. She had a way, that is, of making the drumset sing, exacting an exhortative, oratorical range, a reconnoitering stir in whose arch embrace push and support were indissolubly one. Punch and propulsion complicated by slippage—well-placed hints of erosive wear, erosive retreat—were the dominant threads in the rhythmelodic carpet she wove and rode, the pushy-supportive rug which, even as she threatened to pull it out from under us, carried us along.

The entire night, as I've already said, was a continuous high, though some points, of course, were higher than others. One such point occurred during the second set as we were into a piece Lambert had recently written, "Half-Staff Appetition"—a piece he was moved to write by a quote he rediscovered in one of his college notebooks, a passage from a book he recalled having read for a philosophy course, a book by Alfred North Whitehead: "In each actuality there are two concrescent poles of realization—'enjoyment' and 'appetition,' that is, the 'physical' and the 'conceptual.' For God the conceptual is prior to the physical, for the World the physical poles are prior to the conceptual poles. A physical pole is in its own nature exclusive, bounded by contradiction: a conceptual pole is in its own nature all-embracing, unbounded by contradiction. The former derives its share of infinity from the infinity of appetition; the latter derives its share of limitation from the exclusiveness of enjoyment." Weeks before at a rehearsal, introducing the piece, Lambert had joked that if Whitehead had been a musician he could've let it go with playing "Body and Soul." (He also had some fun with the name, insisting on an emphatic pause between "White" and "head.") We laughed but, joke notwithstanding, the piece does derive in part from "Body and Soul's" chord progressions, Lambert having done with them something like what Mal Waldron does in "Anatomy" with those of "All the Things You Are." It's a simple piece—pointedly, deceptively so, considering the Whitehead quote—on which Lambert imposed a namesake ceiling, writing it entirely in the bottom half of the staff. Never does it go above third-line B, a prohibition we were instructed to observe even in our solos.

"Half-Staff Appetition" speaks of caution and confinement, a near crippling sense of unascendable height bearing down which makes us feel, whenever we play it, as though we stood stooped over. This has in part, of course, to do with Lambert's play on "staff," where with "half" he insists on fractionality and lack, the falling short of its ostensible support. That one makes up the lack oneself seems implied by the stooped-over feeling we can never quite shake, the sense that unascendable height rests on our backs, bearing down with the weight of lowered expectation. Shepherdly cramp, that is, meets shepherded craving, each in its way the splintered remains of a collateral coup and consolidation, the exploited, ever splintering crutch on which prohibitive height itself leans for support.

Lambert appears also, in writing the piece, to have wanted to ask, "What about the enjoyment of appetition?" The low ceiling which is third-line B feeds and fosters a sweet tooth for dialectics, a philosophic appeal which appears intent on insisting on furtherance and frustration as one when it comes to desire. Appeal feeds philosophic aplomb, a recuperative crutch implicating desire in its own obstruction. That any such crutch is only a half-eaten stick, an indebted baton, the implosive receipt of which wants to incite as it offers solace, almost goes without saying. Does "half-staff" thus have to do with "half-eaten," one has reason to ask, a question Lambert left room for us to address in our improvisations. Appetitive earth leaned on by cannibalized height (half-eaten heaven) is thus a motif which comes up each time we play the piece. This particular night, with Drennette sitting in, was no exception.

Drennette is indeed, in many ways, the ideal drummer for such a piece. The intimate terms on which we stood with erosion, thanks to her, underscored its implied embrace of half-eaten height. Splintered support sparked and spiced by slippage, as I've already said, is a key feature of Drennette's approach, an insistent appeal which, in the case of this piece, applied appetitive heat to unascendable height. Thus it was, one was left to infer, that appetition and enjoyment were one, a farther-reaching idea than that the former could be the latter's object. "The consumption of unascendability," I said to myself as I concluded my solo, so taken, as it turned out, was I with this idea. I at once regretted it having occurred to me too late to've been made more explicit, too late to be made a part of my solo. It was luckily an idea which Lambert, who soloed last, after me, had also picked up on.

It was, in fact, Lambert and Drennette's interplay, prohibitive height notwithstanding, which afforded us the quantum-qualitative ascent I'm here labeling "C." Lambert started off somewhat tentatively, with an apprehensiveness and a hesitant, fearful tread which were not inconsistent with the strains of erosive wear and erosive retreat Drennette insisted on. Woven into the rug she invited one to ride was a suspect appeal he had every reason to have qualms about, to be wary of, notwithstanding that he savored its allure. The consumption of unascendability partook of that savor, taking the form, as he espoused and put it forth, of a performative discourse having to do with fugitive breath, tasted breath.

"Half-Staff Appetition," I may not have said, is a ballad. A balladeer to the bone once he got into it, Lambert expounded its ballad marrow as he apportioned its ballad blood with a sound whose breathy/breathless caress brought Ben Webster to mind—the Webster of, say, "Prisoner of Love" or of "Tenderly." This Websterian recourse to subtones made for an accent which fell on wind as rudimentary voice, an insinuative return to basics, as it were, whose flirtatious, make-believe bite—a fugitive lover's blown breath or kiss—one could never not woo the enjoyment of. Thus it was that ballad bone was a now asthmatic, now respirated baton which had made the rounds from time immemorial, a broken, half-staff capacity for aspirate expulsion, aspirate escape.

Lambert's Websterian celebration of breath couldn't help but be infused with a spectre of loss, an intimate acknowledgement if not embrace of expiration's most ominous undertones, in dialogue with which a consoling image of "inspired" leakage came into play. The latter made for a reading of aspirate expulsion (savored aspiration, inverse breathless ascent) as a cushion for what might otherwise have been unbearable, an inspired albeit merely implied pillow talk to soften its blow. Such implicative talk sugarcoated a pill which was hard to swallow, though Drennette, it appeared, was by no means entirely won over. She bit or bought into it only to bargain for something more, keeping up her end of what was a bartered embrace with a not-to-be-bought barrage of post-romantic rescissions played on cymbals and high hat.

The rest of us gradually pulled back. This was obviously between the two of them, an expulsive-appetitive pillow and rug rolled into one.

Being it was a ballad, Drennette used brushes. So it was that rug was already rolled into one with brush. This meant it was also rolled into one with broom, Drennette's brushwork putting us in mind of what had gone on in Griffith Park a few weeks before—not only the sound but, in my case, the "seen," Broom Ex Machina's dance. Her brushed embellishments blended with Lambert's Websterian pillow in such a way as to sound as if she swept up the breath which escaped between the reed and his bottom lip. That such leakage intimated mortality was lost on no one, least of all her, and she made the most of it (dusted broom, dust under the rug) whenever she could.

Remembering what had happened in Griffith Park, I didn't dare, as you can imagine, close my eyes, though Penguin did eventually close his. There was something funereal about Lambert and Drennette's exchange, as though they lamented appetition's death or, if not its death, the dire straits ("half-staff") thru which it passed. This isn't to say there was anything morbid or morose about it so much as that direness and desire walked hand in hand. In keeping with its funereal aspect, Penguin removed his hat (a gray, stingy-brim number he'd picked up in Harlem) and bowed his head. That the air was being let out of something was clear. What that something was would've been considered by some to be common knowledge, by others anybody's guess. My sense was that the air was being let out of enjoyment, of which the swept-under side was that the letting out of air was being enjoyed.

What Lambert and Drennette got into increasingly sounded like a low-register crawl, an eked-out advance which was not uninformed by overtones of encroachment. Drennette peppered their coaxed incursions with intermittent hisses, clipped hisses on high hat—by way of response, this, to Penguin's bowed head and doffed hat. There was nothing, she seemed to insist, to be glum about. The clipped hisses brought the phantom drummer we'd heard in Griffith Park all the more to mind. Whether or not Drennette was aware of this became the question when she took up a slap-and-stir line which, above the thumps thrown in on bass drum, was even more reminiscent of what we'd heard in the park. Aunt Nancy and I evidently asked it of ourselves at the same time, for as our eyes at that moment met we seemed to ask it of one another as well.

Penguin continued to stand motionless, his head still bowed, stingy-brim in hand, though he did ever so noticeably shiver. A chill had run up his back. Djamilaa's eyes were glued to Drennette, posing the question Aunt Nancy and I were likewise posing. We as well were now staring at Drennette, set wondering all the more by the grin she shot us. That the grin was a knowing one there could be no question. The question was did she know (how could she know) what had happened in the park.

The answer was no, though we didn't find it out until later, after the gig, when we asked her outright. At the time, though, it appeared she must have known, so blown away were we by the blend of longstanding simmer and suppositious retreat she resorted to now. This was the insinuative mix, you'll recall, whoever it was we'd heard in Griffith Park had so seductively served up. Drennette's right hand, that is, was rock steady, the snare a pot in which it stirred an endlessly simmering stew. A suggestion of endlessly abiding patience and nonchalance was what one got. Her left, slapping hand intermittently erupted in its turning over, lending itself to the bass drum's equally eruptive thumps. This gave it a sense of suppositious retreat, as though the beat every now and then were backing up, a conflicted sense of being upheld and taken out at the same time. The increasing closeness of this to what we'd heard in the park was uncanny.

That Lambert heard it as well one heard in the change his intonation underwent. Once again the music found itself haunted as he played as if pestered by an appetitive ghost. There was now an ever so audible quaver visited upon each note, a begging off which, albeit slight, said ostensible solidity had by now been seen thru. See-thru quaver bespoke an introvert fierceness whose intuitive simmer agreed in full with Drennette's adroit suppositious retreat. The blue see-thru truth of this was that hollowed-out appetite haunted—having itself been inhabited by—an inauspicious thump or an inostensible thud, putative solidity and soul rolled into one.

It was at this point that Penguin closed his eyes, pushed even deeper into would-be obsequies by Lambert's quantum-qualitative quaver, a sound which even now, rehearing it as I write, I find it hard to not be taken away by. Lambert's eyes, of course, had been closed for some time, him having closed them as his and Drennette's duet grew more and more intimate. Hers remained open and she picked up the tempo a bit when she saw that Penguin's eyes had closed. Once again he shivered. Another chill had run up his back.

Penguin opened his eyes and raised his head once the shiver passed. An incredulous look was on his face. He was impressed. He was so impressed, in fact, he stood staring into empty space. Lambert and Drennette soon wrapped up their duet, getting back to the head, but Penguin, rather than joining us in the cadenza we took the piece out on, continued gazing into empty space. He snapped out of it once the audience began to applaud, to play cheerleader, holding his hat out to them as if bumming a handout ("Don't be stingy"), all the while, with his other hand, gesturing toward Drennette ("Give the drummer some").

The quantum-qualitative climb Lambert and Drennette had pulled off turned out to have been even steeper than it appeared. Both Penguin and Lambert reported afterward that, yes, while their eyes were closed they'd seen the dancing broom.

Yours,
N.

19.XII.81

Dear Angel of Dust,

Sorry I ended my last letter so abruptly. It was all I could do to get it finished and into an envelope, so shaky my hand and my sense of things became the more I wrote. Quantum-qualitative "so much" made for an aliquant reminder which undermined my senses of access and ascertainment, though it pressed me and prodded me as well. Toward the letter's end I began to get lightheaded and to feel a dizziness coming on, what turned out to be another shattered cowrie shell attack. A puff of something I felt must've been sesame dust blew into my face, a new wrinkle which gave the attack an adventitious brunt it shared with Broom Ex Machina's dance. The puff carried an ever so subtle smell of magnolias, an adventitious bouquet whose oblique perfume proposed a synaesthetic unity the shattered cowries threw into harsh, paratactic relief. The advent of angular scent complied with a promise of post-equivalent splash, a compensative hint of perfume which arose out of dues paid in sesame dust. Such a teasingly scented, synaesthetic intervention wasn't something I much expected, though earlier attacks had taught me, if anything, to rule nothing out.

Synaesthetic sweetness notwithstanding, the dancing broom, I felt, had swept dust into my eyes. I blinked a few times to clear them, then I squinted—an austere Rasta Far-Eye squint. What I saw was a pharmacopoeic elsewhere which, no matter how much I blinked, was always a bit blurred and off to the side, tauntingly, it seemed, tangential to the medicinal regard it nonetheless prescribed. Squint was all one could or would ever do, it seemed to say, but, even so, one could never squint enough. I knew "enough" was more a matter of "how" than of "how much," but still I sat around blinking and squinting for days. I sought to see the smell of magnolias, to catch its optic, albeit occult or concealed aspect (what the Dogon call *obia*) offguard. That such a visible olfactivity existed I never once doubted, though looking for it made me all the more dizzy. As if the shattered cowries' whirl wasn't enough, my scent-seeking Far-Eye squint went to my head, made it hard for me to even stand up, let alone walk or do anything else. I was out of it for almost a week. I even considered seeing a doctor again. I waited it out, though, and things are now back to normal.

What I wanted to say before ending my last letter maybe goes without saying but I'll say it anyway: Drennette's the drummer for us. We were ecstatic with the way our third night at NuMu went with her sitting in—"we" here including her, for she too spoke afterward of what a high it was. She said playing with us felt like home, that she couldn't wait to get back to California so we could pick up where we left off. That'll be early next month, after New Year's.

Anyway, enough for now. I'm only, so to speak, checking in.

As ever,

N.

26.XII.81

Dear Angel of Dust,

Remember the letter a long while back in which I spoke of music haunting us like a phantom limb? Well, take a look at what I happened upon a few days ago, something a former slave in South Carolina, one Andy Brice, told a Federal Writer's Project interviewer in the late thirties: "One day I see Marse Thomas a twistin' de ears on a fiddle and rosinin' de bow. Then he pull dat bow 'cross de belly of dat fiddle. Something bust loose in me and sing all thru my head and tingle in my fingers. I made up my mind, right then and dere, to save and buy me a fiddle. I got one dat Christmas, bless God! I learnt and been playin' de fiddle ever since. I pat one foot while I'm playin'. I kept on playin' and pattin' dat foot for thirty years. I lose dat foot in a smash-up wid a highway accident, but I play de old tunes on dat fiddle at night, dat foot seem to be dere at de end of dat leg and pats just de same. Sometime I ketch myself lookin' down to see if it have come back and joined itself up to dat leg, from de very charm of de music I makin' wid de fiddle and de bow."

When I showed it to the other members of the band a subtle glow lit up Aunt Nancy's face, so I wasn't surprised at rehearsal the next day when she announced that it'd moved her to write a new piece. A tape of it you'll find enclosed. As you can see, it's called "Feet, Don't Fail Me Now." She was torn, she says, between that and "Divertimento for Violin and Prepared Feet," a friendly dig, no doubt, at my "Robotic Aria for Prepared and Unprepared Alto." Don't let the title fool you though.

It's a serious piece, featuring some of the headiest writing and playing Aunt Nancy's done, which is all the more amazing in light of the "preparation" referred to in the alternate title. For this piece, that is, she steps into a pair of shoes which are bolted to a concrete block, immobilizing the foot she pats time with, the right, while preventing the left from doing so as well. The piece thus has to do with amputation in a mainly figurative way, being more literally a case of implantation (a word one might wish to hyphenate, im-plantation, to emphasize the auction-block ordeal the piece alludes to). Friendly dig or not, Aunt Nancy has taken my play on Cage a bit farther, investing all the more visibly in the spectre of captivity which haunts the avant-garde. To keep time on cageling feet is to conjure a history in whose light "preparation" looks tame and redundant.

Notice, though, the way a gesture of retrieval works rhythmically throughout the piece, the way retrieved historical trauma syncopates a retrieved "inner" body sense. I say inner to accent the fact that outward constraint ignites recuperative repercussions, a strain of compensatory feints and refractory shifts bent on restoring a somatic disposition which no longer obtains. How rightly we speak of a *body of work*, the torsional propriety of which Aunt Nancy teases with her ingenious conceit of caged or eclipsed extremities (fixed yet insistent feet, "phantom" feet). A new body begins to emerge with this work. Granted, there's something of a setup to it, in that the timekeeping, metronomic foot has by now been internalized. That's a bone I leave to others to pick, though not without noting that the feet have to do with attitude and stance, a dancelike function the bolted-down shoes genuinely get in the way of.

The agitation on the image front I won't belabor. The quote, for example, from "Spooks," one of the tunes on Marion Brown's *Three for Shepp*, speaks for itself. In fact, I won't burden the piece with any further comments except to say that I hope you like it and I hope this letter finds you well.

Sincerely,
N.

30.XII.81

Dear Angel of Dust,

Thank you for your letter. Sorry to hear "Feet, Don't Fail Me Now" didn't do much for you. Maybe one has to see it performed to really appreciate it. Watching Aunt Nancy move like a piece of animate sculpture would break thru your reservations I think, but the questions you raise are nonetheless worth addressing. As to whether the concrete block could be construed as playing on or poking fun at historical-materialist precepts, I suppose I'd have to say yes, why not, to "playing on," though "poking fun at" I'm not so sure about. The word "concrete," like any other, creaks, which may be the best guarantee we've got against the buzzword it could—being subject, like any other, to semantic erosion—and too often already has become. Yes, Aunt Nancy literally plays on concrete, but not, as you put it, "to poke fun at a materialist orientation." We've had this argument before. Why not hear it as a struggle to incarnate abstraction, to bring ideas which were once visualizable back into view? This is why I say one has to see the piece performed. Aunt Nancy's feints, bobs, weaves and what have you body forth an agonistic thrust or displacement up from erosion toward restoration. An element of play, furthermore, needn't be at odds with seriousness. Though I'd be the first to acknowledge the piece lacks ideological solemnity, I'd warn against confusing solemnity with truth.

In emphasizing the visual impact of the piece, I realize, I run the risk of endorsing or appearing to endorse an eye-based bias, the bias which, for example, accounts for "cant," whose root is "to sing," being a putdown, a pejorative term. I've no wish to do so. One looks on with a philosophic eye, "philosophy" being one's fight against the fascination any form of expression tends to exert. Both the creaking and the erosion to which words are prone (the multiplication as well as the depletion or debilitation of meaning) make a certain amount of play inescapable. A complicated mesh of endowments and deprivations, music thrives on an admission of weakness, the lapse into "can't" toward which language tends. The advantage of seeing "Feet, Don't Fail Me Now" played is that the struggle against that lapse gets another dimension. You'd think Aunt Nancy were a flamenco dancer at points, given how a jolt appears to enter her feet from the concrete block, stiffening her body and causing her to wince. It's all one can do not to yell out, "Olé!"

Having said all this, though, I should add that I haven't forgotten that reactions vary. So be it. I wouldn't, even if I could, have it any other way.

Yours,
N.

9.1.82

Dear Angel of Dust,

Drennette's in town. She came down from Santa Barbara two days ago. She's been back for about a week now. We've been playing a lot, which's been going well, extremely well—so well it's hard to believe we ever played without her. Yesterday we did a number in six which'll stay with me forever. Drennette's drumset seemed more like a wagon than a drumset, a rickety, lumbering ride which periodically creaked as it went along, creaked as if to complain of some weight. The weight of ongoingness might've been what it was. More and more we moved as if crossing a desert—a nice, nomadic, loping touch rolling stretch and lack of strain ever so lightly into one. The weight of recurrence might've equally been what it was but in either case complaint included aspects of consolation, shadowy leverages Drennette insistently brought to our attention. Either way, we found relative rest in repetition, recess thru quasi-outages linking caution to repercussion. Too bad we didn't get it on tape.

There's already (though not a second too soon) talk of Drennette moving down here. There's nothing, she says, holding her in Santa Barbara, no reason for her to stay there now that she and the man she moved there to be with have split up. This came up earlier today at lunch. We decided to go out after a late-morning rehearsal, ending up at a place in Venice which is part restaurant and part antique store, a place called The Merchant of Venice. The name fits. Everything in it's for sale. The tables have price tags on them, as do the chairs, the photos and pictures on the walls, the decorative bric-a-brac and even the salt and pepper shakers. Choosing it was a bit cute I have to admit. We made a joke of wondering out loud what would happen if someone wanted to buy our table.

We were talking about the similarities and differences among beach towns when we got on the subject of Santa Barbara—how Drennette liked it, what'd caused her to move there and so forth. She said she moved there a couple of years ago when the man she was living with in Philadelphia, Rick, took a job teaching at the UC campus. "Neither of us had ever lived in California," she explained, "but we'd been out here on a vacation and liked it and thought the change might not be a bad thing. Besides, the only other offer he got was in Minnesota." She went on to talk about him and how things had gone. Though she spoke with a nonchalant, wry detachment, it became evident after a while that this was something about which she needed to talk, something she continued to feel deeply about. You didn't have to be a shrink to see thru the stoic front she put up, to see that grief got its due at some deeper level. She talked a bit, in any event, about what she likes and what she doesn't like about Santa Barbara, as well as about what she liked and what she didn't like about living with Rick. Their breaking up last year she also talked about.

Her account of a bicycle accident she suffered a concussion from got to us most. She and Rick, she explained, had gotten into biking after moving west. When they split up, stopped living together, they agreed to remain friends and one of the things they continued to do was go biking together. "I think he really meant it," she said, "all the talk about friendship, but for me it was only a holding action, a way of holding on to the hope we'd get back together." Her voice was dry, dispassionate. There was a hard-won putting away of hope to the tone she spoke in, a numb, no-nonsense immunity to expectation. "I didn't realize it for a while," she went on, "but eventually I found out the hard way." She then went into what she meant by "the hard way," the accident which had left her concussed. She and Rick, we were told, were out riding one day and were coming to a hill. She challenged him to a race to its top, he said okay and they both began pedaling all-out. They had a way to go before getting to where the road began to rise and by the time they did they were going pretty fast. It was at this point that it happened. The race was close, neck and neck, and just after the road began to rise and the pedaling got harder her right pedal broke off on a downstroke. "It was like walking up a stairway and reaching for a step that isn't there. My foot hit the asphalt and the bike and I went down. The next thing I knew I was lying on my back. Rick was bending over me, cradling my head with his hand and saying something I couldn't make out, though the softness of his voice made me feel happy, secure." She paused, barely a beat, and went on. "It was crazy. I thought we were in bed, lovers again. I closed my eyes and pulled him closer. I felt something warm on the side of my face I thought was him kissing me. I later realized it was blood. It was crazy, me lying on the road bleeding, whispering I loved him, happy to be held and kissed." She went on to explain that it was this which, as she put it, woke her up, made her admit she still harbored hope they'd get back together. "It was an eye-opener," she commented drily. "It made me face how much I clung"—here she paused a moment, reflected on how to put it, gazing around the restaurant/store—"how much I clung to antique sentiment."

Penguin later told me that while she spoke he felt more and more protective, that the more stoic the attitude she took, the more post-expectant, the more he wanted to put his arm around her. It was a worn-out chivalric impulse I warned him, as much a case of "antique sentiment" as any, though I too had found myself moved. What was especially striking was that she spoke of the spill she took as a turning point in her approach to drumming. "That awakening," she said, "that opening of the eyes, really turned me around. Up to then I didn't really know what percussion's about. I knew the letter, you might say, but not the spirit. That broken pedal, more than anything else, made me a drummer." For a time she said no more, returning to the salad which for some time she hadn't touched, leaving it to us to pursue the tie between concussive spill and percussive spirit. She eventually went on to say that move here is what she'll most likely do, a move we encouraged her to make, saying as far as we're concerned she's already in the band.

Otherwise, things have been on the slow side. It's been a while since we've played a gig, though there's a possible stint up north in the works. We'll see.

Have to close now. Hope to hear from you soon.

As ever,

N.

18.I.82

Dear Angel of Dust,

Drennette's now definite about it. She's looking for an apartment here in L.A., staying at Aunt Nancy's until she finds a place of her own. Which, I guess, makes it official: she's now in the band. It didn't take her long to make up her mind. But it's not about that I'm writing to tell you so much as that Penguin seems increasingly taken with her—something I have to admit we saw coming. His wanting to put his arm around her at The Merchant of Venice I've already told you about. Since then it's grown. At rehearsals and also when we're just hanging out he spends more and more time talking to her, more and more asks her what she thinks about this or that, more and more tries to engage her one-on-one. He even offers to help carry and set up her drums though she's made it clear she can manage by herself, that she prefers to. A few days ago he brought a new piece he'd written to rehearsal, a piece he calls "Drennethology."

It's more than that he's a bit sweet on her, more than that he fancies her in the simple sense of likes. It's more that he's eliciting or looking for something (meaning, concept, clue, what have you), as the title he gave the piece he wrote makes clear. This became all the more evident day before yesterday when he and I went out to Poobah's, a hip, fairly new record store in Pasadena. On the way there he began to talk about Drennette. Before mentioning her outright he asked if he was mistaken in recalling that the drumming we heard a few months back in Griffith Park had sounded as if it came from the north. I said my memory wasn't foolproof but I too recalled it sounding that way. He then suggested that Drennette's claim she knew nothing of what had happened in the park shouldn't be trusted, Santa Barbara being where it is, to the north. "The drummer we heard was her," he insisted. "I'm more and more convinced of that."

He didn't stop there. He went on to say that with all due respect to Lambert's talk of smallpox cults he understood the sesame seeds in the light of Sufi doctrine, that he carried them back to the "Earth of sesame" spoken of by Ibn 'Arabī, 'Abd al-Karīm Jīlī and others. "What we saw," he said, "was what's known as 'the sesame left over from the clay of Adam,' the hidden portion of the surplus clay from which the palm tree was made. This tree they call 'Adam's sister.' The sesame seeds, analogous, if you like, to the biblical 'grain of mustard seed,' were a sign that we were on visionary ground." Having said this, he fell silent, as if to let me mull it over. It made a certain sense to me, especially in light of Broom Ex Machina's dance and the synaesthetic squint the sesame dust induced in my last cowrie shell attack. The fact that, given the remainder sesame attests to, Adam and his sister could be said to be aliquant factors of clay, aliquant factors of earth (they don't go into it integrally), also spoke to me. The reverse, earth or clay as aliquant factor of Adam and his sister, did as well. Remainder and thus reminder of what's left over, what's left out, sesame, I saw, blew the lid off totalizing assumptions. "Yeah," I finally said, "I follow you."

We rode in silence a short while, a silence Penguin broke by saying, "There's more to Drennette than meets the eye." He paused, winked at me and added, "Not that what meets the eye's not mighty fine." I grinned, took a hand off the wheel and offered my palm. He slapped it, turned his hand over and I slapped his. "Still," he went on, "what that 'more' is I intend to find out." By this time we were at Poobah's and I pulled over, parked, and we got out. On the sidewalk he surprised me by singing a few lines from "Earth Angel," the song, you may recall, a quartet known as The Penguins had a hit with back in the fifties. He pressed his hands to his chest as he sang, hamming it up, his voice an exaggerated falsetto. He sought, it seemed clear, to get leverage on himself, to make light of what he'd said and how he felt by doing this, but the seriousness of it wasn't that easily effaced. I smiled as he sang, "Earth angel, earth angel, please be mine . . . ," but again I saw him as on the night of his phonological run. Earth angel, albeit jokingly invoked, entered into a two-way conjuration with grounded bird.

This indeed shed light on "Drennethology," to which Penguin had introduced us only a couple of days before. Its allusion to Bird's "Ornithology" appeared all the more appropriate, as did its echoings of the tune Bird based his piece on, "How High the Moon." What was it if not a pathic, problematic incommensurability one meant by "more," a verticality of unassured measure? Locked in sublunar, symbiotic play with earth angel, grounded bird bespoke earth as tautologic base of aspiration, mourning its wings while adoring those of its other. It occurred to me that Penguin had taken Drennette's concussive spill to be grounds for his embrace of her as angel of mended wings—wounded bird and recuperative bounce rolled into one. It even seemed I saw a ball hit the sidewalk as he sang, a ball of crumpled wings not unlike a balled-up sheet of paper which hit but, unlike paper, bounced ahead of us as we walked.

I now had a feel for the piece I hadn't had before, which is the reason for the tape I'm enclosing. It made a difference you'll be able to hear on the two takes of "Drennethology" we recorded during rehearsals—the first three days ago, the second yesterday. My sesame glimpse of injured wing and repercussive bounce's quantum knot brought something to my solo yesterday I won't risk putting into words. As you can hear, it wasn't there two days before.

You're probably wondering how Drennette's reacting to Penguin's attention. Well, she seems to be flattered but, while not put off, a bit cool. She certainly can't be accused of encouraging him. I can't help being afraid he's letting himself in for a big blow. Lambert, Aunt Nancy and Djamilaa feel the same. Djamilaa told me that Aunt Nancy told her Drennette talks about her breakup with Rick a lot, that she doesn't seem to've gotten over it yet, that the last thing she'd want is to get involved with someone again. I hope Penguin doesn't find out the hard way her post-expectancy's for real.

Her response to "Drennethology"? She told Penguin it made her happy he named the piece for her, that it really made her feel welcome in the band, but other than that her approach was businesslike. She changed the rhythm he suggested to something more difficult, more complex, polyrhythmic. “It’s about splitting yourself in two,” she said. As you can hear, that’s what she does.

Sincerely,
N.

22.I.82

Dear Angel of Dust,

Enclosed you'll find a new after-the-fact lecture/libretto. I'm surprised it actually got written since what brought it about appeared to call my antithetical opera into question, made me wonder if I wasn't reinventing the wheel. What brought it about was my going to hear Betty Carter at the Parisian Room the other night. I'd been sitting around somewhat at loose ends, not really into anything and a bit on edge, when I remembered she was in town. I've loved her music for years but never heard her in person, so I decided I'd go over and catch the last set.

What I heard and saw blew me away. I should underline "saw," I suppose, for the facial teasing she applies to a song, especially the ballads, was something I'd heard about but still wasn't quite prepared for the impact of. That combination breathless/easy-as-breathing delivery of hers had long gotten to me on records, a mixed impression of effortlessness and extremity which gives it the sound of an extended sigh, an extended whisper. An extended, endlessly calibrated sigh or whisper I should quickly add, as well as that extremity here gets implied by exactly the act of prolongation. She parcels out and extends each breath as though it might otherwise, that is, be her last. The discrepant play of her precise, near parsimonious delivery against the facial extravagance it's accompanied by is something, however, one doesn't get on records. One of the interesting things is that discrepant play is also ratifying play, insofar as facial extravagance is facial extremity, an extremity every bit as telling as the eking out of sound it runs parallel with. That discrepant/ratifying play, the longer I sat watching and listening, put me in mind of the concept of apt operatic incongruity I tried to discuss in an earlier letter.

It also put me in mind of ventriloquism, for every now and then she achieved a throwing or a displacement of her voice, though with means which radically diverge from the conventionally ventriloquistic. What she did might be called metathetic ventriloquism because of the interchange between vocal and facial roles it rested on. I was struck by her inversion of conventional ventriloquism's motionless lips and expressionless face, by the way the wealth of labial gesture and facial projection she resorted to metathetically altered the ventriloquial formula. Reticent ventriloquial ("silent") face plus projected voice became reticent voice plus projected ("vocal") face:

$$rf + pv \rightarrow rv + pf$$

The discrepant play between facial wealth and vocal reticence, gesture and voice, opened an abyss large enough at times to efface the latter's source. Her voice, that is, on occasion seemed not to be coming from her—an elusiveness of source which created an illusion of sourcelessness. It was eerie.

The next day, talking about it at rehearsal, I tried to describe it by saying that her face had evoked a "voice" one synaesthetically "saw," a "voice" which was not the voice one in fact heard. That spectral, silent "voice," I went on, upstaged every now and then her actual, audible voice and in so doing cultivated a furtiveness of source, a synaesthetic, ventriloquial abyss whose transparency "sang," a synaesthetic, ventriloquial "mask." Lambert took to the phrase "furtiveness of source" and spoke up to that effect, going on to insist on this as what he termed "a utopian foretaste of sourcelessness." That foretaste, he allowed however, was haunted by contested claims to causation, contentious albeit ambiguous historical debris. This, he argued, was where its owning up to furtiveness came in, in regard both to its own subterfuge and to a history of would-be sources which were really subversions, a history it proposed an "unsourced" exit from. He went on to bring up, as an example of historical debris, the minstrel show, making much of what he called "minstrel preemption," the preemption of the black face and voice by derogatory distortions passed off as likenesses. He wondered whether this hadn't instilled in its victims a mistrust of all claims to likeness, whether what one saw in Betty Carter's discrepant/ratifying play might not be, if I understood him correctly, a case in point of a consequent poetics built on suspicion. "Facial extravagance," he said, "revels in distortion to show that it's wise to distortion, immune to presumed equivalence." We broke out laughing when Aunt Nancy put in, "Yeah, like they used to tell us in the church choir: 'You can't sing with a pretty mouth.'"

We went around on this for a while. Afterward, even though the night before I'd ended up feeling there wasn't much point in pursuing my opera, that what I was after Betty Carter had already done, I began to be put upon by an urge to write which resulted in the lecture/libretto I'm enclosing ("after-the-fact," again, to admit that what it does had already been done). Something Lambert said at rehearsal stayed with me: "To steal a person's face as if it were a matter of saving face sets the stage for an aesthetic lynching."

Yours,
N.

AX ME NOW

or, The Creaking of the Word: After-the-Fact Lecture/Libretto (Lambert Version)

Jarred Bottle tottered at bunk's edge, unable to tell whether or not he was dreaming. No longer sure he'd in fact woken up, he pinched himself, only to find himself numb. He felt nothing. Where he was and how he'd gotten there he couldn't say, though the sense that he was there to make a speech wouldn't let him rest. His mind wandered, tugged here and there by an extensibility coincident with feelings he'd have given his right arm to've been able to cut loose—for one, that of being as tall as a redwood tree.

All but overcome by vertigo, he looked down at the bunk at whose edge he stood, a narrow, thin, pitiful affair which appeared to be a world apart, a world away. Was he, he wondered while looking down from mythic height, the tree itself or simply hung from the tree? The question passed almost as soon as it arose, for Jarred Bottle couldn't help noticing—also, it appeared, a world apart, a world away—the scrap of paper he held in his right hand. Raising it too to mythic height, crossing what appeared to be the space between worlds, he brought the scrap of paper up to where he could read what was written on it, the words "Namesake Epigraph" beneath which was a passage in quotes:

When *a* and *b* occurred together as parts of the same total

> object, without being discriminated, the occurrence of one of these, *a*, in a new combination *ax*, favors the discrimination of *a*, *b* and *x* from one another. Elements are withdrawn from their usual settings and combined with one another in a totally unique configuration, the monster. Monsters startle neophytes into thinking about objects, persons, relationships, and features of their environment they have hitherto taken for granted.

Jarred Bottle also couldn't help noticing that the scrap of paper had been pinned to his hand. A pin stuck thru the flesh at the base of his middle finger held it in place. Seeing this, he let out a sigh, thankful that he found himself numb. He also noticed, stamped at the bottom of the scrap of paper, the words "Exhibit B." It now began to come back to him. He was in jail.

Still, he found himself fuzzy, not at all clear as to whether or not he was awake, nowhere near certain what had brought him there. Was it something he had said or intended to say, as the evidential use the scrap of paper was apparently to be put to led one to believe? His thoughts drifted, pushed and put upon by memories and impressions he had a hard time sorting out. He vaguely, one moment, recalled a multicolored snake, only to have its place taken, a moment later, by the red, yellow and green lights of a traffic signal. These in turn, a moment later, became one and the same: a red, yellow and green snake suspended in the air above the intersection. "The Serpent's loose again," he could've sworn he heard someone say. Immediately, though, he shook off the conjunctive image (apocalyptic stoplight, apocalyptic snake). He looked at Exhibit B again. No doubt about it. The handwriting was his.

He reread the passage in quotes. Therein lay the key, he began to be convinced, even though he didn't agree with its tendentious drift. That the monster, rather than arousing thought, might occasion a further phase of mystification seemed a possibility eminently worth considering—so obvious, perhaps, as to go without saying, but that was exactly the danger, the very risk he was there to guard against.

That it emphatically not go without saying, he began to remember, was the point of the speech he was there to make. Neither the Serpent nor the monster was loose but had instead been co-opted by a circuit of promptings and prohibitions. This was the meaning of the poem he now recalled intending to recite at the end of his performance:

Red light, green
light. Yellow
in-between light.

He could already hear the applause.

Indeed, he'd have applauded himself had he not, moving to do so, noticed a scrap of paper pinned to his left hand. Raising it to mythic height so as to read what was written on it, he saw that it too, like the one pinned to his right hand, bore the words "Namesake Epigraph" followed by a quote. He was intrigued by what he read. He stood accused, or so he felt, by the quote's implied critique of having something to say:

> There's nothing like learning to play. I'm not a Master yet, but that's what I'm after—to be able to play whatever I hear at any time. Then I won't have anything to say at all; all I'll be able to do is play. I would like to get everything down that small, where that's all I do, where I become my instrument and my instrument becomes me. I'd like to walk around the streets looking like a trumpet.

Here too the handwriting was his. Stamped at the bottom were the words "Exhibit A."

Exhibit A's announced antiphonal swing away from say toward play made him totter all the more. He swayed from side to side. A big tree about to fall was what he felt like—a big tree, he thought (again glancing at Exhibit B), bit into and brought down by *ax*. Brought to the brink of bearing witness against himself, he wavered, recalling that he was possibly there to sing. Did song imply a forfeiture of speech or was it speech's fulfillment? This he couldn't help wondering. He was bothered by Exhibit A's insinuation that to play was to default on say. He was bothered but fighting back. Could it be that to play was to say by default?

Were he a horn, he reflected, thinking back to Exhibit A, a straight one was the kind he'd be. A flute, a clarinet, an uncurved soprano. What was it, though, that could only be said by default? With him it seemed to come down to *If I fall I fall unbending*, the antithetic play between descent and unbent constituting the default by way of which it was said. He was well aware that in the case of the kinds of horn he wanted to be a lower pitch required curvature. A bass flute was bent, as was a bass clarinet and so forth. Indeed, it seemed that the lower one went the more bent the horn was, especially among the saxophones. He also couldn't help knowing that the very fact of having recourse to a horn, no matter how straight, bespoke a bend in and of itself, a turning away from straightforward say.

Was it also true, he went on to wonder, that say was at best only figuratively straight, a bent, oblique version of do? Were default and detour so rolled into one as to make say, regarding do, the same as play? The truth was he was fed up with both. Obviously play echoed say and was echoed in turn but "So what?" was on the tip of his tongue. He held it back, all but bit his tongue, recalling now that "So what?" was what had landed him in jail. Bit by bit it began to come back to him. "So what?" was what he had said when the cop said, "You're sitting at a green light."

Instead of "So what?," then, he muttered, "So much talk of talk these days." It was true, he inwardly confessed, that say blatantly echoed play and vice versa, but the sense of operatic entrapment to which this led seemed distant, vague, remote, a stage he'd long ago gotten over, long since outgrown. The theoretically-inclined, he realized, would argue that being held for questioning wasn't the same as being invited to give a speech. Those who were less inclined to split hairs, however, knew that under the circumstances to speak and to sing were the same. This was what being in jail was about.

Another bit of the picture now fell into place as "being held for questioning" reminded Jarred Bottle of the song he was there to sing, "Ax Me Now," a variation on one of Monk's tunes, "Ask Me Now." "Ax," anyone could see, was both a blackening and a loosening of the Serpent, the convergence of promptings and prohibitions translated into an inkling of polychromatic permission.

What had attracted him to "Ask Me Now" were its lullabylike inflections. Conciliation compounded with something which bordered on complaint was also partly what he heard, its air one of reasoning resorted to under prolonged emotional duress. The tune's mixing of resolve with resignation (a rare mix in which weariness, the brink of collapse it adroitly wooed, proposed an otherwise inconceivable out) seemed to insist on the persistence of camouflage at the very heart of arbitrated composure, a catch in the breath of arbitrated calm. Charlie Rouse's solo on the 1959 recording had brought exactly this quality of put-upon, threadbare, endlessly abiding patience to the fore, an eloquently tensile willingness to reason in the face of inauspicious odds. The lullabylike inflections were thus not without a sardonic theme and thrust: *world-as-nursery*. It was this undertone, this intimation of stunted growth, "Ax Me Now" would accent all the more—accent in order to alter, he now reminded and reassured himself.

Jarred Bottle swayed from side to side as the opening strains of "Ask Me Now," recollected, rocked him as in a cradle. Thad Jones's cornet made him think of Exhibit A, whose valorization of introverted brass was now entwined with the tune's Ellingtonian suggestion of bright city lights in some way muted so as to've become reflective. The problematics of brass as a medium of reflection (the unlikeliness of so extrovert an instrument turning inward) made him all the more receptive to the traumatization which had brought it about. This too he would underscore in "Ax Me Now," factored into which an accent would fall on streetwise awakenings amid the glare and garish allure of big-city nightlife. This too was what being in jail was about—a Babylonian captivity whereby the shifting terms of incarceration (brazen cage, brazen camouflage) could be chanted down. Brazen cage (urban cage) was brazen cradle (urbane camouflage) and depended mainly on how deep in one's cheek one's tongue was.

Brazen cradle (blatant lull, blatant lure, urbane composure) laid stress on Monk's predilection for the "wrong" note which turns out "right." The trick, though, would be to steer clear of sloganistic investments in black-phonological "ax" and, indeed, in black-malapropistic practice more widely considered. The temptation was to hear a categorically subversive "edge" written into such practice, but a simplistic, knee-jerk inversion of minstrel derogation, he reminded himself, wasn't what was meant by polychromatic permission.

Charlie Rouse's tenor came back into it now, its reserved, meditative entrance built on a phrase in which it appeared he fingered a cut. It was a phrase by way of which he kept in touch with brazen injury, gently probed while gently prodding axiologic blood. Evidently immune to cauterization, brazen cut bled variations on "edge" which went so far as to endorse or seem to endorse categorical victim. It was here that camouflage came in, rescuing blood by equating "ax" with sacrificial fluency, cauterization with cathartic blush.

Jarred Bottle, as he swayed from side to side, reminded himself that if he fell he'd fall unbending, reflecting for an ever so fleeting instant on the early reggae anthem "Small Axe." In his mind, he now recognized, Marley and Monk had become so closely associated as to conflate the former's black-millenarian "edge" with the latter's black-malapropistic "patience" (the conviction that time would tell and that "wrong" would turn out "right"). To what extent was to fall unbending to mix resolve with resignation? Just as practice implied patience, "Ax Me Now" implied redwood height, operatic height. The question wasn't whether or not to fall but how to fall.

Jarred Bottle's bunk took on a monastic look as he closed his eyes and steeled himself against the impending blow to the back of his neck—a blow which, however, failed to materialize. Thus the curtain fell on Act I and immediately rose on Act II: same set, same cell, same bunk at whose edge he tottered looking down from operatic height. The one difference was that projected onto the wall of the cell one now saw newsreel footage of Mussolini's invasion of Abyssinia, Italy's entrance into, as it were, the Ethiopian theater. The source of the implied connections among redwood height, operatic artifice, metathetic "ax" and millenarian "edge" came to light when Jarred Bottle raised his hand to touch the back of his neck. Instead of blood what he found there was a scrap of paper stuck on with a wad of chewing gum. Removing it and bringing it around to where he could see it, he saw that it, like the other two, bore an inscription, the words "Minstrel Entry" under which was a passage in quotes, a passage having apparently to do with a boat ride:

> When we got out a little piece from the shore, de man axed me if I knowed anyting about frenologism. I told him no. Ah, says he, den one quarter of your life's gone. Finally he says, does you know anyting about grammar. I told him no. Ah, says he, den one half ob you life am gone. He axed if I knowed anyting about dickshionary. I told him no and he say tree quarters of your life is gone. We hit a rock and den I axed him if he knowed how to swim. He said no. Den, says I, de whole four quarters of your life am gone.

Again the handwriting was his. The word "tree" had been circled in red. Stamped at the bottom were the words "Exhibit C."

Again Jarred Bottle saw that what he was was what he stood accused of—an atavistic note-bearing bottle set adrift by black-malapropistic shipwreck, black-metathetic survival. The mixed-metaphorical conjunction of bottle with tree more than bore this out. Its recruit of raw suggestibility in the service of a vaccinal dispatch of minstrel "blood" coincided with Kongo-based bottle tree traditions. Thus again he had cause to wonder was he a tree or simply hung from a tree. "Ax Me Now's" catechistic reply was to pose in terms of black-metathetic one-upmanship (ship-inside-a-bottle, bottle-hung-from-a-branch) the answer written wittingly or not into minstrel vengeance, the boat dredged up out of minstrel debris. That the soul was a boat or that it rode in a boat was ancient knowledge.

"Ax Me Now" simultaneously laid stress on Exhibit C's ancestral connection to stories of Shine aboard the Titanic. A fugitive ray of sun, cell notwithstanding, momentarily flashed as it ricocheted off the back of Jarred Bottle's neck, an alchemization of minstrel derision which might have also been the gleam of an axe's blade struck by light. This was the visual counterpart of the composition's recourse to a brighter tempo, its not so subtle way of underscoring flashiness, show, shine. Derisive spit, it wanted to say, inadvertently allied itself with alchemizing polish. Thus it was that "Shine swam on."

The composition, though, sped up only to slow back down. The time for the speech he was there to make was fast approaching, Jarred Bottle knew. He heard Lambert's tenor emerge from the chorus in back of him. It came on with an idiosyncratic rhythmic wiliness and wont which was ever so exactingly "off"—a pointed instance of "malapropistic" precision. Listeners who had heard Billy Harper's croaking, hiccuping solo on "Cry of Hunger" with Gil Evans's band had already heard something akin to the way Lambert started off. Had they also heard Wayne Shorter's solo on "Kryptonite" they'd already heard as well something of which what he went on to play was obliquely reminiscent. This isn't to say that the solo was imitative or slavishly derived but, its original, eccentric accent and slant notwithstanding, there was something familiar about it, an amended fold of predecessor voices whose names he put on the tip of one's tongue yet kept out of reach. "Cry of Hunger" and "Kryptonite" came close but turned out to've been no more than straws one grabbed after.

Lambert stayed in the horn's low register and took what could be called a topologic approach. He played as though speaking under his breath, a hovering, muted buzz which all but outright implicated minstrel eugenics in hegemonic blood. That hemorrhage and hegemony were one established the ground in relation to which each reconnoitering run extrapolated itself. His low-to-the-ground regard for curvature and contour seemed a rebuke to Jarred Bottle's resolve to fall unbending. Jarred Bottle, however, knew that this was no more than a heuristic gesture needed to give his impending lecture operatic relief. Lambert spoke for a literalizing spirit of place whereby confinement bore the brunt of necessary cramp, cramp the brunt of triggerless bend.

Was Lambert's low-to-the-ground reconnaissance run fall as well as flight? Was "ax" what had landed him there? Jarred Bottle gave

Lambert's run relief in turn, beginning his lecture on a questioning note. These two questions, it turned out, were the last coherent utterances he would make in the course of his speech. From that point on he spoke a mix comprised almost wholly of made-up words.

Any speaker worth his or her pocomaniacal salt, it seemed to go without saying, "tore" the language or, as he lately preferred to put it, chopped it up. Jarred Bottle's lecture, that is, took him back to his adopted boyhood in Jamaica. Thus the projection of Italy's invasion of Ethiopia. One of his most vivid and strongest boyhood recollections was the way the news of it had fired people up in Kingston. Likenings of it to the crucifixion of Christ by "the said same Romans" rolled off almost every tongue. Lambert's low-to-the-ground inspection of hostile terrain, his pentecostal run, likewise insisted on prophetic fulfillment, the eventual triumph of Ethiopia, small axe to Mussolini's tall tree. It was this air of providential "patience" which gave Jarred Bottle's pocomaniacal rant operatic relief. It was all the more fitting that it forecast the fall of opera's birthplace, a point the Program Notes made mention of a number of times.*

Act II, then, turned out to be brief, Act III even briefer. At the very moment Jarred Bottle abandoned conventional speech the curtain, which, it was impossible not to see, had been cut to shreds, came down and then rose again—rose not at once but, still, only a moment or so later. (It was clear one was to take that moment to register the fact of its being in shreds.) Act III was briefer than it would otherwise have been had Jarred Bottle not forgotten most of the words to an obscure Rastafarian prayer he now chose to put in place of "Red light, green / light . . . ," chose now to end his performance with.

It was a prayer contemporaneous with the Fascist assault on Abyssinia. Its opening lines Jarred Bottle had no trouble reciting:

---

* The Notes also made reference to what they termed "a case in point of operatic support of minstrel eugenics," the opera *Il deserto tentato* ("The Conquest of the Desert") composed by Alfredo Casella in 1937 to celebrate the invasion. Casella called it a "poetic exaltation of the civilizing mission of a great nation."

To Allah alpha to matta edoo koo
to ganzasngoo roo
Manage anne jabo novy moosoo
hel at ataga gerier
Anne nunia amil nunia gandec annxe
etoza gandec annxe nokeye
Anne etobeph anne enophele anne
yaran anne mantour

At this point, though, his memory failed him. Though the prayer's concluding lines were on the tip of his tongue the numerous lines in-between escaped him. He couldn't, to save his life, recall them. Thinking quickly, missing only a beat, he proceeded to fake it, going on to recite the prayer's concluding lines as though that were, in fact, the way it went, as though the forgotten in-between lines didn't exist:

Halin cebon minz coorooding yan
go annedocoos
Am sawsback anne watie anne
jurah anne apaz
To Allah

Jarred Bottle overstated the concluding "ah," opening his mouth as wide as it would go, a gesture, one reviewer pointed out, worthy of Billy Kersands, the nineteenth-century minstrel known for his "copiousness of mouth."* He stood in the spotlight holding his open-mouth pose as the "ah" decreased in volume, an antithetic play between fade and finish (acoustic subsidence vs. visual gloss) whose latter term recalled the earlier allusion to Shine, its invocation of alchemizing polish.

Jarred Bottle continued to hold his pose even after the "ah" had

* The reviewer informed readers that Kersands's act included filling his mouth with billiard balls and that W. C. Handy recalled an occasion on which he put a cup and saucer inside it.

concluded, standing with his mouth wide open though no sound came out, the accompanying instrumental chorus again coming to the fore, Lambert's tenor the lead voice. They restated "Ax Me Now's" head and after stressing its derivation from "Ask Me Now" by quoting from Charlie Rouse's solo Lambert took brazen cage and brazen camouflage a step further, weaving Grachan Moncur's "Frankenstein" in. The emphasis had obviously returned to "ax" as monster, an acoustic ratification of Jarred Bottle's minstrel artifice, the operatic-malapropistic masquerade he accentuated by standing centerstage with his mouth wide open.

The "Frankenstein" note was the one on which Lambert chose to end. Jarred Bottle, silence notwithstanding, continued to hold his open-mouth pose. The audience came to understand not only that this pose took the place of a final curtain but that this, "Ax Me Now's" finishing touch, gave it an alias. What they'd been watching, they now saw, was "Mask Me Now." No sooner was this understood than the lights went out.

28.1.82

Dear Angel of Dust,

What is it with dreams? Don't they know when they're no longer welcome? Last night I dreamt of Djeannine again. Lambert and Penguin dreamt of her too. The same dream as a few months ago, down to the smallest detail—even, in Penguin's case, the broken tooth. One would think that now that we've decided on Drennette as our drummer the Djeannine dream would leave us alone. On the contrary, it seems to've come back with a vengeance. The dream was exactly the same in every detail but everything was more salient, saltier. Everything was more intense. Djeannine, without being literally larger, loomed larger. The wafting of an imaginary musk was more pungent, more penetrant. The trombone blast was more annunciative, the hill Djeannine stood on higher, the big top bigger. Likewise, the dark blue blouse and skirt she wore were bluer, the crotch of her cotton panties more blindingly white. The mint-flavored liquid even tasted more like mint. Every aspect of the dream had gained in vibrancy, piquancy, sting. I woke up from it sweating, muscles cramping. Lambert and Penguin say they did so too. It felt a little bit like withdrawal, as if Djeannine had been an addiction we sought to kick by choosing Drennette, as if Djeannine were our collective jones.

We wondered if Aunt Nancy and Djamilaa had dreamt of Penny again. We told them about the Djeannine dream and asked but they said no. Actually, they wouldn't let it go at simply saying no. They insisted on teasing us about it, saying boys will be boys and asking when would we ever grow up, when would we outgrow our dreamgirl fixation, get out of our dreamgirl rut. We laughed it off, but them not having dreamt of Penny made our Djeannine dream's return all the more disturbing. Penguin went so far as to accuse them of lying—jokingly, granted, but a bit seriously I suspect—kidded them by saying they really had dreamt of Penny but were too afraid to admit it. To this they made no reply. They simply looked at one another, rolling their eyes.

All of this notwithstanding, I'm impressed by the dream's persistence. I find it disturbing and disconcerting but I'm also attracted to the parallactic play meted out by the reality/dream, Drennette/Djeannine gap. It makes me think of Andrew Hill, the parallactic address with which he approaches a note or a phrase, makes it sound as though one heard it from a number of points at the same time. All evening I've been listening to the records of his I have, hearing them, thanks to the Djeannine dream's return, as if at last I'm *truly* hearing them, hearing them *fully* for the first time. I like the array of adjacent threads he keeps active when he solos, his knack for making loose ends count. One hears a staggered, parallactic disbursement given play to propose an endlessly reinvented horizon. The abstruse, post-expectant tangentiality this lets loose applies the aptest homeopathy I can think of to the way the Djeannine dream's return makes me feel.

How much does this quality in Andrew's music have to do with the modified drummer's stool he sits on when he plays? Critics have written about the percussive aspect of his playing but I haven't read anything which deals with this. I was struck the one time I saw him in person by the disequilibrium—well, maybe not that so much as a precarious, endlessly adjusted equilibrium—the stool appeared to be meant to maintain. Its one fulcrumlike leg isn't only bent toward the piano but it also moves as he plays. It's as if he deliberately sought to destabilize himself. Would it be going too far to say that the stool, moving as he plays, literally keeps him on the edge of his seat, much the way the music does a listener?

Thanks, while I'm at it, for your letter. I'm flattered you think we're ready to make a record, even more by your offer to write the liner notes. I can't say we hadn't already been giving it some thought, but for now it remains wait and see. Most likely we'd have to put it out ourselves and at the moment our money situation's not that good. Anyway, all in due time as they say.

Yours,
N.

PS: Henry Threadgill has a seven-piece band he calls a sextet. He uses two drummers but he counts them as one. I'm wondering if Djeannine and Drennette might not likewise be two halves of a whole, two sides of an otherwise unavailable coin the Penny dream was meant to apprise us of.

10.11.82

Dear Angel of Dust,

I've been hit by a new round of shattered cowrie shell attacks—a round of attacks whose new wrinkle is that their having to do with vision (the shells' eyelike look when whole) seems now to have to do with putting on a lid. The shells have been replaced by bottle caps. The caps line my forehead, held on by a wire which passes thru the holes punched in them but left with enough play to be able to buzz, vibrate in sympathy with the music piped into my head—not Ornette's "Embraceable You" but Lightnin' Hopkins's "Bottle Up and Go." (Lightnin', you may know, died the week before last.) A veritable hive of bottle cap buzzings, my head resonates like a calabash gourd on an mbira. The bottle caps' raspy disbursements make for a cross-accentual "screen," the acoustic rough-equivalent of burlap.

The first attack occurred during the gig we just got back from, a three-night stint at a club called Earl's up north in Albany. It was brought on in part by the news that Monk had suffered a cerebral hemorrhage and was in a coma, which we heard on the local jazz station KJAZ. They were playing a lot of Monk's music, calling it "Monk Watch"—what amounted to a before-the-fact wake. "My God," Penguin muttered, shaking his head, "three years ago Mingus, Marley last May, now Monk." I shook mine as well, saying something about Lightnin' having died the week before. It was then I began to hear "Bottle Up and Go," a faint strain factored into which the play between loose fit and tight fit, bottle cap and coffin lid, conjugated itself at an even fainter, whisperlike remove. It wasn't until later, though, that it hit with full force.

It was Saturday afternoon when we heard the news. We were in Richmond at my cousin Kenny's. He plays baritone mainly, but also alto, soprano and flute, and there'd been talk of him sitting in with us at Earl's. I think it was he who eventually suggested we get something together for the set that night, put together some sort of tribute to Monk. We ended up deciding not to leave it at just Monk but to include the other three who'd come up as well, Mingus, Marley and Lightnin'. We settled on a medley we'd announce under the collective title "Three M's and an H," a medley which would start off with Monk's (yes, you guessed it) "Ask Me Now." From there we'd move on to Marley's "No Woman, No Cry," then to Lambert, *a cappella*, doing "Bottle Up and Go" on harmonica. We'd wrap it up with Mingus's "Free Cell Block F, 'tis Nazi USA." This last we decided to preface with all of us reading in unison the first paragraph of Ellison's novel *Invisible Man*—this to announce an equation of *Nazi* with *not see*.

We didn't have much in the way of rehearsal time but the tunes were all ones we knew so it didn't take much. A quick run-thru during the sound check at the club that evening did it. We deliberately didn't put a lot of polish on it, choosing instead to go after the ragged momentariness the occasion, we felt, required. This we not only went after but largely got. We played the medley during the second set, in the course of which I was hit by the shattered cowrie shell attack, the shattered-cowrie-shell-become-bottle-cap attack.

The medley got off to a good start with Kenny sitting in on alto and doing the soloing on "Ask Me Now." He gave it a sensitive, extended reading which parlayed its lullabylike inflections into inklings and outright glimpses of tensile endurance. This he did largely by way of a tremolo on the spoons to which he resorted every now and then, an abrupt, bothered, headstrong helium-inhalation which made light of all odds or obstruction. The at once wide-eyed, squinting stress on glimpses looked ahead to the Mingus piece, a foreshadowing tack which was lost on none of us. A blue, bruised adumbration of damage done, it was a reading whose wincing regard spoke of loss and resilience. It mourned and put its mourning to rest in the same breath. It etched into its dormant features a see-thru function, the ascendancy of technical-ecstatic squint.

Ever so smoothly, "Ask Me Now" segued into "No Woman, No Cry," another lullaby of sorts. Djamilaa's harmonium gave it a churchical, Eastern feeling, evoked a church or a sacred cave in which it seemed we were gathered. Aunt Nancy had the lead voice on trumpet. She not only saw Kenny's technical-ecstatic squint but raised him a cried-out eye. She let each run break down into a sputter à la Lester Bowie, an extravagant, blubbering collapse whose extravagance mocked itself. Aunt Nancy played sacred clown in the sacred cave it seemed we were in. With each exorbitant, blubbering breakdown more and more people in the audience laughed. Penguin and Lambert on sopraninos and Kenny and I on sopranos comprised a high-pitched, complicit chorus whose giddy insistences complied with Kenny's earlier helium hits. We endorsed and punctuated Aunt Nancy's tragicomic lead with giggly rushes which, a friend who was in the audience told us later, grew possessed of an infectious cartoon quality. We came on—Penguin, Lambert, Kenny and I—like a group of hyperactive chipmunks. What with Aunt Nancy's "quackical" sputter it amounted to a cartoon script and score rolled into one, Donald Duck backed up by Alvin and the Chipmunks.

It was an odd, unexpected treatment of Marley's tune. It caught most of the audience off guard. Chipmunk chatter (chipmunk ecstasy) caught Aunt Nancy a bit off guard as well, though she more than held her own in the fray. Her collapses into "quackical" pathos notwithstanding, she was never long out of touch with the heartfelt resolve and reassurance of the line "Everything's gonna be alright." However much Penguin, Lambert, Kenny and I threatened to take such resolve and reassurance to absurd, overstated heights, she resisted any impulse to follow. Chipmunk sublimity upped the ante on cried-out extravagance but Aunt Nancy had clearly given some thought to these matters, clearly had ideas of her own. More and more she steered a course away from exorbitant collapse as well as away from chipmunk exuberance.

Eventually Aunt Nancy indicated we should back off. We brought "No Woman, No Cry" to a close with a cadenza out of which she emerged with only drum and harmonium accompaniment. She blew nothing but seriously now, a short coda in which when she sputtered she did so poignantly, no longer parodic. She put one in mind of Bill Dixon, so harassed and heartfelt was the winded urgency of her approach, fury so insistently the "note" she resorted to. The dead do live again she implied with an unpitched run of wind which flew like a bat thru the sacred cave. This run she let the piece go out on. Lambert put his harmonica to his mouth, gave the run's echo time to fade and took up from there. The stage lights went down, leaving only a spotlight fixed on him. Sacred cave became deserted crossroads.

So as not to clash with the lullabylike inflections of what had gone before, Lambert gave "Bottle Up and Go" a more laidback reading than usual. He took it slow, gave it a drawn-out feel, made it almost dirgelike. It could've been taps he was playing the way he started out, what with the stage lights going down and all. He gave it a mournful, plaintive sound which spoke of ultimate lights-out, ultimate sleep, reminded us of Lightnin's death. He blew for all he was worth and more, taking deep, gut-swelling inhalations as though breath were both carriage and cure, as though he sought to resuscitate the dead. It was some of the most moving harp we'd ever heard Lambert play. He even threw in a Dixonian touch of his own, interpolating, à la Mingus, Willie Dixon's "I Want You to Love Me" into "Bottle Up and Go," implicitly stressing the rhyme between the latter's title line and the former's "love your baby slow." He thus recalled Aunt Nancy's coda while obliquely anticipating the Mingus piece. Heartfelt for sure but also exquisitely heady stuff, it went to my head. It was here that the shattered-cowrie-shell-become-bottle-cap attack began to come on.

I immediately noticed the impacted feeling in my forehead to be of a more integral and substantive, less brokenly symbolic sort. The cowrie shells had not only become bottle caps, I noticed, but the bottle caps were unbroken, whole. I was surprised, even a little bit shocked, but, true to my new bottle cap aplomb, took it in stride. I began to hear "Bottle Up and Go" not only coming from Lambert's harmonica but also Lightnin's version piped into my head. The bottle caps buzzed in sympathy with both, "fuzzing" or "dirtying" the sound to such an extent I could've sworn the line Lightnin' sang was "Gotta bottle up a ghost." I immediately thought of Jarred Bottle and even murmured the name under my breath, but the memory of Aunt Nancy's bat-winged run of wind whispered, "Djbot Baghostus," correcting me it seemed. I now knew for sure I'd been hit.

Lambert brought his *a cappella* section to a close and the stage lights came back up. It was now time for the unison reading from *Invisible Man*. Though my head was a corrected cave in which Jarred Bottle had taken a new name, a scarred, unsacred cave in which Aunt Nancy's run of wind still flew, I somehow was able to hold myself together—bottle cap aplomb notwithstanding, barely able. We read the Ellison passage, which only two or three people in the audience seemed to recognize. We then leapt into "Free Cell Block F . . . ," the piece Mingus gave its title after reading an *Ebony* article on southern prisons. It's a piece whose uptown flair and good feeling seem at odds with its political prognosis, a time-lapse equation linking before-the-fact tune with after-the-fact title or intent. The post-equivalence aligning before-the-fact elation with titular afterthought or intent gets made more emphatic by the tune's excursions into 5/4. Perhaps it was this alignment I couldn't quite see. Perhaps it was this which woke me up to the astigmatic strain I now saw to be endemic to the nominal politics the piece pursues. Perhaps the *Nazi/not see* homophony ricocheted from wall to wall with too much force and too little correction within the recesses of the bottle cap cave. Perhaps the ascendancy of technical-ecstatic squint to which Kenny had alluded was neither an inverse nor a yielding function so much as a philosophic advocacy of "off-the-wall" inflection. Perhaps it was this which triggered the interception of chimerical wind by chimerical wall inside my head. Whatever it was, I knew I was in trouble after only a few bars.

It all, it seemed, got harder all at once—harder to hold together, harder not to want to, harder to put inside a single frame. The memory of Aunt Nancy's run went on whispering. The air was a delicate fabric her Dixonian tag had made run like a piece of silk. An elated sound that bordered on fanfare, Mingus's piece was a lit-up cave concentric with the one my head had become, a metallic shell whose putative utopia bat-winged wind only made more remote. A bit more metallic with Kenny sitting in, our rendition had a top-heaviness to it Drennette worked overtime keeping afloat. To me it confirmed and gave added conviction to the bottle caps' cowrie shell conceit, the illusion of sewn lids made more durable, the propped-up incumbency of astigmatic squint.

Penguin soloed first and I followed—him on alto, me on tenor. He took a preacherly tack which made the most of the possibilities for chastisement the equation of *Nazi* with *not see* opened up. Refusing to see, as did looking the other way, came under fire. Tending less toward rhapsody than rant, he put uptown flair and good feeling aside. He harangued and exhorted and even opted at points for a screw-loose, loquacious plea for open eyes, a return to Kenny's wide-eyed squint. It was Penguin to the limit—a bittersweet, biting sound à la Jimmy Lyons without Jimmy's trepidatious phrasing. Penguin went for the big, mouthfilling phrase, straightahead but syntactically loose enough to point to particulars where the need arose. The Greensboro killings came up. The Atlanta child murders came up. The lynching last March in Alabama came up, as did a number of other such "incidents" people choose not, Penguin pointed out, to see for what they are.

The audience appeared to be both chastened and charged up by Penguin's solo. Many sat with their heads bowed, eyes fixed on the floor, nodding every now and then in agreement—some in sad, some in grudging, some in gratified agreement. Others were more vocal in their response, a few shouting out, "Right on," another few, "Amen," another few, "Tell it like it is." Church and political rally rolled into one, Penguin's preacherly tack more than paid off—so much so it had me wondering what if any stone he'd left unturned, what if any ground he hadn't covered, at a loss where to go in my solo.

Penguin ended his solo and there was a long, loud round of applause. Still at a loss, my only chance, I saw, was to somehow predicate the very predicament I was in, to somehow make depletion a virtue, to blow as though beginning from scratch. What came out of the horn recalled Frank Lowe somewhat, a bluesy, gutbucket croak of a sound I devoted to a single note. I began by playing the same note, C, over and over again, a back-to-basics move or approach by way of which I underscored my start from scratch. I jumped octaves and varied placement and duration but the only note I played was C. I played it long, I played it short, I played it staccato, I played it spaced, I played it soft, I played it loud. C was my letter to the world.

The world's reply was at first a cool one, almost no reply at all. The audience looked on as if perplexed, not knowing what to make of so stark a contrast to what had gone before. The cooler, more noncommittal their response, though, the more insistent I became, the more "scratchical" my tack, as though C were something caught in my throat. "Scratchical" C grew more and more gruff, more and more abrasive. Still, I kept at it. My mind was made up I'd play nothing but C until the audience responded, showed some sign of catching on. It took a while but finally I saw a few people nod their heads—nod as if to say, "Yeah, I hear you." These few nods proved contagious, or so it seemed, for more and more people began nodding their heads. In no time at all everyone in the club was doing so. A few even yelled out things like "Yeah, break it down" and "That's it, you got it." It was only then that I let go of my "scratchical" fixation, only then that I dared play anything but C, dared acknowledge not-C.

I now played a few other notes. I now extended my insistence on C into a "scratchical" dialectic between it and not-C. Which one would win out I rhetorically asked by way of recourse to a tremolo which "tested" each note. It was then that the audience did something which completely took me by surprise. As if on cue, they each took out a pair of glasses and put them on. They were 3D glasses, the kind made for watching 3D movies. They took them out of bags, they took them out of pocketbooks, they took them out of pockets. Those already wearing glasses took them off to put the 3D glasses on. Almost before I could blink everyone sat bespectacled, staring up at the stage as though "Free Cell Block F . . ." were a 3D movie. I wasn't sure what to make of it. Had they seen my C and raised me a D? What did D mean were that in fact the case? Was 3D the dialectic itself? These and other questions crowded my head.

What I did know, what I couldn't help noticing, was that as soon as they put on the glasses the bottle caps on my forehead gained greater contour. Whereas before they'd been a bit flat, a bit faint, as though they were only a rough draft of themselves, they were now much more sharply defined, were now given greater relief. They were now much more pronounced, more protuberant. (I took a hand off the horn to touch my forehead.) They've been that way ever since.

Yours,
N.

13.11.82

Dear Angel of Dust,

Thank you for your letter. I'm touched by your concern. The buzzing bottle cap attacks have now let up I'm glad to say, but if it's not one thing it's another. They've subsided, that is, though not before rubbing off, it appears, on Penguin. He showed me a poem he wrote for Drennette the other day, a poem whose hive and honey conceit he said has to be connected to my buzzing bottle cap complaint, its mead cup motif's long pedigree notwithstanding. That the Norse poets drank from Odin's mead cup, he admitted, hadn't been lost on him, but the literal buzz which accompanied the poem, he went on to insist, could only've been a contact hit off my bottle cap "hive." The poem's a short one. I'll quote the whole thing:

DRENNETTE'S MEAD CUP

Buzzings grace
the notes inside
my head, re-
call the riff

Swarms as if
of bees about my
head swell
the air

The hum, how
the reeds would
taste on
my lips, when,

honeyheaded, heady,
as if my
tongue were
dipped in mead,

we met

As you can see, he continues to be taken with Drennette. He confided that originally in the fourth line "riff" had been "kiss" and that, "high would" player that he is notwithstanding, he was afraid that might be going too far, might seem too forward. I was quick to agree. In fact, I went on to say I didn't think it was a good idea to show the poem to Drennette, that even in its revised form it might seem he was coming on strong. Not that my saying so mattered. Once Penguin makes up his mind about something it's pretty hard to make him change it. (This is the same guy, remember, who ate three sweet potato pies on Trane's birthday a couple of years ago.) Bent on reading the poem to Drennette, he went ahead to do so, an attempt whose going awry now has him depressed.

It seems he called her on the phone last night. This he did "rather than arrange a tryst," as he put it—his one concession to my advice against coming on strong. He told her he'd found a nut on the floor after rehearsal and that he thought it might've come off of her drumset. After she said that it probably hadn't but that he should hold onto it anyway, just in case, he casually (he says) mentioned that he'd written a poem he wanted her to hear. She said go ahead and read it, which he went to do, but he didn't, as it turned out, get past the title. Instead of "Drennette's Mead Cup" he called it "Djeannine's Mead Cup," a slip he found so disconcerting he couldn't go on. Instead of reading her the poem he coughed, cleared his throat, then told her there was someone at his door, that he had to get off the phone.

Poor Penguin. You'd think he was a man who'd called his wife by his mistress's name. He says he can't bring himself to face Drennette. This afternoon he stayed away from rehearsal. He'll get over it I'm sure, though that that'll be soon we can only hope.

As ever,
N.

14.11.82

Dear Angel of Dust,

I forgot to thank you in yesterday's letter for asking about "Baghostus." What I found out because of your asking deepens its reach. I'd simply taken it to be an Osirian play on Malachi Favors's "Maghostus" (*Ba* being what the Egyptians called the soul), but your question made me give it more thought. The first thing to occur to me was a song on an album I've listened to a lot, *The Real Bahamas*. The song, "Come for Your Dinner," is addressed to someone the album notes identify as "Bynassy" (though they follow it with a parenthesized question mark): "Oh Bynassy (?) come for your dinner. . . ." I wondered if a Bahamian provenance lay beneath what I took to be Egyptian. Did "Baghostus" arise from a less obvious level within the auto-suggestive hive my head had become, a level at which, after repeated hearings, "Bynassy" had ensconced itself? The album notes explain that the song probably comes from a story, so I did some reading on Bahamian folklore. In a book called *I Could Talk Old-Story Good* I found a story in which the trickster-hero B'Anansi (also known as Nansi, Boy Nasty and Gulumbanasi) is sung to—told to come for his dinner—by his three stepdaughters. I also found this: "Some idioms and pronunciations are reserved for the folktale. The foremost example is that most commonly represented by B', but also by Ba, Be, Ber, Bioh, Bra, B'Bra, Brer, Bro, Bra, Bu, Bul and Bulla. This is clearly related to the use of 'Brer' in the Uncle Remus tales of the American South, where it is equated with 'brother.' In the Bahamas it is continually used as a prefix to a name, indicating 'brother' or friend. It seems to have a double root, English 'brother' and a hypothetical 'African' word, 'Bulla,' 'buller,' or 'bullah.'" In Bahamian tales one hears of B'Rabby, B'Book, B'Jack, B'Jenerat, B'Devil, B'Big-Gut, B'Snapper, B'Head, B'Straggle-Leg and others. No mere trick my ears played on me, what the echo of Aunt Nancy's run of wind said rings true: B'Ghostus and Baghostus both, a B'-*Ba* conjunction whose Egypto-Bahamian harmonics plumb the tie between "brother" and "soul." This I probably wouldn't have found out were it not for your question.

No improvement to report on the Penguin front. If anything, he's gotten worse. He's either left his house or simply refuses to come to the door or answer his phone. He's also put a new recording on his answering machine—no spoken message as to what number you've reached and so forth, just The Penguins' recording of "Earth Angel."

Yours,
N.

15.II.82

Dear Angel of Dust,

Still no sign of Penguin. We've repeatedly phoned him, repeatedly gone by his house. He still neither answers the phone nor comes to the door. It's too soon to worry but I can't help wondering what he's up to. I find myself dialing his number more and more often, not so much to see if he'll answer or to leave a message as to listen to the recording of "Earth Angel." Clearly it's meant to say something. Certain sides of that something are blatantly clear. He surely recorded it hoping Drennette would call. I can't help noticing, though, that, no matter how much it may be a song of praise, the tape isn't altogether ingenuous. The more I think about it the more I detect an implied quadratic rejoinder in the fact that four Penguins answer the phone. It's as if he'd upped the ante on "splitting yourself in two," seen Drennette's deuce and raised her another. That a contentious edge, no matter how subtle, infiltrates the lover's ostensible paean also must be meant to say something. Is it possible there's a courtly, coy side to Drennette's blasé, post-expectant cool? Penguin certainly seems to think so.

This, though, doesn't explain why the tape has grown on me so. I'm not sure there's an explanation or that it needs an explanation. All I know is I've increasingly felt that the tape's arch, extravagant aspect, as did the Betty Carter gig last month, offers a clue to the sort of opera I'm working toward. The apt inordinacy of Penguin's retreat (apt if only in that his crush on Drennette has been nothing if not inordinate from the start) endows the doo-wop hyperbolics of "Earth Angel" with further degrees of operatic tilt. Why is it I'm only now noticing doo-wop's grassroots reclamation of operatic extremity? Only now have I begun to see the sugared sweat of insistence to which it resorts as the exponential aria it's always been. What's more, I've been seized by the feeling that I was meant to see it, that I've been set up to see it, that Penguin (maestro absconditus and hidden Imam rolled into one) went into retreat in order to teach me this.

I've had, that is, something like the sense I had the evening of Penguin's phonological run—only here pathos met with brotherly rapport to instigate a salty-sweet shamanic serenade, soul serenade. I can't help feeling him to be a plumb line, his imagino-emotional plunge an attitudinal flight from lateral numbness. I keep feeling his retreat to be an instructive one—so much so it brought forth a new after-the-fact lecture/libretto. I'm enclosing a copy. As I wrote it I could all but feel Penguin's hand guiding mine. My bottle cap buzz having rubbed off on him, it now seemed his retreat was rubbing off on me.

Let me know what you think.

As ever,

N.

E PO PEN

or, The Creaking of the Word: After-the-Fact Lecture/Libretto (Penguin Version)

"Tell them you're not from here. Tell them your father is a wealthy man, that he sang with The Ink Spots before they made it big but that nevertheless he's a very wealthy man. Tell them that's why he named you Djbot. Spell it out for them if you have to: d as in dot, j as in jot, b-o-t as in bottle. Tell them it relates to ink, eponymous ink, namesake ink. Tell them you're not from here, even that you're not really here. Tell them it relates to ink, invisible ink. You can never make too much of it. Tell them you're a ghost." So spoke the grasshopper into Djbot Baghostus's ear.

Djbot Baghostus lay on his bunk staring up at the ceiling, stiff, unbending. The mattress, thin to begin with and pressed even thinner by years of use, might almost have not been missed had it not been there. Likewise the pillow felt like a rock and might as well have been one. The grasshopper spoke to him from under it rather than on it, as if put there (eye of Amma, Ogo's food) by a Dogon diviner.

Djbot Baghostus lay stiff and unmoved even though the grasshopper was his father's ghost. It wasn't the first time his father had assumed a grasshopper guise, nor was it the first time he (Djbot Baghostus) had been accused of having roots in the insect world. He himself had called his father a jitterbug. Thus he lay as motionless as he could, refusing to let it get to him, refusing to let his father faze him a second time. He'd been on his guard ever since he was four, wary of his father's tricks ever since falling for Faze #1.

It was all play, only a play, he told himself, perhaps only a play on words. Grasshopper, were this a dream as he sometimes imagined, was only the dream's oblique way of suggesting glass slipper (though this, to say the least, had its problems as well).

He sometimes wondered had Faze #1 itself been a dream. His mother had said it had to've been, as she had no recollection of his father donning a sheet to play a grasshopper's ghost. Nevertheless it was one of his most vivid childhood memories, so vivid it seemed to have happened only a few nights before. The episode, which had happened when he was four, unfolded regularly before his mind's eye. He had caught and killed a grasshopper one afternoon and showed it to his father, proud of his feat, expecting praise. His father had scolded him instead, asking how he'd like it if he were in the grasshopper's place. That night he was awakened by someone wearing a sheet claiming to be the ghost of the grasshopper he'd killed and saying he was there to get revenge. That someone, his father, eventually removed the sheet, saying, "Let that be a lesson to you," laughing, but not before scaring Djbot Baghostus nearly out of his mind.

He'd felt like running as he lay looking up at the grasshopper's ghost but, rigid with fear, found himself unable to move. His whole life since then, he felt, had been one long sprint, an ongoing after-the-fact flight. It was as if, unable to run then, he'd been running ever since. It felt good to simply lie on his back now, good to lie on his bunk awaiting the trial or the questioning or whatever it was he was to sing or to give a speech at the following day.

The grasshopper, he recognized, meant to be helpful in suggesting what he should say, prompting him before the fact. He had his own ideas, however, as to what his namesake testimony, as he called it, should consist of. He had his own way of thinking about the name he'd assumed (dot, jot, bottle, alibi and alias rolled into one). Clutched in his right hand, for example, was a piece of paper on which he'd copied something he called a Namesake Epigraph, something Mingus had reportedly said to Dannie Richmond:

> You're doing well, but now suppose you had to play a composition alone. How could you play it on the drums? Okay, if you had a dot in the middle of your hand and you were going in a circle, it would have to expand and go round and round, and get larger and larger and larger. And at some point it would have to stop, and then this same circle would have to come back around, around, around to the little dot in the middle of your hand.

This was after Richmond had been in the Mingus band for nine months, a fact and figure Djbot Baghostus had seized on to coin a new name, to claim an alternate birthright.

He took it farther in fact, reading it in light of information he'd presumably picked up during his adopted childhood in Bandiagara. The expanding circle, he planned to explain, was a cosmogonic spiral, the dot in the middle of the hand a fonio seed, the tiny primeval seed the Dogon call *po*. He was prepared to offer in support of such a reading another quote:

> The internal movement of germination was prefigured by this spiral movement in two directions, which is the movement of the *po*. It is said: "The seed grows by turning." Inside, while germinating, it first spins in one direction, then, after bursting, that is, after the emergence of the germ, it spins in the other direction, in order to produce its root and stalk. In addition, the explosion and release of the spiral in the opposite direction produced—in the image of the "word" which it contained—the fundamental twinness of the *po*, as provided for by Amma. It is said: "The *po*, spinning as it came out, became twins." Thus this second creation, that of the *po*, displays a movement that belongs to the universe.

This lent itself to a universalizing bent, to the cosmic pedigree his testimony would seek to establish.

He now couldn't help wondering, as he lay on his bunk, could he get away with punning on "The *po* is the father," a venerable Dogon precept, in order to refute the grasshopper's claim that his father was a wealthy man. He was surprised to hear the voice beneath his pillow say, "No problem." Either the grasshopper had read his mind or, unbeknown to himself, he'd been thinking out loud. In any event, he decided against "My father was po'," crossing it out in his imaginary notebook. "A needless lapse into minstrel tactics," he said out loud.

"No problem," the grasshopper said again.

Djbot Baghostus had to remind himself to ignore him, to continue to lie stiff and unmoving. The agreeable posture his father's ghost was now assuming, he warned himself, was no more than a ploy, an ingratiating tactic meant to put him off guard. Better, he thought, to think about his upcoming day in court, to reflect on and further refine the courtly masque which had begun to take shape, the arch operatic defense he had planned (arch asymptotic aria rolled into one with arch alibi spin). "E Po Pen" he would call it. Spiraling *po* would apprise the court of a "somewhere" one hears within the echo of an expulsion long out of reach. They would then advance to the notion of asymptotic sprint, the idea of an "elsewhere" indigenous to "run," teasingly native to the chase it escapes—so constitutively incident to the reach it evades, he would add, as to be tantamount to the "nowhere" to which one refers when saying, "Nowhere to run." Thus it had been that he saw no point, he would argue, in going when the light turned green.

Part lecture, part demonstration, "E Po Pen" would evoke Mingus in more ways than one, its music resorting to Mingusesque tempo changes, speeding up and then slowing back down. It would thus put one in mind of an abandoned sprint, the inevitably frustrated end of asymptotic pursuit. Djbot Baghostus had arranged for the music to be played by a band which would show up in court, each of its members wearing a placard reading "He Didn't Do It."

Word of this had leaked out somehow and all the trade papers were calling it a "dream band" (even the high-powered big ones like *Billboard*). The phrase irked him to no end. It made him all the more apprehensive as to whether the drummer for the date would show up. It was the drummer, after all, on whom the whole thing hinged, a drummer known for never being on time and, indeed, at times not showing up at all. Her name was Djeannine. Once during an interview he called her "the ideal drummer," a statement the gossip sheets misconstrued under such headlines as "Djbot Baghostus Tells All," "Djbot Baghostus Names the Girl of His Dreams," "Tortured Heart Of A Living Legend" and so forth. He couldn't help fearing, as he lay on his bunk, that the trade papers were now doing the same thing, trying to palm his masque off as a love story, pandering to mass romantic appetite.

"Palm?" he heard the voice beneath his pillow ask, though he pretended not to. He continued to lie stiff, unmoving, refusing to pay the grasshopper any mind. Even so, the point had been made. "Palm," a telling choice of words, betrayed the grain of truth in the gossip sheet stories, a grain to which the Mingus quote as well gave latent support. Wasn't it true, the Namesake Epigraph, if read in a certain way, suggested, that Djeannine had him in the palm of her hand? Why else, he had no choice now but to ask himself, did he put up with her irresponsible comings and goings? "Ideal drummer my eye," the grasshopper piped up. Again Djbot Baghostus outwardly ignored him. "You'd drink her spit from a Dixie cup if she asked you to," the voice beneath his pillow went on. "Gratefully, gladly drink it."

All this, however, he'd foreseen—not only foreseen but found a place for in "E Po Pen." Inoculative inclusion he called it, a technique whereby he incorporated what might otherwise be disturbing, even the story of Djeannine having rejected him for another man. Not a day went by that the gossip sheets didn't carry the latest on her storybook romance with a conga player named Ibo Ben, another living legend. The trade papers had gotten in on it as well, ecstatically reporting on the duets they'd recorded, one of which was not only getting AM airplay but had even made it into the Top 10. The inevitable comparisons with Ashford and Simpson had of course been made.

The lecture part of Djbot Baghostus's lecture-demonstration would suggest that Djeannine's "happily ever after" duets with Ibo Ben were in fact no more than a purely formal consummation, a concession to formulaic endings which, as the trade papers themselves admitted, seemed to be back by popular demand. His avant-garde masque would go so far, in fact, as to imply that Ibo Ben didn't even exist except as projected by narratological demands, a predictably formal/formulaic fixture and/or effect. In his left hand he held a piece of paper on which he'd copied a quote which lent itself to this line of thought, another Namesake Epigraph:

> The formula which started in England as "Be Bow Bended, this story is ended," has received a myriad of transformations in the Bahamas. "Ebo Ben" or "Ebo John" was thought with some justification to be "probably African" . . . in reference to the Ibo people of Nigeria.

So convinced was Djbot Baghostus that Ibo Ben was a "folkloric" effect (narrative curvature and narrative outcome rolled into one) he'd invited Djeannine to bring him along to sit in with the band. Thus his fear was a two-sided one. He was afraid Djeannine wouldn't show up but also afraid that if she did so would Ibo Ben.

This business of bend, however, brought another sense of "palm" to mind. Djbot Baghostus now couldn't help thinking of the palm trees which during his adopted Caribbean youth he saw bent by hurricanes to what appeared to be the breaking point. That they didn't break had impressed him greatly, left him with imprints which now began to feed his apprehensions, causing him to wonder was Ibo Ben an avatar of resilient, unlikely survival, was Ibo Ben therefore bound to show up?

"What about 'The Ibo hang themselves'?" the grasshopper asked.

Again Djbot Baghostus outwardly ignored him, but, yes, there was that, a West Indian saying dating back to slavery times. That was the other side of it, he realized, still pretending to pay the grasshopper no mind. Could "bow" have become "bough," bent by the weight of an Ibo who rather than be a slave chose to hang himself from it? Again it seemed Ibo Ben was only the proverbial sense of an ending. What had appeared to be a choice between bend and break turned out to include aspects of both, as though bend had both a first and a second register, the latter relativizing the former's conflict with break (narrative curvature and narrative conflict rolled into one). Putting tendency in tension's place, second-register bend, his cosmic masque would demonstrate, was asymptotic bend, its theoretical non-embrace of break maintained by the infinitesimal turning known as *po*. A quantum conjunction on the order of particle and wave, bend and break's asymptotic embrace calibrated a refusal to invest in the ultimacy of either, doing so in unendingly altered ways. Thus it was, Djbot Baghostus hoped, that Ibo Ben, never all there though always there, wouldn't show up.

He heaved an inaudible sigh of relief, glad to have escaped his close brush with Ibo bend. His gladness got the best of him however, causing him to gloat, to feel invincible and, in turn, vindictive. Even though the grasshopper had been helpful, reminding him of Ibo break, he turned on him, taunting him out loud (also dropping his guard) with a line from Ibn 'Arabī's *Tarjumān al-Ashwāq*: "May my father be the ransom of the boughs swaying to and fro as they bend." By this he meant to evoke a lynching, to get back at his father for having donned a sheet—Klan-style, he claimed—and scared him almost to death when he was four. It would also give his masque another Mingusesque touch, an apocryphal lynching recalling Mingus's tale that his brother-in-law had been lynched.

"They lynched my father," he would say under oath. "The white people stood around and laughed." It could, of course, have been true. It was, in the best sense of the term, a likely story—more likely, statistically speaking, than that his father ever sang with The Ink Spots, a story his brother had told him but his mother denied. His father, she said, had played their records a lot, frequently singing along, which must've been what his brother meant.

Djbot Baghostus had second thoughts about this line of defense after only a moment's reflection. It was only to be expected that he'd rest his case on a traumatic pedigree. To do so would simply conform to predictable canons of deprivation. This was known in the business as walking the bench, though some called it playing the fool, playing into the system's hands. Thus it was that the court was ready to hear his likely story, that it indeed harbored profound investments in the problematic likeliness "E Po Pen" was meant to uproot. The indictment of apocryphal truth assuming the guise of ingenuous fact would be one of its key motifs, as the whistle he meant to blow on Ibo Ben had already made clear. But how could he do so and at the same time base his defense on a made-up lynching? Wasn't this the same as the minstrel tactic he'd earlier dismissed? Why not also cop to the gossip sheet stories about him and Djeannine, Djeannine and Ibo Ben?

Djbot Baghostus, having let down his guard, was now paying for it, reeling from the repercussions of his vindictive jab at the voice beneath his pillow. The refusal to face facts of which he accused mass romantic appetite would in no way be corrected by appeals to probabilistic paternity, in no strategic way discouraged by the abuse of grasshopper truth. The fractious impasse to which this had brought him simply dramatized all the more the need for the antithetical masque he intended his day in court to be, the out opera the trade papers consistently misportrayed.

Djbot Baghostus regretted having quoted Ibn 'Arabī out of context, the irony that this was routine gossip sheet practice not having escaped him. He would have to put his fight with his father aside. He would be nice to the voice beneath his pillow, which, he had to admit, having now let down his guard, had only been trying to help. He would no longer pretend to ignore the grasshopper. He lay silently now, waiting for him to speak again.

He lay that way for some time—stiff, unmoving, waiting. The grasshopper said nothing. Finally, Djbot Baghostus turned over, a move, the first he'd made since the curtain rose, which took the audience by surprise. They'd been sitting, absorbed, for some time, watching the lack of action onstage. The more action-starved among them, the first to recover from the shock of his turning over, burst into uproarious applause.

Having turned over, Djbot Baghostus now spoke into his pillow. "Speak to me, Hoppergrass. Please, speak to me," he begged, his plea made all the more poignant by the "metathetic" version of "grasshopper" to which he resorted, a children's coinage he hadn't used since he was a kid. So forlorn, so genuinely filled with affection was his voice that several people in the audience, men among them, openly wept.

Djbot Baghostus's asymptotic aria had now begun. His turning over was a *po*-inflected appeal to metathetic emotion ("Put yourself in my place," it implied), to quantum-qualitative leaps, quicksilver changes of heart. It took the audience entirely by surprise, none of whom would've predicted he'd throw himself on the mercy of the court.*

Djbot Baghostus's appeal to metathetic emotion fell on deaf ears. His touching asymptotic aria notwithstanding, the grasshopper was not to be heard from. Obviously the tables had turned. The grasshopper was pretending to pay Djbot Baghostus no mind. This was the retributive trauma which tormented his legendary heart, a tale the gossip sheets, had they been the least bit serious, he fumed, would have eagerly seized upon. One would peruse their pages in vain, however, for news of punitive paternity's grasshopper squint. (Even in the depths of his metathetic ordeal he found a moment to reflect on journalistic incompetence, an occasion to advance his quarrel with the gossip sheets.)

Things, though, otherwise began to move. Djbot Baghostus's turning over was followed by the band being lifted into view, brought ever so slowly to stage level upon a platform which favored stage left and which arose from the orchestra pit. The band members all wore placards reading "He Didn't Do It," which was emblazoned on the bass drum as well. All eyes, of course, sought to see who was on drums. It was, reassuringly, Djeannine. The conga chair was conspicuously empty, however, and a buzz of whispering ran thru the audience when they saw that Ibo Ben was nowhere in sight.

"He Didn't Do It" entered into somewhat ambiguous play not only with the charge against Djbot Baghostus of not having gone on the green light but also with the grasshopper's refusal to speak. As though the grasshopper's non-response were a cue (as if group sound and grasshopper silence enjoyed a profound, albeit implied rapport), the band, a quintet, began playing not long after Djbot Baghostus pleaded

---

* The question on every tongue in the after-theatre cafés was had he gotten grasshopper confused with kangaroo.

with "Hoppergrass," begged him to speak. It was a dirge they played, putting, thereby, the opening tableau to rest.

That the grasshopper parlayed reticence into so resonantly cathartic a sound made for many a scratched head in the audience. Thus it was, though, that the curtain fell on the first act or the first movement, the proemic outset of "E Po Pen." Not so much a curtain as a huge white sheet, it fell slowly as the platform the band played on slowly lowered them into the orchestra pit again.

Djbot Baghostus now turned over again, back the other way. He lay on his back staring up at the ceiling. The strange musical fruit his would-be bough had borne—the odd way the band had of bending notes—made him again reflect on second-register bend. The unimpeachable truth of his made-up tale was not only that trees would never be the same for the preyed-upon African but that nothing would ever again be exactly coincident with itself, that the shock of predatory convergence ultimated an alarmed or an aloof obliquity, an oblique,* bend-assisted resolve. Resonance and resolution were spiraling *po*'s asymmetrical twins. Their incestuous itch reflected the band's tangential squint.

Djbot Baghostus closed his eyes as the curtain rose on the second act or the second movement. He wasn't sure why his day in court had

---

* The Program Notes informed the audience of a play between oblique and opaque one was not to miss. For this they asserted what they termed an "archaeo-avant-garde pedigree." They quoted Ellington's reply to Mingus's proposal that the two of them make "a real avant-garde record" together: "Charles, let's not go back *that* far." They also quoted from Thomas Bowditch's early nineteenth-century account of the music he heard in Gabon: "As regards the words, there was such rhapsody of recitative, or mournful, impetuous, and exhilarated air, wandering through the life of man, throughout the animal and vegetable kingdom for its subjects, without period, without connection, so transient, abrupt, and allegorical, that the Governor of the town could translate a line but occasionally, and I was too much possessed by the music, and the alternate rapture and phrenzy of the performer, to minute the half which he communicated." The grasshopper requiem, the Notes alerted the audience, would appraise and pass this pedigree on.

come so soon but here it was and here he was as well, lying flat on his back in bed. Was this the price he paid, he wondered, for his fear of things going too fast? Wasn't that at bottom the charge he faced, what his failure to go on green was about? Were crime and punishment in this case rolled into one?

He lay pondering these and other questions, thrown back in traumatized recoil as the grasshopper's bent-legged spring brought to the surface the latent slipper which had haunted him for some time. In this, the alternate version of his defense, he built his case on a problematic romance which had driven him insane several years before, now known as Faze #2. What concerned him most at this point was how to stage it, how to comply with its intimations of a post-architectonic design. What he wanted would in a sense walk the bench, albeit a bench, tightrope and bar rolled into one, albeit run would be more like it than walk. What he wanted would run the risk of appearing to concede to the gossip sheets. This, in a sense, it would, although, in theory, only in order to better fight back. Part courtly, confessional masque, part guerrilla theatre, it would ring changes on the oldest tale in the world, Boy meets Girl. Djbot Baghostus, of course, was the Boy in question. Djeannine would leave her drums to play Girl.

Faze #2 made a long story short: Boy sees Girl, who's wearing a pair of glass slippers. Boy falls hopelessly in love and approaches Girl. Girl encourages Boy's advances. Boy thinks they're off to a good start but "good start" comes back to haunt him when Girl begins to play hard to get. Girl wants to be pursued and takes off running. Boy takes off too in hot pursuit. Boy and Girl run for a while, only to be caught up with by an obvious truth: glass slippers make poor running shoes. The slippers, that is, shatter, leaving a trail of broken glass in Girl's wake. Girl, barefooted, continues running—runs faster in fact—but Boy stops to pick up the broken glass. Once the glass is gathered (all but a tiny sliver) Boy looks up, only to find Girl is gone. Boy never sees Girl again.

Thus it was, the defense would argue, that Djbot Baghostus's fear of things going too fast, of getting off to too fast a start, had been born, that for him fast and false were the same. Boy's broken pursuit of Girl had planted the seed (a mere sliver of glass) from which a fear that sprint was inevitably asymptotic had sprouted or sprung. It was this which had kept him from going when the light turned green. Special Dogon counsel brought in for the trial would inform the court that Djbot Baghostus's antisocial behavior not only couldn't be helped but, looked at correctly, could be seen to comply with cosmogonic law. Ogo's disruptive search for his female twin, everyone knew, continued to have resounding repercussions. One of these was Djbot Baghostus's antithetical sprint before the traffic light, the static antithetical run by way of which he would get, he thought, together with Girl again.

Djbot Baghostus lay on his back, entranced by the sliver of glass which, he felt, was lodged in the ball of his right foot. He wondered how Girl had been able to go on running, wondered hadn't her feet been cut by the glass. What he felt in the ball of his foot was something close to couvade, a made-up ordeal he underwent for the sake of metathetic truth, painfully putting himself in Girl's place. The tiny blade of glass had eventually brought her down, he lay there thinking, knowing, however, this probably wasn't so.*

As he lay entranced by the oddly satisfying pain in the ball of his foot, again going over the last-minute arrangements of "E Po Pen," he was suddenly roused from his meditations by the sound of footsteps out in the hall, the sound, it seemed, of someone approaching his cell. He turned and opened his eyes to see Djeannine tiptoe in, a finger held up to her lips to say hush, a wary, fugitive look on her face. Dressed up as Girl, she wore a spandex workout suit and a pair of glass Adidas. She carried a second pair in her left hand. Djbot Baghostus was glad to see her, but also surprised. She was for once not only on time but a bit early. What's more, she'd for some reason come directly to his cell.

Even though she'd shushed him, Djeannine immediately broke into song, into speech which was part spoken, part sung. "The court will turn a deaf ear to your defense," she semisaid, semisang. He was impressed by the force of her voice, a crystalline soprano, but

* "Part couvade, part wishfulfilling revenge" one of the newspaper critics wrote.

gestured for her to lower it some. "The only way out is out," she continued. "We've gotta make a run for it." She handed him the glass Adidas. "Here. Put these on. They'll help."

The pain in the ball of Djbot Baghostus's foot had now gone away. He sat up on the edge of the bunk and took the Adidas Djeannine handed him. He couldn't help but be impressed by the tight, revealing fit of her workout suit. "No doubt about it, Girl, you're a fox," he semisaid, semisang (mythoerotic overture, operatic rap).

"So I'm told," she semisaid, semisang back, absolutely blasé. "No time for that now though. Get those Adidas on."

His come-on rebuffed, he did as he was told. His out-operatic induction was underway. Djeannine was his asymmetrical twin, his asymptotic escort. "You can look if you like but don't touch" was clearly the drift of her blasé retort, the bend away from touch toward looking pointing up the fact that see-thru shoe preempted mythoerotic foot. Once he had the Adidas on he stood up. His legs were a bit rusty but it felt good to be standing again after what seemed like ages of lying down. He felt a change, a sense of transparent advance which hit him almost at once. A rush related to second-register bend worked its way up from his feet, causing him to feel he'd been lifted off the floor when it reached his head. As if the Adidas' transparency were contagious, he now saw thru to the fact that all along he'd been afraid. He'd lain on his bunk putting his masque together, he admitted, scared stiff the entire time. This admission loosened his legs, rid them of rust. He was ready to run.

The audience was again surprised to see the band emerge from the orchestra pit. Their ascent had begun when Djbot Baghostus got the Adidas on and stood up, but it was a moment or two after that before they came into view. The platform on which they stood rose faster than it had the first time and one soon saw that Djeannine's drumset had been replaced by a DMX drum machine. The conga chair was again conspicuously empty but none of the band members wore the "He Didn't Do It" placard. Renamed for the occasion, they stood before a banner on which they were announced to be Drum Ex Machina's Grasshopper Band and Blue Rabbit Revue. Members of the audience now knew why the Program Notes had quoted—calling it a Namesake Epigraph—the line "The blues jumped a rabbit, run him a solid mile."

Once the platform had risen to stage level it turned counterclockwise to the point where the band stood facing Djeannine and Djbot Baghostus. The two of them stood downstage right in what passed for a cell on "E Po Pen's" post-architectonic set. Simultaneously, they too turned counterclockwise, moving with slow, mechanical deliberation to the point where they stood facing the wings, their backs to the band. The band, it presently appeared, was hot on their heels. Once the new tableau was in place the music started and Djeannine and Djbot Baghostus began running in place.

An uptempo romp whose adrenaline-pump approach not only was harmolodic but out-Ornetted Ornette, the music was as far from a dirge as one could imagine. Djeannine and Djbot Baghostus ran in place, lifting their knees high, a quantum-qualitatively accelerated cakewalk and asymptotic sprint rolled into one. Though they ran in place Djbot Baghostus ran for real. No one could've convinced him he wasn't moving. Indeed, true to the universal conception he was after, his flight transcended itself. He ran with Everyman's legs, aboriginal to the future, a synoptic, transhistorical sprint. He was a caveman pursued by a mastodon, a slave with paterollers on his trail, a protester chased by troops in Chile, an intergalactic alien dodging shots from a laser gun. Fear, he knew, had long been afoot. Every reason anyone had ever had for running now seemed to be his. Every reason anyone would ever have was also his.

Djbot Baghostus stole a glance at Djeannine out of the corner of his eye. She was cool, composed, collected, the perfect escort. She ran with excellent, firm, assertive arm action, her head held high, her eyes forward. They ran abreast of one another, evenly matched, stride for stride. Djbot Baghostus couldn't help marveling over the fact that the glass Adidas hadn't shattered and that, indeed, he was able to run even harder in them. No, there was no doubt about it, he ran for real. For him the stage was no artifice. Word was out that an actor had been elected president and already there was talk of war, the spectre of which the DMX's machinegun-like report did nothing to dispel and everything to enhance. He'd heard it would be a war only bugs would survive and he ran as if the grasshopper itself were hot on his heels, the spectre of insect succession. Already, he remembered, wiping his brow, he'd heard of a record called *Thermonuclear Sweat* by a group calling itself Defunkt.

The Grasshopper Band gave no sign of slowing down and, if anything, seemed to be playing faster. The alto player seemed to especially enjoy the pace, playing with a whistle-while-you-work jauntiness and joy, an unflustered facility and fluency which made several audience members' mouths hang open. Djbot Baghostus now sweated more profusely and grew more and more perplexed by Djeannine's cool, sweatless perfection, her ability to stay with him stride for stride without so much as a routine bit of moisture on her brow. It was just as he began to grow anxious for the band to go from harmolodic to Mingusesque, to slow down the pace, that a loud, resounding "Aha!" was heard coming from downstage left. He and Djeannine looked over their shoulders (the first lapse in her otherwise perfect form) to see Ibo Ben running toward them waving a machete. Djeannine, her composure broken, let out a scream before she could help it, a scream which, ad-libbing, she then developed into an impromptu aria whose last, extremely high note shattered the Adidas.

With the shattering of the Adidas Djeannine and Djbot Baghostus began to move, no longer just running in place. It was as if the Adidas had been holding them back. Eyes forward again, they ran into the wings and out the back door of the theatre, the stage behind them littered with shattered glass. All the more now Djbot Baghostus ran for real, as if pursued by the ghost of an appointment (punctual bow, apocalyptic bend). He wondered had Ibo Ben stopped to pick up the broken glass but even so he didn't dare look back.

ATET A.D.

for my sister
Dolores Williams

21.II.82

Dear Angel of Dust,

No doubt by now you've heard the news of Monk's death. What can one say? No doubt there'll now be outpourings of appreciation, much of it from hitherto silent sources, long overdue. It can never amount to more than too little too late. I'm reminded of how I learned of Duke's death in 1974. I was living up north at the time, in Oakland, and was in the habit of listening to the Berkeley Pacifica station, KPFA. Every weekday morning they had a program called "The Morning Concert," two hours of what's commonly called classical. So exclusively was European and Europe-derived "art music" its regimen that when I turned on the program one morning late in May and heard "Black and Tan Fantasy" I knew it could only mean one thing. Well before the announcer came on and said so I knew Duke was dead.

In any event, the way we heard that Monk had died is that Onaje called Lambert the day the news broke to ask if we'd play in a memorial gig at his club that night. It came as no surprise, Monk having been in a coma for more than a week, though that's not to say it had no impact. Still, as I've already said, what can one say? We agreed with no hesitation to take part in the gig, even though Penguin hadn't yet come out of hiding and even though we didn't know when he would. If playing the gig turned out to mean playing without him we were ready to do so.

Penguin's retreat, of course, had given rise to a good deal of comment, concern and speculation among us. Drennette even ventured to wonder out loud one day what kind of trip it was he was on, did he go off that way often and, if so, why do we put up with it. This struck us as a little harsh and to me at least it suggested she had a deeper emotional investment in Penguin's doings than she let on. Aunt Nancy wasted no time speaking up. She called Penguin's "trip" an "occupational hazard," repeating Baraka's line that music makes you think of a lot of weird things and that it can even make you become one of them. Clearly, she suggested, Penguin had.

I spoke up as well. Penguin's retreat, I said, struck me as related to something he once told me about Monk. I recounted his telling me of Monk getting into moods in which he'd answer the phone by grumbling, "Monk's not here," then hang up. Penguin's own telephonically announced retreat, I suggested, amounted to a kind of couvade. It was a case of sympathetic ordeal, him turning away from the world in solidarity with Monk. How it came to me to say this I can't entirely say. It simply popped into my head as I spoke. I can, however, say that I deliberately downplayed Penguin's attraction to Drennette, thinking it might be the source of her annoyance. I steered clear of his would-be rap, the aborted recitation I knew was at the root of his retreat. This doesn't, however, explain the particulars which popped into my head to take its place. Nor does it explain why I persisted along these lines even after I saw that my not mentioning his attraction to her seemed to increase instead of lessen Drennette's annoyance. I'm tempted to say that I could feel Penguin feeding me my lines, just as with "E Po Pen," but it wouldn't be true. All I felt was the pull and the appeal of the Monk angle, the fact that it so perfectly fit. (Indeed, so much so that I wondered, even as I spoke, had I gotten things wrong in "E Po Pen," thought Mingus when I should've thought Monk.)

The impromptu connection I drew between Penguin's retreat and Monk's coma seemed to be borne out by what subsequently occurred, the fact that Penguin chose to make his return at the memorial gig. We had no way, as I've already said, of knowing whether he would emerge in time for the gig. Lambert called and left a message on his machine, giving him the details, but by that night, not having heard from him, we accepted having to play without him.

A good-sized crowd showed up at Onaje's. A small place, it was pretty much packed. Considering the short notice, word had gotten around pretty well. Besides us, a number of other bands from around town took part. We each played what was supposed to be a thirty-minute set, though in most cases it turned out more like forty-five. Our set came fairly late, as we were the fifth group to play. We followed a trio led by Badi Taqsim, a pianist who's been turning a lot of heads lately. He mainly plays other people's compositions, among them a good number of standards, but the touch he puts on them is all his own. They finished up their set with a couple of pieces which really tore the place up—Monk's "Pannonica," followed by a John Lewis piece hardly anyone ever does, "Natural Affection." A wistful strain had run thru the set, held in check or bitten back, however, by Monk's ironic pluck and puckish good humor (all the pieces they played, save the last one, were Monk pieces). "Pannonica" took the standoff between wistful plaint and ironic pluck to an almost unbearable pitch before the Lewis piece exacted a surprising denouement. How piano, bass and drums could effect a breathy timbral suspension worthy of Charlie Rouse himself I'll never know, but they somehow did on the former. All the built-up tension, the austere articulacy and the sense of incomplete release "Natural Affection" then took into another domain. The bossa nova beat, coming after the solemnity of the piece's opening chords, took most of the audience by surprise, introducing an abrupt, dilated liquidity, an agile dilation finessed on several fronts at once. Wistfulness turned into *saudade*.

As I stood there listening I couldn't help remembering that the quality the Brazilians call *saudade* goes back to the homesickness the slaves felt for Africa. A Brazilian friend of mine told me this a few years back and it struck me that Badi must have known it as well, so apt was the evocation of "going home" to the occasion. What got to me was what almost always does with bossa nova, the mix of compliance, complication and complaint it brings off. The piece, that is, was one in which longing, heavily tinged with regret, became complicit with a no-regrets furtherance of itself or beyond itself, a self-possessed rhythmic advance which, when it was on, ran the line between "of" and "beyond."

But I've gotten caught up with something I really didn't mean to go on about so long. Suffice it to say that we were there, Badi's trio reminded us, to see Monk home, that their reading of the piece more than rose to the occasion, so gently thrusted was its mating of tendency with touch, that they more than made it live up to its title. Which is also to say that they put us in just the right mood, just the right frame of mind. They put us in touch with a well of affection we repeatedly had recourse to throughout our set (though "put us in touch" wasn't so much what it was as that they variously apprised us we already were).

Penguin chose to show up at the gig, as I've already said, but we were well into our set by the time he did. We had just finished "Reflections," our rendition of which, though I hate to brag, was a killer. With Aunt Nancy on violin and Djamilaa doubling on harmonium and bandoneon, we gave it an Indo-Argentine reading which, by way of tempo changes here and there, insisted on links between tango and Baul. Lambert and I both played tenor, both of us heavily indebted to Sonny Rollins's Blue Note recording of the piece, most notably the sense of alarm he gets from the leap to high D in the fifth bar. We gave it that same quantum sense of duress but added a touch of our own, pulling back as if to declare the alarm false. If you can imagine the acoustical equivalent of a fadeaway jumpshot you've got a good idea of the approach we took. Aunt Nancy complicated the figure once or twice with a sirenlike shooting-pain bowswipe recalling Piazzolla's violinist Fernando Paz. Anyway, it all added up to murder—so much so Onaje joked with us later he'd considered calling the coroner's office. Things got even more lethal with our next and, as it turned out, final number, "In Walked Bud." I went over to alto, Djamilaa switched to piano and Aunt Nancy went from violin to bass. Djamilaa played the first eight bars unaccompanied, the rest of us joining in on the first repeat. It was at the beginning of the second repeat that we heard an oboe join in from near the club's entrance, perfectly in tune and right on the beat. We looked out over the heads of the audience, all of whom had turned around to see who the oboist was, and there was Penguin playing away while slowly making his way toward the stage. We went into yet another repeat and still another and, before it was over, several more—an impromptu vamp-till-ready as we waited for Penguin to reach the stage.

Once Penguin was onstage one couldn't help noticing how disheveled he was. He hadn't shaved, his hair hadn't been combed and his clothes looked as if he'd slept in them. What's more, he appeared to have slept outdoors. Twigs, bits of dry grass and even leaves clung to his clothes and to his hair. (We later learned he'd spent the time he'd been away camping out near the Hollywood Reservoir.) One also couldn't help noticing how different he sounded, the expansive, magisterial sound he got from the horn, a voluminous thrust and dimensionality which was all the more pronounced now that he blew into a mike. This was a bigger, rounder, more hollowed-out, holier sound than he'd ever gotten, a sound he sought to surround us with. It was as if he sought to house us in a celestial cave. It was what I can't help calling a *world* sound, a ringing sound which went well beyond the pinched, piercing sound the oboe normally has. This Penguin later attributed to the time he spent practicing during his retreat, his time in what he insisted on calling the "wouldshed." (This apparent concession to the "high would" pun which has more and more come to be common coinage among us, given the manifest advance we'd all heard with our own ears, had a not very subtle smirk woven into it.)

Shortly after Penguin made it onstage we brought our vamp to an end. We went on to the next eight bars and then returned to the first eight, after which Djamilaa tore into a solo which honored Monk in so wincingly dexterous a manner it made one's fingers ache just to be in the same room. What hit was its tolling, tangential resonances, the off-to-one-side ringing she coaxed from the keys, the oblique "bell" she had a way of resorting to now and again, a "bell" which confounded alloy with allure (as though "belle" was much more what it was). Aunt Nancy followed with a bass solo which took alloy further toward its limit by accentuating "alien" wood. Her right hand, that is, repeatedly left the strings to give the body of the bass a percussive tap or a number of taps, the play between plucked and percussed her way of having some fun with Penguin's heartthrob Drennette. For her part, however, Drennette showed no sign of noticing, going on in as blasé, matter-of-fact, businesslike a way as ever. Penguin, though, did seem to take note, albeit ever so briefly, recovering quickly, adopting a duck's back's attitude to water.

During Djamilaa's solo Lambert had whispered to each of us that Aunt Nancy would solo next, that I'd follow her and that Penguin would, as he put it, "bat cleanup." Penguin then came over to me and whispered that rather than soloing one after the other he and I should do so at the same time, trade choruses and so forth, make it a dialogue, a duet. This I agreed to. When Aunt Nancy finished her solo the two of us took up what turned out to be an extended, increasingly contentious conversation. Penguin, I quickly found out, took exception to "E Po Pen," felt it trivialized his retreat. It made too much of his aborted rap to Drennette, too much of the torch it alleged he carried for Djeannine. This he insisted by way of a bold, falsetto run which embraced "high would" in order to complain of my "low blow." He ended the run by quoting the stuttering, low-register croak Wayne Shorter gets into toward the end of his solo on "Fee-Fi-Fo-Fum," one of the pieces on the *Speak No Evil* album, the point of neither title missing its mark. With that we were off on what ended up being duet, duel and dozens rolled into one. Though a bit surprised at first, Aunt Nancy, Drennette and Djamilaa egged us on, as tight and on-top-of-it a rhythm section as one could want, and Lambert threw in an exhortative two or three notes every now and then. It was somewhat like Freddie Hubbard and Lee Morgan's exchanges on *The Night of the Cookers*, Hawkins and Rollins's on *Sonny Meets Hawk*, Mingus and Dolphy's on "What Love" or "So Long Eric." What it came down to was an old-time cuttin' session.

I won't attempt to give you a detailed account. Let me let it go at saying that I held my ground as best I could, arguing that "E Po Pen" struck me as being dictated to me by him (to which he replied I was blaming the victim), that, in any case, a little humor never hurt anyone (to which he replied we'd see who'd laugh last), that, even so, it was his Djeannine dream and only his which had the broken-tooth ending (to which he replied so what), and so forth. It was some of the hottest, heaviest going I've ever taken part in. We worked what seemed like a million variations on "In Walked Bud" and by the end had come up with a new tune that you'll find on the tape I've enclosed. Penguin and I recorded it yesterday, just the two of us, unaccompanied. We set out to recapture what we did at Onaje's and, allowing for the inevitable variances, we succeeded. We call the piece "In Walked Pen."

The thing worth pointing out about both the tape and our duel/duet at Onaje's is that Penguin ultimately prevailed by turning my "low blow" against me. Somehow during his retreat he managed to add a full octave to the bottom end of the oboe's range. Toward the end of our duel/duet he lured me into what amounted to a limbo match, a test of who could go lower. (It was this match, in fact, which brought both our duel/duet and the piece to a conclusion. It also, that night at Onaje's, ended our set, "In Walked Bud" having gone on longer than we'd planned as a result of Penguin showing up.) The alto being pitched over half an octave lower than the oboe, I figured I had it made. He surprised me and everyone else, though, by working his way down past the horn's low B-flat to an even lower B-flat, almost half an octave lower than mine. As he did so I could've sworn I heard the rafters rattle and felt the floor shake. I made the futile gesture of putting my knee in the bell of my horn to play A, though I knew that didn't even come close to making up the difference. Penguin had beat me at what he insisted was my own game, deftly augmenting "high would" with "low would," a stunning move to which my A was a lame comeback, next to none at all. Had it been knives rather than horns we battled with I'd have bled to death.

As ever,
N.

27.11.82

Dear Angel of Dust,

Thanks for writing back so soon. What a surprise to receive your "liner notes" to "In Walked Pen." I appreciate your once again encouraging us to put out a record, even more your willingness to write the notes for it. The idea of a "test run" is a good one and I'm glad you thought of it, glad you acted on it as well. I've read your "run" a couple of times and I'm very excited. I particularly like the use you make of narration. Yes, every tune does tell a story. The coy, contingent yarn you spin teases out—instructively so—"In Walked Pen" 's oblique, centrifugal drift. I also like the length you give it. Do you remember those Limelight albums in the sixties, the ones that opened up sort of like a book and had several pages of liner notes? That's the kind of thing I'd want done with what you've written.

There's one thing, though, I have problems with: the way you belabor the relationship of Penguin's boastful, magisterial sound to rap music. It's not that your play on his would-be rap to Drennette is lost on me, nor that rap isn't the latest in a long tradition of black (male mostly) self-praise and contestual display, a tradition of which our duel/duet is obviously a part. No, it's more a matter of scale and perspective. I wouldn't want anyone to get the idea we were pandering to fashion, putting undue emphasis on something simply because it's in. I'd feel more at ease with your notes if you gave more attention to the wider matrix rap's a part of, were you to drop a few of the rap references for some mention of, say, Memphis Slim's "Sweet Root Man,"

Bo Diddley's "Who Do You Love," Dexter Gordon's "Soy Califa" (or, for that matter, Pete "El Conde" Rodriguez's "Soy La Ley"), John Lee Hooker's "I'm Bad Like Jesse James," Lord Invader's "Me One Alone" or any number of others too numerous to list. There's nothing new about swagger.

What *is* new is that since I last wrote there's begun to be talk about changing the name of the band. It was Drennette who brought it up. She complained at rehearsal the other day that "Mystic Horn Society" privileges the horns, emphasizes them at the other instruments' expense. She went on to say that since our sound wouldn't be what it is were any of the instruments missing she saw no reason to single out the horns as in some way worthy of special notice. It was a point none of us could disagree with. Aunt Nancy was quick to chime in that not only was Drennette right but that the problem went farther, that the name smacks of male privilege, given that the horns are played primarily by the men in the group. "To say nothing," she capped it off by saying, "of the phallic associations horns have."

This last remark had a funny effect on me. I had no problem with Drennette's complaint, nor with Aunt Nancy's addendum apropos male privilege. Something inside me, however, instinctively objected to the "phallic associations" bit, the easy, one-sided equation it rested on, the reductiveness of it. The phrase triggered—antithetically triggered—the recollection of a dream I hadn't thought about in years. Almost before I knew it I found myself speaking up to say that while I agreed with almost everything that had been said I thought the phallic bit was going too far. I then proceeded to recount, as a counter example, the dream which had just come back to me again, a dream I'd had when I was about eight, the circumstances surrounding which I recounted as well. I explained that as a kid I was a big fan of rock and roll—Little Richard, Chuck Berry, Bill Haley and the like—and that I was also under the influence of the church, that my mother, at my grandmother's insistence, had started me going to Sunday school when I was five. I explained that I thought about Judgment Day a lot and that having heard that to listen to rock and roll was a sin had me worried. I found it hard to believe it was and different people gave different opinions, but, I explained further, I worried about it anyway. I then recounted how one night I decided to settle the question, how when I said my prayers that night I asked God to send me a sign: to make me dream of pirates if it was true that listening to rock and roll was a sin, to make me dream of cowboys if it wasn't. I went on to how it ended up I dreamt about neither pirates nor cowboys that night but dreamt instead I was in a dark room in which I heard a sinuous, arresting piece of music played on what sounded like a cross between a trumpet and a bassoon; how it went on that way for a while, me standing in the dark, unable to see anything, caught up in the music; how finally a spotlight came on and illumined a figure quite some distance away from me and how with that it became clear that this figure was where the music was coming from; how I knew now I was in a large auditorium and began walking toward the spotlighted figure; how as I got closer I could tell the figure was a woman and, closer yet, that she had no clothes on and that the music was as much a scent as it was a sound, a synaesthetic mix (part music, part musk), a penetrating mist of sound which was earthy, ethereal, refined and funky, all at the same time; how as I got even closer I could tell the music emanated from a horn between the spotlighted woman's thighs, a cornucopic horn without the grapes and so forth, though I couldn't make out whether it was a part of her body or simply held in place by pressure put on it by her legs; how when I reached the stage and finally stood in front of her I couldn't resist sticking my nose up over the lip of the horn to "smell" the music better; how when I did my eyes crossed and rolled around before closing and my head shot back in slow motion as I went into a swoon.

Once I finished there was a silence lasting a moment or two before Aunt Nancy, nonplussed, rolled her eyes in mock motherly amazement and exclaimed, "Such a precocious child! Yes, the Lord does work in mysterious ways." Everyone laughed and I blushed a bit. She went on to add, however, that, all joking aside, even though my dream might simply be the exception which proves the rule she was willing to back off on the phallic business, that that wasn't the main point anyway and that if no one could come up with a reason not to we should start thinking about a new name for the band. No one could. Neither could anyone come up with a new name that all of us liked. We're still thinking about it.

Thanks again for the notes.

Yours,
N.

11.III.82

Dear Angel of Dust,

I found myself going back to your "liner notes" again and again over the past few days. The ipseic surmise they engage the music with kept calling me back—that along with a wish to have my own way with what you'd written, a wish I couldn't quite shake even though I told myself I should. It's not so much that I had quarrels with your take on the piece as that the more I read your notes the more it seemed I stood on revisionary ground, so exponential the seismic suzerainty ipseity served. Sesame squared I'm tempted to call it, Earth of sesame to the second power, ground grown rich with susurrant seed, an open aliquance insisting on emendation. (One of Cecil Taylor's titles, "Chorus of Seed," comes to mind.) Seismic seed not only fed me but, as if I were a muscle, flexed me. I found myself changing words here and there, making notes in the margins, putting my own stylistic spin on this, that and the other. That spin bore an antithetical bent, the ongoing gist or gestation of an *opera contra naturam*. Your notes were clearly lecture/libretto material. The results you'll find enclosed.

As you can see, the changes are not that radical. I followed your lead at all points. Your notes ended up, it seems to me, not so much rewritten as differently pitched. Seismic seed's pneumatic sprout, however much it recast or reconceived your tack, for the most part reconfirmed it.

Anyway, let me know what you think.

Yours,
N.

IN WALKED PEN

or, The Creaking of the Word: After-the-Fact Lecture/Libretto (A.D. Version)

Penguin's return coincided with the news of Monk's death. Newly descended from an ancient line of authority figures, he came back having crowned himself King Pen. Some, he knew, would think of King Oliver, King Pleasure, King Curtis, Nat King Cole. Duke, Pres, Count, Prince Lasha and others would also come to mind. It went, in fact, much further back than any of them, further back than he himself had initially suspected. It went further back than the 'Lection Day fifes and drums he'd heard the moment the crown touched his head, further back than the Pinkster eelpot he'd heard not more than a split-second after that.

King Pen had come into antiphonal play with "monastic flight," Penguin's loose, euphemistic term for Monk's death. A funereal wedding of church and state, nominal kingship heralded the end of charismatic retreat. The quality Lambert once referred to as Monk's "renunciative harmonics" had long struck a mendicant chord deep within. Even so, Penguin seized upon the occasion of "monastic flight" (a further phase of the mock-awkward mantle, the gnostic shrug Monk so regally wore) to inaugurate a new recourse to power, a return to the world.

"I went off," Penguin announced on his return, "to prepare a place. The alternate authority of would-be kings no longer sufficed. Gassire's lute-song notwithstanding, I went after an order of metathetic spin which would, pardon the expression, cash in on a eurhythmic aplomb typically consecrated to forfeiture, debility, loss." He stopped, feeling he sounded too rhetorical. N. had already heard it all anyway.

Penguin had gone off to Wouldly Ridge but he'd kept N. abreast of his thoughts off and on, getting in touch by telepathic dispatch when some such incident of note as his coronation came up. N. too had heard the fifes and drums and the Pinkster eelpot the moment the crown touched Penguin's head. They'd both also heard a voice—a faint, faraway voice which asked, "Who are our true rulers?" Possessed of a strong nineteenth-century accent, the voice, barely pausing a beat, went on to answer, "The Negro poets, to be sure. Do they not set the fashion, and give laws to the public taste? Let one of them, in the swamps of Carolina, compose a new song, and it no sooner reaches the ear of a white amateur, than it is written down, amended (that is, almost spoilt), printed, and then put upon a course of rapid dissemination, to cease only with the utmost bounds of Anglo-Saxondom, perhaps with the world. Meanwhile, the poor author digs away with his hoe, utterly ignorant of his greatness." That they'd both heard it had to do with the odd bond Penguin's retreat had brought to the surface, the otherwise Atlantis-like relational "glue" which took the place of place. It was as if the "place" he'd gone off to prepare was not so much a place as a certain rapport, a "place" neither wholly here nor wholly there. It was a "place" which was more than one place at once, a utopic ubiquity which, though always there, was never all there.

Nonetheless, Penguin's hideaway had indeed been a place. Tucked away in a wooded area near the Hollywood Reservoir, Wouldly Ridge overlooked the L.A. Basin. It was there Penguin had pitched his tent after taking a run around the reservoir. Indian vision quest and early American camp meeting rolled into one, his retreat had begun with an unbased ring shout, the atavistic shuffle he took his jog around the reservoir to be.

Before going off Penguin had suffered a romantic setback. This was widely known to be the reason he went off. Going into hiding near the reservoir was an attempt to get back in touch with something he feared had begun to get away. His womanly thought-soul he called it, adopting the Dogon idea of a female intelligent kikínu held in reserve in the family pool—an idea N. had turned him on to some time ago. Perhaps it was this which had made for the brotherly rapport which telepathically kept the two of them in touch.

"'Cash in,'" Penguin resumed after a pause, "isn't quite the right way to put it." He paused again. His mouth was dry. He was no longer sure he had N.'s attention. Afraid he'd see that he didn't, he looked away, out the living room window, deliberately avoiding eye contact.

As the two of them sat there in N.'s living room the odd, psychosomatic thirst from which he'd suffered while on Wouldly Ridge again, for a moment, parched his mouth and throat. It had been a thirst he couldn't shake no matter how much he drank, a thirst made all the more intransigent, it seemed, by the nearness of the reservoir. It had been as if water was there in too much abundance, as if the thought of so much held in reserve refuted satiety. If, as he'd once read, thirst proves water's existence, wasn't the converse also true? The whole time on Wouldly Ridge he'd felt like a dying man in a desert, his thirst seeming at times, deliriously, like a thirst for diminution, a wish that the reservoir were smaller, the watery, womanly thought-soul he sought to replenish notwithstanding. "A spoonful," he'd found himself muttering, "just a spoonful." "Spoonful" had become a kind of mantra he often resorted to over the course of his retreat. "Spoonful, spoonful," he'd intone from time to time, seeking to soothe (and to some degree succeeding) his parched mouth and throat's insatiate "fling" with proximate water.

N. looked at Penguin, who continued gazing out the window. He wondered what had made him fall silent. No longer telepathically in touch, he had no way of knowing that Penguin's thoughts were on Wouldly Ridge, that he sat absorbed in recollecting the spill he'd suffered three days into his retreat. Even so, he himself felt a slight centrifugal rush as a somewhat stronger centrifugal rush took hold of Penguin, an ultimately phantom centrifugal sense of being swirled or swung or, "ec-" to "centric" water, flung. This was the sense Penguin had had during his run around the reservoir on day three of his retreat—not so much a mere sense, though, as an outright force causing his legs to cross and him to go tumbling to the ground.

"At first I felt it had to be that I was being punished," Penguin muttered, more to himself than to N. but breaking the silence nonetheless. He continued to not make eye contact, gazing out the window. "My centrifugal fling with womanly water had led to a fall. An ever so faint atavistic voice pointed out that my legs had crossed and for a moment I'd been dancing. My head hit the ground and I saw the Big Dipper, the 'drinking gourd' the same voice had said I should follow. It seemed to rebuke the diminution I sought, cosmically magnify the mantric spoonful I'd invoked. Oddly enough, it was then, I think, that my accession to the throne began, adumbrated by the 'starry crown,' to use the voice's expression, I saw swirling right above my head. There was something baptismal about the astral splash my spill brought me abreast of. Yes, my head hit the ground and I saw stars. This was the wet celestial seed of which King Pen appears to've been born."

N. wasn't sure he got Penguin's drift but he went on listening without interrupting. Penguin had sent no telepathic dispatch on this matter. This was the first he'd heard of the spill. It gave him a lot to think about and he was having a hard time keeping up. Did Penguin mean to suggest, he wondered, that he himself (that is, Penguin) had assumed the role of womanly water? Did he mean to say that he'd been dipped into, that the "starry crown," the magnified spoonful, capped an interior, "southern" sky? The long journey from humble gourd to coronal spoonful he could follow, though he'd have wanted it to be a northward one. Was it, after all, merely sublimation, he wondered, couvade?

Drennette, N. remembered, had suffered a spill she credited with revelatory impact, an epiphanous bicycle accident she said had turned her sense of things around. Did Penguin seek to spark some sort of parallel with her by claiming to have similarly suffered a revelatory spill? Did he mean to show that he too could invoke a blow to the head, that the initiatic tie between spill and spirit was an experiential truth to which he too was now privy? If so, in what spirit did he seek to do so? Was it rapport or was it one-upmanship he sought? Did he mean to install himself as King to Drennette's Queen or was he claiming a throne all to himself? Why had he so far made no mention of her? These were the questions N. sat asking himself while Penguin made such pronouncements as: "I gave birth to myself on Wouldly Ridge," "King Pen is for real and it's him I really am," "Monk died so King Pen could be born."

After a while N. could sit quietly no longer. "What about Drennette?" he interrupted to ask.

Penguin stopped talking but went on gazing out the window. He himself realized he'd suffered multiple blows. The blow to his head when he fell while jogging had been followed the next day by the news of Monk's death. The problematic turn his interest in Drennette had taken, he had to admit, was the blow to which those two were like aftershocks. The looped allusion to womanly water to which his run around the reservoir amounted he continued to conceive as a ring shout—unbased because of Drennette's anti-antiphonal silence. Her non-response had sent him off in search of inner resources, the atavistic, "southern" chorus whose antiphonal support placed him on the throne. He caught the point of N.'s question at once and wanted to answer that the throne was solely the King's, that it rested on antiphonal authority which wasn't hers, that Drennette could in no way be said to be his Queen. On the other hand, he quickly admitted to himself, Drennette's non-response had mothered his need to give birth to King Pen, his need to break womanly water to become his own unmatched body of water—to *thirst,* outward water notwithstanding. "Yes," he said, turning at last to look at N., "for a time the throne I sought was the oceanic sway of Drennette's hips. I'm way beyond that now. King Pen sits on his own." It was a surprising way to put it, surprising even to himself, and he paused to reflect a moment before going on. "The fifes and drums and the Pinkster eelpot I heard made it clear I'd made it north, that no matter how compensatory it appeared it was no mirage. No, this was no 'southern' sky lit by an illusory Dipper, no wishful pursuit of illusory depth, no illusory spoonful's putative plunge. No, this was true north."

N. felt he'd been caught out. He himself had heard the fifes and drums and the Pinkster eelpot, a fact which didn't leave much room for the kinds of questions he'd been entertaining. The slight centrifugal rush he'd felt should also have taught him something. What was at stake was the nature of true rule, the circumambular cast of an antiphonal north natively known to be true, quixotic needle notwithstanding. Penguin had apparently picked up on this, apparently read his thoughts or in some other way known that "What about Drennette?" was a loaded question. His powers were not to be dismissed or taken lightly. King Pen had to be reckoned with.

All of this N. already knew. Penguin did nothing more than make him admit it. Native knowledge went a long way to "explain" circumambular north but in the end had not really gone anywhere. What had gone was explanation itself, the tangential demand put on perimetric spill by centric water.

For a short while they sat silently looking at one another. Penguin then turned his head and went back to gazing out the window, whereupon N. once more felt a slight centrifugal rush. The inexplicable sense of having been flung caused a shiver to run up his back, a sharp, anti-explanatory twinge that made him sit up straight. "Explanation," he found himself saying, "is the pail of water we used to dance with atop our heads in slavery times. Would you agree that post-explanatory spillage's 'Hush now, don't' takes the cake nowadays?"

Penguin turned and looked at N. again, a look on his face which seemed to ask what was going on. N.'s tangential comment had touched on the limits of explanatory truth, the perimetric defects of circumambular persuasion, circular trope and treadmill rolled into one. Even so, N. again found himself tempted. An explanatory model proposed itself in which the would-be bond between phallic plunge and philosophic spoonful surfaced again. Before he could stop himself he gave in to it, taking advantage of Penguin's non-response to insist, "You've still got a chance with Drennette if you'll only come down from Would-Be Ridge."

No sooner had N. said this than they both felt a further centrifugal rush, an oblique furtherance of an emergent prospect or principle whose outline remained obscure. The lateral drift accelerated by N.'s pointed play on "Wouldly" was not without a vertical aspect, a sense of tilt, disorientation or erosion which made it feel as though as they slid they lost elevation as well. "Would-Be Ridge"'s intimation of unreliable support, much to N.'s own chagrin, fostered a sense that the floor sank as they slid across it. He himself couldn't shake the feeling that he slid upon a precipitous ledge, inexplicably dependent upon a hypothetic surface which might not have been there. Thus it was that epithetic "Would-Be" boomeranged against him. He found he'd cast a more inclusive net than he'd intended. Not only had he reversed his earlier position regarding Drennette (encouraging Penguin to pursue her whereas before he'd urged him to cool it), he'd also cast aspersions on Wouldly Ridge. Neither of these had he intended to do. It was this, the irrelevance of intention, which undermined his living room floor, made it more and more hypothetic. Hypothetic floor, moreover, might as well have been epithetic Ridge—a reversal which was by no means lost on him.

Penguin, on the other hand, endured the further centrifugal rush and the sense of tilt with the firm conviction that they were evidence of King Pen's power. Tangential drift and the loss of elevation paradoxically bolstered the throne on which he sat. Tilt and slide recalled the oceanic sway he'd spoken of in regard to Drennette's hips, an ironic accession to the "throne" he'd earlier insisted he'd gone beyond. With this he rubbed N.'s innuendo in his face, tilt and slide taking less time than the blinking of an eye, at the end of which he sat grinning with satisfaction. "I didn't come here to be insulted," he told N. He'd made it clear that King Pen didn't play.

N. understood he'd been put in his place. The pail of water crowning the slave's head, he reflected, might as well have been a dunce's cap. Penguin had answered with an antiphonal spoonful, an ever so slight bit of spillage he'd endowed with the movement of a wave about to break. Crest, crown and womanly rump rolled into one, the tilting, sliding sense of a "spilling" floor had brought N. up short. That this had occurred at all would've been wonder enough. That it was done with a mere spoonful of water—spilled water—humbled him all the more.

Having made it clear that King Pen didn't play, Penguin now went on to insist that "What about Monk?" was much more to the point. "Monastic flight," he said, "brought home to me the fact that in retreating to Wouldly Ridge I was looking for a meeting of would-be king with worldly king, the fact that wouldly reign sought to reconcile the two. Monkish, renunciative accent unquenchably thirsted after wouldly rule. That this was the case was all the more obvious now that Monk was gone. When I heard the news I couldn't help thinking of 'New Monastery,' Andrew's piece. The title of the album it's on, *Point of Departure*, ratified my sense of tangential vocation. Call it the rendezvous of *tendency* with *point*, or, better yet, say that the prospect of punctual access *lifted*, possessed of a centrifugal 'high.'"

Penguin fell silent, his head slightly tilted like a bird's. The implications of lifted access caused him to pause and reflect a while. Tendency and point's conjunctive capture, their joint possession by centrifugal "high," felt as if point no longer yielded to explanatory pressure.

N. studied the look on Penguin's face while giving some thought to what he'd said. It was an odd, not entirely convincing take, he thought, having more to do with Monk's name than with the music or the man. Still, the Andrew Hill piece to which Penguin had referred happened to be one of his favorites. The mix of watery verticality and angular surge it pulled off had taken hold of him what seemed like ages ago. The mere mention of it now filled his head with the synaesthetic images of staggered ignition which had filled it the first time he heard the piece—subaquatic fountains and jets, underwater fireworks giving Penguin's pursuit of womanly thought-soul all the more oomph. Even so, N. continued to apply a grain of salt to Penguin's take on Monk's death, a take he increasingly felt to be off base—deliberately so, therapeutically so perhaps, but bordering on disrespect all the same. He had a hard time not meeting disrespect with disrespect, a hard time refraining from asking, "What about Djeannine? What about lilac time?"

Repressing the question hurt the tip of his tongue. It was a question alluding to a song which had recently come to his attention, a song Gene Austin recorded in the twenties, "Jeannine, I Dream of Lilac Time." That the song had been featured in a movie, *Lilac Time*, a movie starring Colleen Moore and Gary Cooper, made the question all the more sarcastic. Behind its dig lay the lines "Jeannine, my queen of lilac time, / When I return, I'll make you mine." Penguin's return, the question implied, was mere fantasy resolution, King Pen's throne a mere would-be seat beside his dream-queen Djeannine.

It was an allusion, however, whose bite would've been lost on Penguin. N. himself had only recently learned of the song, having happened upon Austin's recording on an album he found in a used record store. He had no reason to believe Penguin had ever heard of it. The question was thus one whose dig he'd have to explain—all the more reason, he admitted, not to ask it. Even so, it took an immense effort to hold it back, so immense he literally bit his tongue, applied a steady, clamplike pressure with his teeth. As he did so he couldn't help wondering was reverse bite, boomeranging bite, yet another demonstration of King Pen's power.

N.'s nose now began to twitch. The smell of lilacs wafted in from some abrupt, immediately suspect source he thought of turning his head to try to catch offguard—a thought it took no more than a moment to reject. Years ago he'd read liner notes on an Eric Dolphy album, notes which spoke of Dolphy's "impatience," his wish to "sneak" past limits. "He implies beyond the horn," the notes had asserted. "He tries to sneak through its limitations at some swift, flat angle." The passage had stayed with him, stuck in his mind, more or less verbatim. It was exactly that "swift, flat angle" from which he now felt himself addressed, an obtuse, tangential angle thru which the lilac scent made its way. The resistance of any such angle to attribution argued against turning his head. He knew too well it would've done no good.

The clamplike pressure of his teeth on his tongue and the angular advent of lilac scent made for a synaesthetic wad of apprehension to which the eelpot's return was now added. The sound of it came in loud and clear, entering at exactly the same "swift, flat angle" the smell of lilacs took. Smell, touch and hearing were rolled into one by the lilac vibe, an unsettling mix which made it evident that Penguin had not only read his thoughts but succeeded in turning them against him again. The eelpot completed the combination which took him out, an epiphanous "click" not unlike sesame access except that it was clamp-lilac-eelpot access instead.

Yes, he now knew for sure, reverse bite, boomeranging bite, was another demonstration of King Pen's power. A split-second before he passed out he glimpsed a spoon spinning slowly like the blade of a fan just above Penguin's head, a suspended "crown" which, hovering halo-like, confirmed the now uncontested majesty of King Pen.

26.III.82

Dear Angel of Dust,

What I called clamp-lilac-eelpot access in my lecture/libretto has turned a new page in the band's book. We've all fallen in with a flow we always knew was there, though not as viscerally as we know it now. We've again been apprised of an echoic whir, warned against pre-emptive equivalence. The aliquant register unveiled by Penguin's "low would" run, the kingly descent that put him on his "throne," conferred a false-fingered, winged as well as winded benediction on one and all—a dry, self-appointing anointment both in and out of keeping with a prosaic age. "Low would" run spoke of blown resources, a desultory, deciduous calculus of last resort. Winded, wing-and-a-prayer benediction blew thru from the lips of a desiderative muse.

This has all become increasingly evident as the days have gone by since Penguin's return. What I thought at first was a local hit—what, in fact, was at first a local hit—has turned out to be a sustained buzz, a namesake bud which eventually bloomed. Infectious wind and incongruous wing rolled into one, it carried a spark which didn't stop with me and Penguin but went on to light up Aunt Nancy, Djamilaa, Lambert and Drennette as well. That it took a while to spread takes nothing away from it. It makes it all the more formidable in fact. Part spore, part resuscitated fossil, it's for real. Something new seems to be afoot.

Djamilaa and I were talking about this last night. She spoke of Penguin's epiphany as the realization that "would" works both ways. He came to see, she said, that he'd set himself up to be let down, that the would-be high he projected held hands with would-be low, that Drennette, just like everyone else, was as much the one as she was the other. His "low would" run, she went on, sought to announce this realization triumphantly, to proclaim it as an edict he was the author of. That the bottom falls out to reveal another bottom was clearly the point of the wouldly octave he blew. Wouldly reign, she elaborated, the recognition of "would's" two-way cut, gave welcome relief to ostensible bottom, see-thru bottom. It was here that she got to the part that spoke to me most. To've been taken up, she said, by "low would" run, as we clearly have, is to be seated in a glass-bottom boat.

It was this I was thinking about today at rehearsal when I suggested we give "Sun Ship" a try. I've long been drawn to the percussive, sculptor's approach Trane takes to its iterative head (as though he chipped or hammered away at stone), the rhythmic seizure which translates shock into shapeliness. I knew it would put the visceral flow we've fallen in with to a test, but something told me it was a test we could pass. In any case, the prospect of a glass-bottom ride (wouldly ride) in the company of no less than the Sun was one I couldn't see passing up.

It turned out to be all I'd expected, even more—a ride unlike any we'd ever known. To say that *lapse* was the element we moved in begins to give some sense of what it was like, though to say that a navigable inordinacy opened up begins to as well. A condition of catch-up, that is, with all the turbulence and winded urgency thus implied (wouldly weather), came into complicated play with glass-bottom repose. Iterative head, it seemed, charted a zigzag, serrate course. It was as if we sought to stitch two pieces of cloth together, to close the rift between Wouldly River's two banks, to bite thru the element we rode even though to do so proposed its undoing. It was this bite which brought clamp into the picture, a clenched, mandibular coefficient which, even so, left one's embouchure as open as one could want. One sang thru one's teeth as lilacs bloomed on both banks. Eels wiggled by below.

Mandibular clench was both a courtesy and a caution. I looked around and saw that everyone's jaws were a little tight. It was as if we bit back or fought back further expression even as we gave the piece all the expressive propulsion we could. We each, it seemed, had clenching recourse to the old blues line, "Don't start me talkin'"—a disingenuous disclaimer animating the reservoir it sought to conserve. Consumption and conservation locked hands. Glass-bottom advance insisted on the ultimacy of see-thru bottom, albeit "see-thru" declared ultimacy void.

Reservoir notwithstanding, it was the flow clamp-lilac-eelpot calibrated which was most worth noting. We all hunched forward—a flow-thru posture—as we played. I was relieved, as I looked around, to see it wasn't just me. Djamilaa hunched forward over the piano, as did Drennette over the drumset, Aunt Nancy over the bass, Penguin and Lambert, just like me, over their tenors. The band roared like a three-horned beast. The three tenors played the head in unison, then improvised all at the same time (shades of Trane, Pharoah and Donald Garrett on the *Live in Seattle* date), a tricorn crown to which Penguin alluded at one point with a quote from Rahsaan's "We Free Kings." The relationship of crown to head, as was only to be expected of wouldly reign, grew faint, far-fetched at times—the ravings of thwarted royalty, would-be kings. Wouldly roar's tricorn crown went Alexander the Great, the Two-Horned, one better.

Kings in Exile, a band in Dallas whose record *Music from Ancient Texts* we've been listening to of late, was clearly in the back of our minds—not so much their music as the outcast kingship their name evokes. This went well with the Nilotic rush the rhythm section laid down, the magic, magisterial carpet they rolled out. Pharaonic pariahs we called ourselves, an etymologic accent Drennette introduced with grumbling bass drum patter (Tamil *paraiyan*: drummer).

But I've gone on like this longer than I know why. Don't take my word for any of it, listen for yourself. I'm enclosing a copy of the tape we made.

Yours,
N.

4.IV.82

Dear Angel of Dust,

It's three in the morning and I haven't slept a wink. I tossed and turned for what felt like forever before I finally gave up and got out of bed. What's keeping me up is that there's a piece I'd like to write, a piece which, at least for now, will neither let me write it nor let me rest. It all started earlier today while I was at my mother's in Santa Ana. An old friend I went to junior high school and high school with also happened to be in town and we got together and hung out a while. He's been doing some research on the Indians of the area and we got to talking about that. What especially spoke to me and got me wanting to write this piece were the stories he told me about, stories the Juaneño Indians told regarding a black rock known as Tosaut. This rock was put at the center of the world shortly after Creation by the god Nocuma. This was done to secure the world. At that time the sea was only a small stream running from south to north, so crowded with fish the fish didn't have enough room. They conferred as to what they should do, some proposing they go ashore, others arguing against it. While they were conferring a large fish came along carrying the Tosaut rock, inside which, when they broke it open, they found a ball shaped like a bladder, filled with gall. This they emptied into the water, which turned salty and swelled and overflowed across the earth and came to occupy the space it covers now. The fish were glad to finally have more room and they also found the change in the water's taste to their liking. But that's not all. The part that got me thinking about a new composition is the part where, many years after the creation of the first man and woman, a tyrant by the name of Ouiot comes to power. He starts out fine, ruling peacefully and kindly, but after a few years he's ruling with such cruelty the people plot to get rid of him. The method they decide on is poison. They put a poison made from powdered Tosaut rock on his chest one night while he's asleep. He wakes up to feel a sickness in his limbs and at length dies.

I've been reading *The Black Jacobins,* C. L. R. James's book on Toussaint L'Ouverture and the Haitian Revolution, and I couldn't help thinking of the use of poison he writes about early on, the fact that the slaves resorted to it so often. (The notorious Mackandal, he says, built up his organization for six years, he and his followers poisoning both whites and disobedient members of their own band. They had a plan to launch an uprising by poisoning the water of every house in the capital.) I also couldn't help recalling that the most intractable slaves were the so-called saltwater Negroes, those who'd made the Middle Passage. The title "Tosaut L'Ouverture" popped into my head. Unfortunately, no music popped in with it.

Still, the title wouldn't let me be. The more I thought about it the more that second syllable, "-saut," seemed intent on telling me something, something I vaguely remembered having read having to do with ring shouts. When I got home tonight I followed up on it. It took a while but I finally found what I was looking for in Lydia Parrish's book *Slave Songs of the Georgia Sea Islands.* Concerning the word "shout" (which refers not to the singing but to the circumambular movement the singing accompanies), she uses Lorenzo Turner's work on West African survivals in Gullah to suggest an Arabic provenance: "Dr. L. D. Turner has discovered that the Arabic word *Saut* (pronounced like our word 'shout'), in use among the Mohamedans of West Africa, meant to run and walk around the Kaaba." That clinched it. One black rock had led me to another. The Juaneño had led me to Mecca by way of Haiti and the Georgia coast. "Tosaut L'Ouverture," I now knew, was a piece I *had* to write. It would demand all the syncretistic salt I could muster. Exactly the sort of work I like most.

So far no good. I'm beginning to think I should change the title to

"I Can't Get Started." I sat down before going to bed and tried to work something up. Nothing I came up with worked. What most readily suggested itself was a derivative tack I didn't find at all satisfactory—allusions to "Salt Peanuts," "Haitian Fight Song" and so forth. I finally gave up and went to bed but, as I've said, couldn't get to sleep. My head, it seemed, had become a black rock. I saw notes revolving around it—the notes, I took it, to the Afro-Amerindian dhikr I was after—but the hitching movement they made made it impossible to make them out.

The difficulty might be put this way: By syncretistic salt one means a mix in which adverse traditions relativize one another, relate while applying a grain of salt to one another. Though "while" need not exclude "by way of," what's hard is not to conflate the two, not to foreclose on truth however rightly one recoils from presumed absolutes. The detour thru salt, that is, isn't the same as obstruction. Nor does it argue anything goes. Relativistic salt insists upon a hitch. By way of that hitch it calls its orbit into question, laments its ability to universalize though it employs it nonetheless. Some such hitch, in some way I've yet to figure out, has to advance "Tosaut L'Ouverture."

Writing you, I thought, might help. I'm not sure it has, as far as getting going on the piece is concerned, but it's done some good to put the problem in words. I'll close now and, whichever comes first, either get going or get some sleep.

Sincerely,
N.

PS: (Next day, before I mail this.) Sleep came first.

6.IV.82

Dear Angel of Dust,

Not a whole lot of progress to report on "Tosaut L'Ouverture," except that I've decided there'll be a synthesizer in it. This would be a first for us, though Djamilaa's had a synthesizer for a few months now and is getting to know her way around on it pretty well. What I like is the sense of extrapolative surge one can get from it, the sense of immanent atmosphere, spheric dilation, synaptic expanse. I'd like, running the risk of a lapse into the programmatic, to save it for the last part of the piece, have it come on like a sudden crystallization, a capacious "inwardness" turned unexpectedly "overt." What I'd like to evoke is a psychotropic surge into synthetic air, a synthesized ripening of resident capacity tantamount to a "miracle of the fishes" all its own—etheric, synthetic, yet (in only the most corporeal sense) "inside," an extrapolative sense of streaming viscera (vatic outwardness, visceral sky). This is all, I admit, merely embryonic, a mere beginning.

Here, in any case, are some thoughts I think might move matters further along: 1) Saltwater intransigence translates grain of salt into grain of truth. 2) Black rock is the occult obduracy the pursuit of granular truth revolves around. 3) By salt one means a reminder of waters crossed. 4) Salt returns us to ourselves, brings us back to where we were, wakes us up to sedated senses of who we are. 5) Black salinity thrives on the memory of cramped space, the congestion Tosaut salt opens up.

Somewhere I want it also implied, if not stated outright, that the swept air, the unstrapped immensity of synthesized advent, wipes away chagrin. But that's a bridge we'll cross when we get to it.

You're well I hope.

As ever,

N.

22.IV.82

Dear Angel of Dust,

I've been listening a lot these past few days to "Cyclic Episode," one of the cuts on *Fuchsia Swing Song*, one of Sam Rivers's early albums. Something about it seems to speak all the more pointedly to me these days, something pertinent, I can't help thinking, to "Tosaut L'Ouverture." Perhaps it's the understated way Sam has of opening it up, the way understatement works to further, of all things, the anthem-like way the piece gathers, the seemingly offhand way in which it grows. There's an air of confidentiality he lends the head's ditty-bop assurance, intimations of a ditty-bop conspiracy, some hip, whispered insurgency we sense might be afoot. It all somehow turns on that soft-spoken entrance, the way chagrin seems to've long since been dealt with, digested, qualms verged on but in the end veered away from, the head spun of an element all its own by so close an encounter. Then, too, one mustn't forget the degree to which *grow* gives way to *glide* at crucial points, only then to come back with such ferocity we see that *growl* inhered in what *grow* proposed. I'm struck, that is, by the way soft-spoken entrance opens onto its opposite, as though the likelihood of abrupt, expulsive dilation obtained at all points. I'm reminded of something of Rumi's I once read: "When you have closed your mouth on this side, open it on that, for your shout of triumph will echo in the placeless air."

What Rumi has to say bears not only on "Cyclic Episode" but also on *saut*, the unsounded shout he thus helps us to see as a two-sided shout, the circumambular play of not only voiced but unvoiced endowments.

I'm wondering if this doesn't in some way have something to say about the blank I continue to draw when it comes to "Tosaut L'Ouverture." Could that blank, that is, be the unsounded side of a shout which resounds elsewhere, the unsounded side on which that elsewhere shuts me up? What I like about "Cyclic Episode" is the way Sam seems to've been able to give both sides their due. I'd avail myself of a similar ditty-bop ability to dwell in unplaced as well as placed air, unvoiced as well as voiced investiture, unbased as well as based circumlocution. This would seem to be the challenge I've not yet risen to in my attempts to tap into "Tosaut L'Ouverture," to bring it over from that other side on which I'm now even more convinced it resides. Something like Sam's unhurried assurance might be the soft-spoken key, the "open sesame," I'm after.

As I've already said, I've been listening to that one cut over and over these past few days. It got to where getting up to return the needle to where the cut begins got to be a drag, so I put it on tape in what amounts to a loop, the one cut, repeated, taking up the entire cassette. (What's more, I've got an auto reverse cassette player, so I don't even have to turn it over.) I'm listening to it now, as I write. In fact, something I heard in what went by a few moments ago I have to say something about, for it seemed if I could only reach out at the appropriate angle I'd have been able to take hold of the soft-spoken entry of which the minor sevenths the piece piles up appear intent on telling, literally hold it in my hand. The hovering accretion Sam somehow manages made me think of the air of which we're thus apprised as momentarily so possible it became palpable as well, a teasing hint of tangibility I'm straining my pen to give senses of. (Words may not, as I once heard someone say, go there, but I'm convinced they do come from there.) Though Sam's ditty-bop insistences accent fugitivity, the runaway gist and the apt impropriety of any such attempt, I did in fact attempt to take hold of that air. Evidently I got the angle wrong. Either that or some fickle sense of Tosaut access intervened, inklings of access qualified by salt, cystic regard for what gets away. Hopefully the latter's the case, meaning "Tosaut L'Ouverture" is now at least within range.

Yours,
N.

30.IV.82

Dear Angel of Dust,

I finally got "Tosaut L'Ouverture" written. "Cyclic Episode" turned out, as I suspected it would, to be the key, though you'd never guess the lengths I had to go to to get it to work. Have you ever heard of "Muslim soup"? Probably not. Neither had I until a few days ago when I read about a group of people known as the Nafama, a nonliterate group who live in northwestern Ghana. They've been influenced by the Mande, their Muslim neighbors, and though they've not converted to Islam they believe Arabic script has talismanic power, Koranic verses particularly so. They make a brew they call *siliama-que*, "Muslim soup." This they do by steeping roots and herbs in water used to wash Islamic chalkboards, boards on which verses from the Koran have been written being believed to make the strongest "soup." Their version of holy water, it can be sprinkled on a person to give him or her protection, but it's thought to be most effective when imbibed. They tell stories of invulnerability to bullets being thus induced.

Anyway, my frustrated attempts to get going on "Tosaut L'Ouverture" finally got to where I decided to concoct a chalkboard brew of my own, a talismanic tea or soup (*saut* soup I decided I'd call it) which would assist me toward the breakthrough I sought. What I did was write out the head to "Cyclic Episode" on a chalkboard and wash it away with water, saving the water and adding herbs and roots to make *saut* soup. I couldn't help thinking of the chalk-inscribed head as being something like a vévé in Haitian vodoun, though analogies to football or basketball (plays drawn up in chalk) seemed relevant as well. It was as I drank the chalky concoction that a further parallel suggested itself: the book John eats in *Revelation*. The stomached ordeal the bitter brew induced hit me at once. I felt I'd vomit, so queasy, so conducive to qualms had my stomach become, big with bibliophagous apprehensions it seemed, angst wound up inside it like a scroll. The watery book I'd swallowed meted out emulsified extrusions of what turned out, as in the Djeannine dream, to be emptiness, air, albeit, as in the dream, X-ray emptiness, X-ray air. I looked at my legs and saw bones, looked at my arms and saw bones, looked and saw bones and internal organs when I looked at my torso.

A ring of notes began to revolve around my head, possessed of an intimate spin as though bent (bent by the antipodal itch to hold something which had never been held before). They bobbed like horses on a carousel, made of wood but with a lifelike limberness evocative of blood warmth, heat, hot pursuit. They ran ridden by the hitch which bore them aloft, Haitian horses, winged rule and winged exception rolled into one unruly whir, intimate spur rolled in with warm, unquenchable spin. Each horse was "given its head," as though of each it could have honestly been said, "Everything I know runs within that note." Each note was a Tosaut rock, Tosaut horse, ready to break, run out from inside. Everything I knew ran around my head in a ring which grew so tight, so like a tourniquet, I was afraid my eyes would pop out. I felt as if I'd been poisoned, not unlike Ouiot, the ring of notes part would-be crown, part mark of the beast.

But such, I consoled myself, were the visionary dues one had to pay, bled by what one knew in such fashion even stanching the flow was a pain, an ordeal. The ring of notes did eventually stand still, stop turning, the only problem then being that, pressed as they were to my head, I could no longer see them, much less make them out. The ring loosened a bit, not so much a tourniquet anymore as a sweatband or a bandage, but it still didn't stand away from my head the way it had at first. To see the notes I had no recourse but to look in a mirror. I somehow made my way to the bathroom, where with the help of the mirror on the medicine cabinet I could make out the notes which girded my head, those at the back with the aid of a handheld mirror used in concert, so to speak, with the larger one.

I'm not sure I've made it clear that also girding my head was a staff and that it was on this that the notes were written. Thus it was, in any event, that I finally got going. I got out some staff paper and copied what I saw in the mirror, then got out my tenor and played what I'd written and, liking what I heard, knew "Tosaut L'Ouverture" was at last underway. It obliquely and ever so elusively recalled "Cyclic Episode," though what the resemblance consisted of one would've been extremely hardpressed to say. I've since come to see that it has somewhat the same relationship to "Cyclic Episode" that Frank Wright's "One for John" has to "Naima," except that here there's an even more teasing, immensely more lost-on-the-tip-of-the-tongue sense of (there's no other way to say it) Tosaut opening, Tosaut access.

Anyway, I got the piece written, only to run into a hitch when I took it to rehearsal. After I passed out the charts and we talked about the piece a bit, we gave it a go. Everything went okay for the first few bars but then the time began to drag, this getting worse the farther we went, my gestures to Drennette to pick up the tempo notwithstanding. Soon she quit playing altogether, saying that something about the piece deeply disabled her, that she couldn't say exactly what it was but that her legs and arms had begun to knot up, her body to ache under what felt like added weight. She immediately went on, however, to allow that this made no sense, that it must've been all in her mind, so we gave it another try but the same thing happened. Again, a few bars into the piece she stopped, complaining that her legs and arms were on the verge of cramping, that the sense of added weight had come on again. We gave it several more tries but each time the same thing happened.

We put our heads together as to what was going on. Pressed to go into it, Drennette said the piece reminded her of something she couldn't quite put her finger on, that, more specifically, it brought another piece to mind whose title escaped her. "'Cyclic Episode,'" I suggested. After a moment's reflection she said yes, that was it. This, then, cleared the whole thing up. Our best collective guess was that

"Tosaut L'Ouverture" 's oblique recollection of "Cyclic Episode" spoke, on some deep muscular level, to Drennette's memory of the spill she suffered on her last bike ride with Rick. Oblique namesake recall spoke not only subliminally but physically, percussive spirit bested, here at least, by traumatic spill, Tosaut opening undermined by Tosaut block. The question, then, was—and remains—what to do about it.

Let me know what you think.

Yours,

N.

15.V.82

Dear Angel of Dust,

We took your advice and it works. Drennette swallows a few salt tablets whenever we play "Tosaut L'Ouverture"; her legs and arms no longer knot up. Why none of us thought of this I don't know, but on the very first try, right after I got your last letter, the salt tablets took care of the problem. Drennette swallowed a few, we jumped into "Tosaut L'Ouverture" and for the first time, finally, we got past the first few bars without her dropping out. We played the whole piece in fact. You're on to something in saying that her reaction to the piece has to do with more than her concussive bicycle ride with Rick, that it reaches back to the fishes' predicament in the Juaneño myth. Yes, repercussive cramp, related to crowded, pre-Tosaut conditions, might well be an aspect of the muscular recall Drennette endures by way of torqued, sympathetic attunement, Tosaut block. She herself describes it as "perspiratory interiority." A cyclic equation of loss of salt with torqued exacerbation calibrates couvadelike premises: *saut* sauna, soul sauna, psychic sweat-lodge. "It's as if soul," Drennette says, "were a cavewall dripping with sweat. I'm sweating outside-in rather than inside-out, but the salt's being lost anyway." Which, as you seem to have known, is where the salt tablets come in, Tosaut replenishment rolling duress and durability into one (damping muscular recoil but leaving its recall aspect intact). Drennette says the sense of knottedness and added weight continues, but only as a phantom sensation contrapuntal to the unencumbered extension of arms and legs. Phantom cramp, that is, exacts real yet etheric dues, the evaporative sweat an atmospheric endorsement of repercussive sympathy, prepossessing salt. One of the things I like most about the piece is the confluence of sympathetic and synthetic resonances Drennette and Djamilaa's interplay brings one back to again and again.

I'm enclosing a tape of the piece we made at rehearsal last night. You'll notice from the label that we've settled on a new name for the band. This came about only a few days ago, about the same time, actually, as I got your "prescription." (It seems to've been a week for solutions.) The name is a composite of two names Lambert and Aunt Nancy suggested, both of which we liked but were ultimately unable to decide between. Lambert's idea was that we call ourselves the Molimo Sound Ensemble, a name alluding to the Mbuti Pygmies of the Congo. You may have read *The Forest People*, Colin Turnbull's book about the Mbuti, and, if so, you may remember that the molimo is the name they give the ritual they perform at times of crisis, a ritual consisting mainly of songs sung nightly by the men. It's also the name given to the fire around which they gather, as well as to the musical instrument, a long trumpet, which assumes a central role in the ritual. The trumpet's voice is the voice of the forest, the voice, the men tell the women, of "the animal of the forest," a forest monster women are not allowed to see. But this assertion of male primacy and privilege gets undermined in the course of the performance Turnbull recounts. It comes to light that originally the women owned the molimo. Hence Lambert's reasoning that "Molimo Sound Ensemble" resolves Drennette and Aunt Nancy's objection to "Mystic Horn Society's" male bias. He made his reasoning clear by reading from a book by Evan Zuesse, *Ritual Cosmos,* three of whose chapters deal with the Mbuti. Zuesse refers to what he terms "the molimo spirit," a spirit of mediation or reconciliation, it turns out, characterized by a coincidence of opposites, as in the passage Lambert read to us: "The beginning of the festival seems to suggest the phallic aspect of the molimo; the end equates the molimo with the women. Actually, we may have the answer to the nature of the spirit in concluding that it is both male and female. In almost every area of symbolism the molimo is the unity of opposites."

Aunt Nancy's idea was that we call ourselves the Maatet, or, simply, Maatet, a name the Egyptians gave one of the boats in which the sun sails across the sky, the one it boards at dawn, the morning boat (the other being the one in which it completes its journey, Sektet, the evening boat). Maatet joins Atet, a more common name for the morning boat, with Maat, the name of the goddess of truth: Maat + Atet = Maatet. Aunt Nancy said she likes the suggestion of maternity, matriarchy, in the very sound of it, as well as what she calls its feminization of SunStick's claim, "I play truth." (It was at SunStick's aborted audition, remember, that we made the decision to seek a woman drummer.) She'd gotten intimations of the name, she said, a few weeks back, when we played the clamp-lilac-eelpot rendition of "Sun Ship." The glass-bottom disposition it opened up seems to've been an avatar of see-thru truth, a truth whose translucent body she rode, not yet consciously equating its light touch with Maat's ostrich feather. "Ever since then," she said, "I've had a feeling of namesake encasement, see-thru cartouche, a swift, boat-bodied lightness, light-bodied bigness we'd grow into. It's a name we'll have to fill in, occupy, but I don't have any doubts we can."

As I've said, we liked both names—though not entirely without reservations. Drennette said she thought "Molimo Sound Ensemble's" implicit critique of male bias was too implicit, too subtle, that most people would miss it. Penguin, on the other hand, said he thought "Maatet," ostrich feather notwithstanding, was a bit heavyhanded. There were some other quibbles as well, but these two were the most substantive. The former we decided to address by giving "Molimo," as though it were Spanish, an alternate, feminine ending, "-ma," adding it with the help of a slash, on the model of "his/her"—that is, Molimo/ma. This helped address Penguin's reservation as well, allowing "Maatet" to become "Atet" ("-ma Atet") in the compound/compromise "Molimo/ma Atet." We then dropped the slash, kept the space between "-mo" and "ma," closed the space between "ma" and "Atet," contracting and apostrophizing to get "m'Atet." Hence, the Molimo m'Atet.

As ever,

N.

22.V.82

Dear Angel of Dust,

There's a story John Gilmore tells about the first time he played in New York. It was in 1956 at Birdland, where he'd been hanging out with his horn for about a month without getting a chance to play. Pat Patrick was working there with Willie Bobo's band one night and it was thanks to him that John finally got a chance to sit in. He says he knew right away he wouldn't be able to play with them the way he was used to playing, in the loose, "lag along" Chicago style. They took a stiffer tack, so after he jumped into his solo he decided to play, as he puts it, "contra to them." He played *against* everything they played. Whatever rhythm they played he played its opposite, playing inversions instead of straight eighth or straight sixteenth notes. "Contrary motion" he calls it. He says Trane was in the audience that night and that he liked what he heard so much he came running up to him afterward saying, "John Gilmore, John Gilmore, you've got it, you've got the concept! You've got the concept! You've got to show me how to play some of that stuff."

I bring this up in response to your kind comments on "Tosaut L'Ouverture," your request that I say a bit more regarding "cystic regard for what gets away." You're right, I think, to say that there's a poetics implied, though to call it a prosody makes the point more precisely. You're also right to relate this to the "peculiar sense of weight" you find at work in "Tosaut L'Ouverture," the galled and galling combinatory pace parsed out in rapport (parallactic rapport) with an agile array of inertial constraints. John Gilmore comes to mind because that "sense," to my ears at least, is one which flirts with unwieldiness, gives a feel for unwieldiness in ways which are indebted to my long-time fascination with his approach. I'm struck by the way the tenor, in John's hands, seems to become bulkier, bigger, more dangerous, a volatile beast requiring more effort to simply hold on to. One hears apprehensions of imminent emergency, a strapped, struggling conception of things as though at all points they were on the verge of getting away, getting out of hand. He approaches the horn with a lion trainer's caution and respect, a circumspect "contrary motion" which is endlessly at pains not to be caught out. Maybe it's more an anti-prosodic than a prosodic approach, the "lag along" looseness of it insisting on a resistant lag, a contestatory lag, as if keeping up were a life-or-death struggle and an irrelevance both.

In any event, for "resistant lag" read "regard for what gets away," galled and galling regard. Read "stolen march," "contestatory stagger," "lost step." I'm thinking of Alejo Carpentier's novel *The Lost Steps*, where the search for the origins of music repeatedly turns upon an insistence on fugitivity, a resistance to capture at even the vegetative level. ("'These are the plants which have fled from man since the beginning,' the friar told me, 'the rebel plants, those which refused to serve him as food, which crossed rivers, scaled mountains, leaped the deserts. . . .'") Thinking of the salsa group Orquesta Cimarrón, I relate this to marronage, the runaway tack resorted to by so many slaves. It's as if in our music we honor fugitive roots while paying homage to captive kin, as if, descendants of captives, we come to the beat (punctual capture, captive concurrence) with weightier qualms, weightier qualifications. "Lag along" equivocation speaks to this.

But I don't want to load it up entirely on rhythm. John's intonation has taught me a lot as well. You've no doubt noticed the way he endows his tone, whether in the upper or the lower register, with inklings of tenuous containment, an insinuative touch which makes us imagine a mere twitch of his lip would take the whole thing out. As with the rhythm, he appears to grapple with an extrapolative tonality, a timbral momentum that wants to work loose. Adumbrations of imminent alarm run throughout, the beginnings of a sirenlike escalation, no matter how muffled, never not implicitly there. Think of Clifton Chenier doing "I Can't Stop Loving You," how he lets the accordion begin to scream only to rein it back in, coming right out on the *Bon Ton Roulet* album and saying, "Whoa," the poignant play between "whoa" and "can't stop" addressing runaway love with resistant (would-be resistant) lag.

There's more I could go into, but this, I think, puts it in a nutshell. Thanks for your strong response to "Tosaut L'Ouverture." I hope it's true that with it, as you say, we've turned a corner.

Yours,
N.

5.VI.82

Dear Angel of Dust,

The other shoe finally dropped. We're in Seattle playing a three-night stint at a club called Soulstice. Last night, the first night of the gig, new repercussions on a number of fronts came to light. Foremost among them is that the wouldly subsidence in which Penguin and Drennette's embryonic romance had gotten hung up seems to've given way, exacting a ledge, an atomistic ledge, from the lapse it rescinded. You've no doubt noticed that since Penguin's return from Wouldly Ridge it's been as though his embryonic courtship of Drennette had never occurred. He's not only not pursued it further, he'll neither speak nor hear talk of it. Whenever I've brought it up he's acted like he had no idea what I was talking about, staring at me with a blank, uncomprehending look on his face, as though English were a foreign language, as if I spoke some unheard-of tongue. Aunt Nancy, Lambert and Djamilaa say it's been the same with them. Drennette likewise has acted like nothing ever happened. She and Penguin have been nothing but normal in their dealings with one another.

It's hard to say what it was, why it was wouldly subsidence took this occasion to exact wouldly ledge. My guess is that the air of anticlimactic futurity pervading this town had something to do with it, the datedness of what was once thought of as "things to come." I'm referring, of course, to the Space Needle. That the future has no place in which to arrive but the present, that its arrival is thus oxymoronic, is the sort of reflection one can't help entertaining in the shadow of such a monument as that—a monument, when it was built, to the future, a future it prematurely memorialized, prematurely entombed. Today it's more properly a monument to the past, a reminder of the times in which it was built, tomb to the elapsed expectancy it all turns out to've been. I remember my aunt and uncle driving up for the World's Fair twenty years ago—hopelessly long ago it seems now.

But by no means to be ignored is the reinforcement given elapsed or outmoded future by us happening to hear "Telstar," the early sixties hit by the Tornadoes, on the jukebox in a diner we had lunch in yesterday. The tinny, strained, "futuristic" sound of it said it all, spoke to a sense of lost occasion elapsed future began infusing us with the moment we laid eyes on that Needle. I thought of every wish which had seemed to miss the mark in being fulfilled, though I corrected myself at once, admitting the case to be one of an "it" which could only be projected, never arrived at. Anticlimactic "it," I reminded myself, allotted virtual space, an ironic investiture missed opportunity couldn't help but inhabit. Disappointment, the needling sense of a missed appointment, couldn't help but be there. This we knew before "Telstar" came on. We knew it all the more once it did.

The weather played a part as well. It hasn't rained outright since we've been here but it's been overcast and drizzling, a thin mist coming down pretty much all the time. That mist, it seemed, went with us into the club last night. It adopted a low profile for the occasion, close to the floor like a carpet so intimate with our feet we'd have sworn we dragged it in. What had been of the air was now oddly underfoot. In a way it was like the world had turned upside down, the way the mist, instead of falling from the sky, came up from the floor, ever so lightly addressing the soles of our feet. The difference this would make in our music was evident at once. No sooner had we taken the stage than the low-lying mist was an atomistic ledge we stood on which made our feet feel as though they'd fallen asleep—not entirely numb but (you know the feeling I'm sure) put upon by pins, subject to a sort of pointillist embrace. Point had become a hydra, its pinpoint tactility multiply-pinned. We couldn't help knowing it was "missed" on which we stood (missed mark, missed opportunity, missed appointment), no less real, no less an actual mist even so. What it came down to was an odd, pointillist plank-walk, notwithstanding we walked in place if it can be said we walked at all. The ledge onto which we stepped calibrated a tenuous compound or compaction of low-lying spray with spreading phantasmality (phantom feet and/or the phantom ledge on which "missed" insisted we stood).

We stood on lost, oddly elevated ground, elegiac ledge. This was no mere materialization of loss even so, no glib legitimation of lack, elegy (lapsed eligibility) notwithstanding. We stood upon or perhaps had already stepped across an eccentric threshold, thrust, or so it seemed, into a post-expectant future, the anti-expectant gist of which warned us that "post-" might well turn out to've been premature. What expectant baggage did we weigh ourselves down with even now? What ingenuous out did we disingenuously harbor hopes of having secured? The needling mist which addressed our feet multiply apprised us of an inoculative boon we sought even as we disavowed all promise, all prepossessing "post-." Post-expectant futurity stood accused of harboring hope. Nonetheless we stood by it, one and all, atomistic ledge an exemplary rug allotting endless rapport, unimpeachable aplomb.

Post-expectant futurity stood its ground. It was this of which our feet grew multiply-possessed before we hit a single note. Though its multiply-pinned massage ostensibly comforted the soles of our feet, the needling mist became a goad of sorts. The quantum-qualitative lift it afforded gave an operatic lilt and leverage to the post-expectant ground on which we stood. Ground and goad rolled into one, it coaxed an abrupt, acquiescent grunt from each of our throats, an abrupt, expectorant exhalation whose fishbone urgency furthered itself once we began to play. Part seismic splint, part psychic implant exacting an auto-inscriptive lilt, it put the phrase "inasmuch as what we want is real" on the tip of our tongues, amending our attack and our intonation in ways we'd have not thought possible had it not been so palpably so. What this meant was that "want" walked arm in arm with "real" across bumptious ground. We knew it all at once, it seemed, an instantaneous jolt as though the needling mist were an electric mace.

We were several bars into our opening number before fishbone urgency let go of our throats. The ripped, expectorant permission it apprised us of abruptly left us on our own, ushered albeit we were that much farther along the pointillist plank on which we walked. Djamilaa, Penguin, Aunt Nancy, Lambert and I stood in staggered array, stumbling in place while Drennette sat as though caught in a suspended spill. She looked as if she'd fallen backward, as if her fall had been broken by the stool on which she sat. She too, it appeared, stumbled in place.

Our collective stumble suspended us in time it seemed, notwithstanding the atomistic ledge had a decidedly glide aspect and sense of advance running thru it. This was its odd, contradictory confirmation of post-expectant premises, the odd, post-expectant way it had of rolling promise and prohibition into one. The piece we opened with was Lambert's "Prometheus." The expectorant, post-expectant permission the occasion laced it with put one in mind of Charles Davis's "Half and Half," the rash, rhythmelodic treadmill effect Elvin Jones and Jimmy Garrison's band exact on the *Illumination* album. Still, it went way beyond that in the anticlimactic refractivity, the visionary hiccup we fostered and factored in. It was this which tallied with while taking elsewhere the iterative carpet-ride on which we ran in place. Iterant weave and itinerant rug ran as one. Atomistic ledge came on as though steeped in deep-seated conveyance, *run* so deeply woven into wouldly arrest it was all we could do to keep our feet on the floor. The conveyor-belt bridge and the bedouin breach it addressed introduced a deep, irredentist quiver to the needling mist, an ever so agitant feather's touch tickling our feet.

What struck us most was how quickly we'd moved onto mixed-metaphorical ground. Where was it we stood if stand could be said to be what we did? Where was it we stumbled if stumble said it better? So many different sensations complicated one another: mixed-metaphorical conveyor-belt/carpet-ride, mixed-metaphorical mist/pointillist plank, mixed-metaphorical feather/pinpoint massage, mixed-metaphorical splint/low-lying spray . . .

The other shoe I spoke of to begin with fully partook of this dispensation, a mixed-metaphoricality which brought off being a hammer, a broken pedal and a shoe at the same time. It seemed a Cinderella fit or effect wherein hammer, broken pedal and shoe were now showcase items, encased in or even constituted of glass. Hammer had been placed under glass by the Penny dream. Broken pedal had been placed under glass by Drennette's concussive spill, shoe (slipper, to be more exact) by the presumption of fairy-tale artifice, fairy-tale fit. These three were one, a see-thru insistence upon breakage, atomization, the meaning, however chimeric, of atomistic ledge. The other shoe, the newly shod alterity onto which or into which or invested with which we now stepped, came down with a resounding report it took us a while to realize was us—a new sound which, unbeknown to ourselves, we'd come up with (or which, "unbeknown" being the case, had come up with us).

Other shoe mixed-metaphorically segued into other shore, the floor sliding away like sand when a wave retreats. Suppositious wave, I turned around and saw, was intimated, ever so exactingly meted out, by the drumroll Drennette now sustained, a roll which required all but acrobatic skill, so at odds with the suspended spill it appeared she was in. Suppositious retreat, the spasmic thumps thrown in on bass drum, tended to be consistent with suspended spill, suppositious wave rolling back upon itself so as to pull what ground one thought there was back with it. Thus it was that Drennette played out the mixed-emotional endowment her final bicycle ride with Rick had left her with, the promise and the putting aside of promise her critique of "antique emotion" so insisted on. Promise and resistance to promise rolled pregnancy and post-expectancy into one, the bass drum pedal sounding the post-expectant "floor" the broken pedal had introduced her to.

Drennette's anti-foundational patter recalled the fact (recalled while commenting on the fact) that it was Lambert's debut of "Prometheus" which had launched us on our quest for a drummer. Whatever hope he might have had of bedrock solidity had long since been given an antithetic spin, made to comply with and to confirm or anticipate (or so it seemed in retrospect) the sense of anticlimactic futurity we've been under since getting here. The rhythmic anchor Lambert announced he wanted had turned out to be exactly that, turned out to be a *rhythmic* anchor. Rhythmicity, Drennette insisted, contends with bedrock foundation, the sense of an unequivocal floor anchorage implies.

That the atomistic ledge on which we stood entailed wouldly subsidence having been rescinded became clear the more one listened to Penguin. The piece's "love slave" thematics, the subtextual strain having to do with Epimetheus's "hots" (as Penguin put it) for Pandora, was the thread he pulled out and pursued. It took us a while to realize it, but this was largely what was new about the way we sounded. Never before had we so equated Promethean fire with Epimethean "hots." While at first it was difficult to pick out Penguin's advancement of that equation from the avalanche of sound we put forth, his needling insinuation that "Pandora" was an apter title than "Prometheus" gradually came to the fore. Gradually he blew louder, needling insinuation becoming more blunt, less innuendo than hammerlike assertion. The more assertive he became the more Drennette encouraged the equation he advanced, quickening the pace with rabbitlike rolls as though they were wheels for him to ride. Penguin, in turn, grew bolder, swifter, quickening the pace to play Epimetheus to what he took to be Drennette's Pandora (or took, it turned out, to be Djeannine's Pandora, took to be Drennette's Djeannine).

It was a blistering pace which Penguin handled without the slightest loss of articulacy. With each note he did as he wished. He clearly had something to say, something which all but leapt out of him, so Lambert and I backed away from our mikes, letting him solo first. Drennette's rabbitlike rolls continued to feed the Epimethean heat with which he blew, heat which was all the more astonishing considering the finesse with which he played, the nuanced ability to speak which, notwithstanding the frenzy it appeared he was in, he maintained. His oboe spoke. It not only spoke but did so with outrageous articulacy, so exquisitely so a balloon emerged from its bell. Lambert and I looked at one another. We traded looks with Aunt Nancy, Djamilaa and Drennette as well. It was hard to believe one's eyes but there it was, a comic-strip balloon enclosed in which one read the words Penguin's oboe spoke: *Drennette dreamt I lived on Djeannine Street. I walked from one end to the other everyday, back and forth all day. Having heard flamenco singers early on, I wanted in on duende.* Penguin took a breath and with that the balloon disappeared.

Another balloon took the first balloon's place when Penguin blew again, a balloon in which one read: *A long-toed woman, no respecter of lines, Drennette obliged me by dreaming I walked up and down Djeannine Street, stepping, just as she or Djeannine would, into literality, notwithstanding the littered sidewalk and the unkempt yards.* He took another breath and when he blew again the third balloon read: *Sprung by her long toe, Drennette (part gazelle, part tumbleweed) leapt away as I reached out to embrace Djeannine. Among the weeds in a vacant lot a half-block away, she ran a few steps and turned a cartwheel. All I wanted was to bury my head between her legs, press my nose to the reinforced crotch of her white cotton panties.* He took another breath and when he blew again the fourth balloon read: *Something I saw, thought I saw, some intangible something led me on. Something I saw not so much as in some other way sensed, an audiotactile aroma, the synaesthetic perfume Djeannine wore which was known as Whiff of What Was, a scent like none I'd otherwise have known.*

While this fourth balloon hung in the air several people in the audience stood up and came forward to get a better look, not stopping until they stood in front of Penguin, squinting to make out the last few words. I had already noticed that *a* and *scent* were written somewhat close together, so I took it they were trying to determine whether what was written was *a scent* or *ascent*. They returned to their seats when Penguin took another breath and the fourth balloon disappeared. In its place, when he blew again, was a fifth which read: *The salty-sweet, sweating remembrance of Drennette's long-toed advance animated the street with an astringent allure, a ruttish funk I fell into which was more than mere mood. Drennette's advance made the ground below the sidewalk swell, cracking the concrete to release an atomistic attar, dilating my nostrils that much more.*

This went on for some time, a new balloon appearing each time Penguin blew after taking a breath. There was a sixth, a seventh, an eighth balloon and more. How many there were in all I can't say. I lost count. In any case, I understood them as a ploy by way of which Penguin sought to gain relief, comic relief, from the erotic-elegiac affliction of which the oboe so articulately spoke. By way of the balloons he made light of and sought to get leverage on the pregnant, post-expectant ground Drennette so adamantly espoused or appeared to espouse. The leverage he sought gave all the more torque to the dream-projection he projected onto her, the "street" he later admitted to be based on the projects he lived in as a child. There was a regal touch to it as well, each balloon both cartoon and cartouche, this latter aspect very much in keeping with the stately tone the oboe wove into its erotic-elegiac address. Wounded kingship came thru loud and clear, an amalgam of majesty and misery, salty-sweet. Love lost was as easily loss loved it intimated, a blasé spin the blue funk it announced increasingly came to be amended by. Such grim jest or indifferent gesture increasingly infiltrated courtly ordeal, cap and bells inaugurating an alternate crown, King Pen's cartoon/cartouche. Laughing to keep from crying some would call it, but in fact it went much deeper than that.

Penguin wrapped up his solo with a round of circular breathing which introduced an unexpected wrinkle to what had by then become a pattern: blow/balloon emerge, take a breath/balloon disappear, blow/balloon emerge, take a breath/balloon disappear, blow/balloon emerge, take a breath/balloon disappear. . . The breath he now took was continuous with the one he expelled and the balloon, instead of disappearing, hung in the air above the bell of his horn growing larger the longer he blew. The steady enlargement, however, was only partly what was new about the new wrinkle he introduced. Two-dimensional up to this point, the balloon acquired a third dimension as it grew, becoming a much more literal balloon. What was also new was that there were now no words written inside it. By making it more a literal than a comic-strip balloon Penguin put aside the comic lever he'd made use of up to this point. He was now nothing if not emotionally forthright, the empty balloon all but outright insisting, the way music so often does, that when it came to the crux of the matter, the erotic-elegiac fix one was in, words were beside the point.

The admission that words fail us would normally not have been so unexpected, normally come as no surprise. Music, as I've said, does it all the time. But in this case it seemed a new and unusual twist, so persuasively had the comic-strip balloons insisted it could all be put into words. It's a measure of Penguin's genius that he could endow something so close to cliché with new life. The balloon not only swelled like a pregnant belly but, thanks to the mixed-metaphorical ground onto which we'd moved, it appeared to be a sobriety-test balloon as well. Penguin blew into it intent on proving himself sober even as he extolled the intoxicant virtues of Djeannine's audiotactile perfume. Whiff of What Was notwithstanding, the vacant balloon seemed intended to acquit him of drunken charges, the admission of words' inadequacy a sobering descent from the auto-inscriptive high to which the earlier balloons had lent themselves. Even so, this descent could easily be said to have been further flight, so deciduously winged was the winded ferocity with which Penguin blew, what falling off there was reaching beyond itself with a whistling falsetto—stratospheric screech and a crow's caw rolled into one.

So it was that sobering descent mounted higher and higher. The balloon grew bigger and bigger, a weather balloon pitting post-expectant wind against pregnant air. Penguin put a punning spin on it, wondering out loud whether it might also be the other way around, pregnant wind encountering post-expectant air. With us crescendoing behind him all the while (Lambert and I had now joined back in), he eventually answered his own question when the balloon swelled and swelled and finally burst with a loud bang, pricked by a post-expectant needle, the needling mist which was now not only on the floor. It was with this that he brought his solo to an end, whereupon the audience went crazy, loudly applauding the release he'd had them hungering for, the release he now at last let them have.

Penguin timed it exactly right. The audience couldn't have stood another beat, much less another bar, couldn't have held its collective breath a moment longer. We too, the rest of us in the band, breathed easier now, inwardly applauded the release we too had begun to be impatient for. All of us, that is, except Drennette, who quickly apprised us, with the solo she now insisted upon taking, of the fact that the ground on which we stood was, if anyone's, hers, that impatience had no place where post-expectancy ruled.

Post-expectant futurity brought one abreast of the ground, Drennette announced, annulled, in doing so, any notion of ground as not annexed by an alternate ground. This was the pregnancy, the unimpatient expectancy, she explained, Penguin, albeit put upon and perplexed, had been granted rare speech, rare fluency by. Djeannine Street, alternate ground par excellence, inflected each run of heavy bass drum thumps with ventriloquial spectres, Drennette's recourse to the sock cymbal insistent that she and Djeannine, long spoken for, had spooked (her word was "inspirited") wouldly ledge, atomistic ledge.

It was a wild, outrageous boast, but she had the chops, it turned out, to back it up. The drumset had become a wind instrument by the time she finished her solo. A gust of wind arose from each roll and with each roll the storm she brewed grew more ferocious. We felt it at our backs when we joined in again, pressing as it pestered us toward some occult articulation only Drennette, not looking ahead, saw deep enough to have inklings of. Not so much needling as pounding us now, the needling mist partook of that wind—mystical hammer rolled into one with atomistic pulse. Wouldly ledge, needling mist and Penguin's auto-inscriptive high would all, post-expectancy notwithstanding, turn out to have only been a beginning.

Suffice it to say we made some of the most ontic, unheard-of music we've ever made. Say what one will about unimpatient expectancy, I can't wait to play again tonight.

As ever,
N.

10.VI.82

Dear Angel of Dust,

We're back in L.A. Got back from Seattle a few days ago. The Soulstice gig, all in all, went well, though the last two nights were a little bit disappointing. It's not that we didn't play well or that the music wasn't well received. We played with fluency and fire both nights and both nights the crowd, noticeably larger than the first night, got into it, urged us on. Even so, the post-expectant ground we stepped onto the first night was nowhere to be found on nights two and three. The pointillist tread, the wouldly "one step beyond" with which we'd been blessed, pointedly avoided us the next two nights. No atomistic plank-walk lay before us, no needling mist massaged our feet. It was ground we couldn't get back to no matter how hard we tried, ground we couldn't get back to perhaps because of how hard we tried.

The most conspicuous difference was that no balloons emerged from Penguin's horn. It was this which left the audience a bit disappointed, notwithstanding the applause and the hip exhortations they repeatedly gave the music. Word of the balloons had quickly gotten around town after night number one and it was this which in large part accounted for the larger turnout the next two nights. Clearly, people came hoping to see the balloons emerge again. Though we've never thought of ourselves as crowd-pleasers, never been overly concerned with approbation, we'd have been happy to oblige them had it been up to us. But that the balloons didn't emerge amounted to an anti-expectant lesson which, while not exactly the same, was consistent with the post-expectant premises onto which we had stepped and again hoped to step. The air of anticipation the audience brought with them was so thick that before our final number the second night, the balloons not having reappeared and, clearly, to us in the band, not likely to, Aunt Nancy stepped forward and spoke into the mike. “Remember what Eric said,” she admonished them. “‘When you hear music, after it’s over, it’s gone in the air. You can never capture it again.’”

It was a lesson we ourselves have had to ponder. Post-expectant ground was clearly evaporative ground, but it was hard not to be disappointed we couldn’t find it again. It had been a lapse to expect otherwise, we admitted, but that’s been easier to say than to accept. Lambert, in any event, said it best as we were discussing this at rehearsal the other night. “It’s about digesting what you can’t swallow,” he said at one point.

As ever,
N.

11.VI.82

Dear Angel of Dust,

Penguin phoned Lambert and me early this morning, insisting we three get together, saying there was something he needed to discuss. He asked if Lambert and I could come to his place, explaining that he was a bit shaky after what had happened. What had happened, he promised, he would go into when we got there, but he preferred not to talk about it over the phone. Lambert and I each said okay, despite the early hour, hearing something awry, the note of urgency in Penguin's voice. We got there at more or less the same time, Lambert arriving a minute or two before I did. His car was already there as I drove up. He had already gone inside.

The air of disarray hit me as soon as I walked thru the door. The house was filled with cigarette smoke. Penguin, who doesn't smoke, sat at the kitchen table smoking a cigarette, a saucer full of butts in front of him, Lambert seated at the table as well. I joined them at the table after minimal greetings and Penguin got right to the point. He had dreamt the Penny dream after falling asleep on Drennette's couch last night he said. He asked if Lambert and I had dreamt it as well. When we answered no he sighed and said, "I didn't think so." He said he felt more strongly than ever that there's more to Drennette than meets the eye, snuffing out the cigarette in the saucer of butts and immediately lighting another. "Let me begin at the beginning," he said, going on to relate why he had gone over to Drennette's. After everyone had packed up and left rehearsal, he explained, he saw the leather bag she keeps her drumsticks in lying on the floor underneath a chair. "I gave her a call to tell her she'd forgotten it," he said, pausing to take a drag on the cigarette. A wrought, whimsical look came over his face. "Maybe I had it coming, maybe I was asking for it," he allowed when he resumed talking, going on to relate how he had insisted on taking the bag to her, insisted it would be no trouble when she protested he needn't go to the trouble of driving across town. The phrase "go to the trouble" had come back to haunt him, he confessed, blowing smoke out of his nose and mouth.

Lambert and I listened in silence, despite the pauses Penguin took, no matter how lengthy. We gave him the room he so obviously needed, room enough to say what he had to say at his own pace, tell what he had to tell as best he could. He spoke with increasing deliberateness, as though the effort exacted a growing toll. It seems, in any case, he made the drive across town in record time, getting to Drennette's evidently sooner than she expected. She came to the door dressed in sweats and immediately asked him to excuse her appearance, explaining that at home she dresses for comfort rather than looks and that she had intended to put on something more presentable before he arrived. She invited him in and he handed her the drumstick bag and she asked him to have a seat. He sat on the couch and she followed suit, he at one end, she at the other. They made small talk—nervous talk, he admitted. He recalls the light being on the dim side, turned low, though he allowed that this might merely have been the fuzziness of recollection. He also recalls, more definitively, that the radio was on. "To make a long story short," he said, snuffing out the cigarette and lighting up another, "we gradually felt a bit more relaxed and she asked if I'd like a glass of wine. I said yes and she got up and when she came back she carried a bottle and two glasses. Things got more relaxed after that—eventually, it turned out, *too* relaxed."

Penguin took lengthy, forceful drags on the cigarette, sucking on it like a suffocating man trying to get air. Lambert and I, every now and then, looked at one another out of the corners of our eyes, noting the inordinate strain he increasingly invested in each drag. He went on, between strenuous puffs, to explain that he and Drennette ended up drinking more and more wine, that they slowly and ever more relaxedly sipped several glasses, that in fact she had to open a second bottle. Their conversation, he said, flowed more and more smoothly, the nervousness and awkward talk giving way to "the most incredible, entrancing meeting of minds I've ever known." He described the conversation as "bordering on telepathic," though he admitted he couldn't recall what it was they talked about, let alone anything he or she specifically said. "In a sense," he explained, "it wasn't about words at all. It's as if we spoke in spite of the words. The words were no more than an accoutrement under which the real communication—nuance, insinuation, body language, nonverbal rapport—went its way, more or less autonomous." What he most remembers, he went on, is the extraordinary closeness, the "almost caressive receptivity" he and Drennette addressed one another with. "Indeed," he added, letting the smoke lazily cascade from his mouth, "we sat closer and closer to one another."

The going now seemed to get more difficult, the telling more a test of Penguin's ability not to break down. He spoke in a now laconic, now headlong, now herky-jerk fashion, put upon by an accumulative chagrin. He said the closeness, the caressive receptivity, was infinitely comforting, soothing, ultimately soporific. "I don't know," he said, invisibly throwing his hands up in the air. "Maybe it was the wine, perhaps the low lights (if they were in fact low), perhaps the low, confidential tone our voices assumed, the music on the radio even. Maybe it was all these things together or none of them at all. Maybe it was something I haven't thought of yet, something I may never think of." He paused long enough to snuff out the cigarette and light up another. He resumed speaking by saying that the closeness, the intimacy, the caressive receptivity, was of such palpable presence as to project the imminence of something more physical, that he had the feeling Drennette wanted him to kiss her, that, whatever the case, he couldn't help wanting to kiss her. "Our faces couldn't have been more than two inches apart when it happened," he sighed. "I also remember very distinctly what was on the radio. They were playing 'Funk Underneath,' one of the things Rahsaan did with Jack McDuff. The exhortative insistence of Rahsaan's throaty flute is the last thing I recall being aware of."

Penguin fell silent. He seemed to assume Lambert and I knew what "it" was, the "it" of "when it happened." It was the lengthiest pause to that point, so lengthy we wondered was that the end, would he go on. Finally, Lambert, impatient, said, "Well? What happened?" Penguin started, as if awakened from a trance. He took a drag on the cigarette, blew out the smoke and related with an exasperated sigh what "it" was. On the very verge of initiating a kiss, it turns out, he fell asleep. He not only fell asleep; he slept for a long time, in the course of which he dreamt the Penny dream. "It was exactly the way Aunt Nancy and Djamilaa described it," he elaborated, "except at the end." He went on to explain that rather than concluding with the bit about a twitch in the eye and a hole in time, as in Djamilaa's version, or with the business of an eye made of opera glass, as in Aunt Nancy's, he found himself holding a spyglass up to his eye as the quarters cascaded from the ain'thropologist's empty sockets and Penny continued pounding the floor. He couldn't, he said, believe what he saw. Pulling away from the spyglass, he shook his head as if to clear it, but to no avail. He saw the same scene again upon looking thru the glass, whereupon he pulled away again, shaking the spyglass rather than his head this time. At that point the ain'thropologist, quarters cascading from his empty sockets notwithstanding, spoke. "Shake it, but don't break it," he said. "Without giving it so much as a moment's thought," Penguin went on, "I shot back immediately, ridiculously, 'It's ass, not glass.' Then I woke up."

He woke up to find himself alone on Drennette's couch. He had been asleep for several hours. Dawn was breaking. Draped over him was a blanket Drennette had evidently covered him with. He'd apparently remained sitting the whole time he slept. The two wine bottles, one of them empty, the other near empty, were still on the coffee table in front of him, as were the two glasses from which he and Drennette had drank. "I don't know why, maybe I've seen too many movies," he allowed, pausing to take a drag on the cigarette, "but I picked up each glass and sniffed it. I didn't have any trouble remembering where I was or what had brought me there. My head was as clear as a bell, albeit the fact of having fallen asleep the way I did made me shiver with embarrassment." So much so, he went on to say, that he couldn't bear to face

Drennette, who evidently had gotten up and gone to bed rather than wake him. All he wanted was to get out of there as fast as he could, which is what he did, driving home in a state of increasing dismay, a state of mind which grew increasingly distraught.

"It would have been bad enough," Penguin lamented, "had I simply fallen asleep. The fact that I dreamt the Penny dream was even worse. But what bothers me most is the new wrinkle, the alternate ending I introduced, the 'Shake it, but don't break it' / 'It's ass, not glass' exchange. I know exactly where that came from." He now got up to put water on for coffee, asking Lambert and me would we like some, to which we both said yes. He continued talking as he went about getting the coffee made. He went on to tell us something we already knew, that "Shake it, but don't break it" was something which, when younger, one would say to a passing girl, referring to the way she swung her hips. She would answer, "It's ass, not glass." "It always got to me," Penguin explained, "that they would put it that way. As though ass wasn't an entity, a thing, wasn't, to put it bluntly, the butt. 'It's ass, not glass.' As though ass was a substance, even a condition, a state, atmospheric even—pervious, pervasive, diffuse—even though the tight, compact containment of it stood right there before one's eyes." He paused, as if to get a grip on himself, as if merely thinking about it, talking about it, was enough to get to him, take him out. "It made it more abstract, but all the more erotic, intensified its allure, the play between ass, put so, and blunt butt—the inordinacy, the incommensurateness of it."

Penguin now proceeded to delve deeper into the dream, especially the alternate ending he'd introduced. No hermeneutic stone was left unturned as he teased out the implications and insinuations to be found in it. Worked up, he went on and on, pursuing one interpretive tack after another. He worked it, worried it, wrung every drop of meaning he could from it. He made one think of Lee Morgan and Freddie Hubbard's version of "Pensativa" on *The Night of the Cookers*, the way they light into it and stay on it, picking at it from all angles, refusing to let it rest, pulling out strand after strand of ramification. Still, that looking is made of what one sees was the tautologic truth he couldn't get beyond. What bothered him, got to him, egged him on, was the dream's insistence that he looked at the world with a carnal eye—"not," as he put it, "a glass eye but an ass eye." The dream had him confessing that, for all his talk of there being more to Drennette than meets the eye, the delicate instrument he took himself to be saw no more than blunt butt. Shaken glass, breakable glass, the extended eye thru which he looked and the delicate projection of himself he proposed, turned out to be tantamount to swung rump.

Lambert and I, as I've already said, deferred to Penguin's need to talk, the therapeutic pursuit his going on as he did so unmistakably was. His talk was more agitated now, less prone to pauses, but whereas earlier he had made nothing in the way of overtures for us to join in, he now peppered and punctuated what he had to say by asking, "What do you think? Does that make any sense to you?" and the like. Still, we could only, whether we agreed or disagreed with him, do so in the fewest possible words (a nod of the head or a shaking of the head most often), so quickly was he off and going again. We found ourselves cut off more than a few times—whenever, that is, we tried to get more than our small allotment in. Lambert, I could see, was getting more and more annoyed at this, though Penguin didn't seem to notice. Finally, he refused to be cut off any longer and took an aggressive tack, intruding, with butt-bluntness, on Penguin's increasingly abstruse ruminations. "Why don't you and Drennette just hop in the sack and get it over with?" he snapped.

Penguin, visibly thrown off-balance, missed a beat or two but shot back, "It's not about that," immediately correcting himself by adding, "Not only about that." He would not be backed into a corner by butt-bluntness. He now spoke with less agitation in fact, as if Lambert's intervention freed him of the need to go on so, as if going on so had been a flight from butt-bluntness, a flight Lambert's intervention made it pointless to pursue, no longer possible to pursue. It was almost as if Lambert had *relieved* him of the need to go on so, so relaxedly did he take to a new pace—a slower, more open pace which made room for conversation. Penguin, though he didn't say so outright, had gotten Lambert's point.

Lambert lightened up as well. No, Penguin wasn't making a mountain out of a molehill, he allowed. Yes, these were odd goings-on. There was indeed, he admitted, more to Drennette than meets the eye, but wasn't that, he went on, the case with everyone? Any such "more," he maintained, wasn't something delving deeper into the dream would do much to get to. I also had a few things to say. We kicked it around for a while. Lambert and I both tried to convince Penguin that he should be talking to Drennette rather than talking to us, but I'm not sure we had any real success. He agreed with us readily enough—maybe too readily—but not with much resolve to actually speak with her. It was clear he's afraid to face her again. That'll change, given time, no doubt, but for now she's got him spooked. It was all we could do to talk him out of going off on another retreat.

Yours,
N.

18.VI.82

Dear Angel of Dust,

Drennette says that what went on the other night is that Penguin drank too much. She says he drank much, much more than she did, that he poured himself glass after glass of wine and that she wasn't surprised when he nodded off. She says it seemed he might have already had a drink or two before he got there, that he seemed nervous and worked up and must have taken a drink before coming over, trying to calm himself down. Coming over seems to have been a momentous event for him, she says, something he felt he needed fortification for, a drink or two to steady his nerves. She told this to Aunt Nancy and Djamilaa and Djamilaa told me. Djamilaa says Drennette spoke with a practiced numbness, nonchalant, saying that Penguin seemed to be in a world of his own and that she had no idea why he'd made her out to be some sort of mystery, some sort of muse. His going on about there being more to her than meets the eye she dismissed as "wine talk." "The bottle," she says, "blurs his vision."

Odd, isn't it? It's as if the post-expectant ground we happened onto in Seattle was premonitory ground. Penguin's sobriety-test balloon seems to have anticipated Drennette's flat, no-nonsense dismissal, her deflation of his enchantment with her, the charge of drunkenness her version of what went on the other night amounts to. Was Whiff of What Was a whiff of what would be? Is that even the question so much as was it a perfume or a vintage bouquet? It's an old story—he said, she said—but I tend to believe them both. It was wine Penguin got a whiff of, wine as well as perfume. But the bouquet in question, the bouquet which took Penguin out, wasn't that of the wine he and Drennette drank. The bouquet which mingled with Drennette's perfume, sweats notwithstanding, ushered in by Rahsaan's "Funk Underneath," was of a wine bottled so far back as to be ageless, wine served in the Shard Café.

It's a case of More-Than-Meets-The-Eye meets What-You-See-Is-What-You-Get. Penguin and Drennette comprise a match made in heaven: flat, post-expectant sobriety wooed by wind-afflicted high, epiphanic flight. What the outcome will be is anyone's guess.

As ever,
N.

20.VI.82

Dear Angel of Dust,

We've had to cancel a couple of rehearsals the past few days. Penguin wasn't up to facing Drennette for a while. He's gotten over it now and things are more or less back to normal, though it's not that that I'm writing you about. I don't think I've mentioned, what with everything else that's been going on, that we've begun to move on the idea of cutting a record. We've checked out some studios around town and the money it'll take to get it done looks to be within reach. It'll be our own production, on our own label called Disques m'Atet (a foreign-sounding name should help sales), and we'll get it distributed thru New Music Distribution Service, along with mail-order ads in *Coda*, *Cadence* and the like. It'll be a while still, but we've taken the first few steps at least.

I'm enclosing a new after-the-fact lecture/libretto, "So Dja Seh," a new movement (or at least a new moment) in the antithetic opera I've been working toward. The prospect of cutting a record has made me think of "more than meets the eye" in another light, a "mediumistic" light having to do with audiotactile propensities which de-prioritize the eye, synaesthetic ascendancies of sound and scent of the sort suggested by "funk." It's been something of an elegiac reflection, recognizing that sound more and more doesn't matter, that to more and more people "more than meets the eye" makes no sense. Archie Shepp's been going around calling Michael Jackson "the Coltrane of our time," saying that nowadays it's the image, not the sound, that counts. The recent advent of "music television," visual support to an auditivity understood as insufficient, makes that abundantly clear. Djamilaa calls it "videocy."

An anthropologist once told me that Victor Turner's notion of ritual as a mechanism whereby the obligatory is made to look desirable says more about the society Turner lives in than about the Ndembu, his ostensible subject. MTV bears this out. What are music videos but consumption rituals, soft-porn commercials promoting the purchase of the very thing they help diminish, nonvisual capacity, "blind" capacity (funk underneath)? Purchase of in lieu of purchase upon. Loss of nonvisual capacity, audiotactility understood as lack (less than meets the eye), is the axiomatic obligation lubricating the exchange. Video insists upon a deficit in order to fill it, gives and takes at the same time: obligatory lack, illusory restitution.

Think of "So Dja Seh" as antithetic video, synaesthetic video, one in which "an eye made of opera glass" turns out to be a post-expectant picture tube. Obligatory respect for what gets away—what gets away from visualization itself—promotes a regard for what can only be off-screen, something like the quantum charade or shape-shift which defies illustration (particle/wave). Soft-porn premises, along with soft etymologic focus, blur the line between *off-screen* and *obscene*.

Yours,
N.

SO DJA SEH

or, The Creaking of the Word: After-the-Fact Lecture/Libretto (Drennette Virgin)

ACT ONE

Penny wondered was it a dream the way the mist came down like a diffuse hammer, a dream how the hammer's head, blunt but exploded, unlike a hammer came down so gently she moaned. She lay in bed in her room at Hotel Didjeridoo. She knew it never snowed down under, but no sooner had she dismissed the thought of the mist coming down like a diffuse hammer than she thought of it as coming down like snow. No sooner did she dismiss this thought than she thought of it as coming down like ash.

This had to be someone's doing Penny thought. In telepathic touch only the day before with her sister Djeannine living in Djibouti, she decided that someone had to be her. Why would Djeannine do such a thing, she wondered, just as what sounded like a bass trombone hit a note so low it made the windows rattle.

There was always music at Hotel Didjeridoo—mostly no more than an all but inaudible background growl or hum, but on occasion it rose, as it did now, in volume as well as intensity, an insistent, insinuative thread or threnodic complaint which told of loss, laceration, collapse. The low note, however, was hit not by a bass trombone but by the hotel's namesake axe. It initiated a riff one could only call doo-wop didjeridoo, a funky-sweet rhythmic foray into ditty-bop dreamtime.

Penny wondered again was it a dream the way the mist came down—hammer, snow, ash, the way it was all three of them alternating one by one. Let it be said I saw it all wear down she more thought than said, though, all but inaudibly, under her breath, she said it as well. But there was something overdone, prematurely elegiac, about this. She was glad she hadn't said it louder, glad Penguin, thank God, hadn't heard. But it was just like Djeannine to try to spoil her fun she reflected, changing register from resigned-elegiac to sibling-rival-indignant, letting the mist coming down make her moan again.

Meanwhile Penguin continued licking the soft flesh of her inner thigh, letting his tongue venture tentatively closer to the mat of pubic hair and the lips underneath it which were moist already, ready, salty-sweet. He took the soft flesh of her left inner thigh between his teeth, a pretend bite Penny thought of as being seized by Penguin's beak, the namesake beak he too thought of this way (with the added spin that, austral bird, antarctic bird, he sought mammal warmth, marsupial warmth, in the salty-sweet cleft between Penny's legs).

The low note announcing ditty-bop dreamtime had caught Penguin's ear as well. It only intensified the heat he was in. Penny had dabbed a drop of perfume on each inner thigh and the mix of flower smells and pubic funk made for a scent he'd have given a king's ransom to capture in sound. Thus it was that in taking the flesh of her left inner thigh between his teeth he sought to seize the synaesthetic equation of love-bite with embouchure, music with musk. The low note announcing ditty-bop dreamtime made it maddeningly clear he hadn't even come close.

It seemed only appropriate, though, that namesake beak had taken over. The train of events culminating in this tryst had begun with a photo Penguin received in the mail it seemed ages ago, a photo someone had sent him of Penny sitting on a chair. Shot from a slight angle rather than straight-on, the photo showed her wearing a dark blue blouse and skirt. The skirt was a short one, hem at about mid-thigh, and she sat relaxed, her legs nonchalantly parted—not flagrantly so, albeit open enough to reveal a bit of her panties. This one saw, however, only after lifting a parakeet feather which had been taped to the photograph—

taped at an angle between her legs, covering what little could be seen of her crotch. It was the recollection of this feather which now brought out the bird in Penguin, brought out the beak with which he bit Penny's inner thigh. He thought of his pursuit of marsupial warmth as a return to basics: feather and fur. Florid perfume, pubic funk and recollected feather worked him into a frenzy.

Penguin and Penny were conceptually complicit, giving birth to a feathered-furred amalgam which olfactorily included fish attributes as well. Furred-fish-alighted-on-by-feather spoke to their need for an annunciative mix, a new day which would contend with realist constriction, realist constraint. "The wing praises the root by taking to the limbs" was the motto inscribed above the entrance to the hotel. Both Penny and Penguin thought of it as endorsing the way he now addressed her leg, taking to it by applying namesake beak to soft inner thigh. The motto lent itself to the need for flight in which they were caught up, the need which had brought them to the hotel. It was a need to plumb depths even as one flew, to probe roots as though *plume* and *plumb* shared a common origin. "Plumbage" named a neologistic mix of which furred-fish-alighted-on-by-feather was the announcement. Hence the low note announcing ditty-bop dreamtime.

Penny's moans blended in with the music—so much so that, in a flash, before she could stop herself, she imagined Penguin had lifted his head from between her legs to ask what tune was it she was humming. Quick enough to keep from answering, however, she saw that this was only her mind playing games with her. "I'm not humming, I'm moaning" was on the tip of her tongue, but she opened her eyes and saw Penguin's head still between her thighs just in time to hold it back. Again she thought of Djeannine, that it had to be her behind this, that even Djibouti wasn't far enough away to keep Djeannine from trying to spoil her fun. The flash which had just come over her, she was convinced, was only so much telepathic noise, telepathic static, Djeannine up to no good again.

Having herself had an aborted fling with Penguin, a fledgeling affair which had never quite gotten off the ground, Djeannine, Penny suspected, resented her and Penguin having hit it off. She was now doing whatever she could to interfere, abusing the telepathic sisterly rapport which kept them in touch to make Penny's mind play games with her. Even as Penny thought this, the incongruous, disconcerting image of a penguin perched on the branch of a tree popped into her head, an outrageous reading of "wing . . . taking to the limbs" which played mercilessly upon Penguin's namesake winglessness. Such thoughts and such images were clearly meant to distract her, to destroy the mood, to make Penguin's address of her inner thigh more problematic than pleasurable. It took an effort to shoo them away but she did, moaning all the more loudly to sustain the mood.

Penny's thoughts and momentary discomposure unbeknown to him, Penguin let go of the flesh between his teeth and went back to licking, leaving her left inner thigh to attend to the right after a moment or two. Eventually, having licked and nuzzled the right for some time, he went back and forth between right and left, increasingly possessed by the pungent musk which, "part flower / part rutting beast" (as he had once read in a poem), pervaded the bed, the room, the entire world it increasingly seemed. The increased warmth of Penny's loins and crotch bore the odor aloft. Marsupial warmth, for all its fur evocation, might as well have evoked feather instead. What it did was endow the odor with wings, broadcasting it about, bruiting it about, to where it did indeed fill, if not the world, the entire room.

Broadcasting-bruiting was the way Penguin thought of it, confounding the smell with the music which also filled the room. Broadcasting-bruiting's endowment of wings was indebted to, if not descended from, the parakeet feather which had been taped to the photograph of Penny, the pubic feather which, more than any other single item, had gotten his and Penny's romance off the ground. It was also indebted to doo-wop didjeridoo's winged invitation to arrive at plume thru "plumbage," the rummaging way in which austral bird, one way or another, would find its way to marsupial warmth. The low note's annunciative mix of olfactory fish and marsupial fur with southern flight fueled as it frustrated Penguin's wish to translate scent into synaesthetic sound.

Penguin's tongue stroked the beginnings of pubic hair along Penny's loins, gesturing toward without venturing into the mound of hair and the glistening lips underneath. The evanescent whiff of which the low note had spoken grew endowed with everlasting allure, an amalgam of tease and tentativeness Penguin attempted to emulate in so restrainedly tending toward Penny's cunt. This, though, he persisted in thinking of as her cleft. Lingering allure bred by evanescent access instilled a wary, almost worshipful regard for what Penguin feared would be taken away if too hurriedly pursued. Circumlocutory "cleft" bespoke this fear no less than did the tentative approach to it he took.

It also veiled a musical conceit. Penguin's wish to fuse music and vaginal musk equated cleft with clef, bass clef, cleft and key rolled into one, anagrammatic odor bound up with anagrammatic door. Synaesthetic odor, the low note's allure, spoke of liminal entry, limbed in-betweenness, anagrammatic fissures, cracks, namesake word-creak.*

It befit love in a language-conscious age that he increasingly felt his arms to be fins, namesake fins, anagrammatically related to synaesthetic sniff. He part swam, part flew in the heady space between Penny's legs.

ACT TWO

Djeannine only had eyes for Djibouti. All her life she had wanted to go there. Even as a child she had made up stories about voyages to Djibouti, doing so with what so bordered on obsession it had caused her and Penny's parents to take her to a shrink. Though the psychiatrist had assured them there was no problem, given her "a clean bill of health," Djeannine had never forgotten the way he questioned her, the way it made her feel she had done something wrong.

This was the reason she and Penguin had not hit it off. Early in their courtship, as she more and more talked about Djibouti, Penguin

---

* None of the doors at the hotel opened or closed without creaking. Penguin saw no reason it should be any different with anagrammatic odor, synaesthetic allure.

had made the mistake of "interpreting" her desire to go there. Based on sound and his own thinly veiled wishes, he had said, "It means you want to be mounted from behind while being held by the waist. You want my stomach pressed against your namesake booty, my dick to part the lips of your cunt and come deep inside you." They had not, to that point, gone to bed. So blunt, so unsubtle a way of proposing that they do so meant, it turned out, they never would. Penguin had gambled, taken a chance and lost, chosen to press rather than let things take their course. He succeeded only in turning Djeannine off. She resented his bravado and told him so. She was deeply offended by the propositioning spin he put on Djibouti, the trivialization of her desire to go there. It took her back to her childhood, to being questioned by the shrink, the offensive assumption that her interest in Djibouti was abnormal, something which had to be interpreted, explained.

Penguin was chastened by Djeannine's rebuff. His brash proposal had surprised him even as he spoke and it shocked him more and more in retrospect as time went on. What had gotten into him he didn't know. In advancing his prepossessing "read" on Djibouti he had spoken like a man possessed, as though it were he who had been "mounted," put upon from behind, some blunt, prepossessing spirit's unwitting "horse." It had momentarily made sense at the time—a way of dispensing with courtship ritual, getting around boy/girl games, coy pretenses, getting, albeit bluntly, to the point—but Djeannine had been standoffish ever since. He now blushed whenever he thought of his indelicate "exegesis." This was the reason his tongue so unhurriedly advanced toward Penny's "cleft," the reason he forbade himself to be so bold as to call it her cunt.

Only in oblique, involuntary ways would Penny admit she had gotten Penguin on the rebound. She had seen him as a soon-to-emerge bird balled up inside a shell she grew impatient for him to crack. She had grown so impatient she mailed him the photograph of herself with the parakeet feather taped across her crotch—a way of encouraging him to "emerge" faster, come on stronger, not move so diffidently. She would never admit, even to herself, that she had sent it, though it had worked, had gotten Penguin to move more quickly and with greater assurance. Now, though, as the curtain rose on Act Two, she looked down across her chest and stomach at Penguin's head between her legs and with lids half-closed, half-open, saw it as an indistinct ball of wrinkled wings.

This was the effect of the Djibouti Eye Djeannine telepathically transmitted, a soft-focus endowment which in this particular instance rolled fledgeling flight and recuperative bounce into one. Penny saw the entire room, not only Penguin's head, under its auspices. Djeannine had hijacked Penny's eyes, as it were, installing the Djibouti Eye in their stead. It was this that made for the mist which continued to hit like a diffuse hammer, the at-large, erotizing regard built on contagious premises, the lack of distinct outline which infused everything.

But the Djibouti Eye was no simple flight from sharp definition, however much the soft-porn dispersal it advanced blurred—even bordered on obliterating—the line between this and that. The sonic apprisal of posteriority Penguin had taken Djibouti to be was not irrelevant to the course Penny's Djibouti-Eye-commandeered eyes now took. She let her gaze carry past the ball of wrinkled wings between her legs and alight upon Penguin's ass, the slow, undulatory, humping movement of which excited her so she let out another moan. She not only recognized but validated distinctions between this and that. Notwithstanding the indistinct ball of wrinkled wings his head had become, Penguin's ass was unequivocally his ass, blunt butt. The way it moved up and down as he humped the bed made it difficult for Penny not to grab the ball of wrinkled wings and expedite his tongue's unhurried progress toward her cunt. But she too was intent that, now that their tryst at Hotel Didjeridoo was finally happening, they both go slow, take their time.

Not unrelated to Rasta telescopy, the Djibouti Eye advanced a Far-Eye furtherance of sight. Djibouti's proximity to Ethiopia was lost on no one, least of all Penny. Penguin's ass notwithstanding, she glimpsed Harrar out of one corner of the Djibouti Eye, the Gulf of Aden out of the other. And as if to comply with the synaesthetic premises upon which Penguin sought to establish a foothold, its infiltration of sound, scent, taste and touch added a qualitative increment to its increased reach.

Penny saw, heard, smelled, tasted and felt in a single sensation under the Djibouti Eye's auspices, her commandeered eyes each occupying a separate corner while advancing a unity of image and apprehension nonetheless. Far meant miles, low notes, feel, funk and the taste on Penguin's tongue rolled into one, Harrar and the Gulf of Aden rolled in as well, Djibouti and Didjeridoo rolled in as well, ad infinitum.

Still, all was not bliss with the Djibouti Eye. Factored into the mist of which it apprised Penny was an admission that Djeannine was Penguin's lady of choice, that it was his missed opportunity with her which had brought them to Hotel Didjeridoo. The Djibouti Eye blurred the distinction between mist and "missed," belaboring with the bluntness of a hammer blow a lack so palpable missingness verged upon mystic presence. For a moment the missing lady of choice was there with such blunt subtlety it all but took Penny's breath away. The diffuse descent of Djeannine's pestering play on "missed" made her moan again.

Penguin would have been upset had he known her moans had only partly to do with him. He played the space between her legs like an instrument he thought, licking the soft insides of her thighs with all but unbearable virtuosity, all but unbearable finesse. The audible rapture into which he worked her with his tongue he heard woven in with doo-wop didjeridoo's funky-butt crescendo, the ditty-bop build-up in intensity which increasingly filled the room (an infectious mix of Mingus and Barry White, it seemed). That what he heard as funky-butt rapture was in part funky-butt despair would never have occurred to him.

By now Penny had begun to give up on getting away from Djeannine. She had suspected something was up when only a couple of days after her romance with Penguin got off the ground Djeannine announced that she was finally getting her wish, finally going to Djibouti. This was Djeannine's way, Penny had thought at the time, of upstaging her, stealing her thunder, diminishing the impact of her and Penguin hitting it off. It was her way of saying that she was unfazed (albeit the timing of the announcement said otherwise). By announcing her trip to Djibouti she insisted she had better things to think about than what her sister and a once would-be lover might be up to, that her desires and concerns were deeper than that. Djibouti bespoke longstanding sensitivity, long-lived refinement of feeling, rare depth, rare rectitude of desire.

Penny moaned in despair on realizing how tenacious Djeannine could be. The missing lady of choice's momentary presence had truly taken her aback. Rather than leaving a space in which Penguin and she could pursue their romance, Djeannine's departure had given her greater leverage, endowed her with additional power. From her vantage point in Djibouti she evidently was able to keep track of every move they made. Her ability to get inside Penny's head was a power Penny resolved to go on resisting, even though she'd begun to give up on being able to. Funky-butt rapture and funky-butt despair truly locked horns. Penny herself, out of the corner of her ear, heard it as an orchestral crescendo—dense, deeply insinuative, richly bottomed—not unlike the Aluar horn ensemble she had heard on a record of Ugandan music.

The orchestral crescendo built antithetically upon the low note's namesake root. Woven into it Penny heard a caveat, a cautionary note pitting horn against horn, yes against no. Compounded of yes as well as no, the Djibouti Eye turned inward, translating light into a high, "silent" screech played on a newly invented horn (actually an old horn simply renamed for the occasion), a radically antithetic horn. Funky-butt rapture and funky-butt despair found themselves entwined in a Manichean embrace, namesake root entwined with namesake anti-root, didjeridoo entwined with didjeridon't.

Seduced by the didjeridon't's high, "silent" cry, Penny increasingly said yes to its apparent critique of the times. She increasingly heard it as an antidote to the widespread, facile accent on "do" (the "_____ do it _____" bumperstickers, "Let's do lunch sometime" and so forth). The didjeridon't's flight from such accent she found apt and salutary.*

She began to suspect that her and Penguin's tryst at Hotel Didjeridoo had more to do with facile accent than anything else, that they blindly obeyed the imperative "Do it," that it was this the Djibouti Eye

---

* Penny had gone to a Mingus concert in 1975. After one number, once the applause had subsided, a man in the audience yelled out, "Yeah. Do it, Charlie!" Mingus, annoyed, leaned over the mike and snapped, "Do *what,* man?"

meant her to see. She began to envy Djeannine's rare depth and rectitude of desire, the clean-burning flame and long-lived ardor which had taken her to Djibouti. Compared to such lofty, longstanding passion, her and Penguin's romance amounted to nothing, less than nothing, a tawdry, slapdash affair. Out of the corner of her ear she could hear she no longer moaned. She was withdrawing, increasingly not into it, increasingly unaroused, wishing she were somewhere else. Hotel Didjeridoo had become Hotel Didjeridon't.

Penguin didn't pick up on the change in Penny's mood. He continued addressing the beginnings of pubic hair along her loins, letting his tongue venture a bit closer to the thick, pungent mat and the glistening cleft underneath. This was fortunate. It gave Penny time to recover. It amounted to an unwitting vamp-till-ready while she gathered herself up, got back the excitement Hotel Didjeridon't had taken away. Realizing she was falling into Djeannine's trap, that the didjeridon't was Djeannine's way of sabotaging her romance, Penny began to fight back. She resisted the Djibouti Eye's image of Djeannine's rare depth and rectitude of desire, resisted its derogation of her and Penguin's romance, turned a deaf ear to the didjeridon't.

Penny closed her eyes and immediately opened them again as wide as they would go, closed and opened them again and yet again, washing away the Djibouti Eye's influence and effect. Harrar disappeared. The Gulf of Aden disappeared. She looked down across her chest and stomach at Penguin's head between her legs. It was no longer an indistinct ball of wrinkled wings. Looking past it, she saw his ass going slowly up and down as he humped the bed.

It excited her. She felt the tip of Penguin's tongue stroke the beginnings of pubic hair along her loins. She closed her eyes, happy to be back at Hotel Didjeridoo. She moaned again. "Do it to me, Penguin, do it," she whispered as the curtain fell on Act Two.

ACT THREE

Djeannine held the empty bottle up to her left eye. She held it like a telescope, the open end to her eye, her right eye closed. The curtain had risen on Act Three after falling on the Djibouti Eye, the enabling bottle she continued to hold like a telescope, convinced its Far-Eye reach would soon return. But the bottle, for all she saw, might as well have been a penny on a dead man's eye, the patch over a pirate's eye. She stood on the dock in Djibouti facing southeast. She had lost focus, Far-Eye reach and resolution. She no longer saw all the way to Australia.

The goings-on down under had abruptly faded from view. The ghost had gone out of the bottle, the namesake djinn which had given Djeannine access to Penguin and Penny's tryst at Hotel Didjeridoo. She now waited and waited and waited, not ready to believe the telepathic telescopy she'd been granted would not soon be restored. She held the bottle up to her eye, straining to see what Penguin and Penny were up to, thwarted by the see-thru spirit's departure, the pirate's-patch blackness it had left behind. She was insistent it come back, incensed it would dare to leave, convinced will and resolve were all it would take. She learned otherwise.

Djeannine stood and stood and stood, waiting for the Djibouti Eyes's return, waiting for the namesake djinn, the see-thru spirit, to inhabit the bottle again. She continued holding the bottle up to her eye, turning it from time to time as if to focus it, switching it from eye to eye every so often—all to no avail. Will and resolve, she began to see, were not the same as Far-Eye reach and resolution. Her indignation began to subside, give way to acceptance. The goings-on at Hotel Didjeridoo were off-screen, no longer accessible to the talismanic bottle she held in her hands. This was the sad, accepting realization which moved her to lower the bottle from her eye and to stand, hands at her side, the bottle in her right hand, resignedly staring out across the water. She stood that way for what seemed like eternity though it was only a couple of minutes at most.

She raised the bottle to her lower lip and began to blow across the opening. What moved her to do this was the same sad, accepting realization, only infinitely more mature now owing to eternity's two-minute stay. The sound she made was likewise infinitely mature, as though it had lain within the bottle for aeons, all of time—rich, dark, resonant, mellow beyond belief. It was a sound that bestowed a blessing and a kiss. She blew for every wish that had never been granted, letting all the tense will and resolve go out with each breath.

Djeannine blew without knowing the ghost had returned to the bottle. She had no way of knowing the namesake djinn which had gone away had now come back. No longer the avatar of ocular access it had been before, it endowed the bottle with rare audiotactile reach. She felt a buzz where her bottom lip pressed against the bottle's rim, as though an invisible reed vibrated against it with the rapidity of a hummingbird's wing. She was unable to know it was the see-thru spirit's return in another form, its translation of ocular access into synaesthetic hum. She was equally unable to know that the namesake djinn whose names were legion (Jarred Bottle, Flaunted Fifth, DB, Djbot Baghostus . . .) had now taken a new one, Djbouche. With increasingly caressive insistence, her embouchure altered so as to elicit pitch variations. Djbouche endowed the normally monotone bottle with the ability to render a tune. The tune Djeannine now began to play was "I Cover the Waterfront."

She gave it all she had, more than she had. She hummed as she blew across the opening, à la Yusef Lateef or Rahsaan Roland Kirk, hummed and played the tune at the same time. It was a technique she had seen called *zemzemeh* on an album of music from Luristan in Iran, a technique resorted to by a nay-player accompanying a song whose lyrics complained of "the taste of separation." This was indeed the audiotactile "taste" in Djeannine's mouth, the synaesthetic lament for lost ocular access to the off-screen goings-on at Hotel Didjeridoo. Djeannine covered the waterfront, lamenting the loss not of love but of power, not "in search of my love," as the lyrics insist, but in resigned acceptance of the Djibouti Eye's eclipse. The "desolate docks" on which she stood were desolate not because of "the one I love" having gone away. "Will you return?" was the rhetorical question she asked not of "my love" but of the Far-Eye reach and resolution she had been so abruptly separated from.

Djeannine had no way of knowing how much in touch with Hotel Didjeridoo she continued to be. Penguin noticed, at that very moment, a warm gust of wind caress the small of his back, a warm gust that brushed his skin like an ostrich feather. The blown-bottle effect of the low flute which had just entered the music piped into the room also did not escape his notice. It was an alto or a bass flute—he wasn't sure which—and it lent itself to doo-wop didjeridoo's initiatic riff. The warm gust blew over the small of his back and across his buttocks as he continued slowly humping the bed. His rump's antiphonal rise and fall soon obeyed a rhythm introduced by Djbouche, an onomatopoetic meeting of oomph and whoosh the low flute had become the exponent of.

Penny, whose eyes were still closed, also felt a warm gust of wind. It blew across her face and, as with Penguin, it felt like an ostrich feather brushing her skin. Even so, Djeannine didn't cross her mind. The contact was infinitely more subtle than the Djibouti Eye's intrusion. She felt the warm gust brush her face and she also heard the low flute's blown-bottle accent. It had a way of etherealizing the funky-butt rush woven into the music piped into the room. The way it had its way with her, seized her, sent a shiver running down her back.

Djeannine, still standing on the dock in Djibouti, continued to blow with unwitting reach. Djbouche, unbeknown to her, had long since bid the Djibouti Eye goodbye, long since acceded to the throne emptied by its ouster. Djeannine blew across the bottle's opening, knowing it was an empty socket she blew across, knowing it more than she knew. Djbouche bore the knowing she kept from herself, a way she'd had with knowing—wanting but not wanting to know—ever since she was a child. Djibouti had been the elsewhere knowing would not reach, but now that she was there Hotel Didjeridoo took its place. The off-screen goings-on between Penguin and Penny she both knew and wanted not to know, knew and wanted not to see. She wanted to know and not know, wanted to know and not see, "know" both bound up with and unbound by "see." This was the mixed benediction (blessing and kiss, blessing and curse) borne by Djbouche, oomph woven in with whoosh by their meeting's low logarithmic flute.

Djeannine extracted more music from "I Cover the Waterfront" than anyone ever had. It was all the more miraculous that she did it on a normally monotone bottle. The bottle itself was the "desolate dock" spoken of in the song. Djeannine played upon and made a music of its emptiness, its evacuation by the Djibouti Eye. Vacuity was the voided ground she stood upon, the hollow premises upon which oomph and whoosh rested and relied. Dearth and desolation so eloquently spoke at Djbouche's behest it would have been all anyone within earshot could have done not to burst into tears. There was no one within earshot however. Djeannine stood all alone on the dock.

Djeannine's "I Cover the Waterfront" acknowledged Billie Holiday's version, but only to go on to surpass it. Acknowledgment took the form of an insinuative accent, à la Billie, on the first syllable of the word *cover*. That she blew across a lack of cover came into dialectical play with the very accent she advanced. The bottle got the sound of a gasba, the Arabico-Berber flute, scattered breath suggesting wasted breath, leakage, loss. Djbouche was the genie let out of the lamp, wasted wish as well as wasted breath, an abrasive wind intent on scouring the air. There was no cover, no place to hide, it seemed to insist. The "desolate dock" across which she blew confirmed the "desolate dock" upon which she stood, an abject, abandoned waterfront that offered no cover.

The blown bottle's abrasive wind advanced an audiotactile equivalent of the grainy telescopy that filled Penny and Penguin's room. It was the audible counterpart of the soft-focus mist the Djibouti Eye brought on, the blows of a diffuse hammer translated into sound. It was a warm desert wind. It was a weird, resistant wind, the weirdest wind which had ever blown. Insinuative accent found itself entwined with lost access, a lament for lost ocular access embroidered by the reach of an erotizing foray. It was a wind whose elegiac embrace blew without respite, desolate wind woven in with desolate waterfront, blown blessing and kiss rolled into one.

Djeannine sought refuge, cover, consolation in the bottle she blew. She had begun to blow when telepathic access turned against her, when ocular access turned aural, when something she heard put her on the defensive. Not long after the goings-on down under had gone off-screen Djeannine had become prey to an alternate transmission. As she stood on the dock holding the bottle at her side, resignedly accepting the

Djibouti Eye's eclipse, she had begun to hear what she no longer saw, the goings-on at Hotel Didjeridoo. She heard Penny's moans, heard heavy breathing, heard her whisper, "Do it to me, Penguin, do it," over and over again. It was as if she had become the receiver, Penny the transmitter. It was as if the Djibouti Eye had not simply closed but had boomeranged against her, undergoing a synaesthetic translation on its return. It struck her with the force of an obscene telephone call. It was partly due to this that she had raised the bottle to her mouth and begun to blow. It was partly a way of covering her ears.

Djeannine filled the air with a spray of sound. In part she blew to drown out Penny's "Do it to me, Penguin, do it," to drown out the noise from down under, turn a deaf ear to Penny's pantings and moans. She blew loud, but with no loss of nuance, no collapse of what she played into mere oomph. Djbouche, unbeknown to her, was in the bottle. She blew, not knowing how far.

Off-screen, Penny grew more and more impatient, less and less able to resist expediting Penguin's unhurried progress toward the cleft between her legs. The warm wind continued to blow across her face, an ostrich feather fanning the flames.

Unbeknown to Penny, Penguin grew more impatient as well. A warm wind continued to blow across the small of his back and across his buttocks, insistent he not take so much time, it seemed to him. He resisted, letting his tongue linger as unhurriedly as ever upon the beginnings of pubic hair along her loins. He was relieved, however, when Penny, unable to wait any longer, took hold of the back of his head and gently pulled, causing his mouth to fill with hair, his tongue to part the salty-sweet lips underneath.

Penny, feeling the warmth and the wetness of Penguin's mouth, emitted a mix of moan and sigh, ecstasy and relief. Djeannine blew that much louder as the curtain fell on Act Three.

24.VI.82

Dear Angel of Dust,

Once again I'm writing while convalescing in bed—another round of shattered cowrie shell attacks, shattered-shell-become-buzzing-bottle-cap attacks. My head feels like a calabash wrapped around an mbira. I hear the plucking of metal keys, a slow, methodical plucking which sounds like a leaky faucet at first, then builds and becomes more complicated over time. It's as though the drops of water aren't content simply to drop and go down the drain or to drip and be absorbed in the cup or whatever it is of water they fall into. They insist on living beyond their descent, dancing rather than disappearing, kept alive by cross-accentual ricochet and recurrence.

How much this has to do with Hotel Didjeridoo I can't say. A good deal it would seem, as it's neither Ornette's "Embraceable You" nor Lightnin's "Bottle Up and Go" but "Drennethology," Penguin's piece, I hear piped into my head. An imagino-cathartic edifice built on "Drennethology's" how-high harmonics (Drennette says jump, Penguin asks how high) is what my head seems to have become. Call it a carnival hive, a Junkanoo house worn on my head which *is* my head, a house built in resonant rapport with wouldly reach (wouldly fall as well as wouldly rise). Call it Hotel Didjeridoo if you like, but it's really less a wind axe than a plucked one—Hotel Mbira or, in its lowest wouldly register, Hotel Bagana. At moments of lowest wouldly descent my head is a trapezoidal wooden frame with a skin-covered soundbox at the smaller end, a Davidic harp strung with strings made of sheep gut. U-shaped leather thong buzzers amplify the sound. At such moments my head is nothing if not a hotel, home away from home, an exilic harp, diasporic play upon exile, pitched, like a tent, in transit, peripatetic, plucked. Still, I can't help wondering how home can be away from home. How can home so divide itself as to be other than itself, severed, selfsame, either/and all at once? How can home be in more than one place at the same time?

Yet "home away from home" so succinctly says it I don't know why I go on so. It's clearly an aspect of my condition to go on so. "Home away from home" titrates the entrance and the reintroduction (woof to "Drennethology's" warp) of an mbira piece whose title, "Nhemamusasa," means "The Cutting of Branches for a Temporary Shelter." Nominal hotel notwithstanding, music as movement thru a makeshift succession of huts calibrates while conducing diasporic drift. Each plucked key proffers makeshift shelter, ephemeral "structure" on the order of a shantytown lean-to, exactly the tentlike shelter made of branches the Shona mean by *musasa*. Call it Hotel Musasa-Turned-Junkanoo-Headdress. A succession of huts-worn-atop-the-head file thru my head, a Junkanoo parade, a procession of heads within my head, huts within the hut my head thus becomes. No elaborate house, no stately mansion, my head becomes a warrior's hut, makeshift shelter made of branches on a march into the bush. Call it rickety weave equilibrating "domicility" with romp. Home away from home, in short. Everyone tells me it's all in my head. Moot solace. The problem is that it *is* in my head.

It all came about, this latest round of attacks, yesterday at rehearsal. Lambert suggested we work an early Shepp tune into our book, a tune Shepp recorded with the New York Contemporary Five, "Like a Blessed Baby Lamb." It's a tune no one plays anymore, not even Shepp himself, but it's a tune it took none of us much time to recall. "Oh yeah, I remember that one," Aunt Nancy was the first to say. It's a tune whose infectious head had stayed with all of us over the years, though none of us, other than Lambert, had heard it or given it much thought for quite some time. Advancing a mix of croaked insistence and wry wager, it's a tune whose infectious head all the more infectiously tapers—tapers to assume the contour of an acquiescent growl, a wistful growl. It's a tune we quickly agreed to have a go at.

The namesake aspect of Lambert's suggestion soon made itself clear, so clear it became hard to believe we hadn't seen it right away. Following a couple of aborted starts, we hit on our third try, Drennette and Aunt Nancy laying down the rhythm as straightforwardly as one could want. Drennette kept straightahead time on the cymbal while Aunt Nancy, on bass, walked as if her life, if not all our lives, depended on it. Still, this didn't preclude the introduction of a hesitant or a hasty step every now and then, a fearful, fugitive tread which proved to be the base Lambert built his namesake solo on.

I say namesake solo because after only two or three bars that was clearly what it was. It was clear Lambert took the tune's title to heart, however much he complicated nominal meekness, lamblike meekness, with under-the-breath invective, namesake beatitude, namesake boast. Which is to say that while *lamb* was clearly the facet on which his accent fell, *ram* inflected that accent with under-the-breath bluster, gruff pronouncement, self-praise. The horn's gruff, sandpaper tonalities abraded namesake meekness even as Lambert extolled his lamblike virtues. He resorted to a taut, semisung, semiswallowed moan which was a muffled moan, a moan smothered in lamb's wool, it seemed. So seeming, it made it clear Lambert thereby renamed or nicknamed himself Lamb, recalling the night Djamilaa soothed and consoled Penguin, calling him Pen. He too wished to be babied, consoled, addressed by a motherly voice, a wish Djamilaa took little time to grant him, interjecting a wordless, lullabylike run which put one in mind of a Wagogo soothing song.

Lambert called out to be consoled, however, only to fly from such announcement of need, to flee whatever answering embrace might be forthcoming. In doing so he renamed or nicknamed himself Lam, nicked his name further. This he did by availing himself of the opening advanced by Drennette and Aunt Nancy's fugitive tread—rhythmic permission on which he built the namesake bifurcation he sounded again and again. Fugitive tread's divergence from straightahead lope underwrote Lam's analogous divergence from Lamb. Lamb bleated, cooed, cried, poignantly pleaded for care and understanding. Lam, on the other hand, darted, dashed as though driven, daunted all hope of straightforward access or capture, emotional and otherwise.

It was a devastating one-two punch, Lam in more senses than one. It was all I could do to keep my head on straight, actually more than I could do to keep my head on straight, taken out as I was by Lambert's Lamb/Lam combination. Lamb/Lam, that is, exacted a vibratory tension, so tautly rolling pulse into one with punch as to become corpuscular (part airy, openhanded slap, part haymaker fist).

Not only did I feel I'd been hit upside the head but I understood "upside" in a new epistemic light, saw how deeply, how resonantly, "upside" said it all. "Upside" spoke for angularity, glancing access. More locus than location, "upside" spoke for tendency, tangency, the tease of a play on intangibility, oblique—not straightforwardly inside or outside, not straightforwardly both. No wonder huts-worn-atop-the-head file thru my head. Tenancy, interiority, what was housed, had now to be understood as itineracy, Lamb/Lam's tangential address.

No wonder strings made of sheep gut vibrated. No wonder cowrie-shells-turned-into-bottle-caps buzzed and have gone on buzzing. Threaded in with everything else—"Drennethology," "Nhemamusasa," Junkanoo drums, exilic harp—I still hear Lam telling Lamb to come off it, Lamb purveying its theme of needy innocence nonetheless.

Yours,
N.

26.VI.82

Dear Angel of Dust,

Yesterday as I lay in bed convalescing from the latest bottle cap attacks I heard the sound of something hitting my bedroom window. It sounded as if someone were tossing pebbles at the window, though the sound, a tapping sound, seemed of something lighter and less compact than pebbles, not so solid a sound, a tinnier sound. I didn't pay it much mind at first, not at all sure it wasn't simply a new thread in the cross-accentual cloth my head had become, but after a while I could clearly tell it was coming from outside rather than inside my head. It was clearly the sound of something hitting the window pane. After a dozen or so taps I got up and went to the window to see what was up. I looked out the window and what I saw, about fifteen feet away, was Djamilaa, feet planted firmly on the ground, arched back like a limbo dancer, holding a bottle cap between the middle finger and thumb of her right hand, just behind her shoulder at about the level of her ear. With a flick of her middle finger, a snap, she sent the bottle cap flying, arcing thru the air toward the window. It hit the window with a tap, clearly and exactly the sound I'd been hearing. I looked down at the ground just below the window, where the bottle cap fell, and saw what I already knew, that it wasn't the first.

There were bottle caps which had already been launched lying on the ground just below the window. There were even more which were yet to be launched lying in a paper bag sitting on the ground to Djamilaa's right. No sooner did she launch one than she reached into the bag and took out another. She launched them one right after another, nonstop, shooting them high into the air so that they hit the window on their way down. They spun like tiny flying saucers, cutting a high, hyperbolic arc thru the air. The play of arcs—her body's backward-bending arc and the bottle caps' high, sun-seeking arc—bordered on sublime. I stood at the window transfixed, entranced. Her body seemed a bow, each bottle cap an arrow. I stood captivated by her body's bow-like bottle cap launch. Her backward bend seemed an obverse evocation of early Egyptian sky, taut bow and heavenly bend rolled into one, albeit obverse bow. Her thin body's limbo harmonics not only brought arc into play with arc, how-low into play with how-high, but bow (bo) into play with bow (bau), inverse bow (bau).

Rolling arrow and flying saucer into one, each bottle cap's quantum coalescence effected a head-on, bull's-eye hit and a glancing blow. This, I soon saw, was Djamilaa's answer to the shattered cowrie shell attack, the shattered-shell-turned-bottle-cap attack, her counter-attack. Each bottle cap, as it hit the window and fell to the ground, tugged at and seemed to take with it some of the tension which filled my head, the compacted, full-to-bursting feeling the attacks entail. It was as if my skull relaxed, emitted a subtle sigh of relief, as each bottle cap fell to the ground. Djamilaa seemed to be saying that ridding me of the attack was a snap, child's play, as elementary as the game of shooting bottle caps we played as kids.

It went further than that however. I stared out the window at Djamilaa, entranced by the sculpted grace of her arced body, the way the light cotton dress she wore draped her midriff and thighs. She showed no sign of having noticed me standing there. She too seemed entranced, caught up in the methodical rhythm of shooting bottle caps one after another. Over time she bent farther and farther back, arcing the bottle caps higher and higher. These were the sublimest bottle cap flights I had ever seen. I'd have hoped in vain, I'm sure, had I hoped to see any more sublime. Each bottle cap, at the apex of its arc, seemed to rival the sun, to compete with the sun for suzerainty over an otherwise unlit world. So bright was arced ascendancy it forced me to close my eyes.

Upon closing my eyes I saw myself seated in a bottle cap that had been turned upside down. Whether it was that the bottle cap had grown or that I had shrunk I wasn't sure, but I clearly saw myself seated inside it as it spun. It reminded me of the teacup ride at Disneyland. The bottle cap spun and spun and spun, spinning me with it, so fast I had to hold on to its edge to keep from flying out. It spun thru soundless, oddly unlit space (bottle cap suzerainty, bottle cap eclipse), though the lack of light had no effect on my ability to see. The soundlessness—a malarial deafness it seemed—had more impact on me, a veritable dream of suppressed resonance, older than rhythm, even older than time. I hungered after sound so ravenously I opened my eyes again, hoping to again hear the sound of bottle caps hitting the window.

My eyes were open only long enough to see how dizzy I was. The room—the whole world in fact—was spinning. I immediately lost my legs and fell to the floor, blacking out on my way down. The next thing I knew I was coming to, lying on my back looking up at Djamilaa, who was kneeling over me, shaking me gently, bringing me back. I instinctively went to shake my head to clear it of cobwebs, only to find I didn't need to, that it was the clearest it had been in days—no "Nhemamusasa," no Hotel Bagana, no Junkanoo-huts-worn-atop-the-head and so forth. Djamilaa smiled at the look of surprise on my face. My head's been clear ever since.

As ever,
N.

11.VII.82

Dear Angel of Dust,

What a relief getting out to play can be. I don't subscribe to the putting down of "head trips" (headiness appeals to me as much for its inner as its outer dispatch) but there's something to be said for the notion that you can dwell too long or too much in your own head. The gig we just got back from, three nights in San Francisco at Keystone Korner, makes me think it's this my recent bottle cap attacks were about. It was as if I'd been let out of some place I'd been cooped up in for too long. Djamilaa's curative bottle cap launches notwithstanding, my head had remained more tight than I realized, more subtly compacted thanks to Djamilaa's intervention but compacted still. It was as if getting away for the gig in San Francisco let out what subtle pressure persisted (like letting air out of a balloon one thought was empty). It relieved me of the bottle caps' lingering impact, apprising me of it as it also rid me of it, an all but audible "hiss" announcing bottle cap residuum's heady retreat.

No doubt it was good to get out of town as well. The smog's always worse come summer, which with the heat makes outside so uninviting I tend to pull in – perhaps too far in. In any case, I felt a further release of pressure as we traveled north. Bottle cap impactedness, albeit by now all the more subtle, let up the farther away we got from L.A. Indeed, so subtle did its grip become that it got harder to tell whether it let up or simply held on with greater finesse. It was the lightest touch (if it was a touch) I'd ever felt—so light it seemed to have become light itself by the time we rolled past San Miguel. Bottle cap finesse now so seamlessly sewed touch and intangibility together that the osmotic exchange between inside and out made it feel as if my forehead—all and/or nothing at all—was no longer there, not only the all which wasn't all there but also the nothing which almost was. For a moment I was indeed light-headed in the most fleet, far-reaching sense—a fleet sense which never entirely went away I would later find out.

None of this is to say that outside lost any of the grounded spin which makes it a world. Nor was the gruff interiority of which the shattered cowrie shell and/or bottle cap attacks are an outward sign at all relinquished by bottle cap finesse's furtive stitch. Part cough, part call to prayer, gruff interiority infused earth and sky with an animate glint which appeared to scour them from within. Scoured earth and sky cried out for bottle cap finesse's reconnoitering spin, an umbilical aubade which bid aliquant ambush goodbye, the closest inside and out would ever come to adequation. What was in was also out not so much in that to be either was to be both as in that spin locked arms with spin as in a dance, an embrace whose wrought elasticity made waves, a gruff, corded quiver running back and forth. The brown, undulant hills to the east were such waves, reconnoitering roll made malleable, palpable, possessed. One needed only to reach out the window and grab hold.

Mile after mile went by with those hills to our right. They had the look of sanded wood at times, an elision of crevice and curvature so adroit they appeared to have been molded by a sculptor's hands. At times they had the look of limbless torsos, recumbent flesh coaxed into an obdurate mix of art and unselfconsciousness. It was the grace of that condition or conditionlessness one was tempted to reach out the window and grab, convinced one could reach out and grab, so fleet had in's reconnoitering traverse of out now become, so stolid out's apparent habitation of in. Mound after mound rose and fell, spread and flowed, one into another, the comeliest calibration of rise and recline I've ever seen. Sunlight hit the browned grass they were covered with at just the right angle (it was late afternoon) and made it look as though the hills, like "frosted" lightbulbs, were aglow with their own inner light, muted light. Such light was in fact the synaesthetic variable advancing an equation of sight with sound, a low-key, subterranean hum which was otherwise mute. Strings had been buried underground it seemed, plucked guts parlayed into polyvocalic root, chthonic strum. We all sat in silence looking out the windows as the brown rolling hills promised to go on forever and we ourselves rolled on past San Lucas, King City, Salinas . . .

An aura lay about the hills. It clung without actually touching them, a heaving, low-to-the-ground cover not unlike fog, except that it aided rather than obstructed the eye. One saw what one would otherwise not have seen, the topographic spread if not spillage of a "frosted" effect, summer sun and the hills' torsolike allure notwithstanding. Indeed, such effect abetted every bodily hint the hills possessed, each erogenous crevice, curve and rumpish roll all the more insistent under the soft-focus look it bestowed. The browned grass was an extensive body hair the angular sun lent a matte, oddly lunar light, halo and haunt so deftly rolled into one that the hills were no less ablaze for being "frosted," no less lyric albeit mute. We sat, looked and listened, rolling along, subterranean strum an immaterial web tying us to our seats.

I looked at Djamilaa sitting next to me out of the corner of my eye and I could see that she saw and heard what I saw and heard. Out of the same corner I looked around the van and saw that Drennette, Lambert, Aunt Nancy and Penguin saw and heard it too. This turned out to be a tuning up of sorts and a sound check of sorts, not only previous to those we later did at the club but ontically prior, proto-, fundamental albeit diffuse. There wasn't a note we played during the whole gig that wasn't inflected by subterranean strum, our proto-tune-up-and-sound-check-rolled-into-one's chthonic stir. Having sat, looked and listened for so long, having been so enthralled, we exacted a rolling contour from the music we must've long suspected was there but never so explicitly actualized until this gig. Contour and contagion met one another unawares it appeared, so instinctively threaded, so hypnotically stitched was the cloth we donned, a cloak of sound which heaved and throbbed like involuntary tissue, a living organ.

We were, in that regard, "live at Keystone Korner" in more senses than one. This in fact made for difficulties during the sound check we did once we got to the club. The music, albeit peppered with glottal reports whose flayed cut and cutaneous flap were anything but soporific, had a steadying effect on the sound engineer, induced an awake but oddly adjunct state, a sort of waking sleep. He drifted in and out, his attention not always where it should've been, and getting the levels right, the mix right, the placement of the mikes right and so forth took a lot more time than it normally would've. Over and over one of us had to leave the stage and walk back to the sound booth to rouse him from his rapt adjacency. He apologized each time, saying he was normally much more efficient, asking us to bear with him, mumbling with increasing wonder something about the music's adjunct address.

Were I to say that out followed us in I'd be telling only part of it. Rumpish roll acquired an introspective quiver, a mind-itch deeply enough interred to invest all premises, the club's, not surprisingly, prime among those it endowed on this particular occasion. Cutaneous flap was our attempt at "answering" not only subterranean strum but subcortical irritant, though this turned out, in the sound man's case, to have a different effect. Subcortical irritant, not so much "answered" as accelerated until we got the right mix, invited secretions of adjunct rapture, rapt adjacency's eventual pearl, "answering" pearl. This, at any rate, was the sense I had of it, given that once we got the levels where we wanted them rapt adjacency no longer took the sound man out. Looked at accordingly, in, in the person of the sound man, could be said to have followed us out up until that point. Whatever the case, the story I mean to tell isn't so much that one as another one, that of our first public performance of "Like a Blessed Baby Lamb," an impromptu debut which bears upon what I began this letter talking about—bottle cap finesse's furtive stitch, fugitive stitch.

It was during the first night of the gig, the end of it in fact. All had gone well, exceptionally well, and the audience, at the end of the second set, rose from their seats and insisted on an encore. I was the one who suggested we encore with "Like a Blessed Baby Lamb." It was a throwing down of a gauntlet of sorts, a test and a dare, my resolve to see how far bottle cap impactedness had pulled back, how real its retreat in fact was. My head was light, a see-thru amenity, weightless, but I wondered would it remain so under the brunt of "upside" itineracy, Lamb/Lam's tangential address.

"Why not?" Drennette was quick to say—quick as well to count off the time while tapping it out on the ride cymbal. We were into it before we knew it.

A ride it very much turned out to be, notwithstanding the slow, almost dirgelike pace Drennette meted out. It seemed we dredged whatever ground it was we traversed as we began, as if to unearth the umbilical quiver subterranean strum so insisted on. The accordingly "collapsed" contour of the piece, the staggered eloquence within the ruin of prepossessing traipse it apprised one of, came into arch, enabling play with reconnoitering roll. Lambert put a pestering spin on Shepp's allusion to a train whistle's moan, a frayed lowing which conjured smoke seen receding from afar. The brown rolling hills we'd earlier driven past grew possessed of trails of locomotive smoke, as did the sense of topographic spread the Websterian buzz Lambert resorted to evoked. Topographic spread served a corollary sense of tautologic inclusion while antiphonal qualm and/or qualification brought the other horns in. Penguin, Djamilaa and I formed a tricorn chorus (he on alto, she and I on trumpets) which amended Lambert's gruff semiotic smoke while exhorting him all the more. Lambert blew smoke and we answered with a swart, sway figure, all on behalf of tautologic totality, tautologic inclusion—he as if to say, "Everything is everything," we as if to say, "Except when it's not." We coaxed and called his bluff at the same time.

"So far, so good," I said to myself several bars into the piece, relieved to find my head still unimpacted, unimpaired by "upside" itineracy, though I knew the tough parts were yet to come. Lambert's bluster came into pestering play with nominal meekness, possessed of a ramlike, trainlike power, Lamb notwithstanding, possessed of a leonine ferocity as well. Lamb's wool, ram's horn, train whistle's moan and lion's roar indeed all stood as one, an upstart amalgam only "upside" itineracy could've concocted, but my head's unimpacted amenity held its own. The apparent "pauses to reflect" written into the piece no doubt helped—not only the backpedaling figure our tricorn chorus offered up, but also the slight, strategic rest right before the paradelike passage, the parade-turning-into-car-truck-and-bus-horns-in-mid-Manhattan-traffic passage.

The real test, I knew, would be Lambert's solo coming out of that passage. Indeed, he was on it from note one, inviting any and all who would to rethink the paradelike swell which had gone before. He bellowed, to begin, as if mired in tar, a pestered, put-upon sound evoking prehistoric animals going under in pits, a thick sludge of a sound that unpaved and undermined the paradelike premises on which we'd stood only moments before. Impediment (senses of problematic tread) vied with implied advance, parade elation. Paradelike premises were now decidedly left behind but only partially put away, as the very hope of parade advance turned into spectre, a deferred ghost haunting the hope it otherwise instilled or insisted on. Lambert evidently felt such insistence as prod, prepossessing lope, for he gradually quickened the pace, tar pit premises notwithstanding, sludge notwithstanding, pulling Drennette and Aunt Nancy along. What better reason to run than tar pit premises' rained-on parade, the sense of being stuck, he implicitly asked.

Still, it was anything but an out and out run—less that than a sense of tenuous hold he applied to each note, as if the sound, even the horn itself, were on the verge of getting away. He blew as though he fought to keep up or to catch up. The getaway twist he gave each note was retrospectively the spur that appeared to quicken the pace. Thus, it only seemed he pulled Drennette and Aunt Nancy along. That he effected an appearance of tempo change through ambiguations of pitch, the burred expanse of a note confounding lag with lurch, is a fact which, hard if not impossible to give an account of, there's nonetheless a name for: Lam. It was a beautiful, brilliant move on Lambert's part, given that the overblown, bellowing tack with which he'd set out thereby showed or punningly implied itself to've been an overstated version of Lamb, bellow an overblown version of bleat, prehistoric bleat. The getaway twist he increasingly gave each note not only fled or attempted to flee tar pit premises but tended, more specifically, toward Lamb, stole away to Lamb, again, albeit differently, rolling Lam and Lamb into one.

The sense of strata which both distinguished and linked bellow and bleat, tar pit and pavement, was a new wrinkle no doubt introduced by chthonic strum. Tar pit premises notwithstanding, Aunt Nancy's walking bass was as steady as ever, an assured, insistent tread Lambert chose to take issue with now and again, interjecting reminders of tar pit ordeal, tar pit duress. In so doing, he brought Lam's other side or sense into play, a pugilistic refusal to abide by the bedrock amenities he otherwise invited, a bellowing bone Lam picked with Lamb's wish to be cradled, reassured. Such reassurance came under loud indictment, steal-away wish and intrepid cradle rocked as one albeit kept at a distance, a split, spitting figure Lambert came back to more than once. It was all he could do to contain Lam's bluster, equally all he could do to keep Lamb's bleat from becoming maudlin, melodramatic.

There were two things Lamb/Lam seemed intent on saying. "I'm rough and I'm tough and I don't take no stuff" was Lam's unabashed boast, the gruff bravado which made for a mix with Lamb's low-key disquiet, Lamb's lament that (this was the second thing) we had yet to advance beyond muck, prehistoric mire. Indeed, Lamb, the ostensible baby (namesake baby), came right out and called itself Tar Baby, making explicit what up until then had only been implied. Lam's punches held him (Lam) captive, getaway twist or steal-away wish notwithstanding, Lamb's low-key self-nomination announced.

It was an idea which Penguin, Djamilaa and I ratified at once, offering up an impromptu unison figure whose "we-hear-you" inflection put the finishing touch on Lambert's split, spitting mien or motif. Yes, better to think of history as not yet begun, better to insist on some future inception, that what had passed and continued to pass for it wasn't where we were headed, that the true advent of humanity lay ahead—this was the responsive chord Lambert had touched and with which we now replied. As low-key as Lamb's disquiet, we comprised a sedate chorus, a chaste, oddly sibylline amen corner, dispensing our repeated "we-hear-you" with utmost composure, utmost calm. Lam, on the other hand, thrashed and bellowed boast after boast, spouting threats and spitting out curses, thickening the tar pit preserve its attempt to punch its way out of only made worse, prehistoric premises Lamb would've helped it flee had it only been able.

But so low-key was Lamb's disquiet one wondered at points was Lamb really there. Was its presence no more than promised or implied, a homonymic "twin," semantic twist or detour notwithstanding, conjured by Lam, contrapuntally conjured or constituted, an eponymic arrival ever to arise in the nick of time, the very nick out of which Lam itself had arisen and repeatedly arose? Lambert blew this and other questions our way, more and more insisting we no longer resort to such easy response as our repeated "we-hear-you," upping the ante on post-prehistoric Lamb, presumed human advent.

By now we were well into Lambert's solo and still my head's unimpacted amenity remained intact. Not even the hint of a bottle cap buzz arose to distract me, much less a parade of Junkanoo huts. "Drennethology," "Nhemamusasa," exilic harp and all couldn't have been farther away. Some other world it seemed they were part of when, for one moment, I gave them any thought at all. No, the gauntlet had clearly been thrown down and clearly bottle cap impactedness remained in retreat.

This continued to be the case despite Lam/Lamb's vibratory harmonics growing more and more fierce. Lambert increasingly let us know that unison assent wasn't good enough, that no sedate chorus, no chaste amen corner, came close to being adequate to the task his bleat-within-bellow hopefully prompted or at least proposed. Something more strained or strung out seemed to be in order. Lambert's split, spitting fierceness and fury grew even more split, more splintered, more ferocious, moving Penguin, Djamilaa and me to adopt a split, splintered approach of our own. Unison assent gave way to a staggered, scattered, catch-as-catch-can fray in the fabric which up until then we'd so sedately woven.

Djamilaa was the first to diverge, taking the trumpet from her lips and singing the wordless, lullabylike motif which recalled a Wagogo soothing song. She sought, it seemed, to caress the disconsolate Lamb/

Lam rift away, kiss it with a mother's medicinal kiss, make it all better. Penguin, less than a beat behind, darted off in a different direction, concocting a high run of bittersweet flutter, bird-wing flash, making light of Lambert's tar pit complaint. I let a beat and a half go by before joining in with a split, spitting rush of wind which was all the more spitting and split for being played on trumpet, thereby beating Lambert at his own game or at least aiming to. Our unison assent's uniform fabric was now multiply inflected, multiply frayed, multiply worn if not outright rent, a thin, threadbare cloth caroling dredge and redress. It all made for a wild witches' brew of a sound which was not uninformed by subterranean strum. Subterranean strum, that is, added further undertones of tear, seismic tatter, chthonic rent. Dues went deeper than we thought, it seemed to say.

Lambert's was no longer the dominant voice. We were now into a collectively improvised passage, a cacophonous bridge which was what he'd had in mind when he began to pooh-pooh our unison assent. He let his tenor fade a bit, fall into the fray, not so much resolving Lamb/Lam's dialectics as letting it dissolve, one voice, albeit splintered, split, among several. Lambert refused to disentangle Lamb and Lam but instead let their adhesion infuse the bridge or brew we were concocting, a bridge or brew from which or out of which one of us, we knew, would soon get the nod to launch his or her solo. That nod, when it came, came my way, not exactly catching me unprepared but, even so, caught up in recollecting Djamilaa's bottle-cap-launching bend. That bend, not our cacophonous brew, was the bridge I would cross or which would carry me across I couldn't help feeling—a feeling which made me pause, ever so slightly hesitate before launching my solo.

As it turned out, I knew more than I knew, for Djamilaa did indeed play a peculiar role in my solo, though not a role involving her bottle-cap-launching bend in any literal way. It would be safe to say, however, that a certain articulacy came into my playing, an advanced ability to bend notes I don't normally have when I play trumpet, an ability bestowed by my reflecting on her bottle-cap-launching bend if not by the bend itself. "Stay loose" was the implied advice it gave and this I did, but its impact and/or instruction went much farther than that.

I began with a dilated, hemorrhaging sound, advancing the Lamb aspect of Lambert's solo to insist that brass had something to do with blood, that to bleat was to bleed. Brass Lamb tinctured seepages of widening alarm, bleeding mainly air, titrating the mix whereby what brass had to do with blood gained atmospheric effect. It was a big, epochal sound it seemed—pressured, apocalyptic, as intimate as gossip nonetheless. I stayed loose, holding bottle cap impactedness at bay, doing so without giving it a thought.

Although Penguin and Lambert took their horns from their mouths once I got going, Djamilaa continued singing the wordless, Wagogo-like air she'd woven into the frayed, cacophonous bridge we crossed. This no doubt made it easier to keep bottle cap impactedness at bay, though there's reason to believe it stayed away of its own accord. Whatever the case, we went on, the two of us, for some time, my solo less a solo than a duet, brass Lamb's dilated alarm somewhat sedated by Djamilaa's make-it-all-better remit.

The role I referred to as peculiar came in farther on. It was as I toyed with a string of inverted mordents that Djamilaa, having let her singing fade, raised her trumpet to her lips again. She fingered the valves and blew into the horn, matching what I played note for note, flurry for flurry—miming what I played, to be more exact, for though she fingered and blew not a sound came out. It was an odd, mimed or mute provocation or support which got even odder. Nothing at all came out at first but after a few bars a balloon emerged from the bell of the horn. The trumpet continued to emit no sound, albeit Djamilaa continued fingering and blowing, but a comic-strip balloon came out of the bell as if to show that, even though I thought I gave it little if any thought, bottle cap impact, if not impactedness, would not be denied its due. Inscribed in the balloon were these words: *Bottle cap suzerainty lifted its magic wand, a conductor's baton it tapped me on the shoulders with as if dubbing me a knight. A page, a prompter-in-waiting, arose with each tap, one on my left shoulder, one on my right.* This was greeted with scattered applause and exhortations from the audience, some of whom had no doubt heard about that night in Seattle, the now near-legendary night when Penguin blew such balloons.

Djamilaa and I took a breath at the same time and with that the balloon disappeared. Having taken a breath, we began to blow again at the same time. When we did another balloon emerged from the bell of Djamilaa's horn, a balloon in which one read: *Djbai and Bittabai they were called. Djbai stood on my left shoulder and whispered into my ear—spoke for rising pitch, asymptotic inflection. Bittabai stood on my right shoulder and whispered into my ear, speaking for staccato indentation.* It was still only my horn that any sound came out of and it took next to no thinking about at all to realize, what with the advanced articulacy with which I now blew, that the words enclosed in Djamilaa's balloons were the words my trumpet spoke.

We were all, Djamilaa included, both pleased and taken aback, surprised and taken aback, by the return of the comic-strip balloons. Not a few heads were scratched, Djamilaa's and mine included, as to whether she put words in my mouth or I put words in hers. Whatever the case, we again took a breath at the same time, whereupon the second balloon disappeared. When we again, at the same time, began to blow another balloon emerged, this one, with its Penguin spin, raising further questions as to who had whose two cents' worth in whose mouth: *They vied like devil and angel locked in quantum coalescence, less devil and angel, on deeper inspection, than fire and light. I lay flat on the floor, brought back to life by the bottle cap's hum, but in what the hum said I saw myself run over, having walked all day at loose ends up and down Djeannine Street, the one serious risk I had ever taken or would ever take, it seemed at the time.* I looked at Penguin, who smiled and seemed on the verge of laughing. When Djamilaa and I took a breath the balloon disappeared.

People in the audience were now on the edge of their seats, some of them holding their breath it appeared. Djamilaa and I blew again at the same time and out came a balloon bearing these words: *The car I saw myself run over by was the car Jarred Bottle sat in waiting for the traffic light to change—turn red, yellow and green at the same time. Djbai stood on his left shoulder shouting go, Bittabai on his right shouting stop. He was waiting for them to say the same thing at the same time, the car, unmoving, running over me nonetheless.* Again we took a breath at the same time and the balloon disappeared. Again when we resumed blowing a new balloon emerged: *I was what moved. Flat on my back, I slid along under the car, a quasi-conveyor-belt I could've sworn I saw Djeannine running in place on. I now no longer walked the street, I* was *the street. Bottle cap adamance hummed underneath me, stroked my back, my spine a string struck dulcimerlike by bottle cap suzerainty's magic wand.*

The return of the comic-strip balloons provided more than ample food for thought. Bottle cap impactedness had gone underground it appeared, but only to emerge with all the more finesse, all the more bouyancy, only to rise like a balloon or as a balloon, subterranean strum calibrating the hum of which balloon number three spoke and to which balloon number five returned. As it rose it also evidently picked up or picked up on the gauntlet I had thrown down, dubbing me a knight before extending a chivalrous conveyor-belt street on which Djeannine walked and/or ran in place. Djamilaa's bottle-cap-launching bend had been some sort of grounding device which evidently made her the channel thru which chthonic strum's ventriloquial élan issued forth. I had less than a moment to chew and digest this and what other food the balloons' return provided for thought, for Penguin, I heard and saw, had taken his horn to his mouth and was now preening, punctuating and embroidering the Djeannine Street line I'd ventured upon. This was clearly turf he took to be his or at least turf he took it he knew a thing or two about. Clearly he wanted in—indeed, was already there, I heard his alto insist.

Penguin's tone was a tart, mordacious thing which bit into the latter part of the run I played and continued on when Djamilaa and I again took a breath at the same time. He staked a claim during the pause we took, but the balloons were evidently no respecter of persons, for when Djamilaa and I resumed blowing this time no balloon emerged. Yes, it was true that the balloons' first appearance had been out of the bell of Penguin's horn on that phenomenal night in Seattle, his tart claim now insisted we recall. And, yes, it was at least arguable that Penguin's broken-tooth addendum to the Djeannine dream seemed to single him out, seemed to give him special status, even seemed, as he now contended, to have been the "open sesame" which gave us access to Djeannine Street. Still, the balloons were not to be summoned by Penguin's increasingly proprietary boast, no matter how heartfelt, no matter how heady, no matter that Djamilaa and I went on in the very vein which had been so effective before he jumped in. Proprietary claims had no place on post-expectant ground, the balloons' non-emergence appeared to insist—a caveat whose bearing upon tar pit premises didn't escape one's notice. Tar was indeed the antithesis of post-expectancy's non-attached address—anything but unstuck one saw at once.

Though the wind had been somewhat taken out of our sails we continued to play, press on, the music in a sense all the more inspired in the face of the balloons' reticence and refusal to emerge. Chastened a bit perhaps but clearly undaunted, Penguin played with as much passion and precision as ever, soon indicating that Djamilaa and I should pull back, let him take over. This we did and Penguin went from embellishing voice to solo voice by adopting a somewhat drier tone, picking his way thru a wry, reflective run whose admonitory tag turned proprietary boast on its head but was no less heartfelt and no less heady for doing so. What was most instructive was the way in which dryness gradually grew bittersweet. Penguin, it seemed, wagged a bittersweet, admonishing finger which bordered on tart, recalling Carlos Ward, maybe early Robin Kenyatta somewhat, slurred sweetness tolling the balloons' non-emergence, bidding them goodbye.

Penguin had now embarked on a Lamb/Lam dialectic of his own, bittersweet bleat implicitly vying with proprietary boast, the tart proprietary claims he'd embroidered the latter part of my solo with, the balloonless part. That the balloons had not come out for him he now parlayed into lamblike penance, a sheepish mien which over the long haul, however, built on a dry run of wit as well as on bittersweet bleat. He increasingly accented the fact that in this case the wind taken out of our sails was actually air let out of our balloons. This he did by literalizing lamblike penance (metaphorical boat no match for literal balloon) and by taking dry run literally as well.

It was as if tart giving way to bittersweet wasn't renunciative enough. It reached the point where he took the horn from his mouth, removed the mouthpiece, returned the horn to his mouth and blew, playing the rest of his solo that way, mouthpiece in his pocket. Unlike Djamilaa's balloon-accompanied blowing, which had been silent and to which the mouthpiece removal alluded, Penguin's alto, absent mouthpiece notwithstanding, emitted sound. One heard the air passing thru the horn, as if (the insinuation escaped no one) it was air being let out of a balloon.

Penguin blew and blew and blew—so much so, so taxingly so, one feared he would hyperventilate, pass out. Lost air, let-out air, was his text and he took no prisoners, preaching a long, no-letup sermon while Drennette and Aunt Nancy provided sober, unstinting support. Sackcloth and ashes couldn't have made his point any more graphically, but the audience couldn't quite agree on how to take his penitential tack, invested as it so deftly was with droll insinuation, witty vagary, dry jest. Some sat with long faces, lugubrious, withdrawn. Others wore an all-purpose grin, enjoying the spectacle no less than the wry humor woven into it. Others outright giggled, as though the air being let out of the balloon were laughing gas.

It was wild, for all its lamblike penitence, raucous—as wicked as it was witty. The giggles, in fact, gradually gained the upper hand, spreading throughout the audience, infectious even to the point of seizing those who sat with long faces. It reached the point where everyone in the audience sat giggling. Even Penguin, once it got to this point, looked out over the audience and grinned, notwithstanding the horn was still in his mouth. He seemed pleased, as though his intent had been to arrive at a giggly consensus, but soon it was more than this, soon he did more than grin. It reached the point where he too couldn't help giggling, though he continued blowing even so. His embouchure was now unsteady but he somehow managed to keep hold of the horn and to keep blowing, his blowing broken into by giggles, the infectious tickle which had taken hold.

The giggly vibration which now ran thru the room was hard to resist. It was all the rest of us in the band could do to keep from being swept up in it, but somehow each of us was able to keep a straight face. Drennette and Aunt Nancy went on providing austere, unstinting support, while Djamilaa, Lambert and I looked on without a hint of a giggle or a grin. The contrastive play between Penguin's giggly depletion and the calm, no-nonsense chorus we comprised made the audience giggle all the more, which in turn made it even more difficult for us not to giggle or grin.

Even so, we maintained our calm, no-nonsense aplomb. On the cue from Lambert we restated the head, albeit Penguin went on blowing sans mouthpiece, giggling, and then we brought the piece to an end with the paradelike passage. Notwithstanding so emphatic an ending (not unlike an exclamation point), Penguin went on blowing a bit longer, letting the sound of the air passing thru the horn gradually fade, giving himself the last word, no longer giggling.

Then there was silence for a moment or two. The applause, when it came, was loud and long. I found I couldn't help joining in—applauding, unbeknown to all but myself, my head's newly arrived at unimpactedness having withstood the giddy gauntlet Penguin threw down.

Yours,
N.

17.VII.82

Dear Angel of Dust,

The balloons are words taken out of our mouths, an eruptive critique of predication's rickety spin rewound as endowment. They subsist, if not on excision, on exhaust, abstract-extrapolative strenuousness, tenuity, technical-ecstatic duress. They advance the exponential potency of dubbed excision—plexed, parallactic articulacy, vexed elevation, vatic vacuity, giddy stilt. They speak of overblown hope, loss's learned aspiration, the eventuality of seen-said formula, filled-in equation, vocative imprint, prophylactic bluff. They raise hopes while striking an otherwise cautionary note, warnings having to do with empty authority, habitable indent, housed as well as unhoused vacuity, fecund recess.

The balloons are love's exponential debris, "high would's" atmospheric dispatch. Hyperbolic aubade (love's post-expectant farewell), they arise from the depth we invest in ordeal, chivalric trauma—depth charge and buoy rolled into one. They advance an exchange adumbrating the advent of optic utterance, seen-said exogamous mix of which the coupling of tryst and trial would bear the inaugural brunt. Like Djeannine's logarithmic flute, they obey, in the most graphic imaginable fashion, ocular deficit's oracular ricochet, seen-said remit.

The balloons are thrown-away baggage, oddly sonic survival, sound and sight rolled into one. They map even as they mourn post-appropriative precincts, chthonic or subaquatic residua come to the surface caroling world collapse. They dredge vestiges of premature post-expectancy (overblown arrival, overblown goodbye), seen-said belief's wooed risk of inflation, synaesthetic excess, erotic-elegiac behest. The balloons augur—or, put more modestly, acknowledge—the ascendancy of videotic premises (autoerotic tube, autoerotic test pattern), automatic stigmata bruited as though of the air itself.

Such, at least, was the insistence I heard coming out of Dolphy's horn. "The Madrig Speaks, the Panther Walks" was the cut. I sat down to listen to it only minutes ago and found myself writing what you've just read. Never had Eric's alto sounded so precocious and multiply-tongued, never so filled with foreboding yet buoyant all the same, walk (panther) and talk (madrig) never so disarmingly entwined.

Listening, more deeply than ever, bone-deep, I knew the balloons were evanescent essence, fleet seen-said equivalence, flighty identity, sigil, sigh. This was the horn's bone-deep indenture, wedge and decipherment rolled into one. This could only, I knew, be the very thing whose name I'd long known albeit not yet found its fit, the very thing which, long before I knew it as I now know it, I knew by name—the name of a new piece I'd write if I could.

What I wouldn't give, that is, to compose a piece I could rightly call "Dolphic Oracle." It would indeed ally song (madrig) with speech, as well as with catlike muscularity and sinew—but also with catlike, post-expectant tread, oxymoronically catlike, post-expectant prowl, post-expectant pounce, an aroused, heretofore unheard-of, hopefully seen-said panther-python mix . . .

Yours,
N.

26.VII.82

Dear Angel of Dust,

Could be. Yes, possibly so. The balloons, for all their outward display and apparent address of popular wish (literal access, legible truth) may well, as you say, signal an inward turn. As I've said before, the last thing we want is to be a lonely hearts band, but that may in fact be what, under Penguin and Drennette's influence, we're becoming or may even have already become. Are the balloons' apparent roots in problematic romance, their repeated erotic-elegiac lament, a default on collectivist possibility, a forfeiture of possible bondings greater than two, an obsessed, compensatory return (would-be return) to pre-post-romantic ground?

I don't know. I'm not so sure, for one thing, it can all be laid at Penguin and Drennette's feet. To whatever extent the balloons embody a retreat from more properly collectivist wishes, an introspective move masquerading as wished-for romance, costume-courtly complaint, the larger social, political moment we find ourselves in would have to have had a hand in it, no? I don't much subscribe to the increasing talk, in these dreary times, of "empowerment," "subversion," "resistance" and so forth. I once quoted Bachelard's line, "Thirst proves the existence of water," to a friend, who answered, "No, *water* proves the existence of water." I find myself more and more thinking that way. I find myself—and this goes for everyone else in the band, I think—increasingly unable (albeit not totally unable) to invest in notions of dialectical inevitability, to read the absence of what's manifestly not there as the sign of its eventual presence. To whatever extent hyperbolic aubade appears to have eclipsed collective "could," the balloons' going on about love's inflated goodbye should alert us to the Reaganomic roots of that eclipse.

I drove down to Santa Ana yesterday. An old friend and I went to the store at one point and on our way we passed a neighborhood park which has more and more become a camp for the homeless. Park Avenue, people now call it, irony their one defense. Anyway, as we drove past, my friend, looking out the window, sneered, "Look at them, a bunch of dialects." He meant "derelicts." So much for malaprop speech as oppositional speech, I couldn't help thinking, so much for oppositional *any*thing.

That's how I sometimes feel, how we all sometimes feel. Not all the time, but often enough to nourish what you call an inward turn. I don't altogether buy your inward/outward split, but if you're saying the balloons' erotic-elegiac lament mourns the loss of larger bonding as well, I agree.

Yours,
N.

PS: What the two occasions the balloons have emerged on have in common is the ur-foundational/anti-foundational sense and/or apprehension we had—atomistic ledge/needling mist/pointillist plank-walk in Seattle, subterranean strum/"collapsed" contour/tar pit premises at Keystone Korner. Each entailed an excavation of substrate particles or precincts, erstwhile plummet or plunge. Are the balloons mud we resurface with, mud we situate ourselves upon, heuristic precipitate, axiomatic muck, unprepossessing mire? I ask because of my acquaintance with earth-diver myths—myths in which an animal plunges into primeval waters and brings up a mouthful or a beakful of mud, mud from which the world is then made. In some the animal is a tortoise, in others a boar, in others a duck, in others a loon. Could the balloons, I'm asking, be a pseudo-Bahamian play on the latter, namesake play with B'-*Ba* overtones, the spirit or the embodied soul of namesake play going by the name B'Loon?

I say yes. B'Loon, not unrelated to Djbouche, is our murky, mired cry, a call for world reparation. It muddies our mouths with the way the world is even if only to insist it be otherwise. Such insistence notwithstanding, it implicates us (myth advancing mud, mouth proving mud) in the pit we'd have it extricate us from.

4.VIII.82

Dear Angel of Dust,

Djamilaa says Turner was wrong. We worked on "Tosaut L'Ouverture" at rehearsal last night and I got to talking about how the piece came about. Lately we haven't been getting the sense of subtle, unsounded shout I had in mind when I wrote it. We managed it early on, but the last few times we've played the piece on gigs I've noticed a certain overstatement creeping in, as though the band had read but misread my mind regarding shout, taken it literally, a matter of volume rather than bend (circumambular bend, oblique, steal-away torque). I pointed this out last night after we ran thru the piece once and the overstatement, as on recent gigs, was there again. Hoping it would help, I related in detail what had brought "Tosaut L'Ouverture" about, which I hadn't before to anyone but you. When I got to Turner's idea that the use of the word "shout" to refer to circumambular movement derives from the Arabic word *saut*, Djamilaa said no, that couldn't be, that *saut* isn't pronounced like "shout" and that it doesn't mean to walk around the Ka'aba, it means voice, sound.

I thought about it a while and then said it was no problem, that *saut* not being pronounced like "shout" actually made the point I was trying to make, albeit differently, that *saut*, not sounding like "shout," implies the turn toward unsounded shout I wanted us to bring to "Tosaut L'Ouverture." "Let it be our boat," I found myself saying, "a bend at the heart of sound we ride like an ark, weather like a storm, a calm, contrary eye to see us thru." I said that meaning bent toward movement rather than sound was what whatever shout the piece calls for wants—an arced, inostensible shout, inostensible decree. Inostensible decree, I went on, was a proviso issued at the heart of sound which allowed fertile mistakes like Turner's *saut*/shout derivation, the phonic license which made it possible to imagine *saut* might have been (mis)-pronounced "shout." "Especially," Aunt Nancy chimed in, "given the phonic liberties transported Africans have been known to take."

"Rather than take shout literally," I eventually concluded, "treat it like a mistake that's bound to be made and that one both wants and doesn't want to make. Remember that the 'shout'—the *saut*—in 'Tosaut' has to do with a detour thru relativizing salt. Remember that salt gives its grain of truth a renunciative spin. Remember that shout posed as movement rather than sound is a way of dancing by another name." It was one of my more inspired exhortations, a quick mix of admonition and provocation I wouldn't have thought I could come up with had I not heard myself do so. And it did make a difference. "Tosaut L'Ouverture," when we now ran thru it, was a long devotional song tinctured with inklings of angular remit. Post-expectant distraint, a rare breed of longing, qualified our sound by way of an arced, immaterial itch with which it invested each note. Tosaut horses did indeed run, as though itch were the constituent meat they were made of, not unlike the carousel of notes I saw circling my head after drinking *saut* soup. We were definitely a whole lot closer to my conception of the piece—all the more so the third time we ran thru it, which we got on tape, a copy of which I've enclosed.

I write as well to say that word has been spreading about the balloons. The Seattle gig created a bit of a stir but it seems to have taken the Keystone Korner appearance to convince people the balloons are no fluke. Their second appearance appears to have made the point that they're for real, a force to contend with, and the scene has been more and more abuzz with talk of them over the past three weeks. As you yourself have done, many people have asked questions about them, ranging from technical (how do we do it) to philosophic (what do they mean), some posing them directly to us, others bandying questions as well as theories about on a grapevine which ultimately makes its way to us. We could see something like this coming back when the balloons first appeared on the Seattle gig and we decided the best thing would be to maintain a public silence, not respond to the talk, something we now see we're not able to do.

We've gotten requests for interviews from some of the music journals and have started to get phone calls from newspeople at a few TV and radio stations. We've turned them all down. We've also, however, come under attack by some who say the balloons are a gimmick, a ploy, an attempt to go commercial, that we're turning ourselves into a circus act. It's in the face of this development we find we can't keep quiet. That the balloons are being taken the wrong way, by the well-meaning as well as the not-so-well-meaning, became clear a couple of days ago when we got a call from NuMu in New York, the place we played last November. They wanted us to come back for a two-week stint, but the owner, after talking a while about dates, pay and such, said, "By the way, be sure to bring the balloons"—which would've been funny had he not been serious. He wanted to write it into our contract that the balloons had to appear at least once a night.

How much our silence has had to do with things getting so out of hand we can't say, but their having done so requires we speak up. To that end, we decided to issue a press release. It was agreed I should be the one to write it, which I did, with editorial input from the rest of the band. We've sent it out to all the newspapers, wire services, radio and TV stations, music journals and so forth. I enclose a copy for you.

As ever,
N.

POST-EXPECTANT PRESS RELEASE #1

In view of discussions now going on concerning the balloon sightings at two of our recent performances, we, the Molimo m'Atet, feel impelled to break our silence regarding the matter. We now issue the first in a possible series of press releases. We will issue others if the need arises, as the need arises. There has been a great deal of talk and speculation generated by the two performances and we speak now to respond to questions which have been posed to us and to dispel certain misunderstandings which are going around as to the nature and import of the balloons' emergence. These inquiries dwell on questions of origin and motive, so let us state at the outset that the balloons are not, as some have alleged, a gimmick, a publicity stunt, a cheap trick we hope to cash in on. The charge of sellout is the last we should have to answer, but that there are those who will stop at nothing to explain mystery away comes as no surprise. By this we mean to suggest, to those genuinely interested in where the balloons come from, that their roots, as far as we can tell, are coincident with the world, that they afford no abstraction or extrapolation away from the post-expectant, post-explanatory fact of their being here.

Mystery notwithstanding, post-explanatory fact, in this instance, bears a name—a name which reminds us of certain risks we run with naming, a name which risks inflation as well as tautology: B'Loon. B'Loon is the bird that dives under the water at the beginning of things, fills its beak with mud at the bottom and then comes back up. It's from B'Loon's beakful of mud that the world is made. Rather than explain, B'Loon expands upon murky origins. According to some, for example, B'Loon was once a man, a fisherman in fact. He and another fisherman quarreled one day while out at sea in their canoes. B'Loon had caught several fish and the other fisherman, having caught none, knocked him on the head, cut out his tongue and took his catch. When B'Loon reached shore he could only cry like a loon and the Great Spirit, hearing his cry, turned him into a loon. His quasi-human cry recalls his having once been a man, as well as the wrong he suffered at the other fisherman's hands.

Others, however, insist B'Loon was at first a loon and that he became a man at a certain Kuloscap's behest, having served faithfully as Kuloscap's servant, during which tenure Kuloscap taught him his distinctive quasi-human cry. Still others argue that B'Loon had been a boar before becoming a loon and a tortoise before becoming a boar, that B'Loon's roots go all the way back to Mesopotamia. Some say that B'Loon's footprints inspired cuneiform writing, though others dispute this, arguing that B'Loon didn't become a loon until long after leaving the Fertile Crescent. Even so, the belief persists among some that the world arose not from a founding beakful of mud but from founding footprints left in the mud, that the world began with writ, B'Loon's wedgelike tracks.

We, the Molimo m'Atet, see no reason to choose. B'Loon, true muse of inclusion, rolls earthen writ and airborne whoosh into one, earthen wedge and airborne oomph into one, subaquatic beak and airborne word into one. B'Loon marries flight with mired cry, height with depth, depth with height, heaven-piercing beak with aboriginal mud, fecund muck, footloose, itinerant word with graven earth. Thus it is that B'Loon is said to be intimate with air, the atmosphere's doings, weather, said to be able to forecast rain. This, we now know, cuts both ways. Thus it was that a low-lying mist followed us into Soulstice that night in Seattle—a metathetic prediction auguring B'Loon's imminent advent.

B'Loon's comings and goings, however, we can neither predict nor control. As Byard Lancaster said in the title of one of his albums: it's not up to us. B'Loon indicts presumptions of command as it bestows command, as though command were its own false twin, seeded cloud the false face of rain save that ceded command antithetically intervene. By no means an easy muse or master, B'Loon requires that grasp and relinquishment meet, that they wrestle the angel each takes the other to be, the devil each takes the other to be—a harlequin fray in which debt mires endowment, advancing an ethic of letting go while suggesting letting go might be an ulterior tack aimed at taking hold, taking hold a Pyrrhic seizure not unmixed with letting go, each the other's taint and contagion, ad infinitum. B'Loon ushers the soul of blown seizure, fractured access, reach and retreat.

Whether "man" first and "bird" later or vice versa, B'Loon is both "man" and "bird," an avatar of broken bonds, the break both advance and ordeal. B'Loon's quasi-human cry recalls the attack he suffered but also aligns articulate squawk with legible scratch, inscribed earth with contentious air, wedge with complaint. Whether as wing or as wedge, B'Loon augurs an opportune prodigal opening conducive to broken bond as qualitative breakthrough, quantum slip. Whether as wing or as wedge, squawking slip bridges seen/said chasm—wishfully most often but for real at B'Loon's behest. Squawking slip rolls wing and wedge into one, scrawl and scratch into one, witness and plaintiff into one, wind and writ into one.

Sibling wind and sibling witness (Sun Ra said it years ago: "My Brother the Wind"), B'Loon yields mended kinship, mended membership, mends otherwise broken bonds. B'Loon blows thru every exhaustion, a second wind not unequatable with fugitive spirit, fertile exhaust, bent on depletion being the ground for new growth. We get lucky every now and then and blow with it.

6.VIII.82

Dear Angel of Dust,

Turner was right. Djamilaa and I have gone into the shout/*saut* matter further and the problem turns out to be that the word rendered *Saut* in Parrish's book doesn't appear that way in his. Parrish uses an *S* instead of the phonetic symbol ʃ that Turner uses ("voiceless palato-alveolar fricative, like *sh* in English *shame*"). In the passage she refers to, Turner writes with regard to "shout": "Cf. Ar., *ʃaut* 'to move around the Kaaba (the small stone building at Mecca which is the chief object of the pilgrimage of Mohammedans) until exhausted'; *ʃauwata* 'to run until exhausted.'" There is in fact an Arabic *saut*, which, as Djamilaa pointed out, means voice, sound, but we now see that's not the word Turner meant. The dictionary we consulted says that *ʃaut* is a race to a goal, also the course or the track over which a race takes place. It's not hard to see how it could have come to refer, in idiomatic usage, to the course taken around the Ka'aba. That it was applied to the course taken by participants in the ring shout is also easy to understand, especially given the presence of Muslims in the Sea Islands. In the context of cross-cultural sanction and subterfuge brought about by the slave trade, it makes perfect sense. The phonic distinction between sound and movement in Arabic (*saut* and *ʃaut*) is maintained but all but lost in its intersection with "shout"—to say nothing of its application to a form of movement, the ring shout, which is decidedly not without sound. The distinction is, in effect, silent, as is the admission that the shout isn't only sound but also movement—that is, a dance.

Not that "Tosaut L'Ouverture" would be any less valid had Turner been wrong. Its tenability is one of generative divergence, the bend away from pat equivalence exemplified by nonsonant shout. It was incorrect but not a mistake, a mistake but a fertile mistake, to read the "-saut" in "Tosaut" as though it was Turner's *ſaut*. "The accuracy of the bow is judged by its curve," Ibn 'Arabī says.

Yours,
N.

9.VIII.82

Dear Angel of Dust,

There's a new wrinkle on the balloon front. A photographer has come forth claiming to have been at Keystone Korner the night the balloons made their second appearance. He says he took photos of them or at least thought he had until he developed the film. He says he could find no trace of them on either the negatives or the prints. Everything else—the band, the instruments, the stage and so forth—came out fine, but the balloons were nowhere to be seen. He doesn't question that they were actually there that night—he saw them, no doubt about that, he insists—but this "new revelation," as some are now calling it, has added to the controversy surrounding the balloons. Doubters are calling the sightings a case of mass hysteria, arguing not that none of us saw what we say we saw but that what we saw was a collective hallucination. The camera doesn't lie, they insist.

I wanted to issue another press release addressing this new information and the doubts to which it's given rise, but no one else in the band thought it a good idea. It's too soon after the first release, they told me, and, besides, we can't spend our time arguing with the doubters and the critics, responding every time something new comes up—a view I came around to without much fuss. Still, I'd like to have publicly made the point that the balloons' refusal to show up on the photographs (it's a refusal, not a failure, I'd insist) calibrates a distinction between mechanical gaze and organic sight. This "new revelation" has caused me to rethink my assertion that the balloons "acknowledge the ascendancy of videotic premises." I'm glad they turn out to be camera-shy, and I hope, if they ever show up again, they'll continue to be. That B'Loon is neither photogenic nor, one would assume, telegenic, that, rather than a failing, this augurs the rejection of telecom charisma, is a point which might've been worth pursuing in a "Post-Expectant Press Statement #2," an intermittent feature of which would have been a soft phonologic focus allowing *camera* and *chimera* to blend, bleed into each other, *chimeric* and *charismatic* to do so as well.

I would have started it something like this: "B'Loon stood at the podium holding a pointer—part magic wand, part conductor's baton, a pointer nonetheless. On the blackboard behind him, scrawled in chalk, was the inscription 'B'Lam!,' below which, also scrawled in chalk, was a dash followed by the words 'Namesake Exclamation #1.' B'Loon, charismatic mage, cleared his throat, turned to his left and pointed to the writing on the blackboard, still not having spoken yet." I would have gone on to identify B'Lam as anagrammatic Lamb apostrophized, called out to as kin. I'd have called it a loonlike cry, personified, protesting capture, demanding immediate release. I'd have called it the avatar of onomatopoetic impact (rough-and-ready command, camera-ready chimera), gone on to write something like this: "B'Loon, chimeric bird/man mix, invoked the avatar of onomatopoetic impact, hoping to go over big, hoping he'd be a hit, during this the taping of his appearance on *The Tonight Show*. He'd been nervous for days, weeks, months. It thus came as no surprise that during the drive to Burbank there had been moths, not butterflies, in his stomach and that his stomach might as well have been wool. He stood now, nervous as ever, charismatic albeit camera-shy, all the more chimeric, about to embark upon the lecture he'd been invited to present, or so everyone thought."

I'd have then gone on to devote a good deal of space to B'Loon's inner state, the anxiety and the apprehension that plague him, the qualms, the insistent self-questioning he faces regarding the propriety of such an appearance. I'd have taken my time evoking the fraught vessel he feels himself to be (rough-and-ready charisma, ready-or-not chimera), taken pains to evoke the stage fright he suffers, gone to great lengths to evoke the camera-shy refuge he seeks turning toward the blackboard behind him. With an exactitude approaching camera-shy quanta, chimeric truth, I'd have then dwelt on his moth-eaten stomach, offering image after image aimed at suggesting the vertiginous pit he now feels it to be. I'd have ended this stretch with something like this: "B'Loon teetered on the brink of a precipice, the macrocosmic pit implied by the moth-eaten pit his stomach now was. He would have to dive down, go deep into that pit were he ever to get his feet on new ground, gain a new footing. He would brave the moth-eaten remains both outside and inside himself, raise the muck to higher ground, make of the muck some higher ground."

I'd have gone on to point out that although at its deepest reach macrocosmic pit meets cosmic shiver, the more immediate cause of B'Loon's nervousness needs to be taken into account. I'd have noted that B'Loon, quite private by nature, intends to go public in an even bigger way than appearing on *The Tonight Show* implies, much bigger, in fact, than he'd ever dreamt he would until only a few days before. "B'Loon," I'd have written, "had more in mind than the lecture he'd been invited to present. He had decided only a few days before to put his 'Notes on Capillary Pneumatics' aside, to cash in on his otherwise camera-shy charisma (chimeric readiness) by using his appearance on such a widely viewed program to announce his candidacy for president. He derived a certain pedigree from Lester Young, of course, but the write-in campaign, many years back, for a trumpeter with whom he'd long felt a namesake rapport also bolstered his resolve. The first words out of his mouth, he had decided, would be these: 'I largely owe the decision I'm about to announce to the ballooning cheeks of another bird/man mix's "worthy constituent." It's mainly, that is, because of Dizzy that I'm here to do what I'm about to do.' Only now, having cleared his throat again but still not having spoken, did he see that the debt he owed Dizzy ran deeper than even he knew. Vertiginous pit bespoke such depth, bore capacious witness to the namesake spin B'Loon increasingly felt himself caught up in, the giddy brink the moth-eaten ground on which he stood had brought him to, a giddiness which made him grab the podium for support."

I'd have needed to convey how anxious B'Loon is to get it over with, to get the announcement out of the way and to sit chatting with Johnny. That he actually looks forward to that conversation is a point worth making, one that I'd have pursued at some length. It shows that B'Loon's apprehensions have largely to do with the portentousness of public scale, that the one-on-one conversation format, albeit viewed by millions, offers a semblance of the intimate proportions he feels more comfortable with. B'Loon is there, that is, both to avail himself of and to in some degree temper the advance of telespeak. He's not so sure anymore, however, that he can pull it off, that he can actually, as he likes to put it, feed the beast without it biting off his hand. He feels, that is, less and less camera ready. Chimeric readiness more and more turns camera-shy. "B'Loon's would-be camera-ready charisma," I'd have gone on to write, "let him down. He more and more felt that mass-mediated stump stood in the way of genuine change. He cleared his throat yet again but instead of speaking stepped away from the podium, laid his pointer down, turned his back to the audience and the cameras and took the two steps it took to reach the blackboard. When he didn't feel on the verge of falling he felt on the verge of floating away, yet even so he managed to pick up a stick of chalk and to carefully, albeit a bit shakily, write the word *REVOLUTION*, all in caps, on the board. He also, with his other hand, picked up an eraser, with which, once he'd gotten the word written, he erased the *R*. Having erased the *R*, he now, with his chalk-holding hand, rewrote it, whereupon he promptly, with the eraser-holding hand, erased it again, only to write it again with the chalk-holding hand. He quickly established and sustained a rhythm wherein he alternately erased and rewrote the *R*. He thought of *REVOLUTION* as a neon sign whose *R* flickered off and on. He stood with his back to the audience and the cameras, still not speaking, still not having spoken, though the chalkdust, every now and then, made him ever so gently cough, clear his throat."

That's the way I'd have left him—standing close to the blackboard, slightly hunched over, writing and erasing the *R* again and again. That now he owed less to Dizzy than to Miles might have gone without saying, but most likely I'd have pointed it out anyway. B'Loon, camera-shy chimera, decides that what he's doing is the way it ought to be done.

He continues to stand there, his back to the audience and the cameras, gently coughing or clearing his throat every so often but silent otherwise. He has no interest now in presenting a lecture or in making a speech, no interest in chatting with Johnny afterward. This becomes apparent to everyone present after a while and the cameras stop rolling. B'Loon, intent only upon the *R*, the chalk and the eraser, eventually has to be carried off the stage.

Forgive me. I didn't intend to go on so. It turns out to be something that wouldn't quite let go, our decision not to issue another press statement notwithstanding. Call it "Suppressed Press Release #1."

We've also made another decision, decided to put a record out. The arrangements have all been made, the date set. We go into the recording studio in a month and a half, on Trane's birthday, September 23rd.

As ever,
N.

17.VIII.82

Dear Angel of Dust,

Drennette's blasé facade finally broke. Djamilaa tells me the two of them went for a walk on the beach yesterday, that in the course of that walk it became clear that her apparent post-expectancy is anything but post-. It became apparent, she says, that Drennette's post-expectant pose is just that, a pose. It was Santa Monica Beach they went for the walk on. Drennette had phoned her in the morning saying she felt "at loose ends," had asked if they could get together sometime that afternoon. She looked, when she came by to pick her up, like nothing out of the ordinary had happened, Djamilaa says. She looked no different, showed no signs of distress or disarray, nor did it ever become apparent that anything on the order of an occurrence had caused what she called her being "at loose ends"—anything of recent advent, that is, for it eventually became evident, Djamilaa says, that a longstanding malaise lay beneath her blasé facade, the same longstanding malaise she touched on a bit at the Merchant of Venice a few months back.

They were walking along the beach, close to the water, Djamilaa says. They came to a mound of kelp which had been left there by the tide and Drennette stopped, looking down at it, momentarily lost in thought, contemplating the tangle of branches and stems. After a moment's reflection she all but inaudibly sighed before saying (more to herself than to her, Djamilaa says), "Our legs used to entwine like that. Rick and I used to lie in bed with our legs entwined." She let it go at that as they resumed walking, going back to whatever it was they'd been talking about before she stopped. She let it go only for the time being it turned out. Every so often, Djamilaa says, she went back to it, filling any lull in the conversation by reminiscing out loud, "Rick and I would sleep with our legs tightly entwined. . . ." Tight entwinement, Djamilaa says, came into poignant, retrospective play with "loose ends," limbed entanglement so elegiacally evoked it retroactively lent "loose" a previously absent grist. Limbed reminiscence achieved a rough poetry at points, bordering on "Empty Bed Blues." "Our legs," Drennette announced, "crossed and recrossed each other, less kelp than kindling. We were one another's wood, one another's shed, sought shelter." She went back to this conceit time and again, Djamilaa says. "Rick was my wood," she'd say, "Rick was my shed, sought shelter"—incantatory, almost liturgical, albeit, unlike liturgy or incantation, discontinuous, interrupted, cut up. They'd be walking along, talking about music or clothes or how good it felt to get out to the beach, whatever, and the talk would tail off and they'd walk on in silence for a while. Drennette, after a while, would say, "Rick was my wood, my shed, the wood I schooled my axe on, not knowing I schooled my axe." Or she'd say, "We were each other's fire. Our legs warmed each other like flames, wood to one another's fire." Or she'd say, "Rick's promise of warmth seemed endless," limbed reminiscence's rough poetry bordering on "Someday My Prince Will Come." "Even now," she'd continue, "it's hard not to believe we'll eventually be together again."

Djamilaa says that the oddest thing was that when she'd respond to this, try to pursue Drennette's talk of Rick further, asking a question, voicing her concern, Drennette would change the subject, go back to talking about music or the new skirt she recently bought or how beautifully the gulls flew, whatever. She seemed bent on talking about Rick but resisted talking about Rick. Heartfelt loss vied with affected non-feeling. "What's done's done," was the closest she'd come to engaging Djamilaa's questions or concern. "No point in going on about that." Surface acceptance, Djamilaa says, attempted to fend off depth—deepseated longing, deepseated lament, deep feelings of loss only partly put behind. The mounds of kelp strewn along the beach were depth's reminders, mnemonic triggers translating "loose ends" into revenant limbs, ventral embrace. Limbed reminiscence gained its grain of salt by posing kelp as kindling, its true grain or its gritty truth mixing would-be return with suppositious wood. Rick was wood and seaweed both—revenant body, salt entanglement, ephemeral touch, unravelable embrace. Weed (unwanted growth) complicated wood (revenant flesh-and-blood), an aliquant reminder gotten deep under her skin going even deeper as time went by.

Rick, her fixation on kelp insinuated, was Drennette's Tosaut wood, erstwhile rock. His remembered legs had a hold on her still, entangled her with Tosaut obduracy, Tosaut salt. Not unlike Ouiot's withered limbs, her own legs grew weaker, Tosaut wood become Tosaut toxin, saline immensity's constrictive "twin." Drennette's legs, Djamilaa says, betrayed her. As they walked on, close to the water, wet sand feeling good on their bare feet, Drennette actually fell not long after saying, "No point in going on about that." Her legs buckled, gave out under her, sending her to the sand, knees first. She broke her fall with her knees and her hands, bounding back up at once, as though quickly recovering could erase the fact of her having fallen, upset with herself for having done so but pretending it was no big thing. Djamilaa had let out a cry of some sort as she fell, had made a move to catch hold of her and keep her from falling or, failing that, help her back up off the sand. Drennette shrugged off her offer of help, Djamilaa says, attempting to mask her disarray by resuming her blasé facade. Her rough poetry betrayed her however. "I must have tripped over a strand of kelp," she announced, though a quick perusal of the area where she'd fallen proved otherwise. It was an area bare of kelp. There was nothing there but sand.

Drennette's having tripped over a phantom strand of kelp (if that's what it was) only made the fact that "what's done" wasn't really done more abundantly clear. Her going on to put a positive, compensatory spin on her breakup with Rick, Djamilaa says, was impossible not to see thru. "A drummer uses all four limbs," she said not long after falling. "Rick and me breaking up gave me back my legs. He was the wood I schooled my axe on in more ways than I knew. Disentangling axe from wood was something I needed to do." Tight entwinement, she was now saying, had arrested her growth. It was a bud whose bloom was breakup. Breakup loosened her limbs. It was this that had made her the drummer she now is.

This, as you know, is a claim she's made before. At the Merchant of Venice she implied a link between concussive spill and percussive spirit, suggesting she really didn't get going as a drummer until after that final bike ride with Rick. Here though, Djamilaa says, the hollowness of it couldn't have rung louder. There was a straining, vacuous quality to it, she says, as frayed-edged as nervous laughter. It was clear she sought consolation in the idea that her drumming thrives on solitude. Following as it did upon her fall gave it an almost desperate air.

Our recent attention to "Tosaut L'Ouverture" had a hand in all of this, as I've already suggested (Tosaut wood, erstwhile rock, Tosaut toxin . . .). This became evident tonight when Drennette showed up at rehearsal with a composition she's written, the first time she's done so since joining the band. The name of it is "Tosaut Strut." It shows her bent on bearing out the claim she made at the beach. More lope than strut, it brings Dewey Redman's "Lop-O-Lop" to mind, a deliberate erasure on Drennette's part, one suspects, of the line between lope and lop.

Like Dewey's piece, "Tosaut Strut" brings drums-and-bass interplay to the forefront, an uptempo outing in which spasmic rolls puncture tonic declension, lopped rolls giving way to the bass's low note braiding adventitious furtherance with suppositious fall. Drennette's recourse to the cowbell all but gloats over adventitious furtherance's braided survival, excavating a ruminative in-and-under ebb in which the raveling lines' taut storage unloads. How she and Aunt Nancy manage to create so prodigal a sense of outmaneuvered collapse I don't know. How they pull off the digestive translation of lop into lope they pull off I don't know. Bent-legged lope, which I'm tempted to call it, doesn't do it justice. Nor does (even more tempting) lope-a-dope.

I'd send a tape but we haven't ironed out all the wrinkles yet. The horn parts are particularly tricky, difficult to get down—long, overarching lines pestered by intercalary divagations. Brazilian samba lays reminiscent vocality atop a no-regrets percussive "pillow" in a way Drennette seems to want "Tosaut Strut" to have learned from. She seems to have had a "stratic" attenuation in mind, superstructural stretch undermined and maintained by bittersweet voicings. It's as if she'll admit or acknowledge nostalgia only in the mouths of others. The horns' bittersweet voicings grant a grudging nod to limbed reminiscence, a discreet division of emotional labor whereby she both doffs and dons her blasé facade. But, as I've said, all the wrinkles have yet to be ironed out. For one, Penguin does alright during the unison horn passages but he draws a blank when his turn to solo comes.

I'll send a tape when we've worked it out.

Yours,

N.

25.VIII.82

Dear Angel of Dust,

Penguin continues to draw a blank when it comes to soloing on "Tosaut Strut." Something inside him balks at the revivalist tack written into the piece—the way the mournful chorus the unison passages effect gives way to solos that advance a sense of renascent vigor, born-again legs gaining higher ground. It's not hard to imagine what that something is. The persistence of Drennette's memories of Rick no doubt bothers him, though there's an aspect of it he's encouraged by as well. Such persistence shows her, blasé facade notwithstanding, to be not quite the post-expectant number she pretends to be. He's more than ready to play his part in the mournful chorus, to lament and lay such memories to rest. But the laying-to-rest "Tosaut Strut" intends to advance means to rise above rather than move on. It wants to anaesthetize present feeling rather than make way for it by leaving past feeling behind. It wants to leave all feeling behind, all but a feeling for the drums. It's to that that Penguin balks at lending himself. Thus the blank he draws when it's his turn to solo.

He hasn't come right out and said any of this. "For some reason, I simply draw a blank when it's my turn to solo," he says, declining to elaborate or to venture a guess what that reason might be. He says it in a flat, disinterested tone of voice, his face as devoid of expression as his manner of speaking. Does he don a blasé facade of his own or is it true he has no idea why he draws a blank? Whichever, we've decided not to force the issue. We've decided not to have him solo on "Tosaut Strut."

Since doing so we've made some headway on the other wrinkles which need ironing out. I'll be able to send you a tape of it soon.

And, yes, there continues to be a to-do surrounding the balloons. We're beginning to regret them having come into the music. Maybe undermine is more what they do than underwrite it we've begun to fear. At the very least, in the public eye they've upstaged it of late. A failed embrace of captionless being or a failure to abide by captionless being is a fact of contemporary life they perhaps alert us to by appealing to—nothing, that is, to cheer about.

As ever,

N.

4.IX.82

WIND-ASSISTED DRUM-LAB READOUT (DREAM SOLILOQUY)

In my head I composed a letter I knew by heart. It began in a way I knew by heart but didn't know I knew. I bit my lip not to mouth what I wrote out loud. So it was I resisted adventitious locution, the wafted remit I ran the risk of exacting were it the "open sesame" I wished it would be. "Dear Lag-Leg Vibe," I wrote, biting my lip.

I bit my lip, pressing pen to paper within the cardiognostic chamber my head had become. I erased it, only to write it again, "Dear Lag-Leg Vibe." Biting my lip made the marks on the paper stay put.

Voices told me mud was my middle name but I bore it well. Namesake slippage muddied my mouth as I stood my ground, bitten lip bitten all the more intently, all but bleeding, mud a kind of blood, blood mud's afterthought. I bit my lip so intently it eventually began to bleed. It was then that I finally let up, loosened up.

When I loosened my embouchure, no longer bit my lip, a balloon rose from the page on which I wrote. As it rose it took the words up off the page I wrote them on. *Dear Lag-Leg Vibe*, written in the balloon, floated above the page, as did the rest of what I wrote: *That the balloons embody a wished-for return to primal mud there can be no doubt, but that such return makes mud sublime needs to be remembered. The balloons revisit mud only to take it higher, ostensible ascent so inextricably coincident with going down mud would appear to make sight "say's" recompense.*

Mud would so appear to clarify "say" we see words in the air.

It was a reminder I wrote myself, something one might tape to a refrigerator door. I wrote it while serving customers in the kissing booth, the booth I stood in selling kisses and Kashmiri Cough Drops. Middle name notwithstanding, my name was Djeannine. Mud, my middle name, was the name of the funky lipstick I wore. Mud brought all the way from the Nile, the ads insisted—dark, alluvial lipstick laid on thick like a sloppy kiss.

A dreamer licked my sister's pubic lips a million light-years away and with every kiss I flexed my mouth with that dreamer's abandon, loosening and stretching my lips, jaws and tongue, doing all I could to give my clients their money's worth. My lips covered their lips but would neither stick, stay nor settle, would instead wander past corner-of-the-mouth, stray beyond lip-ridge, kiss less what it was than lip-smear, mouth-smother, leave a snail's trail of spit. Dark, alluvial lipstick muddied their faces. No customer left my booth unsatisfied.

But, no, I was not Djeannine, I only dreamt I was. Dreamt name notwithstanding, my name was Drennette. My tongue was as wet as an old rope. My lips, dry as wood, resisted kisses. My ass was as hard as a man's.

I wrote what I wrote not between customers in the kissing booth but between beats. Stand wasn't what I did; I sat.

A snake's head buried beneath the stool on which I sat would've sunk its fangs into my hips had my ass not been so hard. Long hours at the drumset made it so. Many a hand sought passage up my leg, under my dress, but only the drummer's stool felt my rump, the insides of my thighs, only it got anywhere near my private parts. Many a man tried to look up my dress while I played but the drumset blocked their view.

Mud, on the other hand, occluded speech but in so doing made it more clear, no longer transparent. Mud was loose interstitial cement, my dream's loose translation of the space between beats. It was the hair sticking out from the reinforced crotch of Djeannine's white panties, thetic aria ("air") to their whiteness's antithetic "earth."

Mud, I sang, was all name, only a name. Mud was middleness,

founding glue. Name tied my tongue and tore my tongue, taut cord binding an otherwise unbound "earth," agitational cartwheel, blinding white spin.

My name was Drennette. I dreamt of Djeannine, dreamt I was Djeannine. My loose lips delivered spendthrift kisses, prodigal kisses. My tongue was a leaf of kelp, salty-sweet.

I sang an earthy aria, a foul-mouthed aria, fulfilling every customer's wish to be talked dirty to.

My salty tongue made lewd suggestion after lewd suggestion. My saucy mouth talked as nasty a talk as could ever be talked, notwithstanding my name was Drennette (Drennette Virgin to some, DV, Diva).

My high notes harbored B'Loon's beakful of mud.

Dear Angel of Dust,

Working out all the wrinkles introduced a new wrinkle. Scroll and teleprompted script rolled into one, B'Loon's most recent visit took an unexpected turn. What I wrote above is what it seemed I saw written in the blank Penguin had previously drawn on "Tosaut Strut." It was a blank he no longer drew but which it seemed I saw when I closed my eyes shortly into his solo. Yes, he finally soloed on "Tosaut Strut." How this came to be I could hardly wait to write you about. I could wait to write you the script I saw even less.

It happened at a place in town we played earlier tonight (last night really—it's two in the morning now), a place known as The Studio, over in the Crenshaw. Having finally worked out all the wrinkles, we were anxious to play "Tosaut Strut" before a live audience. Things were going well (nice turnout, serious listeners, everyone's chops up), so we gave it a go late in the second set.

We had ended the first set with "Tosaut L'Ouverture." The "lag along" regard for what gets away I've spoken of before in regard to the piece was very much in evidence in the reading we gave it. I hadn't realized before how much the music of my childhood had made an impact on the composition, but Drennette did something she hadn't done before, a subtle something which made me do just that. Every now and then, that is, she would drag the tip of one of her sticks across the snare drum's head, an explicit "lag along" tack she managed to work in without missing a beat. She worked in more than that, however, more than she knew (though, who can say, maybe not), for the very first time she did it I thought of a dance that was popular when I was ten known as "The Stroll." It was a dance in which dancers formed two parallel lines, down the "aisle" between which, a couple at a time, they promenaded. Part stroll, part extended stagger, the promenade featured a gangly, sideways carriage and a crossover step in which one foot was dragged on its side. "Tosaut L'Ouverture's" resistant lag, I realized, owes as much to this as to anything else. I thought of Chuck Willis's "Betty and Dupree," the way the mournful, coaxing sax appears to lament a lost instinctual rapport of some sort. I knew that lament had no doubt informed my piece's "lag along" chagrin.

The noncalibrated apportionment or appeal of "Tosaut L'Ouverture," the "lag along" vibe it adumbrated or advanced, hung in the air throughout the intermission and hung there as well throughout the second set. It hung with pointed incompletion and weight, albeit ever so lightly, especially so when we lit into "Tosaut Strut." It was as if we'd planned ahead—which, in a sense, we had, though with an odd, unwitting prescience that went well beyond obvious namesake tether. We had a feeling we were in for something special the moment Drennette's drumsticks hit the skins. She wasted no time weaving "lag along" vibe and lop-o-lop resilience together as one, relating, with unheard-of articulacy, blown matrimonial stroll and aborted bike ride, lag-leg encumbrance and renascent strut. Betty to Rick's Dupree, she wove an alternative tale, one of alternativity itself.

Drennette made it clear right away that the phantom strand that had broken her stride at the beach was the pedal which had broken during her final bike ride with Rick. Revenant pedal floated up from the drums as though up from under the sand, an inflated premise bent on regaining lost ground, revenant beachhead, surge cut with imminent sashay. The pedal proved a Pyrrhic encumbrance—aliquant landing and "lag along" limb rolled into one, leapt-over strand (she *leapt,* not fell, she insisted) whereby we became a septet. We were seven, newly membered, paralegged. Doppelganger strut so exacted leg from *leapt* we became a "steptet." Rick ran with us it seemed.

In that sense, Rick running with us, we were back to being six rather than seven. So palpable was his presence, so impressive the music's evocation of theretofore lost but now revenant legs, it made Penguin pretty much bow out, daunted by what he took to be his rival's return (rival memory, revivalist "would"). Rick ran with us, thickly part of the pack, the "steptet," and to the extent that he did Penguin withdrew, blowing so faintly during the unison passage he could hardly be heard. Coming out of that passage, Lambert lit into his solo, a blistering foray in which he took no prisoners. Following that came the next unison passage, a long, labyrinthine excursion in which Penguin blew even more faintly than before. He played as though he wasn't there, as though Rick had taken his place. Him having withdrawn, we were again, "steptet" though we were, only six.

It was during this long, labyrinthine unison passage that Aunt Nancy made a decisive move, a move that brought about results beyond her wildest hopes. Penguin stood not far in front of her and a bit to her right, which made it easy for her, taking a step out from behind her bass while continuing to play, to lean forward and whisper into his ear. He had played his part in the unison passage lethargically up to this point, all but not blowing, all but announcing he wasn't there. After Aunt Nancy whispered into his ear, however, he perked up as if called back from nodding out. He now blew full force, his tone biting and robust. It even seemed his clothes fit him better, that he filled them out in exactly the way that, withdrawn, all but begging off being there, he hadn't since the advent of Rick's revenant legs.

Penguin's rehabilitation went even further, however. As we neared the end of the long unison passage he made eye contact with me, whose turn it was to solo next, taking his right hand from the horn momentarily and pointing to himself, indicating by that that he wanted to solo. This took me by surprise but I gave him the nod to go ahead. When the unison passage ended he hit the upbeat like a diver hitting a springboard, then pulled back a microbeat almost at once, lopped ictus and lag-leg lope rolled into one. Drennette, gratified by his recourse to her lop/lope conceit, splashed a rubber-wrist flourish on cymbals by way of acknowledgement, then quickly got back to making her lag-leg rounds. A gimp-leg dip, that is, came around with the persistence of an oblong wheel, an asymmetric wheel Penguin rolled with at first and then, five bars later, climbed aboard and rode.

A rickety mix of ride and run, "Tosaut Strut" lived up to its name nonetheless. Aunt Nancy played "lag along" tag, a walking figure which caught Drennette's dip every other bar. Walking bass catching oblong wheel's apogee seemed to whoa ride's runaway drift somewhat. It brought containment to a pace which at times bordered on frantic, reining in run's unchecked furtherance of itself. More than that, it asserted a cocksure composure in full accord with eponymic strut.

Penguin plays bari on "Tosaut Strut," a horn he got around on, this time out, as though it were a tenor. It wasn't so much that he spent a good deal of time high up on the horn as that he made one think of Ornette's statement that the tenor is a rhythm instrument, made one think of the bari as a rhythm instrument too. He brought Fred Anderson to mind the way he motored so nimbly, nonchalantly even, in so frequently oblique a rapport with Drennette and Aunt Nancy's in-and-under ebb.

For all the time he spent up high on the horn Penguin more than gave the bottom its due. He had a cascading way of getting there and, once there, proffered a dark, thick sound which, viscosity notwithstanding, moved around with an inflection and fluidity more typical of the horn's middle range. Suggesting sludge without at all seeming sluggish, it was as thick as Turkish coffee, with all the kick of Turkish coffee, a dark, ever advancing bulb of sound.

Drennette ingeniously buffed Penguin's bulb of sound with intermittent strings of hissed rescission on high hat, clipped hisses which became a kind of chatter, an ongoing bug she put in Penguin's ear. Buffed bulb gave a glint or gleam to the otherwise dark, ever advancing brew, a philosophico-metallic sheen which led the way as it illumined our way.

Drennette's hissing chatter recalled the drummer we heard in

Griffith Park somewhat—enough so, at any rate, to make me close my eyes. I was curious not so much to see whether I'd see the dancing broom as simply to see, as Rahsaan once put it, what I could see. Her clipped hisses stirred up fairy dust, it seemed, a pharmacopoeic endowment (closed-eye, open-sesame inducement or endowment) one sensed was now in the air.

The first thing I saw when I closed my eyes was that the blank Penguin had previously drawn when it came to soloing on "Tosaut Strut" was indeed a drawn blank, that it lay within lines drawn horizontally and vertically which marked off a space that was rectangular in shape, less tall than it was wide. These lines merely formed a template, however, a frame for what, now that Penguin was soloing, unfolded or unrolled within the space they circumscribed.

That Penguin now played with new fluency and rare articulacy I already knew. How new and how rare I was about to find out. Drennette's clipped hisses both stirred up dust and splashed or spewed forth mud—dust in my eye, mud in Penguin's ear. She lent a taste of earth to his Turkish coffee, but, more than that, she sustained a burr, a buzz, a ring of resonant chatter, so insistently put the proverbial bug in his ear he rose to new heights—heights of uncanny intelligibility and, I would soon see, ventriloquistic legibility as well.

Penguin, that is, played as though possessed, Drennette as though feeding him his lines. He was her put-upon amanuensis. She was prompter and psychopomp both. He spoke thru the horn as though telling of a dream while still asleep, a waking dream whose theme was dreamt conveyance. Behind the lids of my closed eyes I saw the words he spoke inscribed within the blank he had previously drawn, written out and rolling within the template, rolling scroll and teleprompter into one, ancient and modern into one. *In my head I composed a letter I knew by heart* were the first words to appear.

Drennette's inventiveness made the drums a laboratory of sorts. Penguin rolled actor and lab technician into one, rendering his lines with the attentiveness to detail of a lab report. Drennette's "findings" were anything but clinical, however. She goaded and cursed with a slurred insinuation and a possessed insistence worthy of Elvin's work with Trane. Compelled by and competing with dream, resentful of dream, she thumped out a spate of disconsolate patter on the bass drum. No less compelled by and competing with dream and resentful of dream, but also compelled by and competing with drum and resentful of drum, Penguin soliloquized as if to negotiate between grist and beguilement, ghost and beguilement, rival memory and dreamt revival, dream and drum. Admittedly beholden to Drennette's drum-lab chatter, he had much that was his own to say as well.

As Penguin's bari spoke, the words continued to appear within the template, written out on the teleprompted scroll the music unfurled: *But, no, I was not Djeannine, I only dreamt I was. . . .* It occurred to me that the template amounted to something of a balloon. Given the script's overt reference to balloons, it was clear that what was going on was a B'Loon visit. B'Loon was granting what had become our not so secret wish that the balloons appear, if at all, in a more subtle, less attention-getting way. This latest visit thus took an esoteric turn, removing the words from open view, advancing a script only the closed eye saw. B'Loon had gone underground I understood. We had survived our brief encounter with fame.

B'Loon's presence was further confirmed by the wind which gradually arose from Drennette's drumset as Penguin soloed. As at Soulstice in Seattle, where the balloons made their first appearance, Drennette brewed a spinning wind with each roll she resorted to. Answering Penguin's rhythmic aplomb, the rhythm instrument the bari became, she made the drums a wind instrument, ventilated his grist with beguiling gusts. I felt a breeze at my back, especially so on the back of my neck.

Drennette's drum-driven wind gradually blew with more force as Penguin soloed, peaking, appropriately, just as he concluded, both it and the teleprompted script all the more forcefully announcing B'Loon's presence: *My high notes harbored B'Loon's beakful of mud.*

When Penguin ended his solo I opened my eyes and put my horn to my mouth. He, Lambert and I embarked on the next unison passage, following which Aunt Nancy soloed, as planned. Following Aunt Nancy's solo, we repeated the long, labyrinthine unison passage my solo normally follows. This we did to allow me the solo space Penguin pre-empted, having whispered among ourselves to that effect while Aunt Nancy soloed. I took my solo, after which we returned to the head and ended the piece. We played one more number, "The Slave's Day Off," whereupon we got called back for an encore and offered a short, sololess reading of "Half-Staff Appetition."

As usual, a few friends and fans came backstage afterward. We were curious, of course, as to whether any of them had closed their eyes during Penguin's solo and whether, if they had, they'd seen what I saw. It turned out that a couple of them had closed their eyes and they reported that indeed they had seen the teleprompted script. I spoke with both of them at length, comparing notes, as it were, taking notes. The words the three of us had seen, it became clear, were the same.

The only question now is what was it Aunt Nancy whispered in Penguin's ear. She won't say and neither will he. He says the one thing he will say is that she told him not to.

Yours,
N.

8.IX.82

Dear Angel of Dust,

Today at rehearsal Lambert told us about a dream he had last night. He was in the backyard, he says, to a house he heard a voice coming out of, his mother's voice. He stood before a patch of flowers, the house to his left, not looking toward the house, caught up instead in the flowers in front of him, oddly colored flowers—blue lilies, purple tulips, the hues, moreover, metallic. He stood entranced, he says, by the unusual sheen of the flowers' petals, the various grades of metallic blue or metallic purple on a given petal, burnt burnish to mirror-like bright. He heard his mother's voice coming out of the house and it seemed he heard it from closer to the house than he actually was, though he wasn't looking at the house, he says, and thus can't say how he knew what the distance was. It seemed he partook of two lookings, he says. He looked at the flowers and he also had eyes on the back of his head—not eyes *at* the back of his head, he insists, eyes *on* it. He seemed to be subject to as well as wielding a stare that looked at him from behind, saw him in relation to the house without him looking at the house.

Lambert says he heard his mother, who's been dead five years, talking inside the house, talking in a tone of voice that she used to use with him when he was a child. He knew he was in some unusual realm even as he dreamt, he says, the land of the dead perhaps, that of dream at the very least, possibly both (dream, it crossed his mind even as he dreamt, could play psychopomp). He listened more and more intently, hungrily, happy and sad to again hear that voice—happy to be hearing it at all, sad that it could be heard only there in this unusual realm. He continued looking at the blues and purples of the lilacs' and tulips' petals, looking at the flowers but listening to his mother's voice, listening more intently than looking. So intent was his listening, he says, it seemed he could see her inside the house talking to him as a little boy, see himself as a little boy inside the house. Though it seemed he could see inside the house without looking, he was so happy to hear his mother's voice and so hungry to see more he turned and looked toward the house, at which point the house disappeared, taking her voice with it.

Lambert calls the dream an "Orphic warning." He said it speaks to what he termed "our current situation," that he saw no need to elaborate, that he wouldn't say more.

He didn't need to. We all, without discussing it, saw what he meant.

Yours,
N.

10.IX.82

Dear Angel of Dust,

Penguin couldn't hold it in any longer. He told Lambert and Lambert told me what it was Aunt Nancy whispered in his ear the other night. "Don't tell anyone I told you this" was the first thing she said. She then told him Drennette had dreamt the Djeannine dream the night he fell asleep on her couch, that after putting the blanket on him and going to bed she not only dreamt the Djeannine dream but dreamt the version with the broken-tooth ending, his version, that Drennette herself had told her this.

Not much mystery as to why Penguin perked up as he did, played as he did, after that. It must have hit him like an answered prayer: him and Drennette in adjoining rooms dreaming reciprocal dreams. But this maybe has other ramifications as well. Penguin and Drennette slept in a two-room, his-and-her dreamhouse, each the other's inductee (Penguin into Penny's upper room, Drennette into Djeannine's kissing booth). They played host to alternate drumgirl dreams, guest in each other's ostensible room. Subliminally perhaps but even so, he and she took it on themselves to reapportion the band's his-and-her dreams. They revealed the dreamhouse's his-and-her rooms to be permeable rooms, ostensible walls to be pervious walls, his-and-her partitions, otherwise insisted on, susceptible to traffic, place-trading flow.

That they relieved us, in doing so, of a certain division of oneiric labor is obvious enough. But that their doing so sprang from the very verge of a kiss (if Penguin's account is to be believed), what would have been a first kiss, seems to say something (though I'm not exactly sure what) about the precipitous freight of carnal proof in the his-and-her dreamhouse. What Penguin sought to prove thru the press of lips, a perhaps redundant press of lips it turns out, proves in crucial ways to be the far side of carnal capture, far beyond empirical presence or proof. What he sought to prove (more to himself than to anyone else it would seem) was what he's been saying all along, that there's more to Drennette than meets the eye. But that this could be true of the lip as well as the eye has some bearing I'm not yet altogether clear about on the default on captionless being to which the balloons attest. The advent of intervening sleep at the very moment their lips were poised to meet has something to do with renouncing redundant proof, incongruous proof, with positing a Monk-like renunciative harmonic which, albeit warm with the rub of empirical pressure, remains wise to fallacious equations of pressure with proof. It proposes, instead, an aliquant equation of verge-of-a-kiss with virgin kiss, virgin kiss with virgin cognition. Penguin's intervening sleep adduced an incumbent press of limbs and lips, virgin kiss qua cognizance, alternate embrace, vatic, ostensible embrace as if of nothing and if of nothing only of nothing-to-prove. Duke said something that's relevant here, not once and for all but to be revisited again and again: "Prelude to a Kiss." Penguin's intervening sleep took the accent off of proof and put it on prelude, drawing, as his Aunt Nancy-prompted solo also would, on unmarked as well as marked ambiguations of sexual and sacred, sophic and sacrilegious, secular and sacred, body and soul.

Lambert oscillates between saying it was bound to happen, that Drennette and Penguin were bound to, as he puts it, "get it on dreamwise," and doubting that what Aunt Nancy told Penguin is true, dismissing her talk of Drennette having dreamt the Djeannine dream as a motivating fiction, a lie she told to get Penguin to play. I myself have no doubts. Drennette dreaming the Djeannine dream says to me that Penguin's "ass eye" saw more than it saw, that the see-thru amenities glass affords leaves one nonetheless blind to fraught furtherances of sight, synaesthetic impactednesses only a tactile eye could apprehend. Drennette's "caressive receptivity" and corresponding "ass eye" crossed an otherwise unbridgeable divide to barter broken-tooth resolve with ain'thropologic distraint. The *feel* of Kashmiri Cough Drops in Penguin's mouth took hold of her mouth, a circumlocutious kiss whose virgin precincts ("the hill with the sun behind her," "the meadow at the foot of the hill") boasted waters glass-bottom boats patrol. Derived from a soft-focus, near-homophonous equation of booth with boat, such vessels advanced a dreamt occlusion whereby see-thru bottom concerted glass with ass. Penguin picked up on this in his Aunt Nancy-prompted solo: "Mud brought all the way from the Nile. . . ." Mud from Lake Dal it could just as easily have been. In any case, to so elevate mud signals having grown wise to see-thru pretense.

Glass occlusion, after all, isn't all that far-fetched. I still remember looking at a drop of water under a microscope for the first time in a science class in grammar school. The ostensibly clear water could be seen to be teeming with microorganisms, crowded with tiny forms of life made visible only by arrangements of glass. The lens allowed one to see thru clarity itself, see thru to complicating, occluding forms and features one would otherwise not have seen. Glass put mud in one's eye. Ostensible sheerness's occultation was a glass-enhanced recognition of apparent stillness as recondite motility, apparent stasis as unseen agitation, an endlessly adaptive dance.

The latter phrase is Julius Hemphill's. He says that "A.D." in the title of his piece "Dogon A.D." stands for Adaptive Dance, that it came out of his reading an article about the Dogon deciding to reveal some of their sacred dance rituals to attract the tourist trade. Before hearing this I took it to mean Anno Domini, as most people probably do. The appropriateness of this to an adaptive accord between purity and commerce, compromise, makes each meaning fit, work in more than one way. Penguin and Drennette's dream exchange, virgin kiss though it was, adaptively sustained a default on supposed purity, a default (aka mud) whose compromise with commerce (bought kisses, slot-machine eyes) adumbrated an array of subtle adjustments, a sublime, all but microbic pas de deux.

However personal its reach and whatever its roots, Penguin's Aunt Nancy-prompted solo also aired anxieties we've been feeling about the balloons and, more obliquely, the visibility we can't help hoping to gain by cutting a record. Penguin again proved to be our plumb line. Perhaps it bodes well for our upcoming record date that the spectre of cartoon accessibility could itself, like Bird's Woody Woodpecker quotes, be drawn into the music.

So, yes, it's graduation time, time for us to either put aside our forebodings or consume them, feed ourselves, learn how to use them as fuel. It's time to go forward—with a lag-leg stride if need be, but go forward—burn with a variously adaptive dance and adieu, begin to bid apprehension goodbye. Drennette's tripping over a strand of phantom kelp, freighted, we now see, with the weight of having dreamt the Djeannine dream, may well have been a step in the right direction.

A part of me thinks we should quote "Pomp and Circumstance" at some point in the album, play upon Penguin and Drennette's dreamt, soft-focus coupling of commerce and commencement, a double-aspected walk-down-the-aisle. But that would be going too far.

As ever,
N.

12.IX.82

Dear Angel of Dust,

Thank you for your letter. Yes, you read me right. Drennette stumbling over a phantom strand of kelp, going down, albeit briefly, on all fours to bounce right back up, was an adaptive step in a staggered ballet of which Penguin's "Wind-Assisted Drum-Lab Readout" and she and Penguin dreaming reciprocal dreams were respectively later and earlier steps. Her accidental prostration, moreover, flirts with an evocation of reminiscent entwinement as implicitly prayerful, intimations of limbed entanglement rolling animal and religious fidelities into one. Her and Penguin's courtship, if that's what it is, is an adaptive dance drawn out over disparate points in time, cloistered and courtly both, an eight-limbed enablement proposing retreat as a kind of advance, virtual or virgin clasp as immaterially bound beyond empirical demise. So as to touch without touching, each abdicated his or her dream in the his-and-her dreamhouse, a devotional default that granted them both translative passage between horn and drum, ventriloquial pitch apportioning immaculacy and mud. So, at any rate, it seems to me.

We played at a place in Long Beach called the Blue Light Lounge last night. It was a gig which had its moments, the one that stays with me most being one that occurred as we were playing "Altered Cross." Lambert was soloing on tenor, Aunt Nancy behind him on bass, Djamilaa on piano, Drennette on drums. He was into a deep crouch, bent over, his horn all but grazing the floor, bellowing as though caught in some harsh quandary, as though "altered" were a fractious play on "altared," conflicted claims mixing sanctity and sacrilege. He thrashed and brayed, a voice from the depths, but suddenly Aunt Nancy, Djamilaa and Drennette broke into an uptempo bossa nova, a bounding, waltz-time extenuation for which Drennette's stick on the snare's metal rim kept time with even measures of mirth and residual menace, ambidextrous foil and fellow traveller to Djamilaa's light but elated right hand. Aunt Nancy's bass figure evinced a tidelike ebb and flow, a lusty, recurrent swell and subsidence, the four fingers of her left hand scurrying about the bass's fingerboard like an alarmed half-spider. The bass line, it seemed, said it all, though in this instance "all" meant no saying said enough.

Lambert, taken by surprise, relied at first on a captious, expectorant croon reminiscent of Shepp's way of playing "The Girl from Ipanema," a now abrasive, now caressive growl with which he bought time. However, time bought, new bearings gotten, he took a mellower tack, a forthright ride of the rhythm section's roll and recurrence, a willingness to be carried along, even carried away, a transparent, it-doesn't-bother-me facade by way of which he backed away from his earlier abject air. Punctuating such willingness and the wave it rode, however, was an intermittent pass in which Lambert, meditative, sotto voce, let the rhythm section chime louder behind him. It was a turning to himself that bespoke misgiving, albeit misgiving mixed with guileful resolve. It seemed he reasoned with a troublesome remnant of his earlier disarray, pestered but philosophic, up to the task. It was a good example of what John Gilmore means by "contrary motion." The rhythm section's bodily blare and relentless forwarding were countered by Lambert's reflective step back, such misgiven retreat a clearly fictive sublation whose insinuative trace proffered ghost and body both.

Neither hoarse nor laryngitic, Lambert's sotto voce tack resonated, a soliloquistic aside whose elegiac reflection on the furtherance the rhythm section fostered freighted such furtherance with a bittersweet adamance, as though time were so infectiously marked only to lament its loss. But Drennette, head held high, resolutely tapping the rim of the snare, would have none of this—or would have it, having to, only in such mixed-emotional array as Djamilaa's bright right-hand proclamations and Aunt Nancy's ambulant ebb and flow brewed or brought out. Time slipped away, she allowed, but only to be swung by the track or trail it drew with it. It was frighteningly beautiful the way they brokered so duplicit a peace with the passing of time.

Getting back to your letter: no, we haven't worked out which pieces we'll put on the album. Our book's gotten so big we may have to make it a two-record set to keep the omissions to a minimum. We'd like to include a piece or two not written by one of us, "Sun Ship," say, or "Like a Blessed Baby Lamb," but that makes the question of which of our own to include tougher. Probably what we'll do is spend all day in the studio, record everything in our book and then decide which ones came out best. Anyway, we'll see. You're still interested in writing the liner notes, we hope.

Yours,

N.

PS: No sign of the balloons at last night's gig.

25.IX.82

Dear Angel of Dust,

The recording session went well, much more smoothly than we'd expected. Aside from the minor, inevitable hitch here and there, none of our nervousness and apprehension seems to have been justified. In fact, it may be that our nervousness and apprehension got big enough to be an unexpected boon, a roundabout blessing. It's tempting, at least, to see it that way. We got to where we were rehearsing everyday, some days almost all day, so intent were we on getting everything down, on everything going according to plan, on there being a plan. So impressed were we by the thought of the music being immortalized in wax we wanted to make it perfect, provide for all contingencies, leave as little as possible to chance. The recording session loomed so large, came to be so fraught with ultimacy, we mistakenly wanted it all worked out in advance. The closer we got to the recording date the more obsessed we got. It was Drennette who, in her roundabout way, finally straightened us out.

Four days, that is, before the day we recorded we had to call off a rehearsal because of Drennette not showing up. As it turned out, she was nowhere to be found up until the very day we recorded, showing up at the studio, drumset in tow, ready to play, much to our relief though not entirely to our surprise. Not long after the aborted rehearsal, that very same day in fact, Aunt Nancy, Djamilaa, Lambert, Penguin and I had all found the same "message" on our answering machines. Someone had called each of us and played a line from a song on the *Black*

Orpheus soundtrack album into the receiver, recorded the same line from the same song on all our machines. The song was "A Felicidade," the line "*e cai como uma lágrima*." Whoever it was had made a loop of it, letting it repeat exactly seven times before hanging up, giving it the sound of a needle stuck on a nicked record.

Once we put it together that this was the case, that we'd all gotten the same "message" at what must've been about the same time, and put this together with Drennette, within roughly the same span of time, not having shown up for rehearsal and now being nowhere to be found, we suspected the coincidence was no coincidence, that the *Black Orpheus* "message" and Drennette's disappearance were connected. It took hardly any discussion at all to conclude that Drennette had left the "message" on our machines, that, taking a page out of Penguin's book (or, earlier, Lambert's), she had gone into retreat, a preparatory retreat, a retreat the "message" announced while leaving us food for thought. Drennette, we surmised, had gone off "to prepare a place," a place, premise or permission from which to better leverage our recording venture, leaving the rest of us to reflect on the "message" she'd left on our answering machines.

The line means "and falls like a tear." Was this Drennette's way of admitting that she had fallen, not leapt, the day she and Djamilaa walked along the shore at Santa Monica Beach? Was she now allowing there'd been no phantom strand of kelp over which to trip, only pathos, her own choked-up emotion, that she'd in fact fallen "like a tear"? Was she suggesting, confessing, obliquely but even so, that *leapt* was less what her plummet was tantamount to, amounted to, than *wept*? It surely appeared so, though what we soon enough saw was that the more important, more instructive message for us was that she'd found a way to say this without saying it. Roundabout to the bone, she was saying, we soon enough saw, not so much something about what happened at the beach as about us. Say it without saying it she seemed to insist, yet there was more. Didn't the needle-stuck-on-a-nick accent senses of impairment, imperfection, a recognition she meant to bring us back to in the face of our wished-for immaculacy? That she "spoke" with nicked-record insistence, played upon the wear, the maculation endemic to the premises we extolled, would-be states of recorded grace our obsessed rehearsals prepared for, pursued, by no means escaped our notice.

The decisive thing, though, was that with Drennette gone we couldn't go on rehearsing. This ultimately worked to the recording date's advantage, forcing us to loosen up, to let go of our wish to work everything out in advance. Drennette had taken it upon herself to bring our obsessed rehearsals to an end, get us to relax, going into retreat as if to say to us, "Lighten up. Cool it." This occurred to us readily enough once we saw that she was nowhere to be found. Nudging our thoughts in this direction was the recording on her answering machine. When we called her apartment, that is, we found that she'd replaced her spoken greeting with the recording of Trane's voice on the *Sun Ship* album, the comments he makes to the other musicians right before "Dearly Beloved": "Keep, keep, you know, keep a *thing* happening all thru it." This hit us as being directed our way, meant to say something specifically to us, the permissive indefiniteness of Trane's inclusive "*thing*" pointedly contrasting with our recent, exaggerated wish for definitiveness.

Still, all of this was inferred, shadowed by the risk of being wrong inference runs. We could be wrong, we knew. We could be totally misreading the situation. We couldn't be certain that Drennette hadn't simply gotten fed up with us, that she hadn't broken down (fallen like a tear), unable to function, that things weren't amiss in some other way. We had no way of being sure that all of this had been orchestrated by her as we hoped and suspected, that on the day of the recording she'd show up. Though we were confident, all but certain, even, we'd have said, convinced, we nonetheless knew we could be wrong. Thus it was that when Drennette did show up on the day of the recording we were relieved, albeit not surprised.

It went farther than simple relief though. That we'd read Drennette right, that she'd successfully "said it without saying it," not only taught by example but advanced an angular rapport we felt buoyed up by, buoyed up and newly borne along by. It further loosened us up, helped us lighten up, confirmed a certain chemistry we thereby took into the studio with us, an oblique articulacy's jointure and drape, indirect address. Aunt Nancy later resorted to a basketball metaphor to describe it: "It was as though she threw us a no-look pass." Albeit implicitly disavowed, Drennette's phantom strand of kelp informed us throughout, an exposed nerve or its referred sensation, so persistent a report we needed only abide by the auspice it proffered. Indeed, no-look obliquity blessed us with a prescient, post-optic aptitude in Orphic disguise, Orphic bind borne as roundabout reprieve. Hence the title we've decided on for the album, *Orphic Bend.*

I could say more about the music and the recording session itself, but I won't beyond enclosing a new after-the-fact lecture/libretto, a new installment I found myself writing these past couple of days. Impelled in large part by aliquant reminders of the session's look-without-looking aplomb, its no-look élan, the lecture/libretto may prove of some use as you go about writing your liner notes. Also enclosed are tapes of the music, all of what we recorded. We've no more than begun deciding which pieces and which takes will go on the album. As always, we welcome your thoughts.

Yours,
N.

DOOR PEEP
(SHALL NOT ENTER)

or, The Creaking of the Word: After-the-Fact Lecture/Libretto (Djband Virgin)

The fall of Hotel Didjeridoo reverberated worldwide. In Southern California a wave washed a bottle ashore, a note-bearing bottle, the bottle B'Loon had finally been put into, put back into. Cat-out-of-the-bag, horse-out-of-the-barn and genie-out-of-the-lamp rolled into one, B'Loon, while out of the bottle, had written the note the bottle now bore, a note apprising the world of its whorehouse roots. Dubbed "Namesake Encyclical #1," it was a simple note. Referring to the brothels in which "jazz" was reportedly born, the words it bore were these: "And the girls would come down dressed in the finest evening gowns, just like they were going to the opera." Hotel Didjeridoo, it meant to announce, had been such a house.

The word from down under was thus that the music guests had heard piped into their rooms was overdetermined inversion, a music making fun of its mock-operatic roots, opera making fun of its presumed elevation. That such elevation had a hand in its own undoing was thought by many to have helped bring Hotel Didjeridoo down. The girls, everyone knew, put on their evening gowns only to take them off. To do so they went back up. This was the opera they ascended to.

So, at least, the analysis went. Djbouche, however, had tired of such analysis. The note, he knew, existed at his expense. B'Loon had agreed to go back into the bottle only on the condition that the note go in with him, that room be made for the note by evicting Djbouche, his longtime bottle-mate (drinking buddy, according to some). Thus it was that Djbouche too blew into town, washed ashore in an alternate bottle, a noteless bottle, bent on teaming up again with B'Loon, performing a duet. That "jazz" played low note to opera's high note, he insisted, everybody already knew. What he wanted was to play no note to B'Loon's low note. Thus the noteless bottle he blew into town in.

Still, Djbouche was no angel. It was he who had exposed the goings-on at Hotel Didjeridoo, he who had played Peeping Tom raconteur one time too many, he who had tended the Keyhole Club Convention's no-host bar. Though his "No-Note Samba" had more than fit the occasion, he felt depleted, deprived, deserving of greater recognition, wanting, however much he knew better, to be the commercial lubricant his no-note tack took issue with. It was, after all, he who had put the bug in B'Loon's ear, he who had whispered, "Give them what they want."

What the ubiquitous, indefinite "they" wanted was to see, to be able to say what they saw was what they got. This is what B'Loon had delivered. To dress for the opera was to be at the opera. To undress was to bring opera down. It all but went without saying they'd get no more than what they saw, all but amounted to insisting they could see getting only what they saw. "Show them a good time," Djbouche had whispered in B'Loon's ear.

Djbouche, claiming to be no angel but no Mephistopheles either, now blamed the bug he'd put in B'Loon's ear on the heady spirits he'd had the job of serving at the Keyhole Club Convention's no-host bar. "The fumes must've gotten to me," he told himself, more and more convinced that the mere smell of alcohol had loosened his tongue, caused him to speak too freely. Speakeasy premises, he told himself, had taken hold of him, caused him to speak on behalf of slurred speech, slurred but articulate seen-said merger, seen-said auction-block lubricity fusing lucidity with bottom-line sex.

The effect of the fumes confirmed the power of scent over sound, sound over sight. What the ubiquitous, indefinite "they" saw had been dictated by what B'Loon had to say, what B'Loon had to say by the heady whiff Djbouche couldn't help catching while tending bar. The greater recognition Djbouche was intent on gaining for the alternate bottle in which he washed ashore would in part be gained by the theory he came prepared to advocate. It was a theory that would supplant B'Loon's founding script or founding scratch with a notional/anti-notational elision. Founding nose would elide founding noise as what preceded so-called founding script, *founding nose* anti-notationally rendered *founding no(i)se*. The parenthetic *i* would signify an imaginary operation whereby scent pervaded sound, sound scent.

The complex, multifaceted phenomena known collectively as Hotel Didjeridoo, Djbouche came ready to argue, rested on a submerged, fleetingly recognized bottom line, synaesthetic sniff. Hotel Didjeridoo had gone down like Atlantis, a utopic union of sound and scent whose prelapsarian allure held optic ascendancy in check—a plummet or plunge whose latest report would be the newly arrived "Theory of Founding No(i)se" itself. Founding no(i)se, to which B'Loon's mud was related as table to indentation, had been known in an earlier report as "Funk Underneath." Djbouche, with namesake propriety, would lend no(i)se a Franco-Maghrebi inflection, relating it to the bottle in which he washed ashore by posing between-the-sheets musk as winelike fragrance, *djboudoir-djbouteille-djbouquet* as the chord he'd have struck had the bottle not been noteless, a theoretico-subjunctive chord to which an alternate Namesake Encyclical would attach.

For years Miles Davis had been saying of bebop: "We were like scientists of sound. If a door squeaked we could call out the exact pitch." Had Djbouche's bottle borne a note, a Namesake Encyclical, the words written on it would have been those. However much he insisted on between-the-sheets bouquet, Djbouche wanted most to ally brain with bottom-line sex. "Hotel Didjeridoo had a bar but no lab," he was fond of saying. "That's why it went down." The new edifice his duet with B'Loon would erect would roll bottle and beaker into one, sonance and science (chemical wedding) into one.

B'Loon, however, had bigger plans. The duet, as far as he was concerned, had already begun. The point was to parlay it into a stint with

Djband, an up-and-coming combo he had long admired and on a few occasions even sat in with. Eligible advent was the name he'd given it, the sitting in, but he'd have been the first to say he'd made a mistake, legible advent—the first, had Djbouche not beaten him to it. This was the sense in which the duet had already begun. Djbouche chided him for misread eligibility, legible snafu, an antiphonal rejoinder B'Loon didn't hear so much as feel, nonsonant demur. It was as much duel as duet, a bout between contending ways of being.

Though he'd have been the first to say he'd made a mistake, B'Loon blamed it on his childhood, the Farmer Al Falfa cartoons he'd watched as a child. Backed, as they were, by Ellington's music, they'd made an ineradicable impression it seemed, equating the music with cartoon clarity, an impression that had come back to haunt him as legible advent, presumed hyperintelligibility, pictographic imprint, scripted sense.

The balloon-borne legibility B'Loon had adduced from Djband's music bespoke a misconceived cartoon limpidity he could hardly believe he'd ever imagined, much less introduced on those occasions on which, uninvited by Djband, he'd sat in. Though the term *caption*, strictly speaking, didn't apply to what he'd done, he nonetheless thought of it in that regard, chiding himself for the suggestion of *capture* he couldn't help hearing, the presumed abatement of sound's prodigal behest.

Such misgiving had paved the way for B'Loon agreeing to be put back in the bottle. Self-chiding proved to be the beginning of dialogue, the root of duet. B'Loon's qualms were Djbouche's eligible advent, the foot-in-the-door he awaited, unaware it was already there.

Still, however much self-doubt seeded the duet, the fact was that Djbouche's critique of speakeasy fluidity applied to cartoon limpidity as well. It could not have remained lost for long on either him or B'Loon that the music's presumed whorehouse roots were related to presumptions of cartoon clarity, that bottom-line sex exchanged clarity of aegis and intent for what was otherwise fraught with ambiguity, innuendo, traded redeemed, "operatic" mud for aporetic mud. Born-again mud made common coin of sex, sold it for what it thereby became, explain-all base. Love of sex, everyone knew, was the root of such music. Thus it was that in a well-known cartoon Betty Boop ran with Louis Armstrong in hot pursuit. It was a cartoon B'Loon and Djbouche had both seen as kids.

Aporetic mud nonetheless persisted. Explain-all sex undermined its own foundation, aroused expectations it couldn't fulfill. The bottom it sought to secure slid, shifted, wouldn't stay put. Bottom-line lubricity proved a weak antidote to slippage. All of this B'Loon and Djbouche had on good authority. Drennette Scientist had long ago noted that sex too boasted a prodigal behest. This B'Loon and Djbouche both knew, though neither knew that the other knew, she having spoken to each apart from the other.

Drennette Scientist (also known as Drennette Virgin) had made each of them feel it was more a test tube than a bottle he was in. She advocated carrying funk back to Kikongo *lufuki*, a transitive accord between scent and science, root sense of integrity, sweat invested in the working out of the art. This she did to countervail against reductions of funk to a play for commercial appeal, bottom-line sweat as commercial lubricant, bass-line whiff the market's muscular bouquet (auction-block bouquet). She spoke of "Hard Work," John Handy's big hit, saying that its love of labor was to be endorsed but that there needed to be a concurrent, epistatic unsettling of bottom-line barter, bedrock swap. She spoke on behalf of what she termed "laboratory sweat," an anti-anti-sublime titration aimed at funk no longer precluding perfume.

Perfume, it had struck both B'Loon and Djbouche, was an odd, unessential item for Drennette Virgin to be endorsing, but in light of its synthetic aspect and her Drennette Scientist aspect it all made perfect sense. She sought, they'd come separately to understand, a sublime, no longer sublimated accord between ascetic and synthetic, a concomitant accord between synthetic and synaesthetic, epistatic funk and pheromonal sway.

Such admonitions regarding bedrock swap helped Djbouche prevail against the feeling of being deprived, his intermittent wish for greater recognition, the sort of lapse into commercial aspiration which had led him to tell B'Loon, "Give them what they want." His "No-Note Samba" sought to further the sense of epistatic funk Drennette Scientist had adumbrated. He was her test tube, willingly so, happily so. Samba's characteristic bass-drum thump, under his care, was displaced into what could be called splay disposition, backbeat as vagrancy (vacancy at points), no pat recurrence caroling pulse, pertinence, provision. Djbouche's no-note tack accented nonsonant "bump," a noncorpuscular virtuality whose quantum élan had driven the Keyhole Club Conventioneers wild. What they "heard" (more thought they heard than heard, felt more than thought) was temporality partaken of, made palpable, time's passage saluted and lamented all at once, as though "bump" were a protuberant breach they bought into, bought and bid goodbye in the same breath. Epistasis notwithstanding, pulse, a certain tolling insistence, was very much alive in what Djbouche proposed. How he managed to avail himself of samba's amenities while dispensing with its usual trappings was the cause of many a head being scratched.

How Djbouche was able to tend bar and perform at the same time caused many a head to be scratched as well, so cathartic was the nonsonant "bump" he filled the air with. Indeed, it was feeling more than anything else, a felt filling-up of the air with an unspecified something one sensed would not otherwise have been there. The Keyhole Club Convention had been the last major event to take place at Hotel Didjeridoo before its collapse, a fact that led some to believe Djbouche's felt-fill "bump" had had something to do with its fall, the same unspecified something one had felt fill the air throughout the bar, lobby and lounge. The ascetic-scientific spin Djbouche had visited upon samba, they averred, had had unforeseen, cataclysmic repercussions. It was as if, they ventured further, nonsonant "bump" were to samba what black holes were to stars, a pit of antithetic density and concentration all approach to which proffered collapse as ineluctable egress, bottom-line "get."

Part of Djbouche's job as bartender was to chat with customers, lend a friendly ear and offer entertaining talk. The latter he'd given particular attention during the Keyhole Club Convention, regaling conventioneers at the no-host bar with graphic tales of goings-on upstairs, peepshow accounts of the "operatic" doings in various rooms. What he offered was namesake perspective (keyhole perspective) on the bottom-line sex taking place above their heads. This and the nonsonant "bump" of his "No-Note Samba," to say nothing of the drinks he served, provided a one-two punch which had many a conventioneer reeling—reeling, yet coming back for more.

B'Loon had been surprised when Djbouche told him, "Give them what they want. Show them a good time." He had been even more surprised when, on his way out of the hotel, he'd come upon Djbouche entertaining conventioneers at the no-host bar. The moment they made eye contact he saw a twinge of embarrassment shoot across Djbouche's face. It reminded him of the story Benny Golson tells of happening upon Trane honking atop a bar in a club in Philadelphia one night and of Trane's embarrassment and the sheepish grin he wore afterward, having once told Golson he'd never stoop to "walking the bar." Djbouche, however, wore no sheepish grin. He fought his embarrassment back with bravado, motioning B'Loon over to the bar and answering the question he took it B'Loon wanted to ask but wouldn't (or, if he would, beating him to the punch), whispering in his ear as if resigned to a new, disillusioning truth, "Give them what they want. Show them a good time."

B'Loon had not been unaware of bravado's role in what Djbouche whispered, but the statement had surprised him nonetheless. Even more surprising had been the extent to which it hit home, the extent to which B'Loon took it seriously, heard it as an indictment, a snide condemnation of legible advent, the cartoon-clear, literalizing spirit he'd become on those occasions he sat in with Djband.

B'Loon had in fact been on his way out of the hotel that night to sit in with Djband again. The bug Djbouche put in his ear, the snide exhortation to sell out which he heard as accusing him of having sold out, led him to take a more subtle tack. Yes, he reflected guiltily, the legibility he lent the music not only sold it out but sold it short, relieved its listeners of the brunt of incommensurability it meant them to bear, the prodigal stir it wanted them to abide by, digest. Yes, he admitted, the balloon-borne wordage he'd adduced from the music could be taken the wrong way—not as food for thought but as immediatist instinct, something which obviated thought. Yes, he admitted, it had maybe been naive to hope otherwise, fanciful to think he could prevail against cognitive shortcut, notions of an instinctualist language, an instinctualist people's default on language. Yes, there was a long history of exactly that shortcut, a history not to be easily dismissed or too soon forgotten, easy attributions regarding "a tropical race who typify the life of feeling, deficient in the power of abstract thought." It was disconcerting to find himself possibly perpetuating such attribution, unwittingly complicit with grunt clarity, cartoon articulacy, captive address.

Such qualms had led B'Loon to agree to being put back in the bottle. Like Djbouche, he thought of it more as a test tube than a bottle, happily gave Drennette Scientist his support, hoping by that to undo whatever damage he might have done. The prospects implied by virgin science appealed to him immensely. His, he thought, was a dream (even if only a dream) which befit Djband's imminent trek into the recording studio, an erotic-elegiac wish to revisit firstness, know first knowing again. The contradiction didn't escape him, which is in part what gave the wish its elegiac rub, made it the outcome of sad science perhaps, nescience no. His wish took advantage of the imminent trek being Djband's first, a fact he sought to parlay, should the stint he had in mind materialize, into more than incidental fact, more than mere contingency, more than a bleak choice between metaphor and metonym, more than Djband would otherwise know, firstness notwithstanding.

Perhaps Djband itself was a vain dream of union B'Loon sometimes thought, belated quest for first knowledge, first-known fullness, founding cement. There were those who contended science was inevitably sad, that Hotel Didjeridoo, severed sensation's last resort, had been bound to fall, that this was the crash whose everlasting report sad science rehearsed. Drennette Scientist, however, in a letter to B'Loon dated "Any day now," advocated a virgin science, augured its advent, insisted on sound as a recombinant medium pinning virgin hope on aporetic mud. The thought of this letter, which had arrived a few days before the fall of Hotel Didjeridoo, bolstered B'Loon's hope of teaming up with Djbouche and of him and Djbouche teaming up with Djband.

Djbouche's no-note samba's nonsonant "bump" brushed against him again, a compression effect like a sonic boom without the boom. He felt it fill the bottle in which he washed ashore in much the way it had filled the bar, lounge and lobby as he was on his way out of Hotel

Didjeridoo. The recurrent "bump" seemed likewise to augur a new science, ictic non-sound a cardiognostic virginity of address, as though to be so brushed was to know and be known for the very first time. How such virginity renewed itself had somehow to do with aporetic mud's precipitance, the "how" and the "somehow" the very crux of mud, what made it mud, the aporeticity of aporetic mud.

It was a mystery. "Bumped" recurrence lapped against the glass like water against the pilings of a pier. B'Loon let himself be rocked by it—boat, cradle, baby prophet among the rushes, whatever it took to bear the eviscerating buoyancy "bump" induced.

"Fond elixir," B'Loon muttered, more to himself than to the nonsonant "bump" he ostensibly addressed. Watery trope notwithstanding, "bumped" recurrence remained a dry run, a test run which, for all its undulance, left the liquidity it would eventually effect to some future date, "fond" imminence or impendence a felt-fill solution suffusing the air.

Again he muttered, "Fond elixir," awash with "bumped" recurrence's dry caress. Each arid "bump" wafted evaporative perfume, a nomadic, not-where-one-thought-it-would-be thump that rayed out, expanded, swelling toward a blow that never came or, if it did, dissolved, as its way of coming, into a ubiquitous, felt-fill rush. This was a further sense in which his and Djbouche's duet had already begun. The memory of nonsonant "bump" was no less with him than the note his bottle bore, a "fond" memento of his former bottle-mate and, he insisted, a harbinger of things to come.

Unseen but otherwise there, Drennette Scientist loomed larger than life, backdrop and animating breeze rolled into one, assisting the wave that washed the bottles ashore at Venice Beach, rechristened by the bottles' arrival, Venus Beach. Blown-bottle sonority filled the air, a hoarse but penetrant tone as of an Arabico-Berber flute. Faint, frail, it had the sound of having come a long way, the subtlest felt-fill sonority ever to have entered L.A. Very few of those at Venus Beach showed any sign of having heard it. The skaters went on skating as though nothing had happened, the weightlifters lifting weights as though nothing had happened, tourists taking pictures as though nothing had happened. All but a scattered few went on doing what they were doing as though nothing had happened. Those few, however, heard a frail, faint something endowing the otherwise ordinary sky with elegiac primer, sad-scientific base, virgin patina. Blown-bottle austerity attended by synthesizer strings made for a synthetico-symphonic sky, burgeoning crescendo endlessly all-but-absconded-with, beginning to bid sensation goodbye.

Those few turned their heads to see the source of what they heard but couldn't find it. Some of those who were sitting or who lay on their stomachs or backs stood up to get a better look, to no avail. What they saw was not the source of what they heard but one of its effects, an erotic-elegiac graininess bestowed upon or merely brought out in the surrounding flesh, tanning bodies on display, jogging bodies on display, weightlifting bodies on display, skating bodies on display. Blown-bottle sonority peppered all flesh with a flute-blown abrasion as of wind-blown sand, granted it a buff that was not untouched by weather, bruise, wear (grit-given scour, grit-given scratch).

Up to this point flesh had reclined lazily within itself, even that of those engaged in strenuous exertion. But with the advent of blown-bottle sonority a quality of strain, an aroused, ahead-of-itself nostalgia for bodily abidance pervaded and could be seen on the skin of all those within view—seen with such acuity it seemed one could taste it. Sad-scientific foresight gave skin a spiked, philosophic savor, virgin science a newly provident salt, laboratory sweat.

Here and there the few who heard the blown-bottle sonority pinched or scratched or otherwise touched themselves, rubbed an arm or a leg or massaged a wrist, newly apprised of their bodies' unarrestable transit. The strung sky mourned an insistent furtherance it was also an exponent of, the risen power grit-given scratch had been taken to, "fond," empyrean scrub. The sound, faint and frail as it was, sharpened itself on skin and sky alike. Mimicking flesh or proposing a model for flesh, the sky too got a scoured look, wiped and rubbed with an abrasive agent that gave it a close-to-the-bone burnish (buffed ipseity, high-strung strop).

Faint, increasingly fraught, blown-bottle sonority kept close to the water and, once ashore, close to the ground. It could well have been a broom, so sustained and adnate was the sweep it advanced. It grazed the ocean and the shore with an aspirate slide implying meek persistence, a readiness to sweep them clean of water and sand, lose itself in the effort. Such willingness to indulge futility compounded the press of grainy transit imbued on the sky in the eyes of those who heard it. Its futile willingness or wish to sweep sand and sea away notwithstanding, it proposed itself as a potential coat, a protective cover against vain endeavor.

It was an inoculative indulgence, it turned out, meant to ward off undue expectation. This had to do with the ascetic-scientific tack Djbouche, had his bottle borne a note, would have expounded, been an exponent of. As it was, he found his ostensibly no-note approach complicated by the sonic sweep that bore him and B'Loon ashore. The blown-bottle sonority's willingness to indulge futility warned against a willingness to woo frustration. It was nonetheless hard to know how to read it, implicated as inextricably as he was. Indulgence as antithetic omen bore a mixed message which further mixed his own. This, he was beginning to find out, was what being in a test tube meant.

Venus Beach, that is, had become an experimental site presided over by Drennette Scientist on behalf of Djband, a polyrhythmic lab conciliating erstwhile incongruences. She sought a votive, talismanic solution which would bless Djband's recording date, ward off commercial lubricancy's lure without defaulting on juice.

Venus's in name only, Venus Beach was lab and altar both, votive cabinet, an Afro-Atlantic "ultimate altar" brought to the Pacific. Sea met sand as juice met drought, a borderline vow that Djband's music become neither lubricious nor unduly dry. Votive bottles leaned on test tube racks, around which were test tubes half-immersed in sand. Set in cavities dug deep in the sand to protect against wind were Bunsen burners lit to Iemandjá.*

---

* Djeannine, Drennette Scientist's lab assistant/acolyte, insisted on spelling it with a "d"—this to further advance, by way of allusion, Drennette Scientist's theory of epistatic funk as well as pay respects to her own discographic roots. The cut that follows "Jeannine" on *Donald Byrd at the Half Note Cafe*, she never tired of pointing out, was "Pure D. Funk," the "d" in whose title, contrary to common use, was a mobile, epistatizing "d," one which got around. It had migrated to her name and done the same with Iemandjá.

Many more than the few who heard the blown-bottle sonority were those who had noticed Drennette Scientist's laboratory altar. It caught the eye of all who came near it, set in the sand not very far from the water's edge, an unusual sight even on a beach known for unusual sights. It was as though, for that small area at least, Venus Beach were a beach in Rio de Janeiro on New Year's Eve—an analogy neither lost on nor unintended by Drennette Scientist, who saw Djband's trek into the recording studio as a beginning, a new dawn or day or year which was not to be embarked on without asking for Iemandjá's blessing. A Brazilian would probably not have known what to make of the test tubes, test tube racks and Bunsen burners, but the green grapes, white roses and such would have been right at home at Ipanema or Copacabana—certainly more so than at Venus Beach (where the test tubes, test tube racks and Bunsen burners were no less odd than they'd have been in Brazil).

Beachgoers happening past the laboratory altar walked over to it to get a better look. Some of them stooped or crouched or went down on one knee to take it in closer to ground level, poring over its various details and pondering the obvious attention to detail that had gone into it. Word had spread since the first sighting of the laboratory altar early that morning, so there were those who didn't simply happen upon it but came from elsewhere on the beach expressly to see it. No one having seen Drennette Scientist and her lab assistant/acolyte Djeannine as they worked on it well before dawn, the questions on many a lip was how had it gotten there, who built it, why.

Many were those who had looked at the laboratory altar and some of the few who heard the blown-bottle sonority were among them. Very few were those who wondered was there a connection between the two, but those who did were on to more than they suspected. Had they gone so far as to sniff or taste the liquid held by the test tubes, bowls and beakers, the liquid they assumed to be seawater, they'd have found it to be champagne. The significance of this they wouldn't have gotten without also noticing that the sonority had arisen as two bottles washed ashore, that the tide, flowing farther up the beach than usual, had deposited the bottles at the laboratory altar's very edge, in effect making them a part of it. They would also have needed to notice that the bottles were champagne bottles.

It was a very old story: bottle meets prow. Djband was a boat the bottles were there to christen on this the day of its maiden voyage, though they would not, as was custom, be broken against its prow; the fall of Hotel Didjeridoo had wrought breakage enough. Drennette Scientist, influenced by her Drennette Virgin aspect, proffered a less literal meeting, a sympathetic-parallactic alignment she nonetheless, under the influence of Djeannine, likened to a kiss. Bottle, she decided, would kiss prow from a distance, a dry, laboratory kiss with otherwise overt invocatory overtones—dry but still a kiss, a dry kiss wet with the thought of champagne.

So it was that as B'Loon and Djbouche washed ashore borne by champagne bottles at Venus Beach Djband was in a recording studio on the other side of L.A. Arriving in separate bottles made Djbouche's desire to team up with B'Loon all the more intense. Likewise, the bottles' long-distance address of Djband's prow kept B'Loon's desire to join Djband at peak strength. This was exactly what the Drennette Virgin aspect of Drennette Scientist had in mind, convinced that such impediment as distance purified desire, that such desire would be a boon to Djband, bless its maiden voyage.

Everything had fallen into place. Drennette Scientist/Virgin, a tutelary projection based on one of Djband's members ("It's about cutting yourself in two," she'd been known to say), had taken it upon herself to both contain and garner the commitment of B'Loon and Djbouche, two exemplary souls who, intimate with bottom-line "get," could never be forgotten to be potential gremlins. They were there in the studio with Djband, though not literally so, parallactically present by way of a triangulated tryst whose two other points were Venus Beach and Hotel Didjeridoo. The mathematics had been worked out well in advance.

B'Loon and Djbouche were there in the studio with Djband from note one, beat one. They lent the music an urgency sifted free of undue anxiety, a weathered resilience free of resignation though not unwise to the uses of restraint. The recording engineer, after only a few bars, shook his head in astonishment, disbelief, not sure whether to trust or, if he did, what to make of what his ears reported.

There in the studio from the very first note of the very first take, B'Loon and Djbouche gave the riverine furtherance of Djband's first number a hint of hover, a haloing hint that mingled furtherance and float and which all who heard were at considerable pains to account for, unable to account for. The closest the recording engineer came was to say that it brought to mind and somehow managed to blend the world-weariness-resisting-itself of Ornette Coleman's "Antiques," the extended, oddly relaxed, extrapolative "alas" of Wayne Shorter's "De Pois do Amor, O Vazio" or Paulinho da Viola's "Cidade Submersa" and the plucked, ambulant ictus typical of Malinke music, the sort of thing he'd heard in certain pieces by Les Ambassadeurs du Mali or Les Amazones de Guinée.

B'Loon and Djbouche, there in the studio with Djband from the very moment the tape began to roll, gave riverine furtherance pause, an all but indetectable pause, made a certain peace with not knowing or with the limits of knowing, leaving the sound engineer to admit that it brought to mind and managed to blend all those things he'd named but that it didn't end there, that it blended all those things and more, that it did more than blend.

As did the recording engineer, others would hear that "more," all sides of it ("more" things, "more" than blending), the very "more" Djband's members rode like a boat, an adamant boat, glass-bottomed all the better to see the mud they rode above, borne aloft as though balloons lifted them up.

DISCOGRAPHY

Bedouin Hornbook

3 Archie Shepp, "Cousin Mary," *Four for Trane* (Impulse, 1964).

9 The Bauls of Bengal, *Indian Street Music* (Nonesuch Explorer, 1971).

20 The Cecil Taylor Unit, "Streams," *Dark to Themselves* (Inner City, 1977).
Jair Rodrigues, *Eu Sou O Samba* (Philips, 1975).
Louis Armstrong and His Orchestra, "Star Dust" (Second Master), *The Louis Armstrong Story—Volume 4: Louis Armstrong Favorites* (Columbia, 1956).

22 Jair Rodrigues, "Vai Meu Samba," *Eu Sou O Samba* (Philips, 1975).

51 Al Green, "Love and Happiness," *I'm Still in Love with You* (Hi, 1972).
Charles Mingus, "What Love," *Charles Mingus Presents Charles Mingus* (America, 1960).

52 Sonny Rollins and Coleman Hawkins, "Lover Man," *Sonny Meets Hawk* (RCA Victor, 1963).
Jackie McLean, "I'll Keep Loving You," *Let Freedom Ring* (Blue Note, 1962).
Robin Kenyatta, "Until," *Until* (Vortex, 1968).
Archie Shepp and Philly Joe Jones, "Howling in the Silence," *Archie Shepp and Philly Joe Jones* (Fantasy, 1969).

57 The Roland Kirk Quartet, "No Tonic Pres," *Rip, Rig and Panic* (Limelight, 1965).

63 *Anthologie de la Musique du Tchad* (Ocora, 1968).

66 Earl Zero with the Soul Syndicate, "Get Happy," *Visions of Love* (Epiphany, 1980).

68 Burning Spear, "Jordan River," *Marcus Garvey* (Island, 1975).
Burning Spear, "Man in the Hills," *Live* (Island, 1977).

71 Bob Marley and the Wailers, "Natural Mystic," *Exodus* (Island, 1977).

74 Yusef Lateef, "Love Theme from Spartacus," *Yusef Lateef Plays for Lovers* (Prestige, 1967).
Arthur Prysock, "Someone to Watch Over Me," *Art and Soul* (Verve, 1966).

75 John Coltrane, "My Favorite Things," *Coltrane Live at the Village Vanguard Again!* (Impulse, 1966).

77 Sun Ra, "Space Is the Place," *Space Is the Place* (Blue Thumb, 1972).

78 *Brésil: Musiques du Haut Xingu* (Ocora, 1977).

82 The Clovers, "Devil or Angel," *Their Greatest Recordings: The Early Years* (Atco, 1971).

88 Archie Shepp, "Hambone," *Fire Music* (Impulse, 1965).

92 Joseph Jarman, "Song for Christopher," *As If It Were the Seasons* (Delmark, 1968).

93 Roland Kirk, "Serenade to a Cuckoo," *I Talk With the Spirits* (Limelight, 1964).

95 Sonny Rollins, "Everything Happens to Me," *Sonny Rollins on Impulse* (Impulse, 1965).

100 Olivier Messiaen, *Quatuor pour la Fin du Temps* (Deutsche Grammophon, 1979).

102 The Ornette Coleman Quartet, "Embraceable You," *This Is Our Music* (Atlantic, 1961).

105 Toupouri Wind Ensemble, "Sirléhé," *Anthologie de la Musique du Tchad* (Ocora, 1968).

110 Thelonious Monk Quartet, "In Walked Bud," *Misterioso* (Riverside, 1958).
Bob Marley and the Wailers, *Exodus* (Island, 1977).

117 Charlie Parker, "Confirmation," *The Verve Years (1952–54)* (Verve, 1977).

118 John Coltrane, *Interstellar Space* (Impulse, 1974).
Rashied Ali and Frank Lowe, *Duo Exchange* (Survival, 1973).
Archie Shepp, "The Magic of Ju-Ju," *The Magic of Ju-Ju* (Impulse, 1967).

120 Skip James, "Devil Got My Woman," *Devil Got My Woman* (Vanguard, 1967).

127 Anthony Williams, "Love Song," *Spring* (Blue Note, 1965).

128 Wayne Shorter, "Dindi," *Super Nova* (Blue Note, 1969).

133 Don Cherry, "What's Not Serious," *Symphony for Improvisers* (Blue Note, 1966).

139 Gap Band, "I Can't Get Over You," *Gap Band IV* (Total Experience, 1982).

152 Charles Mingus, "Orange Was the Color of Her Dress, Then Blue Silk," *Mingus at Monterey* (Jazz Workshop, 1967).
Prince Lasha Quintet, "Lost Generation," *The Cry!* (Contemporary, 1963).

155 Frank Wright Quartet, *Center of the World* (Center of the World, 1972).

157 James Brown and the Famous Flames, "Lost Someone," *Live at the Apollo* (King, 1963).

160 John Coltrane, "One Down, One Up," *New Thing at Newport* (Impulse, 1965).

168 Earl Zero with the Soul Syndicate, "Home Sweet Home," *Visions of Love* (Epiphany, 1980).
Muddy Waters, "40 Days and 40 Nights," *The Real Folk Blues* (Chess, 1965).
John Coltrane, "The Promise," *Coltrane Live at Birdland* (Impulse, 1963).

169 Bob Marley and the Wailers, "Lively Up Yourself," *Natty Dread* (Island, 1974).
Bob Marley and the Wailers, "Wake Up and Live," *Survival* (Island, 1979).
Earl Zero with the Soul Syndicate, "Get Happy," *Visions of Love* (Epiphany, 1980).
Max Roach, "Members, Don't Git Weary," *Members, Don't Git Weary* (Atlantic, 1968).
Stanley Turrentine, "Feeling Good," *Rough 'n Tumble* (Blue Note, 1966).
Fela Anikulapo Kuti and Egypt 80 Band, "Original Suffer Head" and "Power Show," *Original Suffer Head* (Lagos International, 1981).
193 Charley Patton, "Pony Blues," *Charley Patton: Founder of the Delta Blues* (Yazoo, 1969).
Muddy Waters, "Long Distance Call," *The Best of Muddy Waters* (Chess, 1957).
Lole y Manuel, "Anta Oumri," *Lole y Manuel* (CBS, 1977).

Djbot Baghostus's Run

203 The Jazz Composer's Orchestra, "Preview," *The Jazz Composer's Orchestra* (JCOA, 1968).
204 Nancy Wilson, "China," *This Mother's Daughter* (Capitol, 1976).
208 Miles Davis, "I Fall in Love too Easily," "So Near So Far," and "Basin Street Blues," *Seven Steps to Heaven* (Columbia, 1963).
209 Charles Mingus, "Solo Dancer," *The Black Saint and the Sinner Lady* (Impulse, 1963).
210 Eddie Jefferson, "Jeannine," *The Main Man* (Inner City, 1977).
Eli Mohammad Shera and Ensemble, "Sufi Love Song," *Folksongs of Kashmir* (Lyrichord, 1972).
211 The Clovers, "One Mint Julep," *Their Greatest Hits: The Early Years* (Atco, 1971).
"The Quintet," "A Night in Tunisia," *Jazz at Massey Hall* (Fantasy, 1953).
Coleman Hawkins, "You Go To My Head," *The Hawk Flies* (Milestone, 1974).
217 Art Blakey, "Ugetsu," *Ugetsu: Art Blakey's Jazz Messengers at Birdland* (Riverside, 1963).
219 Eddie Jefferson, "Jeannine," *The Main Man* (Inner City, 1977).
Donald Byrd, "Jeannine," *Donald Byrd at the Half Note Cafe, Volume 2* (Blue Note, 1960).
220 Sonny Rollins, "Three Little Words," *Sonny Rollins on Impulse* (Impulse, 1965).
231 Eddie Jefferson, "Benny's from Heaven," *The Main Man* (Inner City, 1977).
235 Charlie Parker, "What Is this Thing Called Love?," *The Verve Years (1952-54)* (Verve, 1977).
The Roland Kirk Quartet, "Rip, Rig and Panic," *Rip, Rig and Panic* (Limelight, 1965).

236 Charles Mingus, "Wham Bam Thank You Ma'am," *Oh Yeah* (Atlantic, 1962).
237 Roland Kirk, "The Inflated Tear," *The Inflated Tear* (Atlantic, 1968).
240 Don Cherry and the Jazz Composer's Orchestra, "Desireless," *Relativity Suite* (JCOA, 1973).
245 Frank Wright, "China," *One for John* (BYG, 1969).
246 Pink Anderson, "My Baby Left Me This Morning," *Pink Anderson, Volume 1: Carolina Blues Man* (Prestige/Bluesville, 1961).
248 Thelonious Monk, "April in Paris," *Monk* (Columbia, 1964).
252 Old and New Dreams, "Old and New Dreams" and "Chairman Mao," *Old and New Dreams* (Black Saint, 1977).
255 Ernst Krenek, *Jonny Spielt Auf: Opus 45 (Opera in Two Acts)* (Mace, 1965).
261 Jimmy Reed, "Going to New York," *Jimmy Reed–The Legend–The Man* (Vee-Jay, 1965).
266 Gato Barbieri and Dollar Brand, "Hamba Khale," *Confluence* (Arista, 1975).
268 Etoile de Dakar, *Thiapathioly* (MCA, 1980).
Etoile de Dakar, *Etoile de Dakar* (International Music, 1980).
300 Brother Jack McDuff, "Jive Samba," *Live!* (Prestige, 1965).
Michael Rabin, "Caprice No. 9 in E Major – Allegretto," *Paganini: 24 Caprices, Op. 1* (EMI, 1958).
301 Albert Ayler Trio, "Ghosts: First Variation" and "Ghosts: Second Variation," *Spiritual Unity* (ESP, 1965).
304 Eric Dolphy, "Glad to Be Unhappy," *Outward Bound* (New Jazz, 1960).
John Coltrane, "To Be," *Expression* (Impulse, 1967).
305 Henry Threadgill, *X-75 Volume 1* (Arista/Novus, 1979).
306 Charles Lloyd, "Little Anahid's Day," *Charles Lloyd in Europe* (Atlantic, 1968).
308 Alice Coltrane, "Oh Allah," *Universal Consciousness* (Impulse, 1971).
310 John Coltrane and Paul Quinichette, "Anatomy," *Cattin' with Coltrane and Quinichette* (Prestige, 1957).
312 Ben Webster and Coleman Hawkins, "Prisoner of Love," *Tenor Giants* (Verve, 1977).
Ben Webster, "Tenderly," *King of the Tenors* (Verve, 1953).
319 Marion Brown, "Spooks," *Three for Shepp* (Impulse, 1967).
327 The Penguins, "Earth Angel," *Oldies But Goodies, Volume 1* (Original Sound, 1959).
328 Charlie Parker, "Ornithology," *Charlie Parker on Dial, Volume 1* (Spotlite, 1968).
337 Thelonious Monk, "Ask Me Now," *Five by Monk by Five* (Riverside, 1959).
338 Bob Marley and the Wailers, "Small Axe," *African Herbsman* (Trojan, 1973).
340 Gil Evans, "Cry of Hunger," *Svengali* (Atlantic, 1973).
Wayne Shorter, "Kryptonite," *Schizophrenia* (Blue Note, 1967).
343 Jackie McLean, "Frankenstein," *One Step Beyond* (Blue Note, 1963).
347 Lightnin' Hopkins, "Bottle Up and Go," *Autobiography in Blues* (Tradition, 1960).
348 Bob Marley and the Wailers, "No Woman, No Cry," *Natty Dread* (Island, 1974).

Charles Mingus, "Free Cell Block F, 'tis Nazi USA," *Changes Two* (Atlantic, 1975).

350 Muddy Waters, "I Want You to Love Me," *The Best of Muddy Waters* (Chess, 1957).

358 Frederick McQueen, "Come For Your Dinner," *The Real Bahamas in Music and Song* (Nonesuch Explorer, 1966).

359 The Penguins, "Earth Angel," *Oldies But Goodies, Volume 1* (Original Sound, 1959).

376 Defunkt, *Thermonuclear Sweat* (Hannibal, 1982).

Atet A.D.

379 Duke Ellington and His Orchestra, "Black and Tan Fantasy," *Giants of Jazz: Duke Ellington* (Time-Life, 1978).

381 Thelonious Monk, "Pannonica," *Monk* (Columbia, 1964).

The Modern Jazz Quartet, "Natural Affection," *The Sheriff* (Atlantic, 1964).

382 Sonny Rollins, "Reflections," *Sonny Rollins, Volume 2* (Blue Note, 1957).

384 Wayne Shorter, "Fee-Fi-Fo-Fum," *Speak No Evil* (Blue Note, 1965).

Freddie Hubbard, *The Night of the Cookers: Live at Club La Marchal, Volume 1* (Blue Note, 1965).

Freddie Hubbard, *The Night of the Cookers: Live at Club La Marchal, Volume 2* (Blue Note, 1965).

Sonny Rollins and Coleman Hawkins, *Sonny Meets Hawk* (RCA Victor, 1963).

Charles Mingus, "What Love," *Charles Mingus Presents Charles Mingus* (America, 1960).

Charles Mingus, "So Long Eric," *The Great Concert of Charles Mingus* (America, 1964).

386 Memphis Slim, "Sweet Root Man," *Steady Rolling Blues* (Prestige/Bluesville, 1963).

387 Bo Diddley, "Who Do You Love," *Bo Diddley* (Chess, 1958).

Dexter Gordon, "Soy Califa," *A Swingin' Affair* (Blue Note, 1962).

Pete "El Conde" Rodriguez, "Soy La Ley," *Soy La Ley* (Fania, 1979).

John Lee Hooker, "I'm Bad Like Jesse James," *Live at Cafe au Go-Go* (ABC-Bluesway, 1967).

Lord Invader and His Calypso Group, "Me One Alone," *Calypso Travels* (Folkways, 1960).

390 The Cecil Taylor Unit, "Chorus of Seed," *Dark to Themselves* (Inner City, 1977).

398 Andrew Hill, "New Monastery," *Point of Departure* (Blue Note, 1964).

399 Gene Austin, "Jeannine, I Dream of Lilac Time," *Gene Austin's Great Hits* (Dot, 1960).

Eric Dolphy, *Here and There* (Prestige, 1965).

402 John Coltrane, "Sun Ship," *Sun Ship* (Impulse, 1971).

403 John Coltrane, *Live in Seattle* (Impulse, 1971).

Roland Kirk, "We Free Kings," *We Free Kings* (Mercury, 1962).

Kings in Exile, *Music from Ancient Texts* (Daagnim, 1981).

406 Dizzy Gillespie, "Salt Peanuts," *An Electrifying Evening with the Dizzy Gillespie Quintet* (Verve, 1961).

Charles Mingus, "Haitian Fight Song," *The Clown* (Atlantic, 1957).

409 Sam Rivers, "Cyclic Episode," *Fuchsia Swing Song* (Blue Note, 1965).

413 Frank Wright, "One for John," *One for John* (BYG, 1969).

John Coltrane, "Naima," *Giant Steps* (Atlantic, 1960).

419 Orquesta Cimarrón, *Erupción* (Coco/Lamp, 1977).

420 Clifton Chenier, "I Can't Stop Loving You," *Bon Ton Roulet* (Arhoolie, 1967).

422 The Tornadoes, "Telstar," *The Original Telstar: The Sounds of the Tornadoes* (London, 1962).

424 Elvin Jones/Jimmy Garrison Sextet, "Half and Half," *Illumination!* (Impulse, 1963).

432 Eric Dolphy, "Miss Ann," *Last Date* (Limelight, 1965).

435 Roland Kirk with Jack McDuff, "Funk Underneath," *Kirk's Work* (Prestige, 1966).

437 Freddie Hubbard, "Pensativa," *The Night of the Cookers: Live at Club La Marchal, Volume 1* (Blue Note, 1965).

452 "Aluar Horns," *Africa: Ceremonial and Folk Music* (Nonesuch Explorer, 1975).

455 Billie Holiday, "I Cover the Waterfront," *The Essential Billie Holiday: Carnegie Hall Concert* (Verve, 1961).

"Old Luri Love Song," *Folk Music of Iran: Luristan and Fars Provinces* (Lyrichord, 1972).

459 The Ornette Coleman Quartet, "Embraceable You," *This Is Our Music* (Atlantic, 1961).

Lightnin' Hopkins, "Bottle Up and Go," *Autobiography in Blues* (Tradition, 1960).

"Bagana," *Ethiopian Urban and Tribal Music, Volume 2: Gold from Wax* (Lyrichord, 1972).

460 Cosmas, Alexia and Simon Magaya, "Nhemamusasa," *Africa: Shona Mbira Music* (Nonesuch Explorer, 1977).

Archie Shepp and the New York Contemporary Five, "Like A Blessed Baby Lamb," *Bill Dixon 7-tette/Archie Shepp and the New York Contemporary Five* (Savoy, 1964).

461 "Wagogo Soothing Song," *Africa: Ceremonial and Folk Music* (Nonesuch Explorer, 1975).

482 Eric Dolphy, "The Madrig Speaks, the Panther Walks," *Last Date* (Limelight, 1965).

490 Byard Lancaster, *It's Not Up to Us* (Vortex, 1966).

491 Sun Ra and His Astro-Solar Infinity Arkestra, "My Brother the Wind," *My Brother the Wind* (Saturn Research, 1970).

500 Bessie Smith, "Empty Bed Blues," *The Bessie Smith Story, Volume 4* (Columbia, 1951).

Miles Davis Sextet, "Someday My Prince Will Come," *Someday My Prince Will Come* (Columbia, 1961).

502 Dewey Redman, "Lop-O-Lop," *Tarik* (BYG, 1969).

509 Chuck Willis, "Betty and Dupree," *His Greatest Recordings* (Atco, 1971).

511 Ornette Coleman, *Ornette on Tenor* (Atlantic, 1962).

512 Roland Kirk, "The Monkey Thing," *Kirk in Copenhagen* (Mercury, 1963).

518 Duke Ellington and His Orchestra, "Prelude to a Kiss," *The Best of Duke Ellington and His Famous Orchestra* (Capitol, 1961).

519 Julius Hemphill, "Dogon A.D.," *Dogon A.D.* (Mbari, 1972).

520 Charlie Parker Quintet, "Confirmation," *Bird at St. Nick's* (Jazz Workshop, 1958).

522 Archie Shepp, "The Girl from Ipanema," *Fire Music* (Impulse, 1965).

525 "A Felicidade," *The Original Sound Track from the Film Black Orpheus* (Fontana, 1959).

526 John Coltrane, "Dearly Beloved," *Sun Ship* (Impulse, 1971).

528 Burning Spear, "Door Peep Shall Not Enter," *Studio One Presents Burning Spear* (Coxsone/Studio One, 1973).

530 Roland Kirk with Jack McDuff, "Funk Underneath," *Kirk's Work* (Prestige, 1966).

532 John Handy, "Hard Work," *Hard Work* (Impulse, 1976).

538 Donald Byrd, "Jeannine" and "Pure D. Funk," *Donald Byrd at the Half Note Cafe, Volume 2* (Blue Note, 1960).

541 The Ornette Coleman Trio, "Antiques," *The Ornette Coleman Trio at the "Golden Circle" Stockholm, Volume 2* (Blue Note, 1966).

Wayne Shorter, "De Pois do Amor, O Vazio," *Odyssey of Iska* (Blue Note, 1971).

Paulinho da Viola, "Cidade Submersa," *Nervos de Aço* (EMI-Odeon, 1973).

AUTHOR PHOTO BY NINA SUBIN

NATHANIEL MACKEY is the author of several books of fiction, poetry, and criticism. His poetry book *Splay Anthem* won the 2006 National Book Award. *Atet A.D.* was chosen as one of the best books of 2001 by *Publishers Weekly*: "It has all the charged verve of Henry James encountering Charlie Parker's 'Ko-Ko' and perfectly transcribing every note and nuance." The fourth volume of Mackey's novel, *Bass Cathedral*—also available from New Directions—was chosen by *The New York Times* as one of 100 notable books of 2008.